O. HENRY

SELECTED STORIES

O. HENRY

SELECTED STORIES

Edited and with an Introduction
by Amanda Vaill

BOOK-OF-THE-MONTH CLUB
New York

Printed in the United States of America.

Contents

From **The Gentle Grafter** 1908

From **Roads of Destiny** 1909

From **Options** 1909

From **Whirligigs** 1910

From **Sixes and Sevens** 1911

From **Rolling Stones** 1912

From **Waifs and Strays** 1917

Introduction

How do we assign classic status to a writer? Whatever the hallmarks, William Sydney Porter, a.k.a. O. Henry, has surely exhibited them. His pseudonym has attained that adjectival Olympus where only a handful of other writers' names can be found—one speaks of Dickensian characters, a Hemingwayesque prose style, a Faulknerian sentence . . . and an O. Henry ending. Like Faulkner and Hemingway, he has been memorialized by a major literary prize in his name. Unlike them, he has even been immortalized on a candy bar.

But although his name has become a household expression, O. Henry (as the comedian Rodney Dangerfield used to say) don't get no respect. He's taught to schoolchildren, who learn their first lessons in narrative structure from his surprise endings. He's widely enough read to justify the existence of numerous anthologies of his work (including this one). But you'd never mention his name in the same breath as that of his fellow short story writer Edgar Allan Poe, for instance.

Now why is that? The easy answer is that Poe—or the Nobel Prize winners Faulkner and Hemingway, or the Mark Twain of *Pudd'nhead Wilson* and *The Adventures of Huckleberry Finn*—has a grander vision, a more complex appreciation of the extremes of feeling and experience. In this view, the writer must grapple with the big, dark themes in order to produce Literature, and O. Henry, with his trick endings, his almost made-for-TV emphasis on plot, just doesn't cut it.

In fact, though, O. Henry's endings are no more surprises than the card the magician produces from your ear or your pocket—a card that has been in the magician's hand the whole time. In his best stories, such as "Tobin's Palm," the much-anthologized but evergreen "Gift of the Magi," or "The Cop and the Anthem," they grow organically and inevitably from the characters and situations portrayed. Sometimes they depend on information the author has kept up his sleeve and only produces at the last minute, as in "The Higher Abdication," "Sisters of the Golden Circle," "Hygeia at the Solito," or "The Missing Chord"; sometimes the information is concealed—and revealed—by the confidence man who is the story's hero (as in the Jeff Peters stories).

Always, however, this prestidigitation is meant to entertain, just as the magician's card trick is meant to entertain—and *this,* not the absence of big dark themes, is O. Henry's fatal flaw. As he himself says in the semi-autobiographical story "Confessions of a Humorist,"

> There was a painless stage of incubation that lasted twenty-five years, and then it broke out on me, and people said I was It.
>
> But they called it humor instead of measles.

In this self-portrait, he tells us how, once his gift for comedy had been exposed,

> I was expected to keep it up. Others might speak sanely on business matters and the day's topics, but from me something gamesome and airy was required. . . .
>
> But I soon got the swing of it. Within a month I was turning out copy as regular as shipments of hardware.

We have a long tradition in this country of undervaluing the entertainer, or at least discounting his artistic value—and so O. Henry, "turning out copy" for millions of readers of *Ainslie's Magazine,* is seen as an enjoyable lightweight, less worthy than a more "serious" writer.

But beware. O. Henry's deftness and affability are a front for William Sydney Porter's shadowy and complicated reality. Born to middle-class parents in Greensboro, North Carolina, in 1862, he lost his mother to tuberculosis when he was three. At 20, he went to live on a sheep ranch in Texas (the scene of many of his stories); subsequently he married and got work in a bank—and then the bottom fell out of his life. His first-born child died, and he lost his bank job because money was missing from one of the accounts he managed. Ordered to stand trial for embezzlement, he fled to Honduras by way of New Orleans. Two years later, he learned that his wife had contracted tuberculosis and he returned to Texas; she died in July of 1897, and he was tried and sent to prison at the Ohio State Penitentiary the following spring. Despite the possibility that he'd done nothing wrong and in fact was shielding someone else (some of his stories, including "Friends in San Rosario," involve this scenario), he had to serve a little over three years in prison.

That was where he started to write, turning inmates' anecdotes into casual pieces; it was also where he changed his middle name from Sidney to Sydney (as at least one critic has pointed out, Sydney,

Australia, used to be the penal colony of Botany Bay), and where he evolved a pseudonym that conceals—and reveals—the name of the place where he was imprisoned. As O. Henry, he sold some of his pieces to magazines, and on his release he got the contract with *Ainslie's Magazine* under which he turned out stories "regular as shipments of hardware." Soon he was the most widely read writer in the country—but the audience that laughed at the runaway husband and his hound in "Memoirs of a Yellow Dog" or sighed over the fate of the abandoned sweetheart in "The Furnished Room" never knew how close these charming fables were to the grim truths of their author's life. Certainly they didn't realize that the author of "Hygeia at the Solito"—in which an Irish bum with TB cheats death through a farcical case of mistaken identity—was himself stricken with the disease that would kill him at the age of 47 in 1910.

In these stories—as in almost everything he wrote—O. Henry transforms tragedy and betrayal into pathos and chicanery. Perhaps it was the only way he could bear what had happened to him. By making light of his experiences, he earned himself millions of readers—and talked his way out of serious consideration as a writer of the first rank. But the way he did it gives us a clue to his true place in American literature.

For the distinctive thing about O. Henry, one realizes when one reads a great deal of him, is not the stories' endings but their *voice.* It's a uniquely American voice (this is particularly clear when it tries on a foreign accent, as O. Henry does—unsuccessfully, I think—in the story "Roads of Destiny"); more specifically, it's a *metropolitan* voice, the voice of the polyglot, smart-aleck, Johnny-come-lately city built by Reconstruction and waves of immigration and the industrial revolution. And (like an American tourist abroad) the voice maintains its identity no matter where it finds itself—New York or Texas, Central America or North Carolina.

This isn't a voice for love and death—it's too wised-up, too bittersweet for that. It's teasing, vivid, fond, and funny; it blends the vernacular and the Augustan with a vaudevillian's timing. Articulated by O. Henry, it's a voice that echoes in the books of Damon Runyon and S. J. Perelman, in the cinematic honking of W. C. Fields, and—in our own day—in the work of writers as different as Woody Allen and T. Coraghessan Boyle. Is it a voice for art? O. Henry has a clue for us in the story "Art and the Bronco," in which a cowboy painter destroys a monumental portrait of a steer because of an effete Eastern artist's criticism that it "isn't a picture at all." The disillusioned cowboy launches his pony, Hot Tamales, at the despised work:

> [The horse's] ears pricked up; he snorted. . . . Did Hot Tamales fancy he saw a steer, red and cavorting, that should be headed off and driven back to the herd? . . . With Lonny bending low in the saddle to dodge the top of the frame, [Hot Tamales] ripped through the great canvas like a shell from a mortar, leaving the cloth hanging in ragged shreds about a monstrous hole.

Afterwards the cowboy says to his horse, " 'You was the only one, Tamales, what seen anything in it. It *did* look like a steer, didn't it, old hoss?' " The establishment critics might shrug the cowboy off—but the horse knows better.

In this selection from O. Henry's works, I have grouped his stories as they originally appeared—chronologically, by volume—on the principle that the author's order is better than anything attempted by a later hand. As to those volumes published after the author's death, I've told myself that if he'd wanted those stories to come earlier, he would have published them earlier. In any case, the reader is free to discern linkages—thematic or otherwise—without my interference.

The selection process itself was, of course, a personal one; the criteria for inclusion were that the story should move me, that it should represent the best of what O. Henry can do, and yet that in some way it should push back the boundaries of what we think of when we say the words "O. Henry story." That is why I chose to include, in its entirety, O. Henry's first published book—the complete novel-in-stories, *Cabbages and Kings,* of which only excerpts appear in all other partial anthologies of his work. It shows O. Henry working in an extended way with a complicated set of themes, situations, and characters; and although he characteristically makes light of his efforts in the "Proem" that introduces the book, there's more of Conrad than Mark Twain in this "little tale . . . of many things."

Choosing what to leave out was harder than deciding what to put in. Because it has been anthologized so often, I wanted to cut "The Gift of the Magi"—but there was simply no way *not* to include it. It's too good. On the other hand, the sprightly (and preternaturally deconstructed) "Springtime à la Carte" didn't make it because the ending—indeed, the whole story—seems a little mechanical. Where two stories had similar themes, as in "The Skylight Room" and "The Furnished Room," I chose the grittier, less pretty alternative—O. Henry has an amazingly light touch with bad news. It was hard to dismiss *any* of the hilarious and politically incorrect stories in *The Gentle Grafter,* the volume of tales about the con man Jeff Peters, but there wasn't room for all of them.

Speaking of political incorrectness, perhaps something needs to be said about the attitudes reflected in both the language and intrinsic premises of some of the stories here. We need to remember that the casual prejudices of another era reveal more about the era than about the author's intentions: O. Henry's references to women's wiles, or his use of ethnic epithets, reflect the local color of the time—as do his descriptions of clothing, horse-drawn omnibuses, and gas lamps. They shouldn't distract us from the truth at the heart of his stories. "A Harlem Tragedy," a story about a battered wife and her envious upstairs neighbor, might seem to perpetuate all the hurtful myths about machismo and brutality—but although O. Henry refrains from judging his characters, his description of poor Mame's bruises horrifyingly undercuts the seeming lightheartedness of the ending.

Then there's "The Atavism of John Tom Little Bear," in which a college-educated Indian momentarily sheds his "scholarly verbs and prefixes" for the dialect and ways of the full-blood Cherokee. It's easy to see this tale as a celebration of the patronizing attitude—enunciated by Jeff Peters at the beginning of the story—that "You can't make an Anglo-Saxon of . . . the redman." But I think the real point is more clearly—and poignantly—made by John Tom himself, when he cries out, "What have you done to me? . . . You've taught me to hate the wigwams and love the white man's ways. I can look over into the promised land and see Mrs. Conyers"—the woman he's fallen in love with—"but my place is—on the reservation." This isn't a story about "atavism"—it's a story about the pain of deracination, a cry from the heart of someone who has a foot in two worlds and a place in neither. As always, O. Henry gives it a comic twist, as if to say, "I was only joking." He wasn't, of course. But it was both his gift and his misfortune to make it seem as if he was.

O. HENRY

SELECTED STORIES

From CABBAGES AND KINGS 1904

The Proem: *By the Carpenter*

They will tell you in Anchuria, that President Miraflores, of that volatile republic, died by his own hand in the coast town of Coralio; that he had reached thus far in flight from the inconveniences of an imminent revolution; and that one hundred thousand dollars, government funds, which he carried with him in an American leather valise as a souvenir of his tempestuous administration, was never afterward recovered.

For a *real,* a boy will show you his grave. It is back of the town near a little bridge that spans a mangrove swamp. A plain slab of wood stands at its head. Some one has burned upon the headstone with a hot iron this inscription:

RAMON ANGEL DE LAS CRUZES
Y MIRAFLORES
PRESIDENTE DE LA REPUBLICA
DE ANCHURIA
QUE SEA SU JUEZ DIOS

It is characteristic of this buoyant people that they pursue no man beyond the grave. "Let God be his judge!"—Even with the hundred thousand unfound, though they greatly coveted, the hue and cry went no further than that.

To the stranger or the guest the people of Coralio will relate the story of the tragic end of their former president; how he strove to escape from the country with the public funds and also with Doña Isabel Guilbert, the young American opera singer; and how, being apprehended by members of the opposing political party in Coralio, he shot himself through the head rather than give up the funds, and, in consequence, the Señorita Guilbert. They will relate further that Doña Isabel, her adventurous bark of fortune shoaled by the simultaneous loss of her distinguished admirer and the souvenir hundred thousand, dropped anchor on this stagnant coast, awaiting a rising tide.

They say, in Coralio, that she found a prompt and prosperous tide in the form of Frank Goodwin, an American resident of the town, an inventor who had grown wealthy by dealing in the products of the country—a banana king, a rubber prince, a sarsaparilla, indigo, and mahogany baron. The Señorita Guilbert, you will be told, married Señor Goodwin one month after the president's death, thus, in the very moment when Fortune had ceased to smile, wresting from her a gift greater than the prize withdrawn.

Of the American, Don Frank Goodwin, and of his wife the natives have nothing but good to say. Don Frank has lived among them for years, and has compelled their respect. His lady is easily queen of what social life the sober coast affords. The wife of the governor of the district, herself, who was of the proud Castilian family of Monteleon y Dolorosa de la Santos y Mendez, feels honored to unfold her napkin with olive-hued, ringed hands at the table of Señora Goodwin. Were you to refer (with your northern prejudices) to the vivacious past of Mrs. Goodwin when her audacious and gleeful abandon in light opera captured the mature president's fancy, or to her share in that statesman's downfall and malfeasance, the Latin shrug of the shoulder would be your only answer and rebuttal. What prejudices there were in Coralio concerning Señora Goodwin seemed now to be in her favor, whatever they had been in the past.

It would seem that the story is ended, instead of begun; that the close of tragedy and the climax of a romance have covered the ground of interest; but, to the more curious reader it shall be some slight instruction to trace the close threads that underlie the ingenuous web of circumstances.

The headpiece bearing the name of President Miraflores is daily scrubbed with soap-bark and sand. An old half-breed Indian tends the grave with fidelity and the dawdling minuteness of inherited sloth. He chops down the weeds and ever-springing grass with his machete, he plucks ants and scorpions and beetles from it with his horny fingers, and sprinkles its turf with water from the plaza fountain. There is no grave anywhere so well kept and ordered.

Only by following out the underlying threads will it be made clear why the old Indian, Galvez, is secretly paid to keep green the grave of President Miraflores by one who never saw that unfortunate statesman in life or in death, and why that one was wont to walk in the twilight, casting from a distance looks of gentle sadness upon that unhonored mound.

Elsewhere than at Coralio one learns of the impetuous career of Isabel Guilbert. New Orleans gave her birth and the mingled French and Spanish creole nature that tinctured her life with such turbulence and warmth. She had little education, but a knowledge of men and motives that seemed to have come by instinct. Far beyond the common woman was she endowed with intrepid rashness, with a love for the pursuit of adventure to the brink of danger, and with desire for the pleasures of life. Her spirit was one to chafe under any curb; she was Eve after the fall, but before the bitterness of it was felt. She wore life as a rose in her bosom.

Of the legion of men who had been at her feet it was said that but one was so fortunate as to engage her fancy. To President Miraflores, the brilliant but unstable ruler of Anchuria, she yielded the key to her resolute heart. How, then, do we find her (as the Coralians would have told you) the wife of Frank Goodwin, and happily living a life of dull and dreamy inaction?

The underlying threads reach far, stretching across the sea. Following them out it will be made plain why "Shorty" O'Day, of the Columbia Detective Agency, resigned his position. And, for a lighter pastime, it shall be a duty and a pleasing sport to wander with Momus beneath the tropic stars where Melpomene once stalked austere. Now to cause laughter to echo from those lavish jungles and frowning crags where formerly rang the cries of pirates' victims; to lay aside pike and cutlass and attack with quip and jollity; to draw one saving titter of mirth from the rusty casque of Romance—this were pleasant to do in the shade of the lemon-trees on that coast that is curved like lips set for smiling.

For there are yet tales of the Spanish Main. That segment of continent washed by the tempestuous Caribbean, and presenting to the sea a formidable border of tropical jungle topped by the overweening Cordilleras, is still begirt by mystery and romance. In past times buccaneers and revolutionists roused the echoes of its cliffs, and the condor wheeled perpetually above where, in the green groves, they made food for him with their matchlocks and toledos. Taken and retaken by sea rovers, by adverse powers and by sudden uprising of rebellious factions, the historic 300 miles of adventurous coast has scarcely known for hundreds of years whom rightly to call its master. Pizarro, Balboa, Sir Francis Drake, and Bolivar did what they could to make it a part of Christendom. Sir John Morgan, Lafitte, and other eminent swashbucklers bombarded and pounded it in the name of Abaddon.

The game still goes on. The guns of the rovers are silenced; but the tintype man, the enlarged photograph brigand, the kodaking tourist and the scouts of the gentle brigade of fakirs have found it out, and carry on the work. The hucksters of Germany, France, and Sicily now bag its small change across their counters. Gentleman adventurers throng the waiting-rooms of its rulers with proposals for railways and concessions. The little *opéra-bouffe* nations play at government and intrigue until some day a big, silent gunboat glides into the offing and warns them not to break their toys. And with these changes comes also the small adventurer, with empty pockets to fill, light of heart, busy-brained—the modern fairy prince, bearing an alarm clock with which, more surely than by the sentimental kiss, to awaken the beautiful tropics from their centuries' sleep. Generally he wears a shamrock, which he matches pridefully against the extravagant palms; and it is he who has driven Melpomene to the wings, and set Comedy to dancing before the footlights of the Southern Cross.

So, there is a little tale to tell of many things. Perhaps to the promiscuous ear of the Walrus it shall come with most avail; for in it there are indeed shoes and ships and sealing-wax and cabbage-palms and presidents instead of kings.

Add to these a little love and counterplotting, and scatter everywhere throughout the maze a trail of tropical dollars—dollars warmed no more by the torrid sun than by the hot palms of the scouts of Fortune—and, after all, here seems to be Life, itself, with talk enough to weary the most garrulous of Walruses.

"Fox-in-the-Morning"

Coralio reclined, in the mid-day heat, like some vacuous beauty lounging in a guarded harem. The town lay at the sea's edge on a strip of alluvial coast. It was set like a little pearl in an emerald band. Behind it, and seeming almost to topple, imminent, above it, rose the sea-following range of the Cordilleras. In front the sea was spread, a smiling jailer, but even more incorruptible than the frowning mountains. The waves swished along the smooth beach; the parrots screamed in the orange and ceiba-trees; the palms waved their limber fronds foolishly like an awkward chorus at the prima donna's cue to enter.

Suddenly the town was full of excitement. A native boy dashed down a grass-grown street, shrieking: *"Busca el Señor* Goodwin. "Ha venido en telegramma por él!"

The word passed quickly. Telegrams do not often come to anyone in Coralio. The cry for Señor Goodwin was taken up by a dozen officious voices. The main street running parallel to the beach became populated with those who desired to expedite the delivery of the despatch. Knots of women with complexions varying from palest olive to deepest brown gathered at street corners and plaintively carolled: *"Un telegrama por Señor* Goodwin!" The *comandante,* Don Señor el Coronel Encarnación Rios, who was loyal to the Ins and suspected Goodwin's devotion to the Outs, hissed: "Aha!" and wrote in his secret memorandum book the accusive fact the Señor Goodwin had on that momentous date received a telegram.

In the midst of the hullabaloo a man stepped to the door of a small wooden building and looked out. Above the door was a sign that read "Keogh and Clancy"—a nomenclature that seemed not to be indigenous to that tropical soil. The man in the door was Billy Keogh, scout of fortune and progress and latter-day rover of the Spanish Main. Tintypes and photographs were the weapons with which Keogh and Clancy were at that time assailing the hopeless shores. Outside the shop were set two large frames filled with specimens of their art and skill.

Keogh leaned in the doorway, his bold and humorous countenance wearing a look of interest at the unusual influx of life and sounded into the street. When the meaning of the disturbance became clear to him he placed a hand beside his mouth and shouted:

"Hey! Frank!" in such a robustious voice that the feeble clamor of the natives was drowned and silenced.

Fifty yards away, on the seaward side of the street, stood the abode of the consul for the United States. Out from the door of this building tumbled Goodwin at the call. He had been smoking with Willard Geddie, the consul, on the back porch of the consulate, which was conceeded to be the coolest spot in Coralio.

"Hurry up," shouted Keogh. "There's a riot in town on account of a telegram that's come for you. You want to be careful about these things, my boy. It won't do to trifle with the feelings of the public this way. You'll be getting a pink note some day with violet scent on it; and then the country'll be steeped in the throes of a revolution."

Goodwin had strolled up the street and met the boy with the message. The ox-eyed women gazed at him with shy admiration, for his type drew them. He was big, blond, and jauntily dressed in white linen, with buckskin *zapatos.* His manner was courtly, with a sort of kindly truculence in it tempered by a merciful eye. When the telegram had been delivered, and the bearer of it dismissed with a gratuity, the relieved populace returned to the contiguities of shade from which curiosity had drawn it—the women to their baking in the mud ovens under the orange-trees, or to the interminable combing of their long, straight hair; the men to their cigarettes and gossip in the cantinas.

Goodwin sat on Keogh's doorstep and read his telegram. It was from Bob Englehart, an American, who lived in San Mateo, the capital city of Anchuria, eighty miles in the interior. Englehart was a gold miner, an ardent revolutionist and "good people." That he was a man of resource and imagination was proven by the telegram he had sent. It had been his task to send a confidential message to his friend in Coralio. This could not have been accomplished in either Spanish or English, for the eye politic in Anchuria was an active one. The Ins and the Outs were perpetually on their guard. But Englehart was a diplomatist. There existed but one code upon which he might make requisition with promise of safety—the great and potent code of Slang. So, here is the message that slipped, unconstrued, through the fingers of curious officials, and came to the eye of Goodwin:

> His Nibs skedaddled yesterday per jack-rabbit line with all the coin in the kitty and the bundle of muslin he's spoony about. The boodle is six figures short. Our crowd in good shape, but we need the spondulicks. You collar it. The main guy and the dry goods are headed for the briny. You know what to do.
>
> Bob

This screed, remarkable as it was, had no mystery for Goodwin. He was the most successful of the small advance-guard of speculative Americans that had invaded Anchuria, and he had not reached that enviable pinnacle without having well exercised the arts of foresight and deduction. He had taken up political intrigue as a matter of business. He was acute enough to wield a certain influence among the leading schemers, and he was prosperous enough to be able to purchase the respect of the petty office-holders. There was always a revolutionary party; and to it he had always allied himself; for the adherents of a new administration received the rewards of their labors. There was now a Liberal party seeking to overturn President Miraflores. If the wheel successfully revolved, Goodwin stood to win a concession to 30,000 manzanas of the finest coffee lands in the interior. Certain incidents in the recent career of President Miraflores had excited a shrewd suspicion in Goodwin's mind that the government was near a dissolution from another cause than that of a revolution, and now Englehart's telegram had come as a corroboration of his wisdom.

The telegram, which had remained unintelligible to the Anchurian linguists who had applied to it in vain their knowledge of Spanish and elemental English, conveyed a stimulating piece of news to Goodwin's understanding. It informed him that the president of the republic had decamped from the capital city with the contents of the treasury. Furthermore, that he was accompanied in his flight by that winning adventuress Isabel Guilbert, the opera singer, whose troupe of performers had been entertained by the president at San Mateo during the past month on a scale less modest than that with which royal visitors are often content. The reference to the "jackrabbit line" could mean nothing else than the muleback system of transport that prevailed between Coralio and the capital. The hint that the "boodle" was "six figures short" made the condition of the national treasury lamentably clear. Also it was convincingly true that the ingoing party—its way now made a pacific one—would need the "spondulicks." Unless its pledges should be fulfilled, and the spoils held for the delectation of the victors, precarious indeed would be the position of the new government. Therefore it was exceeding necessary to "collar the main guy," and recapture the sinews of war and government.

Goodwin handed the message to Keogh.

"Read that, Billy," he said. "It's from Bob Englehart. Can you manage the cipher?"

Keogh sat in the other half of the doorway, and carefully perused the telegram.

" 'Tis not a cipher," he said, finally. " 'Tis what they call literature, and that's a system of language put in the mouths of people that they've never been introduced to by writers of imagination. The magazines invented it, but I never knew before that President Norvin Green had stamped it with the seal of his approval. 'Tis now no longer literature, but language. The dictionaries tried, but they couldn't make it go for anything but dialect. Sure, now that the Western Union indorses it, it won't be long till a race of people will spring up that speaks it."

"You're running too much to philology, Billy," said Goodwin. "Do you make out the meaning of it?"

"Sure," replied the philosopher of Fortune. "All languages come easy to the man who must know 'em. I've even failed to misunderstand an order to evacuate in classical Chinese when it was backed up by the muzzle of a breech-loader. This little literary essay I hold in my hands means a game of Fox-in-the-Morning. Ever play that, Frank, when you was a kid?"

"I think so," said Goodwin, laughing. "You join hands all 'round, and ——"

"You do not," interrupted Keogh. "You've got a fine sporting game mixed up in your head with 'All Around the Rosebush.' The spirit of 'Fox-in-the-Morning' is opposed to the holding of hands. I'll tell you how it's played. This president man and his companion in play, they stand up over in San Mateo, ready for the run, and shout: 'Fox-in-the-Morning!' Me and you, standing here, we say: 'Goose and the Gander!' They say: 'How many miles is it to London town?' We say: 'Only a few, if your legs are long enough. How many comes out?' They say: 'More than you're able to catch.' And then the game commences."

"I catch the idea," said Goodwin. "It won't do to let the goose and gander slip through our fingers, Billy; their feathers are too valuable. Our crowd is prepared and able to step into the shoes of the government at once; but with the treasury empty we'd stay in power about as long as a tenderfoot would stick on an untamed bronco. We must play the fox on every foot of the coast to prevent their getting out of the country."

"By the mule-back schedule," said Keogh, "it's five days down from San Mateo. We've got plenty of time to set our outposts. There's only three places on the coast where they can hope to sail from—here and Solitas and Alazan. They're the only points we'll have to guard. It's as easy as a chess problem—fox to play, and mate in three moves. Oh, goosey, goosey, gander, whither do you wander? By the blessing of the literary telegraph the boodle of this benighted fatherland shall be preserved to the honest political party that is seeking to overthrow it."

The situation had been justly outlined by Keogh. The down trail from the capital was at all times a weary road to travel. A jiggety-joggety journey it was; ice-cold and hot, wet and dry. The trail climbed appalling mountains, wound like a rotten string about the brows of breathless precipices, plunged through chilling snow-fed streams, and wriggled like a snake through sunless forests teeming with menacing insect and animal life. After descending to the foothills it turned to a trident, the central prong ending at Alazan. Another branched off to Coralio; the third penetrated to Solitas. Between the sea and the foothills stretched the five miles breadth of alluvial coast. Here was the flora of the tropics in its rankest and most prodigal growth. Spaces here and there had been wrested from the jungle and planted with bananas and cane and orange groves. The rest was a riot of wild vegetation, the home of monkeys, tapirs, jaguars, alligators and prodigious reptiles and insects. Where no road was cut a serpent could scarcely make its way through the tangle of vines and creepers. Across the treacherous mangrove swamps few things without wings could safely pass. Therefore the fugitives could hope to reach the coast only by one of the routes named.

"Keep the matter quiet, Billy," advised Goodwin, "We don't want the Ins to know that the president is in flight. I suppose Bob's information is something of a scoop in the capital as yet. Otherwise he would not have tried to make his message a confidential one; and besides, everybody would have heard the news. I'm going around now to see Dr. Zavalla, and start a man up the trail to cut the telegraph wire."

As Goodwin rose, Keogh threw his hat upon the grass by the door and expelled a tremendous sigh.

"What's the trouble, Billy?" asked Goodwin, pausing. "That's the first time I ever heard you sigh."

" 'Tis the last," said Keogh. "With that sorrowful puff of wind I resign myself to a life of praiseworthy but harassing honesty. What are tintypes, if you please, to the opportunities of the great and hilarious class of ganders and geese? Not that I would be a president, Frank—and the boodle he's got is too big for me to handle—but in some ways I feel my conscience hurting me for addicting myself to photographing a nation instead of running away with it. Frank, did you ever see the 'bundle of muslin' that His Excellency has wrapped up and carried off?"

"Isabel Guilbert?" said Goodwin, laughing. "No, I never did. From what I've heard of her, though, I imagine that she wouldn't stick at anything to carry her point. Don't get romantic, Billy. Sometimes I begin to fear that there's Irish blood in your ancestry."

"I never saw her either," went on Keogh; "but they say she's got all the ladies of mythology, sculpture, and fiction reduced to chromos. They say she can look at a man once, and he'll turn monkey and climb trees to pick cocoanuts for her. Think of that president man with Lord knows how many hundreds of thousands of dollars in one hand, and this muslin siren in the other, galloping down hill on a sympathetic mule amid songbirds and flowers! And here is Billy Keogh, because he is virtuous, condemned to the unprofitable swindle of slandering the faces of missing links on tin for an honest living! 'Tis an injustice of nature."

"Cheer up," said Goodwin. "You are a pretty poor fox to be envying a gander. Maybe the enchanting Guilbert will take a fancy to you and your tintypes after we impoverish her royal escort."

"She could do worse," reflected Keogh; "but she won't. 'Tis not a tintype gallery, but the gallery of the gods that she's fitted to adorn. She's a very wicked lady, and the president man is in luck. But I hear Clancy swearing in the back room for having to do all the work." And Keogh plunged for the rear of the "gallery," whistling gaily in a spontaneous way that belied his recent sigh over the questionable good luck of the flying president.

Goodwin turned from the main street into a much narrower one that intersected it at a right angle.

These side streets were covered by a growth of thick, rank grass, which was kept to a navigable shortness by the machetes of the police. Stone sidewalks, little more than a ledge in width, ran along the base of the mean and monotonous adobe houses. At the outskirts of the village these streets dwindled to nothing; and here were set the palm-thatched huts of the Caribs and the poorer natives, and the shabby cabins of negroes from Jamaica and the West India islands. A few structures raised their heads above the red-tiled roofs of the one-story houses—the bell tower of the *Calaboza,* the Hotel de los Estranjeros, the residence of the Vesuvius Fruit Company's agent, the store and residence of Bernard Brannigan, a ruined cathedral in which Columbus had once set foot, and, most imposing of all, the Casa Morena—the summer "White House" of the President of Anchuria. On the principal street running along the beach—the Broadway of Coralio—were the larger stores, the government *bodega* and postoffice, the *cuartel,* the rum-shops and the market place.

On his way Goodwin passed the house of Bernard Brannigan. It was a modern wooden building, two stories in height. The ground floor was occupied by Brannigan's store, the upper one contained the living apartments. A wide cool porch ran around the house half way up its outer walls. A handsome, vivacious girl neatly dressed in flowing white leaned over the railing and smiled down upon Goodwin. She was no darker than many an Andalusian of high descent, and she sparkled and glowed like a tropical moonlight.

"Good evening, Miss Paula," said Goodwin, taking off his hat, with his ready smile. There was little difference in his manner whether he addressed women or men. Everybody in Coralio like to receive the salutation of the big American.

"Is there any news, Mr. Goodwin? Please don't say no. Isn't it warm? I feel just like Mariana in her moated grange—or was it a range?—it's hot enough."

"No, there's no news to tell, I believe," said Goodwin, with a mischievous look in his eye, "except that old Geddie is getting grumpier and crosser every day. If something doesn't happen to relieve his mind I'll have to quit smoking on his back porch—and there's no other place available that is cool enough."

"He isn't grumpy," said Paula Brannigan, impulsively, "when he——"

But she ceased suddenly, and drew back with a deepening color; for her mother had been a *mestizo* lady, and the Spanish blood had brought to Paula a certain shyness that was an adornment to the other half of her demonstrative nature.

The Lotus and the Bottle

Willard Geddie, consul for the United States in Coralio, was working leisurely on his yearly report. Goodwin, who had strolled in as he did daily for a smoke on the much coveted porch, had found him so absorbed in his work that he departed after roundly abusing the consul for his lack of hospitality.

"I shall complain to the civil service department," said Goodwin;—"or is it a department?—perhaps it's only a theory. One gets neither civility nor service from you. You won't talk; and you won't set out anything to drink. What kind of a way is that of representing your government?"

Goodwin strolled out and across to the hotel to see if he could bully the quarantine doctor into a game on Coralio's solitary billiard table. His plans were completed for the interception of the fugitives from the capital, and now it was but a waiting game that he had to play.

The consul was interested in his report. He was only twenty-four; and he had not been in Coralio long enough for his enthusiasm to cool in the heat of the tropics—a paradox that may be allowed between Cancer and Capricorn.

So many thousand bunches of bananas, so many thousand oranges and cocoanuts, so many ounces of gold dust, pounds of rubber, coffee, indigo and sarsaparilla—actually, exports were twenty percent greater than for the previous year!

A little thrill of satisfaction ran through the consul. Perhaps, he thought, the State Department, upon reading his introduction, would notice—and then he leaned back in his chair and laughed. He was getting as bad as the others. For the moment he had forgotten that Coralio was an insignificant town in an insignificant republic lying along the by-ways of a second-rate sea. He thought of Gregg, the quarantine doctor, who subscribed for the London *Lancet,* expecting to find it quoting his reports to the home Board of Health concerning the yellow fever germ. The consul knew that not one in fifty of his acquaintances in the States had ever heard of Coralio. He knew that two men, at any rate, would have to read his report—some underling in the State Department and a compositor in the Public Printing Office. Perhaps the typesticker would note the increase of commerce in Coralio, and speak of it, over the cheese and beer, to a friend.

He had just written: "Most unaccountable is the supineness of the large exporters in the United States in permitting the French and German houses to practically control the trade interests of this rich and productive country"—when he heard the hoarse notes of a steamer's siren.

Geddie laid down his pen and gathered his Panama hat and umbrella. By the sound he knew it to be the *Valhalla,* one of the line of fruit vessels plying for the Vesuvius Company. Down to *niños* of five years, everyone in Coralio could name you each incoming steamer by the note of her siren.

The consul sauntered by a roundabout, shaded way to the beach. By reason of long practice he gauged his stroll so accurately that by the time he arrived on the sandy shore the boat of the customs officials was rowing back from the steamer, which had been boarded and inspected according to the laws of Anchuria.

There is no harbor at Coralio. Vessels of the draught of the *Valhalla* must ride at anchor a mile from shore. When they take on fruit it is conveyed on lighters and freighter sloops. At Solitas, where there was a fine harbor, ships of many kinds were to be seen, but in the roadstead off Coralio scarcely any save the fruiters paused. Now and then a tramp coaster, or a mysterious brig from Spain, or a saucy French barque would hang innocently for a few days in the offing. Then the custom-house crew would become doubly vigilant and wary. At night a sloop or two would be making strange trips in and out along the shore; and in the morning the stock of Three-Star Hennessey, wines and drygoods in Coralio would be found vastly increased. It has also been said that the customs officials jingled more silver in the pockets of their red-striped trousers, and that the record books showed no increase in import duties received.

The customs boat and the *Valhalla* gig reached the shore at the same time. When they grounded in the shallow water there was still five yards of rolling surf between them and dry sand. Then half-clothed Caribs dashed into the water, and brought in on their backs the *Valhalla's* purser and the little native officials in their cotton undershirts, blue trousers with red stripes, and flapping straw hats.

At college Geddie had been a treasure as a first-baseman. He now closed his umbrella, stuck it upright in the sand, and stooped, with his hands resting upon his knees. The purser, burlesquing the pitcher's contortions, hurled at the consul the heavy roll of newspapers, tied with a string, that the steamer always brought for him. Geddie leaped high and caught the roll with a sounding "thwack."

The loungers on the beach—about a third of the population of the town—laughed and applauded delightedly. Every week they expected to see that roll of papers delivered and received in that same manner, and they were never disappointed. Innovations did not flourish in Coralio.

The consul re-hoisted his umbrella and walked back to the consulate.

This home of a great nation's representative was a wooden structure of two rooms, with a native-built gallery of poles, bamboo and nipa palm running on three sides of it. One room was the official apartment, furnished chastely with a flat-top desk, a hammock, and three uncomfortable cane-seated chairs. Engravings of the first and latest president of the country represented hung against the wall. The other room was the consul's living apartment.

It was eleven o'clock when he returned from the beach, and therefore breakfast time. Chanca, the Carib woman who cooked for him, was just serving the meal on the side of the gallery facing the sea—a spot famous as the coolest in Coralio. The breakfast consisted of shark's fin soup, stew of land crabs, breadfruit, a boiled iguana steak, aguacates, a freshly cut pineapple, claret and coffee.

Geddie took his seat, and unrolled with luxurious laziness his bundle of newspapers. Here in Coralio for two days or longer he would read of goings-on in the world very much as we of the world read those whimsical contributions to inexact science that assume to portray the doings of the Martians. After he had finished with the papers they would be sent on the rounds of the other English-speaking residents of the town.

The paper that came first to his hand was one of those bulky mattresses of printed stuff upon which the readers of certain New York journals are supposed to take their Sabbath literary nap. Opening this the consul rested it upon the table, supporting its weight with the aid of the back of a chair. Then he partook of his meal deliberately, turning the leaves from time to time and glancing half idly at the contents.

Presently he was struck by something familiar to him in a picture—a half-page, badly printed reproduction of a photograph of a vessel. Languidly interested, he leaned for a nearer scrutiny and a view of the florid headlines of the column next to the picture.

Yes; he was not mistaken. The engraving was of the eight-hundred-ton yacht *Idalia,* belonging to "that prince of good fellows, Midas of the money market, and society's pink of perfection, J. Ward Tolliver."

Slowly sipping his black coffee, Geddie read the column of print.

Following a listed statement of Mr. Tolliver's real estate and bonds, came a description of the yacht's furnishings, and then the grain of news no bigger than a mustard seed. Mr. Tolliver, with a party of favored guests, would sail the next day on a six weeks' cruise along the Central American and South American coasts and among the Bahama Islands. Among the guests were Mrs. Cumberland Payne and Miss Ida Payne, of Norfolk.

The writer, with the fatuous presumption that was demanded of him by his readers, had concocted a romance suited to their palates. He bracketed the names of Miss Payne and Mr. Tolliver until he had well-nigh read the marriage ceremony over them. He played coyly and insinuatingly upon the strings of *"on dit"* and "Madame Rumor" and "a little bird" and "no one would be surprised," and ended with congratulations.

Geddie, having finished his breakfast, took his papers to the edge of the gallery, and sat there in his favorite steamer chair with his feet on the bamboo railing. He lighted a cigar, and looked out upon the sea. He felt a glow of satisfaction at finding he was so little disturbed by what he had read. He told himself that he had conquered the distress that had sent him, a voluntary exile, to this far land of the lotus. He could never forget Ida, of course; but there was no longer any pain in thinking about her. When they had had that misunderstanding and quarrel he had impulsively sought his consulship with the desire to retaliate upon her by detaching himself from her world and presence. He had succeeded thoroughly in that. During the twelve months of his life in Coralio no word had passed between them, though he had sometimes heard of her through the dilatory correspondence with the few friends to whom he still wrote. Still he could not repress a little thrill of satisfaction at knowing that she had not yet married Tolliver or any one else. But evidently Tolliver had not yet abandoned hope.

Well, it made no difference to him now. He had eaten of the lotus. He was happy and content in this land of perpetual afternoon. Those old days of life in the States seemed like an irritating dream. He hoped Ida would be as happy as he was. The climate as balmy as that of distant Avalon; the fetterless, idyllic round of enchanted days; the life among this indolent, romantic people—a life full of music, flowers, and low laughter; the influence of the imminent sea and mountains, and the many shapes of love and magic and beauty that bloomed in the white tropic nights—with all he was more than content. Also, there was Paula Brannigan.

Geddie intended to marry Paula—if, of course, she would consent; but he felt rather sure that she would do that. Somehow, he kept postponing his proposal. Several times he had been quite near to it; but a mysterious something always held him back. Perhaps it was only the unconscious, instinctive conviction that the act would sever the last tie that bound him to his old world.

He could be very happy with Paula. Few of the native girls could be compared with her. She had attended a convent school in New Orleans for two years; and when she chose to display her accomplishments no one could detect any difference between her and the girls of Norfolk and Manhattan. But it was delicious to see her at home dressed, as she sometimes was, in the native costume, with bare shoulders and flowing sleeves.

Bernard Brannigan was the great merchant of Coralio. Besides his store, he maintained a train of pack mules, and carried on a lively trade with the interior towns and villages. He had married a native lady of high Castilian descent, but with a tinge of Indian brown showing through her olive cheek. The union of the Irish and the Spanish had produced, as it so often has, an offshoot of rare beauty and variety. They were very excellent people indeed, and the upper story of their house was ready to be placed at the service of Geddie and Paula as soon as he should make up his mind to speak aboout it.

By the time two hours were whiled away the consul tired of reading. The papers lay scattered about him on the gallery. Reclining there, he gazed dreamily out upon an Eden. A clump of banana plants interposed their broad shields between him and the sun. The gentle slope from the consulate to the sea was covered with the dark-green foliage of lemon-trees and orange-trees just bursting into bloom. A lagoon pierced the land like a dark, jagged crystal, and above it a pale ceiba-tree rose almost to the clouds. The waving cocoanut palms on the beach flared their decorative green leaves against the slate of an almost quiescent sea. His senses were cognizant of brilliant scarlet and ochres amid the vert of the coppice, of odors of fruit and bloom and the smoke from Chanca's clay oven under the calabash-tree; of the treble laughter of the native women in their huts, the song of the robin, the salt taste of the breeze, the diminuendo of the faint surf running along the shore—and, gradually, of a white speck, growing to a blur, that introduced itself upon the drab prospect of the sea.

Lazily interested, he watched this blur increase until it became the *Idalia* steaming at full speed, coming down the coast. Without changing his position he kept his eyes upon the beautiful white yacht as she drew swiftly near and came opposite to Coralio. Then, sitting upright, he saw her float steadily past and on. Scarcely a mile of sea had separated her from the shore. He had seen the frequent flash of her polished brass work and the stripes of her deck-awnings—so much, and no more. Like a ship on a magic lantern slide the *Idalia* had crossed the illuminated circle of the consul's little world, and was gone. Save for the tiny cloud of smoke that was left hanging over the brim of the sea, she might have been an immaterial thing, a chimera of his idle brain.

Geddie went into his office and sat down to dawdle over his report. If the reading of the article in the paper had left him unshaken, this silent passing of the *Idalia* had done for him still more. It had brought the calm and peace of a situation from which all uncertainty had been erased. He knew that men sometimes hope without being aware of it. Now, since she had come two thousand miles and had passed without a sign, not even his unconscious self need cling to the past any longer.

After dinner, when the sun was low behind the mountains, Geddie walked on the little strip of beach under the cocoanuts. The wind was blowing mildly landward, and the surface of the sea was rippled by tiny wavelets.

A miniature breaker, spreading with a soft "swish" upon the sand, brought with it something round and shiny that rolled back again as the wave receded. The next influx beached it clear, and Geddie picked it up. The thing was a long-necked wine bottle of colorless glass. The cork had been driven in tightly to the level of the mouth, and the end covered with dark-red sealing-wax. The bottle contained only what seemed to be a sheet of paper, much curled from the manipulation it had undergone while being inserted. In the sealing-wax was the impression of a seal—probably of a signet-ring, bearing the initials of a monogram; but the impression had been hastily made, and the letters were past anything more certain than a shrewd conjecture. Ida Payne had always worn a signet-ring in preference to any other finger decoration. Geddie thought he could make out the familiar "I P"; and a queer sensation of disquietude went over him. More personal and intimate was this reminder of her than had been the sight of the vessel she was doubtless on. He walked back to his house, and set the bottle on his desk.

Throwing off his hat and coat, and lighting a lamp—for the night had crowded precipitately upon the brief twilight—he began to examine his piece of sea salvage.

By holding the bottle near the light and turning it judiciously, he made out that it contained a double sheet of note-paper filled with close writing; further, that the paper was of the same size and shade as that always used by Ida; and that, to the best of his belief, the handwriting was hers. The imperfect glass of the bottle so distorted the rays of light that he could read no word of the writing; but certain capital letters, of which he caught comprehensive glimpses, were Ida's, he felt sure.

There was a little smile both of perplexity and amusement in Geddie's eyes as he set the bottle down, and laid three cigars side by side on his desk. He fetched his steamer chair from the gallery, and stretched himself comfortably. He would smoke those three cigars while considering the problem.

For it amounted to a problem. He almost wished that he had not found the bottle; but the bottle was there. Why should it have drifted in from the sea, whence come so many disquieting things, to disturb his peace?

In this dreamy land, where time seemed so redundant, he had fallen into the habit of bestowing much thought upon even trifling matters.

He began to speculate upon many fanciful theories concerning the story of the bottle, rejecting each in turn.

Ships in danger of wreck or disablement sometimes cast forth such precarious messengers calling for aid. But he had seen the *Idalia* not three hours before, safe and speeding. Suppose the crew had mutinied and imprisoned the passengers below, and the message was one begging for succor! But, premising such an improbable outrage, would the agitated captives have taken the pains to fill four pages of note-paper with carefully penned arguments to their rescue?

Thus by elimination he soon rid the matter of the more unlikely theories, and was reduced—though aversely—to the less assailable one that the bottle contained a message to himself. Ida knew he was in Coralio; she must have launched the bottle while the yacht was passing and the wind blowing fairly toward the shore.

As soon as Geddie reached this conclusion a wrinkle came between his brows and a stubborn look settled around his mouth. He sat looking out through the doorway at the gigantic fire-flies traversing the quiet streets.

If this was a message to him from Ida, what could it mean save an overture toward a reconciliation? And if that, why had she not used the safe methods of the post instead of this uncertain and even flippant means of communication? A note in an empty bottle, cast into the sea! There was something light and frivolous about it, if not actually contemptuous.

The thought stirred his pride and subdued whatever emotions had been resurrected by the finding of the bottle.

Geddie put on his coat and hat and walked out. He followed a street that led him along the border of the little plaza where a band was playing and people were rambling, care-free and indolent. Some timorous *señoritas* scurrying past with fire-flies tangled in the jetty braids of their hair glanced at him with shy, flattering eyes. The air was languorous with the scent of jasmin and orange-blossoms.

The consul stayed his steps at the house of Bernard Brannigan. Paula was swinging in a hammock on the gallery. She rose from it like a bird from its nest. The color came to her cheek at the sound of Geddie's voice.

He was charmed at the sight of her costume—a flounced muslin dress, with a little jacket of white flannel, all made with neatness and style. He suggested a stroll, and they walked out to the old Indian well on the hill road. They sat on the curb, and there Geddie made the expected but long-deferred speech. Certain though he had been that she would not say him nay, he was thrilled with joy at the completeness and sweetness of her surrender. Here was surely a heart made for love and steadfastness. Here was no caprice or questionings or captious standards of convention.

When Geddie kissed Paula at her door that night he was happier than he had ever been before. "Here in this hollow lotus land, ever to live and lie reclined" seemed to him, as it has seemed to many mariners, the best as well as the easiest. His future would be an ideal one. He had attained a Paradise without a serpent. His Eve would be indeed a part of him, unbeguiled, and therefore more beguiling. He had made his decision tonight, and his heart was full of serene, assured content.

Geddie went back to his house whistling that finest and saddest love song, "La Golondrina." At the door his tame monkey leaped down from his shelf, chattering briskly. The consul turned to his desk to get him some nuts he usually kept there. Reaching in the half-darkness, his hand struck against the bottle. He started as if he had touched the cold rotundity of a serpent.

He had forgotten that the bottle was there.

He lighted the lamp and fed the monkey. Then, very deliberately, he lighted a cigar, and took the bottle in his hand, and walked down the path to the beach.

There was a moon, and the sea was glorious. The breeze had shifted, as it did each evening, and was now rushing steadily seaward.

Stepping to the water's edge, Geddie hurled the unopened bottle far out into the sea. It disappeared for a moment, and then shot upward twice its length. Geddie stood still, watching it. The moonlight was so bright that he could see it bobbing up and down with the little waves. Slowly it receded from the shore, flashing and turning as it went. The wind was carrying it out to sea. Soon it became a mere speck, doubtfully discerned at irregular intervals; and then the mystery of it was swallowed up by the greater mystery of the ocean. Geddie stood still upon the beach, smoking and looking out upon the water.

"Simon!—Oh, Simon!—wake up there, Simon!" bawled a sonorous voice at the edge of the water.

Old Simon Cruz was a half-breed fisherman and smuggler who lived in a hut on the beach. Out of his earliest nap Simon was thus awakened.

He slipped on his shoes and went outside. Just landing from one of the *Valhalla's* boats was the third mate of that vessel, who was an acquaintance of Simon's, and three sailors from the fruiter.

"Go up, Simon," called the mate, "and find Dr. Gregg or Mr. Goodwin or anybody that's a friend to Mr. Geddie, and bring 'em here at once."

"Saints of the skies!" said Simon, sleepily, "nothing has happened to Mr. Geddie?"

"He's under that tarpauling," said the mate, pointing to the boat, "and he's rather more than half drowned. We seen him from the steamer nearly a mile out from shore, swimmin' like mad after a bottle that was floatin' in the water, outward bound. We lowered the gig and started for him. He nearly had his hand on the bottle, when he gave out and went under. We pulled him out in time to save him, maybe; but the doctor is the one to decide that."

"A bottle?" said the old man, rubbing his eyes. He was not yet fully awake. "Where is the bottle?"

"Driftin' along out there some'eres," said the mate, jerking his thumb toward the sea. "Get on with you, Simon.

Smith

Goodwin and the ardent patriot, Zavalla, took all the precautions that their foresight could contrive to prevent the escape of President Miraflores and his companion. They sent trusted messengers up the coast to Solitas and Alazan to warn the local leaders of the flight, and to instruct them to patrol the water line and arrest the fugitives at all hazards should they reveal themselves in that territory. After this was done there remained only to cover the district about Coralio and await the coming of the quarry. The nets were well spread. The roads were so few, the opportunities for embarkation so limited, and the two or three probable points of exit so well guarded that it would be strange indeed if there should slip through the meshes so much of the country's dignity, romance, and collateral. The president would, without doubt, move as secretly as possible, and endeavor to board a vessel by stealth from some secluded point along the shore.

On the fourth day after the receipt of Englehart's telegram the *Karlsefin,* a Norwegian steamer chartered by the New Orleans fruit trade, anchored off Coralio with three hoarse toots of her siren. The *Karlsefin* was not one of the line operated by the Vesuvius Fruit Company. She was something of a dilettante, doing odd jobs for a company that was scarcely important enough to figure as a rival to the Vesuvius. The movements of the *Karlsefin* were dependent upon the state of the market. Sometimes she would ply steadily between the Spanish Main and New Orleans in the regular transport of fruit; next she would be making erratic trips to Mobile or Charleston, or even as far north as New York, according to the distribution of the fruit supply.

Goodwin lounged upon the beach with the usual crowd of idlers that had gathered to view the steamer. Now that President Miraflores might be expected to reach the borders of his adjured country at any time, the orders were to keep a strict and unrelenting watch. Every vessel that approached the shores might now be considered a possible means of escape for the fugitives; and an eye was kept even on the sloops and dories that belonged to the sea-going contingent of Coralio. Goodwin and Zavalla moved everywhere, but without ostentation, watching the loopholes of escape.

The customs officials crowded importantly into their boat and rowed out to the *Karlsefin.* A boat from the steamer landed her purser with his papers, and took out the quarantine doctor with his green umbrella and clinical thermometer. Next a swarm of Caribs began to load upon lighters the thousands of bunches of bananas heaped upon the shore and row them out to the steamer. The *Karlsefin* had no passenger list, and was soon done with the attention of the authorities. The purser declared that the steamer would remain at anchor until morning, taking on her fruit during the night. The *Karlsefin* had come, he said, from New York, to which port her latest load of oranges and cocoanuts had been conveyed. Two or three of the freighter sloops were engaged to assist in the work, for the captain was anxious to make a quick return in order to reap the advantage offered by a certain dearth of fruit in the States.

About four o'clock in the afternoon another of those marine monsters, not very familiar in those waters, hove in sight, following the fateful *Idalia*—a graceful steam yacht, painted a light buff, clean-cut as a steel engraving. The beautiful vessel hovered off shore, see-sawing the waves as lightly as a duck in a rain barrel. A swift boat manned by a crew in uniform came ashore, and a stocky-built man leaped to the sands.

The new-comer seemed to turn a disapproving eye upon the rather motley congregation of native Anchurians, and made his way at once toward Goodwin, who was the most conspicuously Anglo-Saxon figure present. Goodwin greeted him with courtesy.

Conversation developed that the newly landed one was named Smith, and that he had come in a yacht. A meagre biography, truly; for the yacht was most apparent; and the "Smith" not beyond a reasonable guess before the revelation. Yet to the eye of Goodwin, who had seen several things, there was a discrepancy between Smith and his yacht. A bullet-headed man Smith was, with an oblique, dead eye and the moustache of a cocktail-mixer. And unless he had shifted costumes before putting off for shore he had affronted the deck of his correct vessel clad in a pearl-gray derby, a gay plaid suit and vaudeville neckwear. Men owning pleasure yachts generally harmonize better with them.

Smith looked business, but he was no advertiser. He commented upon the scenery, remarking upon its fidelity to the pictures in the geography; and then inquired for the United States consul. Goodwin pointed out the starred-and-striped bunting hanging above the little consulate, which was concealed behind the orange-trees.

"Mr. Geddie, the consul, will be sure to be there," said Goodwin. "He was very nearly drowned a few days ago while taking a swim in the sea, and the doctor has ordered him to remain indoors for some time."

Smith plowed his way through the sand to the consulate, his haberdashery creating violent discord against the smooth tropical blues and greens.

Geddie was lounging in his hammock, somewhat pale of face and languid in pose. On that night when the *Valhalla's* boat had brought him ashore apparently drenched to death by the sea, Dr. Gregg and his other friends had toiled for hours to preserve the little spark of life that remained to him. The bottle, with its impotent message, was gone out to sea, and the problem that it had provoked was reduced to a simple sum in addition—one and one make two, by the rule of arithmetic; one by the rule of romance.

There is a quaint old theory that man may have two souls—a peripheral one which serves ordinarily, and a central one which is stirred only at certain times, but then with activity and vigor. While under the domination of the former a man will shave, vote, pay taxes, give money to his family, buy subscription books and comport himself on the average plan. But let the central soul suddenly become dominant, and he may, in the twinkling of an eye, turn upon the partner of his joys with furious execration; he may change his politics while you could snap your fingers; he may deal out deadly insult to his dearest friend; he may get him, instanter, to a monastery or a dance hall; he may elope, or hang himself—or he may write a song or poem, or kiss his wife unasked, or give his funds to the search of a microbe. Then the peripheral soul will return; and we have our safe, sane citizen again. It is but the revolt of the Ego against Order; and its effect is to shake up the atoms only that they may settle where they belong.

Geddie's revulsion had been a mild one—no more than a swim in a summer sea after so inglorious an object as a drifting bottle. And now he was himself again. Upon his desk, ready for the post, was a letter to his government tendering his resignation as consul, to be effective as soon as another could be appointed in his place. For Bernard Brannigan, who never did things in a half-way manner, was to take Geddie at once for a partner in his very profitable and various enterprises; and Paula was happily engaged in plans for refurnishing and decorating the upper story of the Brannigan house.

The consul rose from his hammock when he saw the conspicuous stranger in his door.

"Keep your seat, old man," said the visitor, with an airy wave of his large hand. "My name's Smith; and I've come in a yacht. You are the consul—is that right? A big, cool guy on the beach directed me here. Thought I'd pay my respects to the flag."

"Sit down," said Geddie. "I've been admiring your craft ever since it came in sight. Looks like a fast sailer. What's her tonnage?"

"Search me!" said Smith. "I don't know what she weighs in at. But she's got a tidy gait. The *Rambler*—that's her name—don't take the dust of anything afloat. This is my first trip on her. I'm taking a squint along this coast just to get an idea of the countries where the rubber and red pepper and revolutions come from. I had no idea there was so much scenery down here. Why, Central Park ain't in it with this neck of the woods. I'm from New York. They get monkeys, and cocoanuts, and parrots down here—is that right?"

"We have them all," said Geddie. "I'm quite sure that our fauna and flora would take a prize over Central Park."

"Maybe they would," admitted Smith, cheerfully. "I haven't seen them yet. But I guess you've got us skinned on the animal and vegetation question. You don't have much travel here, do you?"

"Travel?" queried the consul. "I suppose you mean passengers on the steamers. No; very few people land in Coralio. An investor now and then—tourists and sight-seers generally go further down the coast to one of the larger towns where there is a harbor."

"I see a ship out there loading up with bananas," said Smith. "Any passengers come on her?"

"That's the *Karlsefin,*" said the consul. "She's a tramp fruiter—made her last trip to New York, I believe. No; she brought no passengers. I saw her boat come ashore, and there was no one. About the only exciting recreation we have here is watching steamers when they arrive; and a passenger on one of them generally causes the whole town to turn out. If you are going to remain in Coralio a while, Mr. Smith, I'll be glad to take you around to meet some people. There are four or five American chaps that are good to know, besides the native high-fliers."

"Thanks," said the yachtsman, "but I wouldn't put you to the trouble. I'd like to meet the guys you speak of, but I won't be here long enough to do much knocking around. That cool gent on the beach spoke of a doctor; can you tell me where I could find him? The *Rambler* ain't quite as steady on her feet as a Broadway hotel; and a fellow gets a touch of seasickness now and then. Thought I'd strike the croaker for a handful of the little sugar pills, in case I need 'em."

"You will be apt to find Dr. Gregg at the hotel," said the consul. "You can see it from the door—it's that two-story building with the balcony, where the orange-trees are."

The Hotel de los Estranjeros was a dreary hostelry, in great disuse both by strangers and friends. It stood at a corner of the Street of the Holy Sepulchre. A grove of small orange-trees crowded against one side of it, enclosed by a low, rock wall over which a tall man might easily step. The house was of plastered adobe, stained a hundred shades of color by the salt breeze and the sun. Upon its upper balcony opened a central door and two windows containing broad jalousies instead of sashes.

The lower floor communicated by two doorways with the narrow, rock-paved sidewalk. The *pulperia*—or drinking shop—of the proprietress, Madama Timotea Ortiz, occupied the ground floor. On the bottles of brandy, *anisada,* Scotch "smoke" and inexpensive wines behind the little counter the dust lay thick save where the fingers of infrequent customers had left irregular prints. The upper story contained four or five guestrooms which were rarely put to their destined use. Sometimes a fruitgrower, riding in from his plantation to confer with his agent, would pass a melancholy night in the dismal upper story; sometimes a minor native official on some trifling government quest would have his pomp and majesty awed by Madama's sepulchral hospitality. But Madama sat behind her bar content, nor desiring to quarrel with Fate. If any one required meat, drink, or lodging at the Hotel de los Estranjeros they had but to come, and be served. *Está bueno.* If they came not, why, then, they came not. *Está bueno.*

As the exceptional yachtsman was making his way down the precarious sidewalk of the Street of the Holy Sepulchre, the solitary permanent guest of that decaying hotel sat at its door, enjoying the breeze from the sea.

Dr. Gregg, the quarantine physician, was a man of fifty or sixty, with a florid face and the longest beard between Topeka and Terra del Fuego. He held his position by virtue of an appointment by the Board of Health of a seaport city in one of the Southern states. That city feared the ancient enemy of every Southern seaport—the yellow fever—and it was the duty of Dr. Gregg to examine crew and passengers of every vessel leaving Coralio for preliminary symptoms. The duties were light, and the salary, for one who lived in Coralio, ample. Surplus time there was in plenty; and the good doctor added to his gains by a large private practice among the residents of the coast. The fact that he did not know ten words of Spanish was no obstacle; a pulse could be felt and a fee collected without one being a linguist. Add to the description the facts that the doctor had a story to tell concerning the operation of trepanning which no listener had ever allowed him to conclude, and that he believed in brandy as a prophylactic; and the special points of interest possessed by Dr. Gregg will have become exhausted.

The doctor had dragged a chair to the sidewalk. He was coatless, and he leaned back against the wall and smoked, while he stroked his beard. Surprise came into his pale blue eyes when he caught sight of Smith in his unusual and prismatic clothes.

"You're Dr. Gregg—is that right?" said Smith, feeling the dog's head pin in his tie. "The constable—I mean the consul, told me you hung out at this caravansary. My name's Smith; and I came in a yacht. Taking a cruise around, looking at the monkeys and pineapple-trees. Come inside and have a drink, Doc. This café looks on the blink, but I guess it can set out something wet."

"I will join you, sir, in just a taste of brandy," said Dr. Gregg, rising quickly. "I find that as a prophylactic a little brandy is almost a necessity in this climate."

As they turned to enter the *pulperia* a native man, barefoot, glided noiselessly up and addressed the doctor in Spanish. He was yellowish-brown, like an over-ripe lemon; he wore a cotton shirt and ragged linen trousers girded by a leather belt. His face was like an animal's, live and wary, but without promise of much intelligence. This man jabbered with animation and so much seriousness that it seemed a pity that his words were to be wasted.

Dr. Gregg felt his pulse.

"You sick?" he inquired.

"Mi mujer está enferma en la casa," said the man, thus endeavoring to convey the news, in the only language open to him, that his wife lay ill in her palm-thatched hut.

The doctor drew a handful of capsules filled with a white powder from his trousers pocket. He counted out ten of them into the native's hand, and held up his forefinger impressively.

"Take one," said the doctor, "every two hours." He then held up two fingers, shaking them emphatically before the native's face. Next he pulled out his watch and ran his finger round its dial twice. Again the two fingers confronted the patient's nose. "Two—two—two hours," repeated the doctor.

"Si Señor," said the native, sadly.

He pulled a cheap silver watch from his own pocket and laid it in the doctor's hand. "Me bring," said he, struggling painfully with his scant English, "other watchy to-morrow." Then he departed downheartedly with his capsules.

"A very ignorant race of people, sir," said the doctor, as he slipped the watch into his pocket. "He seems to have mistaken my directions for taking the physic for the fee. However, it is all right.

He owes me an account, anyway. The chances are that he won't bring the other watch. You can't depend on anything they promise you. About that drink, now? How did you come to Coralio, Mr. Smith? I was not aware that any boats except the *Karlsefin* had arrived for some days."

The two leaned against the deserted bar; and Madama set out a bottle without waiting for the doctor's order. There was no dust on it.

After they had drank twice Smith said:

"You say there were no passengers on the *Karlsefin,* Doc? Are you sure about that? It seems to me I heard somebody down on the beach say that there was one or two aboard."

"They were mistaken, sir. I myself went out and put all hands through a medical examination, as usual. The *Karlsefin* sails as soon as she gets her bananas loaded, which will be about daylight in the morning, and she got everything ready this afternoon. No, sir, there was no passenger list. Like that Three-Star? A French schooner landed two slooploads of it a month ago. If any customs duties on it went to the distinguished republic of Anchuria you may have my hat. If you won't have another, come out and let's sit in the cool a while. It isn't often we exiles get a chance to talk with somebody from the outside world.

The doctor brought out another chair to the sidewalk for his new acquaintance. The two seated themselves.

"You are a man of the world," said Dr. Gregg; "a man of travel and experience. Your decision in a matter of ethics and, no doubt, on the points of equity, ability, and professional probity should be of value. I would be glad if you will listen to the history of a case that I think stands unique in medical annals.

"About nine years ago, while I was engaged in the practice of medicine in my native city, I was called to treat a case of contusion of the skull. I made the diagnosis that a splinter of bone was pressing upon the brain, and that the surgical operation known as trepanning was required. However, as the patient was a gentleman of wealth and position, I called in for consultation, Dr.——"

Smith rose from his chair, and laid a hand, soft with apology, upon the doctor's shirt sleeve.

"Say, Doc," he said, solemnly, "I want to hear that story. You've got me interested; and I don't want to miss the rest of it. I know it's a loola by the way it begins; and I want to tell it at the next meeting of the Barney O'Flynn Association, if you don't mind. But I've got one or two matters to attend to first. If I get 'em attended to in time I'll come right back and hear you spiel the rest before bedtime—is that right?"

"By all means," said the doctor, "get your business attended to, and then return. I shall wait up for you. You see, one of the most prominent physicians at the consultation diagnosed the trouble as a blood clot; another said it was an abscess, but I——"

"Don't tell me now, Doc. Don't spoil the story. Wait till I come back. I want to hear it as it runs off the reel—is that right?"

The mountains reached up their bulky shoulders to receive the level gallop of Apollo's homing steeds, the day died in the lagoons and in the shadowed banana groves and in the mangrove swamps, where the great blue crabs were beginning to crawl to land for their nightly ramble. And it died, at last, upon the highest peaks. Then the brief twilight, ephemeral as the flight of a moth, came and went; the Southern Cross peeped with its topmost eye above a row of palms, and the fire-flies heralded with their torches the approach of soft-footed night.

In the offing the *Karlsefin* swayed at anchor, her lights seeming to penetrate the water to countless fathoms with their shimmering, lanceolate reflections. The Caribs were busy loading her by means of the great lighters heaped full from the piles of fruit ranged upon the shore.

On the sandy beach, with his back against a cocoanut-tree and the stubs of many cigars lying around him, Smith sat waiting, never relaxing his sharp gaze in the direction of the steamer.

The incongruous yachtsman had concentrated his interest upon the innocent fruiter. Twice had he been assured that no passengers had come to Coralio on board of her. And yet, with a persistence not to be attributed to an idling voyager, he had appealed the case to the higher court of his own eye-sight. Surprisingly like some gay-coated lizard, he crouched at the foot of the cocoanut palm, and with the beady, shifting eyes of the selfsame reptile, sustained his espionage on the *Karlsefin.*

On the white sands a whiter gig belonging to the yacht was drawn up, guarded by one of the white-ducked crew. Not far away in a *pulperia* on the shore-following Calle Grande three other sailors swaggered with their cues around Coralio's solitary billiard-table. The boat lay there as if under orders to be ready for use at any moment. There was in the atmosphere a hint of expectation, of waiting for something to occur, which was foreign to the air of Coralio.

Like some passing bird of brilliant plumage, Smith alights on this palmy shore but to preen his wings for an instant and then to fly away upon silent pinions. When morning dawned there was no Smith, no waiting gig, no yacht in the offing. Smith left no intimation of his mission there, no footprints to show where he had followed the trail of his mystery on the sands of Coralio that night. He came; he spake his strange jargon of the asphalt and the cafés; he sat under the cocoanut-tree, and vanished. The next morning Coralio, Smithless, ate its fried plantain and said: "The man of pictured clothing went himself away." With the *siesta* the incident passed, yawning, into history.

So, for a time, must Smith pass behind the scenes of the play. He comes no more to Coralio nor to Dr. Gregg, who sits in vain, wagging his redundant beard, waiting to enrich his derelict audience with his moving tale of trepanning and jealousy.

But prosperously to the lucidity of these loose pages, Smith shall flutter among them again. In the nick of time he shall come to tell us why he strewed so many anxious cigar stumps around the cocoanut palm that night. This he must do; for, when he sailed away before the dawn in his yacht *Rambler,* he carried with him the answer to a riddle so big and preposterous that few in Anchuria had ventured even to propound it.

Caught

The plans for the detention of the flying President Miraflores and his companion at the coast line seemed hardly likely to fail. Dr. Zavalla himself had gone to the port of Alazan to establish a guard at that point. At Coralio the Liberal patriot Varras could be depended upon to keep close watch. Goodwin held himself responsible for the district about Coralio.

The news of the president's flight had been disclosed to no one in the coast towns save trusted members of the ambitious political party that was desirous of succeeding to power. The telegraph wire running from San Mateo to the coast had been cut far up on the mountain trail by an emissary of Zavalla's. Long before this could be repaired and word received along it from the capital the fugitives would have reached the coast and the question of escape or capture been solved.

Goodwin had stationed armed sentinels at frequent intervals along the shore for a mile in each direction from Coralio. They were instructed to keep a vigilant lookout during the night to prevent Miraflores from attempting to embark stealthily by means of some boat or sloop found by chance at the water's edge. A dozen patrols walked the streets of Coralio unsuspected, ready to intercept the truant official should he show himself there.

Goodwin was very well convinced that no precautions had been overlooked. He strolled about the streets that bore such high-sounding names and were but narrow, grass-covered lanes, lending his own aid to the vigil that had been intrusted to him by Bob Englehart.

The town had begun the tepid round of its nightly diversions. A few leisurely dandies, clad in white duck, with flowing neckties, and swinging slim bamboo canes, threaded the grassy by-ways toward the houses of their favored señoritas. Those who wooed the art of music dragged tirelessly at whining concertinas, or fingered lugubrious guitars at doors and windows. An occasional soldier from the *cuartel,* with flapping straw hat, without coat or shoes, hurried by, balancing his long gun like a lance in one hand. From every density of the foliage the giant tree frogs sounded their loud and irritating clatter. Further out, where the by-ways perished at the brink of the jungle, the guttural cries of marauding baboons and the coughing of the alligators in the black estuaries fractured the vain silence of the wood.

By ten o'clock the streets were deserted. The oil lamps that had burned, a sickly yellow, at random corners, had been extinguished by some economical civic agent. Coralio lay sleeping calmly between toppling mountains and encroaching sea like a stolen babe in the arms of its abductors. Somewhere over in that tropical darkness—perhaps already threading the profundities of the alluvial lowlands—the high adventurer and his mate were moving toward land's end. The game of Fox-in-the-Morning should be coming soon to its close.

Goodwin, at his deliberate gait, passed the long, low *cuartel* where Coralio's contingent of Anchuria's military force slumbered, with its bare toes pointed heavenward. There was a law that no civilian might come so near the headquarters of that citadel of war after nine o'clock, but Goodwin was always forgetting the minor statutes.

"Quién vive?" shrieked the sentinel, wrestling prodigiously with his lengthy musket.

"Americano," growled Goodwin, without turning his head, and passed on, unhalted.

To the right he turned, and to the left up the street that ultimately reached the Plaza Nacional. When within the toss of a cigar stump from the intersecting Street of the Holy Sepulchre, he stopped suddenly in the pathway.

He saw the form of a tall man, clothed in black and carrying a large valise, hurry down the cross-street in the direction of the beach. And Goodwin's second glance made him aware of a woman at the man's elbow on the farther side, who seemed to urge forward, if not even to assist, her companion in their swift but silent progress. They were no Coralians, those two.

Goodwin followed at increased speed, but without any of the artful tactics that are so dear to the heart of the sleuth. The American was too broad to feel the instinct of the detective. He stood as an agent for the people of Anchuria, and but for political reasons he would have demanded then and there the money. It was the design of his party to secure the imperilled fund, to restore it to the treasury of the country, and to declare itself in power without bloodshed or resistance.

The couple halted at the door of the Hotel de los Estranjeros, and the man struck upon the wood with the impatience of one unused to his entry being stayed. Madama was long in response; but after a time her light showed, the door was opened, and the guests housed.

Goodwin stood in the quiet street, lighting another cigar. In two minutes a faint gleam began to show between the slats of the jalousies in the upper story of the hotel. "They have engaged rooms," said Goodwin to himself. "So, then, their arrangements for sailing have yet to be made."

At that moment there came along one Estebán Delgado, a barber, an enemy to existing government, a jovial plotter against stagnation in any form. This barber was one of Coralio's saddest dogs, often remaining out of doors as late as eleven, post meridian. He was a partisan Liberal; and he greeted Goodwin with flatulent importance as a brother in the cause. But he had something important to tell.

"What think you, Don Frank!" he cried, in the universal tone of the conspirator. "I have to-night shaved *la barba*—what you call the 'weeskers' of the *Presidente* himself, of this countree! Consider! He sent for me to come. In the poor *casita* of an old woman he awaited me—in a verree leetle house in a dark place. *Carramba!* el Señor Presidente to make himself thus secret and obscured! I think he desired not to be known—but, *carajo!* can you shave a man and not see his face? This gold piece he gave me, and said it was to be all quite still. I think, Don Frank, there is what you call a chip over the bug."

"Have you ever seen President Miraflores before?" asked Goodwin.

"But once," answered Estebán. "He is tall; and he had weeskers verree black and sufficient."

"Was any one else present when you shaved him?"

"An old Indian woman, Señor, that belonged with the *casa,* and one señorita—a ladee of so much beautee!—*ah, Dios!*"

"All right, Estebán," said Goodwin. "It's very lucky that you happened along with your tonsorial information. The new administration will be likely to remember you for this."

Then in a few words he made the barber acquainted with the crisis into which the affairs of the nation had culminated, and instructed him to remain outside, keeping watch upon the two sides of the hotel that looked upon the street, and observing whether any one should attempt to leave the house by any door or window. Goodwin himself went to the door through which the guests had entered, opened it and stepped inside.

Madama had returned downstairs from her journey above to see after the comfort of her lodgers. Her candle stood upon the bar. She was about to take a thimbleful of rum as a solace for having her rest disturbed. She looked up without surprise or alarm as her third caller entered.

"Ah! it is the Señor Goodwin. Not often does he honor my poor house by his presence."

"I must come oftener," said Goodwin, with the Goodwin smile. "I hear that your cognac is the best between Belize to the north and Rio to the south. Set out the bottle, Madama, and let us have the proof in *un vasito* for each of us."

"My *aguardiente,"* said Madama, with pride, "is the best. It grows, in beautiful bottles, in the dark places among the banana-trees. *Si, Señor.* Only at midnight can they be picked by sailor-men who bring them, before daylight comes, to your back door. Good *aguardiente* is a verree difficult fruit to handle. Señor Goodwin."

Smuggling, in Coralio, was much nearer than competition to being the life of trade. One spoke of it slyly, yet with a certain conceit, when it had been well accomplished.

"You have guests in the house to-night," said Goodwin, laying a silver dollar upon the counter.

"Why not?" said Madama, counting the change. "Two; but the smallest while finished to arrive. One señor, not quite old, and one señorita of sufficient handsomeness. To their rooms they have ascended, not desiring the to-eat nor the to-drink. Two rooms—*Número* 9 and *Número* 10."

"I was expecting that gentleman and that lady," said Goodwin. "I have important *negocios* that must be transacted. Will you allow me to see them?"

"Why not?" sighed Madama, placidly. "Why should not Señor Goodwin ascend and speak to his friends? *Está bueno.* Room *Número* 9 and room *Número* 10."

Goodwin loosened in his coat pocket the American revolver that he carried, and ascended the steep, dark stairway.

In the hallway above, the saffron light from a hanging lamp allowed him to select the gaudy numbers on the doors. He turned the knob of Number 9, entered and closed the door behind him.

If that was Isabel Guilbert seated by the table in that poorly furnished room, report had failed to do her charms justice. She rested her head upon one hand. Extreme fatigue was signified in every line of her figure; and upon her countenance a deep perplexity was written. Her eyes were gray-irised, and of that mould that seems to have belonged to the orbs of all the famous queens of hearts. Their whites were singularly clear and brilliant, concealed above the irises by heavy horizontal lids, and showing a snowy line below them. Such eyes denote great nobility, vigor, and, if you can conceive of it, a most generous selfishness. She looked up when the American entered with an expression of surprised inquiry, but without alarm.

Goodwin took off his hat and seated himself, with his characteristic deliberate ease, upon a corner of the table. He held a lighted cigar between his fingers. He took this familiar course because he was sure that preliminaries would be wasted upon Miss Guilbert. He knew her history, and the small part that the conventions had played in it.

"Good evening," he said. "Now, madame, let us come to business at once. You will observe that I mention no names, but I know who is in the next room, and what he carries in that valise. That is the point which brings me here. I have come to dictate terms of surrender."

The lady neither moved nor replied, but steadily regarded the cigar in Goodwin's hand.

"We," continued the dictator, thoughtfully regarding the neat buckskin shoe on his gently swinging foot—"I speak for a considerable majority of the people—demand the return of the stolen funds belonging to them. Our terms go very little further than that. They are very simple. As an accredited spokesman, I promise that our interference will cease if they are accepted. Give up the money, and you and your companion will be permitted to proceed wherever you will. In fact, assistance will be given you in the matter of securing a passage by any outgoing vessel you may choose. It is on my personal responsibility that I add congratulations to the gentleman in Number 10 upon his taste in feminine charms."

Returning his cigar to his mouth, Goodwin observed her, and saw that her eyes followed it and rested upon it with icy and significant concentration. Apparently she had not heard a word he had said. He understood, tossed the cigar out the window, and, with an amused laugh, slid from the table to his feet.

"That is better," said the lady. "It makes it possible for me to listen to you. For a second lesson in good manners, you might now tell me by whom I am being insulted."

"I am sorry," said Goodwin, leaning one hand on the table, "that my time is too brief for devoting much of it to a course of etiquette. Come, now; I appeal to your good sense. You have shown yourself, in more than one instance, to be well aware of what is to your advantage. This is an occasion that demands the exercise of your undoubted intelligence. There is no mystery here. I am Frank Goodwin; and I have come for the money. I entered this room at a venture. Had I entered the other I would have had it before now. Do you want it in words? The gentleman in Number 10 has betrayed a great trust. He has robbed his people of a large sum, and it is I who will prevent their losing it. I do not say who that gentleman is; but if I should be forced to see him and he should prove to be a certain high official of the republic, it will be my duty to arrest him. The house is guarded. I am offering you liberal terms. It is not absolutely necessary that I confer personally with the gentleman in the next room. Bring me the valise containing the money, and we will call the affair ended."

The lady arose from her chair, and stood for a moment, thinking deeply.

"Do you live here, Mr. Goodwin?" she asked, presently.

"Yes."

"What is your authority for this intrusion?"

"I am an instrument of the republic. I was advised by wire of the movements of the—gentleman in Number 10."

"May I ask you two or three questions? I believe you to be a man more apt to be truthful than—timid. What sort of a town is this—Coralio, I think they call it?"

"Not much of a town," said Goodwin, smiling. "A banana town, as they run. Grass huts, 'dobes, five or six two-story houses, accommodations limited, population half-breed Spanish and Indian, Caribs and blackamoors. No sidewalks to speak of, no amusements. Rather unmoral. That's an offhand sketch, of course."

"Are there any inducements, say in a social or in a business way, for people to reside here?"

"Oh, yes," answered Goodwin, smiling broadly. "There are no afternoon teas, no hand-organs, no department stores—and there is no extradition treaty."

"He told me," went on the lady, speaking as if to herself, and with a slight frown, "that there were towns on this coast of beauty and importance; that there was a pleasing social order—especially an American colony of cultured residents."

"There is an American colony," said Goodwin, gazing at her in some wonder. "Some of the members are all right. Some are fugitives from justice from the States. I recall two exiled bank presidents, one army paymaster under a cloud, a couple of manslayers, and a widow—arsenic, I believe, was the suspicion in her case. I myself complete the colony, but, as yet, I have not distinguished myself by any particular crime."

"Do not lose hope," said the lady, dryly; "I see nothing in your actions to-night to guarantee your further obscurity. Some mistake has been made; I do not know just where. But *him* you shall not disturb to-night. The journey has fatigued him so that he has fallen asleep, I think, in his clothes. You talk of stolen money! I do not understand you. Some mistake has been made. I will convince you.

Remain where you are and I will bring you the valise that you seem to covet so, and show it to you."

She moved toward the closed door that connected the two rooms, but stopped, and half turned and bestowed upon Goodwin a grave searching look that ended in a quizzical smile.

"You force my door," she said, "and you follow your ruffianly behavior with the basest accusations; and yet"—she hesitated, as if to reconsider what she was about to say—"and yet—it is a puzzling thing—I am sure there has been some mistake."

She took a step toward the door, but Goodwin stayed her by a light touch upon her arm. I have said before that women turned to look at him in the streets. He was the viking sort of man, big, good-looking, and with an air of kindly truculence. She was dark and proud, glowing or pale as her mood moved her. I do not know if Eve were light or dark, but if such a woman had stood in the garden I know that the apple would have been eaten. This woman was to be Goodwin's fate, and he did not know it; but he must have felt the first throes of destiny, for, as he faced her, the knowledge of what report named her turned bitter in his throat.

"If there has been any mistake," he said, hotly, "it was yours. I do not blame the man who has lost his country, his honor, and is about to lose the poor consolation of his stolen riches as much as I blame you, for, by Heaven! I can very well see how he was brought to it. I can understand, and pity him. It is such women as you that strew this degraded coast with wretched exiles, that make men forget their trusts, that drag——"

The lady interrupted him with a weary gesture.

"There is no need to continue your insults," she said, coldly, "I do not understand what you are saying, nor do I know what mad blunder you are making; but if the inspection of the contents of a gentleman's portmanteau will rid me of you, let us delay it no longer."

She passed quickly and noiselessly into the other room, and returned with the heavy leather valise, which she handed to the American with an air of patient comtempt.

Goodwin set the valise quickly upon the table and began to unfasten the straps. The lady stood by, with an expression of infinite scorn and weariness upon her face.

The valise opened wide to a powerful, sidelong wrench. Goodwin dragged out two or three articles of clothing, exposing the bulk of its contents—package after package of tightly packed United States bank and treasury notes of large denominations. Reckoning from the high figures written upon the paper bands that bound them, the total must have come closely upon the hundred thousand mark.

Goodwin glanced swiftly at the woman, and saw, with surprise and a thrill of pleasure that he wondered at, that she had experienced an unmistakable shock. Her eyes grew wide, she gasped, and leaned heavily against the table. She had been ignorant, then, he inferred, that her companion had looted the government treasury. But why, he angrily asked himself, should he be so well pleased to think this wandering and unscrupulous singer not so black as report had painted her?

A noise in the other room startled them both. The door swung open, and a tall, elderly, dark complexioned man, recently shaven, hurried into the room.

All the pictures of President Miraflores represent him as the possessor of a luxuriant supply of dark and carefully tended whiskers; but the story of the barber, Estebán, had prepared Goodwin for the change.

The man stumbled in from the dark room, his eyes blinking at the lamplight, and heavy from sleep.

"What does this mean?" he demanded in excellent English, with a keen and perturbed look at the American—"robbery?"

"Very near it," answered Goodwin. "But I rather think I'm in time to prevent it. I represent the people to whom this money belongs, and I have come to convey it back to them." He thrust his hand into a pocket of his loose linen coat.

The other man's hand went quickly behind him.

"Don't draw," called Goodwin, sharply; "I've got you covered from my pocket."

The lady stepped forward, and laid one hand upon the shoulder of her hesitating companion. She pointed to the table. "Tell me the truth—the truth," she said, in a low voice. "Whose money is that?"

The man did not answer. He gave a deep, long-drawn sigh, leaned and kissed her on the forehead, stepped back into the other room and closed the door.

Goodwin foresaw his purpose, and jumped for the door, but the report of the pistol echoed as his hand touched the knob. A heavy fall followed, and some one swept him aside and struggled into the room of the fallen man.

A desolation, thought Goodwin, greater than that derived from the loss of cavalier and gold must have been in the heart of the enchantress to have wrung from her, in that moment, the cry of one turning to the all-forgiving, all-comforting earthly consoler—to have made her call out from that bloody and dishonored room—"Oh, Mother, Mother, Mother!"

But there was an alarm outside. The barber, Estebán, at the sound of the shot, had raised his voice; and the shot itself had aroused half the town. A pattering of feet came up the street, and official orders rang out on the still air. Goodwin had a duty to perform. Circumstances had made him the custodian of his adopted country's treasure. Swiftly cramming the money into the valise, he closed it, leaned far out of the window and dropped it into a thick orange-tree in the little inclosure below.

They will tell you in Coralio, as they delight in telling the stranger, of the conclusion of that tragic flight. They will tell you how the upholders of the law came apace when the alarm was sounded—the *Comandante* in red slippers and a jacket like a head waiter's and girded sword, the soldiers with their interminable guns, followed by outnumbering officers struggling into their gold lace and epaulettes; the bare-footed policemen (the only capables in the lot), and ruffled citizens of every hue and description.

They say that the countenance of the dead man was marred sadly by the effects of the shot; but he was identified as the fallen president by both Goodwin and the barber Estebán. On the next morning messages began to come over the mended telegraph wire; and the story of the flight from the capital was given out to the public. In San Mateo the revolutionary party had seized the sceptre of government, without opposition, and the *vivas* of the mercurial populace quickly effaced the interest belonging to the unfortunate Miraflores.

They will relate to you how the new government sifted the towns and raked the roads to find the valise containing Anchuria's surplus capital, which the president was known to have carried with him, but all in vain. In Coralio Señor Goodwin himself led the searching party which combed that town as carefully as a woman combs her hair; but the money was not found.

So they buried the dead man, without honors, back of the town near the little bridge that spans the mangrove swamp; and for a *real* a boy will show you his grave. They say that the old woman in whose hut the barber shaved the president placed the wooden slab at his head, and burned the inscription upon it with a hot iron.

You will hear also that Señor Goodwin, like a tower of strength, shielded Doña Isabel Guilbert through those subsequent distressful days; and that his scruples as to her past career (if he had any) vanished; and her adventuresome waywardness (if she had any) left her, and they were wedded and were happy.

The American built a home on a little foot hill near the town. It is a conglomerate structure of native woods that, exported, would be worth a fortune, and of brick, palm, glass, bamboo and adobe. There is a paradise of nature about it; and something of the same sort within. The natives speak of its interior with hands uplifted in admiration. There are floors polished like mirrors and covered with hand-woven Indian rugs of silk fibre, tall ornaments and pictures, musical instruments and papered walls—"figure-it-to-yourself!" they exclaim.

But they cannot tell you in Coralio (as you shall learn) what became of the money that Frank Goodwin dropped into the orange-tree. But that shall come later; for the palms are fluttering in the breeze, bidding us to sport and gaiety.

Cupid's Exile Number Two

The United States of America, after looking over its stock of consular timber, selected Mr. John De Graffenreid Atwood, of Dalesburg, Alabama, for a successor to Willard Geddie, resigned.

Without prejudice to Mr. Atwood, it will have to be acknowledged that, in this instance, it was the man who sought the office. As with the self-banished Geddie, it was nothing less than the artful smiles of lovely women that had driven Johnny Atwood to the desperate expedient of accepting office under a despised Federal Government so that he might go far, far away and never see again the false, fair face that had wrecked his young life. The consulship at Coralio seemed to offer a retreat sufficiently removed and romantic enough to inject the necessary drama into the pastoral scenes of Dalesburg life.

It was while playing the part of Cupid's exile that Johnny added his handiwork to the long list of casualties along the Spanish Main by his famous manipulation of the shoe market, and his unparalleled feat of elevating the most despised and useless weed in his own country from obscurity to be a valuable product in international commerce.

The trouble began, as trouble often begins instead of ending with a romance. In Dalesburg there was a man named Elijah Hemstetter, who kept a general store. His family consisted of one daughter called Rosine, a name that atoned much for "Hemstetter." This young woman was possessed of plentiful attractions, so that the young men of the community were agitated in their bosoms. Among the more agitated was Johnny, the son of Judge Atwood, who lived in the big colonial mansion on the edge of Dalesburg.

It would seem that the desirable Rosine should have been pleased to return the affection of an Atwood, a name honored all over the state long before and since the war. It does seem that she should have gladly consented to have been led into that stately but rather empty colonial mansion. But not so. There was a cloud on the horizon, a threatening, cumulus cloud, in the shape of a lively and shrewd young farmer in the neighborhood who dared to enter the lists as a rival to the high-born Atwood.

One night Johnny propounded to Rosine a question that is considered of much importance by the young of the human species. The accessories were all there—moonlight, oleanders, magnolias, the mockbird's song. Whether or no the shadow of Pinkney Dawson, the prosperous young farmer, came between them on that occasion is not known; but Rosine's answer was unfavorable. Mr. John De Graffenreid Atwood bowed till his hat touched the lawn grass, and went away with his head high, but with a sore wound in his pedigree and heart. A Hemstetter refuse an Atwood! Zounds!

Among other accidents of that year was a Democratic president. Judge Atwood was a warhorse of Democracy. Johnny persuaded him to set the wheels moving for some foreign appointment. He would go away—away. Perhaps in years to come Rosine would think how true, how faithful his love had been, and would drop a tear—maybe in the cream she would be skimming for Pink Dawson's breakfast.

The wheels of politics revolved; and Johnny was appointed consul to Coralio. Just before leaving he dropped in at Hemstetter's to say good-bye. There was a queer, pinkish look about Rosine's eyes; and had the two been alone, the United States might have had to cast about for another consul. But Pink Dawson was there, of course, talking about his 400-acre orchard, and the three-mile alfalfa tract, and the 200-acre pasture. So Johnny shook hands with Rosine as coolly as if he were only going to run up to Montgomery for a couple of days. They had the royal manner when they chose, those Atwoods.

"If you happen to strike anything in the way of a good investment down there, Johnny," said Pink Dawson, "just let me know, will you? I reckon I could lay my hands on a few extra thousands 'most any time for a profitable deal."

"Certainly, Pink," said Johnny, pleasantly. "If I strike anything of the sort I'll let you in with pleasure."

So Johnny went down to Mobile and took a fruit steamer for the coast of Anchuria.

When the new consul arrived in Coralio the strangeness of the scenes diverted him much. He was only twenty-two; and the grief of youth is not worn like a garment as it is by older men. It has its seasons when it reigns; and then it is unseated for a time by the assertion of the keen senses.

Billy Keogh and Johnny seemed to conceive a mutual friendship at once. Keogh took the new consul about town and presented him to the handful of Americans and the smaller number of French and Germans who made up the "foreign" contingent. And then, of course, he had to be more formally introduced to the native officials, and have his credentials transmitted through an interpreter.

There was something about the young Southerner that the sophisticated Keogh liked. His manner was simple almost to boyishness; but he possessed the cool carelessness of a man of far greater age and experience. Neither uniforms nor titles, red tape nor foreign languages, mountains nor sea weighed upon his spirits. He was heir to all the ages, an Atwood, of Dalesburg; and you might know every thought conceived in his bosom.

Geddie came down to the consulate to explain the duties and workings of the office. He and Keogh tried to interest the new consul in their description of the work that his government expected him to perform.

"It's all right," said Johnny from the hammock that he had set up as the official reclining place. "If anything turns up that has to be done I'll let you fellows do it. You can't expect a Democrat to work during his first term of holding office."

"You might look over these headings," suggested Geddie, "of the different lines of exports you will have to keep account of. The fruit is classified; and there are the valuable woods, coffee, rubber——"

"That last account sounds all right," interrupted Mr. Atwood. "Sounds as if it could be stretched. I want to buy a new flag, a monkey, a guitar and a barrel of pineapples. Will that rubber account stretch over 'em?"

"That's merely statistics," said Geddie, smiling. "The expense account is what you want. It is supposed to have a slight elasticity. The 'stationery' items are sometimes carelessly audited by the State Department."

"We're wasting our time," said Keogh. "This man was born to hold office. He penetrates to the root of the art at one step of his eagle eye. The true genius of government shows its hand in every word of his speech."

"I didn't take this job with any intention of working," explained Johnny, lazily. "I wanted to go somewhere in the world where they didn't talk about farms. There are none here, are there?"

"Not the kind you are acquainted with," answered the ex-consul. "There is no such art here as agriculture. There never was a plow or a reaper within the boundaries of Anchuria."

"This is the country for me," murmured the consul and immediately he fell asleep.

The cheerful tintypist pursued his intimacy with Johnny in spite of open charges that he did so to obtain a preëmption on a seat in the coveted spot, the rear gallery of the consulate. But whether his designs were selfish or purely friendly, Keogh achieved that desirable privilege. Few were the nights on which the two could not be found reposing there in the sea breeze, with their heels on the railing, and the cigars and brandy conveniently near.

One evening they had sat thus, mainly silent, for their talk had dwindled before the stilling influence of an unusual night.

There was a great, full moon; and the sea was mother-of-pearl. Almost every sound was hushed, for the air was but faintly stirring; and the town lay panting, waiting for the night to cool. Off-shore lay the fruit steamer *Andador,* of the Vesuvius line, full-laden and scheduled to sail at six in the morning. There were no loiterers on the beach. So bright was the moonlight that the two men could see the small pebbles shining on the beach where the gentle surf wetted them.

Then down the coast, tacking close to shore, slowly swam a little sloop, white-winged like some snowy sea fowl. Its course lay within twenty points of the wind's eye; so it veered in and out again in long slow strokes like the movements of a graceful skater.

Again the tactics of its crew brought it close in shore, this time nearly opposite the consulate; and then there blew from the sloop clear and surprising notes as if from a horn of elfland. A fairy bugle it might have been, sweet and silvery and unexpected, playing with spirit the familiar air of "Home, Sweet Home."

It was a scene set for the land of the lotus. The authority of the sea and the tropics, the mustery that attends unknown sails, and the prestige of drifting music on moonlit waters gave it an anodynous charm. Johnny Atwood felt it, and thought of Dalesburg; but as soon as Keogh's mind had arrived at a theory concerning the peripatetic solo he sprang to the railing, and his ear-rending yawp fractured the silence of Coralio like a cannon shot.

"Mel-lin-ger a-hoy!"

The sloop was now on its outward tack; but from it came a clear, answering hail:

"Good-bye, Billy . . . go-ing home—bye!"

The *Andador* was the sloop's destination. No doubt some passenger with a sailing permit from some up-the-coast point had come down in this sloop to catch the regular fruit steamer on its return trip. Like a coquettish pigeon the little boat tacked on its eccentric way until at last its white sail was lost to sight against the larger bulk of the fruiter's side.

"That's old H. P. Mellinger," explained Keogh, dropping back into his chair. "He's going back to New York. He was private secretary of the late hot-foot president of this grocery and fruit stand that they call a country. His job's over now; and I guess old Mellinger is glad."

"Why does he disappear to music, like Zo-zo, the magic queen?" asked Johnny. "Just to show 'em that he doesn't care?"

"That noise you heard is a phonograph," said Keogh. "I sold him that. Mellinger had a graft in this country that was the only thing of its kind in the world. The tooting machine saved it for him once, and he always carried it around with him afterward."

"Tell me about it," demanded Johnny, betraying interest.

"I'm no disseminator of narratives," said Keogh. "I can use language for purposes of speech; but when I attempt a discourse the words come out as they will, and they may make sense when they strike the atmosphere, or they may not."

"I want to hear about that graft," persisted Johnny. "You've got no right to refuse. I've told you all about every man, woman and hitching post in Dalesburg."

"You shall hear it," said Keogh. "I said my instincts of narrative were perplexed. Don't you believe it. It's an art I've acquired along with many other of the graces and sciences."

The Phonograph and the Graft

"What was this graft?" asked Johnny, with the impatience of the great public to whom tales are told.

" 'Tis contrary to art and philosophy to give you the information," said Keogh, calmly. "The art of narrative consists in concealing from your audience everything it wants to know until after you expose your favorite opinions on topics foreign to the subject. A good story is like a bitter pill with the sugar coating inside of it. I will begin, if you please, with a horoscope located in the Cherokee Nation; and end with a moral tune on the phonograph.

"Me and Henry Horsecollar brought the first phonograph to this country. Henry was a quarter-breed, quarter-back Cherokee, educated East in the idioms of football, and West in contraband whisky, and a gentleman, the same as you and me. He was easy and romping in his ways; a man about six foot, with a kind of rubber-tire movement. Yes, he was a little man about five foot five, or five foot eleven. He was what you would call a medium tall man of average smallness. Henry had quit college once, and the Muscogee jail three times—the last-named institution on account of introducing and selling whisky in the territories. Henry Horsecollar never let any cigar stores come up and stand behind him. He didn't belong to that tribe of Indians.

"Henry and me met at Texarkana, and figured out this phonograph scheme. He had $360 which came to him out of a land allotment in the reservation. I had run down from Little Rock on account of a distressful scene I had witnessed on the street there. A man stood on a box and passed around some gold watches, screw case, stem-winders, Elgin movement, very elegant. Twenty bucks they cost you over the counter. At three dollars the crowd fought for the tickets. The man happened to find a valise full of them handy, and he passed them out like putting hot biscuits on a plate. The backs were hard to unscrew, but the crowd put its ear to the case, and they ticked mollifying and agreeable. Three of these watches were genuine tickers; the rest were only kickers. He? Why, empty cases with one of them horny black bugs that fly around electric lights in 'em. Them bugs kick off minutes and seconds industrious and beautiful. So, this man I was speaking of cleaned up $288; and then he went away, because he knew that when it came time to wind watches in Little Rock an entomologist would be needed, and he wasn't one.

"So, as I say, Henry had $360, and I had $288. The idea of introducing the phonograph to South America was Henry's; but I took to it freely, being fond of machinery of all kinds.

" 'The Latin races,' says Henry, explaining easily in the idioms he learned at college, 'are peculiarly adapted to be victims of the phonograph. They have the artistic temperament. They yearn for music and color and gaiety. They give wampum to the hand-organ man and the four-legged chicken in the tent when they're months behind with the grocery and the bread-fruit tree.'

" 'Then,' says I, 'we'll export canned music to the Latins; but I'm mindful of Mr. Julius Cæsar's account of 'em where he says: *"Omnia Gallia in tres partes divisa est";* which is the same as to say, "We will need all of our gall in devising means to tree them parties." '

"I hated to make a show of education; but I was disinclined to be overdone in syntax by a mere Indian, a member of a race to which we owe nothing except the land on which the United States is situated.

"We bought a fine phonograph in Texarkana—one of the best make—and half a trunkful of records. We packed up, and took the T. and P. for New Orleans. From that celebrated centre of molasses and disfranchised coon songs we took a steamer for South America.

"We landed at Solitas, forty miles up the coast from here. 'Twas a palatable enough place to look at. The houses were clean and white; and to look at 'em stuck around among the scenery they reminded you of hard-boiled eggs served with lettuce. There was a block of skyscraper mountains in the suburbs; and they kept pretty quiet, like they had crept up there and were watching the town. And the sea was remarking 'Sh-sh-sh' on the beach; and now and then a ripe cocoanut would drop kerblip in the sand; and that was all there was doing. Yes, I judge that town was considerably on the quiet. I judge that after Gabriel quits blowing his horn, and the car starts, with Philadelphia swinging to the last strap, and Pine Gully, Arkansas, hanging onto the rear step, this town of Solitas will wake up and ask if anybody spoke.

"The captain went ashore with us, and offered to conduct what he seemed to like to call the obsequies. He introduced Henry and me to the United States Consul, and a roan man, the head of the Department of Mercenary and Licentious Dispositions, the way it read upon his sign.

" 'I touch here a week again from to-day,' says the captain.

" 'By that time,' we told him, 'we'll be amassing wealth in the interior towns with our galvanized prima donna and correct imitations of Sousa's band excavating a march from a tin mine.'

" 'Ye'll not,' says the captain. 'Ye'll be hypnotized. Any gentleman in the audience who kindly steps upon the stage and looks this country in the eye will be converted to the hypothesis that he's but a fly in the Elgin creamery. Ye'll be standing knee deep in the surf waiting for me, and your machine for making Hamburger steak out of the hitherto respected art of music will be playing "There's no place like home." '

"Henry skinned a twenty off his roll, and received from the Bureau of Mercenary Dispositions a paper bearing a red seal and a dialect story, and no change.

"Then we got the consul full of red wine, and struck him for a horoscope. He was a thin, youngish kind of a man, I should say past fifty, sort of French-Irish in his affections, and puffed up with disconsolation. Yes, he was a flattened kind of a man, in whom drink lay stagnant, inclined to corpulence and misery. Yes, I think he was a kind of a Dutchman, being very sad and genial in his ways.

" 'The marvelous invention,' he says, 'entitled the phonograph, has never invaded these shores. The people have never heard it. They would not believe it if they should. Simple-hearted children of nature, progress has never condemned them to accept the work of a can-opener as an overture, and rag-time might incite them to a bloody revolution. But you can try the experiment. The best chance you have is that the populace may not wake up when you play. There's two ways,' says the consul, 'they may take it. They may become inebriated with attention, like an Atlanta colonel listening to "Marching Through Georgia," or they will get excited and transpose the key of the music with an axe and yourselves into a dungeon. In the latter case,' says the consul, 'I'll do my duty by cabling to the State Department, and I'll wrap the Stars and Stripes around you when you come to be shot, and threaten them with the vengeance of the greatest gold export and financial reserve nation on earth. The flag is full of bullet holes now,' says the consul, 'made in that way. Twice before,' says the consul, 'I have cabled our government for a couple of gunboats to protect American citizens. The first time the Department sent me a pair of gum boots. The other time was when a man named Pease was going to be executed here. They referred that appeal to the Secretary of Agriculture. Let us now disturb the señor behind the bar for a subsequence of the red wine.'

"Thus soliloquized the consul of Solitas to me and Henry Horsecollar.

"But, notwithstanding, we hired a room that afternoon in the Calle de los Angeles, the main street that runs along the shore, and put our trunks there. 'Twas a good-sized room, dark and cheerful, but small. 'Twas on a various street, diversified by houses and conservatory plants. The peasantry of the city passed to and fro on the fine pasturage between the sidewalks. 'Twas, for the world, like an opera chorus when the Royal Kafoozlum is about to enter.

"We were rubbing the dust off the machine and getting fixed to start business the next day, when a big, fine-looking white man in white clothes stopped at the door and looked in. We extended the invitations, and he walked inside and sized us up. He was chewing a long cigar, and wrinkling his eyes, meditative, like a girl trying to decide which dress to wear to the party.

" 'New York?' he says to me finally.

" 'Originally, and from time to time,' I says. 'Hasn't it rubbed off yet?'

" 'It's simple,' says he, 'when you know how. It's the fit of the vest. They don't cut vests right anywhere else. Coats, maybe, but not vests.'

"The white man looks at Henry Horsecollar and hesitates.

" 'Injun,' says Henry; 'tame Injun.'

" 'Mellinger,' says the man—'Homer P. Mellinger. Boys, you're confiscated. You're babies in the wood without a chaperon or referee, and it's my duty to start you going. I'll knock out the props and launch you proper in the pellucid waters of this tropical mud puddle. You'll have to be christened, and if you'll come with me I'll break a bottle of wine across your bows, according to Hoyle.'

"Well, for two days Homer P. Mellinger did the honors. That man cut ice in Anchuria. He was It. He was the Royal Kafoozlum. If me and Henry was babes in the wood, he was a Robin Redbreast from the topmost bough. Him and me and Henry Horsecollar locked arms, and toted that phonograph around, and had wassail and diversions. Everywhere we found doors open we went inside and set the machine going, and Mellinger called upon the people to observe the artful music and his two lifelong friends, the Señores Americanos. The opera chorus was agitated with esteem, and followed us from house to house. There was a different kind of drink to be had with every tune. The natives had acquirements of a pleasant thing in the way of a drink that gums itself to the recollection. They chop off the end of a green cocoanut, and pour in on the juice of it French brandy and other adjuvants. We had them and other things.

"Mine and Henry's money was counterfeit. Everything was on Homer P. Mellinger. That man could find rolls of bills concealed in places on his person where Hermann the Wizard couldn't have conjured out a rabbit or an omelette. He could have founded universities, and made orchid collections, and then had enough left to purchase the colored vote of his country. Henry and me wondered what his graft was. One evening he told us.

" 'Boys,' said he, 'I've deceived you. You think I'm a painted butterfly; but in fact I'm the hardest worked man in this country. Ten years ago I landed on its shores; and two years ago on the point of its jaw. Yes, I guess I can get the decision over this ginger cake commonwealth at the end of any round I choose. I'll confide in you because you are my countrymen and guests, even if you have assaulted my adopted shores with the worst system of noises ever set to music.

" 'My job is private secretary to the president of this republic; and my duties are running it. I'm not headlined in the bills, but I'm the mustard in the salad dressing just the same. There isn't a law goes before Congress, there isn't a concession granted, there isn't an import duty levied but what H. P. Mellinger he cooks and seasons it. In the front office I fill the president's inkstand and search visiting statesmen for dirks and dynamite; but in the back room I dictate the policy of the government. You'd never guess in the world how I got my pull. It's the only graft of its kind on earth. I'll put you wise. You remember the old top-liner in the copy book—"Honesty is the Best Policy"? That's it. I'm working honesty for a graft. I'm the only honest man in the republic. The government knows it; the people know it; the boodlers know it; the foreign investors know it. I make the government keep its faith. If a man is promised a job he gets it. If outside capital buys a concession it gets the goods. I run a monopoly of square dealing here. There's no competition. If Colonel Diogenes were to flash his lantern in this precinct he'd have my address inside of two minutes. There isn't big money in it, but it's a sure thing, and lets a man sleep of nights.'

"Thus Homer P. Mellinger made oration to me and Henry Horsecollar. And, later, he divested himself of this remark:

" 'Boys, I'm to hold a *soirée* this evening with a gang of leading citizens, and I want your assistance. You bring the musical corn sheller and give the affair the outside appearance of a function. There's important business on hand, but it mustn't show. I can talk to you people. I've been pained for years on account of not having anybody to blow off and brag to. I get homesick sometimes, and I'd swap the entire perquisites of office for just one hour to have a stein and a caviare sandwich somewhere on Thirty-fourth Street, and stand and watch the street cars go by, and smell the peanut roaster at old Giuseppe's fruit stand.'

" 'Yes,' said I, 'there's fine caviare at Billy Renfrow's café, corner of Thirty-fourth and——'

" 'God knows it,' interrupts Mellinger, 'and if you'd told me you knew Billy Renfrow I'd have invented tons of ways of making you happy. Billy was my side-kicker in New York. There is a man who never knew what crooked was. Here I am working Honesty for a graft, but that man loses money on it. Carrambos! I get sick at times of this country. Everything's rotten. From the executive down to the coffee pickers, they're plotting to down each other and skin their friends. If a mule driver takes off his hat to an official, that man figures it out that he's a popular idol, and sets his pegs to stir up a revolution and upset the administration. It's one of my little chores as private secretary to smell out these revolutions and affix the kibosh before they break out and scratch the paint off the government property. That's why I'm down here now in this mildewed coast town. The governor of the district and his crew are plotting to uprise. I've got every one of their names, and they're invited to listen to the phonograph to-night, compliments of H. P. M. That's the way I'll get them in a bunch, and things are on the programme to happen to them.'

"We three were sitting at table in the cantina of the Purified Saints. Mellinger poured out wine, and was looking some worried; I was thinking.

" 'They're a sharp crowd,' he says, kind of fretful. 'They're capitalized by a foreign syndicate after rubber, and they're loaded to the muzzle for bribing. I'm sick,' goes on Mellinger, 'of comic opera. I want to smell East River and wear suspenders again. At times I feel like throwing up my job, but I'm d—n fool enough to be sort of proud of it. "There's Mellinger," they say here. *"Por Dios!* you can't touch him with a million." I'd like to take that record back and show it to Billy Renfrow some day; and that tightens my grip whenever I see a fat thing that I could corral just by winking one eye—and losing my graft. By —, they can't monkey with me. They know it. What money I get I make honest and spend it. Some day I'll make a pile and go back and eat caviare with Billy. To-night I'll show you how to handle a bunch of corruptionists. I'll show them what Mellinger, private secretary, means when you spell it with the cotton and tissue paper off.'

"Mellinger appears shaky, and breaks his glass against the neck of the bottle.

"I says to myself, 'White man, if I'm not mistaken there's been a bait laid out where the tail of your eye could see it.'

"That night, according to arrangements, me and Henry took the phonograph to a room in a 'dobe house in a dirty side street, where the grass was knee high. 'Twas a long room, lit with smoky oil lamps.

There was plenty of chairs, and a table at the back end. We set the phonograph on the table. Mellinger was there, walking up and down, disturbed in his predicaments. He chewed cigars and spat 'em out, and he bit the thumb nail of his left hand.

"By and by the invitations to the musicale came sliding in by pairs and threes and spade flushes. Their color was of a diversity, running from a three-days' smoked meerschaum to a patent-leather polish. They were as polite as wax, being devastated with enjoyments to give Señor Mellinger the good evenings. I understood their Spanish talk—I ran a pumping engine two years in a Mexican silver mine, and had it pat—but I never let on.

"Maybe fifty of 'em had come, and was seated, when in slid the king bee, the governor of the district. Mellinger met him at the door, and escorted him to the grand stand. When I saw that Latin man I knew that Mellinger, private secretary, had all the dances on his card taken. That was a big, squashy man, the color of a rubber overshoe, and he had an eye like a head waiter's.

"Mellinger explained, fluent, in the Castilian idioms, that his soul was disconcerted with joy at introducing to his respected friends America's greatest invention, the wonder of the age. Henry got the cue and run on an elegant brass-band record and the festivities became initiated. The governor man had a bit of English under his hat, and when the music was choked off he says:

" 'Ver-r-ree fine. *Gr-r-r-r-racias,* the American gentleemen, the so esplendeed moosic as to playee.'

"The table was a long one, and Henry and me sat at the end of it next the wall. The governor sat at the other end. Homer P. Mellinger stood at the side of it. I was just wondering how Mellinger was going to handle his crowd, when the home talent suddenly opened the services.

"That governor man was suitable for uprisings and policies. I judge he was a ready kind of man, who took his own time. Yes, he was full of attention and immediateness. He leaned his hands on the table and imposed his face toward the secretary man.

" 'Do the American señores understand Spanish?' he asks in his native accents.

" 'They do not,' says Mellinger.

" 'Then listen,' goes on the Latin man, prompt. "The musics are of sufficient prettiness, but not of necessity. Let us speak of business. I well know why we are here, since I observe my compatriots. You had a whisper yesterday, Señor Mellinger, of our proposals. To-night we will speak out. We know that you stand in the president's favor, and we know your influence. The government will be changed. We know the worth of your services. We esteem your friendship and aid so much that'—Mellinger raises his hand, but the governor man bottles him up. 'Do not speak until I have done.'

"The governor man then draws a package wrapped in paper from his pocket, and lays it on the table by Mellinger's hand.

" 'In that you will find fifty thousand dollars in money of your country. You can do nothing against us, but you can be worth that for us. Go back to the capital and obey our instructions. Take that money now. We trust you. You will find with it a paper giving in detail the work you will be expected to do for us. Do not have the unwiseness of refuse.'

"The governor man paused, with his eyes fixed on Mellinger, full of expressions and observances. I looked at Mellinger, and was glad Billy Renfrow couldn't see him then. The sweat was popping out on his forehead, and he stood dumb, tapping the little package with the ends of his fingers. The colorado-maduro gang was after his graft. He had only to change his politics, and stuff five fingers in his inside pocket.

"Henry whispers to me and wants the pause in the programme interpreted. I whisper back: 'H. P. is up against a bribe, senator's size, and the coons have got him going.' I saw Mellinger's hand moving closer to the package. 'He's weakening,' I whispered to Henry. 'We'll remind him,' says Henry, 'of the peanut-roaster on Thirty-fourth Street, New York.'

"Henry stooped down and got a record from the basketful we'd brought, slid it in the phonograph, and started her off. It was a cornet solo, very neat and beautiful, and the name of it was 'Home, Sweet Home.' Not one of them fifty-odd men in the room moved while it was playing, and the governor man kept his eyes steady on Mellinger. I saw Mellinger's head go up little by little, and his hand came creeping away from the package. Not until the last note sounded did anybody stir. And then Homer P. Mellinger takes up the bundle of boodle and slams it in the governor man's face.

" 'That's my answer,' says Mellinger, private secretary, 'and there'll be another in the morning. I have proofs of conspiracy against every man of you. The show is over, gentlemen.'

" 'There's one more act,' puts in the governor man. 'You are a servant, I believe, employed by the president to copy letters and answer raps at the door. I am governor here. *Señores,* I call upon you in the name of the cause to seize this man.'

"That brindled gang of conspirators shoved back their chairs and advanced in force. I could see where Mellinger had made a mistake in massing his enemy so as to make a grand-stand play. I think he made another one, too; but we can pass that, Mellinger's idea of a graft and mine being different, according to estimations and points of view.

"There was only one window and door in that room, and they were in the front end. Here was fifty-odd Latin men coming in a bunch to obstruct the legislation of Mellinger. You may say there were three of us, for me and Henry, simultaneous, declared New York City and the Cherokee Nation in sympathy with the weaker party.

"Then it was that Henry Horsecollar rose to a point of disorder and intervened, showing, admirable, the advantages of education as applied to the American Indian's natural intellect and native refinement. He stood up and smoothed back his hair on each side with his hands as you have seen little girls do when they play.

" 'Get behind me, both of you,' says Henry.

" 'What's it to be, chief?' I asked.

" 'I'm going to buck centre,' says Henry, in his football idioms. 'There isn't a tackle in the lot of them. Follow me close, and rush the game.'

"Then that cultured Red Man exhaled an arrangement of sounds with his mouth that made the Latin aggregation pause, with thoughtfulness and hesitations. The matter of his proclamation seemed to be a co-operation of the Carlisle war-whoop with the Cherokee college yell. He went at the chocolate team like a bean out of a little boy's nigger shooter. His right elbow laid out the governor man on the gridiron, and he made a lane the length of the crowd so wide that a woman could have carried a step-ladder through it without striking against anything. All Mellinger and me had to do was to follow.

"It took us just three minutes to get out of that street around to military headquarters, where Mellinger had things his own way. A colonel and a battalion of bare-toed infantry turned out and went back to the scene of the musicale with us, but the conspirator gang was gone. But we recaptured the phonograph with honors of war, and marched back to the *cuartel* with it playing 'All Coons Look Alike to Me.'

"The next day Mellinger takes me and Henry to one side, and begins to shed tens and twenties.

" 'I want to buy that phonograph,' says he. "I liked that last tune it played at the *soirée.*'

" 'This is more money than the machine is worth,' says I.

" ' 'Tis government expense money,' says Mellinger. 'The government pays for it, and it's getting the tune-grinder cheap.'

"Me and Henry knew that pretty well. We knew that it had saved

Homer P. Mellinger's graft when he was on the point of losing it; but we never let him know we knew it.

" 'Now you boys better slide off further down the coast for a while,' says Mellinger, 'till I get the screws put on these fellows here. If you don't they'll give you trouble. And if you ever happen to see Billy Renfrow again before I do, tell him I'm coming back to New York as soon as I can make a stake—honest.'

"Me and Henry laid low until the day the steamer came back. When we saw the captain's boat on the beach we went down and stood in the edge of the water. The captain grinned when he saw us.

" 'I told you you'd be waiting,' he says. 'Where's the Hamburger machine?'

" 'It stays behind,' I says, 'to play "Home, Sweet Home." '

" 'I told you so,' says the captain again. 'Climb in the boat.'

"And that," said Keogh, "is the way me and Henry Horsecollar introduced the phonograph into this country. Henry went back to the States, but I've been rummaging around in the tropics ever since. They say Mellinger never travelled a mile after that without his phonograph. I guess it kept him reminded about his graft whenever he saw the siren voice of the boodler tip him the wink with a bribe in its hand."

"I suppose he's taking it home with him as a souvenir," remarked the consul.

"Not as a souvenir," said Keogh. "He'll need two of 'em in New York, running day and night."

Money Maze

The new administration of Anchuria entered upon its duties and privileges with enthusiasm. Its first act was to send an agent to Coralio with imperative orders to recover, if possible, the sum of money ravished from the treasury by the ill-fated Miraflores.

Colonel Emilio Falcon, the private secretary of Losada, the new president, was despatched from the capital upon this important mission.

The position of private secretary to a tropical president is a responsible one. He must be a diplomat, a spy, a ruler of men, a bodyguard to his chief, and a smeller-out of plots and nascent revolutions. Often he is the power behind the throne, the dictator of policy; and a president chooses him with a dozen times the care with which he selects a matrimonial mate.

Colonel Falcon, a handsome and urbane gentleman of Castilian courtesy and débonnaire manners, came to Coralio with the task before him of striking upon the cold trail of the lost money. There he conferred with the military authorities, who had received instructions to cooperate with him in the search.

Colonel Falcon established his headquarters in one of the rooms of the Casa Morena. Here for a week he held informal sittings—much as if he were a kind of unified grand jury—and summoned before him all those whose testimony might illumine the financial tragedy that had accompanied the less momentous one of the late president's death.

Two or three who were thus examined, among whom was the barber Estebán, declared that they had identified the body of the president before its burial.

"Of a truth," testified Estebán before the mighty secretary, "it was he, the president. Consider!—how could I shave a man and not see his face? He sent for me to shave him in a small house. He had a beard very black and thick. Had I ever seen the president before? Why not? I saw him once ride forth in a carriage from the *vapor* in Solitas. When I shaved him he gave me a gold piece, and said there was to be no talk. But I am a Liberal—I am devoted to my country—and I spake of these things to Señor Goodwin."

"It is known," said Colonel Falcon, smoothly, "that the late

President took with him an American leather valise, containing a large amount of money. Did you see that?"

"De veras—no," Estebán answered. "The light in the little house was but a small lamp by which I could scarcely see to shave the President. Such a thing there may have been, but I did not see it. No. Also in the room was a young lady—a señorita of much beauty—that I could see even in so small a light. But the money, señor, or the thing in which it was carried—that I did not see."

The *comandante* and other officers gave testimony that they had been awakened and alarmed by the noise of a pistol-shot in the Hotel de los Estranjeros. Hurrying thither to protect the peace and dignity of the republic, they found a man lying dead, with a pistol clutched in his hand. Beside him was a young woman, weeping sorely. Señor Goodwin was also in the room when they entered it. But of the valise of money they saw nothing.

Madame Timotea Ortiz, the proprietress of the hotel in which the game of Fox-in-the-Morning had been played out, told of the coming of the two guests to her house.

"To my house they came," said she—"one *señor,* not quite old, and one *señorita* of sufficient handsomeness. They desired not to eat or to drink—not even of my *aguardiente,* which is the best. To their rooms they ascended—*Número Nueve* and *Número Diez.* Later came Señor Goodwin, who ascended to speak with them. Then I heard a great noise like that of a *canon,* and they said that the *pobre Presidente* had shot himself. *Está bueno.* I saw nothing of money or of the thing you call *veliz* that you say he carried it in."

Colonel Falcon soon came to the reasonable conclusion that if any one in Coralio could furnish a clue to the vanished money, Frank Goodwin must be the man. But the wise secretary pursued a different course in seeking information from the American. Goodwin was a powerful friend to the new administration, and one who was not to be carelessly dealt with in respect to either his honesty or his courage. Even the private secretary of His Excellency hesitated to have this rubber prince and mahogany baron haled before him as a common citizen of Anchuria. So he sent Goodwin a flowery epistle, each word-petal dripping with honey, requesting the favor of an interview. Goodwin replied with an invitation to dinner at his own house.

Before the hour named the American walked over to the Casa Morena, and greeted his guest frankly and friendly. Then the two strolled, in the cool of the afternoon, to Goodwin's home in the environs.

The American left Colonel Falcon in a big, cool, shadowed room with a floor of inlaid and polished woods that any millionaire in the States would have envied, excusing himself for a few minutes. He crossed a *patio,* shaded with deftly arranged awnings and plants, and entered a long room looking upon the sea in the opposite wing of the house. The broad jalousies were opened wide, and the ocean breeze flowed in through the room, an invisible current of coolness and health. Goodwin's wife sat near one of the windows, making a water-color sketch of the afternoon seascape.

Here was a woman who looked to be happy. And more—she looked to be content. Had a poet been inspired to pen just similes concerning her favor, he would have likened her full, clear eyes, with their white-encircled, gray irises, to moonflowers. With none of the goddesses whose traditional charms have become coldly classic would the discerning rhymester have compared her. She was purely Paradisaic, not Olympian. If you can imagine Eve, after the eviction, beguiling the flaming warriors and serenely re-entering the Garden, you will have her. Just so human, and still so harmonious with Eden seemed Mrs. Goodwin.

When her husband entered she looked up, and her lips curved and parted; her eyelids fluttered twice or thrice—a movement re-mindful (Poesy forgive us!) of the tail-wagging of a faithful dog and a little ripple went through her like the commotion set up in a weeping willow by a puff of wind. Thus she ever acknowledged his coming, were it twenty times a day. If they who sometimes sat over their wine in Coralio, reshaping old, diverting stories of the madcap career of Isabel Guilbert, could have seen the wife of Frank Goodwin that afternoon in the estimable aura of her happy wifehood, they might have disbelieved, or have agreed to forget, those graphic annals of the life of the one for whom their president gave up his country and his honor.

"I have brought a guest to dinner," said Goodwin. "One Colonel Falcon, from San Mateo. He is come on government business. I do not think you will care to see him, so I prescribe for you one of those convenient and indisputable feminine headaches."

"He has come to inquire about the lost money, has he not?" asked Mrs. Goodwin, going on with her sketch.

"A good guess!" acknowledged Goodwin. "He has been holding an inquisition among the natives for three days. I am next on his list of witnesses, but as he feels shy about dragging one of Uncle Sam's subjects before him, he consents to give it the outward appearance of a social function. He will apply the torture over my own wine and provender."

"Has he found any one who saw the valise of money?"

"Not a soul. Even Madame Ortiz, whose eyes are so sharp for the sight of a revenue official, does not remember that there was any baggage."

Mrs. Goodwin laid down her brush and sighed.

"I am so sorry, Frank," she said, "that they are giving you so much trouble about the money. But we can't let them know about it, can we?"

"Not without doing our intelligence a great injustice," said Goodwin, with a smile and a shrug that he had picked up from the natives. *"Americano,* though I am, they would have me in the *calaboza* in half an hour if they knew we had appropriated that valise. No; we must appear as ignorant about the money as the other ignoramuses in Coralio."

"Do you think that this man they have sent suspects you?" she asked, with a little pucker of her brows.

"He'd better not," said the American, carelessly. "It's lucky that no one caught a sight of the valise except myself. As I was in the rooms when the shot was fired, it is not surprising that they should want to investigate my part in the affair rather closely. But there's no cause for alarm. This colonel is down on the list of events for a good dinner, with a dessert of American 'bluff' that will end the matter, I think."

Mrs. Goodwin rose and walked to the window. Goodwin followed and stood by her side. She leaned to him, and rested in the protection of his strength, as she had always rested since that dark night on which he had first made himself her tower of refuge. Thus they stood for a little while.

Straight through the lavish growth of tropical branch and leaf and vine that confronted them had been cunningly trimmed a vista, that ended at the cleared environs of Coralio, on the banks of the mangrove swamp. At the other end of the aërial tunnel they could see the grave and wooden headpiece that bore the name of the unhappy President Miraflores. From this window when the rains forbade the open, and from the green and shady slopes of Goodwin's fruitful lands when the skies were smiling, his wife was wont to look upon that grave with a gentle sadness that was now scarcely a mar to her happiness.

"I loved him so, Frank!" she said, "even after that terrible flight and its awful ending. And you have been so good to me, and have made me so happy. It has all grown into such a strange puzzle. If they were to find out that we got the money do you think they would force you to make the amount good to the government?"

"They would undoubtedly try," answered Goodwin. "You are

right about its being a puzzle. And it must remain a puzzle to Falcon and all his countrymen until it solves itself. You and I, who know more than any one else, only know half of the solution. We must not let even a hint about this money get abroad. Let them come to the theory that the president concealed it in the mountains during his journey, or that he found means to ship it out of the country before he reached Coralio. I don't think that Falcon suspects me. He is making a close investigation, according to his orders, but he will find out nothing."

Thus they spake together. Had any one overheard or overseen them as they discussed the lost funds of Anchuria there would have been a second puzzle presented. For upon the faces and in the bearing of each of them was visible (if countenances are to be believed) Saxon honesty and pride and honorable thoughts. In Goodwin's steady eyes and firm lineaments, moulded into material shape by the inward spirit of kindness and generosity and courage, there was nothing reconcilable with his words.

As for his wife, physiognomy championed her even in the face of their accusive talk. Nobility was in her guise; purity was in her glance. The devotion that she manifested had not even the appearance of that feeling that now and then inspires a woman to share the guilt of her partner out of the pathetic greatness of her love. No, there was a discrepancy here between what the eye would have seen and the ear have heard.

Dinner was served to Goodwin and his guest in the *patio,* under cool foliage and flowers. The American begged the illustrious secretary to excuse the absence of Mrs. Goodwin, who was suffering, he said, from a headache brought on by a slight *calentura.*

After the meal they lingered, according to the custom, over their coffee and cigars. Colonel Falcon, with true Castilian delicacy, waited for his host to open the question that they had met to discuss. He had not long to wait. As soon as the cigars were lighted, the American cleared the way by inquiring whether the secretary's investigations in the town had furnished him with any clue to the lost funds.

"I have found no one yet," admitted Colonel Falcon, "who even had sight of the valise or the money. Yet I have persisted. It has been proven in the capital that President Miraflores set out from San Mateo with one hundred thousand dollars belonging to the government, accompanied by *Señorita* Isabel Guilbert, the opera singer. The Government, officially and personally, is loath to believe," concluded Colonel Falcon, with a smile, "that our last president's tastes would have permitted him to abandon on the route, as excess baggage, either of the desirable articles with which his flight was burdened."

"I suppose you would like to hear what I have to say about the affair," said Goodwin, coming directly to the point. "It will not require many words.

"On that night, with others of our friends here, I was keeping a lookout for the President, having been notified of his flight by a telegram in our national cipher from Englehart, one of our leaders in the capital. About ten o'clock that night I saw a man and a woman hurrying along the streets. They went to the Hotel de los Estranjeros, and engaged rooms. I followed them upstairs, leaving Estebán, who had come up, to watch outside. The barber had told me that he had shaved the beard from the President's face that night therefore I was prepared, when I entered the rooms, to find him with a smooth face. When I apprehended him in the name of the people he drew a pistol and shot himself instantly. In a few minutes many officers and citizens were on the spot. I suppose you have been informed of the subsequent facts."

Goodwin paused. Losada's agent maintained an attitude of waiting, as if he expected a continuance.

"And now," went on the American, looking steadily into the eyes of the other man, and giving each word a deliberate emphasis, "you will oblige me by attending carefully to what I have to add. I saw no valise or receptacle of any kind, or any money belonging to the Republic of Anchuria. If President Miraflores decamped with any funds belonging to the treasury of this country, or to himself, or to any one else, I saw no trace of it in the house or elsewhere, at that time or at any other. Does that statement cover the ground of the inquiry you wished to make of me?"

Colonel Falcon bowed, and described a fluent curve with his cigar. His duty was performed. Goodwin was not to be disputed. He was a loyal supporter of the government, and enjoyed the full confidence of the new president. His rectitude had been the capital that had brought him fortune in Anchuria, just as it had formed the lucrative "graft" of Mellinger, the secretary of Miraflores.

"I thank you, *Señor* Goodwin," said Falcon, "for speaking plainly. Your word will be sufficient for the President. But *Señor* Goodwin, I am instructed to pursue every clue that presents itself in this matter. There is one that I have not yet touched upon. Our friends in France, *señor,* have a saying, *'Cherchez la femme,'* when there is a mystery without a clue. But here we do not have to search. The woman who accompanied the late president in his flight must surely—"

"I must interrupt you there," interposed Goodwin. "It is true that when I entered the hotel for the purpose of intercepting President Miraflores I found a lady there. I must beg of you to remember that that lady is now my wife. I speak for her as I do for myself. She knows nothing of the fate of the valise or of the money that you are seeking. You will say to his excellency that I guarantee her innocence. I do not need to add to you, Colonel Falcon, that I do not care to have her questioned or disturbed."

Colonel Falcon bowed again.

"Por supuesto, no!" he cried. And to indicate that the inquiry was ended he added: "And now, *señor,* let me beg of you to show me that sea view from your *galería* of which you spoke. I am a lover of the sea."

In the early evening Goodwin walked back to the town with his guest, leaving him at the corner of the Calle Grande. As he was returning homeward one "Beelzebub" Blythe, with the air of a courtier and the outward aspect of a scarecrow, pounced upon him hopefully from the door of a *pulpería.*

Blythe had been re-christened "Beelzebub" as an acknowledgment of the greatness of his fall. Once in some distant Paradise Lost, he had foregathered with the angels of the earth. But Fate had hurled him headlong down to the tropics, where flamed in his bosom a fire that was seldom quenched. In Coralio they called him a beachcomber; but he was, in reality, a categorical idealist who strove to anamorphosize the dull verities of life by the means of brandy and rum. As Beelzebub, himself, might have held in his clutch with unwitting tenacity his harp or crown during his tremendous fall, so his namesake had clung to his gold-rimmed eyeglasses as the only souvenir of his lost estate. These he wore with impressiveness and distinction while he combed beaches and extracted toll from his friends. By some mysterious means he kept his drink-reddened face always smoothly shaven. For the rest he sponged gracefully upon whomsoever he could for enough to keep him pretty drunk, and sheltered from the rains and night dews.

"Hallo, Goodwin!" called the derelict, airily. "I was hoping I'd strike you. I wanted to see you particularly. Suppose we go where we can talk. Of course you know there's a chap down here looking up the money old Miraflores lost."

"Yes," said Goodwin, "I've been talking with him. Let's go into Espada's place. I can spare you ten minutes."

They went into the *pulpería* and sat at a little table upon stools with rawhide tops.

"Have a drink?" said Goodwin.

"They can't bring it too quickly," said Blythe. "I've been in a drought ever since morning. Hi—*muchacho!—el aguardiente por acá.*"

"Now, what do you want to see me about?" asked Goodwin, when the drinks were before them.

"Confound it, old man," drawled Blythe, "why do you spoil a golden moment like this with business? I wanted to see you—well, this has the preference." He gulped down his brandy, and gazed longingly into the empty glass.

"Have another?" suggested Goodwin.

"Between gentlemen," said the fallen angel, "I don't quite like your use of that word 'another.' It isn't quite delicate. But the concrete idea that the word represents is not displeasing."

The glasses were refilled. Blythe sipped blissfully from his, as he began to enter the state of a true idealist.

"I must trot along in a minute or two," hinted Goodwin. "Was there anything in particular?"

Blythe did not reply at once.

"Old Losada would make it a hot country," he remarked at length, "for the man who swiped that gripsack of treasury boodle, don't you think?"

"Undoubtedly, he would," agreed Goodwin calmly, as he rose leisurely to his feet. "I'll be running over to the house now, old man. Mrs. Goodwin is alone. There was nothing important you had to say, was there?"

"That's all," said Blythe. "Unless you wouldn't mind sending in another drink from the bar as you go out. Old Espada has closed my account to profit and loss. And pay for the lot, will you, like a good fellow?"

"All right," said Goodwin. *"Buenas noches."*

"Beelzebub" Blythe lingered over his cups, polishing his eyeglasses with a disreputable handkerchief.

"I thought I could do it, but I couldn't," he muttered to himself after a time. "A gentleman can't blackmail the man that he drinks with."

The Admiral

Spilled milk draws few tears from an Anchurian administration. Many are its lacteal sources; and the clocks' hands point forever to milking time. Even the rich cream skimmed from the treasury by the bewitched Miraflores did not cause the newly installed patriots to waste time in unprofitable regrets. The government philosophically set about supplying the deficiency by increasing the import duties and by "suggesting" to wealthy private citizens that contributions according to their means would be considered patriotic and in order. Prosperity was expected to attend the reign of Losada, the new president. The ousted office-holders and military favorites organized a new "Liberal" party, and began to lay their plans for a re-succession. Thus the game on Anchurian politics began, like a Chinese comedy, to unwind slowly its serial length. Here and there Mirth peeps for an instant from the wings and illumines the florid lines.

A dozen quarts of champagne in conjunction with an informal sitting of the president and his cabinet led to the establishment of the navy and the appointment of Felipe Carrera as its admiral.

Next to the champagne the credit of the appointment belongs to Don Sabas Placido, the newly confirmed Minister of War.

The President had requested a convention of his cabinet for the discussion of questions politic and for the transaction of certain routine matters of state. The session had been signally tedious; the business and the wine prodigiously dry. A sudden, prankish humor of Don Sabas, impelling him to the deed, spiced the grave affairs of state with a whiff of agreeable playfulness.

In the dilatory order of business had come a bulletin from the coast department of Orilla del Mar reporting the seizure by the custom-house officers at the town of Coralio of the sloop *Estrella del Noche* and her cargo of drygoods, patent medicines, granulated sugar and three-star brandy. Also six Martini rifles and a barrel of American whisky. Caught in the act of smuggling, the sloop with its cargo was now, according to law, the property of the republic.

The Collector of Customs, in making his report, departed from the conventional forms so far as to suggest that the confiscated vessel be converted to the use of the government. The prize was the first capture to the credit of the department in ten years. The collector took opportunity to pat his department on the back.

It often happened that government officers required transportation from point to point along the coast, and means were usually lacking. Furthermore, the sloop could be manned by a royal crew and employed as a coast guard to discourage the pernicious art of smuggling. The collector also ventured to nominate one to whom the charge of the boat could be safely intrusted—a young man of Coralio, Felipe Carrera—not, be it understood, one of extreme wisdom, but loyal and the best sailor along the coast.

It was upon this hint that the Minister of War acted, executing a rare piece of drollery that so enlivened the tedium of executive session.

In the constitution of this small, maritime banana republic was a forgotten section that provided for the maintenance of a navy. This provision—with many other wiser ones—had lain inert since the establishment of the republic. Anchuria had no navy and had no use for one. It was characteristic of Don Sabas—a man at once merry, learned, whimsical and audacious—that he should have disturbed the dust of this musty and sleeping statute to increase the humor of the world by so much as a smile from his indulgent colleagues.

With delightful mock seriousness the Minister of War proposed the creation of a navy. He argued its need and the glories it might achieve with such gay and witty zeal that the travesty overcame with its humor even the swart dignity of President Losada himself.

The champagne was bubbling trickily in the veins of the mercurial statesmen. It was not the custom of the grave governors of Anchuria to enliven their sessions with a beverage so apt to cast a veil of disparagement over sober affairs. The wine had been a thoughtful compliment tendered by the agent of the Vesuvius Fruit Company as a token of amicable relations—and certain consummated deals—between that company and the republic of Anchuria.

The jest was carried to its end. A formidable, official document was prepared, encrusted with chromatic seals and jaunty with fluttering ribbons, bearing the florid signatures of state. This commission conferred upon el Señor Don Felipe Carrera the title of Flag Admiral of the Republic of Anchuria. Thus within the space of a few minutes and the dominion of a dozen "extra dry," the country took its place among the naval powers of the world, and Felipe Carrera became entitled to a salute of nineteen guns whenever he might enter port.

The southern races are lacking in that particular kind of humor that finds entertainment in the defects and misfortunes bestowed by Nature. Owing to this defect in their constitution they are not moved to laughter (as are their northern brothers) by the spectacle of the deformed, the feeble-minded or the insane.

Felipe Carrera was sent upon earth with but half his wits. Therefore, the people of Coralio called him *"El pobrecito loco"*—"the poor little crazed one"—saying that God had sent but half of him to earth, retaining the other half.

A sombre youth, glowering, and speaking only at the rarest times, Felipe was but negatively "loco." On shore he generally refused all conversation. He seemed to know that he was badly handicapped on land, where so many kinds of understanding are needed; but on the water his only talent set him equal with most men. Few sailors whom God had carefully and completely made could handle a sailboat as well. Five points nearer the wind than even the best of them he could sail his sloop. When the elements raged and set other men to cowering, the deficiencies of Felipe seemed of little importance. He was a perfect sailor, if an imperfect man. He owned no boat, but worked among the crews of the schooners and sloops that skimmed the coast, trading and freighting fruit out to the steamers where there was no harbor. It was through his famous skill and boldness on the sea, as well as for the pity felt for his mental imperfections, that he was recommended by the collector as a suitable custodian of the captured sloop.

When the outcome of Don Sabas' little pleasantry arrived in the form of the imposing and preposterous commission, the collector smiled. He had not expected such prompt and overwhelming response to his recommendation. He despatched a *muchacho* at once to fetch the future admiral.

The collector waited in his official quarters. His office was in the Calle Grande, and the sea breezes hummed through its windows all day. The collector, in white linen and canvas shoes, philandered with papers on an antique desk. A parrot, perched on a pen rack, seasoned the official tedium with a fire of choice Castilian imprecations. Two rooms opened into the collector's. In one the clerical force of young men of variegated complexions transacted with glitter and parade their several duties. Through the open door of the other room could be seen a bronze babe, guiltless of clothing, that rollicked upon the floor. In a grass hammock a thin woman, tinted a pale lemon, played a guitar and swung contentedly in the breeze. Thus surrounded by the routine of his high duties and the visible tokens of agreeable domesticity, the collector's heart was further made happy by the power placed in his hands to brighten the fortunes of the "innocent" Felipe.

Felipe came and stood before the collector. He was a lad of

twenty, not ill-favored in looks, but with an expression of distant and pondering vacuity. He wore white cotton trousers, down the seams of which he had sewed red stripes with some vague aim at military decoration. A flimsy blue shirt fell open at his throat; his feet were bare; he held in his hand the cheapest of straw hats from the States.

"Señor Carrera," said the collector, gravely, producing the showy commission, "I have sent for you at the President's bidding. This document that I present to you confers upon you the title of Admiral of this great republic, and gives you absolute command of the naval forces and fleet of our country. You may think, friend Felipe, that we have no navy—but yes! The sloop the *Estrella del Noche,* that my brave men captured from the coast smugglers, is to be placed under your command. The boat is to be devoted to the services of your country. You will be ready at all times to convey officials of the government to points along the coast where they may be obliged to visit. You will also act as a coast-guard to prevent, as far as you may be able, the crime of smuggling. You will uphold the honor and prestige of your country at sea, and endeavor to place Anchuria among the proudest naval powers of the world. These are your instructions as the Minister of War desires me to convey them to you. *Por Dios!* I do not know how all this is to be accomplished, for not one word did his letter contain in respect to a crew or to the expenses of this navy. Perhaps you are to provide a crew yourself, Señor Admiral—I do not know—but it is a very high honor that has descended upon you. I now hand you your commission. When you are ready for the boat I will give orders that she shall be made over into your charge. That is as far as my instructions go."

Felipe took the commission that the collector handed to him. He gazed through the open window at the sea for a moment, with his customary expression of deep but vain pondering. Then he turned without having spoken a word, and walked swiftly away through the hot sand of the street.

"Pobrecito loco!" sighed the collector; and the parrot on the pen racks screeched "Loco!—loco!—loco!"

The next morning a strange procession filed through the streets to the collector's office. At its head was the admiral of the navy. Somewhere Felipe had raked together a pitiful semblance of a military uniform—a pair of red trousers, a dingy blue short jacket heavily ornamented with gold braid, and an old fatigue cap that must have been cast away by one of the British soldiers in Belize and brought away by Felipe on one of his coasting voyages. Buckled around his waist was an ancient ship's cutlass contributed to his equipment by Pedro Lafitte, the baker, who proudly asserted its inheritance from his ancestor, the illustrious buccaneer. At the admiral's heels tagged his newly shipped crew—three grinning, glossy, black Caribs, bare to the waist, the sand spurting in showers from the spring of their naked feet.

Briefly and with dignity Felipe demanded his vessel of the collector. And now a fresh honor awaited him. The collector's wife, who played the guitar and read novels in the hammock all day, had more than a little romance in her placid yellow bosom. She had found in an old book an engraving of a flag that purported to be the naval flag of Anchuria. Perhaps it had so been designed by the founders of the nation; but, as no navy had ever been established, oblivion had claimed the flag. Laboriously with her own hands she had made a flag after the pattern—a red cross upon a blue-and-white ground. She presented it to Felipe with these words: "Brave sailor, this flag is of your country. Be true, and defend it with your life. Go you with God."

For the first time since his appointment the admiral showed a flicker of emotion. He took the silken emblem, and passed his hand reverently over its surface. "I am the admiral," he said to the collector's lady. Being on land he could bring himself to no more exuberant expression of sentiment. At sea with the flag at the masthead of his navy, some more eloquent exposition of feelings might be forthcoming.

Abruptly the admiral departed with his crew. For the next three days they were busy giving the *Estrella del Noche* a new coat of white paint trimmed with blue. And then Felipe further adorned himself by fastening a handful of brilliant parrot's plumes in his cap. Again he tramped with his faithful crew to the collector's office and formally notified him that the sloop's name had been changed to *El Nacional.*

During the next few months the navy had its troubles. Even an admiral is perplexed to know what to do without any orders. But none came. Neither did any salaries. *El Nacional* swung idly at anchor.

When Felipe's little store of money was exhausted he went to the collector and raised the question of finances.

"Salaries!" exclaimed the collector, with hands raised; *"Valgame Dios!* not one *centavo* of my own pay have I received for the last seven months. The pay of an admiral, do you ask? *Quién sabe?* Should it be less than three thousand *pesos? Mira!* you will see a revolution in this country very soon. A good sign of it is when the government calls all the time for *pesos, pesos, pesos,* and pays none out."

Felipe left the collector's office with a look almost of content on his sombre face. A revolution would mean fighting, and then the government would need his services. It was rather humiliating to be an admiral without anything to do, and have a hungry crew at your heels begging for *reales* to buy plantains and tobacco with.

When he returned to where his happy-go-lucky Caribs were waiting they sprang up and saluted, as he had drilled them to do.

"Come, *muchachos,*" said the admiral; "it seems that the government is poor. It had no money to give us. We will earn what we need to live upon. Thus will we serve our country. Soon"—his heavy eyes almost lighted up—"it may gladly call upon us for help."

Thereafter *El Nacional* turned out with the other coast craft and became a wage-earner. She worked with the lighters freighting bananas and oranges out to the fruit steamers that could not approach nearer than a mile from the shore. Surely a self-supporting navy deserves red letters in the budget of any nation.

After earning enough at freighting to keep himself and his crew in provisions for a week Felipe would anchor the navy and hang about the little telegraph office, looking like one of the chorus of an insolvent comic opera troupe besieging the manager's den. A hope for orders from the capital was always in his heart. That his services as admiral had never been called into requirement hurt his pride and patriotism. At every call he would inquire, gravely and expectantly, for despatches. The operator would pretend to make a search, and then reply:

"Not yet, it seems, *Señor el Almirante—poco tiempo!*"

Outside in the shade of the lime-trees the crew chewed sugar cane or slumbered, well content to serve a country that was contented with so little service.

One day in the early summer the revolution predicted by the collector flamed out suddenly. It had long been smoldering. At the first note of alarm the admiral of the navy force and fleet made all sail for a larger port on the coast of a neighboring republic, where he traded a hastily collected cargo of fruit for its value in cartridges for the five Martini rifles, the only guns that the navy could boast. Then to the telegraph office sped the admiral. Sprawling in his favorite corner, in his fast-decaying uniform, with his prodigious sabre distributed between his red legs, he waited for the long-delayed, but now soon expected, orders.

"Not yet, *Señor el Almirante,*" the telegraph clerk would call to him—*"poco tiempo!"*

At the answer the admiral would plump himself down with a

great rattling of scabbard to await the infrequent tick of the little instrument on the table.

"They will come," would be his unshaken reply; "I am the admiral."

The Flag Paramount

At the head of the insurgent party appeared that Hector and learned Theban of the southern republic, Don Sabas Placido. A traveller, a soldier, a poet, a scientist, a statesman, and a connoisseur—the wonder was that he could content himself with the petty, remote life of his native country.

"It is a whim of Placido's," said a friend who knew him well, "to take up political intrigue. It is not otherwise than as if he had come upon a new *tempo* in music, a new bacillus in the air, a new scent, or rhyme, or explosive. He will squeeze this revolution dry of sensations, and a week afterward will forget it, skimming the seas of the world in his brigantine to add to his already world-famous collections. Collections of what? *Por Dios!* of everything from postage stamps to prehistoric stone idols."

But, for a mere dilettante, the aesthetic Placido seemed to be creating a lively row. The people admired him; they were fascinated by his brilliancy and flattered by his taking an interest in so small a thing as his native country. They rallied to the call of his lieutenants in the capital, where (somewhat contrary to arrangements) the army remained faithful to the government. There was also lively skirmishing in the coast towns. It was rumored that the revolution was aided by the Vesuvius Fruit Company, the power that forever stood with chiding smile and uplifted finger to keep Anchuria in the class of good children. Two of its steamers, the *Traveler* and the *Salvador,* were known to have conveyed insurgent troops from point to point along the coast.

As yet there had been no actual uprising in Coralio. Military law prevailed, and the ferment was bottled for the time. And then came the word that everywhere the revolutionists were encountering defeat. In the capital the president's forces triumphed; and there was a rumor that the leaders of the revolt had been forced to fly, hotly pursued.

In the little telegraph office at Coralio there was always a gathering of officials and loyal citizens, awaiting news from the seat of government. One morning the telegraph key began clicking, and presently the operator called, loudly: "One telegram for *el Almirante,* Don Señor Felipe Carrera!"

There was a shuffling sound, a great rattling of tin scabbard, and the admiral, prompt at his spot of waiting, leaped across the room to receive it.

The message was handed to him. Slowly spelling it out, he found it to be his first official order—thus running:

> Proceed immediately with your vessel to mouth of Rio Ruiz; transport beef and provisions to barracks at Alforan.
>
> Martinez, General

Small glory, to be sure, in this, his country's first call. But it had called, and joy surged in the admiral's breast. He drew his cutlass belt to another buckle hole, roused his dozing crew, and in a quarter of an hour *El Nacional* was tacking swiftly down coast in a stiff landward breeze.

The Rio Ruiz is a small river, emptying into the sea ten miles below Coralio. That portion of the coast is wild and solitary. Through a gorge in the Cordilleras rushes the Rio Ruiz, cold and bubbling, to glide, at last, with breadth and leisure, through an alluvial morass into the sea.

In two hours *El Nacional* entered the river's mouth. The banks were crowded with a disposition of formidable trees. The sumptuous undergrowth of the tropics overflowed the land, and drowned itself in the fallow waters. Silently the sloop entered there, and met a deeper silence. Brilliant with greens and ochres and floral scarlets, the umbrageous mouth of the Rio Ruiz furnished no sound or movement save of the sea-going water as it purled against the prow of the vessel. Small chance there seemed of wresting beef or provisions from that empty solitude.

The admiral decided to cast anchor, and, at the chain's rattle, the forest was stimulated to instant and resounding uproar. The mouth of the Rio Ruiz had only been taking a morning nap. Parrots and baboons screeched and barked in the trees; a whirring and a hissing and a booming marked the awakening of animal life; a dark blue bulk was visible for an instant, as a startled tapir fought his way through the vines.

The navy, under orders, hung in the mouth of the little river for hours. The crew served the dinner of shark's fin soup, plantains, crab gumbo and sour wine. The admiral, with a three-foot telescope, closely scanned the impervious foliage fifty yards away.

It was nearly sunset when a reverberating "hallo-o-o!" came from the forest to their left. It was answered; and three men, mounted upon mules, crashed through the tropic tangle to within a dozen yards of the river's bank. There they dismounted; and one, unbuckling his belt, struck each mule a violent blow with his sword scabbard, so that they, with a fling of heels, dashed back again into the forest.

Those were strange-looking men to be conveying beef and provisions. One was a large and exceedingly active man, of striking presence. He was of the purest Spanish type, with curling, gray-besprinkled, dark hair, blue, sparkling eyes, and the pronounced air of a *caballero grande.* The other two were small, brown-faced men, wearing white military uniforms, high riding boots and swords. The clothes of all were drenched, bespattered and rent by the thicket. Some stress of circumstance must have driven them, *diable à quatre,* through flood, mire and jungle.

"O-hé! Señor Almirante," called the large man. "Send to us your boat."

The dory was lowered, and Felipe, with one of the Caribs, rowed toward the left bank.

The large man stood near the water's brink, waist deep in the curling vines. As he gazed upon the scarecrow figure in the stern of the dory a sprightly interest beamed upon his mobile face.

Months of wageless and thankless service had dimmed the admiral's splendor. His red trousers were patched and ragged. Most of the bright buttons and yellow braid were gone from his jacket. The visor of his cap was torn, and depended almost to his eyes. The admiral's feet were bare.

"Dear admiral," cried the large man, and his voice was like a blast from a horn, "I kiss your hands. I knew we could build upon your fidelity. You had our despatch—from General Martinez. A little nearer with your boat, dear Admiral. Upon these devils of shifting vines we stand with the smallest security."

Felipe regarded him with a stolid face.

"Provisions and beef for the barracks at Alforan," he quoted.

"No fault of the butchers, *Almirante mio,* that the beef awaits you not. But you are come in time to save the cattle. Get us aboard your vessel, señor, at once. You first, *caballeros—á priesa!* Come back for me. The boat is too small."

The dory conveyed the two officers to the sloop, and returned for the large man.

"Have you so gross a thing as food, good admiral?" he cried, when aboard. "And, perhaps, coffee? Beef and provisions! *Nombre de Dios!* a little longer and we could have eaten one of those mules that you, Colonel Rafael, saluted so feelingly with your sword scabbard at parting. Let us have food; and then we will sail—for the barracks at Alforan—no?"

The Caribs prepared a meal, to which the three passengers of *El Nacional* set themselves with famished delight. About sunset, as was its custom, the breeze veered and swept back from the mountains, cool and steady, bringing a taste of the stagnant lagoons and mangrove swamps that guttered the lowlands. The mainsail of the sloop was hoisted and swelled to it, and at that moment they heard shouts and a waxing clamor from the bosky profundities of the shore.

"The butchers, my dear admiral," said the large man, smiling, "too late for the slaughter."

Further than his orders to his crew, the admiral was saying nothing. The topsail and jib were spread, and the sloop glided out of the estuary. The large man and his companions had bestowed themselves with what comfort they could about the bare deck. Belike, the thing big in their minds had been their departure from that critical shore; and now that the hazard was so far reduced their thoughts were loosed to the consideration of further deliverance. But when they saw the sloop turn and fly up coast again they relaxed, satisfied with the course the admiral had taken.

The large man sat at ease, his spirited blue eye engaged in the contemplation of the navy's commander. He was trying to estimate this sombre and fantastic lad, whose impenetrable stolidity puzzled him. Himself a fugitive, his life sought, and chafing under the smart of defeat and failure, it was characteristic of him to transfer instantly his interest to the study of a thing new to him. It was like him, too, to have conceived and risked all upon this last desperate and madcap scheme—this message to a poor, crazed *fanático* cruising about with his grotesque uniform and his farcical title. But his companions had been at their wit's end; escape had seemed incredible; and now he was pleased with the success of the plan they had called crack-brained and precarious.

The brief tropic twilight seemed to slide swiftly into the pearly splendor of a moonlight night. And now the lights of Coralio appeared, distributed against the darkening shore to their right. The admiral stood, silent, at the tiller; the Caribs, like black panthers, held the sheets, leaping noiselessly at his short commands. The three passengers were watching intently the sea before them, and when at length they came in sight of the bulk of a steamer lying a mile out from the town, with her lights radiating deep into the water, they held a sudden voluble and close-headed converse. The sloop was speeding as if to strike midway between ship and shore.

The large man suddenly separated from his companions and approached the scarecrow at the helm.

"My dear admiral," he said, "the government has been exceedingly remiss. I feel all the shame for it that only its ignorance of your devoted service has prevented it from sustaining. An inexcusable oversight has been made. A vessel, a uniform and a crew worthy of your fidelity shall be furnished you. But just now, dear admiral, there is business of moment afoot. The steamer lying there is the *Salvador.* I and my friends desire to be conveyed to her, where we are sent on the government's business. Do us the favor to shape your course accordingly."

Without replying, the admiral gave a sharp command, and put the tiller hard to port. *El Nacional* swerved, and headed straight as an arrow's course for the shore.

"Do me the favor," said the large man, a trifle restively, "to acknowledge, at least, that you catch the sound of my words." It was possible that the fellow might be lacking in senses as well as intellect.

The admiral emitted a croaking, harsh laugh, and spake.

"They will stand you," he said, "with your face to a wall and shoot you dead. That is the way they kill traitors. I knew you when you stepped into my boat. I have seen your picture in a book. You are Sabas Placido, traitor to your country. With your face to a wall. So, you will die. I am the admiral, and I will take you to them. With your face to a wall. Yes."

Don Sabas half turned and waved his hand, with a ringing laugh, toward his fellow fugitives. "To you, *caballeros,* I have related the history of that session when we issued that O! so ridiculous commission. Of a truth our jest has been turned against us. Behold the Frankenstein's monster we have created!"

Don Sabas glanced toward the shore. The lights of Coralio were drawing near. He could see the beach, the warehouse of the *Bodega Nacional,* the long low, *cuartel* occupied by the soldiers, and, behind that, gleaming in the moonlight, a stretch of high adobe wall. He had seen men stood with their faces to that wall and shot dead.

Again he addressed the extravagant figure at the helm.

"It is true," he said, "that I am fleeing the country. But, receive the assurance that I care very little for that. Courts and camps everywhere are open to Sabas Placido. *Vaya!* what is this molehill of a republic—this pig's head of a country—to a man like me? I am a *paisano* of everywhere. In Rome, in London, in Paris, in Vienna, you will hear them say: 'Welcome back, Don Sabas.' Come!—*tonto*—baboon of a boy—admiral, whatever you call yourself, turn your boat. Put us on board the *Salvador,* and here is your pay—five hundred *pesos* in money of the *Estados Unidos*—more than your lying government will pay you in twenty years."

Don Sabas pressed a plump purse against the youth's hand. The admiral gave no heed to the words or the movement. Braced against the helm, he was holding the sloop dead on her shoreward course. His dull face was lit almost to intelligence by some inward conceit that seemed to afford him joy, and found utterance in another parrot-like cackle.

"That is why they do it," he said—"so that you will not see the guns. They fire—boom!—and you fall dead. With your face to the wall. Yes."

The admiral called a sudden order to his crew. The lithe, silent Caribs made fast the sheets they held, and slipped down the hatchway into the hold of the sloop. When the last one had disappeared, Don Sabas, like a big, brown leopard, leaped forward, closed and fastened the hatch and stood, smiling.

"No rifles, if you please, dear admiral," he said. "It was a whimsey of mine once to compile a dictionary of the Carib *lengua.* So, I understood your order. Perhaps now you will—"

He cut short his words, for he heard the dull "swish" of iron scraping along tin. The admiral had drawn the cutlass of Pedro Lafitte, and was darting upon him. The blade descended, and it was only by a display of surprising agility that the large man escaped, with only a bruised shoulder, the glancing weapon. He was drawing his pistol as he sprang, and the next instant he shot the admiral down.

Don Sabas stooped over him, and rose again.

"In the heart," he said briefly. *"Señores,* the navy is abolished."

Colonel Rafael sprang to the helm, and the other officer hastened to loose the mainsail sheets. The boom swung round; *El Nacional* veered and began to tack industriously for the *Salvador.*

"Strike that flag, señor," called Colonel Rafael. "Our friends on the steamer will wonder why we are sailing under it."

"Well said," cried Don Sabas. Advancing to the mast he lowered the flag to the deck, where lay its too loyal supporter. Thus ended the Minister of War's little piece of after-dinner drollery, and by the same hand that began it.

Suddenly Don Sabas gave a great cry of joy, and ran down the slanting deck to the side of Colonel Rafael. Across his arm he carried the flag of the extinguished navy.

"Mire! mire! señor. Ah, *Dios!* Already can I hear that great bear of an *Oestreicher* shout, *'Du hast mein Herz gebrochen!' Mire!* Of my friend, Herr Grunitz, of Vienna, you have heard me relate. That man has travelled to Ceylon for an orchid—to Patagonia for a headdress—to Benares for a slipper—to Mozambique for a spearhead to add to his famous collections. Thou knowest, also, *amigo* Rafael, that

I have been a gatherer of curios. My collection of battle flags of the world's navies was the most complete in existence until last year. Then Herr Grunitz secured two, O! such rare specimens. One of a Barbary state, and one of the Makarooroos, a tribe on the west coast of Africa. I have not those, but they can be procured. But this flag, *señor*—do you know what it is? Name of God! Do you know? See that red cross upon the blue-and-white ground! You never saw it before? *Sequarmente no.* It is the naval flag of your country. *Mire!* This rotten tub we stand upon is its navy—that dead cockatoo lying there was its commander—that stroke of cutlass and single pistol shot a sea battle. All a piece of absurd foolery, I grant you—but authentic. There has never been another flag like this, and there never will be another. No. It is unique in the whole world. Yes. Think of what that means to a collector of flags! Do you know, *Coronel mío,* how many golden crowns Herr Grunitz would give for this flag? Ten thousand, likely. Well, a hundred thousand would not buy it. Beautiful flag! Only flag! Little devil of a most heaven-born flag! *O-hé!* old grumbler beyond the ocean. Wait till Don Sabas comes again to the Königin Strasse. He will let you kneel and touch the folds of it with one finger. *O-hé!* old spectacled ransacker of the world!"

Forgotten was the impotent revolution, the danger, the loss, the gall of defeat. Possessed solely by the inordinate and unparalleled passion of the collector, he strode up and down the little deck, clasping to his breast with one hand the paragon of a flag. He snapped his fingers triumphantly toward the east. He shouted the paean to his prize in trumpet tones, as though he would make old Grunitz hear in his musty den beyond the sea.

They were waiting, on the *Salvador,* to welcome them. The sloop came close alongside the steamer where her sides were sliced almost to the lower deck for the loading of fruit. The sailors of the *Salvador* grappled and held her there.

Captain McLeod leaned over the side.

"Well, *señor,* the jig is up, I'm told."

"The jig is up?" Don Sabas looked perplexed for a moment. "That revolution—ah, yes!" With a shrug of his shoulders he dismissed the matter.

The captain learned of the escape and the imprisoned crew.

"Caribs?" he said; "no harm in them." He slipped down into the sloop and kicked loose the hasp of the hatch. The black fellows came tumbling up, sweating but grinning.

"Hey! black boys!" said the captain, in a dialect of his own; "you sabe, catchy boat and vamos back same place quick."

They saw him point to themselves, the sloop and Coralio. "Yas,

yas!" they cried, with broader grins and many nods.

The four—Don Sabas, the two officers and the captain—moved to quit the sloop. Don Sabas lagged a little behind, looking at the still form of the late admiral, sprawled in his paltry trappings.

"Pobrecito loco," he said softly.

He was a brilliant cosmopolite and a *cognoscente* of high rank; but, after all, he was of the same race and blood and instinct as this people. Even as the simple *paisanos* of Coralio had said it, so said Don Sabas. Without a smile, he looked, and said, "The poor little crazed one!"

Stooping he raised the limp shoulders, drew the priceless and induplicable flag under them and over the breast, pinning it there with the diamond star of the Order of San Carlos that he took from the collar of his own coat.

He followed after the others, and stood with them upon the deck of the *Salvador.* The sailors that steadied *El Nacional* shoved her off. The jabbering Caribs hauled away at the rigging; the sloop headed for the shore.

And Herr Grunitz's collection of naval flags was still the finest in the world.

The Shamrock and the Palm

One night when there was no breeze, and Coralio seemed closer than ever to the gratings of Avernus, five men were grouped about the door of the photograph establishment of Keogh and Clancy. Thus, in all the scorched and exotic places of the earth, Caucasians meet when the day's work is done to preserve the fulness of the heritage by the aspersion of alien things.

Johnny Atwood lay stretched upon the grass in the undress uniform of a Carib, and prated feebly of the cool water to be had in the cucumberwood pumps of Dalesburg. Dr. Gregg, through the prestige of his whiskers and as a bribe against the relation of his imminent professional tales, was conceded the hammock that was swung between the door jamb and a calabash-tree. Keogh had moved out upon the grass a little table that held the instrument for burnishing completed photographs. He was the only busy one of the group. Industriously from between the cylinders of the burnisher rolled the finished depictments of Coralio's citizens. Blanchard, the French mining engineer, in his cool linen viewed the smoke of his cigarette through his calm glasses, impervious to the heat. Clancy sat on the steps, smoking his short pipe. His mood was the gossip's; the others were reduced, by the humidity, to the state of disability desirable in an audience.

Clancy was an American with an Irish diathesis and cosmopolitan proclivities. Many businesses had claimed him, but not for long. The roadster's blood was in his veins. The voice of the tintype was but one of the many callings that had wooed him upon so many roads. Sometimes he could be persuaded to oral construction of his voyages into the informal and egregious. To-night there were symptoms of divulgement in him.

" 'Tis elegant weather for filibusterin'," he volunteered. "It reminds me of the time I struggled to liberate a nation from the poisonous breath of a tyrant's clutch. 'Twas hard work. 'Tis strainin' to the back and makes corns on the hands."

"I didn't know you had ever lent your sword to an oppressed people," murmured Atwood, from the grass.

"I did," said Clancy; "and they turned it into a plowshare."

"What country was so fortunate as to secure your aid?" airily inquired Blanchard.

"Where's Kamchatka?" asked Clancy, with seeming irrelevance.

"Why, off Siberia somewhere in the Arctic regions," somebody answered, doubtfully.

"I thought that was the cold one," said Clancy, with a satisfied nod. "I'm always gettin' the two names mixed. 'Twas Guatemala, then—the hot one—I've been filibusterin' with. Ye'll find that country on the map. 'Tis in the district known as the tropics. By the foresight of Providence, it lies on the coast so the geography man could run the names of the towns off into the water. They're an inch long, small type, composed of Spanish dialects, and, 'tis my opinion, of the same system of syntax that blew up the *Maine.* Yes, 'twas that country I sailed against, single-handed, and endeavored to liberate it from a tyrannical government with a single-barreled pickaxe, unloaded at that. Ye don't understand, of course. 'Tis a statement demandin' elucidation and apologies.

" 'Twas in New Orleans one morning about the first of June; I was standin' down on the wharf, lookin' about at the ships in the river. There was a little steamer moored right opposite me that seemed about ready to sail. The funnels of it were throwin' out smoke, and a gang of roustabouts were carryin' aboard a pile of boxes that was stacked up on the wharf. The boxes were about two feet square, and somethin' like four feet long, and they seemed to be pretty heavy.

"I walked over, careless, to the stack of boxes. I saw one of them had been broken in handlin'. 'Twas curiosity made me pull up the loose top and look inside. The box was packed full of Winchester rifles. 'So, so,' says I to myself; 'somebody's gettin' a twist on the neutrality laws. Somebody's aidin' with munitions of war. I wonder where the popguns are goin'?'

"I heard somebody cough, and I turned around. There stood a little, round, fat man with a brown face and white clothes, a first-class-looking little man, with a four-karat diamond on his finger and his eye full of interrogations and respects. I judged he was a kind of foreigner—may be from Russia or Japan or the archipelagoes.

" 'Hist!' says the round man, full of concealments and confidences. 'Will the señor respect the discoveryments he has made, that the mans on the ship shall not be acquaint? The señor will be a gentleman that shall not expose one thing that by accident occur.'

" 'Monseer,' says I—for I judged him to be a kind of Frenchman—'receive my most exasperated assurances that your secret is safe with James Clancy. Furthermore, I will go so far as to remark, Veev la Liberty—veev it good and strong. Whenever you hear of a

Clancy obstructin' the abolishment of existin' governments you may notify me by return mail.'

"'The señor is good,' says the dark, fat man, smilin' under his black mustache. 'Wish you to come aboard my ship and drink of wine a glass.'

"Bein' a Clancy, in two minutes me and the foreigner man were seated at a table in the cabin of the steamer, with a bottle between us. I could hear the heavy boxes bein' dumped into the hold. I judged that cargo must consist of at least 2,000 Winchesters. Me and the brown man drank the bottle of stuff, and he called the steward to bring another. When you amalgamate a Clancy with the contents of a bottle you practically instigate secession. I had heard a good deal about these revolutions in them tropical localities, and I began to want a hand in it.

"'You goin' to stir things up in your country ain't you, monseer?' says I, with a wink to let him know I was on.

"'Yes, yes,' said the little man, pounding his fist on the table. 'A change of the greatest will occur. Too long have the people been oppressed with the promises and the never-to-happen things to become. The great work it shall be carry on. Yes. Our forces shall in the capital city strike of the soonest. *Carrambos!*'

"'*Carrambos* is the word,' says I, beginning to invest myself with enthusiasm and more wine, 'likewise veeva, as I said before. May the shamrock of old—I mean the banana-vine or the pie-plant, or whatever the imperial emblem may be of your down-trodden country, wave forever.'

"'A thousand thank-yous,' says the round man, 'for your emission of amicable utterances. What our cause needs of the very most is mans who will work do, to lift it along. Oh, for one thousands strong, good mans to aid the General De Vega that he shall to his country bring those success and glory! It is hard—oh, so hard to find good mans to help in the work.'

"'Monseer,' says I, leanin' over the table and graspin' his hand, 'I don't know where your country is, but me heart bleeds for it. The heart of a Clancy was never deaf to the sight of an oppressed people. The family is filibusterers by birth, and foreigners by trade. If you can use James Clancy's arms and his blood in denudin' your shores of the tyrant's yoke they're yours to command.'

"General De Vega was overcome with joy to confiscate my condolence of his conspiracies and predicaments. He tried to embrace me across the table, but his fatness, and the wine that had been in the bottles, prevented. Thus was I welcomed into the ranks of filibustery. Then the general man told me his country had the name of Guatemala, and was the greatest nation laved by any ocean whatever anywhere. He looked at me with tears in his eyes, and from time to time he would emit the remark, 'Ah! big, strong, brave mans! That is what my country need.'

"General De Vega, as was the name by which he denounced himself, brought out a document for me to sign, which I did, makin' a fine flourish and curlycue with the tail of the 'y.'

" 'Your passage-money,' says the general, business-like, 'shall from your pay be deduct.'

" 'Twill not,' says I, haughty. 'I'll pay my own passage.' A hundred and eighty dollars I had in my inside pocket, and 'twas no common filibuster I was goin' to be, filibusterin' for me board and clothes.

"The steamer was to sail in two hours, and I went ashore to get some things together I'd need. When I came aboard I showed the general with pride the outfit. 'Twas a fine Chinchilla overcoat, Arctic over-shoes, fur cap and earmuffs, with elegant fleece-lined gloves and woolen muffler.

" 'Carrambos!' says the little general. 'What clothes are these that shall go to the tropic?' And then the little spalpeen laughs, and he calls the captain, and the captain calls the purser, and they pipe up the chief engineer, and the whole gang leans against the cabin and laughs at Clancy's wardrobe for Guatemala.

"I reflects a bit, serious, and asks the general again to denominate the terms by which his country is called. He tells me, and I see then that 'twas the t'other one, Kamchatka, I had in mind. Since then I've had difficulty in separatin' the two nations in name, climate, and geographic disposition.

"I paid my passage—twenty-four dollars, first cabin—and ate at table with the officer crowd. Down on the lower deck was a gang of second-class passengers, about forty of them, seemin' to be Dagoes and the like. I wondered what so many of them were goin' along for.

"Well, then, in three days we sailed alongside that Guatemala. 'Twas a blue country, and not yellow as 'tis miscolored on the map. We landed at a town on the coast, where a train of cars was waitin' for us on a dinky little railroad. The boxes on the steamer were brought ashore and loaded on the cars. The gang of Dagoes got aboard, too, the general and me in the front car. Yes, me and General De Vega headed the revolution, as it pulled out of the seaport town. That train travelled about as fast as a policeman goin' to a riot. It penetrated the most conspicuous lot of fuzzy scenery ever seen outside a geography. We run some forty miles in seven hours, and the train stopped. There was no more railroad. 'Twas a sort of camp in a damp gorge full of wildness and melancholies. They was gradin' and choppin' out the forests ahead to continue the road. 'Here,' says I to myself, 'is the romantic haunt of the revolutionists. Here will Clancy, by the virtue that is in a superior race and the inculcation of Fenian tactics, strike a tremendous blow for liberty.'

"They unloaded the boxes from the train and begun to knock the tops off. From the first one that was open I saw General De Vega take the Winchester rifles and pass them around to a squad of morbid soldiery. The other boxes was opened next, and, believe me or not, divil another gun was to be seen. Every other box in the load was full of pickaxes and spades.

"And then—sorrow be upon them tropics—the proud Clancy and the dishonored Dagoes, each one of them, had to shoulder a pick or a spade, and march away to work on that dirty little railroad. Yes; 'twas that the Dagoes shipped for, and 'twas that the filibusterin' Clancy signed for, though unbeknownst to himself at the time. In after days I found out about it. It seems 'twas hard to get hands to work on that road. The intelligent natives of the country was too lazy to work. Indeed the saints know, 'twas unnecessary. By stretchin' out one hand, they could seize the most delicate and costly fruits of the earth, and, by stretchin' out the other, they could sleep for days at a time without hearin' a seven-o'clock whistle or the footsteps of the rent man upon the stairs. So, regular, the steamers travelled to the United States to seduce labor. Usually the imported spade-slingers died in two or three months from eatin' the over-ripe water and breathin' the violent tropical scenery. Wherefore they made them sign contracts for a year, when they hired them, and put an armed guard over the poor divils to keep them from runnin' away.

" 'Twas thus I was double-crossed by the tropics through a family failin' of goin' out of the way to hunt disturbances.

"They gave me a pick, and I took it, meditatin' an insurrection on the spot; but there was the guards handlin' the Winchesters careless, and I come to the conclusion that discretion was the best part of filibusterin'. There was about a hundred of us in the gang startin' out to work, and the word was given to move. I steps out of the ranks and goes up to that General De Vega man, who was smokin' a cigar and gazin' upon the scene with satisfactions and glory. He smiles at me polite and devilish. 'Plenty work,' says he, 'for big, strong mans in Guatemala. Yes. T'irty dollars in the month. Good pay. Ah, yes. You strong, brave man. Bimeby we push those railroad in the capital very quick. They want you go work now. *Adios,* strong mans.'

" 'Monseer,' says I, lingerin', 'will you tell a poor little Irishman this: When I set foot on your cockroachy steamer, and breathed liberal and revolutionary sentiments into your sour wine, did you think I was conspirin' to sling a pick on your contemptuous little railroad? And when you answered me with patriotic recitations, humping up the star-spangled cause of liberty, did you have meditations of reducin' me to the ranks of the stump-grubbin' Dagoes in the chain-gangs of your vile and grovelin' country?'

"The general man expanded his rotundity and laughed considerable. Yes, he laughed very long and loud, and I, Clancy, stood and waited.

" 'Comical mans!' he shouts, at last. 'So you will kill me from the laughing. Yes; it is hard to find the brave, strong mans to aid my country. Revolutions? Did I speak of r-r-revolutions? Not one word. I say, big, strong mans is need in Guatemala. So. The mistake is of you. You have looked in those one box containing those gun for the guard. You think all boxes is contain gun? No.

" 'There is not war in Guatemala. But work? Yes. Good. T'irty dollar in the month. You shall shoulder one pickaxe, señor, and dig for the liberty and prosperity of Guatemala. Off to your work. The guard waits for you.'

" 'Little, fat poodle dog of a brown man,' says I, quiet, but full of indignations and discomforts, 'things shall happen to you. Maybe not right away, but as soon as J. Clancy can formulate somethin' in the way of repartee.'

"The boss of the gang orders us to work. I tramps off with the Dagoes, and I hears the distinguished patriot and kidnapper laughin' hearty as we go.

" 'Tis a sorrowful fact, for eight weeks I built railroads for that misbehavin' country. I filibustered twelve hours a day with a heavy pick and a spade, choppin' away the luxurious landscape that grew upon the right of way. We worked in swamps that smelled like there was a leak in the gas mains, trampin' down a fine assortment of the most expensive hot-house plants and vegetables. The scene was tropical beyond the wildest imagination of the geography man. The trees was all sky-scrapers; the under-brush was full of needles and pins; there was monkeys jumpin' around and crocodiles and pink-tailed mockin'-birds, and ye stood knee-deep in the rotten water and grabbed roots for the liberation of Guatemala. Of nights we would build smudges in camp to discourage the mosquitoes, and sit in the smoke, with the guards pacin' all around us. There was two hundred men workin' on the road—mostly Dagoes, nigger-men, Spanish-men and Swedes. Three or four were Irish.

"One old man named Halloran—a man of Hibernian entitlements and discretions, explained it to me. He had been workin' on the road a year. Most of them died in less than six months. He was dried up to gristle and bone and shook with chills every third night.

" 'When you first come,' says he, 'ye think ye'll leave right away. But they hold out your first month's pay for your passage over, and by that time the tropics has its grip on ye. Ye're surrounded by a ragin' forest full of disreputable beasts—lions and baboons and anacondas—waitin' to devour ye. The sun strikes ye hard, and melts the marrow in your bones. Ye get similar to the lettuce-eaters the poetry-book speaks about. Ye forget the elevated sintiments of life, such as patriotism, revenge, disturbances of the peace and the dacint love of a clane shirt. Ye do your work, and ye swallow the kerosene ile and rubber pipestems dished up to ye by the Dago cook for food. Ye light your pipeful, and say to yoursilf, "Nixt week I'll break away," and ye go to sleep and call yersilf a liar, for ye know ye'll never do it.'

" 'Who is this general man,' asks I, 'that calls himself De Vega?'

" ' 'Tis the man,' says Halloran, 'who is tryin' to complete the finishin' of the railroad. 'Twas the project of a private corporation, but it was busted, and then the government took it up. De Vegy is a big politician, and wants to be president. The people want the railroad completed, as they're taxed mighty on account of it. The De Vegy man is pushin' it along as a campaign move.'

" ' 'Tis not my way,' says I, 'to make threats against any man, but there's an account to be settled between the railroad man and James O'Dowd Clancy.'

" ' 'Twas that way I thought, mesilf, at first,' Halloran says, with a big sigh, 'until I got to be a lettuce-eater. The fault's wid these tropics. They rejuices a man's system. 'Tis a land, as the poet says, "Where it always seems to be after dinner." I does me work and smokes me pipe and sleeps. There's little else in life, anyway. Ye'll get that way yersilf, mighty soon. Don't be harborin' any sintiments at all, Clancy.'

" 'I can't help it,' says I; 'I'm full of 'em. I enlisted in the revolutionary army of this dark country in good faith to fight for its liberty, honors and silver candlesticks; instead of which I am set to amputatin' its scenery and grubbin' its roots. 'Tis the general man will have to pay for it.'

"Two months I worked on that railroad before I found a chance to get away. One day a gang of us was sent back to the end of the completed line to fetch some picks that had been sent down to Port Barrios to be sharpened. They were brought on a hand-car, and I noticed, when I started away, that the car was left there on the track.

"That night, about twelve, I woke up Halloran and told him my scheme.

" 'Run away?' says Halloran. 'Good Lord, Clancy, do ye mean it? Why, I ain't got the nerve. It's too chilly, and I ain't slept enough. Run away? I told you, Clancy, I've eat the lettuce. I've lost my grip. 'Tis the tropics that's done it. 'Tis like the poet says: "Forgotten are our friends that we have left behind; in the hollow lettuce-land we will live and lay reclined." You better go on, Clancy, I'll stay, I guess. It's too early and cold, and I'm sleepy.'

"So I had to leave Halloran. I dressed quiet, and slipped out of the tent we were in. When the guard came along I knocked him over, like a ninepin, with a green cocoanut I had, and made for the railroad. I got on that hand-car and made it fly. 'Twas yet a while before daybreak when I saw the lights of Port Barrios about a mile away. I stopped the hand-car there and walked to the town. I stepped inside the corporations of that town with care and hesitations. I was not afraid of the army of Guatemala, but me soul quaked at the prospect of a hand-to-hand struggle with its employment bureau. 'Tis a country that hires its help easy and keeps 'em long. Sure I can fancy Missis America and Missis Guatemala passin' a bit of gossip some fine, still night across the mountains. 'Oh, dear,' says Missis America, 'and it's a lot of trouble I'm havin' ag'in with the help, señora, ma'am.' 'Laws, now!' says Missis Guatemala, 'you don't say so, ma'am! Now, mine never think of leavin' me—te-he! ma'am,' snickers Missis Guatemala.

"I was wonderin' how I was goin' to move away from them tropics without bein' hired again. Dark as it was, I could see a steamer ridin' in the harbor, with smoke emergin' from her stacks. I turned down a little grass street that run down to the water. On the beach I found a little brown nigger-man just about to shove off in a skiff.

" 'Hold on, Sambo,' says I, 'savve English?'

" 'Heap plenty, yes,' says he, with a pleasant grin.

" 'What steamer is that?' I asks him, 'and where is it going? And what's the news, and the good word and the time of day?'

" 'That steamer the *Conchita,*' said the brown man, affable and easy, rollin' a cigarette. 'Him come from New Orleans for load banana. Him got load last night. I think him sail in one, two hour. Verree nice day we shall be goin' to have. You hear some talkee 'bout big battle, maybe so? You think catchee General De Vega, señor? Yes? No?'

" 'How's that, Sambo?' says I. 'Big battle? What battle? Who wants catchee General De Vega? I've been up at my old gold mines in the interior for a couple of months, and haven't heard any news.'

" 'Oh,' says the nigger-man, proud to speak the English, 'verree great revolution in Guatemala one week ago. General De Vega, him try be president. Him raise armee—one—five—ten thousand mans for fight at the government. Those one government send five—forty—hundred thousand soldiers to suppress revolution. They fight big battle yesterday at Lomagrande—that about nineteen or fifty mile in the mountain. That government soldier wheep General De Vega—oh, most bad. Five hundred—nine hundred—two thousand of his mans is kill. That revolution is smash suppress—bust—very quick. General De Vega, him r-r-run away fast on one big mule. Yes, *carrambos!* The general, him r-r-run away, and his armee is kill. That government soldier, they try to find General De Vega verree much. They want catchee him for shoot. You think they catchee that general, señor?'

" 'Saints grant it!' says I. ' 'Twould be the judgment of Providence for settin' the warlike talent of a Clancy to gradin' the tropics with a pick and shovel. But 'tis not so much a question of insurrections now, me little man, as 'tis of the hired-man problem. 'Tis anxious I am to resign a situation of responsibility and trust with the white wings department of your great and degraded country. Row me in your little boat out to that steamer, and I'll give ye five dollars—sinker pacers—sinker pacers,' says I, reducin' the offer to the language and denomination of the tropic dialects.

" '*Cinco pesos,*' repeats the little man. 'Five dollee, you give?'

" 'Twas not such a bad little man. He had hesitations at first, sayin' that passengers leaving the country had to have papers and passports, but at last he took me out alongside the steamer.

"Day was just breakin' as we struck her, and there wasn't a soul to be seen on board. The water was very still, and the nigger-man gave me a lift from the boat, and I climbed onto the steamer where her side was sliced to the deck for loadin' fruit. The hatches was open, and I looked down and saw the cargo of bananas that filled the hold to within six feet of the top. I thinks to myself, 'Clancy, you better go as a stowaway. It's safer. The steamer men might hand you back to the employment bureau. The tropic'll get you, Clancy, if you don't watch out.'

"So I jumps down easy among the bananas and digs out a hole to hide in among the bunches. In an hour or so I could hear the engines goin', and feel the steamer rockin', and I knew we were off to sea. They left the hatches open for ventilation, and pretty soon it was light enough in the hold to see fairly well. I got to feelin' a bit hungry, and thought I'd have a light fruit lunch, by way of refreshment. I creeped out of the hole I'd made and stood up straight. Just then I saw another man crawl up about ten feet away and reach out and skin a banana and stuff it into his mouth. 'Twas a dirty man, black-faced and ragged and disgraceful of aspect. Yes, the man was a ringer for the pictures of the fat Weary Willie in the funny papers. I looked again, and saw it was my general man—De Vega, the great revolutionist, mule-rider and pick-axe importer. When he saw me the general hesitated with his mouth filled with banana and his eyes the size of cocoanuts.

" 'Hist!' I says. 'Not a word, or they'll put us off and make us walk. "Veev la Liberty!" ' I adds, copperin' the sentiment by shovin' a banana into the source of it. I was certain the general wouldn't recognize me. The nefarious work of the tropics had left me lookin' different. There was half an inch of roan whiskers coverin' me face, and me costume was a pair of blue overalls and a red shirt.

" 'How you come in the ship, señor?' asked the general as soon as he could speak.

" 'By the back door—whist!' says I. ' 'Twas a glorious blow for liberty we struck,' I continues; 'but we was overpowered by numbers. Let us accept our defeat like brave men and eat another banana.'

" 'Were you in the cause of liberty fightin', señor?' says the general, sheddin' tears on the cargo.

" 'To the last,' says I. ' 'Twas I led the last desperate charge against the minions of the tyrant. But it made them mad, and we was forced to retreat. 'Twas I, general, procured the mule upon which you escaped. Could you give that ripe bunch a little boost this way, general? It's a bit out of my reach. Thanks.'

" 'Say you so, brave patriot?' said the general, again weepin'. 'Ah, *Dios!* And I have not the means to reward your devotion. Barely did I my life bring away. *Carrambos!* what a devil's animal was that mule, señor! Like ships in one storm was I dashed about. The skin on myself was ripped away with the thorns and vines. Upon the bark of a hundred trees did that beast of the infernal bump, and cause outrage to the legs of mine. In the night to Port Barrios I came. I dispossess myself of that mountain of mule and hasten along the water shore. I find a little boat to be tied. I launch myself and row to the steamer. I cannot see any mans on board, so I climbed one rope which hang at the side. I then myself hide in the bananas. Surely, I say, if the ship captains view me, they shall throw me again to those Guatemala. Those things are not good. Guatemala will shoot General De Vega. Therefore, I am hide and remain silent. Life itself is glorious. Liberty, it is pretty good; but so good as life I do not think.'

"Three days, as I said, was the trip to New Orleans. The general man and me got to be cronies of the deepest dye. Bananas we ate until they were distasteful to the sight and an eyesore to the palate, but to bananas alone was the bill of fare reduced. At night I crawls out, careful, on the lower deck, and gets a bucket of fresh water.

"That General De Vega was a man inhabited by an engorgement of words and sentences. He added to the monotony of the voyage by divestin' himself of conversation. He believed I was a revolutionist of his own party, there bein', as he told me, a good many Americans and other foreigners in its ranks. 'Twas a braggart and a conceited little gabbler it was, though he considered himself a hero. 'Twas on himself he wasted all his regrets at the failin' of his plot. Not a word did the little balloon have to say about the other misbehavin' idiots that had been shot, or run themselves to death in his revolution.

"The second day out he was feelin' pretty braggy and uppish for a stowed-away conspirator that owed his existence to a mule and stolen bananas. He was tellin' me about the great railroad he had been buildin', and he relates what he calls a comic incident about a fool Irishman he inveigled from New Orleans to sling a pick on his little morgue of a narrow-gauge line. 'Twas sorrowful to hear the little, dirty general tell the opprobrious story of how he put salt upon the tail of that reckless and silly bird, Clancy. Laugh, he did, hearty and long. He shook with laughin', the black-faced rebel and outcast, standin' neck-deep in bananas, without friends or country.

" 'Ah, señor,' he snickers, 'to the death you would have laughed at that drollest Irish. I say to him: "Strong, big mans is need very much in Guatemala." "I will blows strike for your down-pressed country," he say. "That shall you do," I tell him. Ah! it was an Irish so comic. He sees one box break upon the wharf that contain for the guard a few gun. He think there is gun in all the box. But that is all pick-axe. Yes. Ah! señor, could you the face of that Irish have seen when they set him to the work!'

" 'Twas thus the ex-boss of the employment bureau contributed to the tedium of the trip with merry jests and anecdote. But now and then he would weep upon the bananas and make oration about the lost cause of liberty and the mule.

" 'Twas a pleasant sound when the steamer bumped against the pier in New Orleans. Pretty soon we heard the pat-a-pat of hundreds of bare feet, and the Dago gang that unloads the fruit jumped on the deck and down into the hold. Me and the general worked a while at passin' up the bunches, and they thought we were part of the gang. After about an hour we managed to slip off the steamer onto the wharf.

" 'Twas a great honor on the hands of an obscure Clancy, havin' the entertainment of the representative of a great foreign filibusterin' power. I first bought for the general and myself many long drinks and things to eat that were not bananas. The general man trotted along at my side, leavin' all the arrangements to me. I led him up to Lafayette Square and set him on a bench in the little park. Cigarettes I had bought for him, and he humped himself down on the seat like a little fat, contented hobo. I look him over as he sets there, and what I see pleases me. Brown by nature and instinct, he is now brindled with dirt and dust. Praise to the mule, his clothes is mostly strings and flaps. Yes, the looks of the general man is agreeable to Clancy.

"I ask him, delicate, if, by any chance, he brought away anybody's money with him from Guatemala. He sighs and bumps his shoulders against the bench. Not a cent. All right. Maybe, he tells me, some of his friends in the tropic outfit will send him funds later. The general was as clear a case of no visible means as I ever saw.

"I told him not to move from the bench, and then I went up to the corner of Poydras and Carondelet. Along there is O'Hara's beat. In five minutes along comes O'Hara, a big, fine man, red-faced, with shinin' buttons, swingin' his club. 'Twould be a fine thing for Guatemala to move into O'Hara's precinct. 'Twould be a fine bit of recreation for Danny to suppress revolutions and uprisin's once or twice a week with his club.

" 'Is 5046 workin' yet, Danny?' says I, walkin' up to him.

" 'Overtime,' says O'Hara, lookin' over me suspicious. 'Want some of it?'

"Fifty-forty-six is the celebrated city ordinance authorizin' arrest, conviction, and imprisonment of persons that succeed in concealin' their crimes from the police.

" 'Don't ye know Jimmy Clancy?' says I. 'Ye pink-gilled monster.' So, when O'Hara recognized me beneath the scandalous exterior bestowed upon me by the tropics, I backed him into a doorway and told him what I wanted, and why I wanted it. 'All right, Jimmy,' says O'Hara. 'Go back and hold the bench. I'll be along in ten minutes.'

"In that time O'Hara strolled through Lafayette Square and spied two Weary Willies disgracin' one of the benches. In ten minutes more J. Clancy and General De Vega, late candidate for the presidency of Guatemala, was in the station house. The general is badly frightened, and calls upon me to proclaim his distinguishments and rank.

" 'The man,' says I to the police, 'used to be a railroad man. He's on the bum now. 'Tis a little bughouse he is, on account of losin' his job.'

" '*Carrambos!*' says the general, fizzin' like a little soda-water fountain, 'you fought, señor, with my forces in my native country. Why do you say the lies? You shall say I am the General De Vega, one soldier, one *caballero—*'

" 'Railroader,' says I again. 'On the hog. No good. Been livin' for three days on stolen bananas. Look at him. Ain't that enough?'

"Twenty-five dollars or sixty days, was what the recorder gave the general. He didn't have a cent, so he took the time. They let me go, as I knew thcy would, for I had money to show, and O'Hara spoke for me. Yes; sixty days he got. 'Twas just so long that I slung a pick for the great country of Kam—Guatemala."

Clancy paused. The bright starlight showed a reminiscent look of happy content on his seasoned features. Keogh leaned in his chair and gave his partner a slap on his thinly-clad back that sounded like the crack of the surf on the sands.

"Tell 'em, you divil," he chuckled, "how you got even with the tropical general in the way of agricultural maneuverings."

"Havin' no money," concluded Clancy, with unction, "they set him to work his fine out with a gang from the parish prison clearing Ursulines Street. Around the corner was a saloon decorated genially with electric fans and cool merchandise. I made that me headquarters, and every fifteen minutes I'd walk around and take a look at the little man filibusterin' with a rake and shovel. 'Twas just such a hot broth of a day as this has been. And I'd call at him 'Hey, monseer!' and he'd look at me black, with the damp showin' through his shirt in places.

" 'Fat, strong mans,' says I to General De Vega, 'is needed in New Orleans. Yes. To carry on the good work. Carrambos! Erin go bragh!' "

The Remnants of the Code

Breakfast in Coralio was at eleven. Therefore the people did not go to market early. The little wooden market-house stood on a patch of short-trimmed grass, under the vivid green foliage of a bread-fruit tree.

Thither one morning the venders leisurely convened, bringing their wares with them. A porch or platform six feet wide encircled the building, shaded from the mid-morning sun by the projecting, grass-thatched roof. Upon this platform the venders were wont to display their goods—newly-killed beef, fish, crabs, fruit of the country, cassava, eggs, *dulces* and high, tottering stacks of native tortillas as large around as the sombrero of a Spanish grandee.

But on this morning they whose stations lay on the seaward side of the market-house, instead of spreading their merchandise formed themselves into a softly jabbering and gesticulating group. For there upon their space of the platform was sprawled, asleep, the unbeautiful figure of "Beelzebub" Blythe. He lay upon a ragged strip of cocoa matting, more than ever a fallen angel in appearance. His suit of coarse flax, soiled, bursting at the seams, crumpled into a thousand diversified wrinkles and creases, inclosed him absurdly, like the garb of some effigy that had been stuffed in sport and thrown there after indignity had been wrought upon it. But firmly upon the high bridge of his nose reposed his gold-rimmed glasses, the surviving badge of his ancient glory.

The sun's rays, reflecting quiveringly from the rippling sea upon his face, and the voices of the marketmen woke "Beelzebub" Blythe. He sat up, blinking, and leaned his back against the wall of the market. Drawing a blighted silk handkerchief from his pocket, he assiduously rubbed and burnished his glasses. And while doing this he became aware that his bedroom had been invaded, and that polite brown and yellow men were beseeching him to vacate in favor of their market stuff.

If the señor would have the goodness—a thousand pardons for bringing to him molestation—but soon would come the *compradores* for the day's provisions—surely they had ten thousand regrets at disturbing him!

In this manner they expanded to him the intimation that he must clear out and cease to clog the wheels of trade.

Blythe stepped from the platform with the air of a prince leaving his canopied couch. He never quite lost that air, even at the lowest point of his fall. It is clear that the college of good breeding does not necessarily maintain a chair of morals within its walls.

Blythe shook out his wry clothing, and moved slowly up the Calle Grande through the hot sand. He moved without a destination in his mind. The little town was languidly stirring to its daily life. Golden-skinned babies tumbled over one another in the grass. The sea breeze brought him appetite, but nothing to satisfy it. Throughout Coralio were its morning odors—those from the heavily fragrant tropical flowers and from the bread baking in the outdoor ovens of clay and the pervading smoke of their fires. Where the smoke cleared, the crystal air, with some of the efficacy of faith, seemed to remove the mountains almost to the sea, bringing them so near that one might count the scarred glades on their wooded sides. The light-footed Caribs were swiftly gliding to their tasks at the waterside. Already along the bosky trails from the banana groves files of horses were slowly moving, concealed, except for their nodding heads and plodding legs, by the bunches of green-golden fruit heaped upon their backs. On doorsills sat women combing their long, black hair and calling, one to another, across the narrow thoroughfares. Peace reigned in Coralio—arid and bald peace; but still peace.

On that bright morning when Nature seemed to be offering the lotus on the Dawn's golden platter "Beelzebub" Blythe had reached rock bottom. Further descent seemed impossible. That last night's slumber in a public place had done for him. As long as he had had a roof to cover him there had remained, unbridged, the space that separates a gentleman from the beasts of the jungle and the fowls of the air. But now he was little more than a whimpering oyster led to be devoured on the sands of a Southern sea by the artful walrus, Circumstance, and the implacable carpenter, Fate.

To Blythe money was now but a memory. He had drained his friends of all that their good-fellowship had to offer; then he had squeezed them to the last drop of their generosity; and at the last, Aaron-like, he had smitten the rock of their hardening bosoms for the scattering, ignoble drops of Charity itself.

He had exhausted his credit to the last *real.* With the minute keenness of the shameless sponger he was aware of every source in Coralio from which a glass of rum, a meal, or a piece of silver could be wheedled. Marshalling each such source in his mind, he considered it with all the thoroughness and penetration that hunger and thirst lent him for the task. All his optimism failed to thresh a grain of hope from the chaff of his postulations. He had played out the game. That one night in the open had shaken his nerves. Until then there had been left to him at least a few grounds upon which he could base his unblushing demands upon his neighbors' stores. Now he must beg instead of borrowing. The most brazen sophistry could not dignify by the name of "loan" the coin contemptuously flung to a beach-comber who slept on the bare boards of the public market.

But on this morning no beggar would have more thankfully received a charitable coin, for the demon thirst had him by the throat—the drunkard's matutinal thirst that requires to be slaked at each morning station on the road to Tophet.

Blythe walked slowly up the street, keeping a watchful eye for any miracle that might drop manna upon him in his wilderness. As he passed the popular eating house of Madama Vasquez, Madama's boarders were just sitting down to freshly-baked bread, *aguacates,* pines and delicious coffee that sent forth odorous guarantee of its quality upon the breeze. Madama was serving; she turned her shy, stolid, melancholy gaze for a moment out the window; she saw Blythe, and her expression turned more shy and embarrassed. "Beelzebub" owed her twenty *pesos.* He bowed as he had once bowed to less embarrassed dames to whom he owed nothing, and passed on.

Merchants and their clerks were throwing open the solid wooden doors of their shops. Polite but cool were the glances they cast upon Blythe as he lounged tentatively by with the remains of his old jaunty air; for they were his creditors almost without exception.

At the little fountain in the *plaza* he made an apology for a toilet with his wetted handkerchief. Across the open square filed the dolorous line of friends of the prisoners in the *calaboza,* bearing the morning meal of the immured. The food in their hands aroused small longing in Blythe. It was drink that his soul craved, or money to buy it.

In the streets he met many with whom he had been friends and equals, and whose patience and liberality he had gradually exhausted. Willard Geddie and Paula cantered past him with the coolest of nods, returning from their daily horseback ride along the old Indian road. Keogh passed him at another corner, whistling cheerfully and bearing a prize of newly-laid eggs for the beakfast of himself and Clancy. The jovial scout of Fortune was one of Blythe's victims who had plunged his hand oftenest into his pocket to aid him. But now it seemed that Keogh, too, had fortified himself against further invasions. His curt greeting and the ominous light in his full gray eye quickened the steps of "Beelzebub," whom desperation had almost incited to attempt an additional "loan."

Three drinking shops the forlorn one next visited in succession.

In all of these his money, his credit, and his welcome had long since been spent; but Blythe felt that he would have fawned in the dust at the feet of an enemy that morning for one draught of *aguardiente.* In two of the *pulperías* his courageous petition for drink was met with a refusal so polite that it stung worse than abuse. The third establishment had acquired something of American methods; and here he was seized bodily and cast out upon his hands and knees.

This physical indignity caused a singular change in the man. As he picked himself up and walked away, an expression of absolute relief came upon his features. The specious and conciliatory smile that had been graven there was succeeded by a look of calm and sinister resolve. "Beelzebub" had been floundering in the sea of improbity, holding by a slender life-line to the respectable world that had cast him overboard. He must have felt that with this ultimate shock the line had snapped, and have experienced the welcome ease of the drowning swimmer who has ceased to struggle.

Blythe walked to the next corner and stood there while he brushed the sand from his garments and repolished his glasses.

"I've got to do it—oh, I've got to do it," he told himself, aloud. "If I had a quart of rum I believe I could stave it off yet—for a little while. But there's no more rum for—'Beelzebub,' as they call me. By the flames of Tartarus! If I'm to sit at the right hand of Satan somebody has got to pay the court expenses. You'll have to pony up, Mr. Frank Goodwin. You're a good fellow; but a gentleman must draw the line at being kicked into the gutter. Blackmail isn't a pretty word, but it's the next station on the road I'm travelling."

With purpose in his steps Blythe now moved rapidly through the town by way of its landward environs. He passed through the squalid quarters of the improvident negroes and on beyond the picturesque shacks of the poorer *mestizos.* From many points along his course he could see, through the umbrageous glades, the house of Frank Goodwin on its wooded hill. And as he crossed the little bridge over the lagoon he saw the old Indian, Galvez, scrubbing at the wooden slab that bore the name of Miraflores. Beyond the lagoon the lands of Goodwin began to slope gently upward. A grassy road, shaded by a munificent and diverse array of tropical flora, wound from the edge of an outlying banana grove to the dwelling. Blythe took this road with long and purposeful strides.

Goodwin was seated on his coolest gallery, dictating letters to his secretary, a sallow and capable native youth. The household adhered to the American plan of breakfast; and that meal had been a thing of the past for the better part of an hour.

The castaway walked to the steps, and flourished a hand.

"Good morning, Blythe," said Goodwin, looking up. "Come in and have a chair. Anything I can do for you?"

"I want to speak to you in private."

Goodwin nodded at his secretary, who strolled out under a mango tree and lit a cigarette. Blythe took the chair that he had left vacant.

"I want some money," he began, doggedly.

"I'm sorry," said Goodwin, with equal directness, "but you can't have any. You're drinking yourself to death, Blythe. Your friends have done all they could to help you to brace up. You won't help yourself. There's no use furnishing you with money to ruin yourself with any longer."

"Dear man," said Blythe, tilting back his chair, "it isn't a question of social economy now. It's past that. I like you, Goodwin; and I've come to stick a knife between your ribs. I was kicked out of Espada's saloon this morning; and Society owes me reparation for my wounded feelings."

"I didn't kick you out."

"No; but in a general way you represent Society; and in a particular way you represent my last chance. I've had to come down to it, old man—I tried to do it a month ago when Losada's man was here turning things over; but I couldn't do it then. Now it's different. I want a thousand dollars, Goodwin; and you have to give it to me."

"Only last week," said Goodwin, with a smile, "a silver dollar was all you were asking for."

"An evidence," said Blythe, flippantly, "that I was still virtuous—though under heavy pressure. The wages of sin should be something higher than a *peso* worth forty-eight cents. Let's talk business. I am the villain in the third act; and I must have my merited, if only temporary, triumph. I saw you collar the late president's valiseful of boodle. Oh, I know it's blackmail; but I'm liberal about the price. I know I'm a cheap villain—one of the regular sawmill-drama kind—but you're one of my particular friends, and I don't want to stick you hard."

"Suppose you go into the details," suggested Goodwin, calmly arranging his letters on the table.

"All right," said "Beelzebub." "I like the way you take it. I despise histrionics; so you will please prepare yourself for the facts without any red fire, calcium or grace notes on the saxophone.

"On the night that His Fly-by-night Excellency arrived in town I was very drunk. You will excuse the pride with which I state that fact; but it was quite a feat for me to attain that desirable state. Somebody had left a cot out under the orange trees in the yard of Madama

Ortiz's hotel. I stepped over the wall, laid down upon it, and fell asleep. I was awakened by an orange that dropped from the tree upon my nose; and I laid there for awhile cursing Sir Isaac Newton, or whoever it was that invented gravitation, for not confining his theory to apples.

"And then along came Mr. Miraflores and his true-love with the treasury in a valise, and went into the hotel. Next you hove in sight, and held a pow-wow with the tonsorial artist who insisted upon talking shop after hours. I tried to slumber again; but once more my rest was disturbed—this time by the noise of the popgun that went off upstairs. Then that valise came crashing down into an orange tree just above my head; and I arose from my couch, not knowing when it might begin to rain Saratoga trunks. When the army and the constabulary began to arrive, with their medals and decorations hastily pinned to their pajamas, and their snickersnees drawn, I crawled into the welcome shadow of a banana plant. I remained there for an hour, by which time the excitement and the people had cleared away. And then, my dear Goodwin—excuse me—I saw you sneak back and pluck that ripe and juicy valise from the orange tree. I followed you, and saw you take it to your own house. A hundred-thousand-dollar crop from one orange tree in a season about breaks the record of the fruit-growing industry.

"Being a gentleman at that time, of course, I never mentioned the incident to any one. But this morning I was kicked out of a saloon, my code of honor is all out at the elbows, and I'd sell my mother's prayer-book for three fingers of *aguardiente.* I'm not putting on the screws hard. It ought to be worth a thousand to you for me to have slept on that cot through the whole business without waking up and seeing anything."

Goodwin opened two more letters, and made memoranda in pencil on them. Then he called "Manuel!" to his secretary, who came, spryly.

"The *Ariel*—when does she sail?" asked Goodwin.

"Señor," answered the youth, "at three this afternoon. She drops downcoast to Punta Soledad to complete her cargo of fruit. From there she sails for New Orleans without delay."

"Bueno!" said Goodwin. "These letters may wait yet awhile."

The secretary returned to his cigarette under the mango tree.

"In round numbers," said Goodwin, facing Blythe squarely, "how much money do you owe in this town, not including the sums you have 'borrowed' from me?"

"Five hundred—at a rough guess," answered Blythe, lightly.

"Go somewhere in the town and draw up a schedule of your

debts," said Goodwin. "Come back here in two hours, and I will send Manuel with the money to pay them. I will also have a decent outfit of clothing ready for you. You will sail on the *Ariel* at three. Manuel will accompany you as far as the deck of the steamer. There he will hand you one thousand dollars in cash. I suppose that we needn't discuss what you will be expected to do in return."

"Oh, I understand," piped Blythe, cheerily. "I was asleep all the time on the cot under Madama Ortiz's orange trees; and I shake off the dust of Coralio forever. I'll play fair. No more of the lotus for me. Your proposition is O. K. You're a good fellow, Goodwin; and I let you off light. I'll agree to everything. But in the meantime—I've a devil of a thirst on, old man—"

"Not a *centavo,*" said Goodwin, firmly, "until you are on board the *Ariel.* You would be drunk in thirty minutes if you had money now."

But he noticed the blood-streaked eyeballs, the relaxed form, and the shaking hands of "Beelzebub"; and he stepped into the dining room through the low window, and brought out a glass and a decanter of brandy.

"Take a bracer, anyway, before you go," he proposed, even as a man to the friend whom he entertains.

"Beelzebub" Blythe's eyes glistened at the sight of the solace for which his soul burned. To-day for the first time his poisoned nerves had been denied their steadying dose; and their retort was a mounting torment. He grasped the decanter and rattled its crystal mouth against the glass in his trembling hand. He flushed the glass, and then stood erect, holding it aloft for an instant. For one fleeting moment he held his head above the drowning waves of his abyss. He nodded easily at Goodwin, raised his brimming glass and murmured a "health" that men had used in his ancient Paradise Lost. And then so suddenly that he spilled the brandy over his hand, he set down his glass, untasted.

"In two hours," his dry lips muttered to Goodwin, as he marched down the steps and turned his face toward the town.

In the edge of the cool banana grove "Beelzebub" halted, and snapped the tongue of his belt buckle into another hole.

"I couldn't do it," he explained, feverishly, to the waving banana fronds. "I wanted to, but I couldn't. A gentleman can't drink with the man that he blackmails."

Shoes

John De Graffenreid Atwood ate of the lotus, root, stem, and flower. The tropics gobbled him up. He plunged enthusiastically into his work, which was to try to forget Rosine.

Now, they who dine on the lotus rarely consume it plain. There is a sauce *au diable* that goes with it; and the distillers are the chefs who prepare it. And on Johnny's menu card it read "brandy." With a bottle between them, he and Billy Keogh would sit on the porch of the little consulate at night and roar out great, indecorous songs, until the natives, slipping hastily past, would shrug a shoulder and mutter things to themselves about the *"Americanos diablos."*

One day Johnny's *mozo* brought the mail and dumped it on the table. Johnny leaned from his hammock, and fingered the four or five letters dejectedly. Keogh was sitting on the edge of the table chopping lazily with a paper knife at the legs of a centipede that was crawling among the stationery. Johnny was in that phase of lotus-eating when all the world tastes bitter in one's mouth.

"Same old thing!" he complained. "Fool people writing for information about the country. They want to know all about raising fruit, and how to make a fortune without work. Half of 'em don't even send stamps for a reply. They think a consul hasn't anything to do but write letters. Slit those envelopes for me, old man, and see what they want. I'm feeling too rocky to move."

Keogh, acclimated beyond all possibility of ill-humor, drew his chair to the table with smiling compliance on his rose-pink countenance, and began to slit open the letters. Four of them were from citizens in various parts of the United States who seemed to regard the consul at Coralio as a cyclopædia of information. They asked long lists of questions, numerically arranged, about the climate, products, possibilities, laws, business chances, and statistics of the country in which the consul had the honor of representing his own government.

"Write 'em, please, Billy," said that inert official, "just a line, referring them to the latest consular report. Tell 'em the State Department will be delighted to furnish the literary gems. Sign my name. Don't let your pen scratch, Billy; it'll keep me awake."

"Don't snore," said Keogh, amiably, "and I'll do your work for you. You need a corps of assistants, anyhow. Don't see how you ever get out a report. Wake up a minute!—here's one more letter—it's from your own town, too—Dalesburg."

"That so?" murmured Johnny, showing a mild obligatory interest. "What's it about?"

"Postmaster writes," explained Keogh. "Says a citizen of the town wants some facts and advice from you. Says the citizen has an idea in his head of coming down where you are and opening a shoe store. Wants to know if you think the business would pay. Says he's heard of the boom along this coast, and wants to get in on the ground floor."

In spite of the heat and his bad temper, Johnny's hammock swayed with his laughter. Keogh laughed too; and the pet monkey on the top shelf of the bookcase chattered in shrill sympathy with the ironical reception of the letter from Dalesburg.

"Great bunions!" exclaimed the consul. "Shoe store! What'll they ask about next, I wonder? Overcoat factory, I reckon. Say, Billy—of our 3,000 citizens, how many do you suppose ever had on a pair of shoes?"

Keogh reflected judicially.

"Let's see—there's you and me and—"

"Not me," said Johnny, promptly and incorrectly, holding up a foot encased in a disreputable deerskin *zapato.* "I haven't been a victim to shoes in months."

"But you've got 'em, though," went on Keogh. "And there's Goodwin and Blanchard and Geddie and old Lutz and Doc Gregg and that Italian that's agent for the banana company, and there's old Delgado—no; he wears sandals. And, oh, yes; there's Madama Ortiz, 'what kapes the hotel'—she had on a pair of red slippers at the *baile* the other night. And Miss Pasa, her daughter, that went to school in the States—she brought back some civilized notions in the way of footgear. And there's the *comandante's* sister that dresses up her feet on feast-days—and Mrs. Geddie, who wears a two with a Castilian instep—and that's about all the ladies. Let's see—don't some of the soldiers at the *cuartel*—no that's so; they're allowed shoes only when on the march. In barracks they turn their little toeses out to grass."

" 'Bout right," agreed the consul. "Not over twenty out of the three thousand ever felt leather on their walking arrangements. Oh, yes; Coralio is just the town for an enterprising shoe store—that doesn't want to part with its goods. Wonder if old Patterson is trying to jolly me! He always was full of things he called jokes. Write him a letter, Billy. I'll dictate it. We'll jolly him back a few."

Keogh dipped his pen, and wrote at Johnny's dictation. With many pauses, filled in with smoke and sundry travellings of the bottle and glasses, the following reply to the Dalesburg communication was perpetrated:

> Mr. Obadiah Patterson,
> Dalesburg, Ala.
>
> *Dear Sir:* In reply to your favor of July 2d, I have the honor to inform you that, according to my opinion, there is no place on the habitable globe that presents to the eye stronger evidence of the need of a first-class shoe store than does the town of Coralio. There are 3,000 inhabitants in the place, and not a single shoe store! The situation speaks for itself. This coast is rapidly becoming the goal of enterprising business men, but the shoe business is one that has been sadly overlooked or neglected. In fact, there are a considerable number of our citizens actually without shoes at present.
>
> Besides the want above mentioned, there is also a crying need for a brewery, a college of higher mathematics, a coal yard, and a clean and intellectual Punch and Judy show. I have the honor to be, sir,
>
> Your Obt. Servant,
> John De Graffenreid Atwood,
> *U. S. Consul at Coralio.*
>
> P. S.—Hello! Uncle Obadiah. How's the old burg racking along? What would the government do without you and me? Look out for a green-headed parrot and a bunch of bananas soon, from your old friend
>
> Johnny

"I throw in that postscript," explained the consul, "so Uncle Obadiah won't take offence at the official tone of the letter! Now, Billy, you get that correspondence fixed up, and send Pancho to the post-office with it. The *Ariadne* takes the mail out to-morrow if they make up that load of fruit to-day."

The night programme in Coralio never varied. The recreations of the people were soporific and flat. They wandered about, barefoot and aimless, speaking lowly and smoking cigar or cigarette. Looking down on the dimly lighted ways one seemed to see a threading maze of brunette ghosts tangled with a procession of insane fire-flies. In some houses the thrumming of lugubrious guitars added to the depression of the *triste* night. Giant tree-frogs rattled in the foliage as loudly as the end man's "bones" in a minstrel troupe. By nine o'clock the streets were almost deserted.

Not at the consulate was there often a change of bill. Keogh would come there nightly, for Coralio's one cool place with the little seaward porch of that official residence.

The brandy would be kept moving; and before midnight sentiment would begin to stir in the heart of the self-exiled consul. Then he would relate to Keogh the story of his ended romance. Each night Keogh would listen patiently to the tale, and be ready with untiring sympathy.

"But don't you think for a minute"—thus Johnny would always conclude his woeful narrative—"that I'm grieving about that girl, Billy. I've forgotten her. She never enters my mind. If she were to enter that door right now, my pulse wouldn't gain a beat. That's all over long ago."

"Don't I know it?" Keogh would answer. "Of course you've forgotten her. Proper thing to do. Wasn't quite O. K. of her to listen to the knocks that—er—Dink Pawson kept giving you."

"Pink Dawson!"—a world of contempt would be in Johnny's tones—"Poor white trash! That's what he was. Had five hundred acres of farming land, though; and that counted. Maybe I'll have a chance to get back at him some day. The Dawsons weren't anybody. Everybody in Alabama knows the Atwoods. Say, Billy—did you know my mother was a De Graffenreid?"

"Why, no," Keogh would say; "is that so?" He had heard it some three hundred times.

"Fact. The De Graffenreids of Hancock County. But I never think of that girl any more, do I, Billy?"

"Not for a minute, my boy," would be the last sounds heard by the conqueror of Cupid.

At this point Johnny would fall into a gentle slumber, and Keogh would saunter out to his own shack under the calabash tree at the edge of the plaza.

In a day or two the letter from the Dalesburg postmaster and its answer had been forgotten by the Coralio exiles. But on the 26th day of July the fruit of the reply appeared upon the tree of events.

The *Andador,* a fruit steamer that visited Coralio regularly, drew into the offing and anchored. The beach was lined with spectators while the quarantine doctor and the custom-house crew rowed out to attend to their duties.

An hour later Bill Keogh lounged into the consulate, clean and cool in his linen clothes, and grinning like a pleased shark.

"Guess what?" he said to Johnny, lounging in his hammock.

"Too hot to guess," said Johnny, lazily.

"Your shoe-store man's come," said Keogh, rolling the sweet morsel on his tongue, "with a stock of goods big enough to supply the continent as far down as Terra del Fuego. They're carting his cases over to the custom-house now. Six barges full they brought ashore and have paddled back for the rest. Oh, ye saints in glory! won't there be regalements in the air when he gets onto the joke and has an interview with Mr. Consul? It'll be worth nine years in the tropics just to witness that one joyful moment."

Keogh loved to take his mirth easily. He selected a clean place on the matting and lay upon the floor. The walls shook with his enjoyment. Johnny turned half over and blinked.

"Don't tell me," he said, "that anybody was fool cnough to take that letter seriously."

"Four-thousand-dollar stock of goods!" gasped Keogh, in ecstasy. "Talk about coals to Newcastle! Why didn't he take a shipload of palm-leaf fans to Spitzbergen while he was about it? Saw the old codger on the beach. You ought to have been there when he put on his specs and squinted at the five hundred or so barefooted citizens standing around."

"Are you telling the truth, Billy?" asked the consul, weakly.

"Am I? You ought to see the buncoed gentleman's daughter he brought along. Looks! She makes the brick-dust señoritas here look like tarbabies."

"Go on," said Johnny, "if you can stop that asinine giggling. I hate to see a grown man make a laughing hyena of himself."

"Name is Hemstetter," went on Keogh. "He's a— Hello! what's the matter now?"

Johnny's moccasined feet struck the floor with a thud as he wriggled out of his hammock.

"Get up, you idiot," he said, sternly, "or I'll brain you with this inkstand. That's Rosine and her father. Gad! what a drivelling idiot old Patterson is! Get up, here, Billy Keogh, and help me. What the devil are we going to do? Has all the world gone crazy?"

Keogh rose and dusted himself. He managed to regain a decorous demeanor.

"Situation has got to be met, Johnny," he said, with some success at seriousness. "I didn't think about its being your girl until you spoke. First thing to do is to get them comfortable quarters. You go down and face the music, and I'll trot out to Goodwin's and see if Mrs. Goodwin won't take them in. They've got the decentest house in town."

"Bless you, Billy!" said the consul. "I knew you wouldn't desert me. The world's bound to come to an end, but maybe we can stave it off for a day or two."

Keogh hoisted his umbrella and set out for Goodwin's house.

Johnny put on his coat and hat. He picked up the brandy bottle, but set it down again without drinking, and marched bravely down to the beach.

In the shade of the custom-house walls he found Mr. Hemstetter and Rosine surrounded by a mass of gaping citizens. The customs officers were ducking and scraping, while the captain of the *Andador* interpreted the business of the new arrivals. Rosine looked healthy and very much alive. She was gazing at the strange scenes around her with amused interest. There was a faint blush upon her round cheek as she greeted her old admirer. Mr. Hemstetter shook hands with Johnny in a very friendly way. He was an oldish, impractical man—one of that numerous class of erratic business men who are forever dissatisfied, and seeking a change.

"I am very glad to see you, John—may I call you John?" he said. "Let me thank you for your prompt answer to our postmaster's letter of inquiry. He volunteered to write to you on my behalf. I was looking about for something different in the way of a business in which the profits would be greater. I had noticed in the papers that this coast was receiving much attention from investors. I am extremely grateful for your advice to come. I sold out everything that I possess, and invested the proceeds in as fine a stock of shoes as could be bought in the North. You have a picturesque town here, John. I hope business will be as good as your letter justifies me in expecting."

Johnny's agony was abbreviated by the arrival of Keogh, who hurried up with the news that Mrs. Goodwin would be much pleased to place rooms at the disposal of Mr. Hemstetter and his daughter. So there Mr. Hemstetter and Rosine were at once conducted and left to recuperate from the fatigue of the voyage, while Johnny went down to see that the cases of shoes were safely stored in the customs warehouse pending their examination by the officials. Keogh, grinning like a shark, skirmished about to find Goodwin, to instruct him not to expose to Mr. Hemstetter the true state of Coralio as a shoe market until Johnny had been given a chance to redeem the situation, if such a thing were possible.

That night the consul and Keogh held a desperate consultation on the breezy porch of the consulate.

"Send 'em back home," began Keogh, reading Johnny's thoughts.

"I would," said Johnny, after a little silence; "but I've been lying to you, Billy."

"All right about that," said Keogh, affably.

"I've told you hundreds of times," said Johnny, slowly, "that I had forgotten that girl, haven't I?"

"About three hundred and seventy-five," admitted the monument of patience.

"I lied," repeated the consul, "every time. I never forget her for one minute. I was an obstinate ass for running away just because she said 'No' once. And I was too proud a fool to go back. I talked with Rosine a few minutes this evening up at Goodwin's. I found out one thing. You remember that farmer fellow who was always after her?"

"Dink Pawson?" asked Keogh.

"Pink Dawson. Well, he wasn't a hill of beans to her. She says she didn't believe a word of the things he told her about me. But I'm sewed up now, Billy. That tomfool letter we sent ruined whatever chance I had left. She'll despise me when she finds out that her old father has been made the victim of a joke that a decent school boy wouldn't have been guilty of. Shoes! Why he couldn't sell twenty pairs of shoes in Coralio if he kept store here for twenty years. You put a pair of shoes on one of these Caribs or Spanish brown boys and what'd he do? Stand on his head and squeal until he'd kicked 'em off. None of 'em ever wore shoes and they never will. If I send 'em back home I'll have to tell the whole story, and what'll she think of me? I want that girl worse than ever, Billy, and now when she's in reach I've lost her forever because I tried to be funny when the thermometer was at 102."

"Keep cheerful," said the optimistic Keogh. "And let 'em open the store. I've been busy myself this afternoon. We can stir up a temporary boom in foot-gear anyhow. I'll buy six pairs when the doors open. I've been around and seen all the fellows and explained the catastrophe. They'll all buy shoes like they was centipedes. Frank Goodwin will take cases of 'em. The Geddies want about eleven pairs between 'em. Clancy is going to invest the savings of weeks, and even old Doc Gregg wants three pairs of alligator-hide slippers if they've got any tens. Blanchard got a look at Miss Hemstetter; and as he's a Frenchman, no less than a dozen pairs will do for him."

"A dozen customers," said Johnny, "for a $4,000 stock of shoes! It won't work. There's a big problem here to figure out. You go home, Billy, and leave me alone. I've got to work at it all by myself. Take that bottle of Three-star along with you—no, sir; not another ounce of booze for the United States consul. I'll sit here to-night and pull out the think stop. If there's a soft place on this proposition anywhere I'll land on it. If there isn't there'll be another wreck to the credit of the gorgeous tropics."

Keogh left, feeling that he could be of no use. Johnny laid a handful of cigars on a table and stretched himself in a steamer chair. When the sudden daylight broke, silvering the harbor ripples, he was still sitting there. Then he got up, whistling a little tune, and took his bath.

At nine o'clock he walked down to the dingy little cable office and hung for half an hour over a blank. The result of his application was the following message, which he signed and had transmitted at a cost of $33:

To Pinkney Dawson,
Dalesburg, Ala.
Draft for $100 comes to you next mail. Ship me immediately 500 pounds stiff, dry cockleburrs. New use here in arts. Market price twenty cents pound. Further orders likely. Rush.

Ships

Within a week a suitable building had been secured in the Calle Grande, and Mr. Hemstetter's stock of shoes arranged upon their shelves. The rent of the store was moderate; and the stock made a fine showing of neat white boxes, attractively displayed.

Johnny's friends stood by him loyally. On the first day Keogh strolled into the store in a casual kind of way about once every hour, and bought shoes. After he had purchased a pair each of extension soles, congress gaiters, button kids, low-quartered calfs, dancing pumps, rubber boots, tans of various hues, tennis shoes and flowered slippers, he sought out Johnny to be prompted as to names of other kinds that he might inquire for. The other English-speaking residents also played their parts nobly by buying often and liberally. Keogh was grand marshal, and made them distribute their patronage, thus keeping up a fair run of custom for several days.

Mr. Hemstetter was gratified by the amount of business done thus far; but expressed surprise that the natives were so backward with their custom.

"Oh, they're awfully shy," explained Johnny, as he wiped his forehead nervously. "They'll get the habit pretty soon. They'll come with a rush when they do come."

One afternoon Keogh dropped into the consul's office, chewing an unlighted cigar thoughtfully.

"Got anything up your sleeve?" he inquired of Johnny. "If you have it's about time to show it. If you can borrow some gent's hat in the audience, and make a lot of customers for an idle stock of shoes come out of it, you'd better spiel. The boys have all laid in enough foot-wear to last 'em ten years; and there's nothing doing in the shoe store but dolcy far nienty. I just came by there. Your venerable victim was standing in the door, gazing through his specs at the bare toes passing by his emporium. The natives here have got the true artistic temperament. Me and Clancy took eighteen tin-types this morning in two hours. There's been but one pair of shoes sold all day. Blanchard went in and bought a pair of fur-lined house-slippers because he thought he saw Miss Hemstetter go into the store. I saw him throw the slippers into the lagoon afterwards."

"There's a Mobile fruit steamer coming in to-morrow or next day," said Johnny. "We can't do anything until then."

"What are you going to do—try to create a demand?"

"Political economy isn't your strong point," said the consul, impudently. "You can't create a demand. But you can create a necessity for a demand. That's what I am going to do."

Two weeks after the consul sent his cable, a fruit steamer brought him a huge, mysterious brown bale of some unknown commodity. Johnny's influence with the custom-house people was sufficiently strong for him to get the goods turned over to him without the usual inspection. He had the bale taken to the consulate and snugly stowed in the back room.

That night he ripped open a corner of it and took out a handful of the cockleburrs. He examined them with the care with which a warrior examines his arms before he goes forth to battle for his lady-love and life. The burrs were the ripe August product, as hard as filberts, and bristling with spines as tough and sharp as needles. Johnny whistled softly a little tune, and went out to find Billy Keogh.

Later in the night, when Coralio was stepped in slumber, he and Billy went forth into the deserted streets with their coats bulging like balloons. All up and down the Calle Grande they went, sowing the sharp burrs carefully in the sand, along the narrow sidewalks, in every foot of grass between the silent houses. And then they took the side streets and byways, missing none. No place where the foot of man, woman or child might fall was slighted. Many trips they made to and from the prickly hoard. And then, nearly at the dawn, they laid themselves down to rest calmly, as great generals do after planning a victory according to the revised tactics, and slept, knowing that they had sowed with the accuracy of Satan sowing tares and the perseverance of Paul planting.

With the rising sun came the purveyors of fruits and meats, and arranged their wares in and around the little market-house. At one end of the town near the seashore the market-house stood; and the sowing of the burrs had not been carried that far. The dealers waited long past the hour when their sales usually began. None came to buy. *"Qué hay?"* they began to exclaim, one to another.

At their accustomed time, from every 'dobe and palm hut and grass-thatched shack and dim *patio* glided women—black women, brown women, lemon-colored women, women dun and yellow and tawny. They were the marketers starting to purchase the family supply of cassava, plantains, meat, fowls, and tortillas. Décolleté they were and bare-armed and bare-footed, with a single skirt reaching below the knee. Stolid and ox-eyed, they stepped from their doorways into the narrow paths or upon the soft grass of the streets.

The first to emerge uttered ambiguous squeals, and raised one foot quickly. Another step and they sat down, with shrill cries of alarm, to pick at the new and painful insects that had stung them upon the feet. *"Qué picadores diablos!"* they screeched to one another across the narrow ways. Some tried the grass instead of the paths, but there they were also stung and bitten by the strange little prickly balls. They plumped down in the grass, and added their lamentations to those of their sisters in the sandy paths. All through the town was heard the plaint of the feminine jabber. The venders in the market still wondered why no customers came.

Then men, lords of the earth, came forth. They, too, began to hop, to dance, to limp, and to curse. They stood stranded and foolish, or stooped to pluck at the scourge that attacked their feet and ankles. Some loudly proclaimed the pest to be poisonous spiders of an unknown species.

And then the children ran out for their morning romp. And now to the uproar was added the howls of limping infants and cockleburred childhood. Every minute the advancing day brought forth fresh victims.

Doña Maria Castillas y Buenventura de las Casas stepped from her honored doorway, as was her daily custom, to procure fresh bread from the *panadería* across the street. She was clad in a skirt of flowered yellow satin, a chemise of ruffled linen, and wore a purple mantilla from the looms of Spain. Her lemon-tinted feet, alas! were bare. Her progress was majestic, for were not her ancestors hidalgos of Aragon? Three steps she made across the velvety grass, and set her aristocratic sole upon a bunch of Johnny's burrs. Doña Maria Castillas y Buenventura de las Casas emitted a yowl even as a wildcat. Turning about, she fell upon hands and knees, and crawled—ay, like a beast of the field she crawled back to her honorable door-sill.

Don Señor Ildefonso Federico Valdazar, *Juez de la Paz,* weighing twenty stone, attempted to convey his bulk to the *pulpería* at the corner of the plaza in order to assuage his matutinal thirst. The first plunge of his unshod foot into the cool grass struck a concealed mine. Don Ildefonso fell like a crumpled cathedral, crying out that he had been fatally bitten by a deadly scorpion. Everywhere were the shoeless citizens hopping, stumbling, limping, and picking from their feet the venomous insects that had come in a single night to harass them.

The first to perceive the remedy was Estebán Delgado, the barber, a man of travel and education. Sitting upon a stone, he plucked burrs from his toes, and made oration:

"Behold, my friend, these bugs of the devil! I know them well. They soar through the skies in swarms like pigeons. These are the dead ones that fell during the night. In Yucatan I have seen them as large as oranges. Yes! There they hiss like serpents, and have wings like bats. It is the shoes—the shoes that one needs! *Zapatos—zapatos para mí!*"

Estebán hobbled to Mr. Hemstetter's store, and bought shoes. Coming out, he swaggered down the street with impunity, reviling loudly the bugs of the devil. The suffering ones sat up or stood upon one foot and beheld the immune barber. Men, women, and children took up the cry: *Zapatos! zapatos!*"

The necessity for the demand had been created. The demand followed. That day Mr. Hemstetter sold three hundred pairs of shoes.

"It is really surprising," he said to Johnny, who came up in the evening to help him straighten out the stock, "how trade is picking up. Yesterday I made but three sales."

"I told you they'd whoop things up when they got started," said the consul.

"I think I shall order a dozen more cases of goods, to keep the stock up," said Mr. Hemstetter, beaming through his spectacles.

"I wouldn't send in any orders yet," advised Johnny. "Wait till you see how the trade holds up."

Each night Johnny and Keogh sowed the crop that grew dollars by day. At the end of ten days two-thirds of the stock of shoes had been sold; and the stock of cockleburrs was exhausted. Johnny cabled to Pink Dawson for another 500 pounds, paying twenty cents per pound as before. Mr. Hemstetter carefully made up an order for $1,500 worth of shoes from Northern firms. Johnny hung about the store until this order was ready for the mail, and succeeded in destroying it before it reached the postoffice.

That night he took Rosine under the mango tree by Goodwin's porch, and confessed everything. She looked him in the eye, and said: "You are a very wicked man. Father and I will go back home. You say it was a joke? I think it is a very serious matter."

But at the end of half an hour's argument the conversation had been turned upon a different subject. The two were considering the respective merits of pale blue and pink wall paper with which the old colonial mansion of the Atwoods in Dalesburg was to be decorated after the wedding.

On the next morning Johnny confessed to Mr. Hemstetter. The shoe merchant put on his spectacles, and said through them: "You strike me as being a most extraordinary young scamp. If I had not managed this enterprise with good business judgment my entire stock of goods might have been a complete loss. Now, how do you propose to dispose of the rest of it?"

When the second invoice of cockleburrs arrived Johnny loaded them and the remainder of the shoes into a schooner, and sailed down the coast to Alazan.

There, in the same dark and diabolical manner, he repeated his success; and came back with a bag of money and not so much as a shoestring.

And then he besought his great Uncle of the waving goatee and starred vest to accept his resignation, for the lotus no longer lured him. He hankered for the spinach and cress of Dalesburg.

The services of Mr. William Terence Keogh as acting consul, *pro tem.,* were suggested and accepted, and Johnny sailed with the Hemstetters back to his native shores.

Keogh slipped into the sinecure of the American consulship with the ease that never left him even in such high places. The tintype establishment was soon to become a thing of the past, although its deadly work along the peaceful and helpless Spanish Main was never effaced. The restless partners were about to be off again, scouting ahead of the slow ranks of Fortune. But now they would take different ways. There were rumors of a promising uprising in Peru; and thither the martial Clancy would turn his adventurous steps. As for Keogh, he was figuring in his mind and on quires of Government letter-heads a scheme that dwarfed the art of misrepresenting the human countenance upon tin.

"What suits me," Keogh used to say, "in the way of a business proposition is something diversified that looks like a longer shot than it is—something in the way of a genteel graft that isn't worked enough for the correspondence schools to be teaching it by mail. I take the long end; but I like to have at least as good a chance to win as a man learning to play poker on an ocean steamer, or running for governor of Texas on the Republican ticket. And when I cash in my winnings, I don't want to find any widows' and orphans' chips in my stack."

The grass-grown globe was the green table on which Keogh gambled. The games he played were of his own invention. He was no grubber after the diffident dollar. Nor did he care to follow it with horn and hounds. Rather he loved to coax it with egregious and brilliant flies from its habitat in the waters of strange streams. Yet Keogh was a business man; and his schemes, in spite of their singularity, were as solidly set as the plans of a building contractor. In Arthur's time Sir William Keogh would have been a Knight of the Round Table. In these modern days he rides abroad, seeking the Graft instead of the Grail.

Three days after Johnny's departure, two small schooners appeared off Coralio. After some delay a boat put off from one of them, and brought a sunburned young man ashore. This young man had a shrewd and calculating eye; and he gazed with amazement at the strange things that he saw. He found on the beach some one who directed him to the consul's office; and thither he made his way at a nervous gait.

Keogh was sprawled in the official chair, drawing caricatures of his uncle's head on an official pad of paper. He looked up at his visitor.

"Where's Johnny Atwood?" inquired the sunburned young man, in a business tone.

"Gone," said Keogh, working carefully at Uncle Sam's necktie.

"That's just like him," remarked the nut-brown one, leaning against the table. "He always was a fellow to gallivant around instead of 'tending to business. Will he be in soon?"

"Don't think so," said Keogh, after a fair amount of deliberation.

"I s'pose he's out at some of his tomfoolery," conjectured the visitor, in a tone of virtuous conviction. "Johnny never would stick to anything long enough to succeed. I wonder how he manages to run his business here, and never be 'round to look after it."

"I'm looking after the business just now," admitted the *pro tem.* consul.

"Are you—then, say!—where's the factory?"

"What factory?" asked Keogh, with a mildly polite interest.

"Why, the factory where they use them cockleburrs. Lord knows what they use 'em for, anyway! I've got the basements of both them ships out there loaded with 'em. I'll give you a bargain in this lot. I've had every man, woman, and child around Dalesburg that wasn't busy pickin' 'em for a month. I hired these ships to bring 'em over. Everybody thought I was crazy. Now, you can have this lot for fifteen cents a pound, delivered on land. And if you want more I guess old Alabam' can come up to the demand. Johnny told me when he left home that if he struck anything down here that there was any money in he'd let me in on it. Shall I drive the ships in and hitch?"

A look of supreme, almost incredulous, delight dawned in Keogh's ruddy countenance. He dropped his pencil. His eyes turned upon the sunburned young man with joy in them mingled with fear lest his ecstasy should prove a dream.

"For God's sake, tell me," said Keogh, earnestly, "are you Dink Pawson?"

"My name is Pinkney Dawson," said the cornerer of the cockleburr market.

Billy Keogh slid rapturously and gently from his chair to his favorite strip of matting on the floor.

There were not many sounds in Coralio on that sultry afternoon. Among those that were may be mentioned a noise of enraptured and unrighteous laughter from a prostrate Irish-American, while a sunburned young man, with a shrewd eye, looked on him with wonder and amazement. Also the "tramp, tramp, tramp" of many well-shod feet in the streets outside. Also the lonesome wash of the waves that beat along the historic shores of the Spanish Main.

Masters of Arts

A two-inch stub of a blue pencil was the wand with which Keogh performed the preliminary acts of his magic. So, with this he covered paper with diagrams and figures while he waited for the United States of America to send down to Coralio a successor to Atwood, resigned.

The new scheme that his mind had conceived, his stout heart indorsed, and his blue pencil corroborated, was laid around the characteristics and human frailties of the new president of Anchuria. These characteristics, and the situation out of which Keogh hoped to wrest a golden tribute, deserve chronicling contributive to the clear order of events.

President Losada—many called him Dictator—was a man whose genius would have made him conspicuous even among Anglo-Saxons, had not that genius been intermixed with other traits that were petty and subversive. He had some of the lofty patriotism of Washington (the man he most admired), the force of Napoleon, and much of the wisdom of the sages. These characteristics might have justified him in the assumption of the title of "The Illustrious Liberator," had they not been accompanied by a stupendous and amazing vanity that kept him in the less worthy ranks of the dictators.

Yet he did his country great service. With a mighty grasp he shook it nearly free from the shackles of ignorance and sloth and the vermin that fed upon it, and all but made it a power in the council of nations. He established schools and hospitals, built roads, bridges, railroads and palaces, and bestowed generous subsidies upon the arts and sciences. He was the absolute despot and the idol of his people. The wealth of the country poured into his hands. Other presidents had been rapacious without reason. Losada amassed enormous wealth, but his people had their share of the benefits.

The joint in his armor was his insatiate passion for monuments and tokens commemorating his glory. In every town he caused to be erected statues of himself bearing legends in praise of his greatness. In the walls of every public edifice, tablets were fixed reciting his splendor and the gratitude of his subjects. His statuettes and portraits were scattered throughout the land in every house and hut. One of the sycophants in his court painted him as St. John, with a halo and a train of attendants in full uniform. Losada saw nothing incongruous in this picture, and had it hung in a church in the capital. He ordered from a French sculptor a marble group including himself with Napoleon, Alexander the Great, and one or two others whom he deemed worthy of the honor.

He ransacked Europe for decorations, employing policy, money and intrigue to cajole the orders he coveted from kings and rulers. On state occasions his breast was covered from shoulder to shoulder with crosses, stars, golden roses, medals and ribbons. It was said that the man who could contrive for him a new decoration, or invent some new method of extolling his greatness, might plunge a hand deep into the treasury.

This was the man upon whom Billy Keogh had his eye. The gentle buccaneer had observed the rain of favors that fell upon those who ministered to the president's vanities, and he did not deem it his duty to hoist his umbrella against the scattering drops of liquid fortune.

In a few weeks the new consul arrived, releasing Keogh from his temporary duties. He was a young man fresh from college, who lived for botany alone. The consulate at Coralio gave him the opportunity to study tropical flora. He wore smoked glasses, and carried a green umbrella. He filled the cool, back porch of the consulate with plants and specimens so that space for a bottle and chair was not to be found. Keogh gazed on him sadly, but without rancour, and began to pack his gripsack. For his new plot against stagnation along the Spanish Main required of him a voyage overseas.

Soon came the *Karlsefin* again—she of the trampish habits—gleaning a cargo of cocoanuts for a speculative descent upon the New York market. Keogh was booked for a passage on the return trip.

"Yes, I'm going to New York," he explained to the group of his countrymen that had gathered on the beach to see him off. "But I'll be back before you miss me. I've undertaken the art education of this piebald country, and I'm not the man to desert it while it's in the early throes of tintypes."

With this mysterious declaration of his intentions Keogh boarded the *Karlsefin.*

Ten days later, shivering, with the collar of his thin coat turned high, he burst into the studio of Carolus White at the top of a tall building in Tenth Street, New York City.

Carolus White was smoking a cigarette and frying sausages over an oil stove. He was only twenty-three, and had noble theories about art.

"Billy Keogh!" exclaimed White, extending the hand that was

not busy with the frying pan. "From what part of the uncivilized world, I wonder!"

"Hello, Carry," said Keogh, dragging forward a stool, and holding his fingers close to the stove. "I'm glad I found you so soon. I've been looking for you all day in the directories and art galleries. The free-lunch man on the corner told me where you were, quick. I was sure you'd be painting pictures yet."

Keogh glanced about the studio with the shrewd eye of a connoisseur in business.

"Yes, you can do it," he declared, with many gentle nods of his head. "That big one in the corner with the angels and green clouds and bandwagon is just the sort of thing we want. What would you call that, Carry—scene from Coney Island, ain't it?"

"That," said White, "I had intended to call 'The Translation of Elijah,' but you may be nearer right than I am."

"Name doesn't matter," said Keogh, largely; "it's the frame and the varieties of paint that does the trick. Now, I can tell you in a minute what I want. I've come on a little voyage of two thousand miles to take you in with me on a scheme. I thought of you as soon as the scheme showed itself to me. How would you like to go back with me and paint a picture? Ninety days for the trip, and five thousand dollars for the job."

"Cereal food or hair-tonic posters?" asked White.

"It isn't an ad."

"What kind of a picture is it to be?"

"It's a long story," said Keogh.

"Go ahead with it. If you don't mind, while you talk I'll just keep my eye on these sausages. Let 'em get one shade deeper than a Vandyke brown and you spoil 'em."

Keogh explained his project. They were to return to Coralio, where White was to pose as a distinguished American portrait painter who was touring in the tropics as a relaxation from his arduous and remunerative professional labors. It was not an unreasonable hope, even to those who had trod in the beaten paths of business, that an artist with so much prestige might secure a commission to perpetuate upon canvas the lineaments of the president, and secure a share of the *pesos* that were raining upon the caterers to his weaknesses.

Keogh had set his price at ten thousand dollars. Artists had been paid more for portraits. He and White were to share the expenses of the trip, and divide the possible profits. Thus he laid the scheme before White, whom he had known in the West before one declared for Art and the other became a Bedouin.

Before long the two machinators abandoned the rigor of the bare studio for a snug corner of a café. There they sat far into the night, with old envelopes and Blythe's stub of blue pencil between them.

At twelve o'clock White doubled up in his chair, with his chin on his fist, and shut his eyes at the unbeautiful wall-paper.

"I'll go you, Billy," he said, in the quiet tones of decision. "I've got two or three hundred saved up for sausages and rent; and I'll take the chance with you. Five thousand! It will give me two years in Paris and one in Italy. I'll begin to pack to-morrow."

"You'll begin in ten minutes," said Keogh. "It's to-morrow now. The *Karlsefin* starts back at four P.M. Come on to your painting shop, and I'll help you."

For five months in the year Coralio is the Newport of Anchuria. Then only does the town possess life. From November to March it is practically the seat of the government. The president with his official family sojourns there; and society follows him. The pleasure-loving people make the season one long holiday of amusement and rejoicing. *Fiestas,* balls, games, sea bathing, processions and small theatres contribute to their enjoyment. The famous Swiss band from the capital plays in the little plaza every evening, while the fourteen carriages and vehicles in the town circle in funereal but complacent procession. Indians from the interior mountains, looking like prehistoric stone idols, come down to peddle their handiwork in the streets. The people throng the narrow ways, a chattering, happy, careless stream of buoyant humanity. Preposterous children rigged out with the shortest of ballet skirts and gilt wings, howl, underfoot, among the effervescent crowds. Especially is the arrival of the presidential party, at the opening of the season, attended with pomp, show and patriotic demonstrations of enthusiasm and delight.

When Keogh and White reached their destination, on the return trip of the *Karlsefin,* the gay winter season was well begun. As they stepped upon the beach they could hear the band playing in the plaza. The village maidens, with fire-flies already fixed in their dark locks, were gliding, barefoot and coy-eyed, along the paths. Dandies in white linen, swinging their canes, were beginning their seductive strolls. The air was full of human essence, of artificial enticement, of coquetry, indolence, pleasure—the man-made sense of existence.

The first two or three days after their arrival were spent in preliminaries. Keogh escorted the artist about town, introducing him to the little circle of English-speaking residents and pulling whatever wires he could to effect the spreading of White's fame as a painter. And then Keogh planned a more spectacular demonstration of the idea he wished to keep before the public.

He and White engaged rooms in the Hotel de los Estranjeros. The two were clad in new suits of immaculate duck, with American straw hats, and carried canes of remarkable uniqueness and inutility. Few caballeros in Coralio—even the gorgeously uniformed officers of the Anchurian army—were as conspicuous for ease and elegance of demeanor as Keogh and his friend, the great American painter, Señor White.

White set up his easel on the beach and made striking sketches of the mountain and sea views. The native population formed at his rear in a vast, chattering semicircle to watch his work. Keogh, with his care for details, had arranged for himself a pose which he carried out with fidelity. His rôle was that of friend to the great artist, a man of affairs and leisure. The visible emblem of his position was a pocket camera.

"For branding the man who owns it," said he, "a genteel dilettante with a bank account and an easy conscience, a steam-yacht ain't in it with a camera. You see a man doing nothing but loafing around making snapshots, and you know right away he reads up well in 'Bradstreet.' You notice these old millionaire boys—soon as they get through taking everything else in sight they go to taking photographs. People are more impressed by a kodak than they are by a title or a four-carat scarf-pin." So Keogh strolled blandly about Coralio, snapping the scenery and the shrinking señoritas, while White posed conspicuously in the higher regions of art.

Two weeks after their arrival, the scheme began to bear fruit. An aide-de-camp of the president drove to the hotel in a dashing victoria. The president desired that Señor White come to the Casa Morena for an informal interview.

Keogh gripped his pipe tightly between his teeth. "Not a cent less than ten thousand," he said to the artist—"remember the price. And in gold or its equivalent—don't let him stick you with this bargain-counter stuff they call money here."

"Perhaps it isn't that he wants," said White.

"Get out!" said Keogh, with splendid confidence. "I know what he wants. He wants his picture painted by the celebrated young American painter and filibuster now sojourning in this down-trodden country. Off you go."

The victoria sped away with the artist. Keogh walked up and down, puffing great clouds of smoke from his pipe, and waited. In an hour the victoria swept again to the door of the hotel, deposited White, and vanished. The artist dashed up the stairs, three at a step. Keogh stopped smoking, and became a silent interrogation point.

"Landed," exclaimed White, with his boyish face flushed with elation. "Billy, you are a wonder. He wants a picture. I'll tell you all about it. By Heavens! that dictator chap is a corker! He's a dictator clear down to his finger-ends. He's a kind of combination of Julius Cæsar, Lucifer and Chauncey Depew done in sepia. Polite and grim—that's his way. The room I saw him in was about ten acres big, and looked like a Mississippi steamboat with its gilding and mirrors and white paint. He talks English better than I can ever hope to. The matter of the price came up. I mentioned ten thousand. I expected him to call the guard and have me taken out and shot. He didn't move an eyelash. He just waved one of his chestnut hands in a careless way, and said, 'Whatever you say.' I am to go back to-morrow and discuss with him the details of the picture."

Keogh hung his head. Self-abasement was easy to read in his downcast countenance.

"I'm failing, Carry," he said, sorrowfully. "I'm not fit to handle these man's-size schemes any longer. Peddling oranges in a push-cart is about the suitable graft for me. When I said ten thousand, I swear I thought I had sized up that brown man's limit to within two cents. He'd have melted down for fifteen thousand just as easy. Say—Carry—you'll see the old man Keogh safe in some nice, quiet idiot asylum, won't you, if he makes a break like that again?"

The Casa Morena, although only one story in height, was a building of brown stone, luxurious as a palace in its interior. It stood on a low hill in a walled garden of splendid tropical flora at the upper edge of Coralio. The next day the president's carriage came again for the artist. Keogh went out for a walk along the beach, where he and his "picture box" were now familiar sights. When he returned to the hotel White was sitting in a steamer-chair on the balcony.

"Well," said Keogh, "did you and His Nibs decide on the kind of chromo he wants?"

White got up and walked back and forth on the balcony a few times. Then he stopped and laughed strangely. His face was flushed, and his eyes were bright with a kind of angry amusement.

"Look here, Billy," he said, somewhat roughly, "when you first came to me in my studio and mentioned a picture, I thought you wanted a Smashed Oats or a Hair Tonic poster painted on a range of mountains or the side of a continent. Well, either of those jobs would have been Art in its highest form compared to the one you've steered me against. I can't paint that picture, Billy. You've got to let me out. Let me try to tell you what that barbarian wants. He had it all planned out and even a sketch made of his idea. The old boy doesn't draw badly at all. But, ye goddesses of Art! listen to the monstrosity he expects me to paint. He wants himself in the centre of the canvas, of course. He is to be painted as Jupiter sitting on Olympus, with the clouds at his feet. At one side of him stands George Washington, in full regimentals, with his hand on the president's shoulder. An angel with outstretched wings hovers overhead, and is placing a laurel wreath on the president's head, crowning him—Queen of the May, I suppose. In the background is to be cannon, more angels and soldiers. The man who would paint that picture would have to have the soul of a dog, and would deserve to go down into oblivion without even a tin can tied to his tail to sound his memory."

Little beads of moisture crept out all over Billy Keogh's brow. The stub of his blue pencil had not figured out a contingency like this. The machinery of his plan had run with flattering smoothness until now. He dragged another chair upon the balcony, and got White back to his heat. He lit his pipe with apparent calm.

"Now, sonny," he said, with gentle grimness, "you and me will have an Art to Art talk. You've got your art and I've got mine. Yours is the real Pierian stuff that turns up its nose at bock-beer signs and oleographs of the Old Mill. Mine's the art of Business. This was my scheme, and it worked out like two-and-two. Paint that president man as Old King Cole, or Venus, or a landscape, or a fresco, or a bunch of lilies, or anything he thinks he looks like. But get the paint on the canvas and collect the spoils. You wouldn't throw me down, Carry, at this stage of the game. Think of that ten thousand."

"I can't help thinking of it," said White, "and that's what hurts. I'm tempted to throw every ideal I ever had down in the mire, and steep my soul in infamy by painting that picture. That five thousand meant three years of foreign study to me, and I'd almost sell my soul for that."

"Now it ain't as bad as that," said Keogh, soothingly. "It's a business proposition. It's so much paint and time against money. I don't fall in with your idea that that picture would so everlasting jolt the art side of the question. George Washington was all right, you know, and nobody could say a word against the angel. I don't think so bad of that group. If you was to give Jupiter a pair of epaulets and a sword, and kind of work the clouds around to look like a blackberry patch, it wouldn't make such a bad battle scene. Why, if we hadn't already settled on the price, he ought to pay an extra thousand for Washington, and the angel ought to raise it five hundred."

"You don't understand, Billy," said White, with an uneasy laugh. "Some of us fellows who try to paint have big notions about Art. I wanted to paint a picture some day that people would stand before and forget that it was made of paint. I wanted it to creep into them like a bar of music and mushroom there like a soft bullet. And

I wanted 'em to go away and ask, 'What else has he done?' And I didn't want 'em to find a thing; not a portrait nor a magazine cover nor an illustration nor a drawing of a girl—nothing but *the* picture. That's why I've lived on fried sausages, and tried to keep true to myself. I persuaded myself to do this portrait for the chance it might give to me to study abroad. But this howling, screaming caricature! Good Lord! can't you see how it is?"

"Sure," said Keogh, as tenderly as he would have spoken to a child, and he laid a long fore-finger on White's knee. "I see. It's bad to have your art all slugged up like that. I know. You wanted to paint a big thing like the panorama of the battle of Gettysburg. But let me kalsomine you a little mental sketch to consider. Up to date we're out $385.50 on this scheme. Our capital took every cent both of us could raise. We've got about enough left to get back to New York on. I need my share of that ten thousand. I want to work a copper deal in Idaho, and make a hundred thousand. That's the business end of the thing. Come down off your art perch, Carry, and let's land that hatful of dollars."

"Billy," said White, with an effort, "I'll try. I won't say I'll do it, but I'll try. I'll go at it, and put it through if I can."

"That's business," said Keogh heartily. "Good boy! Now, here's another thing—rush that picture—crowd it through as quick as you can. Get a couple of boys to help you mix the paint if necessary. I've picked up some pointers around town. The people here are beginning to get sick of Mr. President. They say he's been too free with concessions; and they accuse him of trying to make a dicker with England to sell out the country. We want that picture done and paid for before there's any row."

In the great *patio* of Casa Morena, the president caused to be stretched a huge canvas. Under this White set up his temporary studio. For two hours each day the great man sat to him.

White worked faithfully. But, as the work progressed, he had seasons of bitter scorn, of infinite self-contempt, of sullen gloom and sardonic gaiety. Keogh, with the patience of a great general, soothed, coaxed, argued—kept him at the picture.

At the end of a month White announced that the picture was completed—Jupiter, Washington, angels, clouds, cannon and all. His face was pale and his mouth drawn straight when he told Keogh. He said the president was much pleased with it. It was to be hung in the National Gallery of Statesmen and Heroes. The artist had been requested to return to Casa Morena on the following day to receive payment. At the appointed time he left the hotel, silent under his friend's joyful talk of their success.

An hour later he walked into the room where Keogh was waiting, threw his hat on the floor, and sat upon the table.

"Billy," he said, in strained and laboring tones, "I've a little money out West in a small business that my brother is running. It's what I've been living on while I've been studying art. I'll draw out my share and pay you back what you've lost on this scheme."

"Lost!" exclaimed Keogh, jumping up. "Didn't you get paid for the picture?"

"Yes, I got paid," said White. "But just now there isn't any picture, and there isn't any pay. If you care to hear about it, here are the edifying details. The president and I were looking at the painting. His secretary brought a bank draft on New York for ten thousand dollars and handed it to me. The moment I touched it I went wild. I tore it into little pieces and threw them on the floor. A workman was repainting the pillars inside the *patio.* A bucket of his paint happened to be convenient. I picked up his brush and slapped a quart of blue paint all over that ten-thousand-dollar nightmare. I bowed, and walked out. The president didn't move or speak. That was one time he was taken by surprise. It's tough on you, Billy, but I couldn't help it."

There seemed to be excitement in Coralio. Outside there was a confused, rising murmur pierced by high-pitched cries. *"Abajo el traidor—Muerte al traidor!"* were the words they seemed to form.

"Listen to that!" exclaimed White, bitterly: "I know that much Spanish. They're shouting, 'Down with the traitor!' I heard them before. I felt that they meant me. I was a traitor to Art. The picture had to go."

" 'Down with the blank fool' would have suited your case better, said Keogh with fiery emphasis. "You tear up ten thousand dollars like an old rag because the way you've spread on five dollars' worth of paint hurts your conscience. Next time I pick a side-partner in a scheme the man has got to go before a notary and swear he never even heard the word 'ideal' mentioned."

Keogh strode from the room, white-hot. White paid little attention to his resentment. The scorn of Billy Keogh seemed a trifling thing beside the greater self-scorn he had escaped.

In Coralio the excitement waxed. An outburst was imminent. The cause of this demonstration of displeasure was the presence in the town of a big, pink-cheeked Englishman, who, it was said, was an agent of his government come to clinch the bargain by which the president placed his people in the hands of a foreign power. It was charged that not only had he given away priceless concessions, but that the public debt was to be transferred into the hands of the English, and the custom-houses turned over to them as a guarantee. The long-enduring people had determined to make their protest felt.

On that night, in Coralio and in other towns, their ire found vent. Yelling mobs, mercurial but dangerous, roamed the streets. They overthrew the great bronze statue of the president that stood in the centre of the plaza, and hacked it to shapeless pieces. They tore from public buildings the tables set there proclaiming the glory of the "Illustrious Liberator." His pictures in the government office were demolished. The mobs even attacked the Casa Morena, but were driven away by the military, which remained faithful to the executive. All the night terror reigned.

The greatness of Losada was shown by the fact that by noon the next day order was restored, and he was still absolute. He issued proclamations denying positively that any negotiations of any kind had been entered into with England. Sir Stafford Vaughn, the pink-cheeked Englishman, also declared in placards and in public print that his presence there had no international significance. He was a traveller without guile. In fact (so he stated), he had not even spoken with the president or been in his presence since his arrival.

During this disturbance, White was preparing for his homeward voyage in the steamship that was to sail within two or three days. About noon, Keogh, the restless, took his camera out with the hope of speeding the lagging hours. The town was now as quiet as if peace had never departed from her perch on the red-tiled roofs.

About the middle of the afternoon, Keogh hurried back to the hotel with something decidedly special in his air. He retired to the little room where he developed his pictures.

Later on he came out to White on the balcony, with a luminous, grim, predatory smile on his face.

"Do you know what that is?" he asked, holding up a 4 × 5 photograph mounted on cardboard.

"Snap-shot of a señorita sitting in the sand—alliteration unintentional," guessed White, lazily.

"Wrong," said Keogh with shining eyes. "It's a slung-shot. It's a can of dynamite. It's a gold mine. It's a sight-draft on your president man for twenty thousand dollars—yes, sir—twenty thousand this time, and no spoiling the picture. No ethics of art in the way. Art! You with your smelly little tubes! I've got you skinned to death with a kodak. Take a look at that."

White took the picture in his hand, and gave a long whistle.

"Jove," he exclaimed, "but wouldn't that stir up a row in town if you let it be seen. How in the world did you get it, Billy?"

"You know that high wall around the president man's back garden? I was up there trying to get a bird's-eye of the town. I happened to notice a chink in the wall where a stone and a lot of plaster had slid out. Thinks I, I'll take a peep through to see how Mr. President's cabbages are growing. The first thing I saw was him and this Sir Englishman sitting at a little table about twenty feet away. They had the table all spread over with documents, and they were hobnobbing over them as thick as two pirates. 'Twas a nice corner of the garden, all private and shady with palms and orange trees, and they had a pail of champagne set by handy in the grass. I knew then was the time for me to make my big hit in Art. So I raised the machine up to the crack, and pressed the button. Just as I did so them old boys shook hands on the deal—you see they took that way in the picture."

Keogh put on his coat and hat.

"What are you going to do with it?" asked White.

"Me," said Keogh in a hurt tone, "why, I'm going to tie a pink ribbon to it and hang it on the what-not, of course. I'm surprised at you. But while I'm out you just try to figure out what gingercake potentate would be most likely to want to buy this work of art for his private collection—just to keep it out of circulation."

The sunset was reddening the tops of the cocoanut palms when Billy Keogh came back from Casa Morena. He nodded to the artist's questioning gaze; and lay down on a cot with his hands under the back of his head.

"I saw him. He paid the money like a little man. They didn't want to let me in at first. I told 'em it was important. Yes, that president man is on the plenty-able list. He's got a beautiful business system about the way he uses his brains. All I had to do was to hold up the photograph so he could see it, and name the price. He just smiled, and walked over to a safe and got the cash. Twenty one-thousand-dollar brand-new United States Treasury notes he laid on the table, like I'd pay out a dollar and a quarter. Fine notes, too—they crackled with a sound like burning the brush off a ten-acre lot."

"Let's try the feel of one," said White, curiously. "I never saw a thousand-dollar bill." Keogh did not immediately respond.

"Carry," he said, in an absent-minded way, "you think a heap of your art, don't you?"

"More," said White, frankly, "than has been for the financial good of myself and my friends."

"I thought you were a fool the other day," went on Keogh, quietly, "and I'm not sure now that you wasn't. But if you was, so am I. I've been in some funny deals, Carry, but I've always managed to scramble fair, and match my brains and capital against the other fellow's. But when it comes to—well, when you've got the other fellow cinched, and the screws on him, and he's got to put up—why, it don't strike me as being a man's game. They've got a name for it, you know; it's—confound you, don't you understand? A fellow feels—it's something like that blamed art of yours—he—well, I tore that photograph up and laid the pieces on that stack of money and shoved the whole business back across the table. 'Excuse me, Mr. Losada,' I said, 'but I guess I've made a mistake in the price. You get the photo for nothing.' Now, Carry, you get out the pencil, and we'll do some more figuring. I'd like to save enough out of our capital for you to have some fried sausages in your joint when you get back to New York."

Dicky

There is little consecutiveness along the Spanish Main. Things happen there intermittently. Even Time seems to hang his scythe daily on the branch of an orange tree while he takes a siesta and a cigarette.

After the ineffectual revolt against the administration of President Losada, the country settled again into quiet toleration of the abuses with which he had been charged. In Coralio old political enemies went arm-in-arm, lightly eschewing for the time all differences of opinion.

The failure of the art expedition did not stretch the cat-footed Keogh upon his back. The ups and downs of Fortune made smooth travelling for his nimble steps. His blue pencil stub was at work again before the smoke of the steamer on which White sailed had cleared away from the horizon. He had but to speak a word to Geddie to find his credit negotiable for whatever goods he wanted from the store of Brannigan & Company. On the same day on which White arrived in New York, Keogh, at the rear of a train of five pack mules loaded with hardware and cutlery, set his face toward the grim, interior mountains. There the Indian tribes wash gold dust from the auriferous streams; and when a market is brought to them trading is brisk and *muy bueno* in the Cordilleras.

In Coralio Time folded his wings and paced wearily along his drowsy path. They who had most cheered the torpid hours were gone. Clancy had sailed on a Spanish barque for Colon, contemplating a cut across the isthmus and then a further voyage to end at Calao, where the fighting was said to be on. Geddie, whose quiet and genial nature had once served to mitigate the frequent dull reaction of lotus eating, was now a homeman, happy with his bright orchid, Paula, and never even dreaming of or regretting the unsolved, sealed and monogrammed Bottle whose contents, now inconsiderable, were held safely in the keeping of the sea.

Well may the Walrus, most discerning and eclectic of beasts, place sealing-wax midway on his programme of topics that fall pertinent and diverting upon the ear.

Atwood was gone—he of the hospitable back porch and ingenuous cunning. Dr. Gregg, with his trepanning story smouldering within him, was a whiskered volcano, always showing signs of imminent eruption, and was not to be considered in the ranks of those who might contribute to the amelioration of ennui. The new consul's note chimed with the sad sea waves and the violent tropical greens—he had not a bar of Scheherazade or of the Round Table in his lute. Goodwin was employed with large projects: what time he was loosed from them found him at his home, where he loved to be. Therefore it will be seen that there was a dearth of fellowship and entertainment among the foreign contingent of Coralio.

And then Dicky Maloney dropped down from the clouds upon the town, and amused it.

Nobody knew where Dicky Maloney hailed from or how he reached Coralio. He appeared there one day; and that was all. He afterward said that he came on the fruit steamer *Thor;* but an inspection of the *Thor's* passenger list of that date was found to be Maloneyless. Curiosity, however, soon perished; and Dicky took his place among the odd fish cast up by the Caribbean.

He was an active, devil-may-care, rollicking fellow with an engaging gray eye, the most irresistible grin, a rather dark or much sunburned complexion, and a head of the fieriest red hair ever seen in that country. Speaking the Spanish language as well as he spoke English, and seeming always to have plenty of silver in his pockets, it was not long before he was a welcome companion whithersoever he went. He had an extreme fondness for *vino blanco,* and gained the reputation of being able to drink more of it than any three men in town. Everybody called him "Dicky"; everybody cheered up at the sight of him—especially the natives, to whom his marvellous red hair and his free-and-easy style were a constant delight and envy. Wherever you went in the town you would soon see Dicky or hear his genial laugh, and find around him a group of admirers who appreciated him both for his good nature and the white wine he was always so ready to buy.

A considerable amount of speculation was had concerning the object of his sojourn there, until one day he silenced this by opening a small shop for the sale of tobacco, *dulces* and the handiwork of the interior Indians—fibre-and-silk-woven goods, deerskin *zapatos* and basketwork of *tule* reeds. Even then he did not change his habits; for he was drinking and playing cards half the day and night with the *comandante,* the collector of customs, the *Jefe Político* and other gay dogs among the native officials.

One day Dicky saw Pasa, the daughter of Madama Ortiz, sitting in the side-door of the Hotel de los Estranjeros. He stopped in his tracks, still, for the first time in Coralio; and then he sped, swift as a deer, to find Vasquez, a gilded native youth, to present him.

The young men had named Pasa *"La Santita Naranjadita."* *Naranjadita* is a Spanish word for a certain color that you must go to more trouble to describe in English. By saying "The little saint, tinted the most beautiful delicate-slightly-orange-golden," you will approximate the description of Madama Ortiz's daughter.

La Madama Ortiz sold rum in addition to other liquors. Now, you must know that the rum expiates whatever opprobrium attends upon the other commodities. For rum-making, mind you, is a government monopoly; and to keep a government dispensary assures respectability if not preeminence. Moreover, the saddest of precisions could find no fault with the conduct of the shop. Customers drank there in the lowest of spirits and fearsomely, as in the shadow of the dead; for Madama's ancient and vaunted lineage counteracted even the rum's behest to be merry. For, was she not of the Iglesias, who landed with Pizarro? And had not her deceased husband been *comisionado de caminos y puentes* for the district?

In the evenings Pasa sat by the window in the room next to the one where they drank, and strummed dreamily upon her guitar. And then, by twos and threes, would come visiting young caballeros and occupy the prim line of chairs set against the wall of this room. They were there to besiege the heart of *"La Santita."* Their method (which is not proof against intelligent competition) consisted of expanding the chest, looking valorous, and consuming a gross or two of cigarettes. Even saints delicately oranged prefer to be wooed differently.

Doña Pasa would tide over the vast chasms of nicotinized silence with music from her guitar, while she wondered if the romances she had read about gallant and more—more contiguous cavaliers were all lies. At somewhat regular intervals Madama would glide in from the dispensary with a sort of drought-suggesting gleam in her eye, and there would be a rustling of stiffly-starched white trousers as one of the caballeros would propose an adjournment to the bar.

That Dicky Maloney would, sooner or later, explore this field was a thing to be foreseen. There were few doors in Coralio into which his red head had not been poked.

In an incredibly short space of time after his first sight of her he was there, seated close beside her rocking chair. There were no back-against-the-wall poses in Dicky's theory of wooing. His plan of subjection was an attack at close range. To carry the fortress with one concentrated, ardent, eloquent, irresistible *escalade*—that was Dicky's way.

Pasa was descended from the proudest Spanish families in the country. Moreover, she had had unusual advantages. Two years in a New Orleans school had elevated her ambitions and fitted her for a fate above the ordinary maidens of her native land. And yet here she succumbed to the first red-haired scamp with a glib tongue and a charming smile that came along and courted her properly.

Very soon Dicky took her to the little church in the corner of the plaza, and "Mrs. Maloney" was added to her string of distinguished names.

And it was her fate to sit, with her patient, saintly eyes and figure like a bisque Psyche, behind the sequestered counter of the little shop, while Dicky drank and philandered with his frivolous acquaintances.

The women, with their naturally fine instinct, saw a chance for vivisection, and delicately taunted her with his habits. She turned upon them in a beautiful, steady gaze of sorrowful contempt.

"You meat-cows," she said, in her level, crystal-clear tones; "you know nothing of a man. Your men are *maromeros.* They are fit only to roll cigarettes in the shade until the sun strikes and shrivels them up. They drone in your hammocks and you comb their hair and feed them with fresh fruit. My man is no such blood. Let him drink of the wine. When he has taken sufficient of it to drown one of your *flaccitos* he will come home to me more of a man than one thousand of your *pobrecitos.* My hair he smooths and braids; to me he sings; he himself removes my *zapatos,* and there, there, upon each instep leaves a kiss. He holds—Oh, you will never understand! Blind ones who have never known a *man.*"

Sometimes mysterious things happened at night about Dicky's shop. While the front of it was dark, in the little room back of it Dicky and a few of his friends would sit about a table carrying on some kind of very quiet *negocios* until quite late. Finally he would let them out the front door very carefully, and go upstairs to his little saint. These visitors were generally conspirator-like men with dark clothes and hats. Of course, these dark doings were noticed after a while, and talked about.

Dicky seemed to care nothing at all for the society of the alien residents of the town. He avoided Goodwin, and his skilful escape from the trepanning story of Dr. Gregg is still referred to, in Coralio, as a masterpiece of lightning diplomacy.

Many letters arrived, addressed to "Mr. Dicky Maloney," or "Señor Dickee Maloney," to the considerable pride of Pasa. That so many people should desire to write to him only confirmed her own suspicion that the light from his red head shone around the world. As to their contents she never felt curiosity. There was a wife for you!

The one mistake Dicky made in Coralio was to run out of money at the wrong time. Where his money came from was a puzzle, for the sales of his shop were next to nothing, but that source failed, and at a peculiarly unfortunate time. It was when the *comandante,* Don Señor el Coronel Encarnatión Rios, looked upon the little saint seated in the shop and felt his heart go pitapat.

The *comandante,* who was versed in all the intricate arts of gallantry, first delicately hinted at his sentiments by donning his dress uniform and strutting up and down fiercely before her window. Pasa, glancing demurely with her saintly eyes, instantly perceived his resemblance to her parrot, Chichi, and was diverted to the extent of a smile. The *comandante* saw the smile, which was not intended for him. Convinced of an impression made, he entered the shop, confidently, and advanced to open compliment. Pasa froze; he pranced; she flamed royally; he was charmed to injudicious persistence; she commanded him to leave the shop; he tried to capture her hand,— and Dicky entered, smiling broadly, full of white wine and the devil.

He spent five minutes in punishing the *comandante* scientifically and carefully, so that the pain might be prolonged as far as possible. At the end of that time he pitched the rash wooer out the door upon the stones of the street, senseless.

A barefooted policeman who had been watching the affair from across the street blew a whistle. A squad of four soldiers came running from the *cuartel* around the corner. When they saw that the offender was Dicky, they stopped, and blew more whistles, which brought out reënforcements of eight. Deeming the odds against them sufficiently reduced, the military advanced upon the disturber.

Dicky, being thoroughly imbued with the martial spirit, stooped and drew the *comandante's* sword, which was girded about him, and charged his foe. He chased the standing army four squares, playfully prodding its squealing rear and hacking at its ginger-colored heels.

But he was not so successful with the civic authorities. Six muscular, nimble policemen overpowered him and conveyed him, triumphantly but warily, to jail. *"El Diablo Colorado"* they dubbed him, and derided the military for its defeat.

Dicky, with the rest of the prisoners, could look out through the barred door at the grass of the little plaza, at a row of orange trees and the red tile roofs and 'dobe walls of a line of insignificant stores.

At sunset along a path across this plaza came a melancholy procession of sad-faced women bearing plantains, cassaba, bread and fruit—each coming with food to some wretch behind those bars to whom she still clung and furnished the means of life. Twice a day— morning and evening—they were permitted to come. Water was furnished to her compulsory guests by the republic, but no food.

That evening Dicky's name was called by the sentry, and he stepped before the bars of the door. There stood his little saint, a black mantilla draped about her head and shoulders, her face like glorified melancholy, her clear eyes gazing longingly at him as if they might draw him between the bars to her. She brought a chicken, some oranges, *dulces* and a loaf of white bread. A soldier inspected the food, and passed it in to Dicky. Pasa spoke calmly as she always did, briefly, in her thrilling, flute-like tones. "Angel of my life," she said, "let it not be long that thou art away from me. Thou knowest that life is not a thing to be endured with thou not at my side. Tell me if I can do aught in this matter. If not, I will wait—a little while. I come again in the morning."

Dicky, with his shoes removed so as not to disturb his fellow prisoners, tramped the floor of the jail half the night condemning his lack of money and the cause of it—whatever that might have been. He knew very well that money would have brought his release at once.

For two days succeeding Pasa came at the appointed times and brought him food. He eagerly inquired each time if a letter or package had come for him, and she mournfully shook her head.

On the morning of the third day she brought only a small loaf of bread. There were dark circles under her eyes. She seemed as calm as ever.

"By jingo," said Dicky, who seemed to speak in English or Spanish as the whim seized him, "this is dry provender, *muchachita.* Is this the best you can dig up for a fellow?"

Pasa looked at him as a mother looks at a beloved but capricious babe.

"Think better of it," she said, in a low voice; "since for the next meal there will be nothing. The last *centavo* is spent." She pressed close against the grating.

"Sell the goods in the shop—take anything for them."

"Have I not tried? Did I not offer them for one-tenth their cost? Not even one *peso* would any one give. There is not one *real* in this town to assist Dickee Malonee."

Dicky clenched his teeth grimly. "That's the *comandante,"* he growled. "He's responsible for that sentiment. Wait, oh, wait till the cards are all out."

Pasa lowered her voice to almost a whisper. "And, listen, heart of my heart," she said, "I have endeavored to be brave, but I cannot live without thee. Three days now—"

Dicky caught a faint gleam of steel from the folds of her mantilla. For once she looked in his face and saw it without a smile, stern, menacing and purposeful. Then he suddenly raised his hand and his smile came back like a gleam of sunshine. The hoarse signal of an incoming steamer's siren sounded in the harbor. Dicky called to the sentry who was pacing before the door: "What steamer comes?"

"The *Catarina.*"

"Of the Vesuvius line?"

"Without doubt, of that line."

"Go you, *picarilla,*" said Dicky joyously to Pasa, "to the American consul. Tell him I wish to speak with him. See that he comes at once. And look you! let me see a different look in those eyes, for I promise your head shall rest upon this arm to-night."

It was an hour before the consul came. He held his green umbrella under his arm, and mopped his forehead impatiently.

"Now, see here, Maloney," he began, captiously, "you fellows seem to think you can cut up any kind of row, and expect me to pull you out of it. I'm neither the War Department nor a gold mine. This country has its laws, you know, and there's one against pounding the senses out of the regular army. You Irish are forever getting into trouble. I don't see what I can do. Any thing like tobacco, now, to make you comfortable—or newspapers—"

"Son of Eli," interrupted Dicky, gravely, "you haven't changed an iota. That is almost a duplicate of the speech you made when old Koen's donkeys and geese got into the chapel loft, and the culprits wanted to hide in your room."

"Oh, heavens!" exclaimed the consul, hurriedly adjusting his spectacles. "Are you a Yale man, too? Were you in that crowd? I don't seem to remember any one with red—any one named Maloney. Such a lot of collegemen seem to have misused their advantages. One of the best mathematicians of the class of '91 is selling lottery tickets in Belize. A Cornell man dropped off here last month. He was second steward on a guano boat. I'll write to the department if you like, Maloney. Or if there's any tobacco, or newspa——"

"There's nothing," interrupted Dicky, shortly, "but this. You go tell the captain of the *Catarina* that Dicky Maloney wants to see him as soon as he can conveniently come. Tell him where I am. Hurry. That's all."

The consul, glad to be let off so easily, hurried away. The captain of the *Catarina,* a stout man, Sicilian born, soon appeared, shoving, with little ceremony, through the guards to the jail door. The Vesuvius Fruit Company had a habit of doing things that way in Anchuria.

"I am exceedingly sorry—exceedingly sorry," said the captain, "to see this occur. I place myself at your service, Mr. Maloney. What you need shall be furnished. Whatever you say shall be done."

Dicky looked at him unsmilingly. His red hair could not detract from his attitude of severe dignity as he stood, tall and calm, with his now grim mouth forming a horizontal line.

"Captain De Lucco, I believe I still have funds in the hands of your company—ample and personal funds. I ordered a remittance last week. The money has not arrived. You know what is needed in this game. Money and money and more money. Why has it not been sent?"

"By the *Cristóbal,*" replied De Lucco, gesticulating, "it was despatched. Where is the *Cristóbal?* Off Cape Antonio I spoke her with a broken shaft. A tramp coaster was towing her back to New Orleans. I brought money ashore thinking your need for it might not withstand delay. In this envelope is one thousand dollars. There is more if you need it, Mr. Maloney."

"For the present it will suffice," said Dicky, softening as he crinkled the envelope and looked down at the half-inch thickness of smooth dingy bills.

"The long green!" he said, gently, with a new reverence in his gaze. "Is there anything it will not buy, Captain?"

"I had three friends," replied De Lucco, who was a bit of a philosopher, "who had money. One of them speculated in stocks and made ten million; another is in heaven, and the third married a poor girl whom he loved."

"The answer, then," said Dicky, "is held by the Almighty, Wall Street and Cupid. So, the question remains."

"This," queried the captain, including Dicky's surroundings in a significant gesture of his hand, "is it—it is not—it is not connected with the business of your little shop? There is no failure in your plans?"

"No, no," said Dicky. "This is merely the result of a little private affair of mine, a digression from the regular line of business. They say for a complete life a man must know poverty, love, and war. But they don't go well together, *capitán mío.* No; there is no failure in my business. The little shop is doing very well."

When the captain had departed Dicky called the sergeant of the jail and asked:

"Am I *preso* by the military or the civil authority?"

"Surely there is no martial law in effect now, señor."

"Bueno. Now go or send to the alcalde, the *Juez de la Paz* and the *Jefe de los Policios.* Tell them I am prepared at once to satisfy the demands of justice." A folded bill of the "long green" slid into the sergeant's hands.

Then Dicky's smile came back again, for he knew that the hours of his captivity were numbered; and he hummed, in time with the sentry's tread:

"They're hanging men and women now,
For lacking of the green."

So, that night Dicky sat by the window of the room over his shop and his little saint sat close by, working at something silken and dainty. Dicky was thoughtful and grave. His red hair was in an unusual state of disorder. Pasa's fingers often ached to smooth and arrange it, but Dicky would never allow it. He was poring, to-night, over a great litter of maps and books and papers on his table until that perpendicular line came between his brows that always distressed Pasa. Presently she went and brought his hat, and stood with it until he looked up, inquiringly.

"It is sad for you here," she explained. "Go out and drink *vino blanco.* Come back when you get that smile you used to wear. That is what I wish to see."

Dicky laughed and threw down his paper. "The *vino blanco* stage is past. It has served its turn. Perhaps, after all, there was less entered my mouth and more my ears than people thought. But, there will be no more maps or frowns to-night. I promise you that. Come."

They sat upon a reed *silleta* at the window and watched the quivering gleams from the lights of the *Catarina* reflected in the harbor.

Presently Pasa rippled out one of her infrequent chirrups of audible laughter.

"I was thinking," she began, anticipating Dicky's question, "of the foolish things girls have in their minds. Because I went to school in the States I used to have ambitions. Nothing less than to be the president's wife would satisfy me. And, look, thou red picaroon, to what obscure fate thou hast stolen me!"

"Don't give up hope," said Dicky, smiling. "More than one Irishman has been the ruler of a South American country. There was a dictator of Chili named O'Higgins. Why not a President Maloney, of Anchuria? Say the word, *santita mía,* and we'll make the race."

"No, no, no, thou red-haired, reckless one!" sighed Pasa; "I am content"—she laid her head against his arm—"here."

Rouge et Noir

It has been indicated that disaffection followed the elevation of Losada to the presidency. This feeling continued to grow. Throughout the entire republic there seemed to be a spirit of silent, sullen discontent. Even the old Liberal party to which Goodwin, Zavalla and other patriots had lent their aid was disappointed. Losada had failed to become a popular idol. Fresh taxes, fresh import duties and, more than all, his tolerance of the outrageous oppression of citizens by the military had rendered him the most obnoxious president since the despicable Alforan. The majority of his own cabinet were out of sympathy with him. The army, which he had courted by giving it license to tyrannize, had been his main, and thus far adequate support.

But the most impolitic of the administration's moves had been when it antagonized the Vesuvius Fruit Company, an organization plying twelve steamers and with cash and capital somewhat larger than Anchuria's surplus and debt combined.

Reasonably an established concern like the Vesuvius would become irritated at having a small, retail republic with no rating at all attempt to squeeze it. So when the government proxies applied for a subsidy then encountered a polite refusal. The president at once retaliated by clapping an export duty of one *real* per bunch on bananas—a thing unprecedented in fruit-growing countries. The Vesuvius Company had invested large sums in wharves and plantations along the Anchuria coast, their agents had erected fine homes in the towns where they had their headquarters, and heretofore had worked with the republic in good-will and with advantage to both. It would lose an immense sum if compelled to move out. The selling price of bananas from Vera Cruz to Trinidad was three *reals* per bunch. This new duty of one *real* would have ruined the fruit growers in Anchuria and have seriously discommoded the Vesuvius Company had it declined to pay it. But for some reason, the Vesuvius continued to buy Anchuria fruit, paying four *reals* for it; and not suffering the growers to bear the loss.

This apparent victory deceived His Excellency; and he began to hunger for more of it. He sent an emissary to request a conference with a representative of the fruit company. The Vesuvius sent Mr. Franzoni, a little, stout, cheerful man, always cool, and whistling airs from Verdi's operas. Señor Espiritión, of the office of the Minister of Finance, attempted the sandbagging in behalf of Anchuria. The meeting took place in the cabin of the *Salvador,* of the Vesuvius line.

Señor Espiritión opened negotiations by announcing that the government contemplated the building of a railroad to skirt the alluvial coast lands. After touching upon the benefits such a road would confer upon the interests of the Vesuvius, he reached the definite suggestion that a contribution to the road's expenses of, say, fifty thousand *pesos* would not be more than an equivalent to benefits received.

Mr. Franzoni denied that his company would receive any benefits from a contemplated road. As its representative he must decline to contribute fifty thousand *pesos.* But he would assume the responsibility of offering twenty-five.

Did Señor Espiritión understand Señor Franzoni to mean twenty-five thousand *pesos?*

By no means. Twenty-five *pesos.* And in silver; not in gold.

"Your offer insults my government," cried Señor Espiritión, rising with indignation.

"Then," said Mr. Franzoni, in warning tone, *"we will change it."*

The offer was never changed. Could Mr. Franzoni have meant the government?

This was the state of affairs in Anchuria when the winter season opened at Coralio at the end of the second year of Losada's administration. So, when the government and society made its annual exodus to the seashore it was evident that the presidential advent would not be celebrated by unlimited rejoicing. The tenth of November was the day set for the entrance into Coralio of the gay company from the capital. A narrow-gauge railroad runs twenty miles into the interior from Solitas. The government party travels by carriage from San Mateo to this road's terminal point, and proceeds by train to Solitas. From here they march in grand procession to Coralio where, on the day of their coming, festivities and ceremonies abound. But this season saw an ominous dawning of the tenth of November.

Although the rainy season was over, the day seemed to hark back to reeking June. A fine drizzle of rain fell all during the forenoon. The procession entered Coralio amid a strange silence.

President Losada was an elderly man, grizzly bearded, with a considerable ratio of Indian blood revealed in his cinnamon complexion. His carriage headed the procession, surrounded and guarded by Captain Cruz and his famous troop of one hundred light horse *"El Ciento Huilando."* Colonel Rocas followed, with a regiment of the regular army.

The president's sharp, beady eyes glanced about him for the expected demonstration of welcome; but he faced a stolid, indifferent array of citizens. Sightseers the Anchurians are by birth and habit, and they turned out to their last able-bodied unit to witness the scene; but they maintained an accusive silence. They crowded the streets to the very wheel ruts; they covered the red tile roofs to the eaves, but there was never a *"viva"* from them. No wreaths of palm and lemon branches or gorgeous strings of paper roses hung from thc windows and balconies as was the custom. There was an apathy, a dull, dissenting disapprobation, that was the more ominous because it puzzled. No one feared an outburst, a revolt of the discontents, for they had no leader. The president and those loyal to him had never even heard whispered a name among them capable of crystallizing the dissatisfaction into opposition. No, there could be no danger. The people always procured a new idol before they destroyed an old one.

At length, after a prodigious galloping and curvetting of red-sashed majors, gold-laced colonels and epauletted generals, the procession formed for its annual progress down the Calle Grande to the Casa Morena, where the ceremony of welcome to the visiting president always took place.

The Swiss band led the line of march. After it pranced the local *comandante,* mounted, and a detachment of his troops. Next came a carriage with four members of the cabinet, conspicuous among them the Minister of War, old General Pilar, with his white moustache and his soldierly bearing. Then the president's vehicle, containing also the Ministers of Finance and State; and surrounded by Captain Cruz's light horse formed in a close double file of fours. Following them, the rest of the officials of state, the judges and distinguished military and social ornaments of public and private life.

As the band struck up, and the movement began, like a bird of ill-omen the *Valhalla,* the swiftest steamship of the Vesuvius line, glided into the harbor in plain view of the president and his train. Of course, there was nothing menacing about its arrival—a business firm does not go to war with a nation—but it reminded Señor Espirition and others in those carriages that the Vesuvius Fruit Company was undoubtedly carrying something up its sleeve for them.

By the time the van of the procession had reached the government building, Captain Cronin, of the *Valhalla,* and Mr. Vincenti, member of the Vesuvius Company, had landed and were pushing their way, bluff, hearty, and nonchalant, through the crowd on the narrow sidewalk. Clad in white linen, big, debonair, with an air of good-humored authority, they made conspicuous figures among the dark mass of unimposing Anchurians, as they penetrated to within a few yards of the steps of the Casa Morena. Looking easily above the heads of the crowd, they perceived another that towered above the undersized natives. It was the fiery poll of Dicky Maloney against the wall close by the lower step and his broad, seductive grin showed that he recognized their presence.

Dicky had attired himself becomingly for the festive occasion in a well-fitting black suit. Pasa was close by his side, her head covered with the ubiquitous black mantilla.

Mr. Vincenti looked at her attentively.

"Botticelli's Madonna," he remarked, gravely. "I wonder when she got into the game. I don't like his getting tangled with the women. I hoped he would keep away from them."

Captain Cronin's laugh almost drew attention from the parade.

"With that head of hair! Keep away from the women! And a Maloney! Hasn't he got a license? But, nonsense aside, what do you think of the prospects? It's a species of filibustering out of my line."

Vincenti glanced again at Dicky's head and smiled.

"Rouge et noir," he said. "There you have it. Make your play, gentlemen. Our money is on the red."

"The lad's game," said Cronin, with a commending look at the tall, easy figure by the steps. "But 'tis all like fly-by-night theatricals to me. The talk's bigger than the stage; there's a smell of gasoline in the air, and they're their own audience and scene-shifters."

They ceased talking, for General Pilar had descended from the first carriage and had taken his stand upon the top step of Casa Morena. As the oldest member of the cabinet, custom had decreed that he should make the address of welcome, presenting the keys of the official residence to the president at its close.

General Pilar was one of the most distinguished citizens of the republic. Hero of three wars and innumerable revolutions, he was an honored guest at European courts and camps. An eloquent speaker and a friend to the people, he represented the highest type of the Anchurians.

Holding in his hand the gilt keys of Casa Morena, he began his address in a historical form, touching upon each administration and the advance of civilization and prosperity from the first striving after liberty down to present times. Arriving at the régime of President Losada, at which point, according to the precedent, he should have delivered a eulogy upon its wise conduct and the happiness of the people, General Pilar paused. Then he silently held up the bunch of keys high above his head, with his eyes closely regarding it. The ribbon with which they were bound fluttered in the breeze.

"It still blows," cried the speaker, exultantly. "Citizens of Anchuria, give thanks to the saints this night that our air is still free."

Thus disposing of Losada's administration, he abruptly reverted to that of Olivarra, Anchuria's most popular ruler. Olivarra had been assassinated nine years before while in the prime of life and usefulness. A faction of the Liberal party led by Losada himself had been accused of the deed. Whether guilty or not, it was eight years before the ambitious and scheming Losada had gained his goal.

Upon this theme General Pilar's eloquence was loosed. He drew the picture of the beneficent Olivarra with a loving hand. He reminded the people of the peace, the security, and the happiness they had enjoyed during that period. He recalled in vivid detail and with significant contrast the last winter sojourn of President Olivarra in Coralio, when his appearance at their fiestas was the signal for thundering *vivas* of love and approbation.

The first public expression of sentiment from the people that day followed. A low, sustained murmur went among them like the surf rolling along the shore.

"Ten dollars to a dinner at the Saint Charles," remarked Mr. Vincenti, "that *rouge* wins."

"I never bet against my own interests," said Captain Cronin, lighting a cigar. "Long-winded old boy, for his age. What's he talking about?"

"My Spanish," replied Vincenti, "runs about ten words to the minute; his is something around two hundred. Whatever he's saying, he's getting them warmed up."

"Friends and brothers," General Pilar was saying, "could I reach out my hand this day across the lamentable silence of the grave to Olivarra 'the Good,' to the ruler who was one of you, whose tears fell when you sorrowed, and whose smile followed your joy—I would bring him back to you, but—Olivarra is dead—dead at the hands of a craven assassin!"

The speaker turned and gazed boldly into the carriage of the president. His arm remained extended aloft as if to sustain his peroration. The president was listening, aghast, at this remarkable address of welcome. He was sunk back upon his seat, trembling with rage and dumb surprise, his dark hands tightly gripping the carriage cushions.

Half rising, he extended one arm toward the speaker, and shouted a harsh command at Captain Cruz. The leader of the "Flying Hundred" sat his horse, immovable, with folded arms, giving no sign of having heard. Losada sank back again, his dark features distinctly paling.

"Who says that Olivarra is dead?" suddenly cried the speaker, his voice, old as he was, sounding like a battle trumpet. "His body lies in the grave, but to the people he loved he has bequeathed his spirit—yes, more—his learning, his courage, his kindness—yes, more—his youth, his image—people of Anchuria, have you forgotten Ramon, the son of Olivarra?"

Cronin and Vincenti, watching closely, saw Dicky Maloney suddenly raise his hat, tear off his shock of red hair, leap up the steps and stand at the side of General Pilar. The Minister of War laid his arm across the young man's shoulders. All who had known President Olivarra saw again his same lion-like pose, the same frank, undaunted expression, the same high forehead with the peculiar line of the clustering, crisp black hair.

General Pilar was an experienced orator. He seized the moment of breathless silence that preceded the storm.

"Citizens of Anchuria," he trumpeted, holding aloft the keys to Casa Morena, "I am here to deliver these keys—the keys to your homes and liberty—to your chosen president. Shall I deliver them to Enrico Olivarra's assassin, or to his son?"

"Olivarra! Olivarra!" the crowd shrieked and howled. All vociferated the magic name—men, women, children and the parrots.

And the enthusiasm was not confined to the blood of the plebs. Colonel Rocas ascended the steps and laid his sword theatrically at young Ramon Olivarra's feet. Four members of the cabinet embraced him. Captain Cruz gave a command, and twenty of *El Ciento Huilando* dismounted and arranged themselves in a cordon about the steps of Casa Morena.

But Ramon Olivarra seized that moment to prove himself a born genius and politician. He waved those soldiers aside, and descended the steps to the street. There, without losing his dignity or the distinguished elegance that the loss of his red hair brought him, he took the proletariat to his bosom—the barefooted, the dirty, Indians, Caribs, babies, beggars old, young, saints, soldiers and sinners—he missed none of them.

While this act of the drama was being presented, the scene shifters had been busy at the duties that had been assigned to them. Two of Cruz's dragoons had seized the bridle reins of Losada's horses; others formed a close guard around the carriage; and they galloped off with the tyrant and his two unpopular Ministers. No doubt a place had been prepared for them. There are a number of well-barred stone apartments in Coralio.

"*Rouge* wins," said Mr. Vincenti, calmly lighting another cigar.

Captain Cronin had been intently watching the vicinity of the stone steps for some time.

"Good boy!" he exclaimed suddenly, as if relieved. "I wondered if he was going to forget his Kathleen Mavourneen."

Young Olivarra had reascended the steps and spoken a few words to General Pilar. Then that distinguished veteran descended to the ground and approached Pasa, who still stood, wonder-eyed, where Dicky had left her. With his plumed hat in his hand, and his medals and decorations shining on his breast, the general spoke to her and gave her his arm, and they went up the stone steps of the Casa Morena together. And then Ramon Olivarra stepped forward and took both her hands before all the people.

And while the cheering was breaking out afresh everywhere, Captain Cronin and Mr. Vincenti turned and walked back toward the shore where the gig was waiting for them.

"There'll be another *'presidente proclamada'* in the morning," said Mr. Vincenti, musingly. "As a rule they are not as reliable as the elected ones, but this youngster seems to have some good stuff in him. He planned and manœuvred the entire campaign. Olivarra's widow, you know, was wealthy. After her husband was assassinated she went to the States, and educated her son at Yale. The Vesuvius Company hunted him up, and backed him in the little game."

"It's a glorious thing," said Cronin, half jestingly, "to be able to discharge a government, and insert one of your own choosing, in these days."

"Oh, it is only a matter of business," said Vincenti, stopping and offering the stump of his cigar to a monkey that swung down from a lime tree; "and that is what moves the world of to-day. That extra *real* on the price of bananas had to go. We took the shortest way of removing it."

Two Recalls

There remain three duties to be performed before the curtain falls upon the patched comedy. Two have been promised: the third is no less obligatory.

It was set forth in the programme of this tropic vaudeville that it would be made known why Shorty O'Day, of the Columbia Detective Agency, lost his position. Also that Smith should come again to tell us what mystery he followed that night on the shores of Anchuria when he strewed so many cigar stumps around the cocoanut palm during his lonely night vigil on the beach. These things were promised; but a bigger thing yet remains to be accomplished—the clearing up of a seeming wrong that has been done according to the array of chronicled facts (truthfully set forth) that have been presented. And one voice, speaking, shall do these three things.

Two men sat on a stringer of a North River pier in the City of New York. A steamer from the tropics had begun to unload bananas and oranges on the pier. Now and then a banana or two would fall from an overripe bunch, and one of the two men would shamble forward, seize the fruit and return to share it with his companion.

One of the men was in the ultimate stage of deterioration. As far as rain and wind and sun could wreck the garments he wore, it had been done. In his person the ravages of drink were as plainly visible. And yet, upon his high-bridged, rubicund nose was jauntily perched a pair of shining and flawless gold-rimmed glasses.

The other man was not so far gone upon the descending Highway of the Incompetents. Truly, the flower of his manhood had gone to seed—seed that, perhaps, no soil might sprout. But there were still cross-cuts along where he travelled through which he might yet regain the pathway of usefulness without disturbing the slumbering Miracles. This man was short and compactly built. He had an oblique, dead eye, like that of a sting-ray, and the moustache of a cocktail mixer. We know the eye and the moustache; we know that Smith of the luxurious yacht, the gorgeous raiment, the mysterious mission, the magic disappearance, has come again, though shorn of the accessories of his former state.

At his third banana, the man with the nose glasses spat it from him with a shudder.

"Deuce take all fruit!" he remarked, in a patrician tone of disgust. "I lived for two years where these things grow. The memory of their taste lingers with you. The oranges are not so bad. Just see if you can gather a couple of them, O'Day, when the next broken crate comes up."

"Did you live down with the monkeys?" asked the other, made tepidly garrulous by the sunshine and the alleviating meal of juicy fruit. "I was down there, once myself. But only for a few hours. That was when I was with the Columbia Detective Agency. The monkey people did me up. I'd have my job yet if it hadn't been for them. I'll tell you about it.

"One day the chief sent a note around to the office that read: 'Send O'Day here at once for a big piece of business.' I was the crack detective of the agency at that time. They always handed me the big jobs. The address the chief wrote from was down in the Wall Street district.

"When I got there I found him in a private office with a lot of directors who were looking pretty fuzzy. They stated the case. The president of the Republic Insurance Company had skipped with about a tenth of a million dollars in cash. The directors wanted him back pretty bad, but they wanted the money worse. They said they needed it. They had traced the old gent's movements to where he boarded a tramp fruit steamer bound for South America that same morning with his daughter and a big gripsack—all the family he had.

"One of the directors had his steam yacht coaled and with steam up, ready for the trip; and he turned her over to me, cart blongsh. In four hours I was on board of her, and hot on the trail of the fruit tub. I had a pretty good idea where old Wahrfield—that was his name, J. Churchill Wahrfield—would head for. At that time we had a treaty with about every foreign country except Belgium and that banana republic Anchuria. There wasn't a photo of old Wahrfield to be had in New York—he had been foxy there—but I had his description. And besides, the lady with him would be a dead-give-away anywhere. She was one of the high-flyers in Society—not the kind that have their pictures in the Sunday papers—but the real sort that open chrysanthemum shows and christen battleships.

"Well, sir, we never got a sight of that fruit tub on the road. The ocean is a pretty big place; and I guess we took different paths across it. But we kept going toward this Anchuria, where the fruiter was bound for.

"We struck the monkey coast one afternoon about four. There was a ratty-looking steamer off shore taking on bananas. The monkeys were loading her up with big barges. It might be the one the old man had taken, and it might not. I went ashore to look around. The scenery was pretty good. I never saw any finer on the New York stage. I struck an American on shore, a big, cool chap, standing around with the monkeys. He showed me the consul's office. The consul was a nice young fellow. He said the fruiter was the *Karlsefin,* running generally to New Orleans, but took her last cargo to New York. Then I was sure my people were on board, although everybody told me that no passengers had landed. I didn't think they would land until after dark, for they might have been shy about it on account of seeing that yacht of mine hanging around. So, all I had to do was to wait and nab 'em when they came ashore. I couldn't arrest old Wahrfield without extradition papers, but my play was to get the cash. They generally give up if you strike 'em when they're tired and rattled and short on nerve.

"After dark I sat under a cocoanut tree on the beach for a while, and then I walked around and investigated that town some, and it was enough to give you the lions. If a man could stay in New York and be honest, he'd better do it than to hit that monkey town with a million.

"Dinky little mud houses; grass over your shoe tops in the streets; ladies in low-neck-and-short-sleeves walking around smoking cigars; tree frogs rattling like a hose cart going to a ten blow; big mountains dropping gravel in the back yards; and the sea licking the paint off in front—no, sir—a man had better be in God's country living on free lunch than there.

"The main street ran along the beach, and I walked down it, and then turned up a kind of lane where the houses were made of poles and straw. I wanted to see what the monkeys did when they weren't climbing cocoanut trees. The very first shack I looked in I saw my people. They must have come ashore while I was promenading. A man about fifty, smooth face, heavy eyebrows, dressed in black broadcloth, looking like he was just about to say, 'Can any little boy in the Sunday School answer that?' He was freezing on to a grip that weighed like a dozen gold bricks, and a swell girl—a regular peach, with a Fifth Avenue cut—was sitting on a wooden chair. An old black woman was fixing some coffee and beans on a table. The light they had came from a lantern hung on a nail. I went and stood in the door, and they looked at me, and I said:

" 'Mr. Wahrfield, you are my prisoner. I hope, for the lady's sake, you will take the matter sensibly. You know why I want you.'

" 'Who are you?' says the old gent.

" 'O'Day,' says I, 'of the Columbia Detective Agency. And now, sir, let me give you a piece of good advice. You go back and take your medicine like a man. Hand 'em back the boodle; and maybe they'll let you off light. Go back easy, and I'll put in a word for you. I'll give you five minutes to decide.' I pulled out my watch and waited.

"Then the young lady chipped in. She was one of the genuine high-steppers. You could tell by the way her clothes fit and the style she had that Fifth Avenue was made for her.

" 'Come inside,' she says. 'Don't stand in the door and disturb the whole street with that suit of clothes. Now, what is it you want?'

" 'Three minutes gone,' I said. 'I'll tell you again while the other two tick off.

" 'You'll admit being the president of the Republic, won't you?'

" 'I am,' says he.

" 'Well, then,' says I, 'it ought to be plain to you. Wanted, in New York, J. Churchill Wahrfield, president of the Republic Insurance Company.

" 'Also the funds belonging to said company, now in that grip, in the unlawful possession of said J. Churchill Wahrfield.'

" 'Oh-h-h-h!' says the young lady, as if she was thinking, 'you want to take us back to New York?'

" 'To take Mr. Wahrfield. There's no charge against you, miss. There'll be no objection, of course, to your returning with your father.'

"Of a sudden the girl gave a tiny scream and grabbed the old boy around the neck. 'Oh, father, father!' she says, kind of contralto, 'can this be true? Have you taken money that is not yours? Speak, father!' It made you shiver to hear the tremolo stop she put on her voice.

"The old boy looked pretty bughouse when she first grappled him, but she went on, whispering in his ear and patting his off shoulder till he stood still, but sweating a little.

"She got him to one side and they talked together a minute, and then he put on some gold eyeglasses and walked up and handed me the grip.

" 'Mr. Detective,' he says, talking a little broken. 'I conclude to return with you. I have finished to discover that life on this desolate and displeased coast would be worse than to die, itself. I will go back and hurl myself upon the mercy of the Republic Company. Have you brought a sheep?'

" 'Sheep!' says I; 'I haven't a single——'

" 'Ship,' cut in the young lady. 'Don't get funny. Father is of German birth, and doesn't speak perfect English. How did you come?'

"The girl was all broke up. She had a handkerchief to her face, and kept saying every little bit, 'Oh, father, father!' She walked up to me and laid her lily-white hand on the clothes that had pained her at first. I told her I came in a private yacht.

" 'Mr. O'Day,' she says. 'Oh, take us away from this horrid country at once. Can you! Will you! Say you will.'

" 'I'll try,' I said, concealing the fact that I was dying to get them on salt water before they could change their mind.

"One thing they both kicked against was going through the town to the boat landing. Said they dreaded publicity, and now that they were going to return, they had a hope that the thing might yet be kept out of the papers. They swore they wouldn't go unless I got them out to the yacht without any one knowing it, so I agreed to humor them.

"The sailors who rowed me ashore were playing billiards in a barroom near the water, waiting for orders, and I proposed to have them take the boat down the beach half a mile or so, and take us up there. How to get them word was the question, for I couldn't leave the grip with the prisoner, and I couldn't take it with me, not knowing but what the monkeys might stick me up.

"The young lady says the old colored woman would take them a note. I sat down and wrote it, and gave it to the dame with plain directions what to do, and she grins like a baboon and shakes her head.

"Then Mr. Wahrfield handed her a string of foreign dialect, and she nods her head and says, 'See, señor,' maybe fifty times, and lights out with the note. 'Old Augusta only understands German,' said Miss Wahrfield, smiling at me. 'We stopped in her house to ask where we could find lodging, and she insisted upon our having coffee. She tells us she was raised in a German family in San Domingo.'

" 'Very likely,' I said. 'But you can search me for German words, except *nix verstay* and *noch einst.* I would have called that "See, señor" French, though, on a gamble.'

"Well, we three make a sneak around the edge of town so as not to be seen. We got tangled in vines and ferns and the banana bushes and tropical scenery a good deal. The monkey suburbs was as wild as places in Central Park. We came out on the beach a good half mile below. A brown chap was lying asleep under a cocoanut tree, with a ten-foot musket beside him. Mr. Wahrfield takes up the gun and pitches it into the sea. 'The coast is guarded,' he says. 'Rebellion and plots ripen like fruit.' He pointed to the sleeping man, who never stirred. 'Thus,' he says, 'they perform trusts. Children!'

"I saw our boat coming, and I struck a match and lit a piece of newspaper to show them where we were. In thirty minutes we were on board the yacht.

"The first thing, Mr. Wahrfield and his daughter and I took the grip into the owner's cabin, opened it up and took an inventory. There was one hundred and five thousand dollars, United States treasury notes, in it, beside a lot of diamond jewelry and a couple of hundred Havana cigars. I gave the old man the cigars and a receipt for the rest of the lot, as agent for the company, and locked the stuff up in my private quarters.

"I never had a pleasanter trip than that one. After we got to sea the young lady turned out to be the jolliest ever. The very first time we sat down to dinner, and the steward filled her glass with champagne—that director's yacht was a regular floating Waldorf-Astoria—she winks at me and says, 'What's the use to borrow trouble, Mr. Fly Cop? Here's hoping you may live to eat the hen that scratches on your grave.' There was a piano on board, and she sat down to it and sung better than you give up two cases to hear plenty times. She knew about nine operas clear through. She was sure enough *bon ton* and swell. She wasn't one of the 'among others present' kind; she belonged on the special mention list!

"The old man, too, perked up amazingly on the way. He passed the cigars, and says to me once, quite chipper, out of a cloud of smoke, 'Mr. O'Day, somehow I think the Republic Company will not give me the much trouble. Guard well the gripvalise of the money, Mr. O'Day, for that it must be returned to them that it belongs when we finish to arrive.'

"When we landed in New York I 'phoned to the chief to meet us in that director's office. We got in a cab and went there. I carried the grip, and we walked in, and I was pleased to see that the chief had got together that same old crowd of moneybugs with pink faces and white vests to see us march in. I set the grip on the table. 'There's the money,' I said.

" 'And your prisoner?' said the chief.

"I pointed to Mr. Wahrfield, and he stepped forward and says:

" 'The honor of a word with you, sir, to explain.'

"He and the chief went into another room and stayed ten minutes. When they came back the chief looked as black as a ton of coal.

" 'Did this gentleman,' he says to me, 'have this valise in his possession when you first saw him?'

" 'He did,' said I.

"The chief took up the grip and handed it to the prisoner with a bow, and says to the director crowd: 'Do any of you recognize this gentleman?'

"They all shook their pink faces.

" 'Allow me to present,' he goes on, 'Señor Miraflores, president of the Republic of Anchuria. The señor has generously consented to overlook this outrageous blunder, on condition that we undertake to secure him against the annoyance of public comment. It is a concession on his part to overlook an insult for which he might claim international redress. I think we can gratefully promise him secrecy in the matter.'

"They gave him a pink nod all round.

" 'O'Day,' he says to me. 'As a private detective you're wasted. In a war, where kidnapping governments is in the rules you'd be invaluable. Come down to the office at eleven.'

"I knew what that meant.

" 'So that's the president of the monkeys,' says I 'Well, why couldn't he have said so?'

"Wouldn't it jar you?"

The Vitagraphoscope

Vaudeville is intrinsically episodic and discontinuous. Its audiences do not demand dénouements. Sufficient unto each "turn" is the evil thereof. No one cares how many romances the singing comédienne may have had if she can capably sustain the limelight and a high note or two. The audiences reck not if the performing dogs get to the pound the moment they have jumped through their last hoop. They do not desire bulletins about the possible injuries received by the comic bicyclist who retires head-first from the stage in a crash of (property) china-ware. Neither do they consider that their seat coupons entitle them to be instructed whether or no there is a sentiment between the lady solo banjoist and the Irish monologist.

Therefore let us have no lifting of the curtain upon a tableau of the united lovers, background by defeated villainy and derogated by the comic, osculating maid and butler, thrown in as a sop to the Cerberi of the fifty-cent seats.

But our programme ends with a brief "turn" or two; and then to the exits. Whoever sits the show out may find, if he will, the slender thread that binds together, though ever so slightly, the story that, perhaps, only the Walrus will understand.

Extracts from a letter from the first vice-president of the Republic Insurance Company, of New York City, to Frank Goodwin, of Coralio, Republic of Anchuria.

> My Dear Mr. Goodwin:—Your communication per Messrs. Howland and Fourchet, of New Orleans, has reached us. Also their draft on N. Y. for $100,000, the amount abstracted from the funds of this company by the late J. Churchill Wahrfield, its former president. . . . The officers and directors unite in requesting me to express to you their sincere esteem and thanks for your prompt and much appreciated return of the entire missing sum within two weeks from the time of its disappearance. . . . Can assure you that the matter will not be allowed to receive the least publicity. . . . Regret exceedingly the distressing death of Mr. Wahrfield by his own hand, but. . . . Congratulations on your marriage to Miss Wahrfield . . . many charms,

winning manners, noble and womanly nature and envied position in the best metropolitan society. . . .

Cordially yours,
Lucius E. Applegate
First Vice-President the Republic Insurance Company

The Vitagraphoscope (Moving Pictures)

The Last Sausage

SCENE—*An Artist's Studio.* The artist, a young man of prepossessing appearance, sits in a dejected attitude, amid a litter of sketches, with his head resting upon his hand. An oil stove stands on a pine box in the centre of the studio. The artist rises, tightens his waist belt to another hole, and lights the stove. He goes to a tin bread box, half-hidden by a screen, takes out a solitary link of sausage, turns the box up-side-down to show that there is no more, and chucks the sausage into a frying-pan, which he sets upon the stove. The flame of the stove goes out, showing that there is no more oil. The artist, in evident despair, seizes the sausage, in a sudden access of rage, and hurls it violently from him. At the same time a door opens, and a man who enters receives the sausage forcibly against his nose. He seems to cry out; and is observed to make a dance step or two, vigorously. The newcomer is a ruddy-faced, active, keen-looking man, apparently of Irish ancestry. Next he is observed to laugh immoderately; he kicks over the stove; he claps the artist (who is vainly striving to grasp his hand) vehemently upon the back. Then he goes through a pantomime which to the sufficiently intelligent spectator reveals that he has acquired large sums of money by trading pot-metal hatches and razors to the Indians of the Cordillera Mountains for gold dust. He draws a roll of money as large as a small loaf of bread from his pocket, and waves it above his head, while at the same time he makes pantomime of drinking from a glass. The artist hurriedly secures his hat, and the two leave the studio together.

The Writing on the Sands

SCENE—*The Beach at Nice.* A woman, beautiful, still young, exquisitely clothed, complacent, poised, reclines near the water, idly scrawling letters in the sand with the staff of her silken parasol. The beauty of her face is audacious; her languid pose is one that you feel to be impermanent—you wait, expectant, for her to spring or glide or crawl, like a panther that has unaccountably become stock-still. She idly scrawls in the sand; and the word that she always writes is

"Isabel." A man sits a few yards away. You can see that they are companions, even if no longer comrades. His face is dark and smooth, and almost inscrutable—but not quite. The two speak little together. The man also scratches on the sand with his cane. And the word that he writes is "Anchuria." And then he looks out where the Mediterranean and the sky intermingle with death in his gaze.

The Wilderness and Thou

SCENE—*The Borders of a Gentleman's Estate in a Tropical Land.* An old Indian, with a mahogany-colored face, is trimming the grass on a grave by a mangrove swamp. Presently he rises to his feet and walks slowly toward a grove that is shaded by the gathering, brief twilight. In the edge of the grove stands a man who is stalwart, with a kind and courteous air, and a woman of a serene and clear-cut loveliness. When the old Indian comes up to them the man drops money in his hand. The grave-tender, with the stolid pride of his race, takes it as his due, and goes his way. The two in the edge of the grove turn back along the dim pathway, and walk close, close—for, after all, what is the world at its best but a little round field of the moving pictures with two walking together in it?

CURTAIN

From THE FOUR MILLION 1906

Tobin's Palm

Tobin and me, the two of us, went down to Coney one day, for there was four dollars between us, and Tobin had need of distractions. For there was Katie Mahorner, his sweetheart, of County Sligo, lost since she started for America three months before with two hundred dollars, her own savings, and one hundred dollars from the sale of Tobin's inherited estate, a fine cottage and pig on the Bog Shannaugh. And since the letter that Tobin got saying that she had started to come to him not a bit of news had he heard or seen of Katie Mahorner. Tobin advertised in the papers, but nothing could be found of the colleen.

So, to Coney me and Tobin went, thinking that a turn at the chutes and the smell of the popcorn might raise the heart in his bosom. But Tobin was a hard-headed man, and the sadness stuck in his skin. He ground his teeth at the crying balloons; he cursed the moving pictures; and, though he would drink whenever asked, he scorned Punch and Judy, and was for licking the tintype men as they came.

So I gets him down a side way on a board walk where the attractions were some less violent. At a little six by eight stall Tobin halts, with a more human look in his eye.

" 'Tis here," says he, "I will be diverted. I'll have the palm of me hand investigated by the wonderful palmist of the Nile, and see if what is to be will be."

Tobin was a believer in signs and the unnatural in nature. He possessed illegal convictions in his mind along the subjects of black cats, lucky numbers, and the weather predictions in the papers.

We went into the enchanted chicken coop, which was fixed mysterious with red cloth and pictures of hands with lines crossing 'em like a railroad centre. The sign over the door says it is Madame Zozo the Egyptian Palmist. There was a fat woman inside in a red jumper with pothooks and beasties embroidered upon it. Tobin gives her ten cents and extends one of his hands. She lifts Tobin's hand, which is own brother to the hoof of a drayhorse, and examines it to see whether 'tis a stone in the frog or a cast shoe he has come for.

"Man," says this Madame Zozo, "the line of your fate shows——"

" 'Tis not me foot at all," says Tobin, interrupting. "Sure, 'tis no beauty, but ye hold the palm of me hand."

"The line shows," says the Madame, "that ye've not arrived at your time of life without bad luck. And there's more to come. The mount of Venus—or is that a stone bruise?—shows that ye've been in love. There's been trouble in your life on account of your sweetheart."

" 'Tis Katie Mahorner she has references with," whispers Tobin to me in a loud voice to one side.

"I see," says the palmist, "a great deal of sorrow and tribulation with one whom ye cannot forget. I see the lines of designation point to the letter K and the letter M in her name."

"Whist!" says Tobin to me; "do ye hear that?"

"Look out," goes on the palmist, "for a dark man and a light woman; for they'll both bring ye trouble. Ye'll make a voyage upon the water very soon, and have a financial loss. I see one line that brings good luck. There's a man coming into your life who will fetch ye good fortune. Ye'll know him when ye see him by his crooked nose."

"Is his name set down?" asks Tobin. "'Twill be convenient in the way of greeting when he backs up to dump off the good luck."

"His name," says the palmist, thoughtful looking, "is not spelled out by the lines, but they indicate 'tis a long one, and the letter 'o' should be in it. There's no more to tell. Good-evening. Don't block up the door."

" 'Tis wonderful how she knows," says Tobin as we walk to the pier.

As we squeezed through the gates a nigger man sticks his lighted segar against Tobin's ear, and there is trouble. Tobin hammers his neck, and the women squeal, and by presence of mind I drag the little man out of the way before the police comes. Tobin is always in an ugly mood when enjoying himself.

On the boat going back, when the man calls "Who wants the goodlooking waiter?" Tobin tried to plead guilty, feeling the desire to blow the foam off a crock of suds, but when he felt in his pocket he found himself discharged for lack of evidence. Somebody had disturbed his change during the commotion. So we sat, dry, upon the stools, listening to the Dagoes fiddling on deck. If anything, Tobin was lower in spirits and less congenial with his misfortunes than when we started.

On a seat against the railing was a young woman dressed suitable for red automobiles, with hair the colour on an unsmoked meerschaum. In passing by Tobin kicks her foot without intentions, and, being polite to ladies when in drink, he tries to give his hat a twist while apologizing. But he knocks it off, and the wind carries it overboard.

Tobin came back and sat down, and I began to look out for him, for the man's adversities were becoming frequent. He was apt, when pushed so close by hard luck, to kick the best dressed man he could see, and try to take command of the boat.

Presently Tobin grabs my arm and says, excited: "Jawn," says he, "do ye know what we're doing? We're taking a voyage upon the water."

"There now," says I; "subdue yeself. The boat'll land in ten minutes more."

"Look," says he, "at the light lady upon the bench. And have ye forgotten the nigger man that burned me ear? And isn't the money I had gone—a dollar sixty-five it was?"

I thought he was no more than summing up his catastrophes so as to get violent with good excuse, as men will do, and I tried to make him understand such things was trifles.

"Listen," says Tobin. "Ye've no ear for the gift of prophecy or the miracles of the inspired. What did the palmist lady tell ye out of me hand? 'Tis coming true before your eyes. 'Look out,' says she, 'for a dark man and a light woman; they'll bring ye trouble.' Have ye forgot the nigger man, though he got some of it back from me fist? Can ye show me a lighter woman than the blonde lady that was the cause of me hat falling in the water? And where's the dollar sixty-five I had in me vest when we left the shooting gallery?"

The way Tobin put it, it did seem to corroborate the art of prediction, though it looked to me that these accidents could happen to any one at Coney without the implication of palmistry.

Tobin got up and walked around on deck, looking close at the passengers out of his little red eyes. I asked him the interpretation of his movements. Ye never know what Tobin has in his mind until he begins to carry it out.

"Ye should know," says he, "I'm working out the salvation promised by the lines in me palm. I'm looking for the crooked-nose man that's to bring the good luck. 'Tis all that will save us. Jawn, did ye ever see a straighter-nosed gang of hellions in the days of your life?"

'Twas the nine-thirty boat, and we landed and walked up-town through Twenty-second Street, Tobin being without his hat.

On a street corner, standing under a gas-light and looking over the elevated road at the moon, was a man. A long man he was, dressed decent, with a segar between his teeth, and I saw that his nose made two twists from bridge to end, like the wriggle of a snake. Tobin saw it at the same time, and I heard him breathe hard like a horse when you take the saddle off. He went straight up to the man, and I went with him.

"Good-night to ye," Tobin says to the man. The man takes out a segar and passes the compliments, sociable.

"Would ye hand us your name," asks Tobin, "and let us look at the size of it? It may be our duty to become acquainted with ye."

"My name," says the man, polite, "is Friedenhausman—Maximus G. Friedenhausman."

" 'Tis the right length," says Tobin. "Do you spell it with an 'o' anywhere down the stretch of it?"

"I do not," says the man.

"Can ye spell it with an 'o'?" inquires Tobin, turning anxious.

"If your conscience," says the man with the nose, "is indisposed toward foreign idioms ye might, to please yourself, smuggle the letter into the penultimate syllable."

" 'Tis well," says Tobin. "Ye're in the presence of Jawn Malone and Daniel Tobin."

" 'Tis highly appreciated," says the man, with a bow. "And now since I cannot conceive that ye would hold a spelling bee upon the street corner, will ye name some reasonable excuse for being at large?"

"By the two signs," answers Tobin, trying to explain, "which ye display according to the reading of the Egyptian palmist from the sole of me hand, ye've been nominated to offset with good luck the lines of trouble leading to the nigger man and the blonde lady with her feet crossed in the boat, besides the financial loss of a dollar sixty-five, all so far fulfilled according to Hoyle."

The man stopped smoking and looked at me.

"Have ye any amendments," he asks, "to offer to that statement, or are ye one too? I thought by the looks of ye ye might have him in charge."

"None," says I to him, "except that as one horseshoe resembles another so are ye the picture of good luck as predicted by the hand of me friend. If not, then the lines of Danny's hand may have been crossed, I don't know."

"There's two of ye," says the man with the nose, looking up and down for the sight of a policeman. "I've enjoyed your company immense. Goodnight."

With that he shoves his segar in his mouth and moves across the street, stepping fast. But Tobin sticks close to one side of him and me at the other.

"What!" says he, stopping on the opposite sidewalk and pushing back his hat; "do ye follow me? I tell ye," he says, very loud, "I'm proud to have met ye. But it is my desire to be rid of ye. I am off to me home."

"Do," says Tobin, leaning against his sleeve. "Do be off to your home. And I will sit at the door of it till ye come out in the morning. For the dependence is upon ye to obviate the curse of the nigger man and the blonde lady and the financial loss of the one-sixty-five."

" 'Tis a strange hallucination," says the man, turning to me as a more reasonable lunatic. "Hadn't ye better get him home?"

"Listen, man," says I to him. "Daniel Tobin is as sensible as he ever was. Maybe he is a bit deranged on account of having drink enough to disturb but not enough to settle his wits, but he is no more than following out the legitimate path of his superstitions and predicaments, which I will explain to you." With that I relates the facts about the palmist lady and how the finger of suspicion points to him as an instrument of good fortune. "Now, understand," I concludes, "my position in this riot. I am the friend of me friend Tobin, according to me interpretations. 'Tis easy to be a friend to the prosperous, for it pays; 'tis not hard to be a friend to the poor, for ye get puffed up by gratitude and have your picture printed standing in front of a tenement with a scuttle of coal and an orphan in each hand. But it strains the art of friendship to be true friend to a born fool. And that's what I'm doing," says I, "for, in my opinion, there's no fortune to be read from the palm of me hand that wasn't printed there with the handle of a pick. And, though ye've got the crookedest nose in New York City, I misdoubt that all the fortune-tellers doing business could milk good luck from ye. But the lines of Danny's hand pointed to ye fair, and I'll assist him to experiment with ye until he's convinced ye're dry."

After that the man turns, sudden, to laughing. He leans against a corner and laughs considerable. Then he claps me and Tobin on the backs of us and takes us by an arm apiece.

" 'Tis my mistake," says he. "How could I be expecting anything so fine and wonderful to be turning the corner upon me? I came near being found unworthy. Hard by," says he, "is a café, snug and suitable for the entertainment of idiosyncrasies. Let us go there and have a drink while we discuss the unavailability of the categorical."

So saying, he marched me and Tobin to the back room of a saloon, and ordered the drinks, and laid the money on the table. He looks at me and Tobin like brothers of his, and we have the segars.

"Ye must know," says the man of destiny, "that me walk in life is one that is called the literary. I wander abroad be night seeking idiosyncrasies in the masses and truth in the heavens above. When ye came upon me I was in contemplation of the elevated road in conjunction with the chief luminary of night. The rapid transit is poetry and art: the moon but a tedious, dry body, moving by rote. But these are private opinions, for, in the business of literature, the conditions are reversed. 'Tis me hope to be writing a book to explain the strange things I have discovered in life."

"Ye will put me in a book," says Tobin, disgusted; "will ye put me in a book?"

"I will not," says the man, "for the covers will not hold ye. Not yet. The best I can do is to enjoy ye myself, for the time is not ripe for destroying the limitations of print. Ye would look fantastic in type. All alone by meself must I drink this cup of joy. But, I thank ye, boys; I am truly grateful."

"The talk of ye," says Tobin, blowing through his moustache and pounding the table with his fist, "is an eyesore to me patience. There was good luck promised out of the crook of your nose, but ye bear fruit like the bang of a drum. Ye resemble, with your noise of books, the wind blowing through a crack. Sure, now, I would be thinking the palm of me hand lied but for the coming true of the nigger man and the blonde lady and—"

"Whist!" says the long man; "would ye be led astray by physiognomy? Me nose will do what it can within bounds. Let us have these glasses filled again, for 'tis good to keep idiosyncrasies well moistened, they being subject to deterioration in a dry moral atmosphere."

So, the man of literature makes good, to my notion, for he pays, cheerful, for everything, the capital of me and Tobin being exhausted by prediction. But Tobin is sore, and drinks quiet, with the red showing in his eye.

By and by we moved out, for 'twas eleven o'clock, and stands a bit upon the sidewalk. And then the man says he must be going home, and invites me and Tobin to walk that way. We arrives on a side street two blocks away where there is a stretch of brick houses with high stoops and iron fences. The man stops at one of them and looks up at the top windows which he finds dark.

" 'Tis me humble dwelling," says he, "and I begin to perceive by the signs that me wife has retired to slumber. Therefore I will venture a bit in the way of hospitality. 'Tis me wish that ye enter the basement room, where we dine, and partake of a reasonable refreshment. There will be some fine cold fowl and cheese and a bottle or two of ale. Ye will be welcome to enter and eat, for I am indebted to ye for diversions."

The appetite and conscience of me and Tobin was congenial to the proposition, though 'twas sticking hard in Danny's superstitions to think that a few drinks and a cold lunch should represent the good fortune promised by the palm of his hand.

"Step down the steps," says the man with the crooked nose, "and I will enter by the door above and let ye in. I will ask the new girl we have in the kitchen," says he, "to make ye a pot of coffee to drink before ye go. 'Tis fine coffee Katie Mahorner makes for a green girl just landed three months. Step in," says the man, "and I'll send her down to ye."

The Gift of the Magi

One dollar and eighty-seven cents. That was all. And sixty cents of it was in pennies. Pennies saved one and two at a time by bulldozing the grocer and the vegetable man and the butcher until one's cheeks burned with the silent imputation of parsimony that such close dealing implied. Three times Della counted it. One dollar and eighty-seven cents. And the next day would be Christmas.

There was clearly nothing to do but flop down on the shabby little couch and howl. So Della did it. Which instigates the moral reflection that life is made up of sobs, sniffles, and smiles, with sniffles predominating.

While the mistress of the home is gradually subsiding from the first stage to the second, take a look at the home. A furnished flat at $8 per week. It did not exactly beggar description, but it certainly had that word on the lookout for the mendicancy squad.

In the vestibule below was a letter-box into which no letter would go, and an electric button from which no mortal finger could coax a ring. Also appertaining thereunto was a card bearing the name "Mr. James Dillingham Young."

The "Dillingham" had been flung to the breeze during a former period of prosperity when its possessor was being paid $30 per week. Now, when the income was shrunk to $20, the letters of "Dillingham" looked blurred, as though they were thinking seriously of contracting to a modest and unassuming D. But whenever Mr. James Dillingham Young came home and reached his flat above he was called "Jim" and greatly hugged by Mrs. James Dillingham Young, already introduced to you as Della. Which is all very good.

Della finished her cry and attended to her cheeks with the powder rag. She stood by the window and looked out dully at a gray cat walking a gray fence in a gray backyard. Tomorrow would be Christmas Day, and she had only $1.87 with which to buy Jim a present. She had been saving every penny she could for months, with this result. Twenty dollars a week doesn't go far. Expenses had been greater than she had calculated. They always are. Only $1.87 to buy a present for Jim. Her Jim. Many a happy hour she had spent planning for something nice for him. Something fine and rare and sterling—something just a little bit near to being worthy of the honor of being owned by Jim.

There was a pier-glass between the windows of the room. Perhaps you have seen a pier-glass in an $8 flat. A very thin and very agile person may, by observing his reflection in a rapid sequence of longitudinal strips, obtain a fairly accurate conception of his looks. Della, being slender, had mastered the art.

Suddenly she whirled from the window and stood before the glass. Her eyes were shining brilliantly, but her face had lost its color within twenty seconds. Rapidly she pulled down her hair and let it fall to its full length.

Now, there were two possessions of the James Dillingham Youngs in which they both took a mighty pride. One was Jim's gold watch that had been his father's and his grandfather's. The other was Della's hair. Had the Queen of Sheba lived in the flat across the air-shaft, Della would have let her hair hang out the window some day to dry just to depreciate Her Majesty's jewels and gifts. Had King Solomon been the janitor, with all his treasures piled up in the basement, Jim would have pulled out his watch every time he passed, just to see him pluck at his beard from envy.

So now Della's beautiful hair fell about her rippling and shining like a cascade of brown waters. It reached below her knee and made itself almost a garment for her. And then she did it up again nervously and quickly. Once she faltered for a minute and stood still while a tear or two splashed on the worn red carpet.

On went her old brown jacket; on went her old brown hat. With a whirl of skirts and with the brilliant sparkle still in her eyes, she fluttered out the door and down the stairs to the street.

Where she stopped the sign read: "Mme. Sofronie. Hair Goods of All Kinds." One flight up Della ran, and collected herself, panting. Madame, large, too white, chilly, hardly looked the "Sofronie."

"Will you buy my hair?" asked Della.

"I buy hair," said Madame. "Take yer hat off and let's have a sight at the looks of it."

Down rippled the brown cascade.

"Twenty dollars," said Madame, lifting the mass with a practised hand.

"Give it to me quick," said Della.

Oh, and the next two hours tripped by on rosy wings. Forget the hashed metaphor. She was ransacking the stores for Jim's present.

She found it at last. It surely had been made for Jim and no one else. There was no other like it in any of the stores, and she had turned all of them inside out. It was a platinum fob chain simple and chaste in design, properly proclaiming its value by substance alone and not by meretricious ornamentation—as all good things should do. It was even worthy of The Watch. As soon as she saw it she knew that it must be Jim's. It was like him. Quietness and value—the description applied to both. Twenty-one dollars they took from her for it, and she hurried home with the 87 cents. With that chain on his watch Jim might be properly anxious about the time in any company. Grand as the watch was, he sometimes looked at it on the sly on account of the old leather strap that he used in place of a chain.

When Della reached home her intoxication gave way a little to prudence and reason. She got out her curling irons and lighted the gas and went to work repairing the ravages made by generosity added to love. Which is always a tremendous task, dear friends—a mammoth task.

Within forty minutes her head was covered with tiny, close-lying curls that made her look wonderfully like a truant schoolboy. She looked at her reflection in the mirror long, carefully, and critically.

"If Jim doesn't kill me," she said to herself, "before he takes a second look at me, he'll say I look like a Coney Island chorus girl. But what could I do—oh! what could I do with a dollar and eighty-seven cents?"

At 7 o'clock the coffee was made and the frying-pan was on the back of the stove hot and ready to cook the chops.

Jim was never late. Della doubled the fob chain in her hand and sat on the corner of the table near the door that he always entered. Then she heard his step on the stair away down on the first flight, and she turned white for just a moment. She had a habit of saying little silent prayers about the simplest everyday things, and now she whispered: "Please God, make him think I am still pretty."

The door opened and Jim stepped in and closed it. He looked thin and very serious. Poor fellow, he was only twenty-two—and to be burdened with a family! He needed a new overcoat and he was without gloves.

Jim stopped inside the door, as immovable as a setter at the scent of quail. His eyes were fixed upon Della, and there was an expression in them that she could not read, and it terrified her. It was not anger, nor surprise, nor disapproval, nor horror, nor any of the sentiments that she had been prepared for. He simply stared at her fixedly with that peculiar expression on his face.

Della wriggled off the table and went for him.

"Jim, darling," she cried, "don't look at me that way. I had my hair cut off and sold it because I couldn't have lived through Christmas without giving you a present. It'll grow out again—you won't mind, will you? I just had to do it. My hair grows awfully fast. Say 'Merry Christmas!' Jim, and let's be happy. You don't know what a nice—what a beautiful, nice gift I've got for you."

"You've cut off your hair?" asked Jim, laboriously, as if he had not arrived at that patent fact yet even after the hardest mental labor.

"Cut it off and sold it," said Della. "Don't you like me just as well, anyhow? I'm me without my hair, ain't I?"

Jim looked about the room curiously.

"You say your hair is gone?" he said, with an air almost of idiocy.

"You needn't look for it," said Della. "It's sold, I tell you—sold and gone, too. It's Christmas Eve, boy. Be good to me, for it went for you. Maybe the hairs of my head were numbered," she went on with a sudden serious sweetness, "but nobody could ever count my love for you. Shall I put the chops on, Jim?"

Out of his trance Jim seemed quickly to wake. He enfolded his Della. For ten seconds let us regard with discreet scrutiny some inconsequential object in the other direction. Eight dollars a week or a million a year—what is the difference? A mathematician or a wit would give you the wrong answer. The magi brought valuable gifts, but that was not among them. This dark assertion will be illuminated later on.

Jim drew a package from his overcoat pocket and threw it upon the table.

"Don't make any mistake, Dell," he said, "about me. I don't think there's anything in the way of a haircut or a shave or a shampoo that could make me like my girl any less. But if you'll unwrap that package you may see why you had me going a while at first."

White fingers and nimble tore at the string and paper. And then an ecstatic scream of joy; and then, alas! a quick feminine change to hysterical tears and wails, necessitating the immediate employment of all the comforting powers of the lord of the flat.

For there lay The Combs—the set of combs, side and back, that Della had worshipped for long in a Broadway window. Beautiful combs, pure tortoise shell, with jewelled rims—just the shade to wear in the beautiful vanished hair. They were expensive combs, she knew, and her heart had simply craved and yearned over them without the least hope of possession. And now, they were hers, but the tresses that should have adorned the coveted adornments were gone.

But she hugged them to her bosom, and at length she was able to look up with dim eyes and a smile and say: "My hair grows so fast, Jim!"

And then Della leaped up like a little singed cat and cried, "Oh, oh!"

Jim had not yet seen his beautiful present. She held it out to him eagerly upon her open palm. The dull precious metal seemed to flash with a reflection of her bright and ardent spirit.

"Isn't it a dandy, Jim? I hunted all over town to find it. You'll have to look at the time a hundred times a day now. Give me your watch. I want to see how it looks on it."

Instead of obeying, Jim tumbled down on the couch and put his hands under the back of his head and smiled.

"Dell," said he, "let's put our Christmas presents away and keep 'em a while. They're too nice to use just at present. I sold the watch to get the money to buy your combs. And now supposc you put the chops on."

The magi, as you know, were wise men—wonderfully wise men—who brought gifts to the Babe in the manger. They invented the art of giving Christmas presents. Being wise, their gifts were no doubt wise ones, possibly bearing the privilege of exchange in case of duplication. And here I have lamely related to you the uneventful chronicle of two foolish children in a flat who most unwisely sacrificed for each other the greatest treasures of their house. But in a last word to the wise of these days let it be said that of all who give gifts these two were the wisest. Of all who give and receive gifts, such as they are wisest. Everywhere they are wisest. They are the magi.

A Service of Love

When one loves one's Art no service seems too hard.

That is our premise. This story shall draw a conclusion from it, and show at the same time that the premise is incorrect. That will be a new thing in logic, and a feat in story-telling somewhat older than the great wall of China.

Joe Larrabee came out of the post-oak flats of the Middle West pulsing with a genius for pictorial art. At six he drew a picture of the town pump with a prominent citizen passing it hastily. This effort was framed and hung in the drug-store window by the side of the ear of corn with an uneven number of rows. At twenty he left for New York with a flowing necktie and a capital tied up somewhat closer.

Delia Caruthers did things in six octaves so promisingly in a pine-tree village in the South that her relatives chipped in enough in her chip hat for her to go "North" and "finish." They could not see her f——, but that is our story.

Joe and Delia met in an atelier where a number of art and music students had gathered to discuss chiaroscuro, Wagner, music, Rembrandt's works, pictures, Waldteufel, wall paper, Chopin and Oolong.

Joe and Delia became enamored one of the other, or each of the other, as you please, and in a short time were married—for (see above), when one loves one's Art no service seems too hard.

Mr. and Mrs. Larrabee began housekeeping in a flat. It was a lonesome flat—something like the A sharp way down at the left-hand end of the keyboard. And they were happy; for they had their Art, and they had each other. And my advice to the rich young man would be—sell all thou hast, and give it to the poor—janitor for the privilege of living in a flat with your Art and your Delia.

Flat-dwellers shall indorse my dictum that theirs is the only true happiness. If a home is happy it cannot fit too close—let the dresser collapse and become a billard table; let the mantel turn to a rowing machine, the escritoire to a spare bedchamber, the washstand to an upright piano; let the four walls come together, if they will, so you and your Delia are between. But if home be the other kind, let it be wide and long—enter you at the Golden Gate, hang your hat on Hatteras, your cape on Cape Horn and go out by the Labrador.

Joe was painting in the class of the great Magister—you know his fame. His fees are high; his lessons are light—his high-lights have brought him renown. Delia was studying under Rosenstock—you know his repute as a disturber of the piano keys.

They were mighty happy as long as their money lasted. So is every—but I will not be cynical. Their aims were very clear and defined. Joe was to become capable very soon of turning out pictures that old gentlemen with thin side-whiskers and thick pocketbooks would sandbag one another in his studio for the privilege of buying. Delia was to become familiar and then contemptuous with Music, so that when she saw the orchestra seats and boxes unsold she could have sore throat and lobster in a private dining-room and refuse to go on the stage.

But the best, in my opinion, was the home life in the little flat—the ardent, voluble chats after the day's study; the cozy dinners and fresh, light breakfasts; the interchange of ambitions—ambitions interwoven each with the other's or else inconsiderable—the mutual help and inspiration; and—overlook my artlessness—stuffed olives and cheese sandwiches at 11 P.M.

But after a while Art flagged. It sometimes does, even if some switchman doesn't flag it. Everything going out and nothing coming in, as the vulgarians say. Money was lacking to pay Mr. Magister and Herr Rosenstock their prices. When one loves one's Art no service seems too hard. So, Delia said she must give music lessons to keep the chafing dish bubbling.

For two or three days she went out canvassing for pupils. One evening she came home elated.

"Joe, dear," she said, gleefully, "I've a pupil. And, oh, the loveliest people. General—General A. B. Pinkney's daughter—on Seventy-first Street. Such a splendid house, Joe—you ought to see the front door! Byzantine I think you would call it. And inside! Oh, Joe, I never saw anything like it before.

"My pupil is his daughter Clementina. I dearly love her already. She's a delicate thing—dresses always in white; and the sweetest, simplest manners! Only eighteen years old. I'm to give three lessons a week; and, just think, Joe! $5 a lesson. I don't mind it a bit; for when I get two or three more pupils I can resume my lessons with Herr Rosenstock. Now, smooth out that wrinkle between your brows, dear, and let's have a nice supper."

"That's all right for you, Dele," said Joe, attacking a can of peas with a carving knife and a hatchet, "but how about me? Do you think I'm going to let you hustle for wages while I philander in the regions of high art? Not by the bones of Benvenuto Cellini! I guess I can sell papers or lay cobblestones, and bring in a dollar or two."

Delia came and hung about his neck.

"Joe, dear, you are silly. You must keep on at your studies. It is not as if I had quit my music and gone to work at something else. While I teach I learn. I am always with my music. And we can live as happily as millionaires on $15 a week. You mustn't think of leaving Mr. Magister."

"All right," said Joe, reaching for the blue scalloped vegetable dish. "But I hate for you to be giving lessons. It isn't Art. But you're a trump and a dear to do it."

"When one loves one's Art no service seems too hard," said Delia.

"Magister praised the sky in that sketch I made in the park," said Joe. "And Tinkle gave me permission to hang two of them in his window. I may sell one if the right kind of a moneyed idiot sees them."

"I'm sure you will," said Delia, sweetly. "And now let's be thankful for Gen. Pinkney and this veal roast."

During all of the next week the Larrabees had an early breakfast. Joe was enthusiastic about some morning-effect sketches he was doing in Central Park, and Delia packed him off breakfasted, coddled, praised and kissed at 7 o'clock. Art is an engaging mistress. It was most times 7 o'clock when he returned in the evening.

At the end of the week Delia, sweetly proud but languid, triumphantly tossed three five-dollar bills on the 8 × 10 (inches) centre table of the 8 × 10 (feet) flat parlor.

"Sometimes," she said, a little wearily, "Clementina tries me. I'm afraid she doesn't practise enough, and I have to tell her the same things so often. And then she always dresses entirely in white, and that does get monotonous. But Gen. Pinkney is the dearest old man! I wish you could know him, Joe. He comes in sometimes when I am with Clementina at the piano—he is a widower, you know—and stands there pulling his white goatee. 'And how are the semiquavers and the demisemiquavers progressing?' he always asks.

"I wish you could see the wainscoting in that drawing room, Joe! And those Astrakhan rug portières. And Clementina has such a funny little cough. I hope she is stronger than she looks. Oh, I really am getting attached to her, she is so gentle and high bred. Gen. Pinkney's brother was once Minister to Bolivia."

And then Joe, with the air of Monte Cristo, drew forth a ten, a five, a two and a one—all legal tender notes—and laid them beside Delia's earnings.

"Sold that watercolor of the obelisk to a man from Peoria," he announced, overwhelmingly.

"Don't joke with me," said Delia—"not from Peoria!"

"All the way. I wish you could see him, Dele. Fat man with a woolen muffler and a quill toothpick. He saw the sketch in Tinkle's window and thought it was a windmill at first. He was game, though, and bought it anyhow. He ordered another—an oil sketch of the Lackawanna freight depot—to take back with him. Music lessons! Oh, I guess Art is still in it."

"I'm so glad you've kept on," said Delia, heartily. "You're bound to win, dear. Thirty-three dollars! We never had so much to spend before. We'll have oysters to-night."

"And filet mignon with champignons," said Joe. "Where is the olive fork?"

On the next Saturday evening Joe reached home first. He spread his $18 on the parlor table and washed what seemed to be a great deal of dark paint from his hands.

Half an hour later Delia arrived, her right hand tied up in a shapeless bundle of wraps and bandages.

"How is this?" asked Joe after the usual greetings. Delia laughed, but not very joyously.

"Clementina," she explained, "insisted upon a Welsh rabbit after her lesson. She is such a queer girl. Welsh rabbits at 5 in the afternoon. The General was there. You should have seen him run for the chafing dish, Joe, just as if there wasn't a servant in the house. I know Clementina isn't in good health; she is so nervous. In serving the rabbit she spilled a great lot of it, boiling hot, over my hand and wrist. It hurt awfully, Joe. And the dear girl was so sorry! But Gen. Pinkney!—Joe, that old man nearly went distracted. He rushed downstairs and sent somebody—they said the furnace man or somebody in the basement—out to a drug store for some oil and things to bind it up with. It doesn't hurt so much now."

"What's this?" asked Joe, taking the hand tenderly and pulling at some white strands beneath the bandages.

"It's something soft," said Delia, "that had oil on it. Oh, Joe, did you sell another sketch?" She had seen the money on the table.

"Did I?" said Joe; "just ask the man from Peoria. He got his depot to-day, and he isn't sure but he thinks he wants another parkscape and a view on the Hudson. What time this afternoon did you burn your hand, Dele?"

"Five o'clock, I think," said Dele, plaintively. "The iron—I mean the rabbit came off the fire about that time. You ought to have seen Gen. Pinkney, Joe, when——"

"Sit down here a moment, Dele," said Joe. He drew her to the couch, sat beside her and put his arm across her shoulders.

"What have you been doing for the last two weeks, Dele?" he asked.

She braved it for a moment or two with an eye full of love and stubbornness, and murmured a phrase or two vaguely of Gen. Pinkney; but at length down went her head and out came the truth and tears.

"I couldn't get any pupils," she confessed. "And I couldn't bear to have you give up your lessons; and I got a place ironing shirts in that big Twenty-fourth Street laundry. And I think I did very well to make up both General Pinkney and Clementina, don't you, Joe? And when a girl in the laundry set down a hot iron on my hand this afternoon I was all the way home making up that story about the Welsh rabbit. You're not angry, are you, Joe? And if I hadn't got the work you mightn't have sold your sketches to that man from Peoria."

"He wasn't from Peoria," said Joe, slowly.

"Well, it doesn't matter where he was from. How clever you are, Joe—and—kiss me, Joe—and what made you ever suspect that I wasn't giving music lessons to Clementina?"

"I didn't," said Joe, "until to-night. And I wouldn't have then, only I sent up this cotton waste and oil from the engine-room this afternoon for a girl upstairs who had her hand burned with a smoothing-iron. I've been firing the engine in that laundry for the last two weeks."

"And then you didn't—"

"My purchaser from Peoria," said Joe, "and Gen. Pinkney are both creations of the same art—but you wouldn't call it either painting or music."

And then they both laughed, and Joe began:

"When one loves one's Art no service seems—"

But Delia stopped him with her hand on his lips. "No," she said—"just 'When one loves.' "

The Cop and the Anthem

On his bench in Madison Square Soapy moved uneasily. When wild geese honk high of nights, and when women without sealskin coats grow kind to their husbands, and when Soapy moves uneasily on his bench in the park, you may know that winter is near at hand.

A dead leaf fell in Soapy's lap. That was Jack Frost's card. Jack is kind to the regular denizens of Madison Square, and gives fair warning of his annual call. At the corners of four streets he hands his pasteboard to the North Wind, footman of the mansion of All Outdoors, so that the inhabitants thereof may make ready.

Soapy's mind became cognizant of the fact that the time had come for him to resolve himself into a singular Committee of Ways and Means to provide against the coming rigor. And therefore he moved uneasily on his bench.

The hibernatorial ambitions of Soapy were not of the highest. In them were no considerations of Mediterranean cruises, of soporific Southern skies or drifting in the Vesuvian Bay. Three months on the Island was what his soul craved. Three months of assured board and bed and congenial company, safe from Boreas and bluecoats, seemed to Soapy the essence of things desirable.

For years the hospitable Blackwell's had been his winter quarters. Just as his more fortunate fellow New Yorkers had bought their tickets to Palm Beach and the Riviera each winter, so Soapy had made his humble arrangements for his annual hegira to the Island. And now the time was come. On the previous night three Sabbath newspapers, distributed beneath his coat, about his ankles and over his lap, had failed to repulse the cold as he slept on his bench near the spurting fountain in the ancient square. So the Island loomed big and timely in Soapy's mind. He scorned the provisions made in the name of charity for the city's dependents. In Soapy's opinion the Law was more benign than Philanthropy. There was an endless round of institutions, municipal and eleemosynary, on which he might set out and receive lodging and food accordant with the simple life. But to one of Soapy's proud spirit the gifts of charity are encumbered. If not in coin you must pay in humiliation of spirit for every benefit received at the hands of philanthropy. As Cæsar had his Brutus, every bed of charity must have its toll of a bath, every loaf of bread its compensation of a private and personal inquisition. Wherefore it is better to be a guest of the law, which, though conducted by rules, does not meddle unduly with a gentleman's private affairs.

Soapy, having decided to go to the Island, at once set about accomplishing his desire. There were many easy ways of doing this. The pleasantest was to dine luxuriously at some expensive restaurant; and then, after declaring insolvency, be handed over quietly and without uproar to a policeman. An accommodating magistrate would do the rest.

Soapy left his bench and strolled out of the square and across the level sea of asphalt, where Broadway and Fifth Avenue flow together. Up Broadway he turned, and halted at a glittering café, where are gathered together nightly the choicest products of the grape, the silkworm, and the protoplasm.

Soapy had confidence in himself from the lowest button of his vest upward. He was shaven, and his coat was decent and his neat black, ready-tied four-in-hand had been presented to him by a lady missionary on Thanksgiving Day. If he could reach a table in the restaurant unsuspected success would be his. The portion of him that would show above the table would raise no doubt in the waiter's mind. A roasted mallard duck, thought Soapy, would be about the thing—with a bottle of Chablis, and then Camembert, a demi-tasse and a cigar. One dollar for the cigar would be enough. The total would not be so high as to call forth any supreme manifestation of revenge from the café management; and yet the meat would leave him filled and happy for the journey to his winter refuge.

But as Soapy set foot inside the restaurant door the head waiter's eye fell upon his frayed trousers and decadent shoes. Strong and ready hands turned him about and conveyed him in silence and haste to the sidewalk and averted the ignoble fate of the menaced mallard.

Soapy turned off Broadway. It seemed that his route to the coveted Island was not to be an epicurean one. Some other way of entering limbo must be thought of.

At a corner of Sixth Avenue electric lights and cunningly displayed wares behind plate-glass made a shop window conspicuous. Soapy took a cobblestone and dashed it through the glass. People came running around the corner, a policeman in the lead. Soapy stood still, with his hands in his pockets, and smiled at the sight of brass buttons.

"Where's the man that done that?" inquired the officer, excitedly.

"Don't you figure out that I might have had something to do with it?" said Soapy, not without sarcasm, but friendly, as one greets good fortune.

The policeman's mind refused to accept Soapy even as a clue. Men who smash windows do not remain to parley with the law's minions. They take to their heels. The policeman saw a man halfway down the block running to catch a car. With drawn club he joined in the pursuit. Soapy, with disgust in his heart, loafed along, twice unsuccessful.

On the opposite side of the street was a restaurant of no great pretensions. It catered to large appetites and modest purses. Its crockery and atmosphere were thick; its soup and napery thin. Into this place Soapy took his accusive shoes and telltale trousers without challenge. At a table he sat and consumed beefsteak, flapjacks, doughnuts and pie. And then to the waiter he betrayed the fact that the minutest coin and himself were strangers.

"Now, get busy and call a cop," said Soapy. "And don't keep a gentleman waiting."

"No cop for youse," said the waiter, with a voice like butter cakes and an eye like the cherry in a Manhattan cocktail. "Hey, Con!"

Neatly upon his left ear on the callous pavement two waiters pitched Soapy. He arose joint by joint, as a carpenter's rule opens, and beat the dust from his clothes. Arrest seemed but a rosy dream. The Island seemed very far away. A policeman who stood before a drug store two doors away laughed and walked down the street.

Five blocks Soapy travelled before his courage permitted him to woo capture again. This time the opportunity presented what he fatuously termed to himself a "cinch." A young woman of a modest and pleasing guise was standing before a show window gazing with sprightly interest at its display of shaving mugs and inkstands, and two yards from the window a large policeman of severe demeanor leaned against a water plug.

It was Soapy's design to assume the rôle of the despicable and execrated "masher." The refined and elegant appearance of his victim and the contiguity of the conscientious cop encouraged him to believe that he would soon feel the pleasant official clutch upon his arm that would insure his winter quarters on the right little, tight little isle.

Soapy straightened the lady missionary's ready-made tie, dragged his shrinking cuffs into the open, set his hat at a killing cant and sidled toward the young woman. He made eyes at her, was taken with sudden coughs and "hems," smiled, smirked and went brazenly through the impudent and contemptible litany of the "masher." With half an eye Soapy saw that the policeman was watching him fixedly. The young woman moved away a few steps, and again bestowed her absorbed attention upon the shaving mugs. Soapy followed, boldly stepping to her side, raised his hat and said:

"Ah there, Bedelia! Don't you want to come and play in my yard?"

The policeman was still looking. The persecuted young woman had but to beckon a finger and Soapy would be practically en route for his insular haven. Already he imagined he could feel the cozy warmth of the station-house. The young woman faced him and, stretching out a hand, caught Soapy's coat sleeve.

"Sure, Mike," she said, joyfully, "if you'll blow me to a pail of suds. I'd have spoke to you sooner, but the cop was watching."

With the young woman playing the clinging ivy to his oak Soapy walked past the policeman overcome with gloom. He seemed doomed to liberty.

At the next corner he shook off his companion and ran. He halted in the district where by night are found the lightest streets, hearts, vows and librettos. Women in furs and men in greatcoats moved gaily in the wintry air. A sudden fear seized Soapy that some dreadful enchantment had rendered him immune to arrest. The thought brought a little of panic upon it, and when he came upon another policeman lounging grandly in front of a transplendent theatre he caught at the immediate straw of "disorderly conduct."

On the sidewalk Soapy began to yell drunken gibberish at the top of his harsh voice. He danced, howled, raved, and otherwise disturbed the welkin.

The policeman twirled his club, turned his back to Soapy and remarked to a citizen.

" 'Tis one of them Yale lads celebratin' the goose egg they give to the Hartford College. Noisy; but no harm. We've instructions to lave them be."

Disconsolate, Soapy ceased his unavailing racket. Would never a policeman lay hands on him? In his fancy the Island seemed an unattainable Arcadia. He buttoned his thin coat against the chilling wind.

In a cigar store he saw a well-dressed man lighting a cigar at a swinging light. His silk umbrella he had set by the door on entering. Soapy stepped inside, secured the umbrella and sauntered off with it slowly. The man at the cigar light followed hastily.

"My umbrella," he said, sternly.

"Oh, is it?" sneered Soapy, adding insult to petit larceny. "Well, why don't you call a policeman? I took it. Your umbrella! Why don't you call a cop? There stands one on the corner."

The umbrella owner slowed his steps. Soapy did likewise, with a presentiment that luck would again run against him. The policeman looked at the two curiously.

"Of course," said the umbrella man—"that is—well, you know how these mistakes occur—I—if it's your umbrella I hope you'll excuse me—I picked it up this morning in a restaurant— If you recognize it as yours, why—I hope you'll—"

"Of course it's mine," said Soapy, viciously.

The ex-umbrella man retreated. The policeman hurried to assist a tall blonde in an opera cloak across the street in front of a street car that was approaching two blocks away.

Soapy walked eastward through a street damaged by improvements. He hurled the umbrella wrathfully into an excavation. He muttered against the men who wear helmets and carry clubs. Because he wanted to fall into their clutches, they seemed to regard him as a king who could do no wrong.

At length Soapy reached one of the avenues to the east where the glitter and turmoil was but faint. He set his face down this toward Madison Square, for the homing instinct survives even when the home is a park bench.

But on an unusually quiet corner Soapy came to a standstill. Here was an old church, quaint and rambling and gabled. Through one violet-stained window a soft light glowed, where, no doubt, the organist loitered over the keys, making sure of his mastery of the coming Sabbath anthem. For there drifted out to Soapy's ears sweet music that caught and held him transfixed against the convolutions of the iron fence.

The moon was above, lustrous and serene; vehicles and pedestrians were few; sparrows twittered sleepily in the eaves—for a little while the scene might have been a country churchyard. And the anthem that the organist played cemented Soapy to the iron fence, for he had known it well in the days when his life contained such things as mothers and roses and ambitions and friends and immaculate thoughts and collars.

The conjunction of Soapy's receptive state of mind and the influences about the old church wrought a sudden and wonderful change in his soul. He viewed with swift horror the pit into which he had tumbled, the degraded days, unworthy desires, dead hopes, wrecked faculties and base motives that made up his existence.

And also in a moment his heart responded thrillingly to this novel mood. An instantaneous and strong impulse moved him to battle with his desperate fate. He would pull himself out of the mire; he would make a man of himself again; he would conquer the evil that had taken possession of him. There was time; he was comparatively young yet: he would resurrect his old eager ambitions and pursue them without faltering. Those solemn but sweet organ notes had set up a revolution in him. Tomorrow he would go into the roaring downtown district and find work. A fur importer had once offered him a place as driver. He would find him to-morrow and ask for the position. He would be somebody in the world. He would—

Soapy felt a hand laid on his arm. He looked quickly around into the broad face of a policeman.

"What are you doin' here?" asked the officer.

"Nothin'," said Soapy.

"Then come along," said the policeman.

"Three months on the Island," said the Magistrate in the Police Court the next morning.

Memoirs of a Yellow Dog

I don't suppose it will knock any of you people off your perch to read a contribution from an animal. Mr. Kipling and a good many others have demonstrated the fact that animals can express themselves in remunerative English, and no magazine goes to press nowadays without an animal story in it, except the old-style monthlies that are still running pictures of Bryan and the Mont Pelée horror.

But you needn't look for any stuck-up literature in my piece, such as Bearoo, the bear, and Snakoo, the snake, and Tammanoo, the tiger, talk in the jungle books. A yellow dog that's spent most of his life in a cheap New York flat, sleeping in a corner on an old sateen underskirt (the one she spilled port wine on at the Lady Longshoremen's banquet), mustn't be expected to perform any tricks with the art of speech.

I was born a yellow pup; date, locality, pedigree and weight unknown. The first thing I can recollect, an old woman had me in a basket at Broadway and Twenty-third trying to sell me to a fat lady. Old Mother Hubbard was boosting me to beat the band as a genuine Pomeranian-Hambletonian-Red-Irish-Cochin-China-Stoke-Pogis fox terrier. The fat lady chased a V around among the samples of gros grain flannelette in her shopping bag till she cornered it, and gave up. From that moment I was a pet—a mamma's own wootsey squidlums. Say, gentle reader, did you ever have a 200-pound woman breathing a flavor of Camembert cheese and Peau d'Espagne pick you up and wallop her nose all over you, remarking all the time in an Emma Eames tone of voice: "Oh, oo's um oodlum, doodlum, woodlum, toodlum, bitsy-witsy skoodlums?"

From pedigreed yellow pup I grew up to be an anonymous yellow cur looking like a cross between an Angora cat and a box of lemons. But my mistress never tumbled. She thought that the two primeval pups that Noah chased into the ark were but a collateral branch of my ancestors. It took two policemen to keep her from entering me at the Madison Square Garden for the Siberian bloodhound prize.

I'll tell you about that flat. The house was the ordinary thing in New York, paved with Parian marble in the entrance hall and cobblestones above the first floor. Our flat was three—well, not flights—climbs up. My mistress rented it unfurnished, and put in the regular things—1903 antique upholstered parlor set, oil chromo of geishas in a Harlem tea house, rubber plant and husband.

By Sirius! there was a biped I felt sorry for. He was a little man with sandy hair and whiskers a good deal like mine. Henpecked?—well, toucans and flamingoes and pelicans all had their bills in him. He wiped the dishes and listened to my mistress tell about the cheap, ragged things the lady with the squirrel-skin coat on the second floor hung out on her line to dry. And every evening while she was getting supper she made him take me out on the end of a string for a walk.

If men knew how women pass the time when they are alone they'd never marry. Laura Lean Jibbey, peanut brittle, a little almond cream on the neck muscles, dishes unwashed, half an hour's talk with the iceman, reading a package of old letters, a couple of pickles and two bottles of malt extract, one hour peeking through a hole in the window shade into the flat across the air-shaft—that's about all there is to it. Twenty minutes before time for him to come home from work she straightens up the house, fixes her rat so it won't show, and gets out a lot of sewing for a ten-minute bluff.

I led a dog's life in that flat. 'Most all day I lay there in my corner watching that fat woman kill time. I slept sometimes and had pipe dreams about being out chasing cats into basements and growling at old ladies with black mittens, as a dog was intended to do. Then she would pounce upon me with a lot of that drivelling poodle palaver and kiss me on the nose—but what could I do? A dog can't chew cloves.

I began to feel sorry for Hubby, dog my cats if I didn't. We looked so much alike that people noticed it when we went out; so we shook the streets that Morgan's cab drives down, and took to climbing the piles of last December's snow on the streets where cheap people live.

One evening when we were thus promenading, and I was trying to look like a prize St. Bernard, and the old man was trying to look like he wouldn't have murdered the first organ-grinder he heard play Mendelssohn's wedding-march, I looked up at him and said, in my way:

"What are you looking so sour about, you oakum trimmed lobster? She don't kiss you. You don't have to sit on her lap and listen to talk that would make the book of a musical comedy sound like the maxims of Epictetus. You ought to be thankful you're not a dog. Brace up, Benedick, and bid the blues begone."

The matrimonial mishap looked down at me with almost canine intelligence in his face.

"Why, doggie," says he, "good doggie. You almost look like you could speak. What is it, doggie—cats."

Cats! Could speak!

But, of course, he couldn't understand. Humans were denied the speech of animals. The only common ground of communication upon which dogs and men can get together is in fiction.

In the flat across the hall from us lived a lady with a black-and-tan terrier. Her husband strung it and took it out every evening, but he always came home cheerful and whistling. One day I touched noses with the black-and-tan in the hall, and I struck him for an elucidation.

"See here, Wiggle-and-Skip," I says, "you know that it ain't the nature of a real man to play dry nurse to a dog in public. I never saw one leashed to a bow-wow yet that didn't look like he'd like to lick every other man that looked at him. But your boss comes in every day as perky and set up as an amateur prestidigitator doing the egg trick. How does he do it? Don't tell me he likes it."

"Him?" says the black-and-tan. "Why, he uses Nature's Own Remedy. He gets spifflicated. At first when we go out he's as shy as the man on the steamer who would rather play pedro when they make 'em all jackpots. By the time we've been in eight saloons he don't care whether the thing on the end of his line is a dog or a catfish. I've lost two inches of my tail trying to sidestep those swinging doors."

The pointer I got from that terrier—Vaudeville please copy—set me to thinking.

One evening about 6 o'clock my mistress ordered him to get busy and do the ozone act for Lovey. I have concealed it until now, but that is what she called me. The black-and-tan was called "Tweetness." I consider that I have the bulge on him as far as you could chase a rabbit. Still "Lovey" is something of a nomenclatural tin can on the tail of one's self-respect.

At a quiet place on a safe street I tightened the line of my custodian in front of an attractive, refined saloon. I made a dead-ahead scramble for the doors, whining like a dog in the press despatches that lets the family know that little Alice is bogged while gathering lilies in the brook.

"Why, darn my eyes," says the old man, with a grin; "darn my eyes if the saffron-colored son of a seltzer lemonade ain't asking me in to take a drink. Lemme see—how long's it been since I saved shoe leather by keeping one foot on the foot-rest? I believe I'll—"

I knew I had him. Hot Scotches he took, sitting at a table. For an hour he kept the Campbells coming. I sat by his side rapping for the waiter with my tail, and eating free lunch such as mamma in her flat never equalled with her homemade truck bought at a delicatessen store eight minutes before papa comes home.

When the products of Scotland were all exhausted except the rye bread the old man unwound me from the table leg and played me outside like a fisherman plays a salmon. Out there he took off my collar and threw it into the street.

"Poor doggie," says he; "good doggie. She shan't kiss you any more. 'S a darned shame. Good doggie, go away and get run over by a street car and be happy."

I refused to leave. I leaped and frisked around the old man's legs happy as a pug on a rug.

"You old flea-headed woodchuck-chaser," I said to him—"you moonbaying, rabbit-pointing, egg-stealing old beagle, can't you see that I don't want to leave you? Can't you see that we're both Pups in the Wood and the missis is the cruel uncle after you with the dish towel and me with the flea liniment and a pink bow to tie on my tail. Why not cut that all out and be pards forever more?"

Maybe you'll say he didn't understand—maybe he didn't. But he kind of got a grip on the Hot Scotches, and stood still for a minute, thinking.

"Doggie," says he, finally, "we don't live more than a dozen lives on this earth, and very few of us live to be more than 300. If I ever see that flat any more I'm a flat, and if you do you're flatter; and that's no flattery. I'm offering 60 to 1 that Westward Ho wins out by the length of a dachshund."

There was no string, but I frolicked along with my master to the Twenty-third Street ferry. And the cats on the route saw reason to give thanks that prehensile claws had been given to them.

On the Jersey side my master said to a stranger who stood eating a currant bun:

"Me and my doggie, we are bound for the Rocky Mountains."

But what pleased me most was when my old man pulled both of my ears until I howled, and said:

"You common, monkey-headed, rat-tailed, sulphur-colored son of a door mat, do you know what I'm going to call you?"

I thought of "Lovey," and I whined dolefully.

"I'm going to call you 'Pete,' " says my master; and if I'd had five tails I couldn't have done enough wagging to do justice to the occasion.

An Unfinished Story

We no longer groan and heap ashes upon our heads when the flames of Tophet are mentioned. For, even the preachers have begun to tell us that God is radium, or ether or some scientific compound, and that the worst we wicked ones may expect is a chemical reaction. This is a pleasing hypothesis; but there lingers yet some of the old, goodly terror of orthodoxy.

There are but two subjects upon which one may discourse with a free imagination, and without the possibility of being controverted. You may talk of your dreams; and you may tell what you heard a parrot say. Both Morpheus and the bird are incompetent witnesses; and your listener dare not attack your recital. The baseless fabric of a vision, then, shall furnish my theme—chosen with apologies and regrets instead of the more limited field of pretty Polly's small talk.

I had a dream that was so far removed from the higher criticism that it had to do with the ancient, respectable, and lamented bar-of-judgment theory.

Gabriel had played his trump; and those of us who could not follow suit were arraigned for examination. I noticed at one side a gathering of professional bondsmen in solemn black and collars that buttoned behind; but it seemed there was some trouble about their real estate titles; and they did not appear to be getting any of us out.

A fly cop—an angel policeman—flew over to me and took me by the left wing. Near at hand was a group of very prosperous-looking spirits arraigned for judgment.

"Do you belong with that bunch?" the policeman asked.

"Who are they?" was my answer.

"Why," said he, "they are—"

But this irrelevant stuff is taking up space that the story should occupy.

Dulcie worked in a department store. She sold Hamburg edging, or stuffed peppers, or automobiles, or other little trinkets such as they keep in department stores. Of what she earned, Dulcie received six dollars per week. The remainder was credited to her and debited to somebody else's account in the ledger kept by G— Oh, primal energy, you say, Reverend Doctor— Well, then, in the Ledger of Primal Energy.

During her first year in the store, Dulcie was paid five dollars per week. It would be instructive to know how she lived on that amount. Don't care? Very well; probably you are interested in larger amounts. Six dollars is a larger amount. I will tell you how she lived on six dollars per week.

One afternoon at six, when Dulcie was sticking her hat pin within an eighth of an inch of her *medulla oblongata,* she said to her chum, Sadie—the girl that waits on you with her left side:

"Say, Sade, I made a date for dinner this evening with Piggy."

"You never did!" exclaimed Sadie, admiringly. "Well, ain't you the lucky one? Piggy's an awful swell; and he always takes a girl to swell places. He took Blanche up to the Hoffman House one evening, where they have swell music, and you see a lot of swells. You'll have a swell time, Dulce."

Dulcie hurried homeward. Her eyes were shining, and her cheeks showed the delicate pink of life's—real life's—approaching dawn. It was Friday; and she had fifty cents left of her last week's wages.

The streets were filled with the rush-hour floods of people. The electric lights of Broadway were glowing—calling moths from miles, from leagues, from hundreds of leagues out of darkness around to come in and attend the singeing school. Men in accurate clothes, with faces like those carved on cherry stones by the old salts in sailors' homes, turned and stared at Dulcie as she sped, unheeding, past them. Manhattan, the night-blooming cereus, was beginning to unfold its dead-white, heavy-odored petals.

Dulcie stopped in a store where goods were cheap and bought an imitation lace collar with her fifty cents. That money was to have been spent otherwise—fifteen cents for supper, ten cents for breakfast, ten cents for lunch. Another dime was to be added to her small store of savings; and five cents was to be squandered for licorice drops—the kind that made your cheek look like the toothache, and last as long. The licorice was an extravagance—almost a carouse—but what is life without pleasures?

Dulcie lived in a furnished room. There is this difference between a furnished room and a boarding-house. In a furnished room, other people do not know it when you go hungry.

Dulcie went up to her room—the third-floor-back in a West Side brownstone-front. She lit the gas. Scientists tell us that the diamond is the hardest substance known. Their mistake. Landladies know of a compound beside which the diamond is as putty. They pack it in the tips of gasburners; and one may stand on a chair and dig at it in vain until one's fingers are pink and bruised. A hairpin will not remove it; therefore let us call it immovable.

So Dulcie lit the gas. In its one-fourth-candle-power glow we will observe the room.

Couch-bed, dresser, table, washstand, chair—of this much the landlady was guilty. The rest was Dulcie's. On the dresser were her treasures—a gilt china vase presented to her by Sadie, a calendar issued by a pickle works, a book on the divination of dreams, some rice powder in a glass dish, and a cluster of artificial cherries tied with a pink ribbon.

Against the wrinkly mirror stood pictures of General Kitchener, William Muldoon, the Duchess of Marlborough, and Benvenuto Cellini. Against one wall was a plaster of Paris plaque of an O'Callahan in a Roman helmet. Near it was a violent oleograph of a lemon-colored child assaulting an inflammatory butterfly. This was Dulcie's final judgment in art; but it had never been upset. Her rest had never been disturbed by whispers of stolen copes; no critic had elevated his eyebrows at her infantile entomologist.

Piggy was to call for her at seven. While she swiftly makes ready, let us discreetly face the other way and gossip.

For the room, Dulcie paid two dollars per week. On week-days her breakfast cost ten cents; she made coffee and cooked an egg over the gaslight while she was dressing. On Sunday mornings she feasted royally on veal chops and pineapple fritters at "Billy's" restaurant, at a cost of twenty-five cents—and tipped the waitress ten cents. New York presents so many temptations for one to run into extravagance. She had her lunches in the department-store restaurant at a cost of sixty cents for the week; dinners were $1.05. The evening papers—show me a New Yorker going without his daily paper!—came to six cents; and two Sunday papers—one for the personal column and the other to read—were ten cents. The total amounts to $4.76. Now, one has to buy clothes, and—

I give it up. I hear of wonderful bargains in fabrics, and of miracles performed with needle and thread; but I am in doubt. I hold my pen poised in vain when I would add to Dulcie's life some of those joys that belong to woman by virtue of all the unwritten, sacred, natural, inactive ordinances of the equity of heaven. Twice she had been to Coney Island and had ridden the hobby-horses. 'Tis a weary thing to count your pleasures by summers instead of by hours.

Piggy needs but a word. When the girls named him, an undeserving stigma was cast upon the noble family of swine. The words-of-three-letters lesson in the old blue spelling book begins with Piggy's biography. He was fat; he had the soul of a rat, the habits of a bat, and the magnanimity of a cat. . . . He wore expensive clothes; and was a connoisseur in starvation. He could look at a shop-girl and tell you to an hour how long it had been since she had eaten anything more nourishing than marshmallows and tea. He hung about the shopping districts, and prowled around in department stores with his invitations to dinner. Men who escort dogs upon the streets at the end of a string look down upon him. He is a type; I can dwell upon him no longer; my pen is not the kind intended for him; I am no carpenter.

At ten minutes to seven Dulcie was ready. She looked at herself in the wrinkly mirror. The reflection was satisfactory. The dark blue dress, fitting without a wrinkle, the hat with its jaunty black feather, the but-slightly-soiled gloves—all representing self-denial, even of food itself—were vastly becoming.

Dulcie forgot everything else for a moment except that she was beautiful, and that life was about to lift a corner of its mysterious veil for her to observe its wonders. No gentleman had ever asked her out before. Now she was going for a brief moment into the glitter and exalted show.

The girls said that Piggy was a "spender." There would be a grand dinner, and music, and splendidly dressed ladies to look at and things to eat that strangely twisted the girls' jaws when they tried to tell about them. No doubt she would be asked out again.

There was a blue pongee suit in a window that she knew—by saving twenty cents a week instead of ten in—let's see—— Oh, it would run into years! But there was a second-hand store in Seventh Avenue where——

Somebody knocked at the door. Dulcie opened it. The landlady stood there with a spurious smile, sniffing for cooking by stolen gas.

"A gentleman's downstairs to see you," she said. "Name is Mr. Wiggins."

By such epithet was Piggy known to unfortunate ones who had to take him seriously.

Dulcie turned to the dresser to get her handkerchief; and then she stopped still, and bit her underlip hard. While looking in her mirror she had seen fairyland and herself, a princess, just awakening from a long slumber. She had forgotten one that was watching her with sad, beautiful, stern eyes—the only one there was to approve or condemn what she did. Straight and slender and tall, with a look of sorrowful reproach on his handsome, melancholy face, General Kitchener fixed his wonderful eyes on her out of his gilt photograph frame on the dresser.

Dulcie turned like an automatic doll to the landlady.

"Tell him I can't go," she said, dully. "Tell him I'm sick, or something. Tell him I'm not going out."

After the door was closed and locked, Dulcie fell upon her bed, crushing her black tip, and cried for ten minutes. General Kitchener was her only friend. He was Dulcie's ideal of a gallant knight. He looked as if he might have a secret sorrow, and his wonderful moustache was a dream, and she was a little afraid of that stern yet tender look in his eyes. She used to have little fancies that he would call at the house sometime, and ask for her, with his sword clanking against his high boots. Once, when a boy was rattling a piece of chain against a lamp post she had opened the window and looked out. But there was no use. She knew that General Kitchener was away over in Japan, leading his army against the savage Turks; and he would never step out of his gilt frame for her. Yet one look from him had vanquished Piggy that night. Yes, for that night.

When her cry was over Dulcie got up and took off her best dress, and put on her old blue kimono. She wanted no dinner. She sang two verses of "Sammy." Then she became intensely interested in a little red speck on the side of her nose. And after that was attended to, she drew up a chair to the rickety table, and told her fortune with an old deck of cards.

"The horrid, impudent thing!" she said aloud. "And I never gave him a word or a look to make him think it!"

At nine o'clock Dulcie took a tin box of crackers and a little pot of raspberry jam out of her trunk and had a feast. She offered General Kitchener some jam on a cracker; but he only looked at her as the sphinx would have looked at a butterfly—if there are butterflies in the desert.

"Don't eat if you don't want to," said Dulcie. "And don't put on so many airs and scold so with your eyes. I wonder if you'd be so superior and snippy if you had to live on six dollars a week."

It was not a good sign for Dulcie to be rude to General Kitchener. And then she turned Benvenuto Cellini face downward with a severe gesture. But that was not inexcusable; for she had always thought he was Henry VIII, and she did not approve of him.

At half-past nine Dulcie took a last look at the pictures on the dresser, turned out the light and skipped into bed. It's an awful thing to go to bed with a good-night look at General Kitchener, William Muldoon, the Duchess of Marlborough, and Benvenuto Cellini.

This story doesn't really get anywhere at all. The rest of it comes later—sometime when Piggy asks Dulcie again to dine with him, and she is feeling lonelier than usual, and General Kitchener happens to be looking the other way; and then—

As I said before, I dreamed that I was standing near a crowd of prosperous-looking angels, and a policeman took me by the wing and asked if I belonged with them.

"Who are they?" I asked.

"Why," said he, "they are the men who hired working-girls, and paid 'em five or six dollars a week to live on. Are you one of the bunch?"

"Not on your immortality," said I. "I'm only a fellow that set fire to an orphan asylum, and murdered a blind man for his pennies."

Sisters of the Golden Circle

The Rubberneck Auto was about ready to start. The merry top-riders had been assigned to their seats by the gentlemanly conductor. The sidewalk was blockaded with sightseers who had gathered to stare at sightseers, justifying the natural law that every creature on earth is preyed upon by some other creature.

The megaphone man raised his instrument of torture; the inside of the great automobile began to thump and throb like the heart of a coffee drinker. The top-riders nervously clung to the seats; the old lady from Valparaiso, Indiana, shrieked to be put ashore. But, before a wheel turns, listen to a brief preamble through the cardiaphone, which shall point out to you an object of interest on life's sightseeing tour.

Swift and comprehensive is the recognition of white man for white man in African wilds; instant and sure is the spiritual greeting between mother and babe; unhesitatingly do master and dog commune across the slight gulf between animal and man; immeasurably quick and sapient are the brief messages between one and one's beloved. But all these instances set forth only slow and groping interchange of sympathy and thought beside one other instance which the Rubberneck coach shall disclose. You shall learn (if you have not learned already) what two beings of all earth's living inhabitants most quickly look into each other's hearts and souls when they meet face to face.

The gong whirred, and the Glaring-at-Gotham car moved majestically upon its instructive tour.

On the highest, rear seat was James Williams, of Cloverdale, Missouri, and his Bride.

Capitalize it, friend typo—that last word—word of words in the epiphany of life and love. The scent of the flowers, the booty of the bee, the primal drip of spring waters, the overture of the lark, the twist of lemon peel on the cocktail of creation—such is the bride. Holy is the wife; revered the mother; galliptious is the summer girl—but the bride is the certified check among the wedding presents that the gods send in when man is married to mortality.

The car glided up the Golden Way. On the bridge of the great cruiser the captain stood, trumpeting the sights of the big city to his passengers. Wide-mouthed and open-eared they heard the sights of the metropolis thundered forth to their eyes. Confused, delirious with excitement and provincial longings, they tried to make ocular responses to the megaphonic ritual. In the solemn spires of spreading cathedrals they saw the home of the Vanderbilts; in the busy bulk of the Grand Central depot they viewed, wonderingly, the frugal cot of Russell Sage. Bidden to observe the highlands of the Hudson, they gaped, unsuspecting, at the upturned mountains of a new-laid sewer.

To many the elevated railroad was the Rialto, on the stations of which uniformed men sat and made chop suey of your tickets. And to this day in the outlying districts many have it that Chuck Connors, with his hand on his heart, leads reform; and that but for the noble municipal efforts of one Parkhurst, a district attorney, the notorious "Bishop" Potter gang would have destroyed law and order from the Bowery to the Harlem River.

But I beg you to observe Mrs. James Williams—Hattie Chalmers that was—once the belle of Cloverdale. Pale-blue is the bride's, if she will; and this color she had honored. Willingly had the moss rosebud loaned to her cheeks of its pink—and as for the violet!—her eyes will do very well as they are, thank you. A useless strip of white chaf—oh, no, he was guiding the auto car—of white chiffon—or perhaps it was grenadine or tulle—was tied beneath her chin, pretending to hold her bonnet in place. But you know as well as I do that the hat pins did the work.

And on Mrs. James Williams's face was recorded a little library of the world's best thoughts in three volumes. Volume No. 1 contained the belief that James Williams was about the right sort of thing. Volume No. 2 was an essay on the world, declaring it to be a very excellent place. Volume No. 3 disclosed the belief that in occupying the highest seat in a Rubberneck auto they were travelling the pace that passes all understanding.

James Williams, you would have guessed, was about twenty-four. It will gratify you to know that your estimate was so accurate. He was exactly twenty-three years, eleven months and twenty-nine days old. He was well built, active, strong-jawed, good-natured, and rising. He was on his wedding trip.

Dear kind fairy, please cut out those orders for money and 40 H. P. touring cars and fame and a new growth of hair and the presidency of the boat club. Instead of any of them turn backward—oh, turn backward and give us just a teeny-weeny bit of our wedding trip over again. Just an hour, dear fairy, so we can remember how the grass and poplar trees looked, and the bow of those bonnet strings tied beneath her chin—even if it was the hat pins that did the work.

Can't do it? Very well; hurry up with that touring car and the oil stock, then.

Just in front of Mrs. James Williams sat a girl in a loose tan jacket and a straw hat adorned with grapes and roses. Only in dream and milliners' shops do we, alas! gather grapes and roses at one swipe. This girl gazed with large blue eyes, credulous, when the megaphone man roared his doctrine that millionaires were things about which we should be concerned. Between blasts she resorted to Epictetian philosophy in the form of pepsin chewing gum.

At this girl's right hand sat a young man about twenty-four. He was well built, active, strong-jawed, and good-natured. But if his description seems to follow that of James Williams, divest it of anything Cloverdalian. This man belonged to hard streets and sharp corners. He looked keenly about him, seeming to begrudge the asphalt under the feet of those upon whom he looked down from his perch.

While the megaphone barks at a famous hostelry, let me whisper you through the low-tuned cardiaphone to sit tight; for now things are about to happen, and the great city will close over them again as over a scrap of ticker tape floating down from the den of a Broad Street bear.

The girl in the tan jacket twisted around to view the pilgrims on the last seat. The other passengers she had absorbed; the seat behind her was her Bluebeard's chamber.

Her eyes met those of Mrs. James Williams. Between two ticks of a watch they exchanged their life's experiences, histories, hopes and fancies. And all, mind you, with the eye, before two men could have decided whether to draw steel or borrow a match.

The bride leaned forward low. She and the girl spoke rapidly together, their tongues moving quickly like those of two serpents—a comparison that is not meant to go further. Two smiles and a dozen nods closed the conference.

And now in the broad, quiet avenue in front of the Rubberneck car a man in dark clothes stood with uplifted hand. From the sidewalk another hurried to join him.

The girl in the fruitful hat quickly seized her companion by the arm and whispered in his ear. That young man exhibited proof of ability to act promptly. Crouching low, he slid over the edge of the car, hung lightly for an instant, and then disappeared. Half a dozen of the top-riders observed his feat wonderingly, but made no comment, deeming it prudent not to express surprise at what might be the conventional manner of alighting in this bewildering city. The truant passenger dodged a hansom and then floated past, like a leaf on a stream between a furniture van and a florist's delivery wagon.

The girl in the tan jacket turned again, and looked into the eyes of Mrs. James Williams. Then she faced about and sat still while the Rubberneck auto stopped at the flash of the badge under the coat of the plainclothes man.

"What's eating you?" demanded the megaphonist, abandoning his professional discourse for pure English.

"Keep her at anchor for a minute," ordered the officer. "There's a man on board we want—a Philadelphia burglar called 'Pinky' McGuire. There he is on the back seat. Look out for the side, Donovan."

Donovan went to the hind wheel and looked up at James Williams.

"Come down, old sport," he said pleasantly. "We've got you. Back to Sleepytown for yours. It ain't a bad idea, hidin' on a Rubberneck, though. I'll remember that."

Softly through the megaphone came the advice of the conductor:

"Better step off, sir, and explain. The car must proceed on its tour."

James Williams belonged among the level heads. With necessary slowness he picked his way through the passengers down to the steps at the front of the car. His wife followed, but she first turned her eyes and saw the escaped tourist glide from behind the furniture van and slip behind a tree on the edge of the little park, not fifty feet away.

Descended to the ground, James Williams faced his captors with a smile. He was thinking what a good story he would have to tell in Cloverdale about having been mistaken for a burglar. The Rubberneck coach lingered, out of respect for its patrons. What could be a more interesting sight than this?

"My name is James Williams, of Cloverdale, Missouri," he said, kindly, so that they would not be too greatly mortified. "I have letters here that will show—"

"You'll come with us, please," announced the plainclothes man. " 'Pinky' McGuire's description fits you like flannel washed in hot suds. A detective saw you on the Rubberneck up at Central Park and 'phoned down to take you in. Do your explaining at the stationhouse."

James Williams's wife—his bride of two weeks—looked him in the face with a strange, soft radiance in her eyes and a flush on her cheeks, looked him in the face and said:

"Go with 'em quietly, 'Pinky,' and maybe it'll be in your favor."

And then as the Glaring-at-Gotham car rolled away she turned and threw a kiss—his wife threw a kiss—at some one high up on the seats of the Rubberneck.

"Your girl gives you good advice, McGuire," said Donovan. "Come on now."

And then madness descended upon and occupied James Williams. He pushed his hat far upon the back of his head.

"My wife seems to think I am a burglar," he said, recklessly. "I never heard of her being crazy; therefore I must be. And if I'm crazy, they can't do anything to me for killing you two fools in my madness."

Whereupon he resisted arrest so cheerfully and industriously that cops had to be whistled for, and afterwards the reserves, to disperse a few thousand delighted spectators.

At the station-house the desk sergeant asked for his name.

"McDoodle, the Pink, or Pinky the Brute, I forget which," was James Williams's answer. "But you can bet I'm a burglar; don't leave that out. And you might add that it took five of 'em to pluck the Pink. I'd especially like to have that in the records."

In an hour came Mrs. James Williams, with Uncle Thomas, of Madison Avenue, in a respect-compelling motor car and proofs of the hero's innocence—for all the world like the third act of a drama backed by an automobile mfg. co.

After the police had sternly reprimanded James Williams for imitating a copyrighted burglar and given him as honorable a discharge as the department was capable of, Mrs. Williams rearrested him and swept him into an angle of the station-house. James Williams regarded her with one eye. He always said that Donovan closed the other while somebody was holding his good right hand. Never before had he given her a word of reproach or of reproof.

"If you can explain," he began rather stiffly, "why you—"

"Dear," she interrupted, "listen. It was an hour's pain and trial to you. I did it for her—I mean the girl who spoke to me on the coach. I was so happy, Jim—so happy with you that I didn't dare to refuse that happiness to another. Jim, they were married only this morning—those two; and I wanted him to get away. While they were struggling with you I saw him slip from behind his tree and hurry across the park. That's all of it, dear—I had to do it."

Thus does one sister of the plain gold band know another who stands in the enchanted light that shines but once and briefly for each one. By rice and satin bows does mere man become aware of weddings. But bride knoweth bride at the glance of an eye. And between them swiftly passes comfort and meaning in a language that man and widows wot not of.

The Furnished Room

Restless, shifting, fugacious as time itself is a certain vast bulk of the population of the red brick district of the lower West Side. Homeless, they have a hundred homes. They flit from furnished room to furnished room, transients forever—transients in abode, transients in heart and mind. They sing "Home, Sweet Home" in ragtime; they carry their *lares et penates* in a bandbox; their vine is entwined about a picture hat; a rubber plant is their fig tree.

Hence the houses of this district, having had a thousand dwellers, should have a thousand tales to tell, mostly dull ones, no doubt; but it would be strange if there could not be found a ghost or two in the wake of all these vagrant guests.

One evening after dark a young man prowled among these crumbling red mansions, ringing their bells. At the twelfth he rested his lean handbaggage upon the step and wiped the dust from his hatband and forehead. The bell sounded faint and far away in some remote, hollow depths.

To the door of this, the twelfth house whose bell he had rung, came a housekeeper who made him think of an unwholesome, surfeited worm that had eaten its nut to a hollow shell and now sought to fill the vacancy with edible lodgers.

He asked if there was a room to let.

"Come in," said the housekeeper. Her voice came from her throat; her throat seemed lined with fur. "I have the third-floor back, vacant since a week back. Should you wish to look at it?"

The young man followed her up the stairs. A faint light from no particular source mitigated the shadows of the halls. They trod noiselessly upon a stair carpet that its own loom would have forsworn. It seemed to have become vegetable; to have degenerated in that rank, sunless air to lush lichen or spreading moss that grew in patches to the stair-case and was viscid under the foot like organic matter. At each turn of the stairs were vacant niches in the wall. Perhaps plants had once been set within them. If so they had died in that foul and tainted air. It may be that statues of the saints had stood there, but it was not difficult to conceive that imps and devils had dragged them forth in the darkness and down to the unholy depths of some furnished pit below.

"This is the room," said the housekeeper, from her furry throat.

"It's a nice room. It ain't often vacant. I had some most elegant people in it last summer—no trouble at all, and paid in advance to the minute. The water's at the end of the hall. Sprowls and Mooney kept it three months. They done a vaudeville sketch. Miss B'retta Sprowls—you may have heard of her—Oh, that was just the stage names—right there over the dresser is where the marriage certificate hung, framed. The gas is here, and you see there is plenty of closet room. It's a room everybody likes. It never stays idle long."

"Do you have many theatrical people rooming here?" asked the young man.

"They comes and goes. A good proportion of my lodgers is connected with the theatres. Yes, sir, this is the theatrical district. Actor people never stays long anywhere. I get my share. Yes, they comes and they goes."

He engaged the room, paying for a week in advance. He was tired, he said, and would take possession at once. He counted out the money. The room had been made ready, she said, even to towels and water. As the housekeeper moved away he put, for the thousandth time, the question that he carried at the end of his tongue.

"A young girl—Miss Vashner—Miss Eloise Vashner—do you remember such a one among your lodgers? She would be singing on the stage, most likely. A fair girl, of medium height and slender, with reddish, gold hair and dark mole near her left eyebrow."

"No, I don't remember the name. Them stage people has names they change as often as their rooms. They comes and they goes. No, I don't call that one to mind."

No. Always no. Five months of ceaseless interrogation and the inevitable negative. So much time spent by day in questioning managers, agents, schools and choruses; by night among the audiences of theatres from all-star casts down to music halls so low that he dreaded to find what he most hoped for. He who had loved her best had tried to find her. He was sure that since her disappearance from home this great, water-girt city held her somewhere, but it was like a monstrous quicksand, shifting its particles constantly, with no foundation, its upper granules of to-day buried to-morrow in ooze and slime.

The furnished room received its latest guest with a first glow of pseudo-hospitality, a hectic, haggard, perfunctory welcome like the specious smile of a demirep. The sophistical comfort came in reflected gleams from the decayed furniture, the ragged brocade upholstery of a couch and two chairs, a foot-wide cheap pier glass between the two windows, from one or two gilt picture frames and a brass bedstead in a corner.

The guest reclined, inert, upon a chair, while the room, confused in speech as though it were an apartment in Babel, tried to discourse to him of its divers tenantry.

A polychromatic rug like some brilliant-flowered, rectangular, tropical islet lay surrounded by a billowy sea of soiled matting. Upon the gay-papered wall were those pictures that pursue the homeless one from house to house—The Huguenot Lovers, The First Quarrel, The Wedding Breakfast, Psyche at the Fountain. The mantel's chastely severe outline was ingloriously veiled behind some pert drapery drawn rakishly askew like the sashes of the Amazonian ballet. Upon it was some desolate flotsam cast aside by the room's marooned when a lucky sail had borne them to a fresh port—a trifling vase or two, pictures of actresses, a medicine bottle, some stray cards out of a deck.

One by one, as the characters of a cryptograph became explicit, the little signs left by the furnished rooms' procession of guests developed a significance. The threadbare space in the rug in front of the dresser told that lovely woman had marched in the throng. The tiny fingerprints on the wall spoke of little prisoners trying to feel their way to sun and air. A splattered stain, raying like the shadow of a bursting bomb, witnessed where a hurled glass or bottle had splintered with its contents against the wall. Across the pier glass had been scrawled with a diamond in staggering letters the name "Marie." It seemed that the succession of dwellers in the furnished room had turned in fury—perhaps tempted beyond forbearance by its garish coldness—and wreaked upon it their passions. The furniture was chipped and bruised; the couch, distorted by bursting springs, seemed a horrible monster that had been slain during the stress of some grotesque convulsion. Some more potent upheaval had cloven a great slice from the marble mantel. Each plank in the floor owned its particular cant and shriek as from a separate and individual agony. It seemed incredible that all this malice and injury had been wrought upon the room by those who had called it for a time their home; and yet it may have been the cheated home instinct surviving blindly, the resentful rage at false household gods that had kindled their wrath. A hut that is our own we can sweep and adorn and cherish.

The young tenant in the chair allowed these thoughts to file, softshod, through his mind, while there drifted into the room furnished sounds and furnished scents. He heard in one room a tittering and incontinent, slack laughter; in others the monologue of a scold, the rattling of dice, a lullaby, and one crying dully; above him a banjo tinkled with spirit. Doors banged somewhere; the elevated trains roared intermittently; a cat yowled miserably upon a back fence. And he breathed the breath of the house—a dank savor rather than a smell—a cold, musty effluvium as from underground vaults mingled with the reeking exhalations of linoleum and mildewed and rotten woodwork.

Then suddenly, as he rested there, the room was filled with the strong, sweet odor of mignonette. It came as upon a single buffet of wind with such sureness and fragrance and emphasis that it almost seemed a living visitant. And the man cried aloud: "What, dear?" as if he had been called, and sprang up and faced about. The rich odor clung to him and wrapped him around. He reached out his arms for it, all his senses for the time confused and commingled. How could one be peremptorily called by an odor? Surely it must have been a sound. But, was it not the sound that had touched, that had caressed him?

"She has been in this room," he cried, and he sprang to wrest from it a token, for he knew he would recognize the smallest thing that had belonged to her or that she had touched. This enveloping scent of mignonette, the odor that she had loved and made her own—whence came it?

The room had been but carelessly set in order. Scattered upon the flimsy dresser scarf were half a dozen hairpins—those discreet, indistinguishable friends of womankind, feminine of gender, infinite mood and uncommunicative of tense. These he ignored, conscious of their triumphant lack of identity. Ransacking the drawers of the dresser he came upon a discarded, tiny, ragged handkerchief. He pressed it to his face. It was racy and insolent with heliotrope; he hurled it to the floor. In another drawer he found odd buttons, a theatre programme, a pawnbroker's card, two lost marshmallows, a book on the divination of dreams. In the last was a woman's black satin hair bow, which halted him, poised between ice and fire. But the black satin hair bow also is femininity's demure, impersonal common ornament and tells no tales.

And then he traversed the room like a hound on the scent, skimming the walls, considering the corners of the bulging matting on his hands and knees, rummaging mantel and tables, the curtains and hangings, the drunken cabinet in the corner, for a visible sign, unable to perceive that she was there beside, around, against, within, above him, clinging to him, wooing him, calling him so poignantly through the finer senses that even his grosser ones became cognizant of the call. Once again he answered loudly: "Yes, dear!" and turned, wild-eyed, to gaze on vacancy, for he could not yet discern form and color and love and outstretched arms in the odor of mignonette. Oh,

God! whence that odor, and since when have odors had a voice to call? Thus he groped.

He burrowed in crevices and corners, and found corks and cigarettes. These he passed in passive contempt. But once he found in a fold of the matting a half-smoked cigar, and this he ground beneath his heel with a green and trenchant oath. He sifted the room from end to end. He found dreary and ignoble small records of many a peripatetic tenant; but of her whom he sought, and who may have lodged there, and whose spirit seemed to hover there, he found no trace.

And then he thought of the housekeeper.

He ran from the haunted room downstairs and to a door that showed a crack of light. She came out to his knock. He smothered his excitement as best he could.

"Will you tell me, madam," he besought her, "who occupied the room I have before I came?"

"Yes, sir. I can tell you again. 'Twas Sprowls and Mooney, as I said. Miss B'retta Sprowls it was in the theatres, but Missis Mooney she was. My house is well known for respectability. The marriage certificate hung, framed, on a nail over——"

"What kind of a lady was Miss Sprowls—in looks, I mean?"

"Why, black-haired, sir, short, and stout, with a comical face. They left a week ago Tuesday."

"And before they occupied it?"

"Why, there was a single gentleman connected with the draying business. He left owing me a week. Before him was Missis Crowder and her two children, that stayed four months; and back of them was old Mr. Doyle, whose sons paid for him. He kept the room six months. That goes back a year, sir, and further I do not remember."

He thanked her and crept back to his room. The room was dead. The essence that had vivified it was gone. The perfume of mignonette had departed. In its place was the old, stale odor of mouldy house furniture, of atmosphere in storage.

The ebbing of his hope drained his faith. He sat staring at the yellow, singing gaslight. Soon he walked to the bed and began to tear the sheets into strips. With the blade of his knife he drove them tightly into every crevice around windows and door. When all was snug and taut he turned out the light, turned the gas full on again and laid himself gratefully upon the bed.

It was Mrs. McCool's night to go with the can for beer. So she fetched it and sat with Mrs. Purdy in one of those subterranean retreats where housekeepers foregather and the worm dieth seldom.

"I rented out my third-floor-back this evening," said Mrs. Purdy, across a fine circle of foam. "A young man took it. He went up to bed two hours ago."

"Now, did ye, Mrs. Purdy, ma'am?" said Mrs. McCool, with intense admiration. "You do be a wonder for rentin' rooms of that kind. And did ye tell him, then?" she concluded in a husky whisper laden with mystery.

"Rooms," said Mrs. Purdy, in her furriest tones, "are furnished for to rent. I did not tell him, Mrs. McCool."

" 'Tis right ye are, ma'am; 'tis by renting rooms we kape alive. Ye have the rale sense for business, ma'am. There be many people will rayjict the rentin' of a room if they be tould a suicide has been after dyin' in the bed of it."

"As you say, we has our living to be making," remarked Mrs. Purdy.

"Yis, ma'am; 'tis true. 'Tis just one wake ago this day I helped ye lay out the third-floor-back. A pretty slip of a colleen she was to be killin' herself wid the gas—a swate little face she had, Mrs. Purdy, ma'am."

"She'd a-been called handsome, as you say," said Mrs. Purdy, assenting but critical, "but for that mole she had a-growin' by her left eyebrow. Do fill up your glass again, Mrs. McCool."

From HEART OF THE WEST 1907

The Pimienta Pancakes

While we were rounding up a bunch of the Triangle-O cattle in the Frio bottoms a projecting branch of a dead mesquite caught my wooden stirrup and gave my ankle a wrench that laid me up in camp for a week.

On the third day of my compulsory idleness I crawled out near the grub wagon, and reclined helpless under the conversational fire of Judson Odom, the camp cook. Jud was a monologist by nature, whom Destiny, with customary blundering, had set in a profession wherein he was bereaved, for the greater portion of his time, of an audience.

Therefore, I was manna in the desert of Jud's obmutescence.

Betimes I was stirred by invalid longings for something to eat that did not come under the caption of "grub." I had visions of the maternal pantry "deep as first love, and wild with all regret," and then I asked:

"Jud, can you make pancakes?"

Jud laid down his sixshooter, with which he was preparing to pound an antelope steak, and stood over me in what I felt to be a menacing attitude. He further indorsed my impression that his pose was resentful by fixing upon me with his light blue eyes a look of cold suspicion.

"Say, you," he said, with candid, though not excessive, choler, "did you mean that straight, or was you trying to throw the gaff into me? Some of the boys been telling you about me and that pancake racket?"

"No, Jud," I said, sincerely, "I meant it. It seems to me I'd swap my pony and saddle for a stack of buttered brown pancakes with some first crop, open kettle, New Orleans sweetening. Was there a story about pancakes?"

Jud was mollified at once when he saw that I had not been dealing in allusions. He brought some mysterious bags and tin boxes from the grub wagon and set them in the shade of the hackberry where I lay reclined. I watched him as he began to arrange them leisurely and untie their many strings.

"No, not a story," said Jud, as he worked, "but just the logical disclosures in the case of me and that pink-eyed snoozer from Mired Mule Cañada and Miss Willella Learight. I don't mind telling you.

"I was punching then for old Bill Toomey, on the San Miguel. One day I gets all ensnared up in aspirations for to eat some canned grub that hasn't ever mooed or baaed or grunted or been in peck measures. So, I gets on my bronc and pushes the wind for Uncle Emsley Telfair's store at the Pimienta Crossing on the Neuces.

"About three in the afternoon I throwed my bridle over a mesquite limb and walked the last twenty yards into Uncle Emsley's store. I got up on the counter and told Uncle Emsley that the signs pointed to the devastation of the fruit crop of the world. In a minute I had a bag of crackers and a long-handled spoon, with an open can each of apricots and pineapples and cherries and green-gages beside of me with Uncle Emsley busy chopping away with the hatchet at the yellow clings. I was feeling like Adam before the apple stampede, and was digging my spurs into the side of the counter and working with my twenty-four-inch spoon when I happened to look out of the window into the yard of Uncle Emsley's house, which was next to the store.

"There was a girl standing there—an imported girl with fixings on—philandering with a croquet maul and amusing herself by watching my style of encouraging the fruit canning industry.

"I slid off the counter and delivered up my shovel to Uncle Emsley.

" 'That's my niece,' says he; 'Miss Willella Learight, down from Palestine on a visit. Do you want that I should make you acquainted?'

" 'The Holy Land,' I says to myself, my thought milling some as I tried to run 'em into the corral. 'Why not? There was sure angels in Pales— Why yes, Uncle Emsley,' I says out loud, 'I'd be awful edified to meet Miss Learight.'

"So Uncle Emsley took me out in the yard and gave us each other's entitlements.

"I never was shy about women. I never could understand why some men who can break a mustang before breakfast and shave in the dark, get all left-handed and full of perspiration and excuses when they see a bolt of calico draped around what belongs in it. Inside of eight minutes me and Miss Willella was aggravating the croquet balls around as amiable as second cousins. She gave me a dig about the quantity of canned fruit I had eaten, and I got back at her, flat-footed, about how a certain lady named Eve started the fruit trouble in the first free-grass pasture—'Over in Palestine, wasn't it?' says I, as easy and pat as roping a one-year-old.

"That was how I acquired cordiality for the proximities of Miss Willella Learight; and the disposition grew larger as time passed. She was stopping at Pimienta Crossing for her health, which was very good, and for the climate, which was forty percent hotter than Palestine. I rode over to see her once every week for a while; and then I figured it out that if I doubled the number of trips I would see her twice as often.

"One week I slipped in a third trip; and that's where the pancakes and the pink-eyed snoozer busted into the game.

"That evening, while I set on the counter with a peach and two damsons in my mouth, I asked Uncle Emsley how Miss Willella was.

" 'Why,' says Uncle Emsley, 'she's gone riding with Jackson Bird, the sheep man from over at Mired Mule Cañada.'

"I swallowed the peach seed and the two damson seeds. I guess somebody held the counter by the bridle while I got off; and then I walked out straight ahead till I butted against the mesquite where my roan was tied.

" 'She's gone riding,' I whispered in my bronc's ear, 'with Birdstone Jack, the hired mule from Sheep Man's Cañada. Did you get that, old Leather-and-Gallops?'

"That bronc of mine wept, in his way. He'd been raised a cow pony and he didn't care for snoozers.

"I went back and said to Uncle Emsley: 'Did you say a sheep man?' "

" 'I said a sheep man,' says Uncle again. 'You must have heard tell of Jackson Bird. He's got eight sections of grazing and four thousand head of the finest Merinos south of the Arctic Circle.'

"I went out and sat on the ground in the shade of the store and leaned against a prickly pear. I sifted sand into my boots with unthinking hands while I soliloquized a quantity about this bird with the Jackson plumage to his name.

"I never had believed in harming sheep men. I see one, one day, reading a Latin grammar on hossback, and I never touched him! They never irritated me like they do most cowmen. You wouldn't go to work now, and impair and disfigure snoozers, would you, that eat on tables and wear little shoes and speak to you on subjects? I had always let 'em pass, just as you would a jack-rabbit; with a polite word and a guess about the weather, but no stopping to swap canteens. I never thought it was worth while to be hostile with a snoozer. And because I'd been lenient, and let 'em live, here was one going around riding with Miss Willella Learight!

"An hour by sun they come loping back, and stopped at Uncle Emsley's gate. The sheep person helped her off; and they stood throwing each other sentences all sprightful and sagacious for a while. And then this feathered Jackson flies up in his saddle and raises his little stewpot of a hat, and trots off in the direction of his mutton ranch. By this time I had turned the sand out of my boots and unpinned myself from the prickly pear; and by the time he gets half a mile out of Pimienta, I singlefoots up beside him on my bronc.

"I said that snoozer was pink-eyed, but he wasn't. His seeing arrangement was gray enough, but his eye-lashes was pink and his hair was sandy, and that gave you the idea. Sheep man—he wasn't more than a lamb man, anyhow—a little thing with his neck involved in a yellow silk handkerchief, and shoes tied up in bowknots.

" 'Afternoon!' says I to him. 'You now ride with a equestrian who is commonly called Dead-Moral-Certainty Judson, on account of the way I shoot. When I want a stranger to know me I always introduce myself before the draw, for I never did like to shake hands with ghosts.'

" 'Ah,' says he, just like that—'Ah, I'm glad to know you, Mr. Judson. I'm Jackson Bird, from over at Mired Mule Ranch.'

"Just then one of my eyes saw a roadrunner skipping down the hill with a young tarantula in his bill, and the other eye noticed a rabbit-hawk sitting on a dead limb in a water-elm. I popped over one after the other with my forty-five, just to show him. 'Two out of three,' says I. 'Birds just naturally seem to draw my fire wherever I go.'

" 'Nice shooting,' says the sheep man, without a flutter. 'But don't you sometimes ever miss the third shot? Elegant fine rain that was last week for the young grass, Mr. Judson,' says he.

" 'Willie,' says I, riding over close to his palfrey, 'your infatuated parents may have denounced you by the name of Jackson, but you sure moulted into a twittering Willie—let us slough off this here analysis of rain and the elements, and get down to talk that is outside the vocabulary of parrots. That is a bad habit you have got of riding with young ladies over at Pimienta. I've known birds,' says I, 'to be served on toast for less than that. Miss Willella,' says I, 'don't ever want any nest made out of sheep's wool by a tomtit of the Jacksonian branch of ornithology. Now, are you going to quit, or do you wish for to gallop up against this Dead-Moral-Certainty attachment to my name, which is good for two hyphens and at least one set of funeral obsequies?'

"Jackson Bird flushed up some, and then he laughed.

" 'Why, Mr. Judson,' says he, 'you've got the wrong idea. I've called on Miss Learight a few times; but not for the purpose you imagine. My object is purely a gastronomical one.'

"I reached for my gun.

" 'Any coyote,' says I, 'that would boast of dishonorable—'

" 'Wait a minute,' says this Bird, 'till I explain. What would I do with a wife? If you ever saw that ranch of mine! I do my own cooking and mending. Eating—that's all the pleasure I get out of sheep raising. Mr. Judson, did you ever taste the pancakes that Miss Learight makes?'

" 'Me? No,' I told him. 'I never was advised that she was up to any culinary maneuvers.'

" 'They're golden sunshine,' says he, 'honey-browned by the ambrosial fires of Epicurus. I'd give two years of my life to get the recipe for making them pancakes. That's what I went to see Miss Learight for,' says Jackson Bird, 'but I haven't been able to get it from her. It's an old recipe that's been in the family for seventy-five years. They hand it down from one generation to another, but they don't give it away to outsiders. If I could get that recipe, so I could make them pancakes for myself on my ranch, I'd be a happy man,' says Bird.

" 'Are you sure,' I says to him, 'that it ain't the hand that mixes the pancakes that you're after?'

" 'Sure,' says Jackson. 'Miss Learight is a mighty nice girl, but I can assure you my intentions go no further than the gastro—' but he seen my hand going down to my holster and he changed his similitude—'than the desire to procure a copy of the pancake recipe,' he finishes.

" 'You ain't such a bad little man,' says I, trying to be fair. 'I was thinking some of making orphans of your sheep, but I'll let you fly away this time. But you stick to pancakes,' says I, 'as close as the middle one of a stack; and don't go and mistake sentiments for syrup, or there'll be singing at your ranch, and you won't hear it.'

" 'To convince you that I am sincere,' says the sheep man, 'I'll ask you to help me. Miss Learight and you being closer friends, maybe she would do for you what she wouldn't for me. If you will get me a copy of that pancake recipe, I give you my word that I'll never call upon her again.'

" 'That's fair,' I says, and I shook hands with Jackson Bird. 'I'll get it for you if I can, and glad to oblige.' And he turned off down the big pear flat on the Piedra, in the direction of Mired Mule; and I steered northwest for old Bill Toomey's ranch.

"It was five days afterward when I got another chance to ride over to Pimienta. Miss Willella and me passed a gratifying evening at Uncle Emsley's. She sang some, and exasperated the piano quite a lot with quotations from the operas. I gave imitations of a rattlesnake, and told her about Snaky McFee's new way of skinning cows, and described the trip I made to Saint Louis once. We was getting along in one another's estimations fine. Thinks I, if Jackson can now be persuaded to migrate, I win. I recollect his promise about the pancake receipt, and I thinks I will persuade it from Miss Willella and give it to him; and then if I catches Birdie off of Mired Mule again, I'll make him hop the twig.

"So, along about ten o'clock, I put on a wheedling smile and says to Miss Willella: 'Now, if there's anything I do like better than the sight of a red steer on green grass it's the taste of a nice hot pancake smothered in sugarhouse molasses.'

"Miss Willella gives a little jump on the piano stool, and looked at me curious.

" 'Yes,' says she, 'they're real nice. What did you say was the name of that street in Saint Louis, Mr. Odom, where you lost your hat?'

" 'Pancake Avenue,' says I, with a wink, to show her that I was on about the family receipt, and couldn't be side-corralled off of the subject. 'Come, now, Miss Willella,' I says; 'let's hear how you make 'em. Pancakes is just whirling in my head like wagon wheels. Start her off, now—pound of flour, eight dozen eggs, and so on. How does the catalogue of constituents run?'

" 'Excuse me for a moment, please,' says Miss Willella, and she gives me a quick kind of sideways look, and slides off the stool. She ambled out into the other room, and directly Uncle Emsley comes in in his shirt sleeves, with a pitcher of water. He turns around to get a glass on the table, and I see a forty-five in his hip pocket. 'Great post-holes!' thinks I, 'but here's a family thinks a heap of cooking receipts, protecting it with firearms. I've known outfits that wouldn't do that much by a family feud.'

" 'Drink this here down,' says Uncle Emsley, handing me the glass of water. 'You've rid too far to-day, Jud, and got yourself over-excited. Try to think about something else now.'

" 'Do you know how to make them pancakes, Uncle Emsley?' I asked.

" 'Well, I'm not as apprised in the anatomy of them as some,' says Uncle Emsley, 'but I reckon you take a sifter of plaster of paris and a little dough and saleratus and corn meal, and mix 'em with eggs and buttermilk as usual. Is old Bill going to ship beeves to Kansas City again this spring, Jud?'

"That was all the pancake specifications I could get that night. I didn't wonder that Jackson Bird found it uphill work. So I dropped the subject and talked with Uncle Emsley a while about hollow-horn and cyclones. And then Miss Willella came and said 'Good-night,' and I hit the breeze for the ranch.

'About a week afterward I met Jackson Bird riding out of Pimienta as I rode in, and we stopped in the road for a few frivolous remarks.

" 'Got the bill of particulars for them flap-jacks yet?' I asked him.

" 'Well, no,' says Jackson. 'I don't seem to have any success in getting hold of it. Did you try?'

" 'I did,' says I, 'and 'twas like trying to dig a prairie dog out of his hole with a peanut hull. That pancake receipt must be a jookalorum, the way they hold on to it.'

" 'I'm 'most ready to give it up,' says Jackson, so discouraged in his pronunciations that I felt sorry for him; 'but I did want to know how to make them pancakes to eat on my lonely ranch,' says he. 'I lie awake at nights thinking how good they are.'

" 'You keep on trying for it,' I tells him, 'and I'll do the same. One of us is bound to get a rope over its horns before long. Well, so-long, Jacksy.'

"You see, by this time we was on the peacefullest of terms. When I saw that he wasn't after Miss Willella I had more endurable contemplations of that sandy-haired snoozer. In order to help out the ambitions of his appetite I kept on trying to get that receipt from Miss Willella. But every time I would say 'pancakes' she would get sort of remote and fidgety about the eye, and try to change the subject. If I held her to it she would slide out and round up Uncle Emsley with his pitcher of water and hip-pocket howitzer.

"One day I galloped over to the store with a fine bunch of blue verbenas that I cut out of a herd of wild flowers over on Poisoned Dog Prairie. Uncle Emsley looked at 'em with one eye shut and says:

" 'Haven't ye heard the news?'

" 'Cattle up?' I asks.

" 'Willella and Jackson Bird was married in Palestine yesterday,' says he. 'Just got a letter this morning.'

"I dropped them flowers in a cracker-barrel, and let the news trickle in my ears and down toward my upper left-hand shirt pocket until it got to my feet.

" 'Would you mind saying that over again once more, Uncle Emsley?' says I. 'Maybe my hearing has got wrong, and you only said that prime heifers was 4.80 on the hoof, or something like that.'

" 'Married yesterday,' says Uncle Emsley, 'and gone to Waco and Niagara Falls on a wedding tour. Why, didn't you see none of the signs all along? Jackson Bird has been courting Willella ever since that day he took her out riding.'

" 'Then,' says I, in a kind of a yell, 'what was all this zizzaparoola he gives me about pancakes? Tell me *that.'*

"When I said 'pancakes' Uncle Emsley sort of dodged and stepped back.

" 'Somebody's been dealing me pancakes from the bottom of the deck,' I says, 'and I'll find out. I believe you know. Talk up,' says I, 'or we'll mix a panful of batter right here.'

"I slid over the counter after Uncle Emsley. He grabbed at his gun, but it was in a drawer, and he missed it two inches. I got him by the front of his shirt and shoved him in a corner.

" 'Talk pancakes,' says I, 'or be made into one. Does Miss Willella make 'em?'

" 'She never made one in her life and I never saw one,' says Uncle Emsley, soothing. 'Calm down now, Jud—calm down. You've got excited, and that wound in your head is contaminating your sense of intelligence. Try not to think about pancakes.'

" 'Uncle Emsley,' says I, 'I'm not wounded in the head except so far as my natural cogitative instincts run to runts. Jackson Bird told me he was calling on Miss Willella for the purpose of finding out her system of producing pancakes, and he asked me to help him get the bill of lading of the ingredients. I done so, with the results as you see. Have I been sodded down with Johnson grass by a pink-eyed snoozer, or what?'

" 'Slack up your grip on my dress shirt,' says Uncle Emsley, 'and I'll tell you. Yes, it looks like Jackson Bird has gone and humbugged you some. The day after he went riding with Willella he came back and told me and her to watch out for you whenever you got to talking about pancakes. He said you was in camp once where they was cooking flapjacks, and one of the fellows cut you over the head with a frying pan. Jackson said that whenever you got over-hot or excited that wound hurt you and made you kind of crazy, and you went raving about pancakes. He told us to just get you worked off of the subject and soothed down, and you wouldn't be dangerous. So, me and Willella done the best by you we knew how. Well, well,' says Uncle Emsley, 'that Jackson Bird is sure a seldom kind of a snoozer.' "

During the progress of Jud's story he had been slowly but deftly combining certain portions of the contents of his sacks and cans. Toward the close of it he set before me the finished product—a pair of red-hot, rich-hued pancakes on a tin plate. From some secret hoarding place he also brought a lump of excellent butter and a bottle of golden syrup.

"How long ago did these things happen?" I asked him.

"Three years," said Jud. "They're living on the Mired Mule Ranch now. But I haven't seen either of 'em since. They say Jackson Bird was fixing his ranch up fine with rocking chairs and window curtains all the time he was putting me up the pancake tree. Oh, I got over it after a while. But the boys kept the racket up."

"Did you make these cakes by the famous recipe?" I asked.

"Didn't I tell you there wasn't no receipt?" said Jud. "The boys hollered pancakes till they got pancake hungry, and I cut this receipt out of a newspaper. How does the truck taste?"

"They're delicious," I answered. "Why don't you have some, too, Jud?" I was sure I heard a sigh.

"Me?" said Jud. "I don't never eat 'em."

Hygeia at the Solito

If you are knowing in the chronicles of the ring you will recall to mind an event in the early 'nineties when, for a minute and sundry odd seconds, a champion and a "would-be" faced each other on the alien side of an international river. So brief a conflict had rarely imposed upon the fair promise of true sport. The reporters made what they could of it, but, divested of padding, the action was sadly fugacious. The champion merely smote his victim, turned his back upon him, remarking, "I know what I done to dat stiff," and extended an arm like a ship's mast for his glove to be removed.

Which accounts for a trainload of extremely disgusted gentlemen in uproar of fancy vests and neckwear being spilled from their Pullman in San Antonio in the early morning following the fight. Which also partly accounts for the unhappy predicament in which "Cricket" McGuire found himself as he tumbled from his car and sat upon the depot platform, torn by a spasm of that hollow, racking cough so familiar to San Antonian ears. At that time, in the uncertain light of dawn, that way passed Curtis Raidler, the Nueces County cattleman—may his shadow never measure under six feet two.

The cattleman, out this early to catch the south-bound for his ranch station, stopped at the side of the distressed patron of sport and spoke in the kindly drawl of his ilk and region, "Got it pretty bad, bud?"

"Cricket" McGuire, exfeather-weight prize-fighter, tout, jockey, follower of the "ponies," all-around sport, and manipulator of the gum balls and walnut shells, looked up pugnaciously at the imputation cast by "bud."

"G'wan," he rasped, "telegraph pole. I didn't ring for yer."

Another paroxysm wrung him, and he leaned limply against a convenient baggage truck. Raidler waited patiently, glancing around at the white hats, short overcoats, and big cigars thronging the platform. "You're from the No'th, ain't you, bud?" he asked when the other was partially recovered. "Come down to see the fight?"

"Fight!" snapped McGuire. "Puss-in-the-corner! 'Twas a hypodermic injection. Handed him just one like a squirt of dope, and he's asleep, and no tanbark needed in front of his residence. Fight!" He rattled a bit, coughed, and went on, hardly addressing the cattleman, but rather for the relief of voicing his troubles. "No more dead sure t'ings for me. But Rus Sage himself would have snatched at it. Five to one dat de boy from Cork wouldn't stay t'ree rounds is what I invested in. Put my last cent on, and could already smell the sawdust in dat all-night joint of Jimmy Delaney's on T'irty-seventh Street I was goin' to buy. And den—say, telegraph pole, what a gazaboo a guy is to put his whole roll on one turn of the gaboozlum!"

"You're plenty right," said the big cattleman; "more 'specially when you lose. Son, you get up and light out for a hotel. You got a mighty bad cough. Had it long?"

"Lungs," said McGuire comprehensively. "I got it. The croaker says I'll come to time for six months longer—maybe a year if I hold my gait. I wanted to settle down and take care of myself. Dat's why I speculated on dat five to one perhaps. I had a t'ousand iron dollars saved up. If I winned I was goin' to buy Delaney's café. Who'd a t'ought dat stiff would take a nap in de foist round—say?"

"It's a hard deal," commented Raidler, looking down at the diminutive form of McGuire crumpled against the truck. "But you go to a hotel and rest. There's the Menger and the Maverick, and—"

"And the Fifth Av'noo, and the Waldorf-Astoria," mimicked McGuire. "Told you I went broke. I'm on de bum proper. I've got one dime left. Maybe a trip to Europe or a sail in me private yacht would fix me up—pa'per!"

He flung his dime at a newsboy, got his *Express,* propped his back against the truck, and was at once rapt in the account of his Waterloo, as expanded by the ingenious press.

Curtis Raidler interrogated an enormous gold watch, and laid his hand on McGuire's shoulder.

"Come on, bud," he said. "We got three minutes to catch the train."

Sarcasm seemed to be McGuire's vein.

"You ain't seen me cash in any chips or call a turn since I told you I was broke, a minute ago, have you? Friend, chase yourself away."

"You're going down to my ranch," said the cattleman, "and stay till you get well. Six months'll fix you good as new." He lifted McGuire with one hand, and half-dragged him in the direction of the train.

"What about the money?" said McGuire, struggling weakly to escape.

"Money for what?" asked Raidler, puzzled. They eyed each other, not understanding, for they touched only as at the gear of bevelled cog-wheels—at right angles, and moving upon different axes.

Passengers on the south-bound saw them seated together, and

wondered at the conflux of two such antipodes. McGuire was five feet one, with a countenance belonging to either Yokohama or Dublin. Brightbeady of eye, bony of cheek and jaw, scarred, toughened, broken and reknit, indestructible, grisly, gladiatorial as a hornet, he was a type neither new nor unfamiliar. Raidler was the product of a different soil. Six feet two in height, miles broad, and no deeper than a crystal brook, he represented the union of the West and South. Few accurate pictures of his kind have been made, for art galleries are so small and the mutoscope is as yet unknown in Texas. After all, the only possible medium of portrayal of Raidler's kind would be the fresco—something high and simple and cool and unframed.

They were rolling southward on the International. The timber was huddling into little, dense green motts at rare distances before the inundation of the downright, vert prairies. This was the land of the ranches; the domain of the kings of the kine.

McGuire sat, collapsed into his corner of the seat, receiving with acid suspicion the conversation of the cattleman. What was the "game" of this big "geezer" who was carrying him off? Altruism would have been McGuire's last guess. "He ain't no farmer," thought the captive, "and he ain't no con man, for sure. W'at's his lay? You trail in, Cricket, and see how many cards he draws. You're up against it, anyhow. You get a nickel and gallopin' consumption, and you better lay low. Lay low and see w'at's his game."

At Rincon, a hundred miles from San Antonio, they left the train for a buckboard which was waiting there for Raidler. In this they travelled the thirty miles between the station and their destination. If anything could, this drive should have stirred the acrimonious McGuire to a sense of his ransom. They sped upon velvet wheels across an exhilarant savanna. The pair of Spanish ponies struck a nimble, tireless trot, which gait they occasionally relieved by a wild, untrammelled gallop. The air was wine and seltzer, perfumed, as they absorbed it, with the delicate redolence of prairie flowers. The road perished, and the buckboard swam the uncharted billows of the grass itself, steered by the practised hand of Raidler, to whom each tiny distant mott of trees was a signboard, each convolution of the low hills a voucher of course and distance. But McGuire reclined upon his spine, seeing nothing but a desert, and receiving the cattleman's advances with sullen distrust. "W'at's he up to?" was the burden of his thoughts; "w'at kind of a gold brick has the big guy got to sell?" McGuire was only applying the measure of the streets he had walked to a range bounded by the horizon and the fourth dimension.

A week before, while riding the prairies, Raidler had come upon a sick and weakling calf deserted and bawling. Without dismounting he had reached and slung the distressed bossy across his saddle, and dropped it at the ranch for the boys to attend to. It was impossible for McGuire to know or comprehend that, in the eyes of the cattleman, his case and that of the calf were identical in interest and demand upon his assistance. A creature was ill and helpless; he had the power to render aid—these were the only postulates required for the cattleman to act. They formed his system of logic and the most of his creed. McGuire was the seventh invalid whom Raidler had picked up thus casually in San Antonio, where so many thousand go for the ozone that is said to linger about its contracted streets. Five of them had been guests of Solito Ranch until they had been able to leave, cured or better, and exhausting the vocabulary of tearful gratitude. One came too late, but rested very comfortably, at last, under a ratama tree in the garden.

So, then, it was no surprise to the ranchhold when the buckboard spun to the door, and Raidler took up his debile *protégé* like a handful of rags and set him down upon the gallery.

McGuire looked upon things strange to him. The ranch-house was the best in the country. It was built of brick hauled one hundred miles by wagon, but it was of but one story, and its four rooms were completely encircled by a mud floor "gallery." The miscellaneous setting of horses, dogs, saddles, wagons, guns, and cow-punchers' paraphernalia oppressed the metropolitan eye of the wrecked sportsman.

"Well, here we are at home," said Raidler, cheeringly.

"It's a h—l of a looking place," said McGuire promptly, as he rolled upon the gallery floor, in a fit of coughing.

"We'll try to make it comfortable for you, buddy," said the cattleman, gently. "It ain't fine inside; but it's the outdoors, anyway, that'll do you the most good. This'll be your room, in here. Anything we got, you ask for it."

He led McGuire into the east room. The floor was bare and clean. White curtains waved in the gulf breeze through the open windows. A big willow rocker, two straight chairs, a long table covered with newspapers, pipes, tobacco, spurs, and cartridges stood in the centre. Some well-mounted heads of deer and one of an enormous black javeli projected from the walls. A wide, cool cot-bed stood in a corner. Nueces County people regarded this guest chamber as fit for a prince. McGuire showed his eye teeth at it. He took out his nickel and spun it up to the ceiling.

"T'ought I was lyin' about the money, did ye? Well, you can frisk me if you wanter. Dat's the last simoleon in the treasury. Who's goin' to pay?"

The cattleman's clear gray eyes looked steadily from under his grizzly brows into the huckleberry optics of his guest. After a little he said simply, and not ungraciously, "I'll be much obliged to you, son, if you won't mention money any more. Once was quite a plenty. Folks I ask to my ranch don't have to pay anything, and they very scarcely ever offers it. Supper'll be ready in half an hour. There's water in the pitcher, and some, cooler, to drink in that red jar hanging on the gallery."

"Where's the bell?" asked McGuire, looking about.

"Bell for what?"

"Bell to ring for things. I can't—see here," he exploded in a sudden weak fury, "I never asked you to bring me here. I never held you up for a cent. I never gave you a hard-luck story till you asked me. Here I am fifty mile from a bellboy or a cocktail. I'm sick. I can't hustle. Gee! but I'm up against it!" McGuire fell upon the cot and sobbed shiveringly.

Raidler went to the door and called. A slender, bright-complexioned Mexican youth about twenty came quickly. Raidler spoke to him in Spanish.

"Ylario, it is in my mind that I promised you the position of *vaquero* on the San Carlos range at the fall *rodeo."*

"Sí señor, such was your goodness."

"Listen. This *señorito* is my friend. He is very sick. Place yourself at his side. Attend to his wants at all times. Have much patience and care with him. And when he is well, or—and when he is well, instead of *vaquero* I will make you *mayordomo* of the Rancho de las Piedras. *Está bueno?"*

"Sí, sí—mil gracias, señor." Ylario tried to kneel upon the floor in his gratitude, but the cattleman kicked at him benevolently, growling, "None of your opery-house antics, now."

Ten minutes later Ylario came from McGuire's room and stood before Raidler.

"The little *señor,"* he announced, "presents his compliments" (Raidler credited Ylario with the preliminary) "and desires some pounded ice, one hot bath, one gin feez-z, that the windows be all closed, toast, one shave, one Newyorkheral', cigarettes, and to send one telegram."

Raidler took a quart bottle of whisky from his medicine cabinet. "Here, take him this," he said.

Thus was instituted the reign of terror at the Solito Ranch. For a few weeks McGuire blustered and boasted and swaggered before the cowpunchers who rode in for miles around to see this latest importation of Raidler's. He was an absolutely new experience to them. He explained to them all the intricate points of sparring and the tricks of training and defence. He opened to their minds' view all the indecorous life of a tagger after professional sports. His jargon of slang was a continuous joy and surprise to them. His gestures, his strange poses, his frank ribaldry of tongue and principle fascinated them. He was like a being from a new world.

Strange to say, this new world he had entered did not exist to him. He was an utter egoist of bricks and mortar. He had dropped out, he felt, into open space for a time, and all it contained was an audience for his reminiscences. Neither the limitless freedom of the prairie days nor the grand hush of the close-drawn, spangled nights touched him. All the hues of Aurora could not win him from the pink pages of a sporting journal. "Get something for nothing," was his mission in life; "T'irty-seventh" Street was his goal.

Nearly two months after his arrival he began to complain that he felt worse. It was then that he became the ranch's incubus, its harpy, its Old Man of the Sea. He shut himself in his room like some venomous kobold or flibbertigibbet, whining, complaining, cursing, accusing. The keynote of his plaint was that he had been inveigled into a gehenna against his will; that he was dying of neglect and lack of comforts. With all his dire protestations of increasing illness, to the eye of others he remained unchanged. His currant-like eyes were as bright and diabolic as ever; his voice was as rasping; his callous face, with the skin drawn tense as a drum-head, had no flesh to lose. A flush on his prominent cheek bones each afternoon hinted that a clinical thermometer might have revealed a symptom, and percussion might have established the fact that McGuire was breathing with only one lung, but his appearance remained the same.

In constant attendance upon him was Ylario, whom the coming reward of the *mayordomoship* must have greatly stimulated, for McGuire chained him to a bitter existence. The air—the man's only chance for life—he commanded to be kept out by closed windows and drawn curtains. The room was always blue and foul with cigarette smoke; whosoever entered it must sit, suffocating, and listen to the imp's interminable gasconade concerning his scandalous career.

The oddest thing of all was the relation existing between McGuire and his benefactor. The attitude of the invalid toward the cattleman was something like that of a peevish, perverse child toward an indulgent parent. When Raidler would leave the ranch McGuire would fall into a fit of malevolent, silent sullenness. When he returned, he would be met by a string of violent and stinging reproaches. Raidler's attitude toward his charge was quite inexplicable in its way. The cattleman seemed actually to assume and feel the character assigned him by McGuire's intemperate accusations—the character of tyrant and guilty oppressor. He seemed to have adopted the responsibility of the fellow's condition, and he always met his tirades with a pacific, patient, and even remorseful kindness that never altered.

One day Raidler said to him, "Try more air, son. You can have the buckboard and a driver every day if you'll go. Try a week or two in one of the cow camps. I'll fix you up plum comfortable. The ground, and the air next to it—them's the things to cure you. I knowed a man from Philadelphy, sicker than you are, got lost on the Guadalupe, and slept on the bare grass in sheep camps for two weeks. Well, sir, it started him getting well, which he done. Close to the ground—that's where the medicine in the air stays. Try a little hossback riding now. There's a gentle pony——"

"What've I done to yer?" screamed McGuire. "Did I ever double-cross yer? Did I ask you to bring me here? Drive me out to your camps if you wanter; or stick a knife in me and save trouble. Ride! I can't lift my feet. I couldn't sidestep a jar from a five-year-old kid. That's what you d—d ranch has done for me. There's nothing to eat, nothing to see, and nobody to talk to but a lot of Reubens who don't know a punching bag from a lobster salad."

"It's a lonesome place, for certain," apologized Raidler abashedly. "We got plenty, but it's rough enough. Anything you think of you want, the boys'll ride up and fetch it down for you."

It was Chad Murchison, a cow-puncher from the Circle Bar outfit, who first suggested that McGuire's illness was fraudulent. Chad had brought a basket of grapes for him thirty miles, and four out of his way, tied to his saddle-horn. After remaining in the smoke-tainted room for a while, he emerged and bluntly confided his suspicions to Raidler.

"His arm," said Chad, "is harder'n a diamond. He interduced me to what he called a shore-perplexus punch, and 'twas like being kicked twice by a mustang. He's playin' it low down on you, Curt. He ain't no sicker'n I am. I hate to say it, but the runt's workin' you for range and shelter."

The cattleman's ingenuous mind refused to entertain Chad's view of the case, and when, later, he came to apply the test, doubt entered not into his motives.

One day, about noon, two men drove up to the ranch, alighted, hitched, and came in to dinner; standing and general invitations being the custom of the country. One of them was a great San Antonio doctor, whose costly services had been engaged by a wealthy cowman who had been laid low by an accidental bullet. He was now being driven to the station to take the train back to town. After dinner Raidler took him aside, pushed a twenty-dollar bill against his hand, and said:

"Doc, there's a young chap in that room I guess has got a bad case of consumption. I'd like for you to look him over and see just how bad he is, and if we can do anything for him."

"How much was that dinner I just ate, Mr. Raidler?" said the doctor bluffly, looking over his spectacles. Raidler returned the money to his pocket. The doctor immediately entered McGuire's room, and the cattleman seated himself upon a heap of saddles on the gallery, ready to reproach himself in the event the verdict should be unfavorable.

In ten minutes the doctor came briskly out. "Your man," he said promptly, "is as sound as a new dollar. His lungs are better than mine. Respiration, temperature, and pulse normal. Chest expansion four inches. Not a sign of weakness anywhere. Of course I didn't examine for the bacillus, but it isn't there. You can put my name to the diagnosis. Even cigarettes and a vilely close room haven't hurt him. Coughs, does he? Well, you tell him it isn't necessary. You asked if there is anything we could do for him. Well, I advise you to set him digging post-holes or breaking mustangs. There's our team ready. Good-day, sir." And like a puff of wholesome, blustery wind the doctor was off.

Raidler reached out and plucked a leaf from a mesquite bush by the railing, and began chewing it thoughtfully.

The branding season was at hand, and the next morning Ross Hargis, foreman of the outfit, was mustering his force of some twenty-five men at the ranch, ready to start for the San Carlos range, where the work was to begin. By six o'clock the horses were all saddled, the grub wagon ready, and the cow-punchers were swinging themselves upon their mounts, when Raidler bade them wait. A boy was bringing up an extra pony, bridled and saddled, to the gate. Raidler walked to McGuire's room and threw open the door. McGuire was lying on his cot, not yet dressed, smoking.

"Get up," said the cattleman, and his voice was clear and brassy, like a bugle.

"How's that?" asked McGuire, a little startled.

"Get up and dress. I can stand a rattlesnake, but I hate a liar. Do I have to tell you again?" He caught McGuire by the neck and stood him on the floor.

"Say, friend," cried McGuire wildly, "are you bug-house? I'm sick—see? I'll croak if I got to hustle. What've I done to yer?"—he began his chronic whine—"I never asked yer to——"

"Put on your clothes," called Raidler, in a rising tone.

Swearing, stumbling, shivering, keeping his amazed, shiny eyes upon the now menacing form of the aroused cattleman, McGuire managed to tumble into his clothes. Then Raidler took him by the collar and shoved him out and across the yard to the extra pony hitched at the gate. The cow-punchers lolled in their saddles, open-mouthed.

"Take this man," said Raidler to Ross Hargis, "and put him to work. Make him work hard, sleep hard, and eat hard. You boys know I done what I could for him, and he was welcome. Yesterday the best doctor in San Antone examined him, and says he's got the lungs of a burro and the constitution of a steer. You know what to do with him, Ross."

Ross Hargis only smiled grimly.

"Aw," said McGuire, looking intently at Raidler, with a peculiar expression upon his face, "the croaker said I was all right, did he? Said I was fakin', did he? You put him onto me. You t'ought I wasn't sick. You said I was a liar. Say, friend, I talked rough, I know, but I didn't mean most of it. If you felt like I did—aw! I forgot—I ain't sick, the croaker says. Well, friend, now I'll go work for yer. Here's where you play even."

He sprang into the saddle easily as a bird, got the quirt from the horn, and gave his pony a slash with it. "Cricket," who once brought in Good Boy by a neck at Hawthorne—and a 10 to 1 shot—had his foot in the stirrups again.

McGuire led the cavalcade as they dashed away from San Carlos, and the cow-punchers gave a yell of applause as they closed in behind his dust.

But in less than a mile he had lagged to the rear, and was last man when they struck the patch of high chaparral below the horse pens. Behind a clump of this he drew rein, and held a handkerchief to his mouth. He took it away drenched with bright, arterial blood, and threw it carefully into a clump of prickly pear. Then he slashed with his quirt again, gasped "G'wan" to his astonished pony, and galloped after the gang.

That night Raidler received a message from his old home in Alabama. There had been a death in the family; an estate was to divide, and they called for him to come. Daylight found him in the buckboard, skimming the prairies for the station. It was two months before he returned. When he arrived at the ranch-house he found it well-nigh deserted save for Ylario, who acted as a kind of steward during his absence. Little by little the youth made him acquainted with the work done while he was away. The branding camp, he was informed, was still doing business. On account of many severe storms the cattle had been badly scattered, and the branding had been accomplished but slowly. The camp was now in the valley of the Guadalupe, twenty miles away.

"By the way," said Raidler, suddenly remembering, "that fellow I sent along with them—McGuire—is he working yet?"

"I do not know," said Ylario. "Man's from the camp come verree few times to the ranch. So plentee work with the leetle calves. They no say. Oh, I think that fellow McGuire he dead much time ago."

"Dead!" said Raidler. "What you talking about?"

"Verree sick fellow, McGuire," replied Ylario, with a shrug of his shoulder. "I theenk he no live one, two month when he go away."

"Shucks!" said Raidler. "He humbugged you, too, did he? The doctor examined him and said he was sound as a mesquite knot."

"That doctor," said Ylario, smiling, "he tell you so? That doctor no see McGuire."

"Talk up," ordered Raidler. "What the devil do you mean?"

"McGuire," continued the boy tranquilly, "he getting drink water outside when that doctor come in room. That doctor take me and pound me all over here with his fingers"—putting his hand to his chest—"I not know for what. He put his ear here and here and here, and listen—I not know for what. He put his little glass stick in my mouth. He feel my arm here. He make me count like whisper—so—twenty, *trienta, cuarenta.* Who knows," concluded Ylario, with a deprecating spread of his hands, "for what that doctor do those verree droll and such-like things?"

"What horses are up?" asked Raidler, shortly.

"Paisano is grazing out behind the little corral, *señor.*"

"Saddle him for me at once."

Within a very few minutes the cattleman was mounted and away. Paisano, well named after that ungainly but swift-running bird, struck into his long lope that ate up the road like a strip of macaroni. In two hours and a quarter Raidler, from a gentle swell, saw the branding camp by a water hole in the Guadalupe. Sick with expectancy of the news he feared, he rode up, dismounted, and dropped Paisano's reins. So gentle was his heart that at that moment he would have pleaded guilty to the murder of McGuire.

The only being in the camp was the cook, who was just arranging the hunks of barbecued beef, and distributing the tin coffee cups for supper. Raidler evaded a direct question concerning the one subject in his mind.

"Everything all right in camp, Pete?" he managed to inquire.

"So, so," said Pete, conservatively. "Grub give out twice. Wind scattered the cattle, and we've had to rake the brush for forty mile. I need a new coffee-pot. And the mosquitoes is some more hellish than common."

"The boys—all well?"

Pete was no optimist. Besides, inquiries concerning the health of cow-punchers were not only superfluous, but bordered on flaccidity. It was not like the boss to make them.

"What's left of 'em don't miss no calls to grub," the cook conceded.

"What's left of 'em?' repeated Raidler in a husky voice. Mechanically he began to look around for McGuire's grave. He had in his mind a white slab such as he had seen in the Alabama church-yard. But immediately he knew that was foolish.

"Sure," said Pete; "what's left. Cow camps change in two months Some's gone."

Raidler nerved himself.

"That—chap—I sent along—McGuire—did—he——"

"Say," interrupted Pete, rising with a chunk of corn bread in each hand, "that was a dirty shame, sending that poor, sick kid to a cow camp. A doctor that couldn't tell he was graveyard meat ought to be skinned with a cinch buckle. Game as he was, too—it's a scandal among snakes—lemme tell you what he done. First night in camp the boys started to initiate him in the leather breeches degree. Ross Hargis busted him one swipe with his chaparreras, and what do you reckon the poor child did? Got up, the little skeeter, and licked Ross. Licked Ross Hargis. Licked him good. Hit him plenty and everywhere and hard. Ross'd just get up and pick out a fresh place to lay down on agin.

"Then that McGuire goes off there and lays down with his head in the grass and bleeds. A hem'ridge they calls it. He lays there eighteen hours by the watch, and they can't budge him. Then Ross Hargis, who loves any man who can lick him, goes to work and damns the doctors from Greenland to Poland Chiny; and him and Green Branch Johnson they gets McGuire in a tent, and spells each other feedin' him chopped raw meat and whisky.

"But it looks like the kid ain't got no appetite to git well, for they misses him from the tent in the night and finds him rootin' in the grass, and likewise a drizzle fallin'. 'Gwan,' he says, 'lemme go and die like I wanter. He said I was a liar and a fake and I was playin' sick. Lemme alone.'

"Two weeks," went on the cook, "he laid around, not noticin' nobody, and then——"

A sudden thunder filled the air, and a score of galloping centaurs crashed through the brush into camp.

"Illustrious rattlesnakes!" exclaimed Pete, springing all ways at once: "here's the boys come, and I'm an assassinated man if supper ain't ready in three minutes."

But Raidler saw only one thing. A little brown-faced, grinning chap, springing from his saddle in the full light of the fire. McGuire was not like that, and yet——

In another instant the cattleman was holding him by the hand and shoulder.

"Son, son, how goes it?" was all he found to say.

"Close to the ground, says you," shouted McGuire, crunching Raidler's fingers in a grip of steel; "and dat's where I found it—healt' and strengt', and tumbled to what a cheap skate I been actin'. T'anks fer kickin' me out, old man. And—say! de joke's on dat croaker, ain't it? I looked t'rough the window and see him playin' tag on dat Dago kid's solar plexus."

"You son of a tinker," growled the cattleman, "whyn't you talk up and say the doctor never examined you?"

"Aw—g'wan!" said McGuire, with a flash of his old asperity, "nobody can't bluff me. You never ast me. You made your spiel, and you t'rowed me out, and I let it go at dat. And, say, friend, dis chasin' cows is outer sight. Dis is de whitest bunch of sports I ever travelled with. You'll let me stay, won't yer, old man?"

Raidler looked wonderingly toward Ross Hargis.

"That cussed little runt," remarked Ross tenderly, "is the Jo-dar-tin'est hustler—and the hardest hitter in anybody's cow camp."

The Higher Abdication

Curly the tramp sidled toward the free-lunch counter. He caught a fleeting glance from the bartender's eye, and stood still, trying to look like a business man who had just dined at the Menger and was waiting for a friend who had promised to pick him up in his motor car. Curly's histrionic powers were equal to the impersonation; but his make-up was wanting.

The bartender rounded the bar in a casual way, looking up at the ceiling as though he was pondering some intricate problem of kalsomining, and then fell upon Curly so suddenly that the roadster had no excuses ready. Irresistibly, but so composedly that it seemed almost absentmindedness on his part, the dispenser of drinks pushed Curly to the swinging doors and kicked him out, with a nonchalance that almost amounted to sadness. That was the way of the Southwest.

Curly arose from the gutter leisurely. He felt no anger or resentment toward his ejector. Fifteen years of tramphood spent out of the twenty-two years of his life had hardened the fibres of his spirit. The slings and arrows of outrageous fortune fell blunted from the buckler of his armored pride. With especial resignation did he suffer contumely and injury at the hands of bartenders. Naturally, they were his enemies; and unnaturally, they were often his friends. He had to take his chances with them. But he had not yet learned to estimate these cool, languid, Southwestern knights of the bung-starter, who had the manners of an Earl of Pawtucket, and who, when they disapproved of your presence, moved you with the silence and despatch of a chess automaton advancing a pawn.

Curly stood a few moments in the narrow, mesquite-paved street. San Antonio puzzled and disturbed him. Three days he had been a non-paying guest of the town, having dropped off there from a box car of an I. & G. N. freight, because Greaser Johnny had told him in Des Moines that the Alamo City was manna fallen, gathered, cooked, and served free with cream and sugar. Curly had found the tip partly a good one. There was hospitality in plenty of a careless, liberal, irregular sort. But the town itself was a weight upon his spirits after his experience with the rushing, business-like, systematized cities of the North and East. Here he was often flung a dollar, but too frequently a good-natured kick would follow it. Once a band of hilarious cowboys had roped him on Military Plaza and dragged him across the black soil until no respectable rag-bag would have stood sponsor for his clothes. The winding, doubling streets, leading nowhere, bewildered him. And then there was a little river, crooked as a pot-hook, that crawled through the middle of the town, crossed by a hundred little bridges so nearly alike that they got on Curly's nerves. And the last bartender wore a number nine shoe.

The saloon stood on a corner. The hour was eight o'clock. Homefarers and outgoers jostled Curly on the narrow stone sidewalk. Between the buildings to his left he looked down a cleft that proclaimed itself another thoroughfare. The alley was dark except for one patch of light. Where there was a light there were sure to be human beings. Where there were human beings after nightfall in San Antonio there might be food, and there was sure to be drink. So Curly headed for the light.

The illumination came from Schwegel's Café. On the sidewalk in front of it Curly picked up an old envelope. It might have contained a check for a million. It was empty; but the wanderer read the address, "Mr. Otto Schwegel," and the name of the town and State. The postmark was Detroit.

Curly entered the saloon. And now in the light it could be perceived that he bore the stamp of many years of vagabondage. He had none of the tidiness of the calculating and shrewd professional tramp. His wardrobe represented the cast-off specimens of half a dozen fashions and eras. Two factories had combined their efforts in providing shoes for his feet. As you gazed at him there passed through your mind vague impressions of mummies, wax figures, Russian exiles, and men lost on desert islands. His face was covered almost to his eyes with a curly brown beard that he kept trimmed short with a pocket-knife, and that had furnished him with his *nom de route.* Light-blue eyes, full of sullenness, fear, cunning, impudence, and fawning, witnessed the stress that had been laid upon his soul.

The saloon was small, and in its atmosphere the odors of meat and drink struggled for the ascendency. The pig and the cabbage wrestled with hydrogen and oxygen. Behind the bar Schwegel labored with an assistant whose epidermal pores showed no signs of being obstructed. Hot wienerwurst and sauerkraut were being served to purchasers of beer. Curly shuffled to the end of the bar, coughed hollowly, and told Schwegel that he was a Detroit cabinet-maker out of a job.

It followed as the night the day that he got his schooner and lunch.

"Was you acquainted maybe mit Heinrich Strauss in Detroit?" asked Schwegel.

"Did I know Heinrich Strauss?" repeated Curly, affectionately. "Why, say, 'Bo, I wish I had a dollar for every game of pinochle me and Heine has played on Sunday afternoons."

More beer and a second plate of steaming food was set before the diplomat. And then Curly, knowing to a fluid-drachm how far a "con" game would go, shuffled out into the unpromising street.

And now he began to perceive the inconveniences of this stony Southern town. There was none of the outdoor gaiety and brilliancy and music that provided distraction even to the poorest in the cities of the North. Here, even so early, the gloomy, rock-walled houses were closed and barred against the murky dampness of the night. The streets were mere fissures through which flowed gray wreaths of river mist. As he walked he heard laughter and the chink of coins and chips behind darkened windows, and music coming from every chink of wood and stone. But the diversions were selfish; the day of popular pastimes had not yet come to San Antonio.

But at length Curly, as he strayed, turned the sharp angle of another lost street and came upon a rollicking band of stockmen from the outlying ranches celebrating in the open in front of an ancient wooden hotel. One great roisterer from the sheep country who had just instigated a movement toward the bar, swept Curly in like a stray goat with the rest of his flock. The princes of kine and wool hailed him as a new zoölogical discovery, and uproariously strove to preserve him in the diluted alcohol of their compliments and regards.

An hour afterward Curly staggered from the hotel barroom, dismissed by his fickle friends, whose interest in him had subsided as quickly as it had risen. Full—stoked with alcoholic fuel and cargoed with food, the only question remaining to disturb him was that of shelter and bed.

A drizzling, cold Texas rain had begun to fall—an endless, lazy, unintermittent downfall that lowered the spirits of men and raised a reluctant steam from the warm stones of the streets and houses. Thus comes the "norther" dousing gentle spring and amiable autumn with the chilling salutes and adieux of coming and departing winter.

Curly followed his nose down the first tortuous street into which his irresponsible feet conducted him. At the lower end of it, on the bank of the serpentine stream, he perceived an open gate in a cemented rock wall. Inside he saw camp fires and a row of low wooden sheds built against three sides of the enclosing wall. He entered the enclosure. Under the sheds many horses were champing at their oats and corn. Many wagons and buckboards stood about with their teams' harness thrown carelessly upon the shafts and doubletrees. Curly recognized the place as a wagon yard, such as is provided by merchants for their out-of-town friends and customers. No one was in sight. No doubt the drivers of those wagons were scattered about the town "seeing the elephant and hearing the owl." In their haste to become patrons of the town's dispensaries of mirth and good cheer the last ones to depart must have left the great wooden gate swinging open.

Curly had satisfied the hunger of an anaconda and the thirst of a camel, so he was neither in the mood nor the condition of an explorer. He zigzagged his way to the first wagon that his eyesight distinguished in the semi-darkness under the shed. It was a two-horse wagon with a top of white canvas. The wagon was half filled with loose piles of wool sacks, two or three great bundles of gray blankets, and a number of bales, bundles, and boxes. A reasoning eye would have estimated the load at once as ranch supplies, bound on the morrow for some outlying hacienda. But to the drowsy intelligence of Curly they represented only warmth and softness and protection against the cold humidity of the night. After several unlucky efforts, at last he conquered gravity so far as to climb over a wheel and pitch forward upon the best and warmest bed he had fallen upon in many a day. Then he became instinctively a burrowing animal, and dug his way like a prairie-dog down among the sacks and blankets, hiding himself from the cold air as snug and safe as a bear in his den. For three nights sleep had visited Curly only in broken and shivering doses. So now, when Morpheus condescended to pay him a call, Curly got such a strangle hold on the mythological old gentleman that it was a wonder that any one else in the whole world got a wink of sleep that night.

Six cow-punchers of the Cibolo Ranch were waiting around the door of the ranch store. Their ponies cropped grass near by, tied in the Texas fashion—which is not tied at all. Their bridle reins had been dropped to the earth, which is a more effectual way of securing them (such is the power of habit and imagination) than you could devise out of a half-inch rope and a live-oak tree.

These guardians of the cow lounged about, each with a brown cigarette paper in his hand, and gently but unceasingly cursed Sam Revell, the storekeeper. Sam stood in the door, snapping the red elastic bands on his pink madras shirtsleeves and looking down affectionately at the only pair of tan shoes within a forty-mile radius. His offence had been serious, and he was divided between humble apology and admiration for the beauty of his raiment. He had allowed the ranch stock of "smoking" to become exhausted.

"I thought sure there was another case of it under the counter, boys," he explained. "But it happened to be catterdges."

"You've sure got a case of happendicitis," said Poky Rodgers, fence rider of the Largo Verde *potrero.* "Somebody ought to happen to give you a knock on the head with the butt end of a quirt. I've rode in nine miles for some tobacco; and it don't appear natural and seemly that you ought to be allowed to live."

"The boys was smokin' cut plug and dried mesquite leaves mixed when I left," sighed Mustang Taylor, horse wrangler of the Three Elm camp. "They'll be lookin' for me back by nine. They'll be settin' up, with their papers ready to roll a whiff of the real thing before bedtime. And I've got to tell 'em that this pink-eyed, sheep-headed, sulphur-footed, shirt-waisted son of a calico broncho, Sam Revell, hasn't got no tobacco on hand."

Gregorio Falcon, Mexican vaquero and best thrower of the rope on the Cibolo, pushed his heavy, silver-embroidered straw sombrero back upon his thicket of jet-black curls, and scraped the bottoms of his pockets for a few crumbs of the precious weed.

"Ah, Don Samuel," he said, reproachfully, but with his touch of Castilian manners, "escuse me. Dthey say dthe jackrabbeet and dthe sheep have the most leetle *sesos*—how you call dthem—brain-es? Ah, don't believe dthat, Don Samuel—escuse me. Ah dthink people w'at don't keep esmokin' tobacco, dthey—both you weel escuse me, Don Samuel."

"Now, what's the use of chewin' the rag, boys," said the untroubled Sam, stooping over to rub the toes of his shoes with a red-and-yellow handkerchief. "Ranse took the order for some more smokin' to San Antone with him Tuesday. Pancho rode Ranse's hoss back yesterday; and Ranse is goin' to drive the wagon back himself. There wa'n't much of a load—just some woolsacks and blankets and nails and canned peaches and a few things we was out of. I look for Ranse to roll in to-day sure. He's an early starter and a hell-to-split driver, and he ought to be here not far from sundown."

"What plugs is he drivin'?" asked Mustang Taylor, with a smack of hope in his tones.

"The buckboard grays," said Sam.

"I'll wait a spell, then," said the wrangler. "Them plugs eat up a trail like a road-runner swallowin' a whip snake. And you may bust me open a can of green-gage plums, Sam, while I'm waitin' for somethin' better."

"Open me some yellow clings," ordered Poky Rodgers. "I'll wait, too."

The tobaccoless punchers arranged themselves comfortably on the steps of the store. Inside Sam chopped open with a hatchet the tops of the cans of fruit.

The store, a big, white wooden building like a barn, stood fifty yards from the ranch-house. Beyond it were the horse corrals; and still farther the wool sheds and the brush-topped shearing pens—for the Rancho Cibolo raised both cattle and sheep. Behind the store, at a little distance, were the grass-thatched *jacals* of the Mexicans who bestowed their allegiance upon the Cibolo.

The ranch-house was composed of four large rooms, with plastered adobe walls, and a two-room wooden ell. A twenty-feet-wide "gallery" circumvented the structure. It was set in a grove of immense live-oaks and water-elms near a lake—a long, not very wide, and tremendously deep lake in which, at nightfall, great gars leaped to the surface and plunged with the noise of hippopotamuses frolicking at their bath. From the trees hung garlands and massive pendants of the melancholy gray moss of the South. Indeed, the Cibolo ranch-house seemed more of the South than of the West. It looked as if old "Kiowa" Truesdell might have brought it with him from the lowlands of Mississippi when he came to Texas with his rifle in the hollow of his arm in '55.

But, though he did not bring the family mansion, Truesdell did bring something in the way of a family inheritance that was more lasting than brick or stone. He brought one end of the Truesdell-Curtis family feud. And when a Curtis brought the Rancho de los Olmos, sixteen miles from the Cibolo, there were lively times on the pear flats and in the chaparral thickets off the Southwest. In those days Truesdell cleaned the brush of many a wolf and tiger cat and Mexican lion; and one or two Curtises fell heirs to notches on his rifle stock. Also he buried a brother with a Curtis bullet in him on the bank of the lake at Cibolo. And then the Kiowa Indians made their last raid upon the ranches between the Frio and the Rio Grande, and Truesdell at the head of his rangers rid the earth of them to the last brave, earning his sobriquet. Then came prosperity in the form of waxing herds and broadening lands. And then old age and bitterness, when he sat, with his great mane of hair as white as the Spanish-dagger blossoms and his fierce, pale-blue eyes, on the shaded gallery at Cibolo, growling like the pumas that he had slain. He snapped his fingers at old age; the bitter taste of life did not come from that. The cup that stuck at his lips was that his only son Ransom wanted to carry a Curtis, the last youthful survivor of the other end of the feud.

For a while the only sounds to be heard at the store were the rattling of the tin spoons and the gurgling intake of the juicy fruits by the cowpunchers, the stamping of the grazing ponies, and the singing of a doleful song by Sam as he contentedly brushed his stiff auburn hair for the twentieth time that day before a crinkly mirror.

From the door of the store could be seen the irregular, sloping stretch of prairie to the south, with its reaches of light-green, billowing mesquite flats in the lower places, and its rises crowned with nearly black masses of short chaparral. Through the mesquite flat wound the ranch road that, five miles away, flowed into the old government trail to San Antonio. The sun was so low that the gentlest elevation cast its gray shadow miles into the green-gold of sunshine.

That evening ears were quicker than eyes.

The Mexican held up a tawny finger to still the scraping of tin against tin.

"One waggeen," said he, "cross dthe Arroyo Hondo. Ah hear dthe wheel. Verree rockee place, dthe Hondo."

"You've got good ears, Gregorio," said Mustang Taylor. "I never heard nothin' but the song-bird in the bush and the zephyr skally-hootin' across the peaceful dell."

In ten minutes Taylor remarked: "I see the dust of a wagon risin' right above the fur end of the flat."

"You have verree good eyes, señor," said Gregorio, smiling.

Two miles away they saw a faint cloud dimming the green ripples of the mesquites. In twenty minutes they heard the clatter of horses' hoofs: in five minutes more the gray plugs dashed out of the thicket, whickering for oats and drawing the light wagon behind them like a toy.

From the *jacals* came a cry of: *"El Amo! El Amo!"* Four Mexican youths raced to unharness the grays. The cow-punchers gave a yell of greeting and delight.

Ranse Truesdell, driving, threw the reins to the ground and laughed.

"It's under the wagon sheet, boys," he said. "I know what you're waiting for. If Sam lets it run out again we'll use them yellow shoes of his for a target. There's two cases. Pull 'em out and light up. I know you'll want a smoke."

After striking dry country Ranse had removed the wagon sheet from the bows and thrown it over the goods in the wagon. Six pairs of hasty hands dragged it off and grabbled beneath the sacks and blankets for the cases of tobacco.

Long Collins, tobacco messenger from the San Gabriel outfit, who rode with the longest stirrups west of the Mississippi, delved with an arm like the tongue of a wagon. He caught something harder than a blanket and pulled out a fearful thing—a shapeless, muddy bunch of leather tied together with wire and twine. From its ragged end, like the head and claws of a disturbed turtle, protruded human toes.

"Who-ee!" yelled Long Collins. "Ranse, are you a-packin' around of corpuses? Here's a—howling' grasshoppers!"

Up from his long slumber popped Curly, like some vile worm from its burrow. He clawed his way out and sat blinking like a disreputable, drunken owl. His face was as bluish red and puffed and seamed and crosslined as the cheapest round steak of the butcher. His eyes were swollen slits; his nose a pickled beet; his hair would have made the wildest thatch of a Jack-in-the-box look like the satin poll of a Cléo de Mérode. The rest of him was scarecrow done to the life.

Ranse jumped down from his seat and looked at his strange cargo with wide-open eyes.

"Here, you maverick, what are you doing in my wagon? How did you get in there?"

The punchers gathered around in delight. For the time they had forgotten tobacco.

Curly looked around him slowly in every direction. He snarled like a Scotch terrier through his ragged beard.

"Where is this?" he rasped through his parched throat. "It's a damn farm in an old field. What'd you bring me here for—say? Did I say I wanted to come here? What are you Reubs rubberin' at—hey? G'wan or I'll punch some of your faces."

"Drag him out, Collins," said Ranse.

Curly took a slide and felt the ground rise up and collide with his shoulder blades. He got up and sat on the steps of the store shivering from outraged nerves, hugging his knees and sneering. Taylor lifted out a case of tobacco and wrenched off its top. Six cigarettes began to glow, bringing peace and forgiveness to Sam.

"How'd you come in my wagon?" repeated Ranse, this time in a voice that drew a reply.

Curly recognized the tone. He had heard it used by freight brakemen and large persons in blue carrying clubs.

"Me?" he growled. "Oh, was you talkin' to me? Why, I was on

my way to the Menger, but my valet had forgot to pack my pajamas. So I crawled into that wagon in the wagon-yard—see? I never told you to bring me out to this bloomin' farm—see?"

"What is it, Mustang?" asked Poky Rodgers, almost forgetting to smoke in his ecstasy. "What do it live on?"

"It's a galliwampus, Poky," said Mustang. "It's the thing that hollers 'williwallo' up in ellum trees in the low grounds of nights. I don't know if it bites."

"No, it ain't, Mustang," volunteered Long Collins. "Them galliwampuses has fins on their backs, and eighteen toes. This here is a hicklesnifter. It lives under the ground and eats cherries. Don't stand so close to it. It wipes out villages with one stroke of its prehensile tail."

Sam, the cosmopolite, who called bartenders in San Antone by their first name, stood in the door. He was a better zoölogist.

"Well, ain't that a Willie for your whiskers?" he commented. "Where'd you dig up the hobo, Ranse? Goin' to make an auditorium for inbreviates out of the ranch?"

"Say," said Curly, from whose panoplied breast all shafts of wit fell blunted. "Any of you kiddin' guys got a drink on you? Have your fun. Say, I've been hittin' the stuff till I don't know straight up."

He turned to Ranse. "Say, you shanghaied me on your d—d old prairie schooner—did I tell you to drive me to a farm? I want a drink. I'm goin' all to little pieces. What's doin'?"

Ranse saw that the tramp's nerves were racking him. He despatched one of the Mexican boys to the ranch-house for a glass of whisky. Curly gulped it down; and into his eyes came a brief, grateful glow—as human as the expression in the eye of a faithful setter dog.

"Thanky, boss," he said, quietly.

"You're thirty miles from a railroad, and forty miles from a saloon," said Ranse.

Curly fell back weakly against the steps.

"Since you are here," continued the ranchman, "come along with me. We can't turn you out on the prairie. A rabbit might tear you to pieces."

He conducted Curly to a large shed where the ranch vehicles were kept. There he spread out a canvas cot and brought blankets.

"I don't suppose you can sleep," said Ranse, "since you've been pounding your ear for twenty-four hours. But you can camp here till morning. I'll have Pedro fetch you up some grub."

"Sleep!" said Curly. "I can sleep a week. Say, sport, have you got a coffin nail on you?"

Fifty miles had Ransom Truesdell driven that day. And yet this is what he did.

Old "Kiowa" Truesdell sat in his great wicker chair reading by the light of an immense oil lamp. Ranse laid a bundle of newspapers fresh from town at his elbow.

"Back, Ranse?" said the old man, looking up.

"Son," old "Kiowa" continued, "I've been thinking all day about a certain matter that we have talked about. I want you to tell me again. I've lived for you. I've fought wolves and Indians and worse white men to protect you. You never had any mother that you can remember. I've taught you to shoot straight, ride hard, and live clean. Later on I've worked to pile up dollars that'll be yours. You'll be a rich man, Ranse, when my chunk goes out. I've made you. I've licked you into shape like a leopard cat licks its cubs. You don't belong to yourself—you've got to be a Truesdell first. Now, is there to be any more nonsense about this Curtis girl?"

"I'll tell you once more," said Ranse, slowly. "As I am a Truesdell and as you are my father, I'll never marry a Curtis."

"Good boy," said old "Kiowa." "You'd better go get some supper."

Ranse went to the kitchen at the rear of the house. Pedro, the Mexican cook, sprang up to bring the food he was keeping warm in the stove.

"Just a cup of coffee, Pedro," he said, and drank it standing. And then:

"There's a tramp on a cot in the wagon-shed. Take him something to eat. Better make it enough for two."

Ranse walked out toward the *jacals.* A boy came running.

"Manuel, can you catch Vaminos, in the little pasture, for me?"

"Why not, señor? I saw him near the *puerta* but two hours past. He bears a drag-rope."

"Get him and saddle him as quick as you can."

"Prontito, señor."

Soon mounted, on Vaminos, Ranse leaned in the saddle, pressed with his knees, and galloped eastward past the store, where sat Sam trying his guitar in the moonlight.

Vaminos shall have a word—Vaminos the good dun horse. The Mexicans, who have a hundred names for the colors of a horse, called him *gruyo.* He was a mouse-colored, slate-colored, flea-bitten roan-dun, if you can conceive it. Down his back from his mane to his tail went a line of black. He would live forever; and surveyors have not laid off as many miles in the world as he could travel in a day.

Eight miles east of the Cibolo ranch-house Ranse loosened the pressure of his knees, and Vaminos stopped under a big ratama tree. The yellow ratama blossoms showered fragrance that would have undone the roses of France. The moon made the earth a great concave bowl with a crystal sky for a lid. In a glade five jack-rabbits leaped and played together like kittens. Eight miles farther east shone a faint star that appeared to have dropped below the horizon. Night riders, who often steered their course by it, knew it to be the light in the Rancho de los Olmos.

In ten minutes Yenna Curtis galloped to the tree on her sorrel pony Dancer. The two leaned and clasped hands heartily.

"I ought to have ridden nearer your home," said Ranse. "But you never will let me."

Yenna laughed. And in the soft light you could see her strong white teeth and fearless eyes. No sentimentality there, in spite of the moonlight, the odor of the ratamas, and the admirable figure of Ranse Truesdell, the lover. But she was there, eight miles from her home, to meet him.

"How often have I told you, Ranse," she said, "that I am your half-way girl? Always half-way."

"Well?" said Ranse, with a question in his tones.

"I did," said Yenna, with almost a sigh. "I told him after dinner when I thought he would be in a good humor. Did you ever wake up a lion, Ranse, with the mistaken idea that he would be a kitten? He almost tore the ranch to pieces. It's all up. I love my daddy, Ranse, and I'm afraid—I'm afraid of him, too. He ordered me to promise that I'd never marry a Truesdell. I promised. That's all. What luck did you have?"

"The same," said Ranse, slowly. "I promised him that his son would never marry a Curtis. Somehow I couldn't go against him. He's mighty old. I'm sorry, Yenna."

The girl leaned in her saddle and laid one hand on Ranse's, on the horn of his saddle.

"I never thought I'd like you better for giving me up," she said ardently, "but I do. I must ride back now, Ranse. I slipped out of the house and saddled Dancer myself. Good-night, neighbor."

"Good-night," said Ranse. "Ride carefully over them badger holes."

They wheeled and rode away in opposite directions. Yenna turned in her saddle and called clearly:

"Don't forget I'm your half-way girl, Ranse."

"Damn all family feuds and inherited scraps," muttered Ranse vindictively to the breeze as he rode back to the Cibolo.

Ranse turned his horse into the small pasture and went to his own room. He opened the lowest drawer of an old bureau to get out the packet of letters that Yenna had written him one summer when she had gone to Mississippi for a visit. The drawer stuck, and he yanked at it savagely—as a man will. It came out of the bureau, and bruised both his shins—as a drawer will. An old, folded yellow letter without an envelope fell from somewhere—probably from where it had lodged in one of the upper drawers. Ranse took it to the lamp and read it curiously.

Then he took his hat and walked to one of the Mexican *jacals.*

"Tía Juana," he said, "I would like to talk with you awhile."

An old, old Mexican woman, white-haired and wonderfully wrinkled, rose from a stool.

"Sit down," said Ranse, removing his hat and taking the one chair in the *jacal.* "Who am I, Tía Juana?" he asked, speaking Spanish.

"Don Ransom, our good friend and employer. Why do you ask?" answered the old woman wonderingly.

"Tía Juana, who am I?" he repeated, with his stern eyes looking into hers.

A frightened look came in the old woman's face. She fumbled with her black shawl.

"Who am I, Tía Juana?" said Ranse once more.

"Thirty-two years I have lived on the Rancho Cibolo," said Tía Juana. "I thought to be buried under the coma mott beyond the garden before these things should be known. Close the door, Don Ransom, and I will speak. I see in your face that you know."

An hour Ranse spent behind Tía Juana's closed door. As he was on his way back to the house Curly called to him from the wagon-shed.

The tramp sat on his cot, swinging his feet and smoking.

"Say, sport," he grumbled. "This is no way to treat a man after kidnappin' him. I went up to the store and borrowed a razor from that fresh guy and had a shave. But that ain't all a man needs. Say—can't you loosen up for about three fingers more of that booze? I never asked you to bring me to your d—d farm."

"Stand up out here in the light," said Ranse, looking at him closely.

Curly got up sullenly and took a step or two.

His face, now shaven smooth, seemed transformed. His hair had been combed, and it fell back from the right side of his forehead with a peculiar wave. The moonlight charitably softened the ravages of drink; and his aquiline, well-shaped nose and small, square-cleft chin almost gave distinction to his looks.

Ranse sat on the foot of the cot and looked at him curiously.

"Where did you come from—have you got any home or folks anywhere?"

"Me? Why, I'm a dook," said Curly. "I'm Sir Reginald—oh, cheese it. No; I don't know anything about my ancestors. I've been a tramp ever since I can remember. Say, old pal, are you going to set 'em up again tonight or not?"

"You answer my questions and maybe I will. How did you come to be a tramp?"

"Me?" answered Curly. "Why, I adopted that profession when I was an infant. Case of had to. First thing I can remember, I belonged to a big, lazy hobo called Beefsteak Charley. He sent me around to houses to beg. I wasn't hardly big enough to reach the latch of a gate."

"Did he ever tell you how he got you?" asked Ranse.

"Once when he was sober he said he bought me for an old six-shooter and six bits from a band of drunken Mexican sheep-shearers. But what's the diff? That's all I know."

"All right," said Ranse. "I reckon you're a maverick for certain. I'm going to put the Rancho Cibolo brand on you. I'll start you to work in one of the camps to-morrow."

"Work!" sniffed Curly, disdainfully. "What do you take me for? Do you think I'd chase cows, and hop-skip-and-jump around after crazy sheep like that pink-and-yellow guy at the store says these Reubs do? Forget it."

"Oh, you'll like it when you get used to it," said Ranse. "Yes. I'll send you up one more drink by Pedro. I think you'll make a first-class cowpuncher before I get through with you."

"Me?" said Curly. "I pity the cows you set me to chaperon. They can go chase themselves. Don't forget my nightcap, please, boss."

Ranse paid a visit to the store before going to the house. Sam Revell was taking off his tan shoes regretfully and preparing for bed.

"Any of the boys from the San Gabriel camp riding in early in the morning?" asked Ranse.

"Long Collins," said Sam, briefly. "For the mail."

"Tell him," said Ranse, "to take that tramp out to camp with him and keep him till I get there."

Curly was sitting on his blankets in the San Gabriel camp cursing talentedly when Ranse Truesdell rode up and dismounted on the next afternoon. The cow-punchers were ignoring the stray. He was grimy with dust and black dirt. His clothes were making their last stand in favor of the conventions.

Ranse went up to Buck Rabb, the camp boss, and spoke briefly.

"He's a plum buzzard," said Buck. "He won't work, and he's the low-downest passel of inhumanity I ever see. I didn't know what you wanted done with him, Ranse, so I just let him set. That seems to suit him. He's been condemned to death by the boys a dozen times, but I told 'em maybe you was savin' him for torture."

Ranse took off his coat.

"I've got a hard job before me, Buck, I reckon, but it has to be done. I've got to make a man out of that thing. That's what I've come to camp for."

He went up to Curly.

"Brother," he said, "don't you think if you had a bath it would allow you to take a seat in the company of your fellow-man with less injustice to the atmosphere?"

"Run away, farmer," said Curly, sardonically. "Willie will send for nursery when he feels like having his tub."

The *charco,* or water hole, was twelve yards away. Ranse took one of Curly's ankles and dragged him like a sack of potatoes to the brink. Then with the strength and sleight of a hammer-thrower he hurled the offending member of society far into the lake.

Curly crawled out and up the bank spluttering like a porpoise.

Ranse met him with a piece of soap and a coarse towel in his hands.

"Go to the other end of the lake and use this," he said. "Buck will give you some dry clothes at the wagon."

The tramp obeyed without protest. By the time supper was ready he had returned to camp. He was hardly to be recognized in his new blue shirt and brown duck clothes. Ranse observed him out of the corner of his eye.

"Lordy, I hope he ain't a coward," he was saying to himself. "I hope he won't turn out to be a coward."

His doubts were soon allayed. Curly walked straight to where he stood. His light-blue eyes were blazing.

"Now I'm clean," he said, meaningly, "maybe you'll talk to me. Think you've got a picnic here, do you? You clodhoppers think you can run over a man because you know he can't get away. All right. Now, what do you think of that?"

Curly planted a stinging slap against Ranse's left cheek. The print of his hand stood out a dull red against the tan.

Ranse smiled happily.

The cow-punchers talk to this day of the battle that followed.

Somewhere in his restless tour of the cities Curly had acquired the art of self-defence. The ranchman was equipped only with the splendid strength and equilibrium of perfect health and the endurance conferred by decent living. The two attributes nearly matched. There were no formal rounds. At last the fibre of the clean liver prevailed. The last time Curly went down from one of the ranchman's awkward but powerful blows he remained on the grass, but looking up with an unquenched eye.

Ranse went to the water barrel and washed the red from a cut on his chin in the stream from the faucet.

On his face was a grin of satisfaction.

Much benefit might accrue to educators and moralists if they could know the details of the curriculum of reclamation through which Ranse put his waif during the month that he spent in the San Gabriel camp. The ranchman had no fine theories to work out—perhaps his whole stock of pedagogy embraced only a knowledge of horse-breaking and a belief in heredity.

The cow-punchers saw that their boss was trying to make a man out of the strange animal that he had sent among them; and they tacitly organized themselves into a faculty of assistants. But their system was their own.

Curly's first lesson stuck. He became on friendly and then on intimate terms with soap and water. And the thing that pleased Ranse most was that his "subject" held his ground at each successive higher step. But the steps were sometimes far apart.

Once he got at the quart bottle of whisky kept sacredly in the grub tent for rattlesnake bites, and spent sixteen hours on the grass, magnificently drunk. But when he staggered to his feet his first move was to find his soap and towel and start for the *charco.* And once, when a treat came from the ranch in the form of a basket of fresh tomatoes and young onions, Curly devoured the entire consignment before the punchers reached the camp at supper time.

And then the punchers punished him in their own way. For three days they did not speak to him, except to reply to his own questions or remarks. And they spoke with absolute and unfailing politeness. They played tricks on one another; they pounded one another hurtfully and affectionately; they heaped upon one another's heads friendly curses and obloquy; but they were polite to Curly. He saw it, and it stung him as much as Ranse hoped it would.

Then came a night that brought a cold, wet norther. Wilson, the youngest of the outfit, had lain in camp two days, ill with a fever. When Joe got up at daylight to begin breakfast he found Curly sitting asleep against a wheel of the grub wagon with only a saddle blanket around him, while Curly's blankets were stretched over Wilson to protect him from the rain and wind.

Three nights after that Curly rolled himself in his blanket and went to sleep. Then the other punchers rose up softly and began to make preparations. Ranse saw Long Collins tie a rope to the horn of a saddle. Others were getting out their six-shooters.

"Boys," said Ranse, "I'm much obliged. I was hoping you would. But I didn't like to ask."

Half a dozen six-shooters began to pop—awful yells rent the air—Long Collins galloped wildly across Curly's bed, dragging the saddle after him. That was merely their way of gently awaking their victim. Then they hazed him for an hour, carefully and ridiculously, after the code of cow camps. Whenever he uttered protest they held him stretched over a roll of blankets and thrashed him woefully with a pair of leather leggins.

And all this meant that Curly had won his spurs, that he was receiving the punchers' accolade. Nevermore would they be polite to him. But he would be their "pardner" and stirrup-brother, foot to foot.

When the fooling was ended all hands made a raid on Joe's big coffeepot by the fire for a Java nightcap. Ranse watched the new knight carefully to see if he understood and was worthy. Curly limped with his cup of coffee to a log and sat upon it. Long Collins followed and sat by his side. Buck Rabb went and sat at the other. Curly—grinned.

And then Ranse furnished Curly with mounts and saddle and equipment, and turned him over to Buck Rabb, instructing him to finish the job.

Three weeks later Ranse rode from the ranch into Rabb's camp, which was then in Snake Valley. The boys were saddling for the day's ride. He sought out Long Collins among them.

"How about that bronco?" he asked.

Long Collins grinned.

"Reach out your hand, Ranse Truesdell," he said, "and you'll touch him. And you can shake his'n, too, if you like, for he's plumb white and there's none better in no camp."

Ranse looked again at the clear-faced, bronzed, smiling cowpuncher who stood at Collins's side. Could that be Curly? He held out his hand, and Curly grasped it with the muscles of a broncobuster.

"I want you at the ranch," said Ranse.

"All right, sport," said Curly, heartily. "But I want to come back again. Say, pal, this is a dandy farm. And I don't want any better fun than hustlin' cows with this bunch of guys. They're all to the merry merry."

At the Cibolo ranch-house they dismounted. Ranse bade Curly

wait at the door of the living room. He walked inside. Old "Kiowa" Truesdell was reading at a table.

"Good-morning, Mr. Truesdell," said Ranse.

The old man turned his white head quickly.

"How is this?" he began. "Why do you call me 'Mr.——'?"

When he looked at Ranse's face he stopped, and the hand that held his newspaper shook slightly.

"Boy," he said slowly, "how did you find it out?"

"It's all right," said Ranse, with a smile. "I made Tía Juana tell me. It was kind of by accident, but it's all right."

"You've been like a son to me," said old "Kiowa," trembling.

"Tía Juana told me all about it," said Ranse. "She told me how you adopted me when I was knee-high to a puddle duck out of a wagon train of prospectors that was bound West. And she told me how the kid—your own kid, you know—got lost or was run away with. And she said it was the same day that the sheep-shearers got on a bender and left the ranch."

"Our boy strayed from the house when he was two years old," said the old man. "And then along came these emigrant wagons with a youngster they didn't want; and we took you. I never intended you to know, Ranse. We never heard of our boy again."

"He's right outside, unless I'm mighty mistaken," said Ranse, opening the door and beckoning.

Curly walked in.

No one could have doubted. The old man and the young had the same sweep of hair, the same nose, chin, line of face, and prominent light-blue eyes.

Old "Kiowa" rose eagerly.

Curly looked about the room curiously. A puzzled expression came over his face. He pointed to the wall opposite.

"Where's the tick-tock?" he asked, absentmindedly.

"The clock," cried old "Kiowa" loudly. "The eight-day clock used to stand there. Why——"

He turned to Ranse, but Ranse was not there.

Already a hundred yards away, Vaminos, the good flea-bitten dun, was bearing him eastward like a racer through dust and chaparral towards the Rancho de los Olmos.

The Caballero's Way

The Cisco Kid had killed six men in more or less fair scrimmages, had murdered twice as many (mostly Mexicans), and had winged a larger number whom he modestly forebore to count. Therefore a woman loved him.

The Kid was twenty-five, looked twenty; and a careful insurance company would have estimated the probable time of his demise at, say, twenty-six. His habitat was anywhere between the Frio and the Rio Grande. He killed for the love of it—because he was quick-tempered—to avoid arrest—for his own amusement—any reason that came to his mind would suffice. He had escaped capture because he could shoot five-sixths of a second sooner than any sheriff or ranger in the service, and because he rode a speckled roan horse that knew every cowpath in the mesquite and pear thickets from San Antonio to Matamoras.

Tonia Perez, the girl who loved the Cisco Kid, was half Carmen, half Madonna, and the rest—oh, yes, a woman who is half Carmen and half Madonna can always be something more—the rest, let us say, was humming-bird. She lived in a grass-roofed *jacal* near a little Mexican settlement at the Lone Wolf Crossing of the Frio. With her lived a father or grandfather, a lineal Aztec, somewhat less than a thousand years old, who herded a hundred goats and lived in a continuous drunken dream from drinking *mescal.* Back of the *jacal* a tremendous forest of bristling pear, twenty feet high at its worst, crowded almost to its door. It was along the bewildering maze of this spinous thicket that the speckled roan would bring the Kid to see his girl. And once, clinging like a lizard to the ridgepole, high up under the peaked grass roof, he had heard Tonia, with her Madonna face and Carmen beauty and humming-bird soul, parley with the sheriff's posse, denying knowledge of her man in her soft *mélange* of Spanish and English.

One day the adjutant-general of the State, who is, *ex officio,* commander of the ranger forces, wrote some sarcastic lines to Captain Duval of Company X, stationed at Laredo, relative to the serene and undisturbed existence led by murderers and desperadoes in the said captain's territory.

The captain turned the color of brick dust under his tan, and forwarded the letter, after adding a few comments, per ranger Private Bill Adamson, to ranger Lieutenant Sandridge, camped at a water hole on the Nueces with a squad of five men in preservation of law and order.

Lieutenant Sandridge turned a beautiful *couleur de rose* through his ordinary strawberry complexion, tucked the letter in his hip pocket, and chewed off the end of his gamboge moustache.

The next morning he saddled his horse and rode alone to the Mexican settlement at the Lone Wolf Crossing of the Frio, twenty miles away.

Six feet two, blond as a Viking, quiet as a deacon, dangerous as a machine gun, Sandridge moved among the *Jacales,* patiently seeking news of the Cisco Kid.

Far more than the law, the Mexicans dreaded the cold and certain vengeance of the lone rider that the ranger sought. It had been one of the Kid's pastimes to shoot Mexicans "to see them kick": if he demanded from them moribund Terpsichorean feats, simply that he might be entertained, what terrible and extreme penalties would be certain to follow should they anger him! One and all they lounged with upturned palms and shrugging shoulders, filling the air with *"quién sabes"* and denials of the Kid's acquaintance.

But there was a man named Fink who kept a store at the Crossing—a man of many nationalities, tongues, interests, and ways of thinking.

"No use to ask them Mexicans," he said to Sandridge. "They're afraid to tell. This *hombre* they call the Kid—Goodall is his name, ain't it?—he's been in my store once or twice. I have an idea you might run across him at—but I guess I don't keer to say, myself. I'm two seconds later in pulling a gun than I used to be and the difference is worth thinking about. But this Kid's got a half-Mexican girl at the Crossing that he comes to see. She lives in that *jacal* a hundred yards down the arroyo at the edge of the pear. Maybe she—no, I don't suppose she would, but that *jacal* would be a good place to watch, anyway."

Sandridge rode down to the *jacal* of Perez. The sun was low, and the broad shade of the great pear thicket already covered the grass-thatched hut. The goats were enclosed for the night in a brush corral near by. A few kids walked the top of it, nibbling the chaparral leaves. The old Mexican lay upon a blanket on the grass, already in a stupor from his mescal, and dreaming, perhaps, of the nights when he and Pizarro touched glasses to their New World fortunes—so old his wrinkled face seemed to proclaim him to be. And in the door of the *jacal* stood Tonia. And Lieutenant Sandridge sat in his saddle staring at her like a gannet agape at a sailorman.

The Cisco Kid was a vain person, as all eminent and successful assassins are, and his bosom would have been ruffled had he known that at a simple exchange of glances two persons, in whose minds he had been looming large, suddenly abandoned (at least for the time) all thought of him.

Never before had Tonia seen such a man as this. He seemed to be made of sunshine and blood-red tissue and clear weather. He seemed to illuminate the shadow of the pear when he smiled, as though the sun were rising again. The men she had known had been small and dark. Even the Kid, in spite of his achievements, was a stripling no larger than herself, with black straight hair and a cold marble façe that chilled the noonday.

As for Tonia, though she sends description to the poorhouse, let her make a millionaire of your fancy. Her blue-black hair, smoothly divided in the middle and bound close to her head, and her large eyes full of the Latin melancholy, gave her the Madonna touch. Her motions and air spoke of the concealed fire and the desire to charm that she had inherited from the *gitanas* of the Basque province. As for the humming-bird part of her, that dwelt in her heart; you could not perceive it unless her bright red skirt and dark blue blouse gave you a symbolic hint of the vagarious bird.

The newly lighted sun-god asked for a drink of water. Tonia brought it from the red jar hanging under the brush shelter. Sandridge considered it necessary to dismount so as to lessen the trouble of her ministrations.

I play no spy; nor do I assume to master the thoughts of any human heart; but I assert, by the chronicler's right, that before a quarter of an hour had sped, Sandridge was teaching her how to plait a six-strand rawhide stake-rope, and Tonia had explained to him that were it not for her little English book that the peripatetic *padre* had given her and the little crippled *chivo,* that she fed from a bottle, she would be very, very lonely indeed.

Which leads to a suspicion that the Kid's fences needed repairing, and that the adjutant-general's sarcasm had fallen upon unproductive soil.

In his camp by the water hole Lieutenant Sandridge announced and reiterated his intention of either causing the Cisco Kid to nibble the black loam of the Frio country prairies or of hailing him before a judge and jury. That sounded business-like. Twice a week he rode over to the Lone Wolf Crossing of the Frio, and directed Tonia's slim, slightly lemon-tinted fingers among the intricacies of the slowly growing lariat. A six-strand plait is hard to learn and easy to teach.

The ranger knew that he might find the Kid there at any visit. He kept his armament ready, and had a frequent eye for the pear thicket at the rear of the *jacal.* Thus he might bring down the kite and the humming-bird with one stone.

While the sunny-haired ornithologist was pursuing his studies the Cisco Kid was also attending to his professional duties. He moodily shot up a saloon in a small cow village on Quintana Creek, killed the town marshal (plugging him neatly in the centre of his tin badge), and then rode away, morose and unsatisfied. No true artist is uplifted by shooting an aged man carrying an old-style .38 bulldog.

On his way the Kid suddenly experienced the yearning that all men feel when wrong-doing loses its keen edge of delight. He yearned for the woman he loved to reassure him that she was his in spite of it. He wanted her to call his bloodthirstiness bravery and his cruelty devotion. He wanted Tonia to bring him water from the red jug under the brush shelter, and tell him how the *chivo* was thriving on the bottle.

The Kid turned the speckled roan's head up the ten-mile pear flat that stretches along the Arroyo Hondo until it ends at the Lone Wolf Crossing of the Frio. The roan whickered; for he had a sense of locality and direction equal to that of a belt-line street-car horse; and he knew he would soon be nibbling the rich mesquite grass at the end of a forty-foot stake rope while Ulysses rested his head in Circe's straw-roofed hut.

More weird and lonesome than the journey of an Amazonian explorer is the ride of one through a Texas pear flat. With dismal monotony and startling variety the uncanny and multiform shapes of the cacti lift their twisted trunks and fat, bristly hands to encumber the way. The demon plant, appearing to live without soil or rain, seems to taunt the parched traveler with its lush gray greenness. It warps itself a thousand times about what look to be open and inviting paths, only to lure the rider into blind and impassable spine-defended "bottoms of the bag," leaving him to retreat if he can, with the points of the compass whirling in his head.

To be lost in the pear is to die almost the death of the thief on the cross, pierced by nails and with grotesque shapes of all the fiends hovering about.

But it was not so with the Kid and his mount. Winding, twisting, circling, tracing the most fantastic and bewildering trail ever picked out, the good roan lessened the distance to the Lone Wolf Crossing with every coil and turn that he made.

While they fared the Kid sang. He knew but one tune and he sang it, as he knew but one code and lived it, and but one girl and loved her. He was a single-minded man of conventional ideas. He had a voice like a coyote with bronchitis, but whenever he chose to sing his song he sang it. It was a conventional song of the camps and trail, running at its beginning as near as may be to these words:

Don't you monkey with my Lulu girl
Or I'll tell you what I'll do——

and so on. The roan was inured to it, and did not mind.

But even the poorest singer will, after a certain time, gain his own consent to refrain from contributing to the world's noises. So the Kid, by the time he was within a mile or two of Tonia's *jacal,* had reluctantly allowed his song to die away—not because his vocal performance had become less charming to his own ears, but because his laryngeal muscles were aweary.

As though he were in a circus ring the speckled roan wheeled and danced through the labyrinth of pear until at length his rider knew by certain landmarks that the Lone Wolf Crossing was close at hand. Then, where the pear was thinner, he caught sight of the grass roof of the *jacal* and the hackberry tree on the edge of the arroyo. A few yards farther the Kid stopped the roan and gazed intently through the prickly openings. Then he dismounted, dropped the roan's reins, and proceeded on foot, stooping and silent, like an Indian. The roan, knowing his part, stood still, making no sound.

The kid crept noiselessly to the very edge of the pear thicket and reconnoitered between the leaves of a clump of cactus.

Ten yards from his hiding-place, in the shade of the *jacal,* sat his Tonia calmly plaiting a raw-hide lariat. So far she might surely escape condemnation; women have been known, from time to time, to engage in more mischievous occupations. But if all must be told, there is to be added that her head reposed against the broad and comfortable chest of a tall red-and-yellow man, and that his arm was about her, guiding her nimble small fingers that required so many lessons at the intricate six-strand plait.

Sandridge glanced quickly at the dark mass of pear when he heard a slight squeaking sound that was not altogether unfamiliar. A gun-scabbard will make that sound when one grasps the handle of a six-shooter suddenly. But the sound was not repeated; and Tonia's fingers needed close attention.

And then, in the shadow of death, they began to talk of their love; and in the still July afternoon every word they uttered reached the ears of the Kid.

"Remember, then," said Tonia, "you must not come again until I send for you. Soon he will be here. A *vaquero* at the *tienda* said today he saw him on the Guadalupe three days ago. When he is that near he always comes. If he comes and finds you here he will kill you. So, for my sake, you must come no more until I send you the word."

"All right," said the ranger. "And then what?"

"And then," said the girl, "you must bring your men here and kill him. If not, he will kill you."

"He ain't a man to surrender, that's sure," said Sandridge. "It's kill or be killed for the officer that goes up against Mr. Cisco Kid."

"He must die," said the girl. "Otherwise there will not be any peace in the world for thee and me. He has killed many. Let him so die. Bring your men, and give him no chance to escape."

"You used to think right much of him," said Sandridge.

Tonia dropped the lariat, twisted herself around, and curved a lemon-tinted arm over the ranger's shoulder.

"But then," she murmured in liquid Spanish, "I had not beheld thee, thou great, red mountain of a man! And thou art kind and good, as well as strong. Could one choose him, knowing thee? Let him die; for then I will not be filled with fear by day and night lest he hurt thee or me."

"How can I know when he comes?" asked Sandridge.

"When he comes," said Tonia, "he remains two days, sometimes three. Gregorio, the small son of old Luisa, the *lavandera,* has a swift pony. I will write a letter to thee and send it by him, saying how it will be best to come upon him. By Gregorio will the letter come. And bring many men with thee, and have much care, oh, dear red one, for the rattlesnake is not quicker to strike than is *'El Chivato,'* as they call him, to send a ball from his *pistola."*

"The Kid's handy with his gun, sure enough," admitted Sandridge, "but when I come for him I shall come alone. I'll get him by myself or not at all. The Cap wrote one or two things to me that make me want to do the trick without any help. You let me know when Mr. Kid arrives, and I'll do the rest."

"I will send you the message by the boy Gregorio," said the girl. "I knew you were braver than that small slayer of men who never smiles. How could I ever have thought I cared for him?"

It was time for the ranger to ride back to his camp on the water hole. Before he mounted his horse he raised the slight form of Tonia with one arm high from the earth for a parting salute. The drowsy stillness of the torpid summer air still lay thick upon the dreaming afternoon. The smoke from the fire in the *jacal,* where the *frijoles* blubbered in the iron pot, rose straight as a plumb-line above the clay-daubed chimney. No sound or movement disturbed the serenity of the dense pear thicket ten yards away.

When the form of Sandridge had disappeared, loping his big

dun down the steep banks of the Frio crossing, the Kid crept back to his own horse, mounted him, and rode back along the tortuous trail he had come.

But not far. He stopped and waited in the silent depths of the pear until half an hour had passed. And then Tonia heard the high, untrue notes of his unmusical singing coming nearer and nearer; and she ran to the edge of the pear to meet him.

The Kid seldom smiled; but he smiled and waved his hat when he saw her. He dismounted, and his girl sprang into his arms. The Kid looked at her fondly. His thick black hair clung to his head like a wrinkled mat. The meeting brought a slight ripple of some undercurrent of feeling to his smooth, dark face that was usually as motionless as a clay mask.

"How's my girl?" he asked, holding her close.

"Sick of waiting so long for you, dear one," she answered. "My eyes are dim with always gazing into that devil's pincushion through which you come. And I can see into it such a little way, too. But you are here, beloved one, and I will not scold. *Qué mal muchacho!* not to come to see your *alma* more often. Go in and rest, and let me water your horse and stake him with the long rope. There is cool water in the jar for you."

The Kid kissed her affectionately.

"Not if the court knows itself do I let a lady stake my horse for me," said he. "But if you'll run in, *chica,* and throw a pot of coffee together while I attend to the *caballo,* I'll be a good deal obliged."

Besides his marksmanship the Kid had another attribute for which he admired himself greatly. He was *muy caballero,* as the Mexicans express it, where the ladies were concerned. For them he had always gentle words and consideration. He could not have spoken a harsh word to a woman. He might ruthlessly slay their husbands and brothers, but he could not have laid the weight of a finger in anger upon a woman. Wherefore many of that interesting division of humanity who had come under the spell of his politeness declared their disbelief in the stories circulated about Mr. Kid. One shouldn't believe everything one heard, they said. When confronted by their indignant men folk with proof of the *caballero's* deeds of infamy, they said maybe he had been driven to it, and that he knew how to treat a lady, anyhow.

Considering this extremely courteous idiosyncrasy of the Kid and the pride that he took in it, one can perceive that the solution of the problem that was presented to him by what he saw and heard from his hiding-place in the pear that afternoon (at least as to one of the actors) must have been obscured by difficulties. And yet one could not think of the Kid overlooking little matters of that kind.

At the end of the short twilight they gathered around a supper of *frijoles,* goat steaks, canned peaches, and coffee, by the light of a lantern in the *jacal.* Afterward, the ancestor, his flock corralled, smoked a cigarette and became a mummy in a gray blanket. Tonia washed the few dishes while the Kid dried them with the flour-sacking towel. Her eyes shone; she chatted volubly of the inconsequent happenings of her small world since the Kid's last visit; it was as all his other home-comings had been.

Then outside Tonia swung in a grass hammock with her guitar and sang sad *canciones de amor.*

"Do you love me just the same, old girl?" asked the Kid, hunting for his cigarette papers.

"Always the same, little one," said Tonia, her dark eyes lingering upon him.

"I must go over to Finks," said the Kid, rising, "for some tobacco. I thought I had another sack in my coat. I'll be back in a quarter of an hour."

"Hasten," said Tonia, "and tell me—how long shall I call you my own this time? Will you be gone again to-morrow, leaving me to grieve, or will you be longer with your Tonia?"

"Oh, I might stay two or three days this trip," said the Kid, yawning. "I've been on the dodge for a month, and I'd like to rest up."

He was gone half an hour for his tobacco. When he returned Tonia was still lying in the hammock.

"It's funny," said the Kid, "how I feel. I feel like there was somebody lying behind every bush and tree waiting to shoot me. I never had mully-grubs like them before. Maybe it's one of them presumptions. I've got half a notion to light out in the morning before day. The Guadalupe country is burning up about that old Dutchman I plugged down there."

"You are not afraid—no one could make my brave little one fear."

"Well, I haven't been usually regarded as a jack-rabbit when it comes to scrapping; but I don't want a posse smoking me out when I'm in your *jacal.* Somebody might get hurt that oughtn't to."

"Remain with your Tonia; no one will find you here."

The Kid looked keenly into the shadows up and down the arroyo and toward the dim lights of the Mexican village.

"I'll see how it looks later on," was his decision.

At midnight a horseman rode into the rangers' camp, blazing his way by noisy "halloes" to indicate a pacific mission. Sandridge and one or two others turned out to investigate the row. The rider announced himself to be Domingo Sales, from the Lone Wolf Crossing. He bore a letter for Señor Sandridge. Old Luisa, the *lavandera,* had persuaded him to bring it, he said, her son Gregorio being too ill of a fever to ride.

Sandridge lighted the camp lantern and read the letter. These were its words:

> Dear One: He has come. Hardly had you ridden away when he came out of the pear. When he first talked he said he would stay three days or more. Then as it grew later he was like a wolf or a fox, and walked about without rest, looking and listening. Soon he said he must leave before daylight when it is dark and stillest. And then he seemed to suspect that I be not true to him. He looked at me so strange that I am frightened. I swear to him that I love him, his own Tonia. Last of all he said I must prove to him I am true. He thinks that even now men are waiting to kill him as he rides from my house. To escape he says he will dress in my clothes, my red skirt and the blue waist I wear and the brown mantilla over the head, and thus ride away. But before that he says that I must put on his clothes, his *pantalones* and *camisa* and hat, and ride away on his horse from the *jacal* as far as the big road beyond the crossing and back again. This before he goes, so he can tell if I am true and if men are hidden to shoot him. It is a terrible thing. An hour before daybreak this is to be. Come, my dear one, and kill this man and take me for your Tonia. Do not try to take hold of him alive, but kill him quickly. Knowing all, you should do that. You must come long before the time and hide yourself in the little shed near the *jacal* where the wagon and saddles are kept. It is dark in there. He will wear my red skirt and blue waist and brown mantilla. I send you a hundred kisses. Come surely and shoot quickly and straight.
>
> Thine Own Tonia

Sandridge quickly explained to his men the official part of the missive. The rangers protested against his going alone.

"I'll get him easy enough," said the lieutenant. "The girl's got him trapped. And don't even think he'll get the drop on me."

Sandridge saddled his horse and rode to the Lone Wolf Crossing. He tied his big dun in a clump of brush on the arroyo, took his Winchester from its scabbard, and carefully approached the Perez *jacal.* There was only the half of a high moon drifted over by ragged, milk-white gulf clouds.

The wagon-shed was an excellent place for ambush; and the ranger got inside it safely. In the black shadow of the brush shelter in front of the *jacal* he could see a horse tied and hear him impatiently pawing the hard-trodden earth.

He waited almost an hour before two figures came out of the *jacal.* One, in man's clothes, quickly mounted the horse and galloped past the wagon-shed toward the crossing and village. And then the other figure, in skirt, waist, and mantilla over its head, stepped out into the faint moonlight, gazing after the rider. Sandridge thought he would take his chance then before Tonia rode back. He fancied she might not care to see it.

"Throw up your hands," he ordered, loudly, stepping out of the wagonshed with his Winchester at his shoulder.

There was a quick turn of the figure, but no movement to obey, so the ranger pumped in the bullets—one—two—three—and then twice more; for you never could be too sure of bringing down the Cisco Kid. There was no danger of missing at ten paces, even in that half moonlight.

The old ancestor, asleep on his blanket, was awakened by the shots. Listening further, he heard a great cry from some man in mortal distress or anguish, and rose up grumbling at the disturbing ways of moderns.

The tall, red ghost of a man burst into the *jacal,* reaching one hand, shaking like a *tule* reed, for the lantern hanging on its nail. The other spread a letter on the table.

"Look at this letter, Perez," cried the man. "Who wrote it?"

"Ah, Dios! it is Señor Sandridge," mumbled the old man, approaching, *"Pues, señor,* that letter was written by *'El Chivato,'* as he is called—by the man of Tonia. They say he is a bad man; I do not know. While Tonia slept he wrote the letter and sent it by this old hand of mine to Domingo Sales to be brought to you. Is there anything wrong in the letter? I am very old; and I did not know. *Valgame Dios!* it is a very foolish world; and there is nothing in the house to drink—nothing to drink."

Just then all that Sandridge could think of to do was to go outside and throw himself face downward in the dust by the side of his humming-bird, of whom not a feather fluttered. He was not a *caballero* by instinct, and he could not understand the niceties of revenge.

A mile away the rider who had ridden past the wagon-shed struck up a harsh, untuneful song, the words of which began:

Don't you monkey with my Lulu girl
Or I'll tell you what I'll do——

The Missing Chord

I stopped overnight at the sheep ranch of Rush Kinney, on the Sandy Fork of the Nueces. Mr. Kinney and I had been strangers up to the time when I called "Hallo!" at his hitching-rack; but from that moment until my departure on the next morning we were, according to the Texas code, undeniable friends.

After supper the ranchman and I lugged our chairs outside the two-room house, to its floorless gallery roofed with chaparral and sacuista grass. With the rear legs of our chairs sinking deep into the hard-packed loam, each of us reposed against an elm pillar of the structure and smoked El Toro tobacco, while we wrangled amicably concerning the affairs of the rest of the world.

As for conveying adequate conception of the engaging charm of that prairie evening, despair waits upon it. It is a bold chronicler who will undertake the description of a Texas night in the early spring. An inventory must suffice.

The ranch rested upon the summit of a lenient slope. The ambient prairie, diversified by arroyos and murky patches of brush and pear, lay around us like a darkened bowl at the bottom of which we reposed as dregs. Like a turquoise cover the sky pinned us there. The miraculous air, heady with ozone and made memorably sweet by leagues of wild flowerets, gave tang and savor to the breath. In the sky was a great, round, mellow searchlight which we knew to be no moon, but the dark lantern of summer, who came to hunt northward the cowering spring. In the nearest corral a flock of sheep lay silent until a groundless panic would send a squad of them huddling together with a drumming rush. For other sounds a shrill family of coyotes yapped beyond the shearing-pen, and whippoorwills twittered in the long grass. But even these dissonances hardly rippled the clear torrent of the mocking-birds' notes that fell from a dozen neighboring shrubs and trees. It would not have been preposterous for one to tiptoe and essay to touch the stars, they hung so bright and imminent.

Mr. Kinney's wife, a young and capable woman, we had left in the house. She remained to busy herself with the domestic round of duties in which I had observed that she seemed to take a buoyant and contented pride. In one room we had supped. Presently, from the other, as Kinney and I sat without, there burst a volume of sudden and brilliant music. If I could justly estimate the art of piano-playing, the construer of that rollicking fantasia had creditably mastered the secrets of the keyboard. A piano, and one so well played, seemed to me to be an unusual thing to find in that small and unpromising ranchhouse. I must have looked my surprise at Rush Kinney, for he laughed in his soft Southern way, and nodded at me through the moonlit haze of our cigarettes.

"You don't often hear as agreeable a noise as that on a sheep-ranch," he remarked; "but I never see any reason for not playing up to the arts and graces just because we happen to live out in the brush. It's a lonesome life for a woman; and if a little music can make it any better, why not have it? That's the way I look at it."

"A wise and generous theory," I assented. "And Mrs. Kinney plays well. I am not learned in the science of music, but I should call her an uncommonly good performer. She has technic and more than ordinary power."

The moon was very bright, you will understand, and I saw upon Kinney's face a sort of amused and pregnant expression, as though there were things behind it that might be expounded.

"You came up the trail from the Double-Elm Fork," he said, promisingly. "As you crossed it you must have seen an old deserted *jacal* to your left under a coma mott."

"I did," said I. "There was a drove of *invalis* rooting around it. I could see by the broken corrals that no one lived there."

"That's where this music proposition started," said Kinney. "I don't mind telling you about it while we smoke. That's where old Cal Adams lived. He had about eight hundred graded merinos and a daughter that was solid silk and as handsome as a new stake-rope on a thirty-dollar pony. And I don't mind telling you that I was guilty in the second degree of hanging around old Cal's ranch all the time I could spare away from lambing and shearing. Miss Marilla was her name; and I had figured it out by the rule of two that she was destined to become the chatelaine and lady superior of Rancho Lomito, belonging to R. Kinney, Esq., where you are now a welcome and honored guest.

"I will say that old Cal wasn't distinguished as a sheepman. He was a little, old stoop-shouldered *hombre* about as big as a gun scabbard, with scraggy white whiskers, and condemned to the continuous use of language. Old Cal was so obscure in his chosen profession that he wasn't even hated by the cowmen. And when a sheepman don't get eminent enough to acquire the hostility of the cattlemen, he is mighty apt to die unwept and considerably unsung.

"But that Marilla girl was a benefit to the eye. And she was the most elegant kind of a housekeeper. I was the nearest neighbor, and I used to ride over to the Double-Elm anywhere from nine to sixteen times a week with fresh butter or a quarter of venison or a sample of new sheepdip just as a frivolous excuse to see Marilla. Marilla and me got to be extensively inveigled with each other, and I was pretty sure I was going to get my rope around her neck and lead her over to the Lomito. Only she was so everlastingly permeated with filial sentiments toward old Cal that I never could get her to talk about serious matters.

"You never saw anybody in your life that was as full of knowledge and had less sense than old Cal. He was advised about all the branches of information contained in learning, and he was up to all the rudiments of doctrines and enlightenment. You couldn't advance him any ideas on any of the parts of speech or lines of thought. You would have thought he was a professor of the weather and politics and chemistry and natural history and the origin of derivations. Any subject you brought up old Cal could give you an abundant synopsis of it from the Greek root up to the time it was sacked and on the market.

"One day just after the fall shearing I rides over to the Double-Elm with a lady's magazine about fashions for Marilla and a scientific paper for old Cal.

"While I was tying my pony to a mesquite, out run Marilla, 'tickled to death' with some news that couldn't wait.

" 'Oh, Rush,' she says, all flushed up with esteem and gratification, 'what do you think! Dad's going to buy me a piano. Ain't it grand? I never dreamed I'd ever have one.'

" 'It's sure joyful,' says I. 'I always admired the agreeable uproar of a piano. It'll be lots of company for you. That's mighty good of Uncle Cal to do that.'

" 'I'm all undecided,' says Marilla, 'between a piano and a organ. A parlor organ is nice.'

" 'Either of 'em,' says I, 'is first-class for mitigating the lack of noise around a sheep-ranch. For my part,' I says, 'I shouldn't like anything better than to ride home of an evening and listen to a few waltzes and jigs, with somebody about your size sitting on the piano-stool and rounding up the notes.'

" 'Oh, hush about that,' says Marilla, 'and go on in the house. Dad hasn't rode out to-day. He's not feeling well.'

"Old Cal was inside, lying on a cot. He had a pretty bad cold and cough. I stayed to supper.

" 'Going to get Marilla a piano, I hear,' says I to him.

" 'Why, yes, something of the kind, Rush,' says he. 'She's been hankering for music for a long spell; and I allow to fix her up with something in that line right away. The sheep sheared six pounds all around this fall; and I'm going to get Marilla an instrument if it takes the price of the whole clip to do it.'

" *'Star wayno,'* says I. 'The little girl deserves it.'

" 'I'm going to San Antone on the last load of wool,' says Uncle Cal, 'and select an instrument for her myself.'

" 'Wouldn't it be better,' I suggest, 'to take Marilla along and let her pick out one that she likes?'

"I might have known that would set Uncle Cal going. Of course, a man like him, that knew everything about everything, would look at that as a reflection on his attainments.

" 'No, sir, it wouldn't,' says he, pulling at his white whiskers. 'There ain't a better judge of musical instruments in the whole world than what I am. I had an uncle,' says he, 'that was a partner in a piano-factory, and I've seen thousands of 'em put together. I know all about musical instruments from a pipe-organ to a corn-stalk fiddle. There ain't a man lives, sir, that can tell me any news about any instrument that has to be pounded, blowed, scraped, grinded, picked, or wound with a key.'

" 'You get me what you like, dad,' says Marilla, who couldn't keep her feet on the floor from joy. 'Of course you know what to select. I'd just as lief it was a piano or a organ or what.'

" 'I see in St. Louis once what they call a orchestrion,' says Uncle Cal, 'that I judged was about the finest thing in the way of music ever invented. But there ain't room in this house for one. Anyway, I imagine they'd cost a thousand dollars. I reckon something in the piano line would suit Marilla the best. She took lessons in that respect for two years over at Birdstail. I wouldn't trust the buying of an instrument to anybody else but myself. I reckon if I hadn't took up sheep-raising I'd have been one of the finest composers or piano-and-organ manufacturers in the world.'

"That was Uncle Cal's style. But I never lost any patience with him, on account of his thinking so much of Marilla. And she thought just as much of him. He sent her to the academy over at Birdstail for two years when it took nearly every pound of wool to pay the expenses.

"Along about Tuesday Uncle Cal put out for San Antone on the last wagon-load of wool. Marilla's Uncle Ben, who lived in Birdstail, come over and stayed at the ranch while Uncle Cal was gone.

"It was ninety miles to San Antone, and forty to the nearest railroad-station, so Uncle Cal was gone about four days. I was over at the Double-Elm when he came rolling back one evening about sundown. And up there in the wagon, sure enough, was a piano or a organ—we couldn't tell which—all wrapped up in wool-sacks, with a wagon-sheet tied over it in case of rain. And out skips Marilla, hollering, 'Oh, oh!' with her eyes shining and her hair a-flying. 'Dad—dad,' she sings out, 'have you brought it—have you brought it?'—and it right there before her eyes, as women will do.

" 'Finest piano in San Antone,' says Uncle Cal, waving his hand, proud. 'Genuine rosewood, and the finest, loudest tone you ever listened to. I heard the storekeeper play it, and I took it on the spot and paid cash down.'

"Me and Ben and Uncle Cal and a Mexican lifted it out of the wagon and carried it in the house and set it in a corner. It was one of them upright instruments, and not very heavy or very big.

"And then all of a sudden Uncle Cal flops over and says he's mighty sick. He's got a high fever, and he complains of his lungs. He gets into bed, while me and Ben goes out to unhitch and put the horses in the pasture, and Marilla flies around to get Uncle Cal something hot to drink. But first she puts both arms on that piano and hugs it with a soft kind of a smile, like you see kids doing with their Christmas toys.

"When I came in from the pasture, Marilla was in the room where the piano was. I could see by the strings and woolsacks on the floor that she had had it unwrapped. But now she was tying the wagon-sheet over it again, and there was a kind of solemn, whitish look on her face.

" 'Ain't wrapping up the music again, are you, Marilla?' I asks. 'What's the matter with just a couple of tunes for to see how she goes under the saddle?'

" 'Not to-night, Rush,' says she. 'I don't want to play any to-night. Dad's too sick. Just think, Rush, he paid three hundred dollars for it—nearly a third of what the wool-clip brought!'

" 'Well, it ain't anyways in the neighborhood of a third of what you are worth,' I told her. 'And I don't think Uncle Cal is too sick to hear a little agitation of the piano-keys just to christen the machine.'

" 'Not to-night, Rush,' says Marilla, in a way that she had when she wanted to settle things.

"But it seems that Uncle Cal was plenty sick, after all. He got so bad that Ben saddled up and rode over to Birdstail for Doc Simpson. I stayed around to see if I'd be needed for anything.

"When Uncle Cal's pain let up on him a little he called Marilla and says to her: 'Did you look at your instrument, honey? And do you like it?'

" 'It's lovely, dad,' says she, leaning down by his pillow; 'I never saw one so pretty. How dear and good it was of you to buy it for me!'

" 'I haven't heard you play on it any yet,' says Uncle Cal; 'and I've been listening. My side don't hurt quite so bad now—won't you play a piece, Marilla?'

"But no, she puts Uncle Cal off and soothes him down like you've seen women do with a kid. It seems she's made up her mind not to touch that piano at present.

"When Doc Simpson comes over he tells us that Uncle Cal has pneumonia the worst kind; and as the old man was past sixty and nearly on the lift anyhow, the odds was against his walking on grass any more.

"On the fourth day of his sickness he calls for Marilla again and wants to talk piano. Doc Simpson was there, and so was Ben and Mrs. Ben, trying to do all they could.

" 'I'd have made a wonderful success in anything connected with music,' says Uncle Cal. 'I got the finest instrument for the money in San Antone. Ain't that piano all right in every respect, Marilla?'

" 'It's just perfect, dad,' says she. 'It's got the finest tone I ever heard. But don't you think you could sleep a little now, dad?'

" 'No, I don't,' says Uncle Cal. 'I want to hear that piano. I don't believe you've even tried it yet. I went all the way to San Antone and picked it out for you myself. It took a third of the fall clip to buy it; but I don't mind that if it makes my good girl happier. Won't you play a little bit for dad, Marilla?'

"Doc Simpson beckoned Marilla to one side and recommended her to do what Uncle Cal wanted, so it would get him quieted. And her Uncle Ben and his wife asked her, too.

" 'Why not hit out a tune or two with the soft pedal on?' I asks Marilla. 'Uncle Cal has begged you so often. It would please him a good deal to hear you touch up the piano he's bought for you. Don't you think you might?'

"But Marilla stands there with big tears rolling down from her eyes and says nothing. And then she runs over and slips her arm under Uncle Cal's neck and hugs him tight.

" 'Why, last night, dad,' we heard her say, 'I played ever so much. Honest—I have been playing it. And it's such a splendid instrument, you don't know how I love it. Last night I played "Bonnie Dundee" and the "Anvil Polka" and the "Blue Danube"—and lots of pieces. You must surely have heard me playing a little, didn't you, dad? I didn't like to play loud when you was so sick.'

" 'Well, well,' says Uncle Cal, 'maybe I did. Maybe I did and forgot about it. My head is a little cranky at times. I heard the man in the store play it fine. I'm mighty glad you like it, Marilla. Yes, I believe I could go to sleep a while if you'll stay right beside me till I do.'

"There was where Marilla had me guessing. Much as she thought of that old man, she wouldn't strike a note on that piano that he'd bought her. I couldn't imagine why she told him she'd been playing it, for the wagon-sheet hadn't even been off of it since she put it back on the same day it come. I knew she could play a little anyhow, for I'd once heard her snatch some pretty fair dance-music out of an old piano at the Charco Largo Ranch.

"Well, in about a week the pneumonia got the best of Uncle Cal. They had the funeral over at Birdstail, and all of us went over. I brought Marilla back home in my buckboard. Her uncle Ben and his wife were going to stay there a few days with her.

"That night Marilla takes me in the room where the piano was, while the others were out on the gallery.

" 'Come here, Rush,' says she; 'I want you to see this now.'

"She unties the rope, and drags off the wagon-sheet.

"If you ever rode a saddle without a horse, or fired off a gun that wasn't loaded, or took a drink out of an empty bottle, why, then you might have been able to scare an opera or two out of the instrument Uncle Cal had bought.

"Instead of a piano, it was one of them machines they've invented to play the piano with. By itself it was about as musical as the holes of a flute without the flute.

"And that was the piano that Uncle Cal had selected; and standing by it was the good, fine, all-wool girl that never let him know it.

"And what you heard playing a while ago," concluded Mr. Kinney, "was that same deputy-piano machine; only just at present it's shoved up against a six-hundred-dollar piano that I bought for Marilla as soon as we was married."

From THE TRIMMED LAMP 1907

Brickdust Row

Blinker was displeased. A man of less culture and poise and wealth would have sworn. But Blinker always remembered that he was a gentleman—a thing that no gentleman should do. So he merely looked bored and sardonic while he rode in a hansom to the centre of disturbance, which was the Broadway office of Lawyer Oldport, who was agent for the Blinker estate.

"I don't see," said Blinker, "why I should be always signing confounded papers. I am packed, and was to have left for the North Woods this morning. Now I must wait until to-morrow morning. I hate night trains. My best razors are, of course, at the bottom of some unidentifiable trunk. It is a plot to drive me to bay rum and a monologuing, thumb-handed barber. Give me a pen that doesn't scratch. I hate pens that scratch."

"Sit down," said double-chinned, gray Lawyer Oldport. "The worst has not been told you. Oh, the hardships of the rich! The papers are not yet ready to sign. They will be laid before you to-morrow at eleven. You will miss another day. Twice shall the barber tweak the helpless nose of a Blinker. Be thankful that your sorrows do not embrace a haircut."

"If," said Blinker, rising, "the act did not involve more signing of papers I would take my business out of your hands at once. Give me a cigar, please."

"If," said Lawyer Oldport, "I had cared to see an old friend's son gulped down at one mouthful by sharks I would have ordered you to take it away long ago. Now, let's quit fooling, Alexander. Besides the grinding task of signing your name some thirty times to-morrow, I must impose upon you the consideration of a matter of business—of business, and I may say humanity or right. I spoke to you about this five years ago, but you would not listen—you were in a hurry for a coaching trip, I think. The subject has come up again. The property——"

"Oh, property!" interrupted Blinker. "Dear Mr. Oldport, I think you mentioned to-morrow. Let's have it all at one dose to-morrow—signatures and property and snappy rubber bands and that smelly sealing-wax and all. Have luncheon with me? Well, I'll try to remember to drop in at eleven to-morrow. Morning."

The Blinker wealth was in lands, tenements, and hereditaments, as the legal phrase goes. Lawyer Oldport had once taken Alexander in his little pulmonary gasoline runabout to see the many buildings and rows of buildings that he owned in the city. For Alexander was sole heir. They had amused Blinker very much. The houses looked so incapable of producing the big sums of money that Lawyer Oldport kept piling up in banks for him to spend.

In the evening Blinker went to one of his clubs, intending to dine. Nobody was there except some old fogies playing whist who spoke to him with grave politeness and glared at him with savage contempt. Everybody was out of town. But here he was kept in like a schoolboy to write his name over and over on pieces of paper. His wounds were deep.

Blinker turned his back on the fogies, and said to the club steward who had come forward with some nonsense about cold fresh salmon roe:

"Symons, I'm going to Coney Island." He said it as one might say: "All's off, I'm going to jump into the river."

The joke pleased Symons. He laughed within a sixteenth of a note of the audibility permitted by the laws governing employees.

"Certainly, sir," he tittered. "Of course, sir, I think I can see you at Coney, Mr. Blinker."

Blinker got a paper and looked up at the movements of Sunday steamboats. Then he found a cab at the first corner and drove to a North River pier. He stood in line, as democratic as you or I, and bought a ticket, and was trampled upon and shoved forward until, at last, he found himself on the upper deck of the boat staring brazenly at a girl who sat alone upon a camp stool. But Blinker did not intend to be brazen; the girl was so wonderfully good looking that he forgot for one minute that he was the prince incog, and behaved just as he did in society.

She was looking at him, too, and not severely. A puff of wind threatened Blinker's straw hat. He caught it warily and settled it again. The movement gave the effect of a bow. The girl nodded and smiled, and in another instant he was seated at her side. She was dressed all in white, she was paler than Blinker imagined milkmaids and girls of humble stations to be, but she was as tidy as a cherry blossom, and her steady, supremely frank gray eyes looked out from the intrepid depths of an unshadowed and untroubled soul.

"How dare you raise your hat to me?" she asked, with a smile-redeemed severity.

"I didn't," Blinker said, but he quickly covered the mistake by extending it to "I didn't know how to keep from it after I saw you."

"I do not allow gentlemen to sit by me to whom I have not been introduced," she said with a sudden haughtiness that deceived him. He rose reluctantly, but her clear, teasing laugh brought him down to his chair again.

"I guess you weren't going far," she declared, with beauty's magnificent self-confidence.

"Are you going to Coney Island?" asked Blinker.

"Me?" She turned upon him wide-open eyes full of bantering surprise. "Why, what a question! Can't you see that I'm riding a bicycle in the park?" Her drollery took the form of impertinence.

"And I'm laying bricks on a tall factory chimney," said Blinker. "Mayn't we see Coney together? I'm all alone and I've never been there before."

"It depends," said the girl, "on how nicely you behave. I'll consider your application until we get there."

Blinker took pains to provide against the rejection of his application. He strove to please. To adopt the metaphor of his nonsensical phrase, he laid brick upon brick on the tall chimney of his devoirs until, at length, the structure was stable and complete. The manners of the best society come around finally to simplicity; and as the girl's way was that naturally, they were on a mutual plane of communication from the beginning.

He learned that she was twenty, and her name was Florence; that she trimmed hats in a millinery shop; that she lived in a furnished room with her best chum Ella, who was cashier in a shoe store; and that a glass of milk from the bottle on the window-sill and an egg that boils itself while you twist up your hair makes a breakfast good enough for any one. Florence laughed when she heard "Blinker."

"Well," she said. "It certainly shows that you have imagination. It gives the 'Smiths' a chance for a little rest, anyhow."

They landed at Coney, and were dashed on the crest of a great human wave of mad pleasure-seekers into the walks and avenues of Fairyland gone into vaudeville.

With a curious eye, a critical mind, and a fairly withheld judgment Blinker considered the temples, pagodas and kiosks of popularized delights. Hoi polloi trampled, hustled, and crowded him. Basket parties bumped him; sticky children tumbled, howling, under his feet, candying his clothes. Insolent youths strolling among the booths with hard-won canes under one arm and easily won girls on the other, blew defiant smoke from cheap cigars into his face. The publicity gentlemen with megaphones, each before his own stupendous attraction, roared like Niagara in his ears. Music of all kinds that could be tortured from brass, reed, hide, or string, fought in the air to gain space for its vibrations against its competitors. But what held Blinker in awful fascination was the mob, the multitude, the proletariat shrieking, struggling, hurrying, panting, hurling itself in incontinent frenzy, with unabashed abandon, into the ridiculous sham palaces of trumpery and tinsel pleasures. The vulgarity of it, its brutal overriding of all the tenets of repression and taste that were held by his caste, repelled him strongly.

In the midst of his disgust he turned and looked down at Florence by his side. She was ready with her quick smile and upturned, happy eyes, as bright and clear as the water in trout pools. The eyes were saying that they had the right to be shining and happy, for was their owner not with her (for the present) Man, her Gentleman Friend and holder of the keys to the enchanted city of fun.

Blinker did not read her look accurately, but by some miracle he suddenly saw Coney aright.

He no longer saw a mass of vulgarians seeking gross joys. He now looked clearly upon a hundred thousand true idealists. Their offenses were wiped out. Counterfeit and false though the garish joys of these spangled temples were, he perceived that deep under the gilt surface they offered saving and apposite balm and satisfaction to the restless human heart. Here, at least, was the husk of Romance, the empty but shining casque of Chivalry, the breath-catching though safe-guarded dip and flight of Adventure, the magic carpet that transports you to the realms of fairyland, though its journey be through but a few poor yards of space. He no longer saw a rabble, but his brothers seeking the ideal. There was no magic of poesy here or of art; but the glamour of their imagination turned yellow calico into cloth of gold and the megaphone into the silver trumpets of joy's heralds.

Almost humbled, Blinker rolled up the shirt sleeves of his mind and joined the idealists.

"You are the lady doctor," he said to Florence. "How shall we go about doing this jolly conglomeration of fairy tales, incorporated?"

"We will begin there," said the Princess, pointing to a fun pagoda on the edge of the sea, "and we will take them all in, one by one."

They caught the eight o'clock returning boat and sat, filled with pleasant fatigue, against the rail in the bow, listening to the Italians' fiddle and harp. Blinker had thrown off all care. The North Woods seemed to him an uninhabitable wilderness. What a fuss he had made over signing his name—pooh! he could sign it a hundred times. And her name was as pretty as she was—"Florence," he said it to himself a great many times.

As the boat was nearing its pier in the North River a two-funnelled, drab, foreign-looking sea-going steamer was dropping down toward the bay. The boat turned its nose in towards its slip. The steamer veered as if to seek mid-stream, and then yawned, seemed to increase its speed and struck the Coney boat on the side near the stern, cutting into it with a terrifying shock and crash.

While the six hundred passengers on the boat were mostly tumbling about the decks in a shrieking panic the captain was shouting at the steamer that it should not back off and leave the rent exposed for the water to enter. But the steamer tore its way out like a savage sawfish and cleaved its heartless way, full speed ahead.

The boat began to sink at its stern, but moved slowly toward the slip. The passengers were a frantic mob, unpleasant to behold.

Blinker held Florence tightly until the boat had righted itself. She made no sound or sign of fear. He stood on a camp stool, ripped off the slats above his head and pulled down a number of the life preservers. He began to buckle one around Florence. The rotten canvas split and the fraudulent granulated cork came pouring out in a stream. Florence caught a handful of it and laughed gleefully.

"It looks like breakfast food," she said. "Take it off. They're no good."

She unbuckled it and threw it on the deck. She made Blinker sit down and sat by his side and put her hand in his. "What'll you bet we don't reach the pier all right?" she said, and began to hum a song.

And now the captain moved among the passengers and compelled order. The boat would undoubtedly make her slip, he said, and ordered the women and children to the bow, where they could land first. The boat, very low in the water at the stern, tried gallantly to make his promise good.

"Florence," said Blinker, as she held him close by an arm and hand, "I love you."

"That's what they all say," she replied, lightly.

"I am not one of 'they all,' " he persisted. "I never knew any one I could love before. I could pass my life with you and be happy every day. I am rich. I can make things all right for you."

"That's what they all say," said the girl again, weaving the words into her little, reckless song.

"Don't say that again," said Blinker in a tone that made her look at him in frank surprise.

"Why shouldn't I say it?" she asked, calmly. "They all do."

"Who are 'they'?" he asked, jealous for the first time in his existence.

"Why, the fellows I know."

"Do you know so many?"

"Oh, well, I'm not a wall flower," she answered with modest complacency.

"Where do you see these—these men? At your home?"

"Of course not. I meet them just as I did you. Sometimes on the boat, sometimes in the park, sometimes on the street. I'm a pretty good judge of a man. I can tell in a minute if a fellow is one who is likely to get fresh."

"What do you mean by 'fresh'?"

"Who try to kiss you—me, I mean."

"Do any of them try that?" asked Blinker, clenching his teeth.

"Sure. All men do. You know that."

"Do you allow them?"

"Some. Not many. They won't take you out anywhere unless you do."

She turned her head and looked searchingly at Blinker. Her eyes were as innocent as a child's. There was a puzzled look in them, as though she did not understand him.

"What's wrong about my meeting fellows?" she asked, wonderingly.

"Everything," he answered, almost savagely. "Why don't you entertain your company in the house where you live? Is it necessary to pick up Tom, Dick, and Harry on the streets?"

She kept her absolutely ingenuous eyes upon his.

"If you could see the place where I live you wouldn't ask that. I live in Brickdust Row. They call it that because there's red dust from the bricks crumbling over everything. I've lived there for more than four years. There's no place to receive company. You can't have anybody come to your room. What else is there to do? A girl has got to meet the men, hasn't she?"

"Yes," he said hoarsely. "A girl has got to meet a—has got to meet the men."

"The first time one spoke to me on the street," she continued, "I ran home and cried all night. But you get used to it. I meet a good many nice fellows at church. I go on rainy days and stand in the vestibule until one comes up with an umbrella. I wish there was a parlor, so I could ask you to call, Mr. Blinker—are you really sure it isn't 'Smith,' now?"

The boat landed safely. Blinker had a confused impression of walking with the girl through quiet crosstown streets until she stopped at a corner and held out her hand.

"I live just one more block over," she said. "Thank you for a very pleasant afternoon."

Blinker muttered something and plunged northward till he found a cab. A big, gray church loomed slowly at his right. Blinker shook his fist at it through the window.

"I gave you a thousand dollars last week," he cried under his breath, "and she meets them in your very doors. There is something wrong; there is something wrong."

At eleven the next day Blinker signed his name thirty times with a new pen provided by Lawyer Oldport.

"Now let me get to the woods," he said, surlily.

"You are not looking well," said Lawyer Oldport. "The trip will do you good. But listen, if you will, to that little matter of business of which I spoke to you yesterday, and also five years ago. There are some buildings, fifteen in number, of which there are new five-year leases to be signed. Your father contemplated a change in the lease provisions, but never made it. He intended that the parlors of these houses should not be sublet, but that the tenants should be allowed to use them for reception rooms. These houses are in the shopping districts, and are mainly tenanted by young working girls. As it is they are forced to seek companionship outside. This row of red brick——"

Blinker interrupted him with a loud, discordant laugh.

"Brickdust Row for an even hundred," he cried. "And I own it. Have I guessed right?"

"The tenants have some such name for it," said Lawyer Oldport.

Blinker arose and jammed his hat down to his eyes.

"Do what you please with it," he said, harshly. "Remodel it, burn it, raze it to the ground. But, man, it's too late, I tell you. It's too late. It's too late. It's too late."

A Harlem Tragedy

Harlem.

Mrs. Fink had dropped into Mrs. Cassidy's flat one flight below.

"Ain't it a beaut?" said Mrs. Cassidy.

She turned her face proudly for her friend Mrs. Fink to see. One eye was nearly closed, with a great, greenish-purple bruise around it. Her lip was cut and bleeding a little and there were red finger-marks on each side of her neck.

"My husband wouldn't ever think of doing that to me," said Mrs. Fink, concealing her envy.

"I wouldn't have a man," declared Mrs. Cassidy, "that didn't beat me up at least once a week. Shows he thinks something of you. Say! but that last dose Jack gave me wasn't no homeopathic one. I can see stars yet. But he'll be the sweetest man in town for the rest of the week to make up for it. This eye is good for theater tickets and a silk shirt waist at the very least."

"I should hope," said Mrs. Fink, assuming complacency, "that Mr. Fink is too much of a gentleman ever to raise his hand against me."

"Oh, go on, Maggie!" said Mrs. Cassidy, laughing and applying witch hazel, "you're only jealous. Your old man is too frappéed and slow to ever give you a punch. He just sits down and practises physical culture with a newspaper when he comes home—now ain't that the truth?"

"Mr. Fink certainly peruses of the papers when he comes home," acknowledged Mrs. Fink, with a toss of her head; "but he certainly don't ever make no Steve O'Donnell out of me just to amuse himself—that's a sure thing."

Mrs. Cassidy laughed the contented laugh of the guarded and happy matron. With the air of Cornelia exhibiting her jewels, she drew down the collar of her kimono and revealed another treasured bruise, maroon-colored, edged with olive and orange—a bruise now nearly well, but still to memory dear.

Mrs. Fink capitulated. The formal light in her eye softened to envious admiration. She and Mrs. Cassidy had been chums in the downtown paper-box factory before they had married, one year before. Now she and her man occupied the flat above Mame and her man. Therefore she could not put on airs with Mame.

"Don't it hurt when he soaks you?" asked Mrs. Fink, curiously.

"Hurt!"—Mrs. Cassidy gave a soprano scream of delight. "Well, say—did you ever have a brick house fall on you?—well, that's just the way it feels—just like when they're digging you out of the ruins. Jack's got a left that spells two matinées and a new pair of Oxfords—and his right!—well, it takes a trip to Coney and six pairs of open-work silk lisle threads to make that good."

"But what does he beat you for?" inquired Mrs. Fink, with wide-open eyes.

"Silly!" said Mrs. Cassidy, indulgently. "Why, because he's full. It's generally on Saturday nights."

"But what cause do you give him?" persisted the seeker after knowledge.

"Why, didn't I marry him? Jack comes in tanked up; and I'm here, ain't I? Who else has he got a right to beat? I'd just like to catch him once beating anybody else! Sometimes it's because supper ain't ready; and sometimes it's because it is. Jack ain't particular about causes. He just lushes till he remembers he's married, and then he makes for home and does me up. Saturday nights I just move the furniture with sharp corners out of the way, so I won't cut my head when he gets his work in. He's got a left swing that jars you! Sometimes I take the count in the first round; but when I feel like having a good time during the week or want some new rags I come up again for more punishment. That's what I done last night. Jack knows I've been wanting a black silk waist for a month, and I didn't think just one black eye would bring it. Tell you what, Mag, I'll bet you the ice cream he brings it to-night."

Mrs. Fink was thinking deeply.

"My Mart," she said, "never hit me a lick in his life. It's just like you said, Mame; he comes in grouchy and ain't got a word to say. He never takes me out anywhere. He's a chair-warmer at home for fair. He buys me things, but he looks so glum about it that I never appreciate 'em."

Mrs. Cassidy slipped an arm around her chum.

"You poor thing!" she said. "But everybody can't have a husband like Jack. Marriage wouldn't be no failure if they was all like him. These discontented wives you hear about—what they need is a man to come home and kick their slats in once a week, and then make it up in kisses, and chocolate creams. That'd give 'em some interest in life. What I want is a masterful man that slugs you when he's jagged and hugs you when he ain't jagged. Preserve me from the man that ain't got the sand to do neither!"

Mrs. Fink sighed.

The hallways were suddenly filled with sound. The door flew open at the kick of Mr. Cassidy. His arms were occupied with bundles. Mame flew and hung about his neck. Her sound eye sparkled with the love light that shines in the eye of the Maori maid when she recovers consciousness in the hut of the wooer who has stunned and dragged her there.

"Hello, old girl!" shouted Mr. Cassidy. He shed his bundles and lifted her off her feet in a mighty hug. "I got tickets for Barnum & Bailey's, and if you'll bust the string of one of them bundles I guess you'll find that silk waist—why, good evening, Mrs. Fink—I didn't see you at first. How's old Mart coming along?"

"He's very well, Mr. Cassidy—thanks," said Mrs. Fink. "I must be going along up now. Mart'll be home for supper soon. I'll bring you down the pattern you want to-morrow, Mame."

Mrs. Fink went up to her flat and had a little cry. It was a meaningless cry, the kind of cry that only a woman knows about, a cry from no particular cause, altogether an absurd cry; the most transient and the most hopeless cry in the repertory of grief. Why had Martin never thrashed her? He was as big and strong as Jack Cassidy. Did he not care for her at all? He never quarrelled; he came home and lounged about silent, glum, idle. He was a fairly good provider, but he ignored the spices of life.

Mrs. Fink's ship of dreams was becalmed. Her captain ranged between plum duff and his hammock. If only he would shiver his timbers or stamp his foot on the quarter-deck now and then! And she had thought to sail so merrily, touching at ports in the Delectable Isles! But now, to vary the figure, she was ready to throw up the sponge, tired out, without a scratch to show for all those tame rounds with her sparring partner. For one moment she almost hated Mame—Mame, with her cuts and bruises, her salve of presents and kisses; her stormy voyage with her fighting, brutal, loving mate.

Mr. Fink came home at 7. He was permeated with the curse of domesticity. Beyond the portals of his cozy home he cared not to roam, to roam. He was the man who had caught the street car, the anaconda that had swallowed its prey, the tree that lay as it had fallen.

"Like the supper, Mart?" asked Mrs. Fink, who had striven over it.

"M-m-m-yep," grunted Mr. Fink.

After supper he gathered his newspapers to read. He sat in his stocking feet.

Arise, some new Dante, and sing me the befitting corner of perdition for the man who sitteth in the house in his stockinged feet. Sisters in Patience who by reason of ties or duty have endured it in silk, yarn, cotton, lisle thread or woollen—does not the new canto belong?

The next day was Labor Day. The occupations of Mr. Cassidy and Mr. Fink ceased for one passage of the sun. Labor, triumphant, would parade and otherwise disport itself.

Mrs. Fink took Mrs. Cassidy's pattern down early. Mame had on her new silk waist. Even her damaged eye managed to emit a holiday gleam. Jack was fruitfully penitent, and there was a hilarious scheme for the day afoot, with parks and picnics and Pilsener in it.

A rising, indignant jealousy seized Mrs. Fink as she returned to her flat above. Oh, happy Mame, with her bruises and her quick-following balm! But was Mame to have a monopoly of happiness? Surely Martin Fink was as good a man as Jack Cassidy. Was his wife to go always unbelabored and uncaressed? A sudden, brilliant breathless idea came to Mrs. Fink. She would show Mame that there were husbands as able to use their fists and perhaps to be as tender afterward as any Jack.

The holiday promised to be a nominal one with the Finks. Mrs. Fink had the stationary washtubs in the kitchen filled with a two-weeks' wash that had been soaking overnight. Mr. Fink sat in his stockinged feet reading a newspaper. Thus Labor Day presaged to speed.

Jealousy surged high in Mrs. Fink's heart and higher still surged an audacious resolve. If her man would not strike her—if he would not so far prove his manhood, his prerogative and his interest in conjugal affairs, he must be prompted to do his duty.

Mr. Fink lit his pipe and peacefully rubbed an ankle with a stockinged toe. He reposed in the state of matrimony like a lump of unblended suet in a pudding. This was his level Elysium—to sit at ease vicariously girdling the world in print amid the wifely splashing of suds and the agreeable smells of breakfast dishes departed and dinner ones to come. Many ideas were far from his mind; but the furthest one was the thought of beating his wife.

Mrs. Fink turned on the hot water and set the washboards in the suds. Up from the flat below came the gay laugh of Mrs. Cassidy. It sounded like a taunt, a flaunting of her own happiness in the face of the unslugged bride above. Now was Mrs. Fink's time.

Suddenly she turned like a fury upon the man reading.

"You lazy loafer!" she cried, "must I work my arms off washing and toiling for the ugly likes of you? Are you a man or are you a kitchen hound?"

Mr. Fink dropped his paper, motionless from surprise. She feared that he would not strike—that the provocation had been insufficient. She leaped at him and struck him fiercely in the face with her clenched hand. In that instant she felt a thrill of love for him such as she had not felt for many a day. Rise up, Martin Fink, and come into your kingdom! Oh, she must feel the weight of his hand now—just to show that he cared—just to show that he cared!

Mr. Fink sprang to his feet—Maggie caught him again on the jaw with a wide swing of her other hand. She closed her eyes in that fearful, blissful moment before his blow should come—she whispered his name to herself—she leaned to the expected shock, hungry for it.

In the flat below Mr. Cassidy, with a shamed and contrite face, was powdering Mame's eye in preparation for their junket. From the flat above came the sound of a woman's voice, high-raised, a bumping, a stumbling and a shuffling, a chair overturned—unmistakable sounds of domestic conflict.

"Mart and Mag scrapping?" postulated Mr. Cassidy. "Didn't know they ever indulged. Shall I trot up and see if they need a sponge holder?"

One of Mrs. Cassidy's eyes sparkled like a diamond. The other twinkled at least like paste.

"Oh, oh," she said, softly and without apparent meaning in the feminine ejaculatory manner. "I wonder if—wonder if! Wait, Jack, till I go up and see."

Up the stairs she sped. As her foot struck the hallway above out from the kitchen door of her flat wildly flounced Mrs. Fink.

"Oh, Maggie," cried Mrs. Cassidy, in a delighted whisper; "did he? Oh, did he?"

Mrs. Fink ran and laid her face upon her chum's shoulder and sobbed hopelessly.

Mrs. Cassidy took Maggie's face between her hands and lifted it gently. Tear-stained it was, flushing and paling, but its velvety, pink-and-white, becomingly freckled surface was unscratched, unbruised, unmarred by the recreant fist of Mr. Fink.

"Tell me, Maggie," pleaded Mame, "or I'll go in there and find out. What was it? Did he hurt you—what did he do?"

Mrs. Fink's face went down again despairingly on the bosom of her friend.

"For God's sake don't open that door, Mame," she sobbed. "And don't ever tell nobody—keep it under your hat. He—he never touched me, and—he's—oh, Gawd—he's washin' the clothes—he's washin' the clothes!"

Elsie in New York

No, bumptious reader, this story is not a continuation of the Elsie series. But if your Elsie had lived over here in our big city there might have been a chapter in her books not very different from this.

Especially for the vagrant feet of youth are the roads of Manhattan beset "with pitfall and with gin." But the civic guardians of the young have made themselves acquainted with the snares of the wicked, and most of the dangerous paths are patrolled by their agents, who seek to turn straying ones away from the peril that menaces them And this will tell you how they guided my Elsie safely through all peril to the goal that she was seeking.

Elsie's father had been a cutter for Fox & Otter, cloaks and furs, on lower Broadway. He was an old man, with a slow and limping gait, so a pot-hunter of a newly licensed chauffeur ran him down one day when livelier game was scarce. They took the old man home, where he lay on his bed for a year and then died, leaving $2.50 in cash and a letter from Mr. Otter offering to do anything he could to help his faithful old employee. The old cutter regarded this letter as a valuable legacy to his daughter, and he put it into her hands with pride as the shears of the dread Cleaner and Repairer snipped off his thread of life.

That was the landlord's cue; and forth he came and did his part in the great eviction scene. There was no snowstorm ready for Elsie to steal out into, drawing her little red woollen shawl about her shoulders, but she went out, regardless of the unities. And as for the red shawl—back to Blaney with it! Elsie's fall tan coat was cheap, but it had the style and fit of the best at Fox & Otter's. And her lucky stars had given her good looks, and eyes as blue and innocent as the new shade of note paper, and she had $1 left of the $2.50. And the letter from Mr. Otter. Keep your eye on the letter from Mr. Otter. That is the clue. I desire that everything be made plain as we go. Detective stories are so plentiful now that they do not sell.

And so we find Elsie, thus equipped, starting out in the world to seek her fortune. One trouble about the letter from Mr. Otter was that it did not bear the new address of the firm, which had moved about a month before. But Elsie thought she could find it. She had heard that policemen, when politely addressed, or thumbscrewed by an investigation committee, will give up information and addresses.

So she boarded a downtown car at One Hundred and Seventy-seventh Street and rode south to Forty-second, which she thought must surely be the end of the island. There she stood against the wall undecided, for the city's roar and dash was new to her. Up where she lived was rural New York, so far out that the milkmen awaken you in the morning by the squeaking of pumps instead of the rattling of cans.

A kind-faced, sunburned, young man in a soft-brimmed hat went past Elsie into the Grand Central Depot. That was Hank Ross, of the Sunflower Ranch, in Idaho, on his way home from a visit to the East. Hank's heart was heavy, for the Sunflower Ranch was a lonesome place, lacking the presence of a woman. He had hoped to find one during his visit who would congenially share his prosperity and home, but the girls of Gotham had not pleased his fancy. But, as he passed in, he noted, with a jumping of his pulses, the sweet, ingenuous face of Elsie and her pose of doubt and loneliness. With true and honest Western impulse he said to himself that here was his mate. He could love her, he knew; and he would surround her with so much comfort, and cherish her so carefully that she would be happy, and make two sunflowers grow on the ranch where there grew but one before.

Hank turned and went back to her. Backed by his never-before-questioned honesty of purpose, he approached the girl and removed his soft-brimmed hat. Elsie had but time to sum up his handsome frank face with one shy look of modest admiration when a burly cop hurled himself upon the ranchman, seized him by the collar and backed him against the wall. Two blocks away a burglar was coming out of an apartment-house with a bag of silverware on his shoulder; but that is neither here nor there.

"Carry on yez mashin' tricks right before me eyes will yez?" shouted the cop. "I'll teach yez to speak to ladies on me beat that ye're not acquainted with. Come along."

Elsie turned away with a sigh as the ranchman was dragged away. She had liked the effect of his light blue eyes against his tanned complexion. She walked southward, thinking herself already in the district where her father used to work, and hoping to find some one who could direct her to the firm of Fox & Otter.

But did she want to find Mr. Otter? She had inherited much of the old cutter's independence. How much better it would be if she could find work and support herself without calling on him for aid!

Elsie saw a sign "Employment Agency" and went in. Many girls were sitting against the wall in chairs. Several well-dressed ladies were looking them over. One white-haired, kind-faced old lady in rustling black silk hurried up to Elsie.

"My dear," she said in a sweet, gentle voice, "are you looking for a position? I like your face and appearance so much. I want a young woman who will be half maid and half companion to me. You will have a good home and I will pay you $30 a month."

Before Elsie could stammer forth her gratified acceptance, a young woman with gold glasses on her bony nose and her hands in her jacket pockets seized her arm and drew her aside.

"I am Miss Ticklebaum," said she, "of the Association for the Prevention of Jobs Being Put Up on Working Girls Looking for Jobs. We prevented forty-seven girls from securing positions last week. I am here to protect you. Beware of any one who offers you a job. How do you know that this woman does not want to make you work as a breaker-boy in a coal mine or murder you to get your teeth? If you accept work of any kind without permission of our association you will be arrested by one of our agents."

"But what am I to do?" asked Elsie. "I have no home or money. I must do something. Why am I not allowed to accept this kind lady's offer?"

"I do not know," said Miss Ticklebaum. "That is the affair of our Committee on the Abolishment of Employers. It is my duty simply to see that you do not get work. You will give me your name and address and report to our secretary every Thursday. We have 600 girls on the waiting list who will in time be allowed to accept positions as vacancies occur on our roll of Qualified Employers, which now comprise twenty-seven names. There is prayer, music and lemonade in our chapel the third Sunday of every month."

Elsie hurried away after thanking Miss Ticklebaum for her timely warning and advice. After all, it seemed that she must try to find Mr. Otter.

But after walking a few blocks she saw a sign, "Cashier wanted," in the window of a confectionery store. In she went and applied for the place, after casting a quick glance over her shoulder to assure herself that the job-preventer was not on her trail.

The proprietor of the confectionery was a benevolent old man with a peppermint flavor, who decided, after questioning Elsie pretty closely, that she was the very girl he wanted. Her services were needed at once, so Elsie, with a thankful heart, drew off her tan coat and prepared to mount the cashier's stool.

But before she could do so a gaunt lady wearing steel spectacles and black mittens stood before her, with a long finger pointing, and exclaimed: "Young woman, hesitate!"

Elsie hesitated.

"Do you know," said the black-and-steel lady, "that in accepting this position you may this day cause the loss of a hundred lives in agonizing physical torture and the sending as many souls to perdition?"

"Why, no," said Elsie, in frightened tones. "How could I do that?"

"Rum," said the lady—"the demon rum. Do you know why so many lives are lost when a theatre catches fire? Brandy balls. The demon rum lurking in brandy balls. Our society women while in theatres sit grossly intoxicated from eating these candies filled with brandy. When the fire fiend sweeps down upon them they are unable to escape. The candy stores are the devil's distilleries. If you assist in the distribution of these insidious confections you assist in the destruction of the bodies and souls of your fellow-beings, and in the filling of our jails, asylums and almshouses. Think, girl, ere you touch the money for which brandy balls are sold."

"Dear me," said Elsie, bewildered. "I didn't know there was rum in brandy balls. But I must live by some means. What shall I do?"

"Decline the position," said the lady, "and come with me. I will tell you what to do."

After Elsie had told the confectioner that she had changed her mind about the cashiership she put on her coat and followed the lady to the sidewalk, where awaited an elegant victoria.

"Seek some other work," said the black-and-steel lady, "and assist in crushing the hydra-headed demon rum." And she got into the victoria and drove away.

"I guess that puts it up to Mr. Otter again," said Elsie, ruefully, turning down the street. "And I'm sorry, too, for I'd much rather make my way without help."

Near Fourteenth Street Elsie saw a placard tacked on the side of a doorway that read: "Fifty girls, neat sewers, wanted immediately on theatrical costumes. Good pay."

She was about to enter, when a solemn man, dressed all in black, laid his hand on her arm.

"My dear girl," he said, "I entreat you not to enter that dressing-room of the devil."

"Goodness me!" exclaimed Elsie, with some impatience. "The devil seems to have a cinch on all the business in New York. What's wrong about the place?"

"It is here," said the solemn man, "that the regalia of Satan—in other words, the costumes worn on the stage—are manufactured. The stage is the road to ruin and destruction. Would you imperil your soul by lending the work of your hands to its support? Do you know, my dear girl, what the theatre leads to? Do you know where actors and actresses go after the curtain of the playhouse has fallen upon them for the last time?"

"Sure," said Elsie. "Into vaudeville. But do you think it would be wicked for me to make a little money to live on by sewing? I must get something to do pretty soon."

"The flesh-pots of Egypt," exclaimed the reverend gentleman, uplifting his hands. "I beseech you, my child, to turn away from this place of sin and iniquity."

"But what will I do for a living?" asked Elsie. "I don't care to sew for this musical comedy, if it's as rank as you say it is; but I've got to have a job."

"The Lord will provide," said the solemn man. "There is a free Bible class every Sunday afternoon in the basement of the cigar store next to the church. Peace be with you. Amen. Farewell."

Elsie went on her way. She was soon in the downtown district where factories abound. On a large brick building was a gilt sign, "Posey & Trimmer, Artificial Flowers." Below it was hung a newly stretched canvas bearing the words, "Five hundred girls wanted to learn trade. Good wages from the start. Apply one flight up."

Elsie started toward the door, near which were gathered in groups some twenty or thirty girls. One big girl with a black straw hat tipped down over her eyes stepped in front of her.

"Say, you'se," said the girl, "are you'se goin' in there after a job?"

"Yes," said Elsie; "I must have work."

"Now don't do it," said the girl. "I'm chairman of our Scab Committee. There's 400 of us girls locked out just because we demanded 50 cents a week raise in wages, and ice water, and for the foreman to shave off his mustache. You're too nice a looking girl to be a scab. Wouldn't you please help us along by trying to find a job somewhere else, or would you'se rather have your face pushed in?"

"I'll try somewhere else," said Elsie.

She walked aimlessly eastward on Broadway, and there her heart leaped to see the sign, "Fox & Otter," stretching entirely across the front of a tall building. It was as though an unseen guide had led her to it through the byways of her fruitless search for work.

She hurried into the store and sent in to Mr. Otter by a clerk her name and the letter he had written her father. She was shown directly into his private office.

Mr. Otter arose from his desk as Elsie entered and took both hands with a hearty smile of welcome. He was a slightly corpulent man of nearly middle age, a little bald, gold spectacled, polite, well dressed, radiating.

"Well, well, and so this is Beatty's little daughter! Your father was one of our most efficient and valued employees. He left nothing? Well, well. I hope we have not forgotten his faithful services. I am sure there is a vacancy now among our models. Oh, it is easy work—nothing easier."

Mr. Otter struck a bell. A long-nose clerk thrust a portion of himself inside the door.

"Send Miss Hawkins in," said Mr. Otter. Miss Hawkins came.

"Miss Hawkins," said Mr. Otter, "ring for Miss Beatty to try on one of those Russian sable coats and—let's see—one of those latest model black tulle hats with white tips."

Elsie stood before the full-length mirror with pink cheeks and quick breath. Her eyes shone like faint stars. She was beautiful. Alas! she was beautiful.

I wish I could stop this story here. Confound it! I will. No; it's got to run it out. I didn't make it up. I'm just repeating it.

I'd like to throw bouquets at the wise cop and the lady who rescues Girls from Jobs, and the prohibitionist who is trying to crush brandy balls, and the sky pilot who objects to costumes for stage people (there are others), and all the thousands of good people who are at work protecting young people from the pitfalls of a great city; and then wind up by pointing out how they were the means of Elsie reaching her father's benefactor and her kind friend and rescuer from poverty. This would make a fine Elsie story of the old sort. I'd like to do this; but there's just a word or two to follow.

While Elsie was admiring herself in the mirror, Mr. Otter went to the telephone booth and called up some number. Don't ask me what it was.

"Oscar," said he, "I want you to reserve the same table for me this evening. . . . What? Why, the one in the Moorish room to the left of the shrubbery. . . . Yes; two. . . . Yes, the usual brand; and the '85 Johannisburger with the roast. If it isn't the right temperature I'll break your neck. . . . No; not her . . . No, indeed . . . A new one—a peacherino, Oscar, a peacherino!"

Tired and tiresome reader, I will conclude, if you please, with a paraphrase of a few words that you will remember were written by him—by him of Gad's Hill, before whom, if you doff not your hat, you shall stand with a covered pumpkin—aye, sir, a pumpkin.

Lost, Your Excellency. Lost, Associations, and Societies. Lost,

Right Reverends and Wrong Reverends of every order. Lost, Reformers and Lawmakers, born with heavenly compassion in your hearts, but with the reverence of money in your souls. And lost thus around us every day.

From THE VOICE OF THE CITY 1908

A Lickpenny Lover

There were 3,000 girls in the Biggest Store. Masie was one of them. She was eighteen and a saleslady in the gents' gloves. Here she became versed in two varieties of human beings—the kind of gents who buy their gloves in department stores and the kind of women who buy gloves for unfortunate gents. Besides this wide knowledge of the human species, Masie had acquired other information. She had listened to the promulgated wisdom of the 2,999 other girls and had stored it in a brain that was as secretive and wary as that of a Maltese cat. Perhaps nature, foreseeing that she would lack wise counsellors, had mingled the saving ingredient of shrewdness along with her beauty, as she has endowed the silver fox of the priceless fur above the other animals with cunning.

For Masie was beautiful. She was a deep-tinted blonde, with the calm poise of a lady who cooks butter cakes in a window. She stood behind her counter in the Biggest Store; and as you closed your hand over the tapeline for your glove measure you thought of Hebe; and as you looked again you wondered how she had come by Minerva's eyes.

When the floorwalker was not looking Masie chewed tutti frutti; when he was looking she gazed up as if at the clouds and smiled wistfully.

That is the shopgirl smile, and I enjoin you to shun it unless you are well fortified with callosity of the heart, caramels, and a congeniality for the capers of Cupid. This smile belonged to Masie's recreation hours and not to the store; but the floorwalker must have his own. He is the Shylock of the stores. When he comes nosing around the bridge of his nose is a toll-bridge. It is goo-goo eyes or "git" when he looks toward a pretty girl. Of course not all floorwalkers are thus. Only a few days ago the papers printed news of one over eighty years of age.

One day Irving Carter, painter, millionaire, traveller, poet, automobilist, happened to enter the Biggest Store. It is due to him to add that his visit was not voluntary. Filial duty took him by the collar and dragged him inside, while his mother philandered among the bronze and terra-cotta statuettes.

Carter strolled across to the glove counter in order to shoot a few minutes on the wing. His need for gloves was genuine; he had forgotten to bring a pair with him. But his action hardly calls for apology, because he had never heard of glove-counter flirtations.

As he neared the vicinity of his fate he hesitated, suddenly conscious of this unknown phase of Cupid's less worthy profession.

Three or four cheap fellows, sonorously garbed, were leaning over the counters, wrestling with the mediatorial hand-coverings, while giggling girls played vivacious seconds to their lead upon the strident string of coquetry. Carter would have retreated, but he had gone too far. Masie confronted him behind her counter with a questioning look in eyes as coldly, beautifully, warmly blue as the glint of summer sunshine on an iceberg dirfting in Southern seas.

And then Irving Carter, painter, millionaire, etc., felt a warm flush rise to his aristocratically pale face. But not from diffidence. The blush was intellectual in origin. He knew in a moment that he stood in the ranks of the ready-made youths who wooed the giggling girls at other counters. Himself leaned against the oaken trysting place of a cockney Cupid with a desire in his heart for the favor of a glove salesgirl. He was no more than Bill and Jack and Mickey. And then he felt a sudden tolerance for them, and an elating, courageous contempt for the conventions upon which he had fed, and an unhesitating determination to have this perfect creature for his own.

When the gloves were paid for and wrapped Carter lingered for a moment. The dimples at the corners of Masie's damask mouth deepened. All gentlemen who bought gloves lingered in just that way. She curved an arm, showing like Psyche's through her shirtwaist sleeve, and rested an elbow upon the show-case edge.

Carter had never before encountered a situation of which he had not been perfect master. But now he stood far more awkward than Bill or Jack or Mickey. He had no chance of meeting this beautiful girl socially. His mind struggled to recall the nature and habits of shop-girls as he had read or heard of them. Somehow he had received the idea that they sometimes did not insist too strictly upon the regular channels of introduction. His heart beat loudly at the thought of proposing an unconventional meeting with this lovely and virginal being. But the tumult in his heart gave him courage.

After a few friendly and well-received remarks on general subjects, he laid his card by her hand on the counter.

"Will you please pardon me," he said, "if I seem too bold; but I earnestly hope you will allow me the pleasure of seeing you again. There is my name; I assure you that it is with the greatest respect that I ask the favor of becoming one of your fr—— acquaintances. May I not hope for the privilege?"

Masie knew men—especially men who buy gloves. Without hesitation she looked him frankly and smilingly in the eyes, and said:

"Sure. I guess you're right. I don't usually go out with strange gentlemen, though. It ain't quite ladylike. When should you want to see me again?"

"As soon as I may," said Carter. "If you would allow me to call at your home, I——"

Masie laughed musically. "Oh, gee, no!" she said emphatically. "If you could see our flat once! There's five of us in three rooms. I'd just like to see ma's face if I was to bring a gentleman friend there!"

"Anywhere, then," said the enamored Carter, "that will be convenient to you."

"Say," suggested Masie, with a bright-idea look in her peachblow face; "I guess Thursday night will about suit me. Suppose you come to the corner of Eighth Avenue and Forty-eighth Street at 7:30. I live right near the corner. But I've got to be back home by eleven. Ma never lets me stay out after eleven."

Carter promised gratefully to keep the tryst, and then hastened to his mother, who was looking about for him to ratify her purchase of a bronze Diana.

A salesgirl, with small eyes and an obtuse nose, strolled near Masie, with a friendly leer.

"Did you make a hit with his nobs, Masie?" she asked, familiarly.

"The gentleman asked permission to call," answered Masie, with the grand air, as she slipped Carter's card into the bosom of her waist.

"Permission to call!" echoed small eyes, with a snigger. "Did he say anything about dinner in the Waldorf and a spin in his auto afterward?"

"Oh, cheese it!" said Masie, wearily. "You've been used to swell things, I don't think. You've had a swelled head ever since that hose-cart driver took you out to a chop suey joint. No, he never mentioned the Waldorf; but there's a Fifth Avenue address on his card, and if he buys the supper you can bet your life there won't be no pigtail on the waiter what takes the order."

As Carter glided away from the Biggest Store with his mother in his electric runabout, he bit his lip with a dull pain at his heart. He knew that love had come to him for the first time in all the twenty-nine years of his life. And that the object of it should make so readily an appointment with him at a street corner, though it was a step toward his desires, tortured him with misgivings.

Carter did not know the shopgirl. He did not know that her home is often either a scarcely habitable tiny room or a domicile filled to overflowing with kith and kin. The street corner is her parlor, the park is her drawing room; the avenue is her garden walk; yet for the most part she is as inviolate mistress of herself in them as is my lady inside her tapestried chamber.

One evening at dusk, two weeks after their first meeting, Carter and Masie strolled arm-in-arm into a little, dimly-lit park. They found a bench, tree-shadowed and secluded, and sat there.

For the first time his arm stole gently around her. Her golden-bronze head slid restfully against his shoulder.

"Gee!" sighed Masie, thankfully. "Why didn't you ever think of that before?"

"Masie," said Carter, earnestly, "you surely know that I love you. I ask you sincerely to marry me. You know me well enough by this time to have no doubts of me. I want you, and I must have you. I care nothing for the difference in our stations."

"What is the difference?" asked Masie, curiously.

"Well, there isn't any," said Carter, quickly, "except in the minds of foolish people. It is in my power to give you a life of luxury. My social position is beyond dispute, and my means are ample."

"They all say that," remarked Masie. "It's the kid they all give you. I suppose you really work in a delicatessen or follow the races. I ain't as green as I look."

"I can furnish you all the proofs you want," said Carter, gently. "And I want you, Masie. I loved you the first day I saw you."

"They all do," said Masie, with an amused laugh, "to hear 'em talk. If I could meet a man that got stuck on me the third time he'd seen me I think I'd get mashed on him."

"Please don't say such things," pleaded Carter. "Listen to me, dear. Ever since I first looked into your eyes you have been the only woman in the world for me."

"Oh, ain't you the kidder!" smiled Masie. "How many other girls did you ever tell that?"

But Carter persisted. And at length he reached the flimsy, fluttering little soul of the shopgirl that existed somewhere deep down in her lovely bosom. His words penetrated the heart whose very lightness was its safest armor. She looked up at him with eyes that saw. And a warm glow visited her cool cheeks. Tremblingly, awfully, her moth wings closed, and she seemed about to settle upon the flower of love. Some faint glimmer of life and its possibilities on the other side of her glove counter dawned upon her. Carter felt the change and crowded the opportunity.

"Marry me, Masie," he whispered, softly, "and we will go away from this ugly city to beautiful ones. We will forget work and business, and life will be one long holiday. I know where I should take you—I have been there often. Just think of a shore where summer is eternal, where the waves are always rippling on the lovely beach and the people are happy and free as children. We will sail to those shores and remain there as long as you please. In one of those far-away cities there are grand and lovely palaces and towers full of beautiful pictures and statues. The streets of the city are water, and one travels about in——"

"I know," said Masie, sitting up suddenly. "Gondolas."

"Yes," smiled Carter.

"I thought so," said Masie.

"And then," continued Carter, "we will travel on and see whatever we wish in the world. After the European cities we will visit India and the ancient cities there, and ride on elephants and see the wonderful temples of the Hindoos and the Brahmins and the Japanese gardens and the camel trains and chariot races in Persia, and all the queer sights of foreign countries. Don't you think you would like it, Masie?"

Masie rose to her feet.

"I think we had better be going home," she said, coolly. "It's getting late."

Carter humored her. He had come to know her varying, thistle-down moods, and that it was useless to combat them. But he felt a certain happy triumph. He had held for a moment, though but by a silken thread, the soul of his wild Psyche, and hope was stronger within him. Once she had folded her wings and her cool hand had closed about his own.

At the Biggest Store the next day Masie's chum, Lulu, waylaid her in an angle of the counter.

"How are you and your swell friend making it?" she asked.

"Oh, him?" said Masie, patting her side curls. "He ain't in it any more. Say, Lu, what do you think that fellow wanted me to do?"

"Go on the stage?" guessed Lulu, breathlessly.

"Nit; he's too cheap a guy for that. He wanted me to marry him and go down to Coney Island for a wedding tour!"

Transients in Arcadia

There is a hotel on Broadway that has escaped discovery by the summer-resort promoters. It is deep and wide and cool. Its rooms are finished in dark oak of a low temperature. Home-made breezes and deep-green shrubbery give it the delights without the inconveniences of the Adirondacks. One can mount its broad staircases or glide dreamily upward in its aërial elevators, attended by guides in brass buttons, with a serene joy that Alpine climbers have never attained. There is a chef in its kitchen who will prepare for you brook trout better than the White Mountains ever served, sea food that would turn Old Point Comfort—"by Gad, sah!"—green with envy, and Maine venison that would melt the official heart of the game warden.

A few have found out this oasis in the July desert of Manhattan. During that month you will see the hotel's reduced array of guests scattered luxuriously about in the cool twilight of its lofty dining-room, gazing at one another across the snowy waste of unoccupied tables, silently congratulatory.

Superfluous, watchful, pneumatically moving waiters hover near, supplying every want before it is expressed. The temperature is perpetual April. The ceiling is painted in water colors to counterfeit a summer sky across which delicate clouds drift and do not vanish as those of nature do to our regret.

The pleasing, distant roar of Broadway is transformed in the imagination of the happy guests to the noise of a waterfall filling the woods with its restful sound. At every strange footstep the guests turn an anxious ear, fearful lest their retreat be discovered and invaded by the restless pleasure-seekers who are forever hounding Nature to her deepest lairs.

Thus in the depopulated caravansary the little band of connoisseurs jealously hide themselves during the heated season, enjoying to the uttermost the delights of mountain and seashore that art and skill have gathered and served to them.

In this July came to the hotel one whose card that she sent to the clerk for her name to be registered read "Mme. Héloise D'Arcy Beaumont."

Madame Beaumont was a guest such as the Hotel Lotus loved. She possessed the fine air of the élite, tempered and sweetened by a cordial graciousness that made the hotel employés her slaves. Bell-boys fought for the honor of answering her ring; the clerks, but for the question of ownership, would have deeded to her the hotel and its contents; the other guests regarded her as the final touch of feminine exclusiveness and beauty that rendered the entourage perfect.

This super-excellent guest rarely left the hotel. Her habits were consonant with the customs of the discriminating patrons of the Hotel Lotus. To enjoy that delectable hostelry one must forego the city as though it were leagues away. By night a brief excursion to the nearby roofs is in order; but during the torrid day one remains in the umbrageous fastnesses of the Lotus as a trout hangs poised in the pellucid sanctuaries of his favorite pool.

Though alone in the Hotel Lotus, Madame Beaumont preserved the state of a queen whose loneliness was of position only. She breakfasted at ten, a cool, sweet, leisurely, delicate being who glowed softly in the dimness like a jasmine flower in the dusk.

But at dinner was Madame's glory at its height. She wore a gown as beautiful and immaterial as the mist from an unseen cataract in a mountain gorge. The nomenclature of this gown is beyond the guess of the scribe. Always pale-red roses reposed against its lace-garnished front. It was a gown that the head-waiter viewed with respect and met at the door. You thought of Paris when you saw it, and maybe of mysterious countesses, and certainly of Versailles and rapiers and Mrs. Fiske and rouge-et-noir. There was an untraceable rumor in the Hotel Lotus that Madame was a cosmopolite, and that she was pulling with her slender white hands certain strings between the nations in the favor of Russia. Being a citizeness of the world's smoothest roads it was small wonder that she was quick to recognize in the refined purlieus of the Hotel Lotus the most desirable spot in America for a restful sojourn during the heat of midsummer.

On the third day of Madame Beaumont's residence in the hotel a young man entered and registered himself as a guest. His clothing—to speak of his points in approved order—was quietly in the mode; his features good and regular; his expression that of a poised and sophisticated man of the world. He informed the clerk that he would remain three or four days, inquired concerning the sailing of European steamships, and sank into the blissful inanition of the nonpareil hotel with the contented air of a traveller in his favorite inn.

The young man—not to question the veracity of the register—was Harold Farrington. He drifted into the exclusive and calm current of life in the Lotus so tactfully and silently that not a ripple alarmed his fellow-seekers after rest. He ate in the Lotus and of its patronym, and was lulled into blissful peace with the other fortunate mariners. In one day he acquired his table and his waiter and the fear lest the panting chasers after repose that kept Broadway warm should pounce upon and destroy this contiguous but covert haven.

After dinner on the next day after the arrival of Harold Farrington Madame Beaumont dropped her handkerchief in passing out. Mr. Farrington recovered and returned it without the effusiveness of a seeker after acquaintance.

Perhaps there was a mystic freemasonry between the discriminating guests of the Lotus. Perhaps they were drawn one to another by the fact of their common good fortune in discovering the acme of summer resorts in a Broadway hotel. Words delicate in courtesy and tentative in departure from formality passed between the two. And, as if in the expedient atmosphere of a real summer resort, an acquaintance grew, flowered and fructified on the spot as does the mystic plant of the conjuror. For a few moments they stood on a balcony upon which the corridor ended, and tossed the feathery ball of conversation.

"One tires of the old resorts," said Madame Beaumont, with a faint but sweet smile. "What is the use to fly to the mountains or the seashore to escape noise and dust when the very people that make both follow us there?"

"Even on the ocean," remarked Farrington sadly, "the Philistines be upon you. The most exclusive steamers are getting to be scarcely more than ferry boats. Heaven help us when the summer resorter discovers that the Lotus is further away from Broadway than Thousand Islands or Mackinac."

"I hope our secret will be safe for a week, anyhow," said Madame, with a sigh and a smile. "I do not know where I would go if they should descend upon the dear Lotus. I know of but one place so delightful in summer, and that is the castle of Count Polinski, in the Ural Mountains."

"I hear that Baden-Baden and Cannes are almost deserted this season," said Farrington. "Year by year the old resorts fall in disrepute. Perhaps many others, like ourselves, are seeking out the quiet nooks that are overlooked by the majority."

"I promise myself three days more of this delicious rest," said Madame Beaumont. "On Monday the *Cedric* sails."

Harold Farrington's eyes proclaimed his regret. "I too must leave on Monday," he said, "but I do not go abroad."

Madame Beaumont shrugged one round shoulder in a foreign gesture.

"One cannot hide here forever, charming though it may be. The château has been in preparation for me longer than a month. Those house parties that one must give—what a nuisance! But I shall never forget my week in the Hotel Lotus."

"Nor shall I," said Farrington in a low voice, "and I shall never *forgive* the *Cedric.*"

On Sunday evening, three days afterward, the two sat at a little table on the same balcony. A discreet waiter brought ices and small glasses of claret cup.

Madame Beaumont wore the same beautiful evening gown that she had worn each day at dinner. She seemed thoughtful. Near her hand on the table lay a small chatelaine purse. After she had eaten her ice she opened the purse and took out a one-dollar bill.

"Mr. Farrington," she said, with the smile that had won the Hotel Lotus, "I want to tell you something. I'm going to leave before breakfast in the morning, because I've got to go back to my work. I'm behind the hosiery counter at Casey's Mammoth Store, and my vacation's up at eight o'clock to-morrow. That paper dollar is the last cent I'll see till I draw my eight dollars salary next Saturday night. You're a real gentleman, and you've been good to me, and I wanted to tell you before I went.

"I've been saving up out of my wages for a year just for this vacation. I wanted to spend one week like a lady if I never do another one. I wanted to get up when I please instead of having to crawl out at seven every morning; and I wanted to live on the best and be waited on and ring bells for things just like rich folks do. Now I've done it, and I've had the happiest time I ever expect to have in my life. I'm going back to my work and my little hall bedroom satisfied for another year. I wanted to tell you about it, Mr. Farrington, because I—I thought you kind of liked me, and I—I liked you. But, oh, I couldn't help deceiving you up till now, for it was all just like a fairy tale to me. So I talked about Europe and the things I've read about in other countries, and made you think I was a great lady.

"This dress I've got on—it's the only one I have that's fit to wear—I bought from O'Dowd & Levinsky on the instalment plan.

"Seventy-five dollars is the price, and it was made to measure. I paid $10 down, and they're to collect $1 a week till it's paid for. That'll be about all I have to say, Mr. Farrington, except that my name is Mamie Siviter instead of Madame Beaumont, and I thank you for your attentions. This dollar will pay the instalment due on the dress to-morrow. I guess I'll go up to my room now."

Harold Farrington listened to the recital of the Lotus's loveliest guest with an impassive countenance. When she had concluded he drew a small book like a checkbook from his coat pocket. He wrote upon a blank form in this with a stub of pencil, tore out the leaf, tossed it over to his companion and took up the paper dollar.

"I've got to go to work, too, in the morning," he said, "and I might as well begin now. There's a receipt for the dollar instalment. I've been a collector for O'Dowd & Levinsky for three years. Funny, ain't it, that you and me both had the same idea about spending our vacation? I've always wanted to put up at a swell hotel, and I saved up out of my twenty per, and did it. Say, Mame, how about a trip to Coney Saturday night on the boat—what?"

The face of the pseudo Madame Héloise D'Arcy Beaumont beamed.

"Oh, you bet I'll go, Mr. Farrington. The store closes at twelve on Saturdays. I guess Coney'll be all right even if we did spend a week with the swells."

Below the balcony the sweltering city growled and buzzed in the July night. Inside the Hotel Lotus the tempered, cool shadows reigned, and the solicitous waiter single-footed near the low windows, ready at a nod to serve Madame and her escort.

At the door of the elevator Farrington took his leave, and Madame Beaumont made her last ascent. But before they reached the noiseless cage he said: "Just forget that 'Harold Farrington,' will you?—McManus is the name—James McManus. Some call me Jimmy."

"Good-night, Jimmy," said Madame.

The Memento

Miss Lynnette D'Armande turned her back on Broadway. This was but tit for tat, because Broadway had often done the same thing to Miss D'Armande. Still, the "tats" seemed to have it, for the ex-leading lady of the "Reaping the Whirlwind" company had everything to ask of Broadway, while there was no vice-versa.

So Miss Lynnette D'Armande turned the back of her chair to her window that overlooked Broadway, and sat down to stitch in time the lisle-thread heel of a black silk stocking. The tumult and glitter of the roaring Broadway beneath her window had no charm for her; what she greatly desired was the stifling air of a dressing-room on that fairyland street and the roar of an audience gathered in that capricious quarter. In the meantime, those stockings must not be neglected. Silk does wear out so, but—after all, isn't it just the only goods there is?

The Hotel Thalia looks on Broadway as Marathon looks on the sea. It stands like a gloomy cliff above the whirlpool where the tides of two great thoroughfares clash. Here the player-bands gather at the end of their wanderings to loosen the buskin and dust the sock. Thick in the streets around it are booking-offices, theatres, agents, schools, and the lobster-palaces to which those thorny paths lead.

Wandering through the eccentric halls of the dim and fusty Thalia, you seem to have found yourself in some great ark or caravan about to sail, or fly, or roll away on wheels. About the house lingers a sense of unrest, of expectation, of transientness, even of anxiety and apprehension. The halls are a labyrinth. Without a guide, you wander like a lost soul in a Sam Lloyd puzzle.

Turning any corner, a dressing-sack or a *cul-de-sac* may bring you up short. You meet alarming tragedians stalking in bath-robes in search of rumored bathrooms. From hundreds of rooms come the buzz of talk, scraps of new and old songs, and the ready laughter of the convened players.

Summer has come; their companies have disbanded, and they take their rest in their favorite caravansary, while they besiege the managers for engagements for the coming season.

At this hour of the afternoon the day's work of tramping the rounds of the agents' offices is over. Past you, as you ramble distractedly through the mossy halls, flit audible visions of houris, with veiled, starry eyes, flying tag-ends of things and a swish of silk, bequeathing to the dull hallways an odor of gaiety and a memory of *frangipanni.* Serious young comedians, with versatile Adam's apples, gather in doorways and talk of Booth. Far-reaching from somewhere comes the smell of ham and red cabbage, and the crash of dishes on the American plan.

The indeterminate hum of life in the Thalia is enlivened by the discreet popping—at reasonable and salubrious intervals—of beer-bottle corks. Thus punctuated, life in the genial hostel scans easily—the comma being the favorite mark, semicolons frowned upon, and periods barred.

Miss D'Armande's room was a small one. There was room for her rocker between the dresser and the wash-stand if it were placed longitudinally. On the dresser were its usual accoutrements, plus the ex-leading lady's collected souvenirs of road engagements and photographs of her dearest and best professional friends.

At one of these photographs she looked twice or thrice as she darned, and smiled friendlily.

"I'd like to know where Lee is just this minute," she said, half-aloud.

If you had been privileged to view the photograph thus flattered, you would have thought at the first glance that you saw the picture of a many-petalled white flower, blown through the air by a storm. But the floral kingdom was not responsible for that swirl of petalous whiteness.

You saw the filmy, brief skirt of Miss Rosalie Ray as she made a complete heels-over-head turn in her wistaria-entwined swing, far out from the stage, high above the heads of the audience. You saw the camera's inadequate representation of the graceful, strong kick, with which she, at this exciting moment, sent flying, high and far, the yellow silk garter that each evening spun from her agile limb and descended upon the delighted audience below.

You saw, too, amid the black-clothed, mainly masculine patrons of select vaudeville a hundred hands raised with the hope of staying the flight of the brilliant aërial token.

Forty weeks of the best circuits this act had brought Miss Rosalie Ray, for each of two years. She did other things during her twelve minutes—a song and dance, imitations of two or three actors who are but imitations of themselves, and a balancing feat with a step-ladder and feather-duster; but when the blossom-decked swing was let down from the flies, and Miss Rosalie sprang smiling into the seat, with the golden circlet conspicuous in the place whence it was soon to slide and become a soaring and coveted guerdon—then it was that the audience rose in its seat as a single man—or presumably so—and indorsed the specialty that made Miss Ray's name a favorite in the booking-offices.

At the end of two years Miss Ray suddenly announced to her dear friend, Miss D'Armande, that she was going to spend the summer at an antediluvian village on the north shore of Long Island, and that the stage would see her no more.

Seventeen minutes after Miss Lynnette D'Armande had expressed her wish to know the whereabouts of her old chum, there were sharp raps at her door.

Doubt not that it was Rosalie Ray. At the shrill command to enter she did so, with something of a tired flutter, and dropped a heavy hand-bag on the floor. Upon my word, it was Rosalie, in a loose, travel-stained automobileless coat, closely tied brown veil with yard-long flying ends, gray walking suit, and tan oxfords with lavender over-gaiters.

When she threw off her veil and hat, you saw a pretty enough face, now flushed and disturbed by some unusual emotion, and restless, large eyes with discontent marring their brightness. A heavy pile of dull auburn hair, hastily put up, was escaping in crinkly, waving strands and curling, small locks from the confining combs and pins.

The meeting of the two was not marked by the effusion vocal, gymnastical, osculatory, and catechetical that distinguishes the greetings of their unprofessional sisters in society. There was a brief clinch, two simultaneous labial dabs, and they stood on the same footing of the old days. Very much like the short salutations of soldiers or of travellers in foreign wilds are the welcomes between the strollers at the corners of their criss-cross roads.

"I've got the hall-room two flights up above yours," said Rosalie, "but I came straight to see you before going up. I didn't know you were here till they told me."

"I've been in since the last of April," said Lynnette. "And I'm going on the road with a 'Fatal Inheritance' Company. We open next week in Elizabeth. I thought you'd quit the stage, Lee. Tell me about yourself."

Rosalie settled herself with a skilful wriggle on the top of Miss D'Armande's wardrobe trunk, and leaned her head against the papered wall. From long habit, thus can peripatetic leading ladies and their sisters make themselves as comfortable as though the deepest armchairs embraced them.

"I'm going to tell you, Lynn," she said, with a strangely sardonic and yet carelessly resigned look on her youthful face. "And then tomorrow I'll strike the old Broadway trail again, and wear some more paint off the chairs in the agents' offices. If anybody had told me any time in the last three months up to four o'clock this afternoon that I'd ever listen to that 'Leave-your-name-and-address' rot of the booking bunch again, I'd have given 'em the real Mrs. Fiske laugh. Loan me a handkerchief, Lynn. Gee! but those Long Island trains are fierce. I've got enough soft-coal cinders on my face to go on and play *Topsy* without using the cork. And, speaking of corks—got anything to drink, Lynn?"

Miss D'Armande opened a door of the washstand and took out a bottle.

"There's nearly a pint of Manhattan. There's a cluster of carnations in the drinking glass, but——"

"Oh, pass the bottle. Save the glass for company. Thanks! That hits the spot. The same to you. My first drink in three months!

"Yes, Lynn, I quit the stage at the end of last season. I quit it because I was sick of the life. And especially because my heart and soul were sick of men—of the kind of men we stage people have to be up against. You know what the game is to us—it's a fight against 'em all the way down the line from the manager who wants us to try his new motor-car to the bill-poster who want to call us by our front names.

"And the men we have to meet after the show are the worst of all. The stage-door kind, and the manager's friends who take us to supper and show their diamonds and talk about seeing 'Dan' and 'Dave' and 'Charlie' for us. They're beasts, and I hate 'em.

"I tell you, Lynn, it's the girls like us on the stage that ought to be pitied. It's girls from good homes that are honestly ambitious and work hard to rise in the profession, but never do get there. You hear a lot of sympathy sloshed around on chorus girls and their fifteen dollars a week. Piffle! There ain't a sorrow in the chorus that a lobster cannot heal.

"If there's any tears to shed, let 'em fall for the actress that gets a salary of from thirty to forty-five dollars a week for taking a leading part in a bum show. She knows she'll never do any better; but she hangs on for years, hoping for the 'chance' that never comes.

"And the fool plays we have to work in! Having another girl roll you around the stage by the hind legs in a 'Wheelbarrow Chorus' in a musical comedy is dignified drama compared with the idiotic things I've had to do in the thirty-centers.

"But what I hated most was the men—the men leering and blathering at you across tables, trying to buy you with Würzburger or Extra Dry, according to their estimate of your price. And the men in the audiences, clapping, yelling, snarling, crowding, writhing, gloating—like a lot of wild beasts, with their eyes fixed on you, ready to eat you up if you come in reach of their claws. Oh, how I hate 'em!

"Well, I'm not telling you much about myself, am I, Lynn?

"I had two hundred dollars saved up, and I cut the stage the first of the summer. I went over on Long Island and found the sweetest little village that ever was, called Soundport, right on the water. I was going to spend the summer there, and study up on elocution, and try to get a class in the fall. There was an old widow lady with a cottage near the beach who sometimes rented a room or two just for company, and she took me in. She had another boarder, too—the Reverend Arthur Lyle.

"Yes, he was the head-liner. You're on, Lynn. I'll tell you all of it in a minute. It's only a one-act play.

"The first time he walked on, Lynn, I felt myself going; the first lines he spoke, he had me. He was different from the men in audiences. He was tall and slim, and you never heard him come in the room, but you *felt* him. He had a face like a picture of a knight—like one of that Round Table bunch—and a voice like a 'cello solo. And his manners!

"Lynn, if you'd take John Drew in his best drawing-room scene and compare the two, you'd have John arrested for disturbing the peace.

"I'll spare you the particulars; but in less than month Arthur and I were engaged. He preached at a little one-night stand of a Methodist church. There was to be a parsonage the size of a lunch-wagon, and hens and honeysuckles when we were married. Arthur used to preach to me a good deal about Heaven, but he never could get my mind quite off those honeysuckles and hens.

"No; I didn't tell him I'd been on the stage. I hated the business and all that went with it; I'd cut it out forever, and I didn't see any use of stirring things up. I was a good girl, and I didn't have anything to confess, except being an elocutionist, and that was about all the strain my conscience would stand.

"Oh, I tell you, Lynn, I was happy. I sang in the choir and attended the sewing society, and recited that 'Annie Laurie' thing with the whistling stunt in it, 'in a manner bordering upon the professional,' as the weekly village paper reported it. And Arthur and I went rowing, and walking in the woods, and clamming, and that poky little village seemed to me the best place in the world. I'd have been happy to live there always, too, if——

"But one morning old Mrs. Gurley, the widow lady, got gossipy while I was helping her string beans on the back porch, and began to gush information, as folks who rent out their rooms usually do. Mr.

Lyle was her idea of a saint on her earth—as he was mine, too. She went over all his virtues and graces, and wound up by telling me that Arthur had had an extremely romantic love-affair, not long before, that had ended unhappily. She didn't seem to be on to the details, but she knew that he had been hit pretty hard. He was paler and thinner, she said, and he had some kind of a remembrance or keepsake of the lady in a little rosewood box that he kept locked in his desk drawer in his study.

" 'Several times,' says she, 'I've seen him gloomerin' over that box of evenings, and he always locks it up right away if anybody comes into the room.'

"Well, you can imagine how long it was before I got Arthur by the wrist and led him down stage and hissed in his ear.

"That same afternoon we were lazying around in a boat among the waterlilies at the edge of the bay.

" 'Arthur,' says I, 'you never told me you'd had another love-affair. But Mrs. Gurley did,' I went on, to let him know I knew. I hate to hear a man lie.

" 'Before you came,' says he, looking me frankly in the eye, 'there was a previous affection—a strong one. Since you know of it, I will be perfectly candid with you.'

" 'I am waiting,' says I.

" 'My dear Ida,' says Arthur—of course I went by my real name, while I was in Soundport—'this former affection was a spiritual one, in fact. Although the lady aroused my deepest sentiments, and was, as I thought, my ideal woman, I never met her, and never spoke to her. It was an ideal love. My love for you, while no less ideal, is different. You wouldn't let that come between us.'

" 'Was she pretty?' I asked.

" 'She was very beautiful,' said Arthur.

" 'Did you see her often?' I asked.

" 'Something like a dozen times,' says he.

" 'Always from a distance?' says I.

" 'Always from quite a distance,' says he.

" 'And you loved her?' I asked.

" 'She seemed my ideal of beauty and grace—and soul,' says Arthur.

" 'And this keepsake that you keep under lock and key, and moon over at times, is that a remembrance from her?'

" 'A memento,' says Arthur, 'that I have treasured.'

" 'Did she send it to you?'

" 'It came from her,' says he.

" 'In a roundabout way?' I asked.

" 'Somewhat roundabout,' says he, 'and yet rather direct.'

" 'Why didn't you ever meet her?' I asked. 'Were your positions in life so different?'

" 'She was far above me,' says Arthur. 'Now, Ida,' he goes on, 'this is all of the past. You're not going to be jealous, are you?'

" 'Jealous!' says I. 'Why, man, what are you talking about? It makes me think ten times as much of you as I did before I knew about it.'

"And it did, Lynn—if you can understand it. That ideal love was a new one on me, but it struck me as being the most beautiful and glorious thing I'd ever heard of. Think of a man loving a woman he'd never even spoken to, and being faithful just to what his mind and heart pictured her! Oh, it sounded great to me. The men I'd always known come at you with either diamonds, knock-out drops, or a raise of salary—and their ideals!—well, we'll say no more.

"Yes, it made me think more of Arthur than I did before. I couldn't be jealous of that far-away divinity that he used to worship, for I was going to have him myself. And I began to look upon him as a saint on earth, just as old lady Gurley did.

"About four o'clock this afternoon a man came to the house for Arthur to go and see somebody that was sick among his church bunch. Old lady Gurley was taking her afternoon snore on the couch, so that left me pretty much alone.

"In passing by Arthur's study I looked in, and saw his bunch of keys hanging in the drawer of his desk, where he'd forgotten 'em. Well, I guess we're all to the Mrs. Bluebeard now and then, ain't we, Lynn? I made up my mind I'd have a look at that memento he kept so secret. Not that I cared what it was—it was just curiosity.

"While I was opening the drawer I imagined one or two things it might be. I thought it might be a dried rosebud she'd dropped down to him from a balcony, or maybe a picture of her he'd cut out of a magazine, she being so high up in the world.

"I opened the drawer, and there was the rosewood casket about the size of a gent's collar box. I found the little key in the bunch that fitted it, and raised the lid.

"I took one look at that memento, and then I went to my room and packed my trunk. I threw a few things into my grip, gave my hair a flirt or two with a side-comb, put on my hat, and went in and gave the old lady's foot a kick. I'd tried awfully hard to use proper and correct language while I was there for Arthur's sake, and I had the habit down pat, but it left me then.

" 'Stop sawing gourds,' says I, 'and sit up and take notice. The ghost's about to walk. I'm going away from here, and I owe you eight dollars. The expressman will call for my trunk.'

"I handed her the money.

" 'Dear me, Miss Crosby!' said she. 'Is anything wrong? I thought you were pleased here. Dear me, young women are so hard to understand, and so different from what you expect 'em to be.'

" 'You're damn right,' says I. 'Some of 'em are. But you can't say that about men. *When you know one man you know 'em all!* That settles the human race question.'

"And then I caught the four-thirty-eight, soft-coal unlimited; and here I am."

"You didn't tell me what was in that box, Lee," said Miss D'Armande, anxiously.

"One of those yellow silk garters that I used to kick off my leg into the audience during that old vaudeville swing act of mine. Is there any of the cocktail left, Lynn?"

From THE GENTLE GRAFTER 1908

Modern Rural Sports

Jeff Peters must be reminded. Whenever he is called upon, pointedly, for a story, he will maintain that his life has been as devoid of incident as the longest of Trollope's novels. But lured, he will divulge. Therefore I cast many and divers flies upon the current of his thoughts before I feel a nibble.

"I notice," says I, "that the Western farmers, in spite of their prosperity, are running after their old populistic idols again."

"It's the running season," said Jeff, "for farmers, shad, maple trees and the Connemaugh River. I know something about farmers. I thought I struck one once that had got out of the rut; but Andy Tucker proved to me I was mistaken. 'Once a farmer, always a sucker,' said Andy. 'He's the man that's shoved into the front row among bullets, ballots and the ballet. He's the funny-bone and gristle of the country,' said Andy, 'and I don't know who we would do without him.'

"One morning me and Andy wakes up with sixty-eight cents between us in a yellow pine hotel on the edge of the predigested hoecake belt of Southern Indiana. How we got off the train there the night before I can't tell you; for she went through the village so fast that what looked like a saloon to us through the car window turned out to be a composite view of a drug store and a water tank two blocks apart. Why we got off at the first station we could, belongs to a little oroide gold watch and Alaska diamond deal we failed to pull off the day before, over the Kentucky line.

"When I woke up I heard roosters crowing, and smelt something like the fumes of nitro-muriatic acid and heard something heavy fall on the floor below us, and a man swearing.

" 'Cheer up, Andy,' says I. 'We're in a rural community. Somebody has just tested a gold brick downstairs. We'll go out and get what's coming to us from a farmer; and then yoicks! and away.'

"Farmers was always a kind of reserve fund to me. Whenever I was in hard luck I'd go to the crossroads, hook a finger in a farmer's suspender, recite the prospectus of my swindle in a mechanical kind of a way, look over what he had, give him back his keys, whetstone, and papers that was of no value except to owner, and stroll away without asking any questions. Farmers are not fair game to me as high up in our business as me and Andy was; but there was times when we found 'em useful just as Wall Street does the Secretary of the Treasury now and then.

"When we went downstairs we saw we was in the midst of the finest farming section we ever see. About two miles away on a hill was a big white house in a grove surrounded by a widespread agricultural agglomeration of fields and barns and pastures and outhouses.

" 'Whose house is that?' we asked the landlord.

" 'That,' says he, 'is the domicile and the arboreal, terrestrial and horticultural accessories of Farmer Ezra Plunkett, one of our county's most progressive citizens.'

"After breakfast me and Andy, with eight cents capital left, casts the horoscope of the rural potentate.

" 'Let me go alone,' says I. 'Two of us against one farmer would look as onesided as Roosevelt using both hands to kill a grizzly.'

" 'All right,' says Andy. 'I like to be a true sport even when I'm only collecting rebates from the rutabag raisers. What bait are you going to use for this Ezra thing?' Andy asks me.

" 'Oh,' says I, 'the first thing that come to hand in the suit case. I reckon I'll take along some of the new income tax receipts; and the recipe for making clover honey out of clabber and apple peelings; and the order blanks for the McGuffey's readers, which afterwards turn out to be McCormick reapers; and the pearl necklace found on the train; and a pocket-size goldbrick; and a——"

" 'That'll be enough,' says Andy. 'Any one of the lot ought to land on Ezra. And, say, Jeff, make that succotash fancier give you nice, clean, new bills. It's a disgrace to our Department of Agriculture, Civil Service and Pure Food Law the kind of stuff some of these farmers hand out to us. I've had to take rolls from 'em that looked like bundles of microbe cultures captured out of a Red Cross ambulance.'

"So, I goes to a livery stable and hires a buggy on my looks. I drove out to the Plunkett farm and hitched. There was a man sitting on the front steps of the house. He had on a white flannel suit, a diamond ring, golf cap and a pink ascot tie. 'Summer boarder,' says I to myself.

" 'I'd like to see Farmer Ezra Plunkett,' says I to him.

" 'You see him,' says he. 'What seems to be on your mind?'

"I never answered a word. I stood still, repeating to myself the rollicking lines of that merry jingle, 'The Man with the Hoe.' When I looked at this farmer, the little devices I had in my pocket for buncoing the pushed-back brows seemed as hopeless as trying to shake down the Beef Trust with a mittimus and a parlor rifle.

" 'Well,' says he, looking at me close, 'speak up. I see the left pocket of your coat sags a good deal. Out with the goldbrick first. I'm rather more interested in the bricks than I am in the trick sixty-day notes and the lost silver mine story.'

"I had a kind of cerebral sensation of foolishness in my ideas of ratiocination; but I pulled out the little brick and unwrapped my handkerchief off it.

" 'One dollar and eighty cents,' says the farmer, hefting it in his hand. 'Is it a trade?'

" 'The lead in it is worth more than that,' says I, dignified. I put it back in my pocket.

" 'All right,' says he. 'But I sort of wanted it for the collection I'm starting. I got a $5,000 one last week for $2.10.'

"Just then a telephone bell rings in the house.

" 'Come in, Bunk,' says the farmer, 'and look at my place. It's kind of lonesome here sometimes. I think that's New York calling.'

"We went inside. The room looked like a Broadway stockbroker's—light-oak desks, two 'phones, Spanish leather upholstered chairs and couches, oil paintings in gilt frames a foot deep and a ticker hitting off the news in one corner.

" 'Hello, hello!' says the funny farmer. 'Is that the Regent Theatre? Yes; this is Plunkett, of Woodbine Centre. Reserve four orchestra seats for Friday evening—my usual ones. Yes; Friday—good-bye.'

" 'I run over to New York every two weeks to see a show,' says the farmer, hanging up the receiver. 'I catch the eighteen-hour flyer at Indianapolis, spend ten hours in the heyday of night on the Yappian Way, and get home in time to see the chickens go to roost forty-eight hours later. Oh, the pristine Hubbard squasherino of the cave-dwelling period is getting geared up some for the annual meeting of the Don't-Blow-Out-the-Gas Association, don't you think, Mr. Bunk?'

" 'I seem to perceive,' says I, 'a kind of hiatus in the agrarian traditions in which, heretofore, I have reposed confidence.'

" 'Sure, Bunk,' says he. 'The yellow primrose on the river's brim is getting to look to us Reubs like a holiday edition de luxe of the Language of Flowers with deckle edges and frontispiece.'

"Just then the telephone calls him again.

" 'Hello, hello!' says he. 'Oh, that's Perkins, at Milldale. I told you $800 was too much for that horse. Have you got him there? Good. Let me see him. Get away from the transmitter. Now make him trot in a circle. Faster. Yes, I can hear him. Keep on—faster yet. . . . That'll do. Now lead him up to the phone. Closer. Get his nose nearer. There. Now wait. No; I don't want that horse. What? No; not at any price. He interferes; and he's windbroken. Good-bye.'

" 'Now, Bunk,' says the farmer, 'do you begin to realize that agriculture has had a hair cut? You belong in a bygone era. Why, Tom Lawson himself knows better than to try to catch an up-to-date agriculturist napping. It's Saturday, the Fourteenth, on the farm, you bet. Now, look here, and see how we keep up with the day's doings.'

"He shows me a machine on a table with two things for your cars like the penny-in-the-slot affairs. I puts it on and listens. A female voice starts up reading headlines of murders, accidents, and other political casualties.

" 'What you hear,' says the farmer, 'is a synopsis of to-day's news in the New York, Chicago, St. Louis and San Francisco papers. It is wired in to our Rural News Bureau and served hot to subscribers. On this table you see the principal dailies and weeklies of the country. Also a special service of advance sheets of the monthly magazines.'

"I picks up one sheet and sees that it's headed: 'Special Advance Proofs. In July, 1909, the *Century* will say'—and so forth.

"The farmer rings up somebody—his manager, I reckon—and tells him to let that herd of 15 Jerseys go at $600 a head; and to sow the 900-acre field in wheat: and to have 200 extra cans ready at the station for the milk trolley car. Then he passes the Henry Clays and sets out a bottle of green chartreuse, and goes over and looks at the ticker tape.

" 'Consolidated Gas up two points,' says he. 'Oh, very well.'

" 'Ever monkey with copper?' I asks.

" 'Stand back!' says he, raising his hand, 'or I'll call the dog. I told you not to waste your time.'

"After a while he says: 'Bunk, if you don't mind my telling you, your company begins to cloy slightly. I've got to write an article on the Chimera of Communism for a magazine, and attend a meeting of the Race Track Association this afternoon. Of course you understand by now that you can't get my proxy for your Remedy, whatever it may be.'

"Well, sir, all I could think of to do was to go out and get in the buggy. The horse turned round and took me back to the hotel. I hitched him and went in to see Andy. In his room I told him about this farmer, word for word; and I sat picking at the table cover like one bereft of sagaciousness.

" 'I don't understand it,' say I, humming a sad and foolish little song to cover my humiliation.

"Andy walks up and down the room for a long time, biting the left end of his mustache as he does when in the act of thinking.

" 'Jeff,' says he, finally, 'I believe your story of this expurgated rustic; but I am not convinced. It looks incredulous to me that he could not have inoculated himself against all the preordained systems of bucolic bunco. Now, you never regarded me as a man of special religious proclivities, did you, Jeff?' says Andy.

" 'Well,' says I, 'No. But,' says I, not to wound his feelings, 'I have also observed many church members whose said proclivities were not so outwardly developed that they would show on a white handkerchief if you rubbed 'em with it.'

" 'I have always been a deep student of nature from creation down,' says Andy, 'and I believe in an ultimatum design of Providence. Farmers was made for a purpose; and that was to furnish a livelihood to men like me and you. Else why was we given brains? It is my belief that the manna that the Israelites lived on for forty years in the wilderness was only a figurative word for farmers; and they kept up the practice to this day. And now,' says Andy, 'I am going to test my theory "Once a farmer, always a come-on," in spite of the veneering and the orifices that a spurious civilization has brought to him.'

" 'You'll fail, same as I did,' says I. 'This one's shook off the shackles of the sheep-fold. He's entrenched behind the advantages of electricity, education, literature and intelligence.'

" 'I'll try,' said Andy. 'There are certain Laws of Nature that Free Rural Delivery can't overcome.'

"Andy fumbles around awhile in the closet and comes out dressed in a suit with brown and yellow checks as big as your hand. His vest is red with blue dots, and he wears a high silk hat. I noticed he'd soaked his sandy mustache in a kind of blue ink.

" 'Great Barnums?' says I. 'You're a ringer for a circus thimblerig man.'

" 'Right,' says Andy. 'Is the buggy outside? Wait here till I come back. I won't be long.'

"Two hours afterwards Andy steps in the room and lays a wad of money on the table.

" 'Eight hundred and sixty dollars,' says he. 'Let me tell you. He was in. He looked me over and began to guy me. I didn't say a word, but got out the walnut shells and began to roll the little ball on the table. I whistled a tune or two, and then I started up the old formula.

" 'Step up lively, gentleman,' says I, 'and watch the little ball. It costs you nothing to look. There you see it, and there you don't.

Guess where the little joker is. The quickness of the hand deceives the eye.'

" 'I steals a look at the farmer man. I see the sweat coming out on his forehead. He goes over and closes the front door and watches me some more. Directly he says: "I'll bet you twenty I can pick the shell the ball's under now."

" 'After that,' goes on Andy, 'there is nothing new to relate. He only had $860 in cash in the house. When I left he followed me to the gate. There was tears in his eyes when he shook hands.

" ' "Bunk," ' says he, ' "thank you for the only real pleasure I've had in years. It brings up happy old days when I was only a farmer and not an agriculturist. God bless you." ' "

Here Jeff Peters ceased, and I inferred that his story was done.

"Then you think——" I began.

"Yes," said Jeff. "Something like that. You let the farmers go ahead and amuse themselves with politics. Farming's a lonesome life; and they've been against the shell game before."

The Hand That Riles the World

"Many of our great men," said I (apropos of many things), "have declared that they owe their success to the aid and encouragement of some brilliant woman."

"I know," said Jeff Peters. "I've read in history and mythology about Joan or Arc and Mme. Yale and Mrs. Caudle and Eve and other noted females of the past. But, in my opinion, the woman of to-day is of little use in politics or business. What's she best in, anyway?—men make the best cooks, milliners, nurses, housekeepers, stenographers, clerks, hairdressers and launderers. About the only job left that a woman can beat a man in is female inpersonator in vaudeville."

"I would have thought," said I, "that occasionally, anyhow, you would have found the wit and intuition of woman valuable to you in your lines of-er-business."

"Now, wouldn't you," said Jeff, with an emphatic nod—"wouldn't you have imagined that? But a woman is an absolutely unreliable partner in any straight swindle. She's liable to turn honest on you when you are depending upon her most. I tried 'em once."

"Bill Humble, an old friend of mine in the Territories, conceived the illusion that he wanted to be appointed United States Marshal. At that time me and Andy was doing a square, legitimate business of selling walking canes. If you unscrewed the head of one and turned it up to your mouth a half pint of good rye whiskey would go trickling down your throat to reward you for your act of intelligence. The deputies was annoying me and Andy some, and when Bill spoke to me about his officious aspirations, I saw how the appointment as Marshal might help along the firm of Peters & Tucker.

" 'Jeff,' says Bill to me, 'you are a man of learning and education, besides having knowledge and information concerning not only rudiments but facts and attainments.'

" 'I do,' says I, 'and I have never regretted it. I am not one,' says I, 'who would cheapen education by making it free. Tell me,' says I, 'which is of the most value to mankind, literature or horse racing?'

" 'Why—er—, playing the po—I mean, of course, the poets and the great writers have got the call, of course,' says Bill.

" 'Exactly,' says I. 'Then why do the master minds of finance philanthropy,' says I, 'charge us $2 to get into a race-track and let us into a library free? Is that distilling into the masses,' says I, 'a correct estimate of the relative value of the two means of self-culture and disorder?'

" 'You are arguing outside of my faculties of sense and rhetoric,' says Bill. 'What I wanted you to do is to go to Washington and dig out this appointment for me. I haven't no ideas of cultivation and intrigue. I'm a plain citizen and I need the job. I've killed seven men,' says Bill; 'I've got nine children; I've been a good Republican ever since the first of May; I can't read nor write, and I see no reason why I ain't illegible for the office. And I think your partner, Mr. Tucker,' goes on Bill, 'is also a man of sufficient ingratiation and connected system of mental delinquency to assist you in securing the appointment. I will give you preliminary,' says Bill, '$1,000 for drinks, bribes and carfare in Washington. If you land the job I will pay you $1,000 more, cash down, and guarantee you impunity in boot-legging whiskey for twelve months. Are you patriotic to the West enough to help me put this thing through the White-washed Wigwam of the Great Father of the most eastern flag station of the Pennsylvania Railroad?' says Bill.

"Well, I talked to Andy about it, and he liked the idea immense. Andy was a man of an involved nature. He was never content to plod along, as I was, selling to the peasantry some little tool like a combination steak beater, shoe horn, marcel waver, monkey wrench, nail file, potato masher and Multum in Parvo tuning fork. Andy had the artistic temper, which is not to be judged as a preacher's or a moral man's is by purely commercial deflections. So we accepted Bill's offer, and strikes out for Washington.

"Says I to Andy, when we get located at a hotel on South Dakota Avenue, G.S.S.W. 'Now Andy, for the first time in our lives we've got to do a real dishonest act. Lobbying is something we've never been used to; but we've got to scandalize ourselves for Bill Humble's sake. In a straight and legitimate business,' says I, 'we could afford to introduce a little foul play and chicanery, but in a disorderly and heinous piece of malpractice like this it seems to me that the straightforward and aboveboard way is the best. I propose,' says I, 'that we hand over $500 of this money to the chairman of the national campaign committee, get a receipt, lay the receipt on the President's desk and tell him about Bill. The President is a man who would appreciate a candidate who went about getting office that way instead of pulling wires.

"Andy agreed with me, but after we talked the scheme over with the hotel clerk we give that plan up. He told us that there was only one way to get an appointment in Washington, and that was through a lady lobbyist. He gave us the address of one he recommended, a Mrs. Avery, who he said was high up in sociable and diplomatic rings and circles.

"The next morning at 10 o'clock me and Andy called at her hotel, and was shown up to her reception room.

"This Mrs. Avery was a solace and a balm to the eyesight. She had hair the color of the back of a twenty-dollar gold certificate, blue eyes and a system of beauty that would make the girl on the cover of a July magazine look like a cook on a Monongahela coal barge.

"She had on a low necked dress covered with silver spangles, and diamond rings and ear bobs. Her arms was bare; and she was using a desk telephone with one hand, and drinking tea with the other.

" 'Well, boys,' says she after a bit, 'what is it?'

"I told her in as few words as possible what we wanted for Bill, and the price we could pay.

" 'Those western appointments,' says she, 'are easy. Le'me see, now,' says she, 'who could put that through for us. No use fooling with Territorial delegates. I guess,' says she, 'that Senator Sniper would be about the man. He's from somewheres in the West. Let's see how he stands on my private menu card.' She takes some papers out of a pigeonhole with the letter 'S' over it.

" 'Yes,' says she, 'he's marked with a star; that means "ready to serve." Now, let's see. "Age 55; married twice; Presbyterian, likes blondes, Tolstoi, poker and stewed terrapin; sentimental at third bottle of wine." Yes,' she goes on, 'I am sure I can have your friend, Mr. Bummer, appointed Minister to Brazil.'

" 'Humble,' says I: 'And United States Marshal was the berth.'

" 'Oh, yes,' says Mrs. Avery. 'I have so many deals of this sort I sometimes get them confused. Give me all the memoranda you have of the case, Mr. Peters, and come back in four days. I think it can be arranged by then.'

"So me and Andy goes back to our hotel and waits. Andy walks up and down and chews the left end of his mustache.

" 'A woman of high intellect and perfect beauty is the rare thing, Jeff,' says he.

" 'As rare,' says I, 'as an omelet made from the eggs of the fabulous bird known as the epidermis,' says I.

" 'A woman like that,' says Andy, 'ought to lead a man to the highest positions of opulence and fame.'

" 'I misdoubt,' says I, 'if any woman ever helped a man to secure a job any more than to have his meals ready promptly and spread a report that the other candidate's wife had once been a shoplifter. They are no more adapted for business and politics,' says I, 'than

Algernon Charles Swinburne is to be floor manager at one of Chuck Connor's annual balls. I know,' says I to Andy, 'that sometimes a woman seems to step out into the kalsomine light as the charge d'affaires of her man's political job. But how does it come out? Say, they have a neat little berth somewhere as foreign consul of record to Afghanistan or lockkeeper on the Delaware and Raritan Canal. One day this man finds his wife putting on her overshoes and three months' supply of bird seed into the canary's cage. "Sioux Falls?" he asks with a kind of hopeful look in his eye. "No, Arthur," says she, "Washington. We're wasted here," says she. "You ought to be Toady Extraordinary to the Court of St. Bridget or Head Porter of the Island of Porto Rico. I'm going to see about it."

" 'Then this lady,' I says to Andy, 'moves against the authorities at Washington with her baggage and munitions, consisting of five dozen indiscriminating letters written to her by a member of the Cabinet when she was 15; a letter of introduction from King Leopold to the Smithsonian Institution, and a pink silk costume with canary colored spats.

" 'Well, and then what?' I goes. 'She has the letters printed in the evening papers that match her costume, she lectures at an informal tea given in the palm room of the B. & O. Depot and then calls on the President. The ninth Assistant Secretary of Commerce and Labor, the first aide-de-camp of the Blue Room and an unidentified colored man are waiting there to grasp her by the hands—and feet. They carry her out to S.W.B. street and leave her on a cellar door. That ends it. The next time we hear of her she is writing postal cards to the Chinese Minister asking him to get Arthur a job in a tea store.'

" 'Then,' says Andy, 'you don't think Mrs. Avery will land the Marshalship for Bill?'

" 'I do not, says I. 'I do not wish to be a septic, but I doubt if she can do as well as you and me could have done.'

" 'I don't agree with you,' says Andy. 'I'll bet you she does. I'm proud of having a higher opinion of the talent and the powers of negotiation of ladies.'

"We was back at Mrs. Avery's hotel at the time she appointed. She was looking pretty and fine enough, as far as that went, to make any man let her name every officer in the country. But I hadn't much faith in looks, so I was certainly surprised when she pulls out a document with the great seal of the United States on it, and 'William Henry Humble' in a fine, big hand on the back.

" 'You might have had it the next day, boys,' says Mrs. Avery, smiling. 'I hadn't the slightest trouble in getting it,' says she. 'I just asked for it, that's all. Now, I'd like to talk to you a while,' she goes on, 'but I'm awfully busy, and I know you'll excuse me. I've got an Ambassadorship, two Consulates and a dozen other minor applications to look after. I can hardly find time to sleep at all. You'll give my compliments to Mr. Humble when you get home, of course.'

"Well, I handed her the $500, which she pitched into her desk drawer without counting. I put Bill's appointment in my pocket and me and Andy made our adieus.

"We started back for the Territory the same day. We wired Bill: 'Job landed; get the tall glasses ready,' and we felt pretty good.

"Andy joshed me all the way about how little I knew about women.

" 'All right,' says I. 'I'll admit that she surprised me. But it's the first time I ever knew one of 'em to manipulate a piece of business on time without getting it bungled up in some way,' says I.

"Down about the edge of Arkansas I got out Bill's appointment and looked it over, and then I handed it to Andy to read. Andy read it, but didn't add any remarks to my silence.

"The paper was for Bill, all right, and a genuine document, but it appointed him post-master of Dade City, Fla.

"Me and Andy got off the train at Little Rock and sent Bill's appointment to him by mail. Then we struck northeast toward Lake Superior.

"I never saw Bill Humble after that."

The Exact Science of Matrimony

"As I have told you before," said Jeff Peters, "I never had much confidence in the perfidiousness of woman. As partners or coeducators in the most innocent line of graft they are not trustworthy."

"They deserve the compliment," said I. "I think they are entitled to be called the honest sex."

"Why shouldn't they be?" said Jeff. "They've got the other sex either grafting or working overtime for 'em. They're all right in business until they get their emotions or their hair touched up too much. Then you want to have a flat-footed, heavy-breathing man with sandy whiskers, five kids and a building and loan mortgage ready as an understudy to take her desk. Now there was that widow lady that me and Andy Tucker engaged to help us in that little matrimonial agency scheme we floated out in Cairo.

"When you've got enough advertising capital—say a roll as big as the little end of a wagon tongue—there's money in matrimonial agencies. We had about $6,000 and we expected to double it in two months, which is about as long as a scheme like ours can be carried on without taking out a New Jersey charter.

"We fixed up an advertisement that read about like this:

> "Charming widow, beautiful, home loving, 32 years, possessing $3,000 cash and owning valuable country property, would remarry. Would prefer a poor man with affectionate disposition to one with means, as she realizes that the solid virtues are oftenest to be found in the humble walks of life. No objection to elderly man or one of homely appearance if faithful and true and competent to manage property and invest money with judgment. Address, with particulars.
>
> Lonely,
> Care of Peters & Tucker, agents, Cairo, Ill

" 'So far, so pernicious,' says I, when we had finished the literary concoction. 'And now,' says I, 'where is the lady?'

"Andy gives me one of his looks of calm irritation.

" 'Jeff,' says he, 'I thought you had lost them ideas of realism in your art. Why should there be a lady? When they sell a lot of watered stock on Wall Street would you expect to find a mermaid in it? What has a matrimonial ad got to do with a lady?"

" 'Now listen,' says I. 'You know my rule, Andy, that in all my illegitimate inroads against the legal letter of the law the article sold must be existent, visible, producible. In that way and by a careful study of city ordinances and train schedules I have kept out of all trouble with the police that a five-dollar bill and a cigar could not square. Now, to work this scheme we've got to be able to produce bodily a charming widow or its equivalent with or without the beauty, hereditaments and appurtenances set forth in the catalogue and writ of errors, or hereafter be held by a justice of the peace.'

" 'Well,' says Andy, reconstructing his mind, 'maybe it would be safer in case the post office or the peace commission should try to investigate our agency. But where,' he says, 'could you hope to find a widow who would waste time on a matrimonial scheme that had no matrimony in it?'

"I told Andy that I thought I knew of the exact party. An old friend of mine, Zeke Trotter, who used to draw soda water and teeth in a tent show, had made his wife a widow a year before by drinking some dyspepsia cure of the old doctor's instead of the liniment that he always got boozed up on. I used to stop at their house often, and I thought we could get her to work with us.

" 'Twas only sixty miles to the little town where she lived, so I jumped out on the I.C. and finds her in the same cottage with the same sunflowers and roosters standing on the washtub. Mrs. Trotter fitted our ad first rate except, maybe, for beauty and age and property valuation. But she looked feasible and praiseworthy to the eye, and it was a kindness to Zeke's memory to give her the job.

" 'Is this an honest deal you are putting on, Mr. Peters?' she asks me when I tell her what we want.

" 'Mrs. Trotter?' says I, 'Andy Tucker and me have computed the calculation that 3,000 men in this broad and fair country will endeavor to secure your fair hand and ostensible money and property through our advertisement. Out of that number something like thirty hundred will expect to give you in exchange, if they should win you, the carcass of a lazy and mercenary loafer, a failure in life, a swindler and contemptible fortune seeker.

" 'Me and Andy,' says I, 'propose to teach these preyers upon society a lesson. It was with difficulty,' says I, 'that me and Andy could refrain from forming a corporation under the title of the Great Moral and Millennial Malevolent Matrimonial Agency. Does that satisfy you?'

" 'It does, Mr. Peters,' says she. 'I might have known you

wouldn't have gone into anything that wasn't opprobrious. But what will my duties be? Do I have to reject personally these 3,000 ramscallions you speak of, or can I throw them out in bunches?'

" 'Your job, Mrs. Trotter,' says I, 'will be practically a cynosure. You will live at a quiet hotel and will have no work to do. Andy and I will attend to all the correspondence and business end of it.

" 'Of course,' says I, 'some of the more ardent and impetuous suitors who can raise the railroad fare may come to Cairo to personally press their suit or whatever fraction of a suit they may be wearing. In that case you will be probably put to the inconvenience of kicking them out face to face. We will pay you $25 per week and hotel expenses.'

" 'Give me five minutes,' says Mrs. Trotter, 'to get my powder rag and leave the front door key with a neighbor and you can let my salary begin.'

"So I conveys Mrs. Trotter to Cairo and establishes her in a family hotel far enough away from mine and Andy's quarters to be unsuspicious and available, and I tell Andy.

" 'Great,' says Andy. 'And now that your conscience is appeased as to the tangibility and proximity of the bait, and leaving mutton aside, suppose we revenoo a noo fish.'

"So, we began to insert our advertisement in newspapers covering the country far and wide. One ad was all we used. We couldn't have used more without hiring so many clerks and marcelled paraphernalia that the sound of the gum chewing would have disturbed the postmaster-General.

"We placed $2,000 in a bank to Mrs. Trotter's credit and gave her the book to show in case anybody might question the honesty and good faith of the agency. I knew Mrs. Trotter was square and reliable and it was safe to leave it in her name.

"With that one ad Andy and me put in twelve hours a day answering letters.

"About one hundred a day was what came in. I never knew there was so many large hearted but indigent men in the country who were willing to acquire a charming widow and assume the burden of investing her money.

"Most of them admitted that they ran principally to whiskers and lost jobs and were misunderstood by the world, but all of 'em were sure that they were so chock full of affection and manly qualities that the widow would be making the bargain of her life to get 'em.

"Every applicant got a reply from Peters & Tucker informing him that the widow had been deeply impressed by his straightforward and interesting letter and requesting them to write again stating more particulars; and enclosing photograph if convenient. Peters & Tucker also informed the applicant that their fee for handling over the second letter to their fair client would be $2, enclosed therewith.

"There you see the simple beauty of the scheme. About 90 per-cent of them domestic foreign noblemen raised the price somehow and sent it in. That was all there was to it. Except that me and Andy complained an amount about being put to the trouble of slicing open them envelopes, and taking the money out.

"Some few clients called in person. We sent 'em to Mrs. Trotter and she did the rest; except for three or four who came back to strike us for carfare. After the letters began to get in from the r.f.d. districts Andy and me were taking in about $200 a day.

"One afternoon when we were busiest and I was stuffing the two and ones into cigar boxes and Andy was whistling 'No Wedding Bells for Her' a small, slick man drops in and runs his eye over the walls like he was on the trail of a lost Gainesborough painting or two. As soon as I saw him I felt a glow of pride, because we were running our business on the level.

" 'I see you have quite a large mail to-day,' says the man.

"I reached and got my hat.

" 'Come on,' says I. 'We've been expecting you. I'll show you the goods. How was Teddy when you left Washington?'

"I took him down to the Riverview Hotel and had him shake hands with Mrs. Trotter. Then I showed him her bank book with the $2,000 to her credit.

" 'It seems to be all right,' says the Secret Service.

" 'It is,' says I. 'And if you're not a married man I'll leave you to talk a while with the lady. We won't mention the two dollars.'

" 'Thanks,' says he. 'If I wasn't, I might. Good day, Mr. Peters.'

" 'Toward the end of three months we had taken in something over $5,000, and we saw it was time to quit. We had a good many complaints made to us; and Mrs. Trotter seemed to be tired of the job. A good many suitors had been calling to see her, and she didn't seem to like that.

"So we decides to pull out, and I goes down to Mrs. Trotter's hotel to pay her last week's salary and say farewell and get her check for $2,000.

"When I get there I found her crying like a kid that don't want to go to school.

" 'Now, now,' says I, 'what's it all about? Somebody sassed you or you getting homesick?"

" 'No, Mr. Peters,' says she. 'I'll tell you. You was always a friend of Zeke's, and I don't mind. Mr. Peters, I'm in love. I just love a man so hard I can't bear not to get him. He's just the ideal I've always had in mind.'

" 'Then take him,' says I. 'That is, if it's a mutual case. Does he return the sentiment according to the specifications and painfulness you have described?'

" 'He does,' says she. 'But he's one of the gentlemen that's been coming to see me about the advertisement and he won't marry me unless I give him the $2,000. His name is William Wilkinson.' And then she goes off again in the agitations and hysterics of romance.

" 'Mrs. Trotter,' says I, 'there's no man more sympathizing with a woman's affections than I am. Besides, you was once a life partner of one of my best friends. If it was left to me I'd say take this $2,000 and the man of your choice and be happy.

" 'We could afford to do that, because we have cleaned up over $5,000 from these suckers that wanted to marry you. But,' says I, 'Andy Tucker is to be consulted.

" 'He is a good man, but keen in business. He is my equal partner financially. I will talk to Andy,' says I, 'and see what can be done.'

"I goes back to our hotel and lays the case before Andy.

" 'I was expecting something like this all the time,' says Andy. 'You can't trust a woman to stick by you in any scheme that involves her emotions and preferences.'

" 'It's a sad thing, Andy,' says I, 'to think that we've been the cause of the breaking of a woman's heart.'

" 'It is,' says Andy, 'and I tell you what I'm willing to do, Jeff. You've always been a man of a soft and generous disposition. Perhaps I've been too hard and worldly and suspicious. For once I'll meet you half way. Go to Mrs. Trotter and tell her to draw the $2,000 from the bank and give it to this man she's infatuated with and be happy.'

"I jumps and shakes Andy's hand for five minutes, and then I goes back to Mrs. Trotter and tells her, and she cries as hard for joy as she did for sorrow.

"Two days afterward me and Andy packed to go.

" 'Wouldn't you like to go down and meet Mrs. Trotter once before we leave?' I asks him. 'She'd like mightily to know you and express her encomiums and gratitude.'

" 'Why, I guess not,' says Andy. 'I guess we'd better hurry and catch that train.'

"I was strapping our capital around me in a memory belt like we always carried it, when Andy pulls a roll of large bills out of his pocket and asks me to put 'em with the rest.

" 'What's this?' says I.

" 'It's Mrs. Trotter's two thousand,' says Andy.

" 'How do you come to have it?' I asks.

" 'She gave it to me,' says Andy. 'I've been calling on her three evenings a week for more than a month.'

" 'Then you are William Wilkinson?' says I.

" 'I was,' says Andy."

Shearing the Wolf

Jeff Peters was always eloquent when the ethics of his profession were under discussion.

"The only times," said he, "that me and Andy Tucker ever had any hiatuses in our cordial intents was when we differed on the moral aspects of grafting. Andy had his standards and I had mine. I didn't approve of all of Andy's schemes for levying contributions from the public, and he thought I allowed my conscience to interfere too often for the financial good of the firm. We had high arguments sometimes. Once one word led on to another till he said I reminded him of Rockefeller.

" 'I know how you mean that, Andy,' says I, 'but we have been friends too long for me to take offense, at a taunt that you will regret when you cool off. I have yet,' says I, 'to shake hands with a subpoena server.'

"One summer me and Andy decided to rest up a spell in a fine little town in the mountains of Kentucky called Grassdale. We was supposed to be horse drovers, and good decent citizens besides, taking a summer vacation. The Grassdale people like us, and me and Andy declared a secession of hostilities, never so much as floating the fly leaf of a rubber concession prospectus or flashing a Brazilian diamond while we was there.

"One day the leading hardware merchant of Grassdale drops around to the hotel where me and Andy stopped, and smokes with us, sociable, on the side porch. We knew him pretty well from pitching quoits in the afternoons in the court house yard. He was a loud, red man, breathing hard, but fat and respectable beyond all reason.

"After we talk on all the notorious themes of the day, this Murkison—for such was his entitlements—takes a letter out of his coat pocket in a careful, careless way and hands it to us to read.

" 'Now, what do you think of that?' he says laughing—'a letter like that to ME!'

"Me and Andy sees at a glance what it is; but we pretend to read it through. It was one of them old-time typewritten green goods letters explaining how for $1,000 you could get $5,000 in bills that an expert couldn't tell from the genuine; and going on to tell how they were made from plates stolen by an employee of the Treasury at Washington.

" 'Think of 'em sending a letter like that to ME!' says Murkison again.

" 'Lots of good men get 'em,' says Andy. 'If you don't answer the first letter they let you drop. If you answer it they write again asking you to come on with your money and do business.'

" 'But think of 'em writing to ME!' says Murkison.

"A few days later he drops around again.

" 'Boys,' says he, 'I know you are all right or I wouldn't confide in you. I wrote to them rascals again just for fun. They answered and told me to come on to Chicago. They said telegraph to J. Smith when I would start. When I get there I'm to wait on a certain street corner till a man in a gray suit comes along and drops a newspaper in front of me. Then I am to ask how the water is, and he knows it's me and I know it's him.'

" 'Ah, yes,' says Andy, gaping, 'it's the same old game. I've often read about it in the papers. Then he conducts you to the private abattoir in the hotel, where Mr. Jones is already waiting. They show you brand-new real money and sell you all you want at five to one. You see 'em put it in a satchel for you and know it's there. Of course it's brown paper when you come to look at it afterward.'

" 'Oh, they couldn't switch it on me,' says Murkison. 'I haven't built up the best paying business in Grassdale without having witticisms about me. You say it's real money they show you, Mr. Tucker?'

" 'I've always—I see by the papers that it always is,' says Andy.

" 'Boys,' says Murkison, 'I've got it in my mind that them fellows can't fool me. I think I'll put a couple of thousand in my jeans and go up there and put it all over 'em. If Bill Murkison gets his eyes once on them bills they show him he'll never take 'em off of 'em. They offer $5 for $1, and they'll have to stick to the bargain if I tackle 'em. That's the kind of trader Bill Murkison is. Yes, I jist believe I'll drop up Chicago way and take a 5 to 1 shot on J. Smith. I guess the water'll be fine enough.'

"Me and Andy tries to get this financial misquotation out of Murkison's head, but we might as well have tried to keep the man who rolls peanuts with a toothpick from betting on Bryan's election. No, sir; he was going to perform a public duty by catching these green goods swindlers at their own game. Maybe it would teach 'em a lesson.

"After Murkison left us me and Andy sat a while prepondering over our silent meditations and heresies of reason. In our idle hours we always improved our higher selves my ratiocination and mental thought.

" 'Jeff,' says Andy after a long time, 'quite unseldom I have seen fit to impugn your molars when you have been chewing the rag with me about your conscientious way of doing business. I may have been often wrong. But here is a case where I think we can agree. I feel that it would be wrong for us to allow Mr. Murkison to go alone to meet those Chicago green goods men. There is but one way it can end. Don't you think we would both feel better if we was to intervene in some way and prevent the doing of this deed?'

"I got up and shook Andy Tucker's hand hard and long.

" 'Andy,' says I, 'I may have had one or two hard thoughts about the heartlessness of your corporation, but I retract 'em now. You have a kind nucleus at the interior of your exterior after all. It does you credit. I was just thinking the same thing that you have expressed. It would not be honorable or praiseworthy,' says I, 'for us to let Murkison go on with this project he has taken up. If he is determined to go let us go with him and prevent this swindle from coming off.'

"Andy agreed with me; and I was glad to see that he was in earnest about breaking up this green goods scheme.

" 'I don't call myself a religious man,' says I, 'or a fanatic in moral bigotry, but I can't stand still and see a man who has built up a business by his own efforts and brains and risk be robbed by an unscrupulous trickster who is a menace to the public good.'

" 'Right, Jeff,' says Andy. 'We'll stick right along with Murkison if he insist on going and block this funny business. I'd hate to see any money dropped in it as bad as you would.'

"Well, we went to see Murkison.

" 'No, boys,' says he. 'I can't consent to let the song of this Chicago siren waft by me on the summer breeze. I'll fry some fat out of this ignis fatuus or burn a hole in the skillet. But I'd be plumb diverted to death to have you all go along with me. Maybe you could help some when it comes to cashing in the ticket to that 5 to 1 shot. Yes, I'd really take it as a pastime and regalement if you boys would go along too.'

"Murkison gives it out in Grassdale that he is going for a few days with Mr. Peters and Mr. Tucker to look over some iron ore property in West Virginia. He wires J. Smith that he will set foot in the spider web on a given date; and the three of us lights out for Chicago.

"On the way Murkison amuses himself with premonitions and advance pleasant recollections.

" 'In a gray suit,' says he, 'on the southwest corner of Wabash Avenue and Lake Street. He drops the paper, and I ask how the water is. Oh, my, my, my!' And then he laughs all over for five minutes.

"Sometimes Murkison was serious and tried to talk himself out of his cogitations, whatever they was.

" 'Boys,' says he, 'I wouldn't have this to get out in Grassdale for ten times a thousand dollars. It would ruin me there. But I know you all are all right. I think it's the duty of every citizen,' says he, 'to try to do up these robbers that prey upon the public. I'll show 'em whether the water's fine. Five dollars for one—that's what J. Smith offers, and he'll have to keep his contract if he does business with Bill Murkison.'

"We got into Chicago about 7 P.M. Murkison was to meet the gray man at half-past 9. We had dinner at a hotel and then went up to Murkison's room to wait for the time to come.

" 'Now boys,' says Murkison, 'let's get our gumption together and inoculate a plan for defeating the enemy. Suppose while I'm exchanging airy bandage with the gray capper you gents come along, by accident, you know, and holler: "Hello, Murk!!" and shake hands with symptoms of surprise and familiarity. Then I take the capper aside and tell him you all are Jenkins and Brown of Grassdale, groceries and feed, good men and maybe willing to take a chance while away from home.'

" 'Bring 'em along," he'll say, of course, "if they care to invest." Now, how does that scheme strike you?'

" 'What do you say, Jeff?' says Andy, looking at me.

" 'Why, I'll tell you what I say,' says I. 'I say let's settle this thing right here now. I don't see any use of wasting any more time.' I took a nickel-plated .38 out of my pocket and clicked the cylinder around a few times.

" 'You undevout, sinful, insidious hog,' says I to Murkison, 'get out that two thousand and lay it on the table. Obey with velocity,' says I, 'for otherwise alternatives are impending. I am preferably a man of mildness, but now and then I find myself in the middle of extremities. Such men as you,' I went on after he had laid the money out, 'is what keeps the jails and court houses going. You come up here to rob these men of their money. Does it excuse you?' I asks, 'that they were trying to skin you? No, sir; you was going to rob Peter to stand off Paul. You are ten times worse,' says I, 'than that green goods man. You go to church at home and pretend to be a decent citizen, but you'll come to Chicago and commit larceny from men that have built up a sound and profitable business by dealing with such contemptible scoundrels as you have tried to be to-day. How do you know,' says I, 'that that green goods man hasn't a large family dependent upon his extortions? It's you supposedly respectable citizens who are always on the lookout to get something for nothing,' says I, 'that support the lotteries and wild-cat mines and stock exchanges and wire tappers of this country. If it wasn't for you they'd go out of business. The green goods man you was going to rob,' says I, 'studied maybe for years to learn his trade. Every turn he makes he risks his money and liberty and maybe his life. You come up here all sanctified and vanoplied with respectability and a pleasing post office address to swindle him. If he gets the money you can squeal to the police. If you get it he hocks the gray suit to buy supper and says nothing. Mr. Tucker and me sized you up,' says I, 'and came along to see that you got what you deserved. Hand over the money,' says I, 'you grass-fed hypocrite.'

"I put the two thousand, which was all in $20 bills, in my inside pocket.

" 'Now get out your watch,' says I to Murkison. 'No, I don't want it,' says I. 'Lay it on the table and you sit in that chair till it ticks off an hour. Then you can go. If you make any noise or leave any sooner we'll hand-bill you all over Grassdale. I guess your high position there is worth more than $2,000 to you.'

"Then me and Andy left.

"On the train Andy was a long time silent. Then he says: 'Jeff, do you mind my asking you a question?'

" 'Two,' says I, 'or forty.'

" 'Was that the idea you had,' says he, 'when we started out with Murkison?'

" 'Why certainly,' says I. 'What else could it have been? Wasn't it yours, too?'

"In about half an hour Andy spoke again. I think there are times when Andy don't exactly understand my system of ethics and moral hygiene.

" 'Jeff,' says he, 'some time when you have the leisure I wish you'd draw off a diagram and footnotes of that conscience of yours. I'd like to have it to refer to occasionally.' "

Innocents of Broadway

"I hope some day to retire from business," said Jeff Peters; "and when I do I don't want anybody to be able to say that I ever got a dollar of any man's money without giving him a quid pro rata for it. I've always managed to leave a customer some little gewgaw to paste in his scrapbook or stick between his Seth Thomas clock and the wall after we are through trading.

"There was one time I came near having to break this rule of mine and do a profligate and illaudable action, but I was saved from it by the laws and statutes of our great and profitable country.

"One summer me and Andy Tucker, my partner, went to New York to lay in our annual assortment of clothes and gents' furnishings. We was always pompous and regardless dressers, finding that looks went further than anything else in our business, except maybe our knowledge of railroad schedules and an autograph photo of the President that Loeb sent us, probably by mistake. Andy wrote a nature letter once and sent it in about animals that he had seen caught in a trap lots of times. Loeb must have read it 'triplets,' instead of 'trap lots,' and sent the photo. Anyhow, it was useful to us to show people as a guarantee of good faith.

"Me and Andy never cared much to do business in New York. It was too much like pothunting. Catching suckers in that town, is like dynamiting a Texas lake for bass. All you have to do anywhere between the North and East rivers is to stand in the street with an open bag marked, 'Drop packages of money here. No checks or loose bills taken.' You have a cop handy to club pikers who try to chip in post office orders and Canadian money, and that's all there is to New York for a hunter who loves his profession. So me and Andy used to just nature fake the town. We'd get out our spyglasses and watch the woodcocks along the Broadway swamps putting plaster casts on their broken legs, and then we'd sneak away without firing a shot.

"One day in the papier mâché palm room of a chloral hydrate and hops agency in a side street about eight inches off Broadway me and Andy had thrust upon us the acquaintance of a New Yorker. We had beer together until we discovered that each of us knew a man named Hellsmith, travelling for a stove factory in Duluth. This caused us to remark that the world was a very small place, and then this New Yorker busts his string and takes off his tin foil and excelsior packing and starts in giving us his Ellen Terris, beginning with the time he used to sell shoelaces to the Indians on the spot where Tammany Hall now stands.

"This New Yorker had made his money keeping a cigar store in Beekman Street, and he hadn't been above Fourteenth Street in ten years. Moreover, he had whiskers, and the time has gone by when a true sport will do anything to a man with whiskers. No grafter except a boy who is soliciting subscribers to an illustrated weekly to win the prize air rifle, or a widow, would have the heart to tamper with the man behind with the razor. He was a typical city Reub—I'd bet the man hadn't been out of sight of a skyscraper in twenty-five years.

"Well, presently this metropolitan backwoodsman pulls out a roll of bills with an old blue sleeve elastic fitting tight around it and opens it up.

" 'There's $5,000, Mr. Peters,' says he, shoving it over the table to me, 'saved during my fifteen years of business. Put that in your pocket and keep it for me, Mr. Peters. I'm glad to meet you gentlemen from the West, and I may take a drop too much. I want you to take care of my money for me. Now, let's have another beer.'

" 'You'd better keep this yourself,' says I. 'We are strangers to you, and you can't trust everybody you meet. Put your roll back in your pocket,' says I. 'And you'd better run along home before some farmhand from the Kaw River bottoms strolls in here and sells you a copper mine.'

" 'O, I don't know,' says Whiskers, 'I guess Little Old New York can take care of herself. I guess I know a man that's on the square when I see him. I've always found the Western people all right. I ask you as a favor, Mr. Peters,' says he, 'to keep that roll in your pocket for me. I know a gentleman when I see him. And now let's have some more beer.'

"In about ten minutes this fall of manna leans back in his chair and snores. Andy looks at me and says: 'I reckon I'd better stay with him for five minutes or so, in case the waiter comes in.'

"I went out the side door and walked half a block up the street. And then I came back and sat down at the table.

" 'Andy,' says I, 'I can't do it. It's too much like swearing off taxes. I can't go off with this man's money without doing something to earn it like taking advantage of the Bankrupt act or leaving a bottle of eczema lotion in his pocket to make it look more like a square deal.'

" 'Well,' says Andy, 'it does seem kind of hard on one's professional pride to lope off with a bearded pard's competency, especially after he has nominated you custodian of his bundle in the sappy insouciance of his urban indiscrimination. Suppose we wake him up and see if we can formulate some commercial sophistry by which he will be enabled to give us both his money and a good excuse.'

"We wakes up Whiskers. He stretches himself and yawns out the hypothesis that he must have dropped off for a minute. And then he says he wouldn't mind sitting in at a little gentleman's game of poker. He used to play some when he attended high school in Brooklyn; and as he was out for a good time, why—and so forth.

"Andy brights up a little at that, for it looks like it might be a solution to our financial troubles. So we all three go to our hotel further down Broadway and have the cards and chips brought up to Andy's room. I tried once more to make this Babe in the Horticultural Gardens take his five thousand. But no.

" 'Keep that little roll for me, Mr. Peters,' says he, 'and oblige. I'll ask you fer it when I want it. I guess I know when I'm among friends. A man that's done business on Beekman Street for twenty years, right in the heart of the wisest little old village on earth, ought to know what he's about. I guess I can tell a gentleman from a con man or a flimflammer when I meet him. I've got some odd change, in my clothes—enough to start the game with, I guess.'

"He goes through his pockets and rains $20 gold certificates on the table till it looked like a $10,000 'Autumn Day in a Lemon Grove' picture by Turner in the salons. Andy almost smiled.

"The first round that was dealt, this boulevardier slaps down his hand, claims low and jack and big casino and rakes in the pot.

"Andy always took a pride in his poker playing. He got up from the table and looked sadly out of the window at the street cars.

" 'Well, gentlemen,' says the cigar man, 'I don't blame you for not wanting to play. I've forgotten the fine points of the game, I guess, it's been so long since I indulged. Now, how long are you gentlemen going to be in the city?'

"I told him about a week longer. He says that'll suit him fine. His cousin is coming over from Brooklyn that evening and they are going to see the sights of New York. His cousin, he says, is in the artificial limb and lead casket business, and hasn't crossed the bridge in eight years. They expect to have the time of their lives, and he winds up by asking me to keep his roll of money for him till next day. I tried to make him take it, but it only insulted him to mention it.

" 'I'll use what I've got in loose change,' says he. 'You keep the rest for me. I'll drop in on you and Mr. Tucker to-morrow afternoon about 6 or 7,' says he, 'and we'll have dinner together. Be good.'

"After Whiskers had gone Andy looked at me curious and doubtful.

" 'Well, Jeff,' says he, 'it looks like the ravens are trying to feed us two Elijahs so hard that if we turned 'em down again we ought to have the Audubon society after us. It won't do to put the crown aside too often. I know this is something like paternalism, but don't you think Opportunity has skinned its knuckles about enough knocking at our door?'

"I put my feet on the table and my hands in my pockets, which is an attitude unfavorable to frivolous thoughts.

" 'Andy,' says i, 'this man with the hirsute whiskers has got us in a predicament. We can't move hand or foot with his money. You and me have got a gentleman's agreement with Fortune that we can't break. We've done business in the West where it's more of a fair game. Out there the people we skin are trying to skin us, even the farmers and the remittance men that the magazines send out to write up Goldfields. But there's little sport in New York City for rod, reel or gun. They hunt here with either one of two things—a slungshot or a letter of introduction. The town has been stocked so full of carp that the game fish are all gone. If you spread a net here, do you catch legitimate suckers in it, such as the Lord intended to be caught—fresh guys who know it all, sports with a little coin and the nerve to play another man's game, street crowds out for the fun of dropping a dollar or two and village smarties who know just where the little pea is? No, sir,' says I. 'What the grafters live on here is widows and orphans, and foreigners who save up a bag of money and hand it over the first counter they see with an iron railing to it, and factory girls and little shopkeepers that never leave the block they do business on. That's what they call suckers here. They're nothing but canned sardines, and all the bait you need to catch 'em is a pocket-knife and a soda cracker.

" 'Now, this cigar man,' I went on, 'is one of the types. He's lived twenty years on one street without learning as much as you would in getting a once-over shave from a lockjawed barber in a Kansas cross-roads town. But he's a New Yorker, and he'll brag about that all the time when he isn't picking up live wires or getting in front of street cars or paying out money to wire-tappers or standing under a safe that's being hoisted into a sky-scraper. When a New Yorker does loosen up,' says I, 'it's like the spring decomposition of the ice jam in the Allegheny River. He'll swamp you with cracked ice and back-water if you don't get out of the way.

" 'It's mighty lucky for us, Andy,' says I, 'that this cigar exponent with the parsley dressing saw fit to bedeck us with his childlike trust and altruism. For,' says I, 'this money of his is an eyesore to my sense of rectitude and ethics. We can't take it, Andy; you know we can't,' says I, 'for we haven't a shadow of a title to it—not a shadow. If there was the least bit of a way we could put in a claim to it I'd be willing to see him start in for another twenty years and make another $5,000 for himself, but we haven't sold him anything, we haven't been embroiled in a trade or anything commercial. He approached us friendly,' says I, 'and with blind and beautiful idiocy laid the stuff in our hands. We'll have to give it back to him when he wants it.'

" 'Your arguments,' says Andy, 'are past criticism or comprehension. No, we can't walk off with the money—as things now stand. I admire your conscious way of doing business, Jeff,' says Andy, 'and I wouldn't propose anything that wasn't square in line with your theories of morality and initiative.

" 'But I'll be away to-night and most of to-morrow, Jeff,' says Andy, 'I've got some business affairs that I want to attend to. When this free greenbacks party comes in to-morrow afternoon hold him here till I arrive. We've all got an engagement for dinner, you know.'

"Well, sir, about 5 the next afternoon in trips the cigar man, with his eyes half open.

" 'Been having a glorious time, Mr. Peters,' says he. 'Took in all the sights. I tell you New York is the onliest only. Now if you don't mind,' says he, 'I'll lie down on that couch and doze off for about nine minutes before Mr. Tucker comes. I'm not used to being up all night. And to-morrow, if you don't mind, Mr. Peters, I'll take that five thousand. I met a man last night that's got a sure winner at the race-track to-morrow. Excuse me for being so impolite as to go asleep, Mr. Peters.'

"And so this inhabitant of the second city in the world reposes himself and begins to snore, while I sit there musing over things and wishing I was back in the West, where you could always depend on a customer fighting to keep his money hard enough to let your conscience take it from him.

"At half-past 5 Andy come in and sees the sleeping form.

" 'I've been over to Trenton,' says Andy, pulling a document out of his pocket, 'I think I've got this matter fixed up all right, Jeff. Look at that.'

"I open the paper and see that it is a corporation charter issued by the State of New Jersey to 'The Peters & Tucker Consolidated and Amalgamated Aërial Franchise Development Company, Limited.'

" 'It's to buy up rights of way for airship lines,' explained Andy.

'The Legislature wasn't in session, but I found a man at a postcard stand in the lobby that kept a stock of charters on hand. There are 100,000 shares,' says Andy, 'expected to reach a par value of $1. I had one blank certificate of stock printed.'

"Andy takes out the blank and begins to fill it in with a fountain pen.

" 'The whole bunch,' says he, 'goes to our friend in dreamland for $5,000. Did you learn his name?'

" 'Make it out to bearer,' says I.

"We put the certificate of stock in the cigar man's hand and went out to pack our suit cases.

"On the ferryboat Andy says to me: 'Is your conscience easy about taking the money now, Jeff?'

" 'Why shouldn't it be?' says I. 'Are we any better than any other Holding Corporation?' "

The Discounters of Money

The spectacle of the money-caliphs of the present day going about Bagdad-on-the-Subway trying to relieve the wants of the people is enough to make the great Al Raschid turn Haroun in his grave. If not so, then the assertion should do so, the real caliph having been a wit and a scholar and therefore a hater of puns.

How properly to alleviate the troubles of the poor is one of the greatest troubles of the rich. But one thing agreed upon by all professional philanthropists is that you must never hand over any cash to your subject. The poor are notoriously temperamental; and when they get money they exhibit a strong tendency to spend it for stuffed olives and enlarged crayon portraits instead of giving it to the installment man.

And still, old Haroun had some advantages as an eleemosynarian. He took around with him on his rambles his vizier, Giafar (a vizier is a composite of a chauffeur, a secretary of state, and a night-and-day bank), and old Uncle Mesrour, his executioner, who toted a snickersnee. With this entourage a caliphing tour could hardly fail to be successful. Have you noticed lately any newspaper articles headed, "What Shall We Do With Our Ex-Presidents?" Well, now, suppose that Mr. Carnegie should engage *him* and Joe Gans to go about assisting in the distribution of free libraries? Do you suppose any town would have the hardihood to refuse one? That caliphalous combination would cause two libraries to grow where there had been only one set of E. P. Roe's works before.

But, as I said, the money-caliphs are handicapped. They have the idea that earth has no sorrow that dough cannot heal; and they rely upon it solely. Al Raschid administered justice, rewarded the deserving, and punished whomsoever he disliked on the spot. He was the originator of the short-story contest. Whenever he succored any chance pick-up in the bazaars he always made the succoree tell the sad story of his life. If the narrative lacked construction, style, and *esprit* he commanded his vizier to dole him out a couple of thousand ten-dollar notes of the First National Bank of the Bosphorus, or else gave him a soft job as Keeper of the Bird Seed for the Bulbuls in the Imperial Gardens. If the story was a crackerjack, he had Mesrour, the executioner, whack off his head. The report that Haroun Al Raschid is yet alive and is editing the magazine that your grandmother used to subscribe for lacks confirmation.

And now follows the Story of the Millionaire, the Inefficacious Increment, and the Babes Drawn from the Wood.

Young Howard Pilkins, the millionaire, got his money ornithologically. He was a shrewd judge of storks, and got in on the ground floor at the residence of his immediate ancestors, the Pilkins Brewing Company. For his mother was a partner in the business. Finally old man Pilkins died from a torpid liver, and then Mrs. Pilkins died from worry on account of torpid delivery-wagons—and there you have young Howard Pilkins with 4,000,000, and a good fellow at that. He was an agreeable, modestly arrogant young man, who implicitly believed that money could buy anything that the world had to offer. And Bagdad-on-the-Subway for a long time did everything possible to encourage his belief.

But the Rat-trap caught him at last; he heard the spring snap, and found his heart in a wire cage regarding a piece of cheese whose other name was Alice von der Ruysling.

The von der Ruyslings still live in that little square about which so much has been said, and in which so little has been done. To-day you hear of Mr. Tilden's underground passage, and you hear of Mr. Gould's elevated passage, and that about ends the noise in the world made by Gramercy Square. But once it was different. The von der Ruyslings live there yet, and they received *the first key ever made to Gramercy Park.*

You shall have no description of Alice v. d. R. Just call up in your mind the picture of your own Maggie or Vera or Beatrice, straighten her nose, soften her voice, tone her down and then tone her up, make her beautiful and unattainable—and you have a faint dry-point etching of Alice. The family owned a crumbly brick house and a coachman named Joseph in a coat of many colors, and a horse so old that he claimed to belong to the order of the Perissodactyla, and had toes instead of hoofs. In the year 1898 the family had to buy a new set of harness for the Perissodactyl. Before using it they made Joseph smear it over with a mixture of ashes and soot. It was the von der Ruysling family that bought the territory between the Bowery and East River and Rivington Street and the Statue of Liberty, in the year 1649, from an Indian chief for a quart of passementerie and a pair of Turkey-red portières designed for a Harlem flat. I have always admired that Indian's perspicacity and good taste. All this is merely to convince you that the von der Ruyslings were exactly the kind of poor aristocrats that turn down their noses at people who have money. Oh, well, I don't mean that; I mean people who have *just* money.

One evening Pilkins went down to the red brick house in Gramercy Square, and made what he thought was a proposal to Alice v. d. R. Alice, with her nose turned down, and thinking of his money, considered it a proposition, and refused it and him. Pilkins, summoning all his resources as any good general would have done, made an indiscreet reference to the advantages that his money would provide. That settled it. The lady turned so cold that Walter Wellman himself would have waited until spring to make a dash for her in a dog-sled.

But Pilkins was something of a sport himself. You can't fool all the millionaires every time the ball drops on the Western Union Building.

"If, at any time," he said to A. v. d. R., "you feel that you would like to reconsider your answer, send me a rose like that."

Pilkins audaciously touched a Jacque rose that she wore loosely in her hair.

"Very well," said she. "And when I do, you will understand by it that either you or I have learned something new about the purchasing power of money. You've been spoiled, my friend. No, I don't think I could marry you. To-morrow I will send you back the presents you have given me."

"Presents!" said Pilkins in surprise. "I never gave you a present in my life. I would like to see a full-length portrait of the man that you would take a present from. Why, you never would let me send you flowers or candy or even art calendars."

"You've forgotten," said Alice v. d. R., with a little smile. "It was a long time ago when our families were neighbors. You were seven, and I was trundling my doll on the sidewalk. You gave me a little gray, hairy kitten, with shoe-buttony eyes. Its head came off and it was full of candy. You paid five cents for it—you told me so. I haven't the candy to return to you—I hadn't developed a conscience at three, so I ate it. But I have the kitten yet, and I will wrap it up neatly to-night and send it to you to-morrow."

Beneath the lightness of Alice v. d. R.'s talk the steadfastness of her rejection showed firm and plain. So there was nothing left for him but to leave the crumbly red brick house, and be off with his abhorred millions.

On his way back, Pilkins walked through Madison Square. The hour hand on the clock hung about eight; the air was stingingly cool, but not at the freezing point. The dim little square seemed like a great, cold, unroofed room, with its four walls of houses, spangled with thousands of insufficient lights. Only a few loiterers huddled here and there on the benches.

But suddenly Pilkins came upon a youth brave and, as if conflicting with summer sultriness, coatless, his white shirt-sleeves conspicuous in the light from the globe of an electric. Close at his side was a girl, smiling, dreamy, happy. Around her shoulders was, palpably, the missing coat of the cold-defying youth. It appeared to be a modern panorama of the Babes in the Wood, revised and brought up to date, with the exception that the robins hadn't turned up yet with the protecting leaves.

With delight the money-caliphs view a situation that they think is relievable while you wait.

Pilkins sat on the bench, one seat removed from the youth. He glanced cautiously and saw (as men do see; and women—oh! never can) that they were of the same order.

Pilkins leaned over after a short time and spoke to the youth, who answered smilingly, and courteously. From general topics the conversation concentrated to the bed-rock of grim personalities. But Pilkins did it as delicately and heartily as any caliph could have done. And when it came to the point, the youth turned to him soft-voiced and with his undiminished smile.

"I don't want to seem unappreciative, old man," he said, with a youth's somewhat too-early spontaneity of address, "but, you see, I can't accept anything from a stranger. I know you're all right, and I'm tremendously obliged, but I couldn't think of borrowing from anybody. You see, I'm Marcus Clayton—the Claytons of Roanoke County, Virginia, you know. The young lady is Miss Eva Bedford—I reckon you've heard of the Bedfords. She's seventeen and one of the Bedfords of Bedford County. We've eloped from home to get married, and we wanted to see New York. We got in this afternoon. Somebody got my pocketbook on the ferry-boat, and I had only three cents in change outside of it. I'll get some work somewhere to-morrow, and we'll get married."

"But, I say, old man," said Pilkins, in confidential low tones, "you can't keep the lady out here in the cold all night. Now, as for hotels——"

"I told you," said the youth, with a broader smile, "that I didn't have but three cents. Besides, if I had a thousand, we'd have to wait here until morning. You can understand that, of course. I'm much obliged, but I can't take any of your money. Miss Bedford and I have lived an outdoor life, and we don't mind a little cold. I'll get work of some kind to-morrow. We've got a paper bag of cakes and chocolates, and we'll get along all right."

"Listen," said the millionaire, impressively. "My name is Pilkins, and I'm worth several million dollars. I happen to have in my pockets about $800 or $900 in cash. Don't you think you are drawing it rather fine when you decline to accept as much of it as will make you and the young lady comfortable at least for the night?"

"I can't say, sir, that I do think so," said Clayton of Roanoke County. "I've been raised to look at such things differently. But I'm mightily obliged to you, just the same."

"Then you force me to say good-night," said the millionaire.

Twice that day had his money been scorned by simple ones to whom his dollars had appeared as but tin tobacco-tags. He was no worshipper of the actual minted coin or stamped paper, but he had always believed in its almost unlimited power to purchase.

Pilkins walked away rapidly, and then turned abruptly and returned to the bench where the young couple sat. He took off his hat and began to speak. The girl looked at him with the same sprightly glowing interest that she had been giving to the lights and statuary and sky-reaching buildings that made the old square seem so far away from Bedford County.

"Mr—er—Roanoke," said Pilkins, "I admire your—your indepen—your idiocy so much that I'm going to appeal to your chivalry. I believe that's what you Southerners call it when you keep a lady sitting outdoors on a bench on a cold night just to keep your old, out-of-date pride going. Now, I've a friend—a lady—whom I have known all my life—who lives a few blocks from here—with her parents and sisters and aunts, and all that kind of endorsement, of course. I am sure this young lady would be happy and pleased to put up—that is, to have Miss—er—Bedford give her the pleasure of having her as a guest for the night. Don't you think, Mr. Roanoke, of—er—Virginia, that you could unbend your prejudices that far?"

Clayton of Roanoke rose and held out his hand.

"Old man," he said, "Miss Bedford will be much pleased to accept the hospitality of the lady you refer to."

He formally introduced Mr. Pilkins to Miss Bedford. The girl looked at him sweetly and comfortably. "It's a lovely evening, Mr. Pilkins—don't you think so?" she said slowly.

Pilkins conducted them to the crumbly red brick house of the von der Ruyslings. His card brought Alice downstairs wondering. The runaways were sent into the drawing-room, while Pilkins told Alice all about it in the hall.

"Of course, I will take her in," said Alice. "Haven't those Southern girls a thoroughbred air? Of course, she will stay here. You will look after Mr. Clayton, of course."

"Will I?" said Pilkins, delightedly. "Oh, yes, I'll look after him! As a citizen of New York, and therefore a part owner of its public parks, I'm going to extend to him the hospitality of Madison Square tonight. He's going to sit there on a bench till morning. There's no use arguing with him. Isn't he wonderful? I'm glad you'll look after the little lady, Alice. I tell you those Babes in the Wood made my—that is, er—made Wall Street and the Bank of England look like penny arcades."

Miss von der Ruysling whisked Miss Bedford of Bedford County up to restful regions upstairs. When she came down, she put an oblong small pasteboard box into Pilkins' hands.

"Your present," she said, "that I am returning to you."

"Oh, yes, I remember," said Pilkins, with a sigh, "the woolly kitten."

He left Clayton on a park bench, and shook hands with him heartily.

"After I get work," said the youth, "I'll look you up. Your address is on your card, isn't it? Thanks. Well, good-night. I'm awfully obliged to you for your kindness. No, thanks, I don't smoke. Good-night."

In his room, Pilkins opened the box and took out the staring, funny kitten, long ago ravaged of his candy and minus one shoe-button eye. Pilkins looked at it sorrowfully.

"After all," he said, "I don't believe that just money alone will——"

And then he gave a shout and dug into the bottom of the box for something else that had been the kitten's resting-place—a crushed but red, red, fragrant, glorious, promising Jacqueminot rose.

From OPTIONS 1909

Art and the Bronco

Out of the wilderness had come a painter. Genius, whose coronations alone are democratic, had woven a chaplet of chaparral for the brow of Lonny Briscoe. Art, whose divine woven expression flows impartially from the fingertips of a cowboy or a dilettante emperor, had chosen for a medium the Boy Artist of the San Saba. The outcome, seven feet by twelve of besmeared canvas, stood, gilt-framed, in the lobby of the Capitol.

The legislature was in session; the capital city of that great Western state was enjoying the season of activity and profit that the congregation of the solons bestowed. The boarding houses were corralling the easy dollars of the gamesome lawmakers. The greatest state in the West, an empire in area and resources, had arisen and repudiated the old libel or barbarism, lawbreaking, and bloodshed. Order reigned within her borders. Life and property were as safe there, sir, as anywhere among the corrupt cities of the effete East. Pillow-shams, churches, strawberry feasts and *habeas corpus* flourished. With impunity might the tenderfoot ventilate his "stovepipe" or his theories of culture. The arts and sciences receive nurture and subsidy. And, therefore, it behooved the legislature of this great state to make appropriation for the purchase of Lonny Briscoe's immortal painting.

Rarely has the San Saba country contributed to the spread of the fine arts. Its sons have excelled in the soldier graces, in the throw of the lariat, the manipulation of the esteemed .45, the intrepidity of the one-card draw, and the nocturnal stimulation of towns from undue lethargy; but, hitherto, it had not been famed as a stronghold of æsthetics. Lonny Briscoe's brush had removed that disability. Here, among the limestone rocks, the succulent cactus, and the drought-parched grass of that arid valley, had been born the Boy Artist. Why he came to woo art is beyond postulation. Beyond doubt, some spore of the afflatus must have sprung up within him in spite of the desert soil of San Saba. The tricksy spirit of creation must have incited him to attempted expression and then have sat hilarious among the white-hot sands of the valley, watching its mischievous work. For Lonny's picture, viewed as a thing of art, was something to have driven away dull care from the bosoms of the critics.

The painting—one might almost say panorama—was designed

to portray a typical Western scene, interest culminating in a central animal figure, that of a stampeding steer, life-size, wild-eyed, fiery, breaking away in a mad rush from the herd that, close-ridden by a typical cowpuncher, occupied a position somewhat in the right background of the picture. The landscape presented fitting and faithful accessories. Chaparral, mesquite, and pear were distributed in just proportions. A Spanish dagger-plant, with its waxen blossoms in a creamy aggregation as large as a water-bucket, contributed floral beauty and variety. The distance was undulating prairie, bisected by stretches of the intermittent streams peculiar to the region lined with the rich green of live-oak and water-elm. A richly mottled rattlesnake lay coiled beneath a pale green clump of prickly pear in the foreground. A third of the canvas was ultramarine and lake white—the typical Western sky and the flying clouds, rainless and feathery.

Between two plastered pillars in the commodious hallway near the door of the chamber of representatives stood the painting. Citizens and lawmakers passed there by twos and groups and sometimes crowds to gaze upon it. Many—perhaps a majority of them—had lived the prairie life and recalled easily the familiar scene. Old cattlemen stood, reminiscent and candidly pleased, chatting with brothers of former camps and trails of the days it brought back to mind. Art critics were few in the town, and there was heard none of that jargon of color, perspective, and feeling such as the East loves to use as a curb and a rod to the pretensions of the artist. 'Twas a great picture, most of them agreed, admiring the gilt frame—larger than any they had ever seen.

Senator Kinney was the picture's champion and sponsor. It was he who so often stepped forward and asserted, with the voice of a bronco buster, that it would be a lasting blot, sir, upon the name of this great state if it should decline to recognize in a proper manner the genius that had so brilliantly transferred to imperishable canvas a scene so typical of the great sources of our state's wealth and prosperity, land—and—er—live-stock.

Senator Kinney represented a section of the state in the extreme West—400 miles from the San Saba country—but the true lover of art is not limited by metes and bounds. Nor was Senator Mullens, representing the San Saba country, lukewarm in his belief that the state should purchase the painting of his constituent. He was advised that the San Saba country was unanimous in its admiration of the great painting by one of its own denizens. Hundreds of connoisseurs had straddled their broncos and ridden miles to view it before its removal to the capital. Senator Mullens desired reëlection, and he knew the importance of the San Saba vote. He also knew that with the help of Senator Kinney—who was a power in the legislature—the thing could be put through. Now, Senator Kinney had an irrigation bill that he wanted passed for the benefit of his own section, and he knew Senator Mullens could render him valuable aid and information, the San Saba country already enjoying the benefits of similar legislation. With these interests happily dovetailed, wonder at the sudden interest in art at the state capital must, necessarily, be small. Few artists have uncovered their first picture to the world under happier auspices than did Lonny Briscoe.

Senators Kinney and Mullens came to an understanding in the matter of irrigation and art while partaking of long drinks in the café of the Empire Hotel.

"H'm!" said Senator Kinney, "I don't know. I'm no art critic, but it seems to me the thing won't work. It looks like the worst kind of a chromo to me. I don't want to cast any reflections upon the artistic talent of your constituent, Senator, but I, myself, wouldn't give six bits for the picture—without the frame. How are you going to cram a thing like that down the throat of a legislature that kicks about a little item in the expense bill of six hundred and eighty-one dollars for rubber erasers for only one term? It's wasting time. I'd like to help you, Mullens, but they'd laugh us out of the Senate chamber if we were to try it."

"But you don't get the point," said Senator Mullens, in his deliberate tones, tapping Kinney's glass with his long forefinger. "I have my own doubts as to what the picture is intended to represent, a bullfight or a Japanese allegory, but I want this legislature to make an appropriation to purchase. Of course, the subject of the picture should have been in the state historical line, but it's too late to have the paint scraped off and changed. The state won't miss the money and the picture can be stowed away in a lumber-room where it won't annoy any one. Now, here's the point to work on, leaving art to look after itself—the chap that painted the picture is the grandson of Lucien Briscoe."

"Say it again," said Kinney, leaning his head thoughtfully. "Of the old, original Lucien Briscoe?"

"Of him. 'The man who,' you know. The man who carved the state out of the wilderness. The man who settled the Indians. The man who cleaned out the horse thieves. The man who refused the crown. The state's favorite son. Do you see the point now?"

"Wrap up the picture," said Kinney. "It's as good as sold. Why didn't you say that at first, instead of philandering along about art. I'll resign my seat in the Senate and go back to chain-carrying for the county surveyor the day I can't make this state buy a picture calcimined by a grandson of Lucien Briscoe. Did you ever hear of a special appropriation for the purchase of a home for the daughter of One-Eyed Smothers? Well, that went through like a motion to adjourn, and old One-Eyed never killed half as many Indians as Briscoe did. About what figure had you and the calciminer agreed upon to sandbag the treasury for?"

"I thought," said Mullens, "that maybe five hundred——"

"Five hundred!" interrupted Kinney, as he hammered on his glass for a lead pencil and looked around for a waiter. "Only five hundred for a red steer on the hoof delivered by a grandson of Lucien Briscoe! Where's your state pride, man? Two thousand is what it'll be. You'll introduce the bill and I'll get up on the floor of the Senate and wave the scalp of every Indian old Lucien ever murdered. Let's see, there was something else proud and foolish he did, wasn't there? Oh, yes; he declined all emoluments and benefits he was entitled to. Refused his head-right and veteran donation certificates. Could have been governor, but wouldn't. Declined a pension. Now's the state's chance to pay up. It'll have to take the picture, but then it deserves some punishment for keeping the Briscoe family waiting so long. We'll bring this thing up about the middle of the month, after the tax bill is settled. Now, Mullens, you send over, as soon as you can, and get me the figures on the cost of those irrigation ditches and the statistics about the increased production per acre. I'm going to need you when that bill of mine comes up. I reckon we'll be able to pull along pretty well together this session and maybe others to come, eh, Senator?"

Thus did fortune elect to smile upon the Boy Artist of the San Saba. Fate had already done her share when she arranged his atoms in the cosmogony of creation as the grandson of Lucien Briscoe.

The original Briscoe had been a pioneer both as to territorial occupation and in certain acts prompted by a great and simple heart. He had been one of the first settlers and crusaders against the wild forces of nature, the savage and the shallow politician. His name and memory were revered equally with any upon the list comprising Houston, Boone, Crockett, Clark, and Green. He had lived simply, independently, and unvexed by ambition. Even a less shrewd man than Senator Kinney could have prophesied that his state would hasten to honor and reward his grandson, come out of the chaparral at even so late a day.

And so, before the great picture by the door of the chamber of representatives at frequent times for many days could be found the breezy, robust form of Senator Kinney and he heard his clarion voice reciting the past deeds of Lucien Briscoe in connection with the handiwork of his grandson. Senator Mullens's work was more subdued in sight and sound, but directed along identical lines.

Then, as the day for the introduction of the bill for appropriation draws nigh, up from the San Saba country rides Lonny Briscoe and a loyal lobby of cowpunchers, bronco-back, to boost the cause of art and glorify the name of friendship, for Lonny is one of them, a knight of stirrup and chaparreras, as handy with the lariat and .45 as he is with brush and palette.

On a March afternoon the lobby dashed with a whoop, into town. The cowpunchers had adjusted their garb suitable from that prescribed for the range to the more conventional requirements of town. They had conceded their leather chaparreras and transferred their six-shooters and belts from their persons to the horns of their saddles. Among them rode Lonny, a youth of twenty-three, brown, solemn-faced, ingenuous, bowlegged, reticent, bestriding Hot Tamales, the most sagacious cow pony west of the Mississippi. Senator Mullens had informed him of the bright prospects of the situation; had even mentioned—so great was his confidence in the capable Kinney—the price that the state would, in all likelihood, pay. It seemed to Lonny that fame and fortune were in his hands. Certainly, a spark of the divine fire was in the little brown centaur's breast, for he was counting the two thousand dollars as but a means to future development of his talent. Some day he would paint a picture even greater than this—one, say, twelve feet by twenty, full of scope and atmosphere and action.

During the three days that yet intervened before the coming of the date fixed for the introduction of the bill, the centaur lobby did valiant service. Coatless, spurred, weather-tanned, full of enthusiasm expressed in bizarre terms, they loafed in front of the painting with tireless zeal. Reasoning not unshrewdly, they estimated that their comments upon its fidelity to nature would be received as expert evidence. Loudly they praised the skill of the painter whenever there were ears near to which such evidence might be profitably addressed. Lem Perry, the leader of the claque, had a somewhat set speech, being uninventive in the construction of new phrases.

"Look at the two-year-old, now," he would say, waving a cinnamon-brown hand toward the salient point of the picture. "Why, dang my hide, the critter's alive. I can jest hear him 'lumpety-lump,' a-cuttin' away from the herd, pretendin' he's skeered. He's a mean scamp, that there steer. Look at his eyes a-wallin' and his tail a-wavin'. He's true and nat'ral to life. He's jest hankerin' fur a cow pony to round him up and send him scootin' back to the bunch. Dang my hide! jest look at that tail of his'n a-wavin'. Never knowed a steer to wave his tail any other way, dang my hide ef I did."

Jud Shelby, while admitting the excellence of the steer, resolutely confined himself to open admiration of the landscape, to the end that the entire picture receive its meed of praise.

"That piece of range," he declared, "is a dead ringer for Dead Hoss Valley. Same grass, same lay of the land, same old Whipper-will Creek skallyhootin' in and out of them moots of timber. Them buzzards on the left is circlin' 'round over Sam Kildrake's old paint hoss that killed hisself over-drinkin' on a hot day. You can't see the hoss for that mott of ellums on the creek, but he's thar. Anybody that was goin' to look for Dead Hoss Valley and come across this picture, why, he'd jest light off'n his bronco and hunt a place to camp."

Skinny Rogers, wedded to comedy, conceived a complimentary little piece of acting that never failed to make an impression. Edging quite near to the picture, he would suddenly, at favorable moments, emit a piercing and awful "Yi-yi!" leap high and away, coming down with a great stamp of heels and whirring of rowels upon the stone-flagged floor.

"Jeeming Christopher!"—so ran his lines—"thought that rattler was a gin-u-ine one. Ding baste my skin if I didn't. Seemed to me I heard him rattle. Look at the blamed, unconverted insect a-layin' under that pear. Little more, and somebody would a-been snake-bit."

With these artful dodges, contributed by Lonny's faithful coterie, with the sonorous Kinney perpetually sounding the picture's merits, and with the solvent prestige of the pioneer Briscoe covering it like a precious varnish, it seemed that the San Saba country could not fail to add a reputation as an art centre to its well-known superiority in steer-roping contests and achievements with the precarious busted flush. Thus was created for the picture an atmosphere, due rather to externals than to the artist's brush, but through it the people seemed to gaze with more admiration. There was a magic in the name of Briscoe that counted high against faulty technique and crude coloring. The old Indian fighter and wolf slayer would have smiled grimly in his happy hunting grounds had he known that his dilettante ghost was thus figuring as an art patron two generations after his uninspired existence.

Came the day when the Senate was expected to pass the bill of Senator Mullens appropriating two thousand dollars for the purchase of the picture. The gallery of the Senate chamber was early pre-empted by Lonny and the San Saba lobby. In the front row of chairs they sat, wild-haired, self-conscious, jingling, creaking, and rattling, subdued by the majesty of the council hall.

The bill was introduced, went to the second reading, and then Senator Mullens spoke for it dryly, tediously, and at length. Senator Kinney then arose, and the welkin seized the bell-rope preparatory to ringing. Oratory was at that time a living thing; the world had not quite come to measure its questions by geometry and the multiplication table. It was the day of the silver tongue, the sweeping gesture, the decorative apostrophe, the moving peroration.

The Senator spoke. The San Saba contingent sat, breathing hard, in the gallery, its disordered hair hanging down to its eyes, its sixteen-ounce hats shifted restlessly from knee to knee. Below, the distinguished Senators either lounged at their desks with the abandon of proven statesmanship or maintained correct attitudes indicative of a first term.

Senator Kinney spoke for an hour. History was his theme—history mitigated by patriotism and sentiment. He referred casually to the picture in the outer hall—it was unnecessary, he said, to dilate upon its merits—the Senators had seen for themselves. The painter of the picture was the grandson of Lucien Briscoe. Then came the word-pictures of Briscoe's life set forth in thrilling colors. His rude and venturesome life, his simple-minded love for the commonwealth he helped to upbuild, his contempt for rewards and praise, his extreme and sturdy independence, and the great services he had rendered the state. The subject of the oration was Lucien Briscoe; the painting stood in the background serving simply as a means, now happily brought forward, through which the state might bestow a tardy recompense upon the descendant of its favorite son. Frequent enthusiastic applause from the Senators testified to the well reception of the sentiment.

The bill passed without an opposing vote. To-morrow it would be taken up by the House. Already was it fixed to glide through that body on rubber tires, Blandford, Grayson, and Plummer, all wheelhorses and orators, and provided with plentiful memoranda concerning the deeds of pioneer Briscoe, had agreed to furnish the motive power.

The San Saba lobby and its *protégé* stumbled awkwardly down the stairs and out into the Capitol yard. Then they herded closely and gave one yell of triumph. But one of them—Buck-Kneed Summers it was—hit the key with the thoughtful remark:

"She cut the mustard," he said, "all right. I reckon they're goin' to buy Lon's steer. I ain't right much on the parlyment'ry but I gather that's what the signs added up. But she seems to me, Lonny, the argyment ran principal to grandfather, instead of paint. It's reasonable calculatin' that you want to be glad you got the Briscoe brand on you, my son."

That remark clinched in Lonny's mind an unpleasant, vague suspicion to the same effect. His reticence increased, and he gathered grass from the ground, chewing it pensively. The picture as a picture had been humiliatingly absent from the Senator's arguments. The painter had been held up as a grandson, pure and simple. While this was gratifying on certain lines, it made art look little and slab-sided. The Boy Artist was thinking.

The hotel Lonny stopped at was near the Capitol. It was near to the one o'clock dinner hour when the appropriation had been passed by the Senate. The hotel clerk told Lonny that a famous artist from New York had arrived in town that day and was in the hotel. He was on his way westward to New Mexico to study the effect of sunlight upon the ancient walls of the Zuñis. Modern stone reflects light. Those ancient building materials absorb it. The artist wanted this effect in a picture he was painting and was travelling two thousand miles to get it.

Lonny sought this man out after dinner and told his story. The artist was an unhealthy man, kept alive by genius and indifference to life. He went with Lonny to the Capitol and stood there before the picture. The artist pulled his beard and looked unhappy.

"Should like to have your sentiments," said Lonny, "just as they run out of the pen."

"It's the way they'll come," said the painter man. "I took three different kinds of medicine before dinner—by the tablespoonful. The taste still lingers. I am primed for telling the truth. You want to know if the picture is, or if it isn't?"

"Right," said Lonny. "Is it wool or cotton? Should I paint some more or cut it out and ride herd a-plenty?"

"I heard a rumor during pie," said the artist, "that the state is about to pay you two thousand dollars for this picture."

"It's passed the Senate," said Lonny, "and the House rounds it up to-morrow."

"That's lucky," said the pale man. "Do you carry a rabbit's foot?"

"No," said Lonny, "but it seems I had a grandfather. He's considerable mixed up in the color scheme. It took me a year to paint that picture. Is she entirely awful or not? Some says, now, that that steer's tail ain't badly drawed. They think it's proportioned nice. Tell me."

The artist glanced at Lonny's wiry figure and nut-brown skin. Something stirred him to a passing irritation.

"For Art's sake, son," he said fractiously, "don't spend any more money for paint. It isn't a picture at all. It's a gun. You hold up the state with it, if you like, and get your two thousand, but don't get in front of any more canvas. Live under it. Buy a couple of hundred ponies with the money—I'm told they're that cheap—and ride, ride, ride. Fill your lungs and eat and sleep and be happy. No more pictures. You look healthy. That's genius. Cultivate it." He looked at his watch. "Twenty minutes to three. Four capsules and one tablet at three. That's all you wanted to know, isn't it?"

At three o'clock the cowpunchers rode up for Lonny, bringing Hot Tamales, saddled. Traditions must be observed. To celebrate the passage of the bill by the Senate the gang must ride wildly through the town, creating uproar and excitement. Liquor must be partaken of, the suburbs shot up, and the glory of the San Saba country vociferously proclaimed. A part of the programme had been carried out in the saloons on the way up.

Lonny mounted Hot Tamales, the accomplished little beast prancing with fire and intelligence. He was glad to feel Lonny's bow-legged grip against his ribs again. Lonny was his friend, and he was willing to do things for him.

"Come on, boys," said Lonny, urging Hot Tamales into a gallop with his knees. With a whoop, the inspired lobby tore after him through the dust. Lonny led his cohorts straight for the Capitol. With a wild yell, the gang indorsed his now evident intention of riding into it. Horray for San Saba!

Up the six broad, limestone steps clattered the broncos of the cow-punchers. Into the resounding hallway they pattered, scattering in dismay those passing on foot. Lonny, in the lead, shoved Hot Tamales direct for the great picture. At that hour a downpouring, soft light from the second-story windows bathed the big canvas. Against the darker background of the hall the painting stood out with valuable effect. In spite of the defects of the art you could almost fancy that you gazed out upon a landscape. You might well flinch a step from the convincing figure of the life-sized steer stampeding across the grass. Perhaps it thus seemed to Hot Tamales. The scene was in his line. Perhaps he only obeyed the will of his rider. His ears pricked up; he snorted. Lonny leaned forward in the saddle and elevated his elbows, wing-like. Thus signals the cow-puncher to his steed to launch himself full speed ahead. Did Hot Tamales fancy he saw a steer, red and cavorting, that should be headed off and driven back to herd? There was a fierce clatter of hoofs, a rush, a gathering of steely flank muscles, a leap to the jerk of the bridle rein, and Hot Tamales, with Lonny bending low in the saddle to dodge the top of the frame, ripped through the great canvas like a shell from a mortar, leaving the cloth hanging in ragged shreds about a monstrous hole.

Quickly Lonny pulled up his pony, and rounded the pillars. Spectators came running, too astounded to add speech to the commotion. The sergeant-at-arms of the House came forth, frowned, looked ominous, and then grinned. Many of the legislators crowded out to observe the tumult. Lonny's cowpunchers were stricken to silent horror by his mad deed.

Senator Kinney happened to be among the earliest to emerge. Before he could speak Lonny leaned in his saddle as Hot Tamales pranced, pointed his quirt at the Senator, and said, calmly:

"That was a fine speech you made to-day, mister, but you might as well let up on that 'propriation business. I ain't askin' the state to give me nothin'. I thought I had a picture to sell to it, but it wasn't one. You said a heap of things about Grandfather Briscoe that makes me kind of proud I'm his grandson. Well, the Briscoes ain't takin' presents from the state yet. Anybody can have the frame that wants it. Hit her up, boys."

Away scuttled the San Saba delegation out of the hall, down the steps, along the dusty street.

Halfway to the San Saba country they camped that night. At bedtime Lonny stole away from the campfire and sought Hot Tamales, placidly eating grass at the end of his stake rope. Lonny hung upon his neck, and his art aspirations went forth forever in one long, regretful sigh. But as he thus made renunciation his breath formed a word or two.

"You was the only one, Tamales, what seen anything in it. It *did* look like a steer, didn't it, old hoss?"

A Double-Dyed Deceiver

The trouble began in Laredo. It was the Llano Kid's fault, for he should have confined his habit of manslaughter to Mexicans. But the Kid was past twenty; and to have only Mexicans to one's credit at twenty is to blush unseen on the Rio Grande border.

It happened in old Justo Valdo's gambling house. There was a poker game at which sat players who were not all friends, as happens often where men ride in from afar to shoot Folly as she gallops. There was a row over so small a matter as a pair of queens; and when the smoke had cleared away it was found that the Kid had committed an indiscretion, and his adversary had been guilty of a blunder. For, the unfortunate combatant, instead of being a Greaser, was a high-blooded youth from the cow ranches, of about the Kid's own age and possessed of friends and champions. His blunder in missing the Kid's right ear only a sixteenth of an inch when he pulled his gun did not lessen the indiscretion of the better marksman.

The Kid, not being equipped with a retinue, nor bountifully supplied with personal admirers and supporters—on account of a rather umbrageous reputation, even for the border—considered it not incompatible with his indisputable gameness to perform that judicious tractional act known as "pulling his freight."

Quickly the avengers gathered and sought him. Three of them overtook him within a rod of the station. The Kid turned and showed his teeth in that brilliant but mirthless smile that usually preceded his deeds of insolence and violence, and his pursuers fell back without making it necessary for him even to reach for his weapon.

But in this affair the Kid had not felt the grim thirst for encounter that usually urged him on to battle. It had been a purely chance row, born of the cards and certain epithets impossible for a gentleman to brook that had passed between the two. The Kid had rather liked the slim, haughty, brown-faced young chap whom his bullet had cut off in the first pride of manhood. And now he wanted no more blood. He wanted to get away and have a good long sleep somewhere in the sun on the mesquite grass with his handkerchief over his face. Even a Mexican might have crossed his path in safety while he was in this mood.

The Kid openly boarded the north-bound passenger train that departed five minutes later. But at Webb, a few miles out, where it was flagged to take on a traveller, he abandoned that manner of escape. There were telegraph stations ahead; and the Kid looked askance at electricity and steam. Saddle and spur were his rocks of safety.

The man whom he had shot was a stranger to him. But the Kid knew that he was of the Coralitos outfit from Hidalgo; and that the punchers from that ranch were more relentless and vengeful than Kentucky feudists when wrong or harm was done to one of them. So, with the wisdom that has characterized many great fighters, the Kid decided to pile up as many leagues as possible of chaparral and pear between himself and the retaliation of the Coralitos bunch.

Near the station was a store; and near the store, scattered among the mesquite and elms, stood the saddled horses of the customers. Most of them waited, half asleep, with sagging limbs and drooping heads. But one, a long-legged roan with a curved neck, snorted and pawed the turf. Him the Kid mounted, gripped with his knees, and slapped gently with the owner's own quirt.

If the slaying of the temerarious card-player had cast a cloud over the Kid's standing as a good and true citizen, this last act of his veiled his figure in the darkest shadows of disrepute. On the Rio Grande border if you take a man's life you sometimes take trash; but if you take his horse, you take a thing the loss of which renders him poor, indeed, and which enriches you not—if you are caught. For the Kid there was no turning back now.

With the springing roan under him he felt little care or uneasiness. After a five-mile gallop he drew into the plainsman's jogging trot, and rode north-eastward toward the Nueces River bottoms. He knew the country well—its most tortuous and obscure trails through the great wilderness of brush and pear, and its camps and lonesome ranches where one might find safe entertainment. Always he bore to the east; for the Kid had never seen the ocean, and he had a fancy to lay his hand upon the mane of the great Gulf, the gamesome colt of the greater waters.

So after three days he stood on the shore at Corpus Christi, and looked out across the gentle ripples of a quiet sea.

Captain Boone, of the schooner *Flyaway,* stood near his skiff, which one of his crew was guarding in the surf. When ready to sail he had discovered that one of the necessaries of life, in the parallelogrammatic shape of plug tobacco, had been forgotten. A sailor had been dispatched for the missing cargo. Meanwhile the captain paced the sands, chewing profanely at his pocket store.

A slim, wiry youth in high-heeled boots came down to the water's edge. His face was boyish, but with a premature severity that hinted at a man's experience. His complexion was naturally dark; and the sun and wind of an outdoor life had burned it to a coffee-brown. His hair was as black and straight as an Indian's; his face had not yet been upturned to the humiliation of a razor; his eyes were a cold and steady blue. He carried his left arm somewhat away from his body, for pearl-handled .45s are frowned upon by town marshals, and are a little bulky when packed in the left armhole of one's vest. He looked beyond Captain Boone at the gulf with the impersonal and expressionless dignity of a Chinese emperor.

"Thinkin' of buyin' that 'ar gulf, buddy?" asked the captain, made sarcastic by his narrow escape from the tobaccoless voyage.

"Why, no," said the Kid gently, "I reckon not. I never saw it before. I was just looking at it. Not thinking of selling it, are you?"

"Not this trip," said the captain. "I'll send it to you C.O.D. when I get back to Buenas Tierras. Here comes that capstan-footed lubber with the chewin'. I ought to've weighed anchor an hour ago."

"Is that your ship out there?" asked the Kid.

"Why, yes," answered the captain, "if you want to call a schooner a ship, and I don't mind lyin'. But you better say Miller and Gonzales, owners, and ordinary plain, Billy-be-damned old Samuel K. Boone, skipper."

"Where are you going to?" asked the refugee.

"Buenas Tierras, coast of South America—I forget what they called the country the last time I was there. Cargo—lumber, corrugated iron, and machetes."

"What kind of a country is it?" asked the Kid—"hot or cold?"

"Warmish, buddy," said the captain. "But a regular Paradise Lost for elegance of scenery and be-yooty of geography. Ye're wakened every morning by the sweet singin' of red birds with seven purple tails, and the sighin' of breezes in the posies and roses. And the inhabitants never work, for they can reach out and pick steamer baskets of the choicest hothouse fruit without gettin' out of bed. And there's no Sunday and no ice and no rent and no troubles and no use and no nothin'. It's a great country for a man to go to sleep with, and wait for somethin' to turn up. The bananys and oranges and hurricanes and pineapples that ye eat comes from there."

"That sounds to me!" said the Kid, at last betraying interest. "What'll the expressage be to take me out there with you?"

"Twenty-four dollars," said Captain Boone; "grub and transportation. Second cabin. I haven't got a first cabin."

"You've got my company," said the Kid, pulling out a buckskin bag.

With three hundred dollars he had gone to Laredo for his regular "blowout." The duel in Valdo's had cut short his season of hilarity, but it had left him with nearly $200 for aid in the flight that it had made necessary.

"All right, buddy," said the captain. "I hope your ma won't blame me for this little childish escapade of yours." He beckoned to one of the boat's crew. "Let Sanchez lift you out to the skiff so you won't get your feet wet."

Thacker, the United States consul at Buenas Tierras, was not yet drunk. It was only eleven o'clock; and he never arrived at his desired state of beatitude—a state where he sang ancient maudlin vaudeville songs and pelted his screaming parrot with banana peels—until the middle of the afternoon. So, when he looked up from his hammock at the sound of a slight cough, and saw the Kid standing in the door of the consulate, he was still in a condition to extend the hospitality and courtesy due from the representative of a great nation. "Don't disturb yourself," said the Kid easily. "I just dropped in. They told me it was customary to light at your camp before starting in to round up the town. I just came in on a ship from Texas."

"Glad to see you, Mr.——," said the consul.

The Kid laughed.

"Sprague Dalton," he said. "It sounds funny to me to hear it. I'm called the Llano Kid in the Rio Grande country."

"I'm Thacker," said the consul. "Take that cane-bottom chair. Now if you've come to invest, you want somebody to advise you. These dingies will cheat you out of the gold in your teeth if you don't understand their ways. Try a cigar?"

"Much obliged," said the Kid, "but if it wasn't for my corn shucks and the little bag in my back pocket I couldn't live a minute." He took out his "makings," and rolled a cigarette.

"They speak Spanish here," said the consul. "You'll need an interpreter. If there's anything I can do, why, I'd be delighted. If you're buying fruit lands or looking for a concession of any sort, you'll want somebody who knows the ropes to look out for you."

"I speak Spanish," said the Kid, "about nine times better than I do English. Everybody speaks it on the range where I come from. And I'm not in the market for anything."

"You speak Spanish?" said Thacker, thoughtfully. He regarded the Kid absorbedly.

"You look like a Spaniard, too," he continued. "And you're from Texas. And you can't be more than twenty or twenty-one. I wonder if you've got any nerve."

"You got a deal of some kind to put through?" asked the Texan, with unexpected shrewdness.

"Are you open to a proposition?" said Thacker.

"What's the use to deny it?" said the Kid. "I got into a little gun frolic down in Laredo, and plugged a white man. There wasn't any Mexican handy. And I come down to your parrot-and-monkey range just for to smell the morning-glories and marigolds. Now, do you *sabe?"*

Thacker got up and closed the door.

"Let me see your hand," he said.

He took the Kid's left hand, and examined the back of it closely.

"I can do it," he said, excitedly. "Your flesh is as hard as wood and as healthy as a baby's. It will heal in a week."

"If it's a fist fight you want to back me for," said the Kid, "don't put your money up yet. Make it gun work, and I'll keep you company. But no bare-handed scrapping, like ladies at a tea-party, for me."

"It's easier than that," said Thacker. "Just step here, will you?"

Through the window he pointed to a two-story white-stuccoed house with wide galleries rising amid the deep-green tropical foliage on a wooded hill that sloped gently from the sea.

"In that house," said Thacker, "a fine old Castilian gentleman and his wife are yearning to gather you into their arms and fill your pockets with money. Old Santos Urique lives there. He owns half the gold-mines in the country."

"You haven't been eating loco weed, have you?" asked the Kid.

"Sit down again," said Thacker, "and I'll tell you. Twelve years ago they lost a kid. No, he didn't die—although most of 'em here do from drinking the surface water. He was a wild little devil, even if he wasn't but eight years old. Everybody knows about it. Some Americans who were through here prospecting for gold had letters to Señor Urique, and the boy who was a favorite with them. They filled his head with big stories about the States; and about a month after they left, the kid disappeared, too. He was supposed to have stowed himself away among the banana bunches on a fruit steamer, and gone to New Orleans. He was seen once afterward in Texas, it was thought, but they never heard anything more of him. Old Urique has spent thousands of dollars having him looked for. The madam was broken up worst of all. The kid was her life. She wears mourning yet. But they say she believes he'll come back to her some day, and never gives up hope. On the back of the boy's left hand was tattooed a flying eagle carrying a spear in his claws. That's old Urique's coat of arms or something that he inherited in Spain."

The Kid raised his left hand slowly and gazed at it curiously.

"That's it," said Thacker, reaching behind the official desk for his bottle of smuggled brandy. "You're not so slow. I can do it. What was I consul at Sandakan for? I never knew till now. In a week I'll have the eagle bird with the frog-sticker blended in so you'd think you were born with it. I brought a set of the needles and ink just because I was sure you'd drop in some day, Mr. Dalton."

"Oh, hell," said the Kid. "I thought I told you my name!"

"All right, 'Kid,' then. It won't be that long. How docs 'Señorito Urique' sound, for a change?"

"I never played son any that I remember of," said the Kid. "If I had any parents to mention they went over the divide about the time I gave my first bleat. What is the plan of your round-up?"

Thacker leaned back against the wall and held his glass up to the light.

"We've come now," said he, "to the question of how far you're willing to go in a little matter of the sort."

"I told you why I came down here," said the Kid simply.

"A good answer," said the consul. "But you won't have to go that far. Here's the scheme. After I get the trade-mark tattooed on your hand I'll notify old Urique. In the meantime I'll furnish you with all of the family history I can find out, so you can be studying up points to talk about. You've got the looks, you speak the Spanish, you know the facts, you can tell about Texas, you've got the tattoo mark. When I notify them that the rightful heir has returned and is waiting to know whether he will be received and pardoned what will happen? They'll simply rush down here and fall on your neck, and the curtain goes down for refreshments and a stroll in the lobby."

"I'm waiting," said the Kid. "I haven't had my saddle off in your camp long, pardner, and I never met you before; but if you intend to let it go at a parental blessing, why, I'm mistaken in my man, that's all."

"Thanks," said the consul. "I haven't met anybody in a long time that keeps up with an argument as well as you do. The rest of it is simple. If they take you in only for a while it's long enough. Don't give 'em time to hunt up the strawberry mark on your left shoulder. Old Urique keeps anywhere from $50,000 to $100,000 in his house all the time in a little safe that you could open with a shoe buttoner. Get it. My skill as a tattooer is worth half the boodle. We go halves and catch a tramp steamer for Rio Janeiro. Let the United States go to pieces if it can't get along without my services. *Qué dice, señor?"*

"It sounds to me!" said the Kid, nodding his head. "I'm out for the dust."

"All right, then," said Thacker. "You'll have to keep close until we get the bird on you. You can live in the back room here. I do my own cooking, and I'll make you as comfortable as a parsimonious government will allow me."

Thacker had set the time at a week, but it was two weeks before the design that he patiently tattooed upon the Kid's hand was to his notion. And then Thacker called a *muchacho,* and dispatched this note to the intended victim:

El Señor Don Santos Urique,
La Casa Blanca,
My Dear Sir:
I beg permission to inform you that there is in my house as a temporary guest a young man who arrived in Buenas Tierras from the United States some days ago. Without wishing to excite any hopes that may not be realized, I think there is a possibility of his being your long-absent son. It might be well for you to call and see him. If he is, it is my opinion that his intention was to return to his home, but upon arriving here, his courage failed him from doubts as to how he would be received. Your true servant,
Thompson Thacker

Half an hour afterward—quick time for Buenas Tierras—Señor Urique's ancient landau drove to the consul's door, with the barefooted coachman beating and shouting at the team of fat, awkward horses.

A tall man with a white moustache alighted, and assisted to the ground a lady who was dressed and veiled in unrelieved black.

The two hastened inside, and were met by Thacker with his best diplomatic bow. By his desk stood a slender young man with clear-cut, sunbrowned features and smoothly brushed black hair.

Señora Urique threw back her heavy veil with a quick gesture. She was past middle age, and her hair was beginning to silver, but her full, proud figure and clear olive skin retained traces of the beauty peculiar to the Basque province. But, once you had seen her eyes, and comprehended the great sadness that was revealed in their deep shadows and hopeless expression, you saw that the woman lived only in some memory.

She bent upon the young man a long look of the most agonized questioning. Then her great black eyes turned, and her gaze rested upon his left hand. And then with a sob, not loud, but seeming to shake the room, she cried *"Hijo mío!"* and caught the Llano Kid to her heart.

A month afterward the Kid came to the consulate in response to a message sent by Thacker.

He looked the young Spanish caballero. His clothes were imported, and the wiles of the jewellers had not been spent upon him in vain. A more than respectable diamond shone on his finger as he rolled a shuck cigarette.

"What's doing?" asked Thacker.

"Nothing much," said the Kid calmly. "I eat my first iguana steak to-day. They're them big lizards, you *sabe?* I reckon, though, that frijoles and side bacon would do me about as well. Do you care for iguanas, Thacker?"

"No, nor for some other kinds of reptiles," said Thacker.

It was three in the afternoon, and in another hour he would be in his state of beatitude.

"It's time you were making good, sonny," he went on, with an ugly look on his reddened face. "You're not playing up to me square. You've been the prodigal son for four weeks now, and you could have had veal for every meal on a gold dish if you'd wanted it. Now, Mr. Kid, do you think it's right to leave me out so long on a husk diet? What's the trouble? Don't you get your filial eyes on anything that looks like cash in the Casa Blanca? Don't tell me you don't. Everybody knows where old Urique keeps his stuff. It's U. S. currency, too; he don't accept anything else. What's doing? Don't say 'nothing' this time."

"Why, sure," said the Kid, admiring his diamond, "there's plenty of money up there. I'm no judge of collateral in bunches, but I will undertake for to say that I've seen the rise of $50,000 at a time in that tin grub box that my adopted father calls his safe. And he lets me carry the key sometimes just to show me that he knows I'm the real little Francisco that strayed from the herd a long time ago."

"Well, what are you waiting for?" asked Thacker angrily. "Don't you forget that I can upset your apple-cart any day I want to. If old Urique knew you were an impostor, what sort of things would happen to you? Oh, you don't know this country, Mr. Texas Kid. The laws here have got mustard spread between 'em. These people here'd stretch you out like a frog that had been stepped on, and give you about fifty sticks at every corner of the plaza. And they'd wear every stick out, too. What was left of you they'd feed to alligators."

"I might as well tell you now, pardner," said the Kid, sliding down low on his steamer chair, "that things are going to stay just as they are. They're about right now."

"What do you mean?" asked Thacker, rattling the bottom of his glass on his desk.

"The scheme's off," said the Kid. "And whenever you have the pleasure of speaking to me address me as Don Francisco Urique. I'll guarantee I'll answer to it. We'll let Colonel Urique keep his money. His little tin safe is as good as the time-locker in the First National Bank of Laredo as far as you and me are concerned."

"You're going to throw me down, then, are you?" said the consul.

"Sure," said the Kid, cheerfully. "Throw you down. That's it. And now I'll tell you why. The first night I was up at the colonel's house they introduced me to a bedroom. No blankets on the floor—a real room, with a bed and things in it. And before I was asleep, in comes this artificial mother of mine and tucks in the covers. 'Panchito,' she says, 'my little lost one, God has brought you back to me. I bless His name forever.' It was that, or some truck like that, she said. And down comes a drop or two of rain and hits me on the nose. And all that stuck by me, Mr. Thacker. And it's been that way ever since. And it's got to stay that way. Don't you think that it's for what's in it for me, either, that I say so. If you have any such ideas keep 'em to yourself. I haven't had much truck with women in my life, and no mothers to speak of, but here's a lady that we've got to keep fooled. Once she stood it; twice she won't. I'm a lowdown wolf, and the devil may have sent me on this trail instead of God, but I'll travel it to the end. And now, don't forget that I'm Don Francisco Urique whenever you happen to mention my name."

"I'll expose you to-day, you—you double-dyed traitor," stammered Thacker.

The Kid arose and, without violence, took Thacker by the throat with a hand of steel, and shoved him slowly into a corner. Then he drew from under his left arm his pearl-handled .45 and poked the cold muzzle of it against the consul's mouth.

"I told you why I come here," he said, with his old freezing smile. "If I leave here, you'll be the reason. Never forget it, pardner. Now, what is my name?"

"Er—Don Francisco Urique," gasped Thacker.

From outside came a sound of wheels, and the shouting of someone, and the sharp thwacks of a wooden whipstock upon the backs of fat horses.

The Kid put up his gun, and walked toward the door. But he turned again and came back to the trembling Thacker, and held up his left hand with its back toward the consul.

"There's one more reason," he said, slowly, "why things have got to stand as they are. The fellow I killed in Laredo had one of them same pictures on his left hand."

Outside, the ancient landau of Don Santos Urique rattled to the door. The coachman ceased his bellowing. Señor Urique, in a voluminous gay gown of white lace and flying ribbons, leaned forward with a happy look in her great soft eyes.

"Are you within, dear son?" she called, in the rippling Castilian.

"Madre mía, yo vengo [mother, I come]," answered the young Don Francisco Urique.

A Retrieved Reformation

A guard came to the prison shoe-shop, where Jimmy Valentine was assiduously stitching uppers, and escorted him to the front office. There the warden handed Jimmy his pardon, which had been signed that morning by the governor. Jimmy took it in a tired kind of way. He had served nearly ten months of a four-year sentence. He had expected to stay only about three months, at the longest. When a man with as many friends on the outside as Jimmy Valentine had is received in the "stir" it is hardly worth while to cut his hair.

"Now, Valentine," said the warden, "you'll go out in the morning. Brace up, and make a man of yourself. You're not a bad fellow at heart. Stop cracking safes, and live straight."

"Me?" said Jimmy, in surprise. "Why, I never cracked a safe in my life."

"Oh, no," laughed the warden. "Of course not. Let's see, now. How was it you happened to get sent up on that Springfield job? Was it because you wouldn't prove an alibi for fear of compromising somebody in extremely high-toned society? Or was it simply a case of a mean old jury that had it in for you? It's always one or the other with you innocent victims."

"Me?" said Jimmy, still blankly virtuous. "Why, warden, I never was in Springfield in my life!"

"Take him back, Cronin," smiled the warden, "and fix him up with outgoing clothes. Unlock him at seven in the morning, and let him come to the bull-pen. Better think over my advice, Valentine."

At a quarter past seven on the next morning Jimmy stood in the warden's outer office. He had on a suit of the villainously fitting, ready-made clothes and a pair of the stiff, squeaky shoes that the state furnishes to its discharged compulsory guests.

The clerk handed him a railroad ticket and the five-dollar bill with which the law expected him to rehabilitate himself into good citizenship and prosperity. The warden gave him a cigar, and shook hands. Valentine, 9762, was chronicled on the books "Pardoned by Governor," and Mr. James Valentine walked out into the sunshine.

Disregarding the song of the birds, the waving green trees, and the smell of the flowers, Jimmy headed straight for a restaurant. There he tasted the first sweet joys of liberty in the shape of a broiled chicken and a bottle of white wine—followed by a cigar a grade better than the one the warden had given him. From there he proceeded leisurely to the depot. He tossed a quarter into the hat of a blind man sitting by the door, and boarded his train. Three hours set him down in a little town near the state line. He went to the café of one Mike Dolan and shook hands with Mike, who was alone behind the bar.

"Sorry we couldn't make it sooner, Jimmy, me boy," said Mike. "But we had that protest from Springfield to buck against, and the governor nearly balked. Feeling all right?"

"Fine," said Jimmy. "Got my key?"

He got his key and went upstairs, unlocking the door of a room at the rear. Everything was just as he had left it. There on the floor was still Ben Price's collar-button that had been torn from that eminent detective's shirt-band when they had overpowered Jimmy to arrest him.

Pulling out from the wall a folding-bed, Jimmy slid back a panel in the wall and dragged out a dust-covered suitcase. He opened this and gazed fondly at the finest set of burglar's tools in the East. It was a complete set, made of specially tempered steel, the latest designs in drills, punches, braces and bits, jimmies, clamps, and augers, with two or three novelties invented by Jimmy himself, in which he took pride. Over nine hundred dollars they had cost him to have made at ——, a place where they make such things for the profession.

In half an hour Jimmy went downstairs and through the café. He was now dressed in tasteful and well-fitting clothes, and carried his dusted and cleaned suitcase in his hand.

"Got anything on?" asked Mike Dolan, genially.

"Me?" said Jimmy, in a puzzled tone. "I don't understand. I'm representing the New York Amalgamated Short Snap Biscuit Cracker and Frazzled Wheat Company."

This statement delighted Mike to such an extent that Jimmy had to take a seltzer-and-milk on the spot. He never touched "hard" drinks.

A week after the release of Valentine, 9762, there was a neat job of safe-burglary done in Richmond, Indiana, with no clue to the author. A scant eight hundred dollars was all that was secured. Two weeks after that a patented, improved, burglar-proof safe in Logansport was opened like a cheese to the tune of fifteen hundred dollars, currency; securities and silver untouched. That began to interest the rogue-catchers. Then an old-fashioned bank-safe in Jefferson City became active and threw out of its crater an eruption of bank-notes amounting to five thousand dollars. The losses were now high enough to bring the matter up into Ben Price's class of work. By comparing notes, a remarkable similarity in the methods of the burglaries was noticed. Ben Price investigated the scenes of the robberies, and was heard to remark:

"That's Dandy Jim Valentine's autograph. He's resumed business. Look at that combination knob—jerked out as easy as pulling up a radish in wet weather. He's got the only clamps that can do it. And look how clean those tumblers were punched out! Jimmy never has to drill but one hole. Yes, I guess I want Mr. Valentine. He'll do his bit next time without any short-time or clemency foolishness."

Ben Price knew Jimmy's habits. He had learned them while working up the Springfield case. Long jumps, quick get-aways, no confederates, and a taste for good society—these ways had helped Mr. Valentine to become noted as a successful dodger of retribution. It was given out that Ben Price had taken up the trail of the elusive cracksman, and other people with burglar-proof safes felt more at ease.

One afternoon Jimmy Valentine and his suitcase climbed out of the mail-hack in Elmore, a little town five miles off the railroad down in the black-jack country of Arkansas. Jimmy, looking like an athletic young senior just home from college, went down the board sidewalk toward the hotel.

A young lady crossed the street, passed him at the corner and entered a door over which was the sign "The Elmore Bank." Jimmy Valentine looked into her eyes, forgot what he was, and became another man. She lowered her eyes and colored slightly. Young men of Jimmy's style and looks were scarce in Elmore.

Jimmy collared a boy that was loafing on the steps of the bank as if he were one of the stock-holders, and began to ask him questions about the town, feeding him dimes at intervals. By and by the young lady came out, looking royally unconscious of the young man with the suitcase, and went her way.

"Isn't that young lady Miss Polly Simpson?" asked Jimmy, with specious guile.

"Naw," said the boy. "She's Annabel Adams. Her pa owns this bank. What'd you come to Elmore for? Is that a gold watch-chain? I'm going to get a bulldog. Got any more dimes?"

Jimmy went to the Planters' Hotel, registered as Ralph D. Spencer, and engaged a room. He leaned on the desk and declared his platform to the clerk. He said he had come to Elmore to look for a location to go into business. How was the shoe business, now, in the town? He had thought of the shoe business. Was there an opening?

The clerk was impressed by the clothes and manner of Jimmy. He, himself, was something of a pattern of fashion to the thinly gilded youth of Elmore, but he now perceived his shortcomings.

While trying to figure out Jimmy's manner of tying his four-in-hand he cordially gave information.

Yes, there ought to be a good opening in the shoe line. There wasn't an exclusive shoe-store in the place. The dry-goods and general stores handled them. Business in all lines was fairly good. Hoped Mr. Spencer would decide to locate in Elmore. He would find it a pleasant town to live in, and the people very sociable.

Mr. Spencer thought he would stop over in the town a few days and look over the situation. No, the clerk needn't call the boy. He would carry up his suitcase, himself; it was rather heavy.

Mr. Ralph Spencer, the phœnix that arose from Jimmy Valentine's ashes—ashes left by the flame of a sudden and alternative attack of love—remained in Elmore, and prospered. He opened a shoe-store and secured a good run of trade.

Socially he was also a success, and made many friends. And he accomplished the wish of his heart. He met Miss Annabel Adams, and became more and more captivated by her charms.

At the end of a year the situation of Mr. Ralph Spencer was this: he had won the respect of the community, his shoe-store was flourishing, and he and Annabel were engaged to be married in two weeks. Mr. Adams, the typical, plodding, country banker, approved of Spencer. Annabel's pride in him almost equalled her affection. He was as much at home in the family of Mr. Adams and that of Annabel's married sister as if he were already a member.

One day Jimmy sat down in his room and wrote this letter, which he mailed to the safe address of one of his old friends in St. Louis:

Dear Old Pal:

I want you to be at Sullivan's place, in Little Rock, next Wednesday night at nine o'clock. I want you to wind up some little matters for me. And, also, I want to make you a present of my kit of tools. I know you'll be glad to get them—you couldn't duplicate the lot for a thousand dollars. Say, Billy, I've quit the old business—a year ago. I've got a nice store. I'm making an honest living, and I'm going to marry the finest girl on earth two weeks from now. It's the only life, Billy—the straight one. I wouldn't touch a dollar of another man's money now for a million. After I get married I'm going to sell out and go West, where there won't be so much danger of having old scores brought up against me. I tell you, Billy, she's an angel. She believes in me; and I wouldn't do another crooked thing for the whole world. Be sure to be at Sully's, for I must see you. I'll bring along the tools with me.

Your old friend,
Jimmy

On the Monday night after Jimmy wrote this letter, Ben Price jogged unobtrusively into Elmore in a livery buggy. He lounged about town in his quiet way until he found out what he wanted to know. From the drug-store across the street from Spencer's shoe-store he got a good look at Ralph D. Spencer.

"Going to marry the banker's daughter are you, Jimmy?" said Ben to himself, softly. "Well, I don't know!"

The next morning Jimmy took breakfast at the Adamses. He was going to Little Rock that day to order his wedding-suit and buy something nice for Annabel. That would be the first time he had left town since he came to Elmore. It had been more than a year now since those last professional "jobs," and he thought he could safely venture out.

After breakfast quite a family party went down town together—Mr. Adams, Annabel, Jimmy, and Annabel's married sister with her two little girls, aged five and nine. They came by the hotel where Jimmy still boarded, and he ran up to his room and brought along his suitcase. Then they went on to the bank. There stood Jimmy's horse and buggy and Dolph Gibson, who was going to drive him over to the railroad station.

All went inside the high, carved oak railings into the banking-room—Jimmy included, for Mr. Adams's future son-in-law was welcome anywhere. The clerks were pleased to be greeted by the good-looking, agreeable young man who was going to marry Miss Annabel. Jimmy set his suitcase down. Annabel, whose heart was bubbling with happiness and lively youth, put on Jimmy's hat and picked up the suitcase. "Wouldn't I make a nice drummer?" said Annabel. "My! Ralph, how heavy it is. Feels like it was full of gold bricks."

"Lot of nickel-plated shoe-horns in there," said Jimmy, coolly, "that I'm going to return. Thought I'd save express charges by taking them up. I'm getting awfully economical."

The Elmore Bank had just put in a new safe and vault. Mr. Adams was very proud of it, and insisted on an inspection by every one. The vault was a small one, but it had a new patented door. It fastened with three solid steel bolts thrown simultaneously with a single handle, and had a time-lock. Mr. Adams beamingly explained its workings to Mr. Spencer, who showed a courteous but not too intelligent interest. The two children, May and Agatha, were delighted by the shining metal and funny clock and knobs.

While they were thus engaged Ben Price sauntered in and leaned on his elbow, looking casually inside between the railings. He told the teller that he didn't want anything; he was just waiting for a man he knew.

Suddenly there was a scream or two from the women, and a commotion. Unperceived by the elders, May, the nine-year-old girl, in a spirit of play, had shut Agatha in the vault. She had then shot the bolts and turned the knob of the combination as she had seen Mr. Adams do.

The old banker sprang to the handle and tugged at it for a moment. "The door can't be opened," he groaned. "The clock hasn't been wound nor the combination set."

Agatha's mother screamed again, hysterically.

"Hush!" said Mr. Adams, raising his trembling hand. "All be quiet for a moment, Agatha!" he called as loudly as he could: "Listen to me." During the following silence they could just hear the faint sound of the child wildly shrieking in the dark vault in a panic of terror.

"My precious darling!" wailed the mother. "She will die of fright! Open the door! Oh, break it open! Can't you men do something?"

"There isn't a man nearer than Little Rock who can open that door," said Mr. Adams, in a shaky voice. "My God! Spencer, what shall we do? That child—she can't stand it long in there. There isn't enough air, and, besides, she'll go into convulsions from fright."

Agatha's mother, frantic now, beat the door of the vault with her hands. Somebody wildly suggested dynamite. Annabel turned to Jimmy, her large eyes full of anguish, but not yet despairing. To a woman nothing seems quite impossible to the powers of the man she worships.

"Can't you do something, Ralph—*try,* won't you?"

He looked at her with a queer, soft smile on his lips and in his keen eyes.

"Annabel," he said, "give me that rose you are wearing, will you?"

Hardly believing that she heard him aright, she unpinned the bud from the bosom of her dress, and placed it in his hand. Jimmy stuffed it into his vest-pocket, threw off his coat and pulled up his shirt-sleeves. With that act Ralph D. Spencer passed away and Jimmy Valentine took his place.

"Get away from the door, all of you," he commanded, shortly.

He set his suitcase on the table, and opened it out flat. From that time on he seemed to be unconscious of the presence of any one else. He laid out the shining, queer implements swiftly and orderly, whistling softly to himself as he always did when at work. In a deep silence and immovable, the others watched him as if under a spell.

In a minute Jimmy's pet drill was biting smoothly into the steel door. In ten minutes—breaking his own burglarious record—he threw back the bolts and opened the door.

Agatha, almost collapsed, but safe, was gathered into her mother's arms.

Jimmy Valentine put on his coat, and walked outside the railings toward the front door. As he went he thought he heard a far-away voice that he once knew call "Ralph!" But he never hesitated.

At the door a big man stood somewhat in his way.

"Hello, Ben!" said Jimmy, still with his strange smile. "Got around at last, have you? Well, let's go. I don't know that it makes much difference, now."

And then Ben Price acted rather strangely.

"Guess you're mistaken, Mr. Spencer," he said. "Don't believe I recognize you. Your buggy's waiting for you, ain't it?"

And Ben Price turned and strolled down the street.

Friends in San Rosario

The west-bound stopped at San Rosario on time at 8:20 A.M. A man with a thick black-leather wallet under his arm left the train and walked rapidly up the main street of the town. There were other passengers who also got off at San Rosario, but they either slouched limberly over to the railroad eating-house or the Silver Dollar saloon, or joined the groups of idlers about the station.

Indecision had no part in the movements of the man with the wallet. He was short in stature, but strongly built, with very light, closely trimmed hair, smooth, determined face, and aggressive, gold-rimmed nose glasses. He was well dressed in the prevailing Eastern style. His air denoted a quiet but conscious reserve force, if not actual authority.

After walking a distance of three squares he came to the center of the town's business area. Here another street of importance crossed the main one, forming the hub of San Rosario's life and commerce. Upon one corner stood the postoffice. Upon another Rubensky's Clothing Emporium. The other two diagonally opposing corners were occupied by the town's two banks, the First National and the Stockmen's National. Into the First National Bank of San Rosario the newcomer walked, never slowing his brisk step until he stood at the cashier's window. The bank opened for business at nine, and the working force was already assembled, each member preparing his department for the day's business. The cashier was examining the mail when he noticed the stranger standing at his window.

"Bank doesn't open 'til nine," he remarked, curtly, but without feeling. He had had to make that statement so often to early birds since San Rosario adopted city banking hours.

"I am well aware of that," said the other man, in cool, brittle tones. "Will you kindly receive my card?"

The cashier drew the small, spotless parallelogram inside the bars of his wicket, and read:

J. F. C. NETTLEWICK
NATIONAL BANK EXAMINER

"Oh—er—will you walk around inside, Mr.—er—Nettlewick. Your first visit—didn't know your business, of course. Walk right around, please."

The examiner was quickly inside the sacred precincts of the bank, where he was ponderously introduced to each employee in turn by Mr. Edlinger, the cashier—a middle-aged gentleman of deliberation, discretion, and method.

"I was kind of expecting Sam Turner round again, pretty soon," said Mr. Edlinger. "Sam's been examining us now for about four years. I guess you'll find us all right, though considering the tightness in business. Not overly much money on hand, but able to stand the storms, sir, stand the storms."

"Mr. Turner and I have been ordered by the Comptroller to exchange districts," said the examiner, in his decisive, formal tones. "He is covering my old territory in southern Illinois and Indiana. I will take the cash first, please."

Perry Dorsey, the teller, was already arranging his cash on the counter for the examiner's inspection. He knew it was right to a cent, and he had nothing to fear, but he was nervous and flustered. So was every man in the bank. There was something so icy and swift, so impersonal and uncompromising about this man that his very presence seemed an accusation. He looked to be a man who would never make nor overlook an error.

Mr. Nettlewick first seized the currency, and with a rapid, almost juggling motion, counted it by packages. Then he spun the sponge cup toward him and verified the count by bills. His thin, white fingers flew like some expert musician's upon the keys of a piano. He dumped the gold upon the counter with a crash, and the coins whined and sang as they skimmed across the marble slab from the tips of his nimble digits. The air was full of fractional currency when he came to the halves and quarters. He counted the last nickel and dime. He had the scales brought, and he weighed every sack of silver in the vault. He questioned Dorsey concerning each of the cash memoranda—certain checks, charge slips, etc., carried over from the previous day's work—with unimpeachable courtesy, yet with something so mysteriously momentous in his frigid manner, that the teller was reduced to pink cheeks and a stammering tongue.

This newly imported examiner was so different from Sam Turner. It had been Sam's way to enter the bank with a shout, pass the cigars, and tell the latest stories he had picked up on his rounds. His customary greeting to Dorsey had been, "Hello, Perry! Haven't skipped out with the boodle yet, I see." Turner's way of counting the cash had been different too. He would finger the packages of bills in a tired kind of way, and then go into the vault and kick over a few sacks of silver, and the thing was done. Halves and quarters and dimes? Not for Sam Turner. "No chicken feed for me," he would say when they were set before him. "I'm not in the agricultural department." But, then, Turner was a Texan, an old friend of the bank's president, and had known Dorsey since he was a baby.

While the examiner was counting the cash, Major Thomas B. Kingman—known to every one as "Major Tom"—the president of the First National, drove up to the side door with his old dun horse and buggy, and came inside. He saw the examiner busy with the money, and, going into the little "pony corral," as he called it, in which his desk was railed off, he began to look over his letters.

Earlier, a little incident had occurred that even the sharp eyes of the examiner had failed to notice. When he had begun his work at the cash counter, Mr. Edlinger had winked significantly at Roy Wilson, the youthful bank messenger, and nodded his head slightly toward the front door. Roy understood, got his hat and walked leisurely out, with his collector's book under his arm. Once outside, he made a beeline for the Stockmen's National. That bank was also getting ready to open. No customers had, as yet, presented themselves.

"Say, you people!" cried Roy, with the familiarity of youth and long acquaintance, "you want to get a move on you. There's a new bank examiner over at the First, and he's a stem-winder. He's counting nickels on Perry, and he's got the whole outfit bluffed. Mr. Edlinger gave me the tip to let you know."

Mr. Buckley, president of the Stockmen's National—a stout, elderly man, looking like a farmer dressed for Sunday—heard Roy from his private office at the rear and called him.

"Has Major Kingman come down to the bank yet?" he asked of the boy.

"Yes, sir, he was just driving up as I left," said Roy.

"I want you to take him a note. Put it into his own hands as soon as you get back."

Mr. Buckley sat down and began to write.

Roy returned and handed to Major Kingman the envelope containing the note. The major read it, folded it, and slipped it into his vest pocket. He leaned back in his chair for a few moments as if he were meditating deeply, and then rose and went into the vault. He came out with the bulky, old-fashioned leather note case stamped on the back in gilt letters, "Bills Discounted." In this were the notes due the bank with their attached securities, and the major, in his rough way, dumped the lot upon his desk and began to sort them over.

By this time Nettlewick had finished his count of the cash. His pencil fluttered like a swallow over the sheet of paper on which he had set his figures. He opened his black wallet, which seemed to be also a kind of secret memorandum book, made a few rapid figures in it, wheeled and transfixed Dorsey with the glare of his spectacles. That look seemed to say: "You're safe this time, but——"

"Cash all correct," snapped the examiner. He made a dash for the individual bookkeeper, and, for a few minutes there was a fluttering of ledger leaves and a sailing of balance sheets through the air.

"How often do you balance your pass-books?" he demanded, suddenly.

"Er—once a month," faltered the individual bookkeeper, wondering how many years they would give him.

"All right," said the examiner, turning and charging upon the general bookkeeper, who had the statements of his foreign banks and their reconcilement memoranda ready. Everything there was found to be all right. Then the stub book of the certificates of deposit. Flutter—flutter—zip—zip—check! All right, list of overdrafts, please. Thanks. H'm-m. Unsigned bills of the bank next. All right.

Then came the cashier's turn, and easy-going Mr. Edlinger rubbed his nose and polished his glasses nervously under the quick fire of questions concerning the circulation, undivided profits, bank real estate, and stock ownership.

Presently Nettlewick was aware of a big man towering above him at his elbow—a man sixty years of age, rugged and hale, with a rough, grizzled beard, a mass of gray hair, and a pair of penetrating blue eyes that confronted the formidable glasses of the examiner without a flicker.

"Er—Major Kingman, our president—er—Mr. Nettlewick," said the cashier.

Two men of very different types shook hands. One was a finished product of the world of straight lines, conventional methods, and formal affairs. The other was something freer, wider, and nearer to nature. Tom Kingman had not been cut to any pattern. He had been mule-driver, cowboy, ranger, soldier, sheriff, prospector and cattleman. Now, when he was bank president, his old comrades from the prairies, of the saddle, tent, and trail, found no change in him. He had made his fortune when Texas cattle were at the high tide of value, and had organized the First National Bank of San Rosario. In spite of his largeness of heart and sometimes unwise generosity toward his old friends, the bank had prospered, for Major Tom Kingman knew men as well as he knew cattle. Of late years the cattle business had known a depression, and the major's bank was one of the few whose losses had not been great.

"And now," said the examiner, briskly, pulling out his watch, "the last thing is the loans. We will take them up now, if you please."

He had gone through the First National at almost record-breaking speed—but thoroughly, as he did everything. The running order of the bank was smooth and clean, and that had facilitated his work. There was but one other bank in the town. He received from the Government a fee of twenty-five dollars for each bank that he examined. He should be able to go over those loans and discounts in half an hour. If so, he could examine the other bank immediately afterward, and catch the 11:45, the only other train that day in the direction he was working. Otherwise, he would have to spend the night and Sunday in this uninteresting Western town. That was why Mr. Nettlewick was rushing matters.

"Come with me, sir," said Major Kingman, in his deep voice, that united the Southern drawl with the rhythmic twang of the West. "We will go over them together. Nobody in the bank knows those notes as I do. Some of 'em are a little wobbly on their legs, and some are mavericks without extra many brands on their backs, but they'll 'most all pay out at the round-up."

The two sat down at the president's desk. First, the examiner went through the notes at lightning speed, and added up their total, finding it to agree with the amount of loans carried on the book of daily balances. Next, he took up the larger loans, inquiring scrupulously into the condition of their endorsers or securities. The new examiner's mind seemed to course and turn and make unexpected dashes hither and thither like a bloodhound seeking a trail. Finally he pushed aside all the notes except a few, which he arranged in a neat pile before him, and began a dry, formal little speech.

"I find, sir, the condition of your bank to be very good, considering the poor crops and the depression in the cattle interests of your state. The clerical work seems to be done accurately and punctually. Your past-due paper is moderate in amount, and promises only a small loss. I would recommend the calling in of your large loans, and the making of only sixty and ninety day or call loans until general business revives. And now, there is one thing more, and I will have finished with the bank. Here are six notes aggregating something like $40,000. They are secured, according to their faces, by various stocks, bonds, shares, etc., to the value of $70,000. Those securities are missing from the notes to which they should be attached. I suppose you have them in the safe or vault. You will permit me to examine them."

Major Tom's light-blue eyes turned unflinchingly toward the examiner.

"No, sir," he said, in a low but steady tone; "those securities are neither in the safe nor the vault. I have taken them. You may hold me personally responsible for their absence."

Nettlewick felt a slight thrill. He had not expected this. He had struck a momentous trail when the hunt was drawing to a close.

"Ah!" said the examiner. He waited a moment, and then continued: "May I ask you to explain more definitely?"

"The securities were taken by me," repeated the major. "It was not for my own use, but to save an old friend in trouble. Come in here, sir, and we'll talk it over."

He led the examiner into the bank's private office at the rear, and closed the door. There was a desk, and a table, and half-a-dozen leather-covered chairs. On the wall was the mounted head of a Texas steer with horns five feet from tip to tip. Opposite hung the major's old cavalry saber that he had carried at Shiloh and Fort Pillow.

Placing a chair for Nettlewick, the major seated himself by the window, from which he could see the post-office and the carved limestone front of the Stockmen's National. He did not speak at once, and Nettlewick felt, perhaps, that the ice should be broken by something so near its own temperature as the voice of official warning.

"Your statement," he began, "since you have failed to modify it, amounts, as you must know, to a very serious thing. You are aware, also, of what my duty must compel me to do. I shall have to go before the United States Commissioner and make——"

"I know, I know," said Major Tom, with a wave of his hand. "You don't suppose I'd run a bank without being posted on national banking laws and the revised statutes! Do your duty. I'm not asking any favors. But I spoke of my friend. I did want you to hear me tell about Bob."

Nettlewick settled himself in his chair. There would be no leaving San Rosario for him that day. He would have to telegraph to the Comptroller of the Currency; he would have to swear out a warrant before the United States Commissioner for the arrest of Major Kingman; perhaps he would be ordered to close the bank on account of the loss of the securities. It was not the first crime the examiner had unearthed. Once or twice the terrible upheaval of human emotions that his investigations had loosed had almost caused a ripple in his official calm. He had seen bank men kneel and plead and cry like women for a chance—an hour's time—the overlooking of a single error. One cashier had shot himself at his desk before him. None of them had taken it with the dignity and coolness of this stern old Westerner. Nettlewick felt that he owed it to him at least to listen if he wished to talk. With his elbow on the arm of his chair, and his square chin resting upon the fingers of his right hand, the bank examiner waited to hear the confession of the president of the First National Bank of San Rosario.

"When a man's your friend," began Major Tom, somewhat didactically, "for forty years, and tried by water, fire, earth, and cyclones, when you can do him a little favor you feel like doing it."

("Embezzle for him $70,000 worth of securities," thought the examiner.)

"We were cowboys together, Bob and I," continued the major, speaking slowly, and deliberately, and musingly, as if his thoughts were rather with the past than the critical present, "and we prospected together for gold and silver over Arizona, New Mexico, and a good part of California. We were both in the war of sixty-one, but in different commands. We've fought Indians and horse thieves side by side; we've starved for weeks in a cabin in the Arizona mountains, buried twenty feet deep in snow; we've ridden herd together when the wind blew so hard the lightning couldn't strike—well, Bob and I have been through some rough spells since the first time we met in the branding camp of the old Anchor-Bar ranch. And during that time we've found it necessary more than once to help each other out of tight places. In those days it was expected of a man to stick to his friend, and he didn't ask any credit for it. Probably next day you'd need him to get at your back and help stand off a band of Apaches, or put a tourniquet on your leg above a rattlesnake bite and ride for whisky. So, after all, it was give and take, and if you didn't stand square with your pardner, why, you might be shy one when you needed him. But Bob was a man who was willing to go further than that. He never played a limit.

"Twenty years ago I was sheriff of this county and I made Bob my chief deputy. That was before the boom in cattle when we both made our stake. I was sheriff and collector, and it was a big thing for me then. I was married, and we had a boy and a girl—a four and a six year old. There was a comfortable house next to the courthouse, furnished by the county, rent free, and I was saving some money. Bob did most of the office work. Both of us had seen rough times and plenty of rustling and danger, and I tell you it was great to hear the rain and the sleet dashing against the windows of nights, and be warm and safe and comfortable, and know you could get up in the morning and be shaved and have folks call you 'mister.' And then, I had the finest wife and kids that ever struck the range, and my old friend with me enjoying the first fruits of prosperity and white shirts, and I guess I was happy. Yes, I was happy about that time."

The major sighed and glanced casually out of the window. The bank examiner changed his position, and leaned his chin upon his other hand.

"One winter," continued the major, "the money for the county taxes came pouring in so fast that I didn't have time to take the stuff to the bank for a week. I just shoved the checks into a cigar box and the money into a sack, and locked them in the big safe that belonged in the sheriff's office.

"I had been overworked that week, and was about sick, anyway. My nerves were out of order, and my sleep at night didn't seem to rest me. The doctor had some scientific name for it, and I was taking medicine. And so, added to the rest, I went to bed at night with that money on my mind. Not that there was much need of being worried, for the safe was a good one, and nobody but Bob and I knew the combination. On Friday night there was about $6,500 in cash in the bag. On Saturday morning I went to the office as usual. The safe was locked, and Bob was writing at his desk. I opened the safe, and the money was gone. I called Bob, and roused everybody in the courthouse to announce the robbery. It struck me that Bob took it pretty quiet, considering how much it reflected upon both him and me.

"Two days went by and we never got a clew. It couldn't have been burglars, for the safe had been opened by the combination in the proper way. People must have begun to talk, for one afternoon in comes Alice—that's my wife—and the boy and girl, and Alice stamps her foot, and her eyes flash, and she cries out, 'The lying wretches—Tom, Tom!' and I catch her in a faint, and bring her 'round little by little, and she lays her head down and cries and cries for the first time since she took Tom Kingman's name and fortunes. And Jack and Zilla—the youngsters—they were always wild as tigers clubs to rush at Bob and climb all over him whenever they were allowed to come to the courthouse—they stood and kicked their little shoes, and herded together like scared partridges. They were having their first trip down into the shadows of life. Bob was working at his desk, and he got up and went out without a word. The grand jury was in session then, and the next morning Bob went before them and confessed that he stole the money. He said he lost it in a poker game. In fifteen minutes they had found a true bill and sent me the warrant to arrest the man with whom I'd been closer than a thousand brothers for many a year.

"I did it, and then I said to Bob, pointing: 'There's my house, and here's my office, and up there's Maine, and out that way is California, and over there is Florida—and that's your range 'til court meets. You're in my charge, and I take the responsibility. You be here when you're wanted.'

" 'Thanks, Tom,' he said, kind of carelessly; 'I was sort of hoping you wouldn't lock me up. Court meets next Monday, so, if you don't object, I'll just loaf around the office until then. I've got one favor to ask, if it isn't too much. If you'd let the kids come out in the yard once in a while and have a romp I'd like it.'

" 'Why not?' I answered him. 'They're welcome, and so are you. And come to my house the same as ever.' You see, Mr. Nettlewick, you can't make a friend of a thief, but neither can you make a thief of a friend, all at once."

The examiner made no answer. At that moment was heard the shrill whistle of a locomotive pulling into the depot. That was the train on the little, narrow-gauge road that struck into San Rosario from the south. The major cocked his ear and listened for a moment, and looked at his watch. The narrow-gauge was in on time—10:35. The major continued.

"So Bob hung around the office, reading the papers and smoking. I put another deputy to work in his place, and, after a while, the first excitement of the case wore off.

"One day when we were alone in the office Bob came over to where I was sitting. He was looking sort of grim and blue—the same look he used to get when he'd been up watching for Indians all night or herd-riding.

" 'Tom,' says he, 'it's harder than standing off redskins; it's harder than lying in the lava desert forty miles from water; but I'm going to stick it out to the end. You know that's been my style. But if you'd tip me the smallest kind of a sign—if you'd just say, "Bob I understand," why, it would make it lots easier.'

"I was surprised. 'I don't know what you mean, Bob,' I said. 'Of course, you know that I'd do anything under the sun to help you that I could. But you've got me guessing.'

" 'All right, Tom,' was all he said, and he went back to his newspaper and lit another cigar.

"It was the night before the court met when I found out what he meant. I went to bed that night with the same old, light-headed, nervous feeling come back upon me. I dropped off to sleep about midnight. When I woke I was standing half dressed in one of the courthouse corridors. Bob was holding one of my arms, our family doctor the other and Alice was shaking me and half crying. She had sent for the doctor without my knowing it, and when he came they had found me out of bed and missing, and had begun a search.

" 'Sleep-walking,' said the doctor.

"All of us went back to the house, and the doctor told us some remarkable stories about the strange things people had done while in that condition. I was feeling rather chilly after my trip out, and, as my wife was out of the room at the time, I pulled open the door of an old wardrobe that stood in the room and dragged out a big quilt I had seen in there. With it tumbled out the bag of money for stealing which Bob was to be tried—and convicted—in the morning.

" 'How the jumping rattlesnakes did that get there?' I yelled, and all hands must have seen how surprised I was. Bob knew in a flash.

" 'You darned old snoozer,' he said, with the old-time look on his face, 'I saw you put it there. I watched you open the safe and take it out, and I followed you. I looked through the window and saw you hide it in that wardrobe.'

" 'Then, you blankety-blank, flop-eared, sheep-headed coyote, what did you say you took it for?'

" 'Because,' said Bob, simply, 'I didn't know you were asleep.'

"I saw him glance toward the door of the room where Jack and Zilla were, and I knew then what it meant to be a man's friend from Bob's point of view."

Major Tom paused, and again directed his glance out of the window. He saw someone in the Stockmen's National Bank reach and draw a yellow shade down the whole length of its plate-glass, big front window, although the position of the sun did not seem to warrant such a defensive movement against its rays.

Nettlewick sat up straight in his chair. He had listened patiently, but without consuming interest, to the major's story. It had impressed him as irrelevant to the situation, and it could certainly have no effect upon the consequences. Those Western people, he thought, had an exaggerated sentimentality. They were not businesslike. They needed to be protected from their friends. Evidently the major had concluded. And what he had said amounted to nothing.

"May I ask," said the examiner, "if you have anything further to say that bears directly upon the question of those abstracted securities?"

"Abstracted securities, sir!" Major Tom turned suddenly in his chair, his blue eyes flashing upon the examiner. "What do you mean, sir?"

He drew from his coat pocket a batch of folded papers held together by a rubber band, tossed them into Nettlewick's hands, and rose to his feet.

"You'll find those securities there, sir, every stock, bond, and share of 'em. I took them from the notes while you were counting the cash. Examine and compare them for yourself."

The major led the way back into the banking room. The examiner, astounded, perplexed, nettled, at sea, followed. He felt that he had been made the victim of something that was not exactly a hoax, but that left him in the shoes of one who had been played upon, used, and then discarded, without even an inkling of the game. Perhaps, also, his official position had been irreverently juggled with. But there was nothing he could take hold of. An official report of the matter would be an absurdity. And, somehow, he felt that he would never know anything more about the matter than he did then.

Frigidly, mechanically, Nettlewick examined the securities, found them to tally with the notes, gathered his black wallet, and rose to depart.

"I will say," he protested, turning the indignant glare of his glasses upon Major Kingman, "that your statements—your misleading statements, which you have not condescended to explain—do not appear to be quite the thing, regarded either as business or humor. I do not understand such motives or actions."

Major Tom looked down at him serenely and not unkindly.

"Son," he said, "there are plenty of things in the chaparral, and on the prairies, and up the cañons that you don't understand. But I want to thank you for listening to a garrulous old man's prosy story. We old Texans love to talk about our adventures and our old comrades, and the home folks have long ago learned to run when we begin with 'Once upon a time,' so we have to spin our yarns to the stranger within our gates."

The major smiled, but the examiner only bowed coldly, and abruptly quitted the bank. They saw him travel diagonally across the street in a straight line and enter the Stockmen's National Bank.

Major Tom sat down at his desk and drew from his vest pocket the note Roy had given him. He had read it once, but hurriedly, and now, with something like a twinkle in his eyes, he read it again. These were the words he read:

> Dear Tom:
>
> I hear there's one of Uncle Sam's greyhounds going through you, and that means that we'll catch him inside of a couple of hours, maybe. Now, I want you to do something for me. We've got just $2,200 in the bank, and the law requires that we have $20,000. I let Ross and Fisher have $18,000 late yesterday afternoon to buy up that Gibson bunch of cattle. They'll realize

$40,000 in less than thirty days on the transaction, but that won't make my cash on hand look any prettier to that bank examiner. Now, I can't show him those notes, for they're just plain notes of hand without any security in sight, but you know very well that Pink Ross and Jim Fisher are two of the finest white men God ever made, and they'll do the square thing. You remember Jim Fisher—he was the one who shot that faro dealer in El Paso. I wired Sam Bradshaw's bank to send me $20,000, and it will get in on the narrow-gauge at 10:35. You can't let a bank examiner in to count $2,200 and close your doors. Tom, you hold that examiner. Hold him. Hold him if you have to rope him and sit on his head. Watch our front window after the narrow-gauge gets in, and when we've got the cash inside we'll pull down the shade for a signal. Don't turn him loose till then. I'm counting on you, Tom.

Your Old Pard,
Bob Buckley,
Prest. Stockmen's National

The major began to tear the note into small pieces and throw them into his waste basket. He gave a satisfied little chuckle as he did so.

"Confounded old reckless cowpuncher!" he growled, contentedly, "that pays him some on account for what he tried to do for me in the sheriff's office twenty years ago."

Two Renegades

In the Gate City of the South the Confederate Veterans were reuniting; and I stood to see them march, beneath the tangled flags of the great conflict, to the hall of their oratory and commemoration.

While the irregular and halting line was passing I made onslaught upon it and dragged forth from the ranks my friend Barnard O'Keefe, who had no right to be there. For he was a Northerner born and bred; and what should he be doing hallooing for the Stars and Bars among those gray and moribund veterans? And why should he be trudging, with his shining, martial, humorous, broad face, among those warriors of a previous and alien generation?

I say I dragged him forth, and held him till the last hickory leg and waving goatee had stumbled past. And then I hustled him out of the crowd into a cool interior; for the Gate City was stirred that day, and the hand-organs wisely eliminated "Marching Through Georgia" from their repertories.

"Now, what deviltry are you up to?" I asked of O'Keefe when there were a table and things in glasses between us.

O'Keefe wiped his heated face and instigated a commotion among the floating ice in his glass before he chose to answer.

"I am assisting at the wake," said he, "of the only nation on earth that ever did me a good turn. As one gentleman to another, I am ratifying and celebrating the foreign policy of the late Jefferson Davis, as fine a statesman as ever settled the financial question of a country. Equal ratio—that was his platform—a barrel of money for a barrel of flour—a pair of $20 bills for a pair of boots—a hatful of currency for a new hat—say, ain't that simple compared with W. J. B.'s little old oxidized plank?"

"What talk is this?" I asked. "Your financial digression is merely a subterfuge. Why were you marching in the ranks of the Confederate Veterans?"

"Because, my lad," answered O'Keefe, "the Confederate Government in its might and power interposed to protect and defend Barnard O'Keefe against immediate and dangerous assassination at the hands of a blood-thirsty foreign country after the United States of America had overruled his appeal for protection, and had instructed Private Secretary Cortelyou to reduce his estimate of the Republican majority for 1905 by one vote."

"Come, Barney," said I, "the Confederate States of America has been out of existence nearly forty years. You do not look older yourself. When was it that the deceased government exerted its foreign policy in your behalf?"

"Four months ago," said O'Keefe, promptly. "The infamous foreign power I alluded to is still staggering from the official blow dealt it by Mr. Davis's contraband aggregation of states. That's why you see me cake-walking with the ex-rebs to the illegitimate tune about 'simmon-seels and cotton. I vote for the Great Father in Washington, but I am not going back on Mars' Jeff. You say the Confederacy has been dead forty years? Well, if it hadn't been for it, I'd have been breathing today with soul so dead I couldn't have whispered a single cussword about my native land. The O'Keefes are not overburdened with ingratitude."

I must have looked bewildered. "The war was over," I said vacantly, "in——"

O'Keefe laughed loudly, scattering my thoughts.

"Ask old Doc Millikin if the war is over!" he shouted, hugely diverted. "Oh, no! Doc hasn't surrendered yet. And the Confederate States! Well, I just told you they bucked officially and solidly and nationally against a foreign government four months ago and kept me from being shot. Old Jeff's country stepped in and brought me off under its wing while Roosevelt was having a gunboat painted and waiting for the National Campaign Committee to look up whether I had ever scratched the ticket."

"Isn't there a story in this, Barney?" I asked.

"No," said O'Keefe; "but I'll give you the facts. You know I went down to Panama when this irritation about a canal began. I thought I'd get in on the ground floor. I did, and had to sleep on it, and drink water with little zoos in it; so, of course, I got the Chagres fever. That was in a little town called San Juan on the coast.

"After I got the fever hard enough to kill a Port-au-Prince nigger, I had a relapse in the shape of Doc Millikin.

"There was a doctor to attend a sick man! If Doc Millikin had your case, he made the terrors of death seem like an invitation to a donkey-party. He had the bedside manners of a Piute medicine-man and the soothing presence of a dray loaded with iron bridge-girders. When he laid his hand on your fevered brow you felt like Cap John Smith just before Pocahontas went his bail.

"Well, this old medical outrage floated down to my shack when I sent for him. He was built like a shad, and his eyebrows was black, and his white whiskers trickled down from his chin like milk coming out of a sprinkling-pot. He had a nigger boy along carrying an old tomato-can full of calomel, and a saw.

"Doc felt my pulse, and then he began to mess up some calomel with an agricultural implement that belonged to the trowel class.

" 'I don't want any death-mask made yet, Doc,' I says, 'nor my liver put in a plaster-of-paris cast. I'm sick; and it's medicine I need, not frescoing.'

" 'You're a blame Yankee, ain't you?' asked Doc, going on mixing up his Portland cement.

" 'I'm from the North,' says I, 'but I'm a plain man, and don't care for mural decorations. When you get the Isthmus all asphalted over with that boll-weevil prescription, would you mind giving me a dose of pain-killer, or a little strychnine on toast to ease up this feeling of unhealthiness that I have got?'

" 'They was all sassy, just like you,' says old Doc, 'but we lowered their temperature considerable. Yes, sir, I reckon we sent a good many of ye over to old *mortuis nisi bonum.* Look at Antietam and Bull Run and Seven Pines and around Nashville! There never was a battle where we didn't lick ye unless you was ten to our one. I knew you were a blame Yankee the minute I laid eyes on you.'

" 'Don't reopen the chasm, Doc,' I begs him. 'Any Yankeeness I may have is geographical; and, as far as I am concerned a Southerner is as good as a Filipino any day. I'm feeling too bad to argue. Let's have secession without misrepresentation, if you say so; but what I need is more laudanum and less Lundy's Lane. If you're mixing that compound gefloxide of gefloxicum for me, please fill my ears with it before you get around to the battle of Gettysburg, for there is a subject full of talk.'

"By this time Doc Millikin had thrown up a line of fortifications on square pieces of paper; and he says to me: 'Yank, take one of these powders every two hours. They won't kill you. I'll be around again about sundown to see if you're alive.'

"Old Doc's powders knocked the Chagres. I stayed in San Juan, and got to knowing him better. He was from Mississippi, and the red-hottest Southerner that ever smelled mint. He made Stonewall Jackson and R. E. Lee look like Abolitionists. He had a family somewhere down near Yazoo City; but he stayed away from the States on account of an uncontrollable liking he had for the absence of a Yankee government. Him and me got as thick personally as the Emperor of Russia and the dove of peace, but sectionally we didn't amalgamate.

" 'Twas a beautiful system of medical practice introduced by old

Doc into that isthmus of land. He'd take that bracket-saw and the mild chloride and his hypodermic, and treat anything from yellow fever to a personal friend.

"Besides his other liabilities Doc could play a flute for a minute or two. He was guilty of two tunes—'Dixie' and another one that was mighty close to the 'Suwanee River'—you might say one of its tributaries. He used to come down and sit with me while I was getting well, and aggrieve his flute and say unreconstructed things about the North. You'd have thought the smoke from the first gun at Fort Sumter was still floating around in the air.

"You know that was about the time they staged them property revolutions down there, that wound up in the fifth act with the thrilling canal scene where Uncle Sam has nine curtain-calls holding Miss Panama by the hand, while the bloodhounds keep Senator Morgan treed up in a cocoanut-palm.

"That's the way it wound up; but at first it seemed as if Colombia was going to make Panama look like one of the $3.98 kind, with dents made in it in the factory, like they wear at North Beach fish fries. For mine, I played the straw-hat crowd to win; and they gave me a colonel's commission over a brigade of twenty-seven men in the left wing and second joint of the insurgent army.

"The Colombian troops were awfully rude to us. One day when I had my brigade in a sandy spot, with its shoes off doing a battalion drill by squads, the Government army rushed from behind a bush at us, acting as noisy and disagreeable as they could.

"My troops enfiladed, left-faced, and left the spot. After enticing the enemy for three miles or so we struck a brier-patch and had to sit down. When we were ordered to throw up our toes and surrender we obeyed. Five of my best staff-officers fell, suffering extremely with stone-bruised heels.

"Then and there those Colombians took your friend Barney, sir, stripped him of the insignia of his rank, consisting of a pair of brass knuckles and a canteen of rum, and dragged him before a military court. The presiding general went through the usual legal formalities that sometimes cause a case to hang on the calendar of a South American military court as long as ten minutes. He asked me my age, and then sentenced me to be shot.

"They woke up the court interpreter, an American named Jenks, who was in the rum business and vice versa, and told him to translate the verdict.

"Jenks stretched himself and took a morphine tablet.

" 'You've got to back up against th' 'dobe, old man,' says he to me. "Three weeks, I believe, you get. Haven't got a chew of fine-cut on you, have you?'

" 'Translate that again, with footnotes and a glossary,' says I. 'I don't know whether I'm discharged, condemned, or handed over to the Gerry Society.'

" 'Oh,' says Jenks, 'don't you understand? You're to be stood up against a 'dobe wall and shot in two or three weeks—three, I think, they said.'

" 'Would you mind asking 'em which?' says I. 'A week don't amount to much after you are dead, but it seems a real nice long spell while you are alive.'

" 'It's two weeks,' says the interpreter, after inquiring in Spanish of the court. 'Shall I ask 'em again?'

" 'Let be,' says I. 'Let's have a stationary verdict. If I keep on appealing this way they'll have me shot about ten days before I was captured. No, I haven't got any fine-cut.'

"They sends me over to the *calaboza* with a detachment of colored postal-telegraph boys carrying Enfield rifles, and I am locked up in a kind of brick bakery. The temperature in there was just about the kind mentioned in the cooking recipes that call for a quick oven.

"Then I gives a silver dollar to one of the guards to send for the United States consul. He comes around in pajamas with a pair of glasses on his nose and a dozen or two inside of him.

" 'I'm to be shot in two weeks,' says I. 'And although I've made a memorandum of it, I don't seem to get it off my mind. You want to call up Uncle Sam on the cable as quick as you can and get him all worked up about it. Have 'em send the *Kentucky* and the *Kearsarge* and the *Oregon* down right away. That'll be about enough battleships; but it wouldn't hurt to have a couple of cruisers and a torpedo-boat destroyer, too. And—say, if Dewey isn't busy, better have him come along on the fastest one of the fleet.'

" 'Now, see here, O'Keefe,' says the consul, getting the best of a hiccup, 'what do you want to bother the State Department about this matter for?'

" 'Didn't you hear me?' says I; 'I'm to be shot in two weeks. Did you think I said I was going to a lawn-party? And it wouldn't hurt if Roosevelt could get the Japs to send down the *Yellowyamstiskookum* or the *Ogotosingsing* or some other first-class cruiser to help. It would make me feel safer.'

" 'Now, what you want,' says the consul, 'is not to get excited. I'll send you over some chewing tobacco and some banana fritters when I go back. The United States can't interfere in this. You know you were caught insurging against the government, and you're subject to the laws of this country. Tell you the truth, I've had an intimation from the State Department—unofficially, of course—that whenever a soldier of fortune demands a fleet of gunboats in a case of revolutionary *katzenjammer,* I should cut the cable, give him all the tobacco he wants, and after he's shot take his clothes, if they fit me, for part payment of my salary.'

" 'Consul,' says I to him, 'this is a serious question. You are representing Uncle Sam. This ain't any little international tomfoolery, like a universal peace congress or the christening of the *Shamrock IV.* I'm an American citizen and I demand protection. I demand the Mosquito fleet, and Schley, and the Atlantic squadron, and Bob Evans, and General E. Byrd Grubb, and two or three protocols. What are you going to do about it?'

" 'Nothing doing,' says the consul.

" 'Be off with you, then,' says I, out of patience with him, 'and send me Doc Millikin. Ask Doc to come and see me.'

"Doc comes and looks through the bars at me, surrounded by dirty soldiers, with even my shoes and canteen confiscated, and he looks mightily pleased.

" 'Hello, Yank,' says he, 'getting a little taste of Johnson's Island, now, ain't ye?'

" 'Doc,' says I, 'I've just had an interview with the U.S. consul. I gather from his remarks that I might just as well have been caught selling suspenders in Kishineff under the name of Rosenstein as to be in my present condition. It seems that the only maritime aid I am to receive from the United States is some navy-plug to chew. Doc,' says I, 'can't you suspend hostilities on the slavery question long enough to do something for me?'

" 'It ain't been my habit,' Doc Millikin answers, 'to do any painless dentistry when I find a Yank cutting an eyetooth. So the Stars and Stripes ain't landing any marines to shell the huts of the Colombian cannibals, hey? Oh, say, can you see by the dawn's early light the star-spangled banner has fluked in the fight? What's the matter with the War Department, hey? It's a great thing to be a citizen of a gold-standard nation, ain't it?'

" 'Rub it in, Doc, all you want,' says I. 'I guess we're weak on foreign policy.'

" 'For a Yank,' says Doc, putting on his specs and talking more mild, you ain't so bad. If you had come from below the line I reckon I would have liked you right smart. Now since your country has gone back on you, you have to come to the old doctor whose cotton you burned and whose mules you stole and whose niggers you freed to help you. Ain't that so, Yank?'

" 'It is,' says I heartily, 'and let's have a diagnosis of the case right away, for in two weeks' time all you can do is to hold an autopsy and I don't want to be amputated if I can help it.'

" 'Now,' says Doc, business-like, 'it's easy enough for you to get out of this scrape. Money'll do it. You've got to pay a long string of 'em from General Pomposo down to this anthropoid ape guarding your door. About $10,000 will do the trick. Have you got the money?'

" 'Me?' says I. 'I've got one Chili dollar, two *real* pieces, and a *medio.*'

" 'Then if you've any last words, utter 'em,' says that old reb. 'The roster of your financial budget sounds quite much to me like the noise of a requiem.'

" 'Change the treatment,' says I. 'I admit that I'm short. Call a consultation or use radium or smuggle me in some saws or something.'

" 'Yank,' says Doc Millikin, 'I've a good notion to help you. There's only one government in the world that can get you out of this difficulty; and that's the Confederate States of America, the grandest nation that ever existed.'

"Just as you said to me I says to Doc; 'Why, the Confederacy ain't a nation. It's been absolved forty years ago.'

" 'That's a campaign lie,' says Doc. 'She's running along as solid as the Roman Empire. She's the only hope you've got. Now, you, being a Yank, have got to go through with some preliminary obsequies before you can get official aid. You've got to take the oath of allegiance to the Confederate Government. Then I'll guarantee she does all she can for you. What do you say, Yank?—it's your last chance.'

" 'If you're fooling with me, Doc,' I answered, 'you're no better than the United States. But as you say it's the last chance, hurry up and swear me. I always did like corn whisky and 'possum anyhow. I believe I'm half Southerner by nature. I'm willing to try the Ku Klux in place of the khaki. Get brisk.'

"Doc Millikin thinks awhile, and then he offers me this oath of allegiance to take without any kind of a chaser:

" 'I, Barnard O'Keefe, Yank, being of sound body but a Republican mind, hereby swear to transfer my fealty, respect, and allegiance to the Confederate States of America, and the Government thereof, in consideration of said government, through its official acts and powers, obtaining my freedom and release from confinement and sentence of death brought about by the exuberance of my Irish proclivities and my general pizenness as a Yank.'

"I repeated these words after Doc, but they seemed to me a kind of hocus-pocus; and I don't believe any life-insurance company in the country would have issued me a policy on the strength of 'em.

"Doc went away saying he would communicate with his government immediately.

"Say—you can imagine how I felt—me to be shot in two weeks and my only hope for help being a government that's been dead so long that it isn't even remembered except on Decoration Day and when Joe Wheeler signs the voucher for his pay-check. But it was all there was in sight; and somehow I thought Doc Milliken had something up his old alpaca sleeve that wasn't all foolishness.

"Around to the jail comes old Doc again in about a week. I was flea-bitten, a mite sarcastic, and fundamentally hungry.

" 'Any Confederate ironclads in the offing?' I asks. 'Do you notice any sounds resembling the approach of Jeb Stewart's cavalry overland or Stonewall Jackson sneaking up in the rear? If you do, I wish you'd say so.'

" 'It's too soon yet for help to come,' says Doc.

" 'The sooner the better,' says I. 'I don't care if it gets in fully fifteen minutes before I am shot; and if you happen to lay eyes on Beauregard or Albert Sidney Johnson or any of the relief corps, wig-wag 'em to hike along.'

" 'There's been no answer received yet,' says Doc.

" 'Don't forget,' says I, 'that there's only four days more. I don't know how you propose to work this thing, Doc,' I says to him; 'but it seems to me I'd sleep better if you had got a government that was alive and on the map—like Afghanistan or Great Britain, or old man Kruger's kingdom, to take this matter up. I don't mean any disrespect to your Confederate States, but I can't help feeling that my chances of being pulled out of this scrape was decidedly weakened when General Lee surrendered.'

" 'It's your only chance,' said Doc; 'don't quarrel with it. What did your own country do for you?'

"It was only two days before the morning I was to be shot when Doc Millikin came around again.

" 'All right, Yank,' says he. 'Help's come. The Confederate States of America is going to apply for your release. The representatives of the government arrived on a fruit-steamer last night.'

" 'Bully!' says I—'bully for you, Doc! I suppose it's marines with a Gatling. I'm going to love your country all I can for this.'

" 'Negotiations,' says old Doc, 'will be opened between the two governments at once. You will know later on to-day if they are successful.'

"About four in the afternoon a soldier in red trousers brings a paper round to the jail, and they unlocks the door and I walks out. The guard at the door bows and I bows, and I steps into the grass and wades around to Doc Millikin's shack.

"Doc was sitting in his hammock playing 'Dixie,' soft and low and out of tune, on his flute. I interrupted him at 'Look away! look away!' and shook his hand for five minutes.

" 'I never thought,' says Doc, taking a chew fretfully, 'that I'd ever try to save any blame Yank's life. But, Mr. O'Keefe, I don't see but what you are entitled to be considered part human, anyhow. I never thought Yanks had any of the rudiments of decorum and laudability about them. I reckon I might have been too aggregative in my tabulation. But it ain't me you want to thank—it's the Confederate States of America.'

" 'And I'm much obliged to 'em,' says I. 'It's a poor man that wouldn't be patriotic with a country that's saved his life. I'll drink to the Stars and Bars whenever there's a flag-staff and a glass convenient. But where,' says I, 'are the rescuing troops? If there was a gun fired or a shell burst, I didn't hear it.'

"Doc Millikin raises up and points out the window with his flute at the banana-steamer loading with fruit.

" 'Yank,' says he, 'there's a steamer that's going to sail in the morning. If I was you, I'd sail on it. The Confederate Government's done all it can for you. There wasn't a gun fired. The negotiations was carried on secretly between the two nations by the purser of that steamer. I got him to do it because I didn't want to appear in it. Twelve thousand dollars was paid to the officials in bribes to let you go.'

" 'Man!' says I, sitting down hard—'twelve thousand—how will I ever—who could have—where did the money come from?'

" 'Yazoo City,' says Doc Millikin; 'I've got a little bit saved up there. Two barrels full. It looks good to these Colombians. 'Twas Confederate money, every dollar of it. Now do you see why you'd better leave before they try to pass some of it on an expert?'

" 'I do,' says I.

" 'Now, let's hear you give the password,' says Doc Millikin.

" 'Hurrah for Jeff Davis!' says I.

" 'Correct,' says Doc. 'And let me tell you something. The next tune I learn on my flute is going to be "Yankee Doodle." I reckon there's some Yanks that are not so pizen. Or, if you was me, would you try "The Red, White, and Blue"?' "

"The Rose of Dixie"

When *The Rose of Dixie* magazine was started by a stock company in Toombs City, Georgia, there was never but one candidate for its chief editorial position in the minds of its owners. Col. Aquila Telfair was the man for the place. By all the rights of learning, family, reputation, and Southern traditions, he was its foreordained, fit, and logical editor. So, a committee of the patriotic Georgia citizens who had subscribed the founding fund of $100,000 called upon Colonel Telfair at his residence, Cedar Heights, fearful lest the enterprise and the South should suffer by his possible refusal.

The colonel received them in his great library, where he spent most of his days. The library had descended to him from his father. It contained ten thousand volumes, some of which had been published as late as the year 1861. When the deputation arrived, Colonel Telfair was seated at his massive white-pine centre-table, reading Burton's "Anatomy of Melancholy." He arose and shook hands punctiliously with each member of the committee. If you were familiar with *The Rose of Dixie* you will remember the colonel's portrait, which appeared in it from time to time. You could not forget the long, carefully brushed white hair, the hooked, highbridged nose, slightly twisted to the left; the keen eyes under the still black eyebrows; the classic mouth beneath the drooping white mustache, slightly frazzled at the ends.

The committee solicitously offered him the position of managing editor, humbly presenting an outline of the field that the publication was designed to cover and mentioning a comfortable salary. The colonel's lands were growing poorer each year and were much cut up by red gullies. Besides, the honor was not one to be refused.

In a forty-minute speech of acceptance, Colonel Telfair gave an outline of English literature from Chaucer to Macaulay, re-fought the battle of Chancellorsville, and said that, God helping him, he would so conduct *The Rose of Dixie* that its fragrance and beauty would permeate the entire world, hurling back into the teeth of the Northern minions their belief that no genius or good could exist in the brains and hearts of the people whose property they had destroyed and whose rights they had curtailed.

Offices for the magazine were partitioned off and furnished in the second floor of the First National Bank building; and it was for the colonel to cause *The Rose of Dixie* to blossom and flourish or to wilt in the balmy air of the land of flowers.

The staff of assistants and contributors that Editor-Colonel Telfair drew about him was a peach. It was a whole crate of Georgia peaches. The first assistant editor, Tolliver Lee Fairfax, had had a father killed during Pickett's charge. The second assistant, Keats Unthank, was the nephew of one of Morgan's Raiders. The book reviewer, Jackson Rockingham, had been the youngest soldier in the Confederate army, having appeared on the field of battle with a sword in one hand and a milk-bottle in the other. The art editor, Roncesvalles Sykes, was a third cousin to a nephew of Jefferson Davis. Miss Lavinia Terhune, the colonel's stenographer and typewriter, had an aunt who had once been kissed by Stonewall Jackson. Tommy Webster, the head office boy, got his job by having recited Father Ryan's poems, complete, at the commencement exercises of the Toombs City High School. The girls who wrapped and addressed the magazines were members of old Southern families in Reduced Circumstances. The cashier was a scrub named Hawkins, from Ann Arbor, Michigan, who had recommendations and a bond from a guarantee company filed with the owners. Even Georgia stock companies sometimes realize that it takes live ones to bury the dead.

Well, sir, if you believe me, *The Rose of Dixie* blossomed five times before anybody heard of it except the people who buy their hooks and eyes in Toombs City. Then Hawkins climbed off his stool and told on 'em to the stock company. Even in Ann Arbor he had been used to having his business propositions heard of at least as far away as Detroit. So an advertising manager was engaged—Beauregard Fitzhugh Banks—a young man in a lavender necktie, whose grandfather had been the Exalted High Pillow-slip of the Ku Klux Klan.

In spite of which *The Rose of Dixie* kept coming out every month. Although in every issue it ran photos of either the Taj Mahal or the Luxembourg Gardens, or Carmencita or La Follette, a certain number of people bought it and subscribed for it. As a boom for it, Editor-Colonel Telfair ran three different views of Andrew Jackson's old home, "The Hermitage," a full-page engraving of the second battle of Manassas, entitled "Lee to the Rear!" and a five-thousand-word biography of Belle Boyd in the same number. The subscription list that month advanced 118. Also there were poems in the same issue by Leonina Vashti Haricot (pen-name), related to the Haricots of Charleston, South Carolina, and Bill Thompson, nephew of one of the stockholders. And an article from a special society correspondent describing a tea-party given by the swell Boston and English set, where a lot of tea was spilled overboard by some of the guests masquerading as Indians.

One day a person whose breath would easily cloud a mirror, he was so much alive, entered the office of *The Rose of Dixie.* He was a man about the size of a real-estate agent, with a self-tied tie and a manner that he must have borrowed conjointly from W. J. Bryan, Hackenschmidt, and Hetty Green. He was shown into the editor-colonel's *pons asinorum.* Colonel Telfair rose and began a Prince Albert bow.

"I'm Thacker," said the intruder, taking the editor's chair—"T. T. Thacker, of New York."

He dribbled hastily upon the colonel's desk some cards, a bulk manila envelope, and a letter from the owners of *The Rose of Dixie.* This letter introduced Mr. Thacker, and politely requested Colonel Telfair to give him a conference and whatever information about the magazine he might desire.

"I've been corresponding with the secretary of the magazine owners for some time," said Thacker, briskly. "I'm a practical magazine man myself, and a circulation booster as good as any, if I do say it. I'll guarantee an increase of anywhere from ten thousand to a hundred thousand a year for any publication that isn't printed in a dead language. I've had my eye on *The Rose of Dixie* ever since it started. I know every end of the business from editing to setting up the classified ads. Now, I've come down here to put a good bunch of money in the magazine, if I can see my way clear. It ought to be made to pay. The secretary tells me it's losing money. I don't see why a magazine in the South, if it's properly handled, shouldn't get a good circulation in the North, too."

Colonel Telfair leaned back in his chair and polished his gold-rimmed glasses.

"Mr. Thacker," said he, courteously but firmly, "*The Rose of Dixie* is a publication devoted to the fostering and the voicing of Southern genius. Its watchword, which you may have seen on the cover, is 'Of, For, and By the South.' "

"But you wouldn't object to a Northern circulation, would you?" asked Thacker.

"I suppose," said the editor-colonel, "that it is customary to open the circulation lists to all. I do not know. I have nothing to do with the business affairs of the magazine. I was called upon to assume editorial control of it, and I have devoted to its conduct such poor literary talents as I may possess and whatever store of erudition I may have acquired."

"Sure," said Thacker. "But a dollar is a dollar anywhere, North, South, or West—whether you're buying codfish, goober peas, or Rocky Ford cantaloupes. Now, I've been looking over your November number. I see one here on your desk. You don't mind running over it with me?

"Well, your leading article is all right. A good write-up of the cotton-belt with plenty of photographs is a winner any time. New York is always interested in the cotton crop. And this sensational account of the Hatfield-McCoy feud, by a schoolmate of a niece of the Governor of Kentucky, isn't such a bad idea. It happened so long ago that most people have forgotten it. Now, here's a poem three pages long called 'The Tyrant's Foot,' by Lorella Lascelles. I've pawed around a good deal over manuscripts, but I never saw her name on a rejection slip."

"Miss Lascelles," said the editor, "is one of our most widely recognized Southern poetesses. She is closely related to the Alabama Lascelles family, and made with her own hands the silken Confederate banner that was presented to the governor of that state at his inauguration."

"But why," persisted Thacker, "is the poem illustrated with a view of the M. & O. Railroad depot at Tuscaloosa?"

"The illustration," said the colonel, with dignity, "shows a corner of the fence surrounding the old homestead where Miss Lascelles was born."

"All right," said Thacker. "I read the poem, but I couldn't tell whether it was about the depot or the battle of Bull Run. Now, here's a short story called 'Rosie's Temptation,' by Fosdyke Piggott. It's rotten. What is a Piggott, anyway?"

"Mr. Piggott," said the editor, "is a brother of the principal stockholder of the magazine."

"All's right with the world—Piggott passes," said Thacker. "Well, this article on Arctic exploration and the one on tarpon fishing might go. But how about this write-up of the Atlanta, New Orleans, Nashville, and Savannah breweries? It seems to consist mainly of statistics about their output and the quality of their beer. What's the chip over the bug?"

"If I understand your figurative language," answered Colonel Telfair, "it is this: the article you refer to was handed to me by the owners of the magazine with instructions to publish it. The literary quality of it did not appeal to me. But, in a measure, I feel impelled to conform, in certain matters, to the wishes of the gentlemen who are interested in the financial side of *The Rose.*"

"I see," said Thacker. "Next we have two pages of selections from 'Lalla Rookh,' by Thomas Moore. Now, what Federal prison did Moore escape from, or what's the name of the F. F. V. family that he carries as a handicap?"

"Moore was an Irish poet who died in 1852," said Colonel Telfair, pityingly. "He is a classic. I have been thinking of reprinting his translation of Anacreon serially in the magazine."

"Look out for the copyright laws," said Thacker, flippantly. "Who's Bessie Belleclair, who contributes the essay on the newly completed waterworks plant in Milledgeville?"

"The name, sir," said Colonel Telfair, "is the *nom de guerre* of Miss Elvira Simpkins. I have not the honor of knowing the lady; but her contribution was sent us by Congressman Brower, of her native state. Congressman Brower's mother was related to the Polks of Tennessee."

"Now, see here, Colonel," said Thacker, throwing down the magazine, "this won't do. You can't successfully run a magazine for one particular section of the country. You've got to make a universal appeal. Look how the Northern publications have catered to the South and encouraged the Southern writers. And you've got to go far and wide for your contributors. You've got to buy stuff according to its quality, without any regard to the pedigree of the author. Now, I'll bet a quart of ink that this Southern parlor organ you've been running has never played a note that originated above Mason & Hamlin's line. Am I right?"

"I have carefully and conscientiously rejected all contributions from that section of the country—if I understand your figurative language aright," replied the colonel.

"All right. Now, I'll show you something."

Thacker reached for his thick manila envelope and dumped a mass of typewritten manuscript on the editor's desk.

"Here's some truck," said he, "that I paid cash for, and brought along with me."

One by one he folded back the manuscripts and showed their first pages to the colonel.

"Here are four short stories by four of the highest priced authors in the United States—three of 'em living in New York, and one commuting. There's a special article on Vienna-bred society by Tom Vampson. Here's an Italian serial by Captain Jack—no—it's the other Crawford. Here are three separate exposés of city governments by Sniffings, and here's a dandy entitled 'What Women Carry in Dress-Suit Cases'—a Chicago newspaper woman hired herself out for five years as a lady's maid to get that information. And here's a Synopsis of Preceding Chapters of Hall Caine's new serial to appear next June. And here's a couple of pounds of *vers de société* that I got at a rate from the clever magazines. That's the stuff that people everywhere want. And now here's a write-up with photographs at the ages of four, twelve, twenty-two, and thirty of George B. McClellan. It's a prognostication. He's bound to be elected Mayor of New York. It'll make a big hit all over the country. He——"

"I beg your pardon," said Colonel Telfair, stiffening in his chair. "What was the name?"

"Oh, I see," said Thacker, with half a grin. "Yes, he's a son of the General. We'll pass that manuscript up. But, if you'll excuse me, Colonel, it's a magazine we're trying to make go off—not the first gun at Fort Sumter. Now, here's a thing that's bound to get next to you. It's an original poems by James Whitcomb Riley. J. W. himself. You know what that means to a magazine. I won't tell you what I had to pay for that poem; but I'll tell you this—Riley can make more money writing with a fountain-pen than you or I can with one that lets the ink run. I'll read you the last two stanzas:

"Pa lays around 'n' loafs all day,
'N' reads and makes us leave him be.
He lets me do just like I please,
'N' when I'm bad he laughs at me,
'N' when I holler loud 'n' say
Bad words 'n' then begin to tease
The cat, 'n' pa just smiles, ma's mad
'N' gives me Jesse crost her knees.
I always wondered why that wuz—
I guess it's cause
Pa never does.

" 'N' after all the lights are out
I'm sorry 'bout it; so I creep
Out of my trundle bed to ma's
'N' say I love her a whole heap,
'N' kiss her, 'n' I hug her tight.
'N' it's too dark to see her eyes,
But every time I do I know
She cries 'n' cries 'n' cries 'n' cries.
I always wondered why that wuz—
I guess it's cause
Pa never does.

"That's the stuff," continued Thacker. "What do you think of that?"

"I am not unfamiliar with the works of Mr. Riley," said the colonel deliberately. "I believe he lives in Indiana. For the last ten years I have been somewhat of a literary recluse, and am familiar with nearly all the books in the Cedar Heights library. I am also of the opinion that a magazine should contain a certain amount of poetry. Many of the sweetest singers of the South have already contributed to the pages of *The Rose of Dixie.* I, myself, have thought of translating from the original for publication in its pages the works of the great Italian poet Tasso. Have you ever drunk from the fountain of this immortal poet's lines, Mr. Thacker?"

"Not even a demi-Tasso," said Thacker. "Now, let's come to the point, Colonel Telfair. I've already invested some money in this as a flyer. That bunch of manuscripts cost me $4,000. My object was to try a number of them in the next issue—I believe you make up less than a month ahead—and see what effect it has on the circulation. I believe that by printing the best stuff we can get in the North, South, East, or West we can make the magazine go. You have there the letter from the owning company asking you to coöperate with me in the plan. Let's chuck out some of this slush that you've been publishing just because the writers are related to the Skoopdoodles of Skoopdoodle County. Are you with me?"

"As long as I continue to be the editor of *The Rose,*" said Colonel Telfair, with dignity, "I shall be its editor. But I desire also to conform to the wishes of its owners if I can do so conscientiously."

"That's the talk," said Thacker, briskly. "Now, how much of this stuff I've brought can we get into the January number? We want to begin right away."

"There is yet space in the January number," said the editor, "for about eight thousand words, roughly estimated."

"Great!" said Thacker. "It isn't much, but it'll give the readers some change from goobers, governors, and Gettysburg. I'll leave the selection of the stuff I brought to fill the space to you, as it's all good. I've got to run back to New York, and I'll be down again in a couple of weeks."

Colonel Telfair slowly swung his eye-glasses by their broad, black ribbon.

"The space in the January number that I referred to," said he, measuredly, "has been held open purposely, pending a decision that I have not yet made. A short time ago a contribution was submitted to *The Rose of Dixie* that is one of the most remarkable literary efforts that has ever come under my observation. None but a master mind and talent could have produced it. It would about fill the space that I have reserved for its possible use."

Thacker looked anxious.

"What kind of stuff is it?" he asked. "Eight thousand words sounds suspicious. The oldest families must have been collaborating. Is there going to be another secession?"

"The author of the article," continued the colonel, ignoring Thacker's allusions, "is a writer of some reputation. He has also distinguished himself in other ways. I do not feel at liberty to reveal to you his name—at least not until I have decided whether or not to accept his contribution."

"Well," said Thacker, nervously, "is it a continued story, or an account of the unveiling of the new town pump in Whitmire, South Carolina, or a revised list of General Lee's body-servants, or what?"

"You are disposed to be facetious," said Colonel Telfair, calmly. "The article is from the pen of a thinker, a philosopher, a lover of mankind, a student, and a rhetorician of high degree."

"It must have been written by a syndicate," said Thacker. "But, honestly, Colonel, you want to go slow. I don't know of any eight-thousand-word single doses of written matter that are read by anybody these days, except Supreme Court briefs and reports of murder trials. You haven't by any accident gotten hold of a copy of one of Daniel Webster's speeches, have you?"

Colonel Telfair swung a little in his chair and looked steadily from under his bushy eyebrows at the magazine promoter.

"Mr. Thacker," he said, gravely, "I am willing to segregate the somewhat crude expression of your sense of humor from the solicitude that your business investments undoubtedly have conferred upon you. But I must ask you to cease your jibes and derogatory comments upon the South and the Southern people. They, sir, will not be tolerated in the office of *The Rose of Dixie* for one moment. And before you proceed with more of your covert insinuations that I, the editor of this magazine, am not a competent judge of the merits of the matter submitted to its consideration, I beg that you will first present some evidence or proof that you are my superior in any way, shape, or form relative to the question in hand."

"Oh, come, Colonel," said Thacker, good-naturedly. "I didn't do anything like that to you. It sounds like an indictment by the fourth assistant attorney-general. Let's get back to business. What's this 8,000 to I shot about?"

"The article," said Colonel Telfair, acknowledging the apology by a slight bow, "covers a wide area of knowledge. It takes up theories and questions that have puzzled the world for centuries, and disposes of them logically and concisely. One by one it holds up to view the evils of the world, points out the way of eradicating them, and then conscientiously and in detail commends the good. There is hardly a phase of human life that it does not discuss wisely, calmly, and equitably. The great policies of governments, the duties of private citizens, the obligations of home life, ethics, morality—all these important subjects are handled with a calm wisdom and confidence that I must confess has captured my admiration."

"It must be a crackerjack," said Thacker, impressed.

"It is a great contribution to the world's wisdom," said the colonel. "The only doubt remaining in my mind as to the tremendous advantage it would be to us to give it publication in *The Rose of Dixie* is that I have not yet sufficient information about the author to give his work publicity in our magazine."

"I thought you said he is a distinguished man," said Thacker.

"He is," replied the colonel, "both in literary and in other more diversified and extraneous fields. But I am extremely careful about the matter that I accept for publication. My contributors are people of unquestionable repute and and connections, which fact can be verified at any time. As I said, I am holding this article until I can acquire more information about its author. I do not know whether I will publish it or not. If I decide against it, I shall be much pleased, Mr. Thacker, to substitute the matter that you are leaving with me in its place."

Thacker was somewhat at sea.

"I don't seem to gather," said he, "much about the gist of this inspired piece of literature. It sounds more like a dark horse than Pegasus to me."

"It is a human document," said the colonel-editor, confidently, "from a man of great accomplishments who, in my opinion, has obtained a stronger grasp on the world and its outcomes than that of any man living to-day."

Thacker rose to his feet excitedly.

"Say!" he said. "It isn't possible that you've cornered John D. Rockefeller's memoirs, is it? Don't tell me that all at once."

"No, sir," said Colonel Telfair. "I am speaking of mentality and literature, not of the less worthy intricacies of trade."

"Well, what's the trouble about running the article," asked Thacker, a little impatiently, "if the man's well known and has got the stuff?"

Colonel Telfair sighed.

"Mr. Thacker," said he, "for once I have been tempted. Nothing has yet appeared in *The Rose of Dixie* that has not been from the pen of one of its sons or daughters. I know little about the author of this article except that he has acquired prominence in a section of the country that has always been inimical to my heart and mind. But I recognize his genius; and, as I have told you, I have instituted an investigation of his personality. Perhaps it will be futile. But I shall pursue the inquiry. Until that is finished, I must leave open the question of filling the vacant space in our January number."

Thacker arose to leave.

"All right, Colonel," he said, as cordially as he could. "You use your own judgment. If you've really got a scoop or something that will make 'em sit up, run it instead of my stuff. I'll drop in again in about two weeks. Good luck!"

Colonel Telfair and the magazine promoter shook hands.

Returning a fortnight later, Thacker dropped off a very rocky Pullman at Toombs City. He found the January number of the magazine made up and the forms closed.

The vacant space that had been yawning for type was filled by an article that was headed thus:

SECOND MESSAGE TO CONGRESS
Written for
"THE ROSE OF DIXIE"
BY
A Member of the Well-Known
BULLOCH FAMILY, OF GEORGIA
T. Roosevelt

The Third Ingredient

The (so-called) Vallambrosa Apartment House is not an apartment house. It is composed of two old-fashioned, brownstone-front residences welded into one. The parlor floor of one side is gay with the wraps and headgear of a modiste; the other is lugubrious with the sophistical promises and grisly display of a painless dentist. You may have a room there for two dollars a week or you may have one for twenty dollars. Among the Vallambrosa's roomers are stenographers, musicians, brokers, shopgirls, spacerate writers, art students, wire-tappers, and other people who lean far over the banister-rail when the door-bell rings.

This treatise shall have to do with but two of the Vallambrosians—though meaning no disrespect to the others.

At six o'clock one afternoon Hetty Pepper came back to her third-floor rear $3.50 room in the Vallambrosa with her nose and chin more sharply pointed than usual. To be discharged from the department store where you have been working four years, and with only fifteen cents in your purse, does have a tendency to make your features appear more finely chiselled.

And now for Hetty's thumb-nail biography while she climbs the two flights of stairs.

She walked into the Biggest Store one morning four years before, with seventy-five other girls, applying for a job behind the waist department counter. The phalanx of wage-earners formed a bewildering scene of beauty, carrying a total mass of blond hair sufficient to have justified the horseback gallops of a hundred Lady Godivas.

The capable, cool-eyed, impersonal, young, bald-headed man, whose task it was to engage six of the contestants, was aware of a feeling of suffocation as if he were drowning in a sea of frangipani, while white clouds, hand-embroidered, floated about him. And then a sail hove in sight. Hetty Pepper, homely of countenance, with small, contemptuous green eyes and chocolate-colored hair, dressed in a suit of plain burlap and a common-sense hat, stood before him with every one of her twenty-nine years of life unmistakably in sight.

"You're on!" shouted the bald-headed young man, and was saved. And that is how Hetty came to be employed in the Biggest Store. The story of her rise to an eight-dollar-a-week salary is the combined stories of Hercules, Joan of Arc, Una, Job, and Little-Red-

Riding-Hood. You shall not learn from me the salary that was paid her as a beginner. There is a sentiment growing about such things, and I want no millionaire store-proprietors climbing the fire-escape of my tenement-house to throw dynamite bombs into my skylight boudoir.

The story of Hetty's discharge from the Biggest Store is so nearly a repetition of her engagement as to be monotonous.

In each department of the store there is an omniscient, omnipresent, and omnivorous person carrying always a mileage book and a red necktie, and referred to as a "buyer." The destinies of the girls in his department who live on (see Bureau of Victual Statistics)—so much per week are in his hands.

This particular buyer was a capable, cool-eyed, impersonal, young, bald-headed man. As he walked along the aisles of his department he seemed to be sailing on a sea of frangipani, while white clouds, machine-embroidered, floated around him. Too many sweets bring surfeit. He looked upon Hetty Pepper's homely countenance, emerald eyes, and chocolate-colored hair as a welcome oasis of green in a desert of cloying beauty. In a quiet angle of a counter he pinched her arm kindly, three inches above the elbow. She slapped him three feet away with one good blow of her muscular and not especially lily-white right. So, now you know why Hetty Pepper came to leave the Biggest Store at thirty minutes' notice, with one dime and a nickel in her purse.

This morning's quotations list the price of rib beef at six cents per (butcher's) pound. But on the day that Hetty was "released" by the B. S. the price was seven and one half cents. That fact is what makes this story possible. Otherwise, the extra four cents would have——

But the plot of nearly all the good stories in the world is concerned with shorts who were unable to cover; so, you can find no fault with this one.

Hetty mounted with her rib beef to her $3.50 third-floor-back. One hot, savory beef-stew for supper, a night's good sleep, and she would be fit in the morning to apply again for the tasks of Hercules, Joan of Arc, Una, Job, and Little-Red-Riding-Hood.

In her room she got the graniteware stew-pan out of the 2 × 4 foot china—er—I mean earthenware closet, and began to dig down in a rat's-nest of paper bags for the potatoes and onions. She came out with her nose and chin just a little sharper pointed.

There was neither a potato nor an onion. Now, what kind of a beef-stew can you make out of simply beef? You can make oyster-soup without oysters, turtle-soup without turtles, coffee-cake without coffee, but you can't make beef-stew without potatoes and onions.

But rib beef alone, in an emergency, can make an ordinary pine door look like a wrought-iron gambling-house portal to the wolf. With salt and pepper and a tablespoonful of flour (first well stirred in a little cold water) 'twill serve—'tis not so deep as a lobster à la Newburgh, nor so wide as a church festival doughnut; but 'twill serve.

Hetty took her stew-pan to the rear of the third-floor hall. According to the advertisements of the Vallambrosa there was running water to be found there. Between you and me and the water-meter, it only ambled or walked through the faucets; but technicalities have no place here. There was also a sink where housekeeping roomers often met to dump their coffee grounds and glare at one another's kimonos.

At this sink Hetty found a girl with heavy, gold-brown, artistic hair and plaintive eyes washing two large "Irish" potatoes. Hetty knew the Vallambrosa as well as any one not owning "double hextra-magnifying eyes" could compass its mysteries. The kimonos were her encyclopædia, her "Who's What?" her clearing-house of news, of goers and comers. From a rose-pink kimono edged with Nile green she had learned that the girl with the potatoes was a miniature-painter living in a kind of attic—or "studio," as they prefer to call it—on the top floor. Hetty was not certain in her mind what a miniature was; but it certainly wasn't a house; because house-painters, although they wear splashy overalls and poke ladders in your face on the street, are known to indulge in a riotous profusion of food at home.

The potato girl was quite slim and small, and handled her potatoes as an old bachelor uncle handles a baby who is cutting teeth. She had a dull shoemaker's knife in her right hand, and she had begun to peel one of the potatoes with it.

Hetty addressed her in the punctiliously formal tone of one who intends to be cheerfully familiar with you in the second round.

"Beg pardon," she said, "for butting into what's not my business, but if you peel them potatoes you lose out. They're new Bermudas. You want to scrape 'em. Lemme show you."

She took a potato and the knife, and began to demonstrate.

"Oh, thank you," breathed the artist. "I didn't know. And I *did* hate to see the thick peeling go; it seemed such a waste. But I thought they always had to be peeled. When you've got only potatoes to eat, the peelings count, you know."

"Say, kid," said Hetty, staying her knife, "you ain't up against it, too, are you?"

The miniature artist smiled starvedly.

"I suppose I am. Art—or, at least, the way I interpret it—doesn't seem to be much in demand. I have only these potatoes for my dinner. But they aren't so bad boiled and hot, with a little butter and salt."

"Child," said Hetty, letting a brief smile soften her rigid features, "Fate has sent me and you together. I've had it handed to me in the neck, too; but I've got a chunk of meat in my room as big as a lap-dog. And I've done everything to get potatoes except pray for 'em. Lets me and you bunch our commissary departments and make a stew of 'em. We'll cook it in my room. If we only had an onion to go in it! Say, kid, you haven't got a couple of pennies that've slipped down into the lining of your last winter's sealskin, have you? I could step down to the corner and get one at old Giuseppe's stand. A stew without an onion is worse'n a matinée without candy."

"You may call me Cecilia," said the artist. "No; I spent my last penny three days ago."

"Then we'll have to cut the onion out instead of slicing it in," said Hetty. "I'd ask the janitress for one, but I don't want 'em hep just yet to the fact that I'm pounding the asphalt for another job. But I wish we did have an onion."

In the shop-girl's room the two began to prepare their supper. Cecilia's part was to sit on the couch helplessly and beg to be allowed to do something, in the voice of a cooing ring-dove. Hetty prepared the rib beef, putting it in cold salted water in the stew-pan and setting it on the one-burner gas-stove.

"I wish we had an onion," said Hetty, as she scraped the two potatoes.

On the wall opposite the couch was pinned a flaming, gorgeous advertising picture of one of the new ferryboats of the P.U.F.F. Railroad that had been built to cut down the time between Los Angeles and New York City one eighth of a minute.

Hetty, turning her head during her continuous monologue, saw tears running from her guest's eyes as she gazed on the idealized presentment of the speeding, foam-girdled transport.

"Why, say, Cecilia, kid," said Hetty, poising her knife, "is it as bad art as that? I ain't a critic, but I thought it kind of brightened up the room. Of course, a manicure-painter could tell it was a bum picture in a minute. I'll take it down if you say so. I wish to the holy Saint Potluck we had an onion."

But the miniature miniature-painter had tumbled down, sobbing, with her nose indenting the hard-woven drapery of the couch. Something was here deeper than the artistic temperament offended at crude lithography.

Hetty knew. She had accepted her rôle long ago. How scant the words with which we try to describe a single quality of a human being! When we reach the abstract we are lost. The nearer to Nature that the babbling of our lips comes, the better do we understand. Figuratively (let us say), some people are Bosoms, some are Hands, some are Heads, some are Muscles, some are Feet, some are Backs for burdens.

Hetty was a Shoulder. Hers was a sharp, sinewy shoulder; but all her life people had laid their heads upon it, metaphorically or actually, and had left there all or half their troubles. Looking at Life anatomically, which is as good a way as any, she was preordained to be a Shoulder. There were few truer collar-bones anywhere than hers.

Hetty was only thirty-three, and she had not yet outlived the little pang that visited her whenever the head of youth and beauty leaned upon her for consolation. But one glance in her mirror always served as an instantaneous painkiller. So she gave one pale look into the crinkly old looking-glass on the wall above the gas-stove, turned down the flame a little lower from the bubbling beef and potatoes, went over to the couch, and lifted Cecilia's head to its confessional.

"Go on and tell me, honey," she said. "I know now that it ain't art that's worrying you. You met him on a ferry-boat, didn't you? Go on, Cecilia, kid, and tell your—your Aunt Hetty about it."

But youth and melancholy must first spend the surplus of sighs and tears that waft and float the barque of romance to its harbor in the delectable isles. Presently, through the stringy tendons that formed the bars of the confessional, the penitent—or was it the glorified communicant of the sacred flame?—told her story without art or illumination.

"It was only three days ago. I was coming back on the ferry from Jersey City. Old Mr. Schrum, an art dealer, told me of a rich man in Newark who wanted a miniature of his daughter painted. I went to see him and showed him some of my work. When I told him the price would be fifty dollars he laughed at me like a hyena. He said an enlarged crayon twenty times the size would cost him only eight dollars.

"I had just enough money to buy my ferry ticket back to New York. I felt as if I didn't want to live another day. I must have looked as I felt, for I saw *him* on the row of seats opposite me, looking at me as if he understood. He was nice-looking, but, oh, above everything else, he looked kind. When one is tired or unhappy or hopeless, kindness counts more than anything else.

"When I got so miserable that I couldn't fight against it any longer, I got up and walked slowly out the rear door of the ferry-boat cabin. No one was there, and I slipped quickly over the rail, and dropped into the water. Oh, friend Hetty, it was cold, cold!

"For just one moment I wished I was back in the old Vallambrosa, starving and hoping. And then I got numb, and didn't care. And then I felt that somebody else was in the water close by me, holding me up. He had followed me, and jumped in to save me.

"Somebody threw a thing like a big, white doughnut at us, and he made me put my arms through the hole. Then the ferry-boat backed, and they pulled us on board. Oh, Hetty, I was so ashamed of my wickedness in trying to drown myself; and, besides, my hair had all tumbled down and was sopping wet, and I was such a sight.

"And then some men in blue clothes came around; and *he* gave them his card, and I heard him tell them he had seen me drop my purse on the edge of the boat outside the rail, and in leaning over to get it I had fallen overboard. And then I remembered having read in the papers that people who try to kill themselves are locked up in cells with people who try to kill other people, and I was afraid.

"But some ladies on the boat took me downstairs to the furnace-room and got me nearly dry and did up my hair. When the boat landed, *he* came and put me in a cab. He was all dripping himself, but laughed as if he thought it was all a joke. He begged me, but I wouldn't tell him my name nor where I lived, I was so ashamed."

"You were a fool, child," said Hetty, kindly. "Wait till I turn the light up a bit. I wish to Heaven we had an onion."

"Then he raised his hat," went on Cecilia, "and said: 'Very well. But I'll find you, anyhow. I'm going to claim my rights of salvage.' Then he gave money to the cab-driver and told him to take me where I wanted to go, and walked away. What is 'salvage,' Hetty?"

"The edge of a piece of goods that ain't hemmed," said the shop-girl. "You must have looked pretty well frazzled out to the little hero boy."

"It's been three days," moaned the miniature-painter, "and he hasn't found me yet."

"Extend the time," said Hetty. "This is a big town. Think of how many girls he might have to see soaked in water with their hair down before he would recognize you. The stew's getting on fine—but, oh, for an onion! I'd even use a piece of garlic if I had it."

The beef and potatoes bubbled merrily, exhaling a mouth-watering savor that yet lacked something, leaving a hunger on the palate, a haunting, wistful desire for some lost and needful ingredient.

"I came near drowning in that awful river," said Cecilia, shuddering.

"It ought to have more water in it," said Hetty; "the stew, I mean. I'll go get some at the sink."

"It smells good," said the artist.

"That nasty old North River?" objected Hetty. "It smells to me like soap factories and wet setter-dogs—oh, you mean the stew. Well, I wish we had an onion for it. Did he look like he had money?"

"First he looked kind," said Cecilia. "I'm sure he was rich; but that matters so little. When he drew out his bill-folder to pay the cabman you couldn't help seeing hundreds and thousands of dollars in it. And I looked over the cab doors and saw him leave the ferry station in a motor-car; and the chauffeur gave him his bearskin to put on, for he was sopping wet. And it was only three days ago."

"What a fool!" said Hetty, shortly.

"Oh, the chauffeur wasn't wet," breathed Cecilia. "And he drove the car away very nicely."

"I mean *you,*" said Hetty. "For not giving him your address."

"I never give my address to chauffeurs," said Cecilia, haughtily.

"I wish we had one," said Hetty, disconsolately.

"What for?"

"For the stew, of course—Oh, I mean an onion."

Hetty took a pitcher and started to the sink at the end of the hall.

A young man came down the stairs from above just as she was opposite the lower step. He was decently dressed, but pale and haggard. His eyes were dull with the stress of some burden of physical or mental woe. In his hand he bore an onion—a pink, smooth, solid, shining onion, as large around as a ninety-eight-cent alarm clock.

Hetty stopped. So did the young man. There was something Joan of Arc-ish, Herculean and Una-ish in the look and pose of the shop-lady—she had cast off the rôles of Job and Little-Red-Riding-Hood. The young man stopped at the foot of the stairs and coughed distractedly. He felt marooned, held up, attacked, assailed, levied upon, sacked, assessed, pan-handled, brow-beaten, though he knew not why. It was the look in Hetty's eyes that did it. In them he saw the Jolly Roger fly to the masthead and an able seaman with a dirk between his teeth scurry up the ratlines and nail it there. But as yet he did not know that the cargo he carried was the thing that had caused him to be so nearly blown out of the water without even a parley.

"Beg your pardon," said Hetty, as sweetly as her dilute acetic acid tones permitted, "but did you find that onion on the stairs?

There was a hole in the paper bag; and I've just come out to look for it."

The young man coughed for half a minute. The interval may have given him the courage to defend his own property. Also, he clutched his pungent prize greedily, and, with a show of spirit, faced his grim way-layer.

"No," he said, huskily, "I didn't find it on the stairs. It was given to me by Jack Bevens, on the top floor. If you don't believe it, ask him. I'll wait until you do."

"I know about Bevens," said Hetty, sourly. "He writes books and things up there for the paper-and-rags man. We can hear the postman guy him all over the house when he brings them thick envelopes back. Say—do you live in the Vallambrosa?"

"I do not," said the young man. "I come to see Bevens sometimes. He's my friend. I live two blocks west."

"What are you going to do with the onion?—*begging* your pardon," said Hetty.

"I'm going to eat it."

"Raw?"

"Yes: as soon as I get home."

"Haven't you got anything else to eat with it?"

The young man considered briefly.

"No," he confessed; "there's not another scrap of anything in my diggins to eat. I think old Jack is pretty hard up for grub in his shack, too. He hated to give up the onion, but I worried him into parting with it."

"Man," said Hetty, fixing him with her world-sapient eyes, and laying a bony but impressive finger on his sleeve, "you've known trouble, too, haven't you?"

"Lots," said the onion owner, promptly. "But this onion is my own property, honestly come by. If you will excuse me, I must be going."

"Listen," said Hetty, paling a little with anxiety. "Raw onion is a mighty poor diet. And so is a beef-stew without one. Now, if you're Jack Bevens' friend, I guess you're nearly right. There's a little lady—a friend of mine—in my room there at the end of the hall. Both of us are out of luck; and we had just potatoes and meat between us. They're stewing now. But it ain't got any soul. There's something lacking to it. There's certain things in life that are naturally intended to fit and belong together. One is pink cheese-cloth and green roses, and one is ham and eggs, and one is Irish and trouble. And the other one is beef and potatoes *with* onions. And still another one is people who are up against it and other people in the same fix."

The young man went into a protracted paroxysm of coughing. With one hand he hugged his onion to his bosom.

"No doubt; no doubt," said he, at length. "But, as I said, I must be going because—"

Hetty clutched his sleeve firmly.

"Don't be a Dago, Little Brother. Don't eat raw onions. Chip in toward the dinner and line yourself inside with the best stew you ever licked a spoon over. Must two ladies knock a young gentleman down and drag him inside for the honor of dining with 'em? No harm shall befall you, Little Brother. Loosen up and fall into line."

The young man's pale face relaxed into a grin.

"Believe I'll go you," he said, brightening. "If my onion is as good as a credential, I'll accept the invitation gladly."

"It's as good as that, but better as seasoning," said Hetty. "You come and stand outside the door till I ask my lady friend if she has any objections. And don't run away with that letter of recommendation before I come out."

Hetty went into her room and closed the door. The young man waited outside.

"Cecilia, kid," said the shop-girl, oiling the sharp saw of her voice as well as she could, "there's an onion outside. With a young man attached. I've asked him in to dinner. You ain't going to kick, are you?"

"Oh, dear!" said Cecilia, sitting up and patting her artistic hair. She cast a mournful glance at the ferry-boat poster on the wall.

"Nit," said Hetty. "It ain't him. You're up against real life now. I believe you said your hero friend had money and automobiles. This is a poor skeezicks that's got nothing to eat but an onion. But he's easy-spoken and not a freshy. I imagine he's been a gentleman, he's so low down now. And we need the onion. Shall I bring him in? I'll guarantee his behavior."

"Hetty, dear," sighed Cecilia, "I'm so hungry. What difference does it make whether he's a prince or a burglar? I don't care. Bring him in if he's got anything to eat with him."

Hetty went back into the hall. The onion man was gone. Her heart missed a beat, and a gray look settled over her face except on her nose and cheek-bones. And then the tides of life flowed in again, for she saw him leaning out of the front window at the other end of the hall. She hurried there. He was shouting to someone below. The noise of the street overpowered the sound of her footsteps. She looked down over his shoulder, saw whom he was speaking to, and heard his words. He pulled himself in from the window-sill and saw her standing over him.

Hetty's eyes bored into him like two steel gimlets.

"Don't lie to me," she said, calmly. "What were you going to do with that onion?"

The young man suppressed a cough and faced her resolutely. His manner was that of one who had been bearded sufficiently.

"I was going to eat it," said he, with emphatic slowness; "just as I told you before."

"And you have nothing else to eat at home?"

"Not a thing."

"What kind of work do you do?"

"I am not working at anything just now."

"Then why," said Hetty, with her voice set on its sharpest edge, "do you lean out of a window and give orders to chauffeurs in green automobiles in the street below?"

The young man flushed, and his dull eyes began to sparkle.

"Because, madam," said he, in *accelerando* tones, "I pay the chauffeur's wages and I own the automobile—and also this onion—this onion, madam."

He flourished the onion within an inch of Hetty's nose. The shoplady did not retreat a hair's-breadth.

"Then why do you eat onions," she said, with biting contempt, "and nothing else?"

"I never said I did," retorted the young man, heatedly. "I said I had nothing to eat where I live. I am not a delicatessen storekeeper."

"Then why," pursued Hetty, inflexibly, "were you going to eat a raw onion?"

"My mother," said the young man, "always made me eat one for a cold. Pardon my referring to a physical infirmity; but you may have noticed that I have a very, very severe cold. I was going to eat the onion and go to bed. I wonder why I am standing here and apologizing to you for it."

"How did you catch this cold?" went on Hetty, suspiciously.

The young man seemed to have arrived at some extreme height of feeling. There were two modes of descent open to him—a burst of rage or a surrender to the ridiculous. He chose wisely; and the empty hall echoed his hoarse laughter.

"You're a dandy," said he. "And I don't blame you for being careful. I don't mind telling you. I got wet. I was on a North River ferry a few days ago when a girl jumped overboard. Of course, I—"

Hetty extended her hand, interrupting his story.

"Give me the onion," she said.

The young man set his jaw a trifle harder.

"Give me the onion," she repeated.

He grinned, and laid it in her hand.

Then Hetty's infrequent, grim, melancholy smile showed itself. She took the young man's arm and pointed with her other hand to the door of her room.

"Little Brother," she said, "go in there. The little fool you fished out of the river is there waiting for you. Go on in. I'll give you three minutes before I come. Potatoes is in there, waiting. Go on in, Onions."

After he had tapped at the door and entered, Hetty began to peel and wash the onion at the sink. She gave a gray look at the gray roofs outside and the smile on her face vanished by little jerks and twitches.

"But it's us," she said, grimly, to herself, "it's *us* that furnished the beef."

Schools and Schools

Old Jerome Warren lived in a hundred-thousand-dollar house at 35 East Fifty-Soforth Street. He was a downtown broker, so rich that he could afford to walk—for his health—a few blocks in the direction of his office every morning and then call a cab.

He had an adopted son, the son of an old friend named Gilbert—Cyril Scott could play him nicely—who was becoming a successful painter as fast as he could squeeze the paint out of his tubes. Another member of the household was Barbara Ross, a step-niece. Man is born to trouble; so, as old Jerome had no family of his own, he took up the burdens of others.

Gilbert and Barbara got along swimmingly. There was a tacit and tactical understanding all round that the two would stand up under a floral bell some high noon, and promise the minister to keep old Jerome's money in a state of high commotion. But at this point complications must be introduced.

Thirty years before, when old Jerome was young Jerome, there was a brother of his named Dick. Dick went West to seek his or somebody else's fortune. Nothing was heard of him until one day old Jerome had a letter from his brother. It was badly written on ruled paper that smelled of salt bacon and coffee-grounds. The writing was asthmatic and the spelling St. Vitusy.

It appeared that instead of Dick having forced Fortune to stand and deliver, he had been held up himself, and made to give hostages to the enemy. That is, as his letter disclosed, he was on the point of pegging out with a complication of disorders that even whiskey had failed to check. All that his thirty years of prospecting had netted him was one daughter, nineteen years old, as per invoice, whom he was shipping East, charges prepaid, for Jerome to clothe, feed, educate, comfort, and cherish for the rest of her natural life or until matrimony should them part.

Old Jerome was a board-walk. Everybody knows that the world is supported by the shoulders of Atlas; and that Atlas stands on a rail-fence; and that the rail-fence is built on a turtle's back. Now, the turtle has to stand on something; and that is a board-walk made of men like old Jerome.

I do not know whether immortality shall accrue to man; but if not so, I would like to know when men like old Jerome get what is due them?

They met Nevada Warren at the station. She was a little girl, deeply sunburned and wholesomely good-looking, with a manner that was frankly unsophisticated, yet one that not even a cigar-drummer would intrude upon without thinking twice. Looking at her, somehow you would expect to see her in a short skirt and leather leggings, shooting glass balls or taming mustangs. But in her plain white waist and black skirt she sent you guessing again. With an easy exhibition of strength she swung along a heavy valise, which the uniformed porters tried in vain to wrest from her.

"I am sure we shall be the best of friends," said Barbara, pecking at the firm, sunburned cheek.

"I hope so," said Nevada.

"Dear little niece," said old Jerome, "you are as welcome to my house as if it were your father's own."

"Thanks," said Nevada.

"And I am going to call you 'cousin,' " said Gilbert, with his charming smile.

"Take the valise, please," said Nevada. "It weighs a million pounds. It's got samples from six of dad's old mines in it," she explained to Barbara. "I calculate they'd assay about nine cents to the thousand tons, but I promised him to bring them along."

II It is a common custom to refer to the usual complications between one man and two ladies, or one lady and two men, or a lady and a man and a nobleman, or—well, any of these problems—as the triangle. But they are never unqualified triangles. They are always isosceles—never equilateral. So, upon the coming of Nevada Warren, she and Gilbert and Barbara Ross lined up into such a figurative triangle; and of that triangle Barbara formed the hypotenuse.

One morning old Jerome was lingering long after breakfast over the dullest morning paper in the city before setting forth to his downtown fly-trap. He had become quite fond of Nevada, finding in her much of his dead brother's quiet independence and unsuspicious frankness.

A maid brought in a note for Miss Nevada Warren.

"A messenger-boy delivered it at the door, please," she said. "He's waiting for an answer."

Nevada, who was whistling a Spanish waltz between her teeth, and watching the carriages and autos roll by in the street, took the envelope. She knew it was from Gilbert, before she opened it, by the little gold palette in the upper left-hand corner.

After tearing it open she pored over the contents for a while, absorbedly. Then, with a serious face, she went and stood at her uncle's elbow.

"Uncle Jerome, Gilbert is a nice boy, isn't he?"

"Why, bless the child!" said old Jerome, crackling his paper loudly; "of course he is. I raised him myself."

"He wouldn't write anything to anybody that wasn't exactly—I mean that everybody couldn't know and read, would he?"

"I'd just like to see him try it," said uncle, tearing a handful from his newspaper. "Why, what—"

"Read this note he just sent me, uncle, and see if you think it's all right and proper. You see, I don't know much about city people and their ways."

Old Jerome threw his paper down and set both his feet upon it. He took Gilbert's note and fiercely perused it twice, and then a third time.

"Why, child," said he, "you had me almost excited, although I was sure of that boy. He's a duplicate of his father, and he was a gilt-edged diamond. He only asks if you and Barbara will be ready at four o'clock this afternoon for an automobile drive over to Long Island. I don't see anything to criticize in it except the stationery. I always did hate that shade of blue."

"Would it be all right to go?" asked Nevada, eagerly.

"Yes, yes, yes, child, of course. Why not? Still, it pleases me to see you so careful and candid. Go, by all means."

"I didn't know," said Nevada, demurely. "I thought I'd ask you. Couldn't you go with us, uncle?"

"I? No, no, no, no! I've ridden once in a car that boy was driving. Never again! But it's entirely proper for you and Barbara to go. Yes, yes. But I will not. No, no, no, no!"

Nevada flew to the door, and said to the maid:

"You bet we'll go. I'll answer for Miss Barbara. Tell the boy to say to Mr. Warren, 'You bet we'll go.' "

"Nevada," called old Jerome, "pardon me, my dear, but wouldn't it be as well to send him a note in reply? Just a line would do."

"No, I won't bother about that," said Nevada, gayly. "Gilbert will understand—he always does. I never rode in an automobile in my life; but I've paddled a canoe down Little Devil River through the Lost Horse Cañon, and if it's any livelier than that I'd like to know!"

III Two months are supposed to have elapsed.

Barbara sat in the study of the hundred-thousand-dollar house. It was a good place for her. Many places are provided in the world where men and women may repair for the purpose of extricating themselves from divers difficulties. There are cloisters, wailing-places, watering-places, confessionals, hermitages, lawyers' offices, beauty-parlors, air-ships, and studies; and the greatest of these are studies.

It usually takes a hypotenuse a long time to discover that it is the longest side of a triangle. But it's a long line that has no turning.

Barbara was alone. Uncle Jerome and Nevada had gone to the theatre. Barbara had not cared to go. She wanted to stay at home and study in the study. If you, miss, were a stunning New York girl, and saw every day that a brown, ingenuous Western witch was getting hobbles and a lasso on the young man you wanted for yourself, you, too, would lose taste for the oxidized silver setting of a musical comedy.

Barbara sat by the quartered-oak library table. Her right arm rested upon the table, and her dextral fingers nervously manipulated a sealed letter. The letter was addressed to Nevada Warren; and in the upper left-hand corner of the envelope was Gilbert's little gold palette. It had been delivered at nine o'clock, after Nevada had left.

Barbara would have given her pearl necklace to know what that letter contained; but she could not open and read it by the aid of steam, or a pen-handle, or a hair-pin, or any of the generally approved methods, because her position in society forbade such an act. She had tried to read some of the lines of the letter by holding the envelope up to a strong light and pressing it hard against the paper, but Gilbert had too good a taste in stationery to make that possible.

At eleven-thirty the theatre-goers returned. It was a delicious winter night. Even so far as from the cab to the door they were powdered thickly with the big flakes downpouring diagonally from the east. Old Jerome growled good-naturedly about villainous cab service and blockaded streets. Nevada, colored like a rose, with sapphire eyes, babbled of the stormy nights in the mountains around dad's cabin. During all these wintry apostrophes, Barbara, cold at heart, sawed wood—the only appropriate thing she could think of to do.

Old Jerome went immediately upstairs to hot-water-bottles and quinine. Nevada fluttered into the study, the only cheerfully lighted room, subsided into an armchair, and, while at the interminable task of unbuttoning her elbow gloves, gave oral testimony as to the demerits of the "show."

"Yes, I think Mr. Fields is really amusing—sometimes," said Barbara. "Here is a letter for you, dear, that came by special delivery just after you had gone."

"Who is it from?" asked Nevada, tugging at a button.

"Well, really," said Barbara, with a smile, "I can only guess. The envelope has that queer little thing in one corner that Gilbert calls a palette, but which looks to me rather like a gilt heart on a schoolgirl's valentine."

"I wonder what he's writing to me about," remarked Nevada, listlessly.

"We're all alike," said Barbara; "all women. We try to find out what is in a letter by studying the postmark. As a last resort we use scissors, and read it from the bottom upward. Here it is."

She made a motion as if to toss the letter across the table to Nevada.

"Great catamounts!" exclaimed Nevada. "These centre-fire buttons are a nuisance. I'd rather wear buckskins. Oh, Barbara, please shuck the hide off that letter and read it. It'll be midnight before I get these gloves off!"

"Why, dear, you don't want me to open Gilbert's letter to you? It's for you, and you wouldn't wish any one else to read it, of course!"

Nevada raised her steady, calm, sapphire eyes from her gloves.

"Nobody writes me anything that everybody mightn't read," she said. "Go on, Barbara. Maybe Gilbert wants us to go out in his car again tomorrow."

Curiosity can do more things than kill a cat; and if emotions, well recognized as feminine, are inimical to feline life, then jealousy would soon leave the whole world catless. Barbara opened the letter, with an indulgent, slightly bored air.

"Well, dear," she said, "I'll read it if you want me to."

She slit the envelope, and read the missive with swift-travelling eyes; read it again, and cast a quick, shrewd glance at Nevada, who, for the time, seemed to consider gloves as the world of her interest, and letters from rising artists as no more than messages from Mars.

For a quarter of a minute Barbara looked at Nevada with a strange steadfastness; and then a smile so small that it widened her mouth only the sixteenth part of an inch, and narrowed her eyes no more than a twentieth flashed like an inspired thought across her face.

Since the beginning no woman has been a mystery to another

woman. Swift as light travels, each penetrates the heart and mind of another, sifts her sister's words of their cunningest disguises, reads her most hidden desires, and plucks the sophistry from her wiliest talk like hairs from a comb, twiddling them sardonically between her thumb and fingers before letting them float away on the breezes of fundamental doubt. Long ago Eve's son rang the door-bell of the family residence in Paradise Park, bearing a strange lady on his arm, whom he introduced. Eve took her daughter-in-law aside and lifted a classic eyebrow.

"The Land of Nod," said the bride, languidly flirting the leaf of a palm. "I suppose you've been there, of course?"

"Not lately," said Eve, absolutely unstaggered. "Don't you think the applesauce they serve over there is execrable? I rather like that mulberryleaf tunic effect, dear; but, of course, the real fig goods are not to be had over there. Come over behind this lilac-bush while the gentlemen split a celery tonic. I think the caterpillar-holes have made your dress open a little in the back."

So, then and there—according to the records—was the alliance formed by the only two who's-who ladies in the world. Then it was agreed that women should forever remain as clear as a pane of glass—though glass was yet to be discovered—to other women, and that she should palm herself off on a man as a mystery.

Barbara seemed to hesitate.

"Really, Nevada," she said, with a little show of embarrassment, "you shouldn't have insisted on my opening this. I—I'm sure it wasn't meant for any one else to know."

Nevada forgot her gloves for a moment.

"Then read it aloud," she said. "Since you've already read it, what's the difference? If Mr. Warren has written to me something that any one else oughtn't to know, that is all the more reason why everybody should know it."

"Well," said Barbara, "this is what it says: 'Dearest Nevada—Come to my studio at twelve o'clock to-night. Do not fail.' " Barbara rose and dropped the note in Nevada's lap. "I'm awfully sorry," she said, "that I knew. It isn't like Gilbert. There must be some mistake. Just consider that I am ignorant of it, will you, dear? I must go upstairs now, I have such a headache. I'm sure I don't understand the note. Perhaps Gilbert has been dining too well, and will explain. Good night!"

IV Nevada tiptoed to the hall, and heard Barbara's door close upstairs. The bronze clock in the study told the hour of twelve was fifteen minutes away. She ran swiftly to the front door, and let herself out into the snowstorm. Gilbert Warren's studio was six squares away.

By aërial ferry the white, silent forces of the storm attacked the city from beyond the sullen East River. Already the snow lay a foot deep on the pavements, the drifts heaping themselves like scaling-ladders against the walls of the besieged town. The Avenue was as quiet as a street in Pompeii. Cabs now and then skimmed past like white-winged gulls over a moonlit ocean; and less frequent motor-cars—sustaining the comparison—hissed through the foaming waves like submarine boats on their jocund, perilous journeys.

Nevada plunged like a wind-driven storm-petrel on her way. She looked up at the ragged sierras of cloud-capped buildings that rose above the streets, shaded by the night lights and the congealed vapors to gray, drab, ashen, lavender, dun, and cerulean tints. They were so like the wintry mountains of her Western home that she felt a satisfaction such as the hundred-thousand-dollar house had seldom brought her.

A policeman caused her to waver on a corner, just by his eye and weight.

"Hello, Mabel!" said he. "Kind of late for you to be out, ain't it?"

"I—I am just going to the drug store," said Nevada, hurrying past him.

The excuse serves as a passport for the most sophisticated. Does it prove that woman never progresses, or that she sprang from Adam's rib, full-fledged in intellect and wiles?

Turning eastward, the direct blast cut down Nevada's speed one half. She made zigzag tracks in the snow; but she was as tough as a piñon sapling, and bowed to it as gracefully. Suddenly the studio-building loomed before her, a familiar landmark, like a cliff above some well-remembered cañon. The haunt of business and its hostile neighbor, art, was darkened and silent. The elevator stopped at ten.

Up eight flights of Stygian stairs Nevada climbed, and rapped firmly at the door numbered "89." She had been there many times before, with Barbara and Uncle Jerome.

Gilbert opened the door. He had a crayon pencil in one hand, a green shade over his eyes, and a pipe in his mouth. The pipe dropped to the floor.

"Am I late?" asked Nevada. "I came as quick as I could. Uncle and me were at the theatre this evening. Here I am, Gilbert!"

Gilbert did a Pygmalion-and-Galatea act. He changed from a statue of stupefaction to a young man with a problem to tackle. He admitted Nevada, got a whiskbroom, and began to brush the snow from her clothes. A great lamp, with a green shade, hung over an easel, where the artist had been sketching in crayon.

"You wanted me," said Nevada, simply, "and I came. You said so in your letter. What did you send for me for?"

"You read my letter?" inquired Gilbert, sparring for wind.

"Barbara read it to me. I saw it afterward. It said: 'Come to my studio at twelve to-night, and do not fail.' I thought you were sick, of course, but you don't seem to be."

"Aha!" said Gilbert, irrelevantly. "I'll tell you why I asked you to come, Nevada. I want you to marry me immediately—to-night. What's a little snowstorm? Will you do it?"

"You might have noticed that I would, long ago," said Nevada. "And I'm rather stuck on the snowstorm idea, myself. I surely would hate one of those flowery church noon-weddings. Gilbert, I didn't know you had grit enough to propose in this way. Let's shock 'em—it's our funeral, ain't it?"

"You bet!" said Gilbert. "Where did I hear that expression?" he added to himself. "Wait a minute, Nevada; I want to do a little 'phoning."

He shut himself up in a little dressing-room, and called upon the lightnings of the heavens—condensed into unromantic numbers and districts.

"That you, Jack? You confounded sleepy-head! Yes, wake up; this is me—or I—oh, bother the difference in grammar! I'm going to be married right away. Yes! Wake up your sister—don't answer me back; bring her along, too—you *must.* Remind Agnes of the time I saved her from drowning in Lake Ronkonkoma—I know it's caddish to refer to it, but she *must* come with you. Yes! Nevada is here, waiting. We've been engaged quite a while. Some opposition among the relatives, you know, and we have to pull it off this way. We're waiting here for you. Don't let Agnes out-talk you—bring her! You will? Good old boy! I'll order a carriage to call for you, double-quick time. Confound you, Jack, you're all right!"

Gilbert returned to the room where Nevada waited.

"My old friend, Jack Peyton, and his sister were to have been here at a quarter to twelve," he explained; "but Jack is so confoundedly slow. I've just 'phoned them to hurry. They'll be here in a few minutes. I'm the happiest man in the world, Nevada! What did you do with the letter I sent you to-day?"

"I've got it cinched here," said Nevada, pulling it out from beneath her opera-cloak.

Gilbert drew the letter from the envelope and looked it over carefully. Then he looked at Nevada thoughtfully.

"Didn't you think it rather queer that I should ask you to come to my studio at midnight?" he asked.

"Why, no," said Nevada, rounding her eyes. "Not if you needed me. Out West, when a pal sends you a hurry call—ain't that what you say here?—we get there first and talk about it after the row is over. And it's usually snowing there, too, when things happen. So I didn't mind."

Gilbert rushed into another room, and came back burdened with overcoats warranted to turn wind, rain, or snow.

"Put this raincoat on," he said, holding it for her. "We have a quarter of a mile to go. Old Jack and his sister will be here in a few minutes." He began to struggle into a heavy coat. "Oh, Nevada," he said, "just look at the headlines on the front page of that evening paper on the table, will you? It's about your section of the West, and I know it will interest you."

He waited a full minute, pretending to find trouble in the getting on of his overcoat, and then turned. Nevada had not moved. She was looking at him with strange and pensive directness. Her cheeks had a flush on them beyond the color that had been contributed by the wind and snow; but her eyes were steady.

"I was going to tell you," she said, "anyhow, before you—before we—before—well, before anything. Dad never gave me a day of schooling. I never learned to read or write a darned word. Now if—"

Pounding their uncertain way upstairs, the feet of Jack, the somnolent, and Agnes, the grateful, were heard.

V When Mr. and Mrs. Gilbert Warren were spinning softly homeward in a closed carriage, after the ceremony, Gilbert said:

"Nevada, would you really like to know what I wrote you in the letter that you received to-night?"

"Fire away!" said his bride.

"Word for word," said Gilbert, "it was this: 'My dear Miss Warren—You were right about the flower. It was a hydrangea, and not a lilac.' "

"All right," said Nevada. "But let's forget it. The joke's on Barbara, anyway!"

From WHIRLIGIGS 1910

The World and the Door

A favorite dodge to get your story read by the public is to assert that it is true, and then add that Truth is stranger than Fiction. I do not know if the yarn I am anxious for you to read is true; but the Spanish purser of the fruit steamer *El Carrero* swore to me by the shrine of Santa Guadalupe that he had the facts from the U.S. vice-consul at La Paz—a person who could not possibly have been cognizant of half of them.

As for the adage quoted above, I take pleasure in puncturing it by affirming that I read in a purely fictional story the other day the line:

" 'Be it so,' said the policeman." Nothing so strange has yet cropped out in Truth.

When H. Ferguson Hedges, millionaire promoter, investor, and man-about-New-York, turned his thoughts upon matters convivial, and word of it went "down the line," bouncers took a precautionary turn at the Indian clubs, waiters put ironstone china on his favorite tables, cab drivers crowded close to the curbstone in front of all-night cafés, and careful cashiers in his regular haunts charged up a few bottles to his account by way of preface and introduction.

As a money power a one-millionaire is of small account in a city where the man who cuts your slice of beef behind the free-lunch counter rides to work in his own automobile. But Hedges spent his money as lavishly, loudly, and showily as though he were only a clerk squandering a week's wages. And, after all, the bartender takes no interest in your reserve fund. He would rather look you up on his cash register than in Bradstreet.

On the evening that the material allegation of facts begins, Hedges was bidding dull care begone in the company of five or six good fellows—acquaintances and friends who had gathered in his wake.

Among them were two younger men—Ralph Merriam, a broker, and Wade, his friend.

Two deep-sea cabmen were chartered. At Columbus Circle they hove to long enough to revile the statue of the great navigator, unpatriotically rebuking him for having voyaged in search of land instead of liquids. Midnight overtook the party marooned in the rear of a cheap café far uptown.

Hedges was arrogant, overriding, and quarrelsome. He was burly and tough, iron-gray but vigorous, "good" for the rest of the night. There was a dispute—about nothing that matters—and the five-fingered words were passed—the words that represent the glove cast into the lists. Merriam played the rôle of the verbal Hotspur.

Hedges rose quickly, seized his chair, swung it once and smashed wildly down at Merriam's head. Merriam dodged, drew a small revolver and shot Hedges in the chest. The leading roysterer stumbled, fell in a wry heap, and lay still.

Wade, a commuter, had formed that habit of promptness. He juggled Merriam out a side door, walked him to the corner, ran him a block and caught a hansom. They rode five minutes and then got out on a dark corner and dismissed the cab. Across the street the lights of a small saloon betrayed its hectic hospitality.

"Go in the back room of that saloon," said Wade, "and wait. I'll go find out what's doing and let you know. You may take two drinks while I am gone—no more."

At ten minutes to one o'clock Wade returned.

"Brace up, old chap," he said. "The ambulance got there just as I did. The doctor says he's dead. You may have one more drink. You let me run this thing for you. You've got to skip. I don't believe a chair is legally a deadly weapon. You've got to make tracks, that's all there is to it."

Merriam complained of the cold querulously, and asked for another drink. "Did you notice what big veins he had on the back of his hands?" he said. "I never could stand—I never could——"

"Take one more," said Wade, "and then come on. I'll see you through."

Wade kept his promise so well that at eleven o'clock the next morning Merriam, with a new suit case full of new clothes and hair-brushes, stepped quietly on board a little 500-ton fruit steamer at an East River pier. The vessel had brought the season's first cargo of limes from Port Limon, and was homeward bound. Merriam had his bank balance of $2,800 in his pocket in large bills, and brief instructions to pile up as much water as he could between himself and New York. There was no time for anything more.

From Port Limon Merriam worked down the coast by schooner and sloop to Colon, thence across the isthmus to Panama, where he caught a tramp bound for Callao and such intermediate ports as might tempt the discursive skipper from his course.

It was at La Paz that Merriam decided to land—La Paz the Beautiful, a little harborless town smothered in a living green ribbon that banded the foot of a cloud-piercing mountain. Here the little steamer stopped to tread water while the captain's dory took him ashore that he might feel the pulse of the cocoanut market. Merriam went too, with his suit case, and remained.

Kalb, the vice-consul, a Græco-Armenian citizen of the United States, born in Hesse-Darmstadt, and educated in Cincinnati ward primaries, considered all Americans his brothers and bankers. He attached himself to Merriam's elbow, introduced him to every one in La Paz who wore shoes, borrowed ten dollars and went back to his hammock.

There was a little wooden hotel in the edge of a banana grove, facing the sea, that catered to the tastes of the few foreigners that had dropped out of the world into the *triste* Peruvian town. At Kalb's introductory: "Shake hands with ——," he had obediently exchanged manual salutations with a German doctor, one French and two Italian merchants, and three or four Americans who were spoken of as gold men, rubber men, mahogany men—anything but men of living tissue.

After dinner Merriam sat in a corner of the broad front *galería* with Bibb, a Vermonter interested in hydraulic mining, and smoked and drank Scotch "smoke." The moonlit sea, spreading infinitely before him, seemed to separate him beyond all apprehension from his old life. The horrid tragedy in which he had played such a disastrous part now began, for the first time since he stole on board the fruiter, a wretched fugitive, to lose its sharper outlines. Distance lent assuagement to his view. Bibb had opened the flood-gates of a stream of long-dammed discourse, overjoyed to have captured an audience that had not suffered under a hundred repetitions of his views and theories.

"One year more," said Bibb, "and I'll go back to God's country. Oh, I know it's pretty here, and you get *dolce far niente* handed to you in chunks, but this country wasn't made for a white man to live in. You've got to have to plug through snow now and then, and see a game of baseball and wear a stiff collar and have a policeman cuss you. Still, La Paz is a good sort of a pipe-dreamy old hole. And Mrs. Conant is here. When any of us feels particularly like jumping into the sea we rush around to her house and propose. It's nicer to be rejected by Mrs. Conant than it is to be drowned. And they say drowning is a delightful sensation."

"Many like her here?" asked Merriam.

"Not anywhere," said Bibb, with a comfortable sigh. "She's the only white woman in La Paz. The rest range from a dappled dun to the color of a b-flat piano key. She's been here a year. Comes from—well, you know how a woman can talk—ask 'em to say 'string' and they'll say 'crow's foot' or 'cat's cradle.' Sometimes you'd think she was from Oshkosh, and again from Jacksonville, Florida, and the next day from Cape Cod."

"Mystery?" ventured Merriam.

"M—well, she looks it; but her talk's translucent enough. But that's a woman. I suppose if the Sphinx were to begin talking she'd merely say: 'Goodness me! more visitors coming for dinner, and nothing to eat but the sand which is here.' But you won't think about that when you meet her, Merriam. You'll propose to her too."

To make a hard story soft, Merriam did meet her and propose to her. He found her to be a woman in black with hair the color of a bronze turkey's wings, and mysterious, *remembering* eyes that—well, that looked as if she might have been a trained nurse looking on when Eve was created. Her words and manner, though, were translucent, as Bibb had said. She spoke, vaguely, of friends in California and some of the lower parishes in Louisiana. The tropical climate and indolent life suited her; she had thought of buying an orange grove later on; La Paz, all in all, charmed her.

Merriam's courtship of the Sphinx lasted three months, although he did not know that he was courting her. He was using her as an antidote for remorse, until he found, too late, that he had acquired the habit. During that time he had received no news from home. Wade did not know where he was; and he was not sure of Wade's exact address, and was afraid to write. He thought he had better let matters rest as they were for a while.

One afternoon he and Mrs. Conant hired two ponies and rode out along the mountain trail as far as the little cold river that came tumbling down the foothills. There they stopped for a drink, and Merriam spoke his piece—he proposed, as Bibb had prophesied.

Mrs. Conant gave him one glance of brilliant tenderness, and then her face took on such a strange, haggard look that Merriam was shaken out of his intoxication and back to his senses.

"I beg your pardon, Florence," he said, releasing her hand; "but I'll have to hedge on part of what I said. I can't ask you to marry me, of course. I killed a man in New York—a man who was my friend—shot him down—in quite a cowardly manner, I understand. Of course, the drinking didn't excuse it. Well, I couldn't resist having my say; and I'll always mean it. I'm here as a fugitive from justice, and—I suppose that ends our acquaintance."

Mrs. Conant plucked little leaves assiduously from the low-hanging branch of a lime tree.

"I suppose so," she said, in low and oddly uneven tones; "but that depends upon you. I'll be as honest as you were. I poisoned my husband. I am a self-made widow. A man cannot love a murderess. So I suppose that ends our acquaintance."

She looked up at him slowly. His face turned a little pale, and he stared at her blankly, like a deaf-and-dumb man who was wondering what it was all about.

She took a swift step toward him, with stiffened arms and eyes blazing.

"Don't look at me like that!" she cried, as though she were in acute pain. "Curse me, or turn your back on me, but don't look that way. Am I a woman to be beaten? If I could show you—here on my arms, and on my back are scars—and it has been more than a year—scars that he made in his brutal rages. A holy nun would have risen and struck the fiend down. Yes, I killed him. The foul and horrible words that he hurled at me the last day are repeated in my ears every night when I sleep. And then came his blows, and the end of my endurance. I got the poison that afternoon. It was his custom to drink every night in the library before going to bed a hot punch made of rum and wine. Only from my fair hands would he receive it—because he knew that the fumes of spirits always sickened me. That night when the maid brought it to me I sent her downstairs on an errand. Before taking him his drink I went to my little private cabinet and poured into it more than a teaspoonful of tincture of aconite—enough to kill three men, so I had learned. I had drawn $6,000 that I had in bank, and with that and a few things in a satchel I left the house without any one seeing me. As I passed the library I heard him stagger up and fall heavily on a couch. I took a night train for New Orleans, and from there I sailed to the Bermudas. I finally cast anchor in La Paz. And now what have you to say? Can you open your mouth?"

Merriam came back to life.

"Florence," he said, earnestly, "I want you. I don't care what you've done. If the world——"

"Ralph," she interrupted, almost with a scream, "be my world!"

Her eyes melted; she relaxed magnificently and swayed toward Merriam so suddenly that he had to jump to catch her.

Dear me! in such scenes how the talk runs into artificial prose. But it can't be helped. It's the subconscious smell of the footlights' smoke that's in all of us. Stir the depths of your cook's soul sufficiently and she will discourse in Bulwer-Lyttonese.

Merriam and Mrs. Conant were very happy. He announced their engagement at the Hotel Orilla del Mar. Eight foreigners and four native Astors pounded his back and shouted insincere congratulations at him. Pedrito, the Castilian-mannered barkeep, was goaded to extra duty until his agility would have turned a Boston cherry-phosphate clerk a pale lilac with envy.

They were both very happy. According to the strange mathematics of the god of mutual affinity, the shadows that clouded their pasts when united became only half as dense instead of darker. They shut the world out and bolted the doors. Each was the other's world. Mrs. Conant lived again. The remembering look left her eyes. Merriam was with her every moment that was possible. On a little plateau under a grove of palms and calabash trees they were going to build a fairy bungalow. They were to be married in two months. Many hours of the day they had their heads together over the house plans. Their joint capital would set up a business in fruit or woods that would yield a comfortable support. "Good-night, my world," would say Mrs. Conant every evening when Merriam left her for his hotel. They were very happy. Their love had, circumstantially, that element of melancholy in it that it seems to require to attain its supremest elevation. And it seemed that their mutual great misfortune or sin was a bond that nothing could sever.

One day a steamer hove in the offing. Bare-legged and bare-shouldered La Paz scampered down to the beach, for the arrival of a steamer was their loop-the-loop, circus, Emancipation Day, and four-o'clock tea.

When the steamer was near enough, wise ones proclaimed that she was the *Pájaro,* bound up-coast from Callao to Panama.

The *Pájaro* put on brakes a mile off shore. Soon a boat came bobbing shoreward. Merriam strolled down on the beach to look on. In the shallow water the Carib sailors sprang out and dragged the boat with a mighty rush to the firm shingle. Out climbed the purser, the captain, and two passengers ploughing their way through the deep sand toward the hotel. Merriam glanced toward them with the mild interest due to strangers. There was something familiar to him in the walk of one of the passengers. He looked again, and his blood seemed to turn to strawberry ice cream in his veins. Burly, arrogant, debonair as ever, H. Ferguson Hedges, the man he had killed, was coming toward him ten feet away.

When Hedges saw Merriam his face flushed a dark red. Then he shouted in his old, bluff way: "Hello, Merriam. Glad to see you. Didn't expect to find you out here. Quinby, this is my old friend Merriam, of New York—Merriam, Mr. Quinby."

Merriam gave Hedges and then Quinby an ice-cold .nd.

"Br-r-r-r!" said Hedges. "But you've got a frappéed flipper!

Man, you're not well. You're as yellow as a Chinaman. Malarial here? Steer us to a bar if there is such a thing, and let's take a prophylactic."

Merriam, still half comatose, led them toward the Hotel Orilla del Mar.

"Quinby and I," explained Hedges, puffing through the slippery sand, "are looking out along the coast for some investments. We've just come up from Concepción and Valparaiso and Lima. The captain of this subsidized ferry boat told us there was some good picking around here in silver mines. So we got off. Now, where is that café, Merriam? Oh, in this portable soda-water pavilion?"

Leaving Quinby at the bar, Hedges drew Merriam aside.

"Now, what does this mean?" he said, with gruff kindness. "Are you sulking about that fool row we had?"

"I thought," stammered Merriam—"I heard—they told me you were—that I had——"

"Well, you didn't, and I'm not," said Hedges. "That fool young ambulance surgeon told Wade I was a candidate for a coffin just because I'd got tired and quit breathing. I laid up in a private hospital for a month; but here I am, kicking as hard as ever. Wade and I tried to find you, but couldn't. Now, Merriam, shake hands and forget it all. I was as much to blame as you were; and the shot really did me good—I came out of the hospital as healthy and fit as a cab horse. Come on; that drink's waiting."

"Old man," said Merriam, brokenly, "I don't know how to thank you—I—well, you know——"

"Oh, forget it," boomed Hedges. "Quinby'll die of thirst if we don't join him."

Bibb was sitting on the shady side of the gallery waiting for the eleven-o'clock breakfast. Presently Merriam came out and joined him. His eye was strangely bright.

"Bibb, my boy," said he, slowly waving his hand, "do you see those mountains and that sea and sky and sunshine?—they're mine, Bibbsy—all mine."

"You go in," said Bibb, "and take eight grains of quinine, right away. It won't do in this climate for a man to get to thinking he's Rockefeller, or James O'Neill either."

Inside, the purser was untying a great roll of newspapers, many of them weeks old, gathered in the lower ports by the *Pájaro* to be distributed at casual stopping-places. Thus do the beneficent voyagers scatter news and entertainment among the prisoners of sea and mountains.

Tío Pancho, the hotel proprietor, set his great silver-rimmed *an-*

teojos upon his nose and divided the papers into a number of smaller rolls. A barefooted *muchacho* dashed in, desiring the post of messenger.

"Vien venido," said Tío Pancho. "This to Señora Conant; that to el Doctor S-S-Schlegel—*Dios!* what a name to say! that to Señor Davis—one for Don Alberto. These two for the *Casa de Huéspedes, Numero 6, en la calle de las Buenas Gracias.* And say to them all, *muchacho,* that the *Pájaro* sails for Panama at three this afternoon. If any have letters to send by the post, let them come quickly, that they may first pass through the *correo.*"

Mrs. Conant received her roll of newspapers at four o'clock. The boy was late in delivering them, because he had been deflected from his duty by an iguana that crossed his path and to which he immediately gave chase. But it made no hardship, for she had no letters to send.

She was idling in a hammock in the *patio* of the house that she occupied, half awake, half happily dreaming of the paradise that she and Merriam had created out of the wrecks of their pasts. She was content now for the horizon of that shimmering sea to be the horizon of her life. They had shut out the world and closed the door.

Merriam was coming to her house at seven, after his dinner at the hotel. She would put on a white dress and an apricot-colored lace mantilla, and they would walk an hour under the cocoanut palms by the lagoon. She smiled contentedly, and chose a paper at random from the roll the boy had brought.

At first the words of a certain headline of a Sunday newspaper meant nothing to her; they conveyed only a visualized sense of familiarity. The largest type ran thus: "Lloyd B. Conant secures divorce." And then the sub headings: "Well-known Saint Louis paint manufacturer wins suit, pleading one year's absence of wife." "Her mysterious disappearance recalled." "Nothing has been heard of her since."

Twisting herself quickly out of the hammock, Mrs. Conant's eye soon traversed the half-column of the *Recall.* It ended thus: "It will be remembered that Mrs. Conant disappeared one evening in March of last year. It was freely rumored that her marriage with Lloyd B. Conant resulted in much unhappiness. Stories were not wanting to the effect that his cruelty toward his wife had more than once taken the form of physical abuse. After her departure a full bottle of tincture of aconite, a deadly poison, was found in a small medicine cabinet in her bedroom. This might have been an indication that she meditated suicide. It is supposed that she abandoned such an intention if she possessed it, and left her home instead."

Mrs. Conant slowly dropped the paper, and sat on a chair, clasping her hands tightly.

"Let me think—O God!—let me think," she whispered. "I took the bottle with me . . . I threw it out of the window of the train . . . I——. . . there was another bottle in the cabinet . . . there were two, side by side—the aconite—and the valerian that I took when I could not sleep . . . If they found the aconite bottle full, why—but, he is alive, of course—I gave him a harmless dose of valerian . . . I am not a murderess in fact . . . Ralph, I—O God, don't let this be a dream!"

She went into the part of the house that she rented from the old Peruvian man and his wife, shut the door, and walked up and down her room swiftly and feverishly for half an hour. Merriam's photograph stood in a frame on a table. She picked it up, looked at it with a smile of exquisite tenderness, and—dropped four tears on it. And Merriam only twenty rods away! Then she stood still for ten minutes, looking into space. She looked into space through a slowly opening door. On her side of the door was the building material for a castle of Romance—love, an Arcady of waving palms, a lullaby of waves on the shore of a haven of rest, respite, peace, a lotus land of dreamy ease and security—a life of poetry and heart's ease and refuge. Romanticist, will you tell me what Mrs. Conant saw on the other side of the door? You cannot?—that is, you will not? Very well; then listen.

She saw herself go into a department store and buy five spools of silk thread and three yards of gingham to make an apron for the cook. "Shall I charge it, ma'am?" asks the clerk. As she walked out a lady whom she met greeted her cordially. "Oh, where did you get the pattern for those sleeves, dear Mrs. Conant?" she said. At the corner a policeman helped her across the street and touched his helmet. "Any callers?" she asked the maid when she reached home. "Mrs. Waldron," answered the maid, "and the two Misses Jenkinson." "Very well," she said. "You may bring me a cup of tea, Maggie."

Mrs. Conant went to the door and called Angela, the old Peruvian woman. "If Mateo is there send him to me." Mateo, a half-breed, shuffling and old but efficient, came.

"Is there a steamer or a vessel of any kind leaving this coast to-night or to-morrow that I can get passage on?" she asked.

Mateo considered.

"At Punta Reina, thirty miles down the coast, señora," he answered, "there is a small steamer loading with cinchona and dye-woods. She sails for San Francisco to-morrow at sunrise. So says my brother, who arrived in his sloop to-day, passing by Punta Reina."

"You must take me in that sloop to the steamer to-night. Will you do that?"

"Perhaps——" Mateo shrugged a suggestive shoulder. Mrs. Conant took a handful of money from a drawer and gave it to him.

"Get the sloop ready behind the little point of land below the town," she ordered. "Get sailors, and be ready to sail at six o'clock. In half an hour bring a cart partly filled with straw into the *patio* here, and take my trunk to the sloop. There is more money yet. Now, hurry."

For one time Mateo walked away without shuffling his feet.

"Angela," cried Mrs. Conant, almost fiercely, "come and help me pack. I am going away. Out with this trunk. My clothes first. Stir yourself. Those dark dresses first. Hurry."

From the first she did not waver from her decision. Her view was clear and final. Her door had opened and let the world in. Her love for Merriam was not lessened; but it now appeared a hopeless and unrealizable thing. The visions of their future that had seemed so blissful and complete had vanished. She tried to assure herself that her renunciation was rather for his sake than for her own. Now that she was cleared of her burden—at least, technically—would not his own weigh too heavily upon him? If she should cling to him, would not the difference forever silently mar and corrode their happiness? Thus she reasoned; but there were a thousand little voices calling to her that she could feel rather than hear, like the hum of distant, powerful machinery—the little voices of the world, that, when raised in unison, can send their insistent call through the thickest door.

Once, while packing, a brief shadow of the lotus dream came back to her. She held Merriam's picture to her heart with one hand, while she threw a pair of shoes into the trunk with her other.

At six o'clock Mateo returned and reported the sloop ready. He and his brother lifted the trunk into the cart, covered it with straw, and conveyed it to the point of embarkation. From there they transferred it on board in the sloop's dory. Then Mateo returned for additional orders.

Mrs. Conant was ready. She had settled all business matters with Angela, and was impatiently waiting. She wore a long, loose black-silk duster that she often walked about in when the evenings were chilly. On her head was a small round hat, and over it the apricot-colored lace mantilla.

Dusk had quickly followed the short twilight. Mateo led her by dark and grass-grown streets toward the point behind which the sloop was anchored. On turning a corner they beheld the Hotel Orilla del Mar three streets away, nebulously aglow with its array of kerosene lamps.

Mrs. Conant paused, with streaming eyes. "I must, *I must* see him once before I go," she murmured in anguish. But even then she did not falter in her decision. Quickly she invented a plan by which she might speak to him, and yet make her departure without his knowing. She would walk past the hotel, ask some one to call him out, and talk a few moments on some trivial excuse, leaving him expecting to see her at her home at seven.

She unpinned her hat and gave it to Mateo. "Keep this, and wait here till I come," she ordered. Then she draped the mantilla over her head as she usually did when walking after sunset, and went straight to the Orilla del Mar.

She was glad to see the bulky, white-clad figure of Tío Pancho standing alone on the gallery.

"Tío Pancho," she said, with a charming smile, "may I trouble you to ask Mr. Merriam to come out for just a few moments that I may speak with him?"

Tío Pancho bowed as an elephant bows.

"Buenas tardes, Señora Conant," he said, as a cavalier talks. And then he went on, less at his ease:

"But does not the señora know that Señor Merriam sailed on the *Pájaro* for Panama at three o'clock of this afternoon?"

The Theory and the Hound

Not many days ago my old friend from the tropics, J. P. Bridger, United States consul on the island of Ratona, was in the city. We had wassail and jubilee and saw the Flatiron building, and missed seeing the Bronxless menagerie by about a couple of nights. And then, at the ebb tide, we were walking up a street that parallels and parodies Broadway.

A woman with a comely and mundane countenance passed us, holding in leash a wheezing, vicious, waddling brute of a yellow pug. The dog entangled himself with Bridger's legs and mumbled his ankles in a snarling, peevish, sulky bite. Bridger, with a happy smile, kicked the breath out of the brute; the woman showered us with a quick rain of well-conceived adjectives that left us in no doubt as to our place in her opinion, and we passed on. Ten yards farther an old woman with disordered white hair and her bankbook tucked well hidden beneath her tattered shawl begged. Bridger stopped and disinterred for her a quarter from his holiday waistcoat.

On the next corner a quarter of a ton of well-clothed man with a rice-powdered, fat, white jowl, stood holding the chain of a devil-born bulldog whose forelegs were strangers by the length of a dachshund. A little woman in a last-season's hat confronted him and wept, which was plainly all she could do, while he cursed her in low, sweet, practised tones.

Bridger smiled again—strictly to himself—and this time he took out a little memorandum book and made a note of it. This he had no right to do without due explanation, and I said so.

"It's a new theory," said Bridger, "that I picked up down in Ratona. I've been gathering support for it as I knock about. The world isn't ripe for it yet, but—well, I'll tell you; and then you run your mind back along the people you've known and see what you make of it."

And so I cornered Bridger in a place where they have artificial palms and wine; and he told me the story which is here in my words and on his responsibility.

One afternoon at three o'clock, on the island of Ratona, a boy raced along the beach screaming, "*Pájaro,* ahoy!"

Thus he made known the keenness of his hearing and the justice of his discrimination in pitch.

He who first heard and made oral proclamation concerning the toot of an approaching steamer's whistle, and correctly named the steamer, was a small hero in Ratona—until the next steamer came. Wherefore, there was rivalry among the barefoot youth of Ratona, and many fell victims to the softly blown conch shells of sloops which, as they enter harbor, sound surprisingly like a distant steamer's signal. And some could name you the vessel when its call, in your duller ears, sounded no louder than the sigh of the wind through the branches of the cocoanut palms.

But to-day he who proclaimed the *Pájaro* gained his honors. Ratona bent its ear to listen; and soon the deep-tongued blast grew louder and nearer, and at length Ratona saw above the line of palms on the low "point" the two black funnels of the fruiter slowly creeping toward the mouth of the harbor.

You must know that Ratona is an island twenty miles off the south of a South American republic. It is a port of that republic; and it sleeps sweetly in a smiling sea, toiling not nor spinning; fed by the abundant tropics where all things "ripen, cease and fall toward the grave."

Eight hundred people dream life away in a green-embowered village that follows the horseshoe curve of its bijou harbor. They are mostly Spanish and Indian mestizos, with a shading of San Domingo Negroes, a lightening of pure-blood Spanish officials, and a slight leavening of the froth of three or four pioneering white races. No steamers touch at Ratona save the fruit steamers which take on their banana inspectors there on their way to the coast. They leave Sunday newspapers, ice, quinine, bacon, watermelons, and vaccine matter at the island and that is about all the touch Ratona gets with the world.

The *Pájaro* paused at the mouth of the harbor, rolling heavily in the swell that sent the whitecaps racing beyond the smooth water inside. Already two dories from the village—one conveying fruit inspectors, the other going for what it could get—were halfway out to the steamer.

The inspector's dory was taken on board with them, and the *Pájaro* steamed away for the mainland for its load of fruit.

The other boat returned to Ratona bearing a contribution from the *Pájaro's* store of ice, the usual roll of newspapers, and one passenger—Taylor Plunkett, sheriff of Chatham County, Kentucky.

Bridger, the United States consul at Ratona, was cleaning his rifle in the official shanty under a bread-fruit tree twenty yards from the water of the harbor. The consul occupied a place somewhat near the tail of his political party's procession. The music of the band wagon sounded very faintly to him in the distance. The plums of office went to others. Bridger's share of the spoils—the consulship at Ratona—was little more than a prune—a dried prune from the boarding-house department of the public crib. But $900 yearly was opulence in Ratona. Besides, Bridger had contracted a passion for shooting alligators in the lagoons near his consulate, and he was not unhappy.

He looked up from a careful inspection of his rifle lock and saw a broad man filling his doorway. A broad, noiseless, slow-moving man sunburned almost to the brown of Vandyke. A man of forty-five, neatly clothed in homespun, with scanty light hair, a close-clipped brown-and-gray beard and pale-blue eyes expressing mildness and simplicity.

"You are Mr. Bridger, the consul," said the broad man. "They directed me here. Can you tell me what those big bunches of things like gourds are in those trees that look like feather dusters along the edge of the water?"

"Take that chair," said the consul, reoiling his cleaning rag. "No, the other one—that bamboo thing won't hold you. Why, they're cocoanuts—green cocoanuts. The shell of 'em is always a light green before they're ripe."

"Much obliged," said the other man, sitting down carefully. "I didn't quite like to tell the folks at home they were olives unless I was sure about it. My name is Plunkett. I'm sheriff of Chatham County, Kentucky. I've got extradition papers in my pocket authorizing the arrest of a man on this island. They've been signed by the President of this country, and they're in correct shape. The man's name is Wade Williams. He's in the cocoanut raising business. What he's wanted for is the murder of his wife two years ago. Where can I find him?"

The consul squinted an eye and looked through his rifle barrel.

"There's nobody on the island who calls himself 'Williams,' " he remarked.

"Didn't suppose there was," said Plunkett mildly. "He'll do by any other name."

"Besides myself," said Bridger, "there are only two Americans on Ratona—Bob Reeves and Henry Morgan."

"The man I want sells cocoanuts," suggested Plunkett.

"You see that cocoanut walk extending up to the point?" said the consul, waving his hand toward the open door. "That belongs to Bob Reeves. Henry Morgan owns half the trees to loo'ard on the island."

"One month ago," said the sheriff, "Wade Williams wrote a confidential letter to a man in Chatham County, telling him where he was and how he was getting along. The letter was lost; and the person that found it gave it away. They sent me after him, and I've got the papers. I reckon he's one of your cocoanut men for certain."

"You've got his picture, of course," said Bridger. "It might be Reeves or Morgan, but I'd hate to think it. They're both as fine fellows as you'd meet in an all-day auto ride."

"No," doubtfully answered Plunkett; "there wasn't any picture of Williams to be had. And I never saw him myself. I've been sheriff only a year. But I've got a pretty accurate description of him. About 5 feet 11; dark hair and eyes; nose inclined to be Roman; heavy about the shoulders; strong, white teeth, with none missing; laughs a good deal, talkative; drinks considerably but never to intoxication; looks you square in the eye when talking; age thirty-five. Which one of your men does that description fit?"

The consul grinned broadly.

"I'll tell you what you do," he said, laying down his rifle and slipping on his dingy black alpaca coat. "You come along, Mr. Plunkett, and I'll take you up to see the boys. If you can tell which one of 'em your description fits better than it does the other you have the advantage of me."

Bridger conducted the sheriff out and along the hard beach close to which the tiny houses of the village were distributed. Immediately back of the town rose sudden, small, thickly wooded hills. Up one of these, by means of steps cut in the hard clay, the consul led Plunkett. On the very verge of an eminence was perched a two-room wooden cottage with a thatched roof. A Carib woman was washing clothes outside. The consul ushered the sheriff to the door of the room that overlooked the harbor.

Two men were in the room, about to sit down, in their shirt sleeves, to a table spread for dinner. They bore little resemblance one to the other in detail; but the general description given by Plunkett could have been justly applied to either. In height, color of hair, shape of nose, build, and manners each of them tallied with it. They were fair types of jovial, ready-witted, broad-gauged Americans who had gravitated together for companionship in an alien land.

"Hello, Bridger!" they called in unison at sight of the consul. "Come and have dinner with us!" And then they noticed Plunkett at his heels, and came forward with hospitable curiosity.

"Gentlemen," said the consul, his voice taking an unaccustomed formality, "this is Mr. Plunkett. Mr. Plunkett—Mr. Reeves and Mr. Morgan."

The cocoanut barons greeted the newcomer joyously. Reeves seemed about an inch taller than Morgan, but his laugh was not quite as loud. Morgan's eyes were deep brown; Reeves's were black.

Reeves was the host and busied himself with fetching other chairs and calling to the Carib woman for supplemental table ware. It was explained that Morgan lived in a bamboo shack to "loo'ard," but that every day the two friends dined together. Plunkett stood still during the preparations, looking about mildly with his pale-blue eyes. Bridger looked apologetic and uneasy.

At length two other covers were laid and the company was assigned to places. Reeves and Morgan stood side by side across the table from the visitors. Reeves nodded genially as a signal for all to seat themselves. And then suddenly Plunkett raised his hand with a gesture of authority. He was looking straight between Reeves and Morgan.

"Wade Williams," he said quietly, "you are under arrest for murder."

Reeves and Morgan instantly exchanged a quick, bright glance, the quality of which was interrogation, with a seasoning of surprise. Then, simultaneously they turned to the speaker with a puzzled and frank deprecation in their gaze.

"Can't say that we understand you, Mr. Plunkett," said Morgan, cheerfully. "Did you say 'Williams'?"

"What's the joke, Bridgy?" asked Reeves, turning to the consul with a smile.

Before Bridger could answer, Plunkett spoke again.

"I'll explain," he said, quietly. "One of you don't need any explanation, but this is for the other one. One of you is Wade Williams of Chatham County, Kentucky. You murdered your wife on May 5, two years ago, after ill-treating and abusing her continually for five years. I have the proper papers in my pocket for taking you back with me, and you are going. We will return on the fruit steamer that comes back by this island to-morrow to leave its inspectors. I acknowledge, gentlemen, that I'm not quite sure which one of you is Williams. But Wade Williams goes back to Chatham County to-morrow. I want you to understand that."

A great sound of merry laughter from Morgan and Reeves went out over the still harbor. Two or three fishermen in the fleet of sloops anchored there looked up at the house of the *diablos Americanos* on the hill and wondered.

"My dear Mr. Plunkett," cried Morgan, conquering his mirth, "the dinner is getting cold. Let us sit down and eat. I am anxious to get my spoon into that shark-fin soup. Business afterward."

"Sit down, gentlemen, if you please," added Reeves, pleasantly. "I am sure Mr. Plunkett will not object. Perhaps a little time may be of advantage to him in identifying—the gentleman he wishes to arrest."

"No objections, I'm sure," said Plunkett, dropping into his chair heavily. "I'm hungry myself. I didn't want to accept the hospitality of you folks without giving you notice; that's all."

Reeves set bottles and glasses on the table.

"There's cognac," he said, "and anisada, and Scotch 'smoke,' and rye. Take your choice."

Bridger chose rye, Reeves poured three fingers of Scotch for himself, Morgan took the same. The sheriff, against much protestation, filled his glass from the water bottle.

"Here's to the appetite," said Reeves, raising his glass, "of Mr. Williams!" Morgan's laugh and his drink encountering sent him into a choking-splutter. All began to pay attention to the dinner, which was well cooked and palatable.

"Williams!" called Plunkett, suddenly and sharply.

All looked up wonderingly. Reeves found the sheriff's mild eye resting upon him. He flushed a little.

"See here," he said, with some asperity, "my name's Reeves, and I don't want you to——" But the comedy of the thing came to his rescue and he ended with a laugh.

"I suppose, Mr. Plunkett," said Morgan, carefully seasoning an alligator pear, "that you are aware of the fact that you will import a good deal of trouble for yourself into Kentucky if you take back the wrong man—that is, of course, if you take anybody back?"

"Thank you for the salt," said the sheriff. "Oh, I'll take somebody back. It'll be one of you two gentlemen. Yes, I know I'll get stuck for damages if I make a mistake. But I'm going to try to get the right man."

"I'll tell you what you do," said Morgan, leaning forward with a jolly twinkle in his eyes. "You take me. I'll go without any trouble. The cocoanut business hasn't panned out well this year, and I'd like to make some extra money out of your bondsmen."

"That's not fair," chimed in Reeves. "I got only $16 a thousand for my last shipment. Take me, Mr. Plunkett."

"I'll take Wade Williams," said the sheriff, patiently, "or I'll come pretty close to it."

"It's like dining with a ghost," remarked Morgan, with a pretended shiver. "The ghost of a murderer, too! Will somebody pass the toothpicks to the shade of the naughty Mr. Williams?"

Plunkett seemed as unconcerned as if he were dining at his own table in Chatham County. He was a gallant trencherman, and the strange tropic viands tickled his palate. Heavy, commonplace, almost slothful in his movements, he appeared to be devoid of all the cunning and watchfulness of the sleuth. He even ceased to observe, with any sharpness or attempted discrimination, the two men, one of whom he had undertaken with surprising self-confidence to drag away upon the serious charge of wife-murder. Here, indeed, was a problem set before him that if wrongly solved would have amounted to his serious discomfiture, yet there he sat puzzling his soul (to all appearances) over the novel flavor of a broiled iguana cutlet.

The consul felt a decided discomfort. Reeves and Morgan were his friends and pals; yet the sheriff from Kentucky had a certain right to his official aid and moral support. So Bridger sat the silentest around the board and tried to estimate the peculiar situation. His conclusion was that both Reeves and Morgan, quickwitted, as he knew them to be, had conceived at the moment of Plunkett's disclosure of his mission—and in the brief space of a lightning flash—the idea that the other might be the guilty Williams; and that each of them had decided in that moment loyally to protect his comrade against the doom that threatened him. This was the consul's theory, and if he had been a bookmaker at a race of wits for life and liberty he would have offered heavy odds against the plodding sheriff from Chatham County, Kentucky.

When the meal was concluded the Carib woman came and removed the dishes and cloth. Reeves strewed the table with excellent cigars, and Plunkett, with the others, lighted one of these with evident gratification.

"I may be dull," said Morgan, with a grin and a wink at Bridger; "but I want to know if I am. Now, I say this is all a joke of Mr. Plunkett's concocted to frighten two babes-in-the-woods. Is this Williamson to be taken seriously or not?"

" 'Williams,' " corrected Plunkett, gravely. "I never got off any jokes in my life. I know I wouldn't travel 2,000 miles to get off a poor one as this would be if I didn't take Wade Williams back with me. Gentlemen!" continued the sheriff, now letting his mild eyes travel impartially from one of the company to another, "see if you can find any joke in this case. Wade Williams is listening to the words I utter now; but out of politeness I will speak of him as a third person. For five years he made his wife lead the life of a dog—No; I'll take that back. No dog in Kentucky was ever treated as she was. He spent the money that she brought him—spent it at races, at the card table, and on horses and hunting. He was a good fellow to his friends, but a cold, sullen demon at home. He wound up the five years of neglect by striking her with his closed hand—a hand as hard as a stone—

when she was ill and weak from suffering. She died the next day; and he skipped. That's all there is to it. It's enough. I never saw Williams; but I knew his wife. I'm not a man to tell half. She and I were keeping company when she met him. She went to Louisville on a visit and saw him there. I'll admit that he spoilt my chances in no time. I lived then on the edge of the Cumberland Mountains. I was elected sheriff of Chatham County a year after Wade Williams killed his wife. My official duty sends me out here after him; but I'll admit that there's personal feeling, too. And he's going back with me. Mr.—er—Reeves, will you pass me a match?"

"Awfully imprudent of Williams," said Morgan, putting his feet up against the wall, "to strike a Kentucky lady. Seems to me I've heard they were scrappers."

"Bad, bad Williams," said Reeves, pouring out more "Scotch."

The two men spoke lightly, but the consul saw and felt the tension and the carefulness in their actions and words. "Good old fellows," he said to himself; "they're both all right. Each of 'em is standing by the other like a little brick church."

And then a dog walked into the room where they sat—a black-and-tan hound, long-eared, lazy, confident of welcome.

Plunkett turned his head and looked at the animal, which halted, confidently, within a few feet of his chair.

Suddenly the sheriff, with a deep-mouthed oath, left his seat and bestowed upon the dog a vicious and heavy kick, with his ponderous shoe.

The hound, heart-broken, astonished, with flapping ears and incurved tail, uttered a piercing yelp of pain and surprise.

Reeves and the consul remained in their chairs, saying nothing, but astonished at the unexpected show of intolerance from the easy-going man from Chatham County.

But Morgan, with a suddenly purpling face, leaped to his feet and raised a threatening arm above the guest.

"You—brute!" he shouted, passionately; "why did you do that?"

Quickly the amenities returned, Plunkett muttered some indistinct apology and regained his seat. Morgan with a decided effort controlled his indignation and also returned to his chair.

And then Plunkett, with the spring of a tiger, leaped around the corner of the table and snapped handcuffs on the paralyzed Morgan's wrists.

"Hound-lover and woman-killer!" he cried; "get ready to meet your God."

When Bridger had finished I asked him:

"Did he get the right man?"

"He did," said the consul.

"And how did he know?" I inquired, being in a kind of bewilderment.

"When he put Morgan in the dory," answered Bridger, "the next day to take him aboard the *Pájaro,* this man Plunkett stopped to shake hands with me and I asked him the same question.

" 'Mr. Bridger,' said he. 'I'm a Kentuckian, and I've seen a great deal of both men and animals. And I never yet saw a man that was overfond of horses and dogs but what was cruel to women.' "

The Ransom of Red Chief

It looked like a good thing: but wait till I tell you. We were down South, in Alabama—Bill Driscoll and myself—when this kidnapping idea struck us. It was, as Bill afterward expressed it, "during a moment of temporary mental apparition"; but we didn't find that out till later.

There was a town down there, as flat as a flannel-cake, and called Summit, of course. It contained inhabitants of as undeleterious and self-satisfied a class of peasantry as ever clustered around a Maypole.

Bill and me had a joint capital of about six hundred dollars, and we needed just two thousand dollars more to pull off a fraudulent town-lot scheme in Western Illinois with. We talked it over on the front steps of the hotel. Philoprogenitoveness, says we, is strong in semi-rural communities; therefore, and for other reasons, a kidnapping project ought to do better there than in the radius of newspapers that send reporters out in plain clothes to stir up talk about such things. We knew that Summit couldn't get after us with anything stronger than constables and, maybe, some lackadaisical bloodhounds and a diatribe or two in the *Weekly Farmers' Budget.* So, it looked good.

We selected for our victim the only child of a prominent citizen named Ebenezer Dorset. The father was respectable and tight, a mortgage fancier and a stern, upright collection-plate passer and forecloser. The kid was a boy of ten, with bas-relief freckles, and hair the color of the cover of the magazine you buy at the news-stand when you want to catch a train. Bill and me figured that Ebenezer would melt down for a ransom of two thousand dollars to a cent. But wait till I tell you.

About two miles from Summit was a little mountain, covered with a dense cedar brake. On the rear elevation of this mountain was a cave. There we stored provisions.

One evening after sundown, we drove in a buggy past old Dorset's house. The kid was in the street, throwing rocks at a kitten on the opposite fence.

"Hey, little boy!" says Bill, "would you like to have a bag of candy and a nice ride?"

The boy catches Bill neatly in the eye with a piece of brick.

"That will cost the old man an extra five hundred dollars," says Bill, climbing over the wheel.

That boy put up a fight like a welter-weight cinnamon bear; but, at last, we got him down in the bottom of the buggy and drove away. We took him up to the cave, and I hitched the horse in the cedar brake. After dark I drove the buggy to the little village, three miles away, where we had hired it, and walked back to the mountain.

Bill was pasting court-plaster over the scratches and bruises on his features. There was a fire burning behind the big rock at the entrance of the cave, and the boy was watching a pot of boiling coffee, with two buzzard tail-feathers stuck in his red hair. He points a stick at me when I come up, and says:

"Ha! cursed paleface, do you dare to enter the camp of Red Chief, the terror of the plains?"

"He's all right now," says Bill, rolling up his trousers and examining some bruises on his shins. "We're playing Indian. We're making Buffalo Bill's show look like magic-lantern views of Palestine in the town hall. I'm Old Hank, the Trapper, Red Chief's captive, and I'm to be scalped at daybreak. By Geronimo! that kid can kick hard."

Yes, sir, that boy seemed to be having the time of his life. The fun of camping out in a cave had made him forget that he was a captive himself. He immediately christened me Snake-eye, the Spy, and announced that, when his braves returned from the warpath, I was to be broiled at the stake at the rising of the sun.

Then we had supper; and he filled his mouth full of bacon and bread and gravy, and began to talk. He made a during-dinner speech something like this:

"I like this fine. I never camped out before; but I had a pet 'possum once, and I was nine last birthday. I hate to go to school. Rats ate up sixteen of Jimmy Talbot's aunt's speckled hen's eggs. Are there any real Indians in these woods? I want some more gravy. Does the trees moving make the wind blow? We had five puppies. What makes your nose so red, Hank? My father has lots of money. Are the stars hot? I whipped Ed Walker twice, Saturday. I don't like girls. You dassent catch toads unless with a string. Do oxen make any noise? Why are oranges round? Have you got beds to sleep on in this cave? Amos Murray has got six toes. A parrot can talk, but a monkey or a fish can't. How many does it take to make twelve?"

Every few minutes he would remember that he was a pesky redskin, and pick up his stick rifle and tiptoe to the mouth of the cave to rubber for the scouts of the hated paleface. Now and then he would let out a war-whoop that made Old Hank the Trapper shiver. That boy had Bill terrorized from the start.

"Red Chief," says I to the kid, "would you like to go home?"

"Aw, what for?" says he. "I don't have any fun at home. I hate to go to school. I like to camp out. You won't take me back home again, Snake-eye, will you?"

"Not right away," says I. "We'll stay here in the cave awhile."

"All right!" says he. "That'll be fine. I never had such fun in all my life."

We went to bed about eleven o'clock. We spread down some wide blankets and quilts and put Red Chief between us. We weren't afraid he'd run away. He kept us awake for three hours, jumping up and reaching for his rifle and screeching: "Hist! pard," in mine and Bill's ears, as the fancied crackle of a twig or the rustle of a leaf revealed to his young imagination the stealthy approach of the outlaw band. At last, I fell into a troubled sleep, and dreamed that I had been kidnapped and chained to a tree by a ferocious pirate with red hair.

Just at daybreak, I was awakened by a series of awful screams from Bill. They weren't yells, or howls, or shouts, or whoops, or yawps, such as you'd expect from a manly set of vocal organs—they were simply indecent, terrifying, humiliating screams, such as women emit when they see ghosts or caterpillars. It's an awful thing to hear a strong, desperate, fat man scream incontinently in a cave at daybreak.

I jumped up to see what the matter was. Red Chief was sitting on Bill's chest, with one hand twined in Bill's hair. In the other he had the sharp case-knife we used for slicing bacon; and he was industriously and realistically trying to take Bill's scalp, according to the sentence that had been pronounced upon him the evening before.

I got the knife away from the kid and made him lie down again. But, from that moment, Bill's spirit was broken. He laid down on his side of the bed, but he never closed an eye again in sleep as long as that boy was with us. I dozed off for a while, but along toward sun-up I remembered that Red Chief had said I was to be burned at the stake at the rising of the sun. I wasn't nervous or afraid; but I sat up and lit my pipe and leaned against a rock.

"What you getting up so soon for, Sam?" asked Bill.

"Me?" says I. "Oh, I got a kind of pain in my shoulder. I thought sitting up would rest it."

"You're a liar!" says Bill. "You're afraid. You was to be burned at sunrise, and you was afraid he'd do it. And he would, too, if he could find a match. Ain't it awful, Sam? Do you think anybody will pay out money to get a little imp like that back home?"

"Sure," said I. "A rowdy kid like that is just the kind that parents dote on. Now, you and the Chief get up and cook breakfast, while I go up on the top of this mountain and reconnoitre."

I went up on the peak of the little mountain and ran my eye over the contiguous vicinity. Over towards Summit I expected to see the sturdy yeomanry of the village armed with scythes and pitchforks beating the countryside for the dastardly kidnappers. But what I saw was a peaceful landscape dotted with one man ploughing with a dun mule. Nobody was dragging the creek; no couriers dashed hither and yon, bringing tidings of no news to the distracted parents. There was a sylvan attitude of somnolent sleepiness pervading that section of the external outward surface of Alabama that lay exposed to my view. "Perhaps," says I to myself, "it has not yet been discovered that the wolves have borne away the tender lambkin from the fold. Heaven help the wolves!" says I, and I went down the mountain to breakfast.

When I got to the cave I found Bill backed up against the side of it, breathing hard, and the boy threatening to smash him with a rock half as big as a cocoanut.

"He put a red-hot boiled potato down my back," explained Bill, "and then mashed it with his foot; and I boxed his ears. Have you got a gun about you, Sam?"

I took the rock away from the boy and kind of patched up the argument. "I'll fix you," says the kid to Bill. "No man ever yet struck the Red Chief but he got paid for it. You better beware!"

After breakfast the kid takes a piece of leather with strings wrapped around it out of his pocket and goes outside the cave unwinding it.

"What's he up to now?" says Bill, anxiously. "You don't think he'll run away, do you, Sam?"

"No fear of it," says I. "He don't seem to be much of a home body. But we've got to fix up some plan about the ransom. There don't seem to be much excitement around Summit on account of his disappearance; but maybe they haven't realized yet that he's gone. His folks may think he's spending the night with Aunt Jane or one of the neighbors. Anyhow, he'll be missed to-day. To-night we must get a message to his father demanding the two thousand dollars for his return."

Just then we heard a kind of war-whoop, such as David might have emitted when he knocked out the champion Goliath. It was a sling that Red Chief had pulled out of his pocket, and he was whirling it around his head.

I dodged, and heard a heavy thud and a kind of a sigh from Bill, like a horse gives out when you take his saddle off. A niggerhead rock the size of an egg had caught Bill just behind his left ear. He loosened himself all over and fell in the fire across the frying pan of hot water for washing the dishes. I dragged him out and poured cold water on his head for half an hour.

By and by, Bill sits up and feels behind his ear and says: "Sam, do you know who my favorite Biblical character is?"

"Take it easy," says I. "You'll come to your senses presently."

"King Herod," says he. "You won't go away and leave me here alone, will you, Sam?"

I went out and caught that boy and shook him until his freckles rattled.

"If you don't behave," says I, "I'll take you straight home. Now, are you going to be good, or not?"

"I was only funning," says he, sullenly. "I didn't mean to hurt Old Hank. But what did he hit me for? I'll behave, Snake-eye, if you won't send me home, and if you'll let me play the Black Scout today."

"I don't know the game," says I. "That's for you and Mr. Bill to decide. He's your playmate for the day. I'm going away for a while, on business. Now, you come in and make friends with him and say you are sorry for hurting him, or home you go, at once."

I made him and Bill shake hands, and then I took Bill aside and told him I was going to Poplar Grove, a little village three miles from the cave, and find out what I could about how the kidnapping had been regarded in Summit. Also, I thought it best to send a peremptory letter to old man Dorset that day, demanding the ransom and dictating how it should be paid.

"You know, Sam," says Bill, "I've stood by you without batting an eye in earthquakes, fire and flood—in poker games, dynamite outrages, police raids, train robberies, and cyclones. I never lost my nerve yet till we kidnapped that two-legged skyrocket of a kid. He's got me going. You won't leave me long with him, will you, Sam?"

"I'll be back some time this afternoon," says I. "You must keep the boy amused and quiet till I return. And now we'll write the letter to old Dorset."

Bill and I got paper and pencil and worked on the letter while Red Chief, with a blanket wrapped around him, strutted up and down, guarding the mouth of the cave. Bill begged me tearfully to make the ransom fifteen hundred dollars instead of two thousand. "I ain't attempting," says he, "to decry the celebrated moral aspect of parental affection, but we're dealing with humans, and it ain't human for anybody to give up two thousand dollars for that forty-pound chunk of freckled wildcat. I'm willing to take a chance at fifteen hundred dollars. You can charge the difference up to me."

So, to relieve Bill, I acceded, and we collaborated a letter that ran this way:

> Ebenezer Dorset, Esq.:
>
> We have your boy concealed in a place far from Summit. It is useless for you or the most skilful detectives to attempt to find him. Absolutely, the only terms on which you can have him restored to you are these: We demand fifteen hundred dollars in large bills for his return; the money to be left at midnight to-night at the same spot and in the same box as your reply—as hereinafter described. If you agree to these terms, send your answer in writing by a solitary messenger to-night at half-past eight o'clock. After crossing Owl Creek on the road to Poplar Grove, there are three large trees about a hundred yards apart, close to the fence of the wheat field on the right-hand side. At the bottom of the fence-post, opposite the third tree, will be found a small pasteboard box.
>
> The messenger will place the answer in this box and return immediately to Summit.
>
> If you attempt any treachery or fail to comply with our demand as stated, you will never see your boy again.
>
> If you pay the money as demanded, he will be returned to you safe and well within three hours. These terms are final, and if you do not accede to them no further communication will be attempted.
>
> Two Desperate Men

I addressed this letter to Dorset, and put it in my pocket. As I was about to start, the kid comes up to me and says:

"Aw, Snake-eye, you said I could play the Black Scout while you was gone."

"Play it, of course," says I. "Mr. Bill will play with you. What kind of a game is it?"

"I'm the Black Scout," says Red Chief, "and I have to ride to the stockade to warn the settlers that the Indians are coming. I'm tired of playing Indian myself. I want to be the Black Scout."

"All right," says I. "It sounds harmless to me. I guess Mr. Bill will help you foil the pesky savages."

"What am I to do?" asks Bill, looking at the kid suspiciously.

"You are the hoss," says Black Scout. "Get down on your hands and knees. How can I ride to the stockade without a hoss?"

"You'd better keep him interested," said I, "till we get the scheme going. Loosen up."

Bill gets down on his all fours, and a look comes in his eye like a rabbit's when you catch it in a trap.

"How far is it to the stockade, kid?" he asks, in a husky manner of voice.

"Ninety miles," says the Black Scout. "And you have to hump yourself to get there on time. Whoa, now!"

The Black Scout jumps on Bill's back and digs his heels in his side.

"For Heaven's sake," says Bill, "hurry back, Sam, as soon as you can. I wish we hadn't made the ransom more than a thousand. Say, you quit kicking me or I'll get up and warm you good."

I walked over to Poplar Grove and sat around the post-office and store, talking with the chaw-bacons that came in to trade. One whiskerando says that he hears Summit is all upset on account of Elder Ebenezer Dorset's boy having been lost or stolen. That was all I wanted to know. I bought some smoking tobacco, referred casually to the price of black-eyed peas, posted my letter surreptitiously, and came away. The postmaster said the mail-carrier would come by in an hour to take the mail to Summit.

When I got back to the cave Bill and the boy were not to be found. I explored the vicinity of the cave, and risked a yodel or two, but there was no response.

So I lighted my pipe and sat down on a mossy bank to await developments.

In about half an hour I heard the bushes rustle, and Bill wabbled out into the little glade in front of the cave. Behind him was the kid, stepping softly like a scout, with a broad grin on his face. Bill stopped, took off his hat, and wiped his face with a red handkerchief. The kid stopped about eight feet behind him.

"Sam," says Bill, "I suppose you'll think I'm a renegade, but I couldn't help it. I'm a grown person with masculine proclivities and habits of self-defense, but there is a time when all systems of egotism and predominance fail. The boy is gone. I sent him home. All is off. There was martyrs in old times," goes on Bill, "that suffered death rather than give up the particular graft they enjoyed. None of 'em ever was subjugated to such supernatural tortures as I have been. I tried to be faithful to our articles of depredation; but there came a limit."

"What's the trouble, Bill?" I asks him.

"I was rode," says Bill, "the ninety miles to the stockade, not barring an inch. Then, when the settlers was rescued, I was given oats. Sand ain't a palatable substitute. And then, for an hour I had to try to explain to him why there was nothin' in holes, how a road can run both ways, and what makes the grass green. I tell you, Sam, a human can only stand so much. I takes him by the neck of his clothes and drags him down the mountain. On the way he kicks my legs black and blue from the knees down; and I've got to have two or three bites on my thumb and hand cauterized.

"But he's gone"—continues Bill—"gone home. I showed him the road to Summit and kicked him about eight feet nearer there at one kick. I'm sorry we lose the ransom; but it was either that or Bill Driscoll to the madhouse."

Bill is puffing and blowing, but there is a look of ineffable peace and growing content on his rose-pink features.

"Bill," says I, "there isn't any heart disease in your family, is there?"

"No," says Bill, "nothing chronic except malaria and accidents. Why?"

"Then you might turn around," says I, "and have a look behind you."

Bill turns and sees the boy, and loses his complexion and sits down plump on the ground and begins to pluck aimlessly at grass and little sticks. For an hour I was afraid of his mind. And then I told him that my scheme was to put the whole job through immediately and that we would get the ransom and be off with it by midnight if old Dorset fell in with our proposition. So Bill braced up enough to give the kid a weak sort of a smile and a promise to play the Russian in a Japanese war with him as soon as he felt a little better.

I had a scheme for collecting that ransom without danger of being caught by counterplots that ought to commend itself to professional kidnappers. The tree under which the answer was to be left—and the money later on—was close to the road fence with big, bare fields on all sides. If a gang of constables should be watching for any one to come for the note, they could see him a long way off crossing the fields or in the road. But no, sirree! At half-past eight I was up in that tree as well hidden as a tree toad, waiting for the messenger to arrive.

Exactly on time, a half-grown boy rides up the road on a bicycle, locates the pasteboard box at the foot of the fence-post, slips a folded piece of paper into it, and pedals away again back toward Summit.

I waited an hour and then concluded the thing was square. I slid down the tree, got the note, slipped along the fence till I struck the woods, and was back at the cave in another half an hour. I opened the note, got near the lantern, and read it to Bill. It was written with a pen in a crabbed hand, and the sum and substance of it was this:

> Two Desperate Men.
> Gentlemen: I received your letter to-day by post, in regard to the ransom you ask for the return of my son. I think you are a little high in your demands, and I hereby make you a counter-proposition, which I am inclined to believe you will accept. You bring Johnny home and pay me two hundred and fifty dollars in cash, and I agree to take him off your hands. You had better come at night, for the neighbors believe he is lost, and I couldn't be responsible for what they would do to anybody they saw bringing him back. Very respectfully,
> Ebenezer Dorset

"Great pirates of Penzance," says I; "of all the impudent——"

But I glanced at Bill, and hesitated. He had the most appealing look in his eyes I ever saw on the face of a dumb or a talking brute.

"Sam," says he, "what's two hundred and fifty dollars, after all? We've got the money. One more night of this kid will send me to a bed in Bedlam. Besides being a thorough gentleman, I think Mr. Dorset is a spendthrift for making us such a liberal offer. You ain't going to let the chance go, are you?"

"Tell you the truth, Bill," says I, "this little he ewe lamb has somewhat got on my nerves too. We'll take him home, pay the ransom, and make our getaway."

We took him home that night. We got him to go to telling him that his father had bought a silver-mounted rifle and a pair of moccasins for him, and we were to hunt bears the next day.

It was just twelve o'clock when we knocked at Ebenezer's front door. Just at the moment when I should have been abstracting the fifteen hundred dollars from the box under the tree, according to the original proposition, Bill was counting out two hundred and fifty dollars into Dorset's hand.

When the kid found out we were going to leave him at home he started up a howl like a calliope and fastened himself as tight as a leech to Bill's leg. His father peeled him away gradually, like a porous plaster.

"How long can you hold him?" asks Bill.

"I'm not as strong as I used to be," says old Dorset, "but I think I can promise you ten minutes."

"Enough," says Bill. "In ten minutes I shall cross the Central,

Southern, and Middle Western States, and be legging it trippingly for the Canadian border."

And, as dark as it was, and as fat as Bill was, and as good a runner as I am, he was a good mile and a half out of Summit before I could catch up with him.

Makes the Whole World Kin

The burglar stepped inside the window quickly, and then he took his time. A burglar who respects his art always takes his time before taking anything else.

The house was a private residence. By its boarded front door and untrimmed Boston ivy the burglar knew that the mistress of it was sitting on some oceanside piazza telling a sympathetic man in a yachting cap that no one had ever understood her sensitive, lonely heart. He knew by the light in the third-story front windows, and by the lateness of the season, that the master of the house had come home, and would soon extinguish his light and retire. For it was September of the year and of the soul, in which season the house's good man comes to consider roof gardens and stenographers as vanities, and to desire the return of his mate and the more durable blessings of decorum and the moral excellencies.

The burglar lighted a cigarette. The guarded glow of the match illuminated his salient points for a moment. He belonged to the third type of burglars.

This third type has not yet been recognized and accepted. The police have made us familiar with the first and second. Their classification is simple. The collar is the distinguishing mark.

When a burglar is caught who does not wear a collar he is described as a degenerate of the lowest type, singularly vicious and depraved, and is suspected of being the desperate criminal who stole the handcuffs out of Patrolman Hennessy's pocket in 1878 and walked away to escape arrest.

The other well-known type is the burglar who wears a collar. He is always referred to as a Raffles in real life. He is invariably a gentleman by daylight, breakfasting in a dress suit, and posing as a paperhanger, while after dark he plies his nefarious occupation of burglary. His mother is an extremely wealthy and respected resident of Ocean Grove, and when he is conducted to his cell he asks at once for a nail file and the *Police Gazette.* He always has a wife in every State in the Union and fiancées in all the Territories, and the newspapers print his matrimonial gallery out of their stock of cuts of the ladies who were cured by only one bottle after having been given up by five doctors, experiencing great relief after the first dose.

The burglar wore a blue sweater. He was neither a Raffles nor one of the chefs from Hell's Kitchen. The police would have been baffled had they attempted to classify him. They have not yet heard of the respectable, unassuming burglar who is neither above nor below his station.

This burglar of the third class began to prowl. He wore no masks, dark lanterns, or gum shoes. He carried a 38-calibre revolver in his pockets, and he chewed peppermint gum thoughtfully.

The furniture of the house was swathed in its summer dust protectors. The silver was far away in safe-deposit vaults. The burglar expected no remarkable "haul." His objective point was that dimly lighted room where the master of the house should be sleeping heavily after whatever solace he had sought to lighten the burden of his loneliness. A "touch" might be made there to the extent of legitimate, fair professional profits—loose money, a watch, a jeweled stick-pin—nothing exorbitant or beyond reason. He had seen the window left open and had taken the chance.

The burglar softly opened the door of the lighted room. The gas was turned low. A man lay in the bed asleep. On the dresser lay many things in confusion—a crumpled roll of bills, a watch, keys, three poker chips, crushed cigars, a pink silk hair bow, and an unopened bottle of bromoseltzer for a bulwark in the morning.

The burglar took three steps toward the dresser. The man in the bed suddenly uttered a squeaky groan and opened his eyes. His right hand slid under his pillow, but remained there.

"Lay still," said the burglar in conversational tone. Burglars of the third type do not hiss. The citizen in the bed looked at the round end of the burglar's pistol and lay still.

"Now hold up both your hands," commanded the burglar.

The citizen had a little, pointed, brown-and-gray beard, like that of a painless dentist. He looked solid, esteemed, irritable, and disgusted. He sat up in bed and raised his right hand above his head.

"Up with the other one," ordered the burglar. "You might be amphibious and shoot with your left. You can count two, can't you? Hurry up, now."

"Can't raise the other one," said the citizen with a contortion of his lineaments.

"What's the matter with it?"

"Rheumatism in the shoulder."

"Inflammatory?"

"Was. The inflammation has gone down."

The burglar stood for a moment or two, holding his gun on the afflicted one. He glanced at the plunder on the dresser and then, with a half-embarrassed air back at the man in the bed. Then he, too, made a sudden grimace.

"Don't stand there making faces," snapped the citizen, bad-humoredly. "If you've come to burgle why don't you do it? There's some stuff lying around."

" 'Scuse me," said the burglar, with a grin; "but it just socked me one, too. Its good for you that rheumatism and me happens to be old pals. I got it in my left arm, too. Most anybody but me would have popped you when you wouldn't hoist that left claw of yours."

"How long have you had it?" inquired the citizen.

"Four years. I guess that ain't all. Once you've got it, it's you for a rheumatic life—that's my judgment."

"Ever try rattlesnake oil?" asked the citizen interestedly.

"Gallons," said the burglar. "If all the snakes I've used the oil of was strung out in a row they'd reach eight times as far as Saturn, and the rattles could be heard at Valparaiso, Indiana, and back."

"Some use Chiselum's Pills," remarked the citizen.

"Fudge!" said the burglar. "Took 'em five months. No good. I had some relief the year I tried Finkelham's Extract, Balm of Gilead poultices, and Pott's Pain Pulverizer; but I think it was the buckeye I carried in my pocket what done the trick."

"Is yours worse in the morning or at night?" asked the citizen.

"Night," said the burglar; "just when I'm busiest. Say, take down that arm of your—I guess you won't—— Say! did you ever try Blickerstaff's Blood Builder?"

"I never did. Does yours come in paroxysms or is it a steady pain?"

The burglar sat down on the foot of the bed and rested his gun on his crossed knee.

"It jumps," said he. "It strikes me when I ain't looking for it. I had to give up second-story work because I got stuck sometimes half-way up. Tell you what—I don't believe the bloomin' doctors know what is good for it."

"Same here. I've spent a thousand dollars without getting any relief. Yours swell any?"

"Of mornings. And when it's goin' to rain—great Christopher!"

"Me, too," said the citizen. "I can tell when a streak of humidity the size of a tablecloth starts from Florida on its way to New York. And if I pass a theatre where there's an 'East Lynne' matinée going on, the moisture starts my left arm jumping like a toothache."

"It's undiluted—hades!" said the burglar.

"You're dead right," said the citizen.

The burglar looked down at his pistol and thrust it into his pocket with an awkward attempt at ease.

"Say, old man," he said, constrainedly, "ever try opodeldoc?"

"Slop!" said the citizen angrily. "Might as well rub on restaurant butter."

"Sure," concurred the burglar. "It's a salve suitable for little Minnie when the kitty scratches her finger. I'll tell you what! We're up against it. I only find one thing that eases her up. Hey? Little old sanitary, ameliorating, lest-we-forget Booze. Say—this job's off—'scuse me—get on your clothes and let's go out and have some. 'Scuse the liberty, but—ouch! There she goes again!"

"For a week," said the citizen, "I haven't been able to dress myself without help. I'm afraid Thomas is in bed, and——"

"Climb out," said the burglar, "I'll help you get into your duds."

The conventional returned as a tidal wave and flooded the citizen. He stroked his brown-and-gray beard.

"It's very unusual——" he began.

"Here's your shirt," said the burglar, "fall out. I know a man who said Omberry's Ointment fixed him in two weeks so he could use both hands in tying his four-in-hand."

As they were going out the door the citizen turned and started back.

"'Liked to forget my money," he explained; "laid it on the dresser last night."

The burglar caught him by the right sleeve.

"Come on," he said, bluffly. "I ask you. Leave it alone. I've got the price. Ever try witch hazel and oil of wintergreen?"

A Ghost of a Chance

"Actually, a *hod!*" repeated Mrs. Kinsolving, pathetically.

Mrs. Bellamy Bellmore arched a sympathetic eyebrow. Thus she expressed condolence and a generous amount of apparent surprise.

"Fancy her telling everywhere," recapitulated Mrs. Kinsolving, "that she saw a ghost in the apartment she occupied here—our choicest guestroom—a ghost, carrying a hod on its shoulder—the ghost of an old man in overalls, smoking a pipe and carrying a hod! The very absurdity of the thing shows her malicious intent. There never was a Kinsolving that carried a hod. Every one knows that Mr. Kinsolving's father accumulated his money by large building contracts, but he never worked a day with his own hands. He had this house built from his own plans; but—oh, a hod! Why need she have been so cruel and malicious?"

"It is really too bad," murmured Mrs. Bellmore, with an approving glance of her fine eyes about the vast chamber done in lilac and old gold. "And it was in this room she saw it. Oh, no, I'm not afraid of ghosts. Don't have the least fear on my account. I'm glad you put me in here. I think family ghosts so interesting. But, really, the story does sound a little inconsistent. I should have expected something better from Mrs. Fischer-Suympkins. Don't they carry bricks in hods? Why should a ghost bring bricks into a villa built of marble and stone? I'm so sorry, but it makes me think that age is beginning to tell upon Mrs. Fischer-Suympkins."

"This house," continued Mrs. Kinsolving, "was built upon the site of an old one used by the family during the Revolution. There wouldn't be anything strange in its having a ghost. And there was a Captain Kinsolving who fought in General Greene's army, though we've never been able to secure any papers to vouch for it. If there is to be a family ghost, why couldn't it have been his, instead of a bricklayer's?"

"The ghost of a Revolutionary ancestor wouldn't be a bad idea," agreed Mrs. Bellmore; "but you know how arbitrary and inconsiderate ghosts can be. Maybe, like love, they are 'engendered in the eye.' One advantage of those who see ghosts is that their stories can't be disproved. By a spiteful eye, a Revolutionary knapsack might easily be construed to be a hod. Dear Mrs. Kinsolving, think no more of it. I am sure it was a knapsack."

"But she told everybody!" mourned Mrs. Kinsolving inconsolable. "She insisted upon the details. There is the pipe. And how are you going to get out of the overalls?"

"Sha'n't get into them," said Mrs. Bellmore, with a prettily suppressed yawn; "too stiff and wrinkly. Is that you, Felice? Prepare my bath, please. Do you dine at seven at Clifftop, Mrs. Kinsolving? So kind of you to run in for a chat before dinner! I love those little touches of informality with a guest. They give such a home flavor to a visit. So sorry; I must be dressing. I am so indolent I always postpone it until the last moment."

Mrs. Fischer-Suympkins had been the first large plum that the Kinsolvings had drawn from the social pie. For a long time, the pie itself had been out of reach on a top shelf. But the purse and the pursuit had at last lowered it. Mrs. Fischer-Suympkins was the heliograph of the smart society parading corps. The glitter of her wit and actions passed along the line, transmitting whatever was latest and most daring in the game of peep-show. Formerly, her fame and leadership had been secure enough not to need the support of such artifices as handing around live frogs for favors at a cotillion. But, now, these things were necessary to the holding of her throne. Besides, middle age had come to preside, incongruous, at her capers. The sensational papers had cut her space from a page to two columns. Her wit developed a sting; her manners became more rough and inconsiderate, as if she felt the royal necessity of establishing her autocracy by scorning the conventionalities that bound lesser potentates.

To some pressure at the command of the Kinsolvings, she had yielded so far as to honor their house by her presence, for an evening and night. She had her revenge upon her hostess by relating, with grim enjoyment and sarcastic humor, her story of the vision carrying the hod. To that lady, in raptures at having penetrated thus far toward the coveted inner circle, the result came as a crushing disappointment. Everybody either sympathized or laughed, and there was little to choose between the two modes of expression.

But, later on, Mrs. Kinsolving's hopes and spirits were revived by the capture of a second and greater prize.

Mrs. Bellamy Bellmore had accepted an invitation to visit at Clifftop, and would remain for three days. Mrs. Bellmore was one of the younger matrons, whose beauty, descent, and wealth gave her a reserved seat in the holy of holies that required no strenuous bolstering. She was generous enough thus to give Mrs. Kinsolving the accolade that was so poignantly desired; and, at the same time, she thought how much it would please Terence. Perhaps it would end by solving him.

Terence was Mrs. Kinsolving's son, aged twenty-nine, quite good-looking enough, and with two or three attractive and mysterious traits. For one, he was very devoted to his mother, and that was sufficiently odd to deserve notice. For others, he talked so little that it was irritating, and he seemed either very shy or very deep. Terence interested Mrs. Bellmore, because she was not sure which it was. She intended to study him a little longer unless she forgot the matter. If he was only shy, she would abandon him, for shyness is a bore. If he was deep, she would also abandon him, for depth is precarious.

On the afternoon of the third day of her visit, Terence hunted up Mrs. Bellmore, and found her in a nook actually looking at an album.

"It's so good of you," said he, "to come down here and retrieve the day for us. I suppose you have heard that Mrs. Fischer-Suympkins scuttled the ship before she left. She knocked a whole plank out of the bottom with a hod. My mother is grieving herself ill about it. Can't you manage to see a ghost for us while you are here, Mrs. Bellmore—a bang-up, swell ghost, with a coronet on his head and a cheque book under his arm?"

"That was a naughty old lady, Terence," said Mrs. Bellmore, "to tell such stories. Perhaps you gave her too much supper. Your mother doesn't really take it seriously, does she?"

"I think she does," answered Terence. "One would think every brick in the hod had dropped on her. It's a good mammy, and I don't like to see her worried. It's to be hoped that the ghost belongs to the hodcarriers' union, and will go out on a strike. If he doesn't there will be no peace in this family."

"I'm sleeping in the ghost-chamber," said Mrs. Bellmore, pensively. "But it's so nice I wouldn't change it, even if I were afraid, which I'm not. It wouldn't do for me to submit a counter story of a desirable, aristocratic shade, would it? I would do so, with pleasure, but it seems to me that it would be too obviously an antidote for the other narrative to be effective."

"True," said Terence, running two fingers thoughtfully into his crisp brown hair; "that would never do. How would it work to see the same ghost again, minus the overalls, and have gold bricks in the hod? That would elevate the spectre from degrading toil to a financial plane. Don't you think that would be respectable enough?"

"There was an ancestor who fought against the Britishers, wasn't there? Your mother said something to that effect."

"I believe so; one of those old chaps in raglan vests and golf trousers. I don't care a continental for a Continental, myself. But the mother has set her heart on pomp and heraldry and pyrotechnics, and I want her to be happy."

"You are a good boy, Terence," said Mrs. Bellmore, sweeping her silks close to one side of her; "not to beat your mother. Sit here by me, and let's look at the album, just as people used to do twenty years ago. Now, tell me about every one of them. Who is this tall, dignified gentleman leaning against the horizon, with one arm on the Corinthian column?"

"That old chap with the big feet?" inquired Terence, craning his neck. "That's great-uncle O'Brannigan. He used to keep a rathskeller on the Bowery."

"I asked you to sit down, Terence. If you are not going to amuse, or obey me, I shall report in the morning that I saw a ghost wearing an apron and carrying schooners of beer. Now, that is better. To be shy, at your age, Terence, is a thing that you should blush to acknowledge."

At breakfast on the last morning of her visit, Mrs. Bellmore startled and entranced every one present by announcing positively that she had seen the ghost.

"Did it have a-a-a—?" Mrs. Kinsolving, in her suspense and agitation, could not bring out the word.

"No, indeed—far from it."

There was a chorus of questions from others at the table. "Weren't you frightened?" "What did it do?" "How did it look?" "How was it dressed?" "Did it say anything?" "Didn't you scream?"

"I'll try to answer everything at once," said Mrs. Bellmore, heroically, "although I'm frightfully hungry. Something awakened me—I'm not sure whether it was a noise or a touch—and there stood the phantom. I never burn a light at night, so the room was quite dark, but I saw it plainly. I wasn't dreaming. It was a tall man all misty white from head to foot. It wore the full dress of the old Colonial days—powdered hair, baggy coat skirts, lace ruffles, and a sword. It looked intangible and luminous in the dark, and moved without a sound. Yes, I was a little frightened at first—or startled, I should say. It was the first ghost I had ever seen. No, it didn't say anything. I didn't scream. I raised up on my elbow, and then it glided silently away, and disappeared when it reached the door."

Mrs. Kinsolving was in the seventh heaven. "The description is that of Captain Kinsolving, of General Greene's army, one of our ancestors," she said, in a voice that trembled with pride and relief. "I really think I must apologize for our ghostly relative, Mrs. Bellmore.

I am afraid he must have badly disturbed your rest."

Terence sent a smile of pleased congratulation toward his mother. Attainment was Mrs. Kinsolving's, at last, and he loved to see her happy.

"I suppose I ought to be ashamed to confess," said Mrs. Bellmore, who was now enjoying her breakfast, "that I wasn't very much disturbed. I presume it would have been the customary thing to scream and faint, and have all of you running about in picturesque costumes. But, after the first alarm was over, I really couldn't work myself up to a panic. The ghost retired from the stage quietly and peacefully, after doing its little turn, and I went to sleep again."

Nearly all listened, politely accepted Mrs. Bellmore's story as a made-up affair, charitably offered as an offset to the unkind vision seen by Mrs. Fischer-Suympkins. But one or two present perceived that her assertions bore the genuine stamp of her own convictions. Truth and candor seemed to attend upon every word. Even a scoffer at ghosts—if he were very observant—would have been forced to admit that she had, at least in a very vivid dream, been honestly aware of the weird visitor.

Soon Mrs. Bellmore's maid was packing. In two hours the auto would come to convey her to the station. As Terence was strolling upon the east piazza, Mrs. Bellmore came up to him, with a confidential sparkle in her eye.

"I didn't wish to tell the others all of it," she said, "but I will tell you. In a way, I think you should be held responsible. Can you guess in what manner that ghost awakened me last night?"

"Rattled chains," suggested Terence, after some thought, "or groaned? They usually do one or the other."

"Do you happen to know," continued Mrs. Bellmore, with sudden irrelevancy, "if I resemble any one of the female relatives of your restless ancestor, Captain Kinsolving?"

"Don't think so," said Terence, with an extremely puzzled air. "Never heard of any of them being noted beauties."

"Then, why," said Mrs. Bellmore, looking the young man gravely in the eye, "should that ghost have kissed me, as I'm sure it did?"

"Heavens!" exclaimed Terence, in wide-eyed amazement; "you don't mean that, Mrs. Bellmore! Did he actually kiss you?"

"I said *it,*" corrected Mrs. Bellmore. "I hope the impersonal pronoun is correctly used."

"But why did you say I was responsible?"

"Because you are the only living male relative of the ghost."

"I see. 'Unto the third and fourth generation.' But, seriously, did he—did it—how do you——?"

"Know? How does any one know? I was asleep, and that is what awakened me, I'm almost certain."

"Almost?"

"Well, I awoke just as—oh, can't you understand what I mean? When anything arouses you suddenly you are not positive whether you dreamed, or—and yet you know that—— Dear me. Terence, must I dissect the most elementary sensations in order to accommodate your extremely practical intelligence?"

"But, about kissing ghosts, you know," said Terence, humbly, "I require the most primary instruction. I never kissed a ghost. Is it—is it——?"

"The sensation," said Mrs. Bellmore, with deliberate, but slightly smiling, emphasis, "since you are seeking instruction, is a mingling of the material and the spiritual."

"Of course," said Terence, suddenly growing serious, "it was a dream or some kind of an hallucination. Nobody believes in spirits, these days. If you told the tale out of kindness of heart, Mrs. Bellmore, I can't express how grateful I am to you. It has made my mother supremely happy. That Revolutionary ancestor was a stunning idea."

Mrs. Bellmore sighed. "The usual fate of ghost-seers is mine," she said, resignedly. "My privileged encounter with a spirit is attributed to lobster salad or mendacity. Well, I have, at least, one memory left from the wreck—a kiss from the unseen world. Was Captain Kinsolving a very brave man, do you know, Terence?"

"He was licked at Yorktown, I believe," said Terence, reflecting. "They say he skedaddled with his company, after the first battle there."

"I thought he must have been timid," said Mrs. Bellmore, absently. "He might have had another."

"Another battle?" asked Terence, dully.

"What else could I mean? I must go and get ready now; the auto will be here in an hour. I've enjoyed Clifftop immensely. Such a lovely morning, isn't it, Terence?"

On her way to the station, Mrs. Bellmore took from her bag a silk handkerchief, and looked at it with a little peculiar smile. Then she tied it in several very hard knots, and threw it, at a convenient moment, over the edge of the cliff along which the road ran.

In his room, Terence was giving some directions to his man, Brooks. "Have this stuff done up in a parcel," he said, "and ship it to the address on that card."

The card was that of a New York costumer. The "stuff" was a gentleman's costume of the days of '76, made of white satin, with silver buckles, white silk stockings, and white kid shoes. A powdered wig and a sword completed the dress.

"And look about, Brooks," added Terence, a little anxiously, "for a silk handkerchief with my initials in one corner. I must have dropped it somewhere."

It was a month later when Mrs. Bellmore and one or two others of the smart crowd were making up a list of names for a coaching trip through the Catskills. Mrs. Bellmore looked over the list for a final censoring. The name of Terence Kinsolving was there. Mrs. Bellmore ran her prohibitive pencil lightly through the name.

"Too shy!" she murmured, sweetly, in explanation.

From ROLLING STONES 1912

The Atavism of John Tom Little Bear

I saw a light in Jeff Peters's room over the Red Front Drug Store. I hastened toward it, for I had not known that Jeff was in town. He is a man of the Hadji breed, of a hundred occupations, with a story to tell (when he will) of each one.

I found Jeff repacking his grip for a run down to Florida to look at an orange grove for which he had traded, a month before, his mining claim on the Yukon. He kicked me a chair, with the same old humorous, profound smile on his seasoned countenance. It had been eight months since we had met, but his greeting was such as men pass from day to day. Time is Jeff's servant, and the continent is a big lot across which he cuts to his many roads.

For a while we skirmished along the edges of unprofitable talk which culminated in that unquiet problem of the Philippines.

"All them tropical races," said Jeff, "could be run out better with their own jockeys up. The tropical man knows what he wants. All he wants is a season ticket to the cock-fights and a pair of Western Union climbers to go up the bread-fruit tree. The Anglo-Saxon man wants him to learn to conjugate and wear suspenders. He'll be happiest in his own way."

I was shocked.

"Education man," I said, "is the watchword. In time they will rise to our standard of civilization. Look at what education has done for the Indian."

"O-ho!" sang Jeff, lighting his pipe (which was a good sign). "Yes, the Indian! I'm looking. I hasten to contemplate the redman as a standard bearer of progress. He's the same as the other brown boys. You can't make an Anglo-Saxon of him. Did I ever tell you about the time my friend John Tom Little Bear bit off the right ear of the arts of culture and education and spun the teetotum back round to where it was when Columbus was a little boy? I did not?

"John Tom Little Bear was an educated Cherokee Indian and an old friend of mine when I was in the Territories. He was a graduate of one of them Eastern football colleges that have been so successful in teaching the Indian to use the gridiron instead of burning his victims at the stake. As an Anglo-Saxon, John Tom was copper-colored in spots. As an Indian, he was one of the whitest men I ever knew. As a Cherokee, he was a gentleman on the first ballot. As a ward of the nation, he was mighty hard to carry at the primaries.

"John Tom and me got together and began to make medicine—how to get up some lawful, genteel swindle which we might work in a quiet way so as not to excite the stupidity of the police or the cupidity of the larger corporations. We had close upon $500 between us, and we pined to make it grow, as all respectable capitalists do.

"So we figured out a proposition which seems to be as honorable as a gold mine prospectus and as profitable as a church raffle. And inside of thirty days you find us swarming into Kansas with a pair of fluent horses and a red camping wagon on the European plan. John Tom is Chief Wish-Heap-Dough, the famous Indian medicine man and Samaritan Sachem of the Seven Tribes. Mr. Peters is business manager and half owner. We needed a third man, so we looked around and found J. Conyngham Binkly leaning against the want column of a newspaper. This Binkly has a disease for Shakespearian rôles, and an hallucination about a 200 nights' run on the New York stage. But he confesses that he never could earn the butter to spread on his William S. rôles, so he is willing to drop to the ordinary baker's kind, and be satisfied with a 200-mile run behind the medicine ponies. Besides Richard III, he could do twenty-seven coon songs and banjo specialties, and was willing to cook, and curry the horses. We carried a fine line of excuses for taking money. One was a magic soap for removing grease spots and quarters from clothes. One was a Sum-wah-tah, the great Indian Remedy made from a prairie herb revealed by the Great Spirit in a dream to his favorite medicine men, the great chiefs McGarrity and Siberstein, bottlers, Chicago. And the other was a frivolous system of pick-pocketing the Kansasters that had the department stores reduced to a decimal fraction. Look ye! A pair of silk garters, a dream book, one dozen clothespins, a gold tooth, and 'When Knighthood Was in Flower' all wrapped up in a genuine Japanese silkarina handkerchief and handed to the handsome lady by Mr. Peters for the trivial sum of fifty cents, while Professor Binkly entertains us in a three-minute round with the banjo.

" 'Twas an eminent graft we had. We ravaged peacefully through the State, determined to remove all doubt as to why 'twas called bleeding Kansas. John Tom Little Bear, in full Indian chief's costume, drew crowds away from the parchesi sociables and government ownership conversaziones. While at the football college in the East he had acquired quantities of rhetoric and the art of calisthenics and sophistry in his classes, and when he stood up in the red wagon and explained to the farmers, eloquent, about chilblains and hyperæsthesia of the cranium, Jeff couldn't hand out the Indian Remedy fast enough for 'em.

"One night we was camped on the edge of a little town out west of Salina. We always camped near a stream, and put up a little tent. Sometimes we sold out of the Remedy unexpected, and then Chief Wish-Heap-Dough would have a dream in which the Manitou commanded him to fill up a few bottles of Sum-wah-tah at the most convenient place. 'Twas about ten o'clock, and we'd just got in from a street performance. I was in the tent with a lantern, figuring up the day's profits. John Tom hadn't taken off his Indian make-up, and was sitting by the campfire minding a fine sirloin steak in the pan for the Professor till he finished his hair-raising scene with the trained horses.

"All at once out of dark bushes comes a pop like a fire-cracker, and John Tom gives a grunt and digs out of his bosom a little bullet that has dented itself against his collar-bone. John Tom makes a dive in the direction of the fireworks, and comes back dragging by the collar a kid about nine or ten years young, in a velveteen suit, with a little nickel-mounted rifle in his hand about as big as a fountain-pen.

" 'Here, you papoose,' says John Tom, 'what are you gunning for with that howitzer? You might hit somebody in the eye. Come out, Jeff, and mind the steak. Don't let it burn, while I investigate this demon with the pea shooter.'

" 'Cowardly redskin,' says the kid like he was quoting from a favorite author. 'Dare to burn me at the stake and the paleface will sweep you from the prairies like—like everything. Now, you lemme go, or I'll tell Mamma.'

"John Tom plants the kid on a camp-stool, and sits down by him. 'Now, tell the big chief,' he says, 'why you try to shoot pellets into your Uncle John's system. Didn't you know it was loaded?'

" 'Are you a Indian?' asks the kid, looking up cute as you please at John Tom's buckskin and eagle feathers. 'I am,' says John Tom. 'Well, then, that's why,' answered the boy, swinging his feet. I nearly let the steak burn watching the nerve of the youngster.

" 'O-ho!' says John Tom, 'I see. You're the Boy Avenger. And you've sworn to rid the continent of the savage redman. Is that about the way of it, son?'

"The kid halfway nodded his head. And then he looked glum. 'Twas indecent to wring his secret from his bosom before a single brave had fallen before his parlor-rifle.

" 'Now, tell us where your wigwam is, papoose,' says John Tom—'where you live? Your mamma will be worrying about your being out so late. Tell me, and I'll take you home.'

"The kid grins. 'I guess not,' he says. 'I live thousands and thousands of miles over there.' He gyrated his hand toward the horizon. 'I come on the train,' he says, 'by myself. I got off here because the conductor said my ticket had ex-pirated.' He looks at John Tom with sudden suspicion. 'I bet you ain't a Indian,' he says. 'You don't talk like an Indian. You look like one, but all a Indian can say is "heap good" and "paleface die." Say, I bet you are one of them make-believe Indians that sell medicine on the streets. I saw one once in Quincy.'

" 'You never mind,' says John Tom, 'whether I'm a cigar-sign or a Tammany cartoon. The question before the council is what's to be done with you. You've run away from home. You've been reading Howells. You've disgraced the profession of boy avengers by trying to shoot a tame Indian, and never saying: "Die, dog of a redskin! You have crossed the path of the Boy Avenger nineteen times too often." What do you mean by it?'

"The kid thought for a minute. 'I guess I made a mistake,' he says. 'I ought to have gone farther west. They find 'em wild out there in the cañons.' He holds out his hand to John Tom, the little rascal. 'Please excuse me, sir,' says he, 'for shooting at you. I hope it didn't hurt you. But you ought to be more careful. When a scout sees a Indian in his war-dress, his rifle must speak.' Little Bear gave a big laugh with a whoop at the end of it, and swings the kid ten feet high and sets him on his shoulder, and the runaway fingers the fringe and the eagle feathers and is full of the joy the white man knows when he dangles his heels against an inferior race. It is plain that Little Bear and that kid are chums from that on. The little renegade has already smoked the pipe of peace with the savage; and you can see in his eye that he is figuring on a tomahawk and a pair of moccasins, children's size.

"We have supper in the tent. The youngster looks upon me and the Professor as ordinary braves, only intended as a background to the camp scene. When he is seated on a box of Sum-wah-tah, with the edge of the table sawing his neck, and his mouth full of beefsteak, Little Bear calls for his name. 'Roy,' says the kid, with a sirloiny sound to it. But when the rest of it and his post-office address is referred to, he shakes his head. 'I guess not,' he says. 'You'll send me back. I want to stay with you. I like this camping out. At home, we fellows had a camp in our back yard. They called me Roy, the Red Wolf! I guess that'll do for a name. Gimme another piece of beefsteak, please.'

"We had to keep that kid. We knew there was a hullabaloo

about him somewheres, and that Mamma, and Uncle Harry, and Aunt Jane, and the Chief of Police were hot after finding his trail, but not another word would he tell us. In two days he was the mascot of the Big Medicine outfit, and all of us had a sneaking hope that his owners wouldn't turn up. When the red wagon was doing business he was in it, and passed up the bottles to Mr. Peters as proud and satisfied as a prince that's abjured a two-hundred-dollar crown for a million-dollar parvenuess. Once John Tom asked him something about his papa. 'I ain't got any papa,' he says. 'He runned away and left us. He made my mamma cry. Aunt Lucy says he's a shape.' 'A what?' somebody asks him. 'A shape,' says the kid; 'some kind of a shape—lemme see—oh, yes, a feendenuman shape. I don't know what it means.' John Tom was for putting our brand on him, and dressing him up like a little chief, with wampum and beads, but I vetoes it. 'Somebody's lost that kid, is my view of it, and they may want him. You let me try him with a few stratagems, and see if I can't get a look at his visiting-card.'

"So that night I goes up to Mr. Roy Blank by the camp-fire, and looks at him contemptuous and scornful. 'Snickenwitzel!' says I, like the word made me sick; 'Snickenwitzel! Bah! Before I'd be named Snickenwitzel!'

" 'What's the matter with you, Jeff?' says the kid, opening his eyes wide.

" 'Snickenwitzel!' I repeats, and I spat the word out. 'I saw a man to-day from your town and he told me your name. I'm not surprised you was ashamed to tell it. Snickenwitzel! Whew!'

" 'Ah, here, now,' says the boy, indignant and wriggling all over, 'what's the matter with you? That ain't my name. It's Conyers. What's the matter with you?'

" 'And that's not the worst of it,' I went on quick, keeping him hot and not giving him time to think. 'We thought you was from a nice, well-to-do family. Here's Mr. Little Bear, a chief of the Cherokee, entitled to wear nine otter tails on his Sunday blanket, and Professor Binkly, who plays Shakespeare and the banjo, and me, that's got hundreds of dollars in that black tin box in the wagon, and we've got to be careful about the company we keep. That man tells me your folks live 'way down in little old Hencoop Alley, where there are no sidewalks, and the goats eat off the table with you.'

"That kid was almost crying now. ' 'Tain't so,' he splutters. 'He—he don't know what he's talking about. We live on Poplar Av'-noo. I don't 'sociate with goats. What's the matter with you?'

" 'Poplar Avenue,' says I, sarcastic. 'Poplar Avenue! That's a street to live on! It only runs two blocks and then falls off a bluff.

You can throw a keg of nails the whole length of it. Don't talk to me about Poplar Avenue.'

" 'It's—it's miles long,' says the kid. 'Our number's 862 and there are lots of houses after that. What's the matter with—aw, you make me tired, Jeff.'

" 'Well, well, now,' says I. 'I guess that man made a mistake. Maybe it was some other boy he was talking about. If I catch him I'll teach him to go around slandering people.' And after supper I goes up town and telegraphs to Mrs. Conyers, 862 Poplar Avenue, Quincy, Ill., that the kid is safe and sassy with us, and will be held for further orders. In two hours an answer comes to hold him tight, and she'll start for him by next train.

"The next train was due at 6 P.M. the next day, and me and John Tom was at the depot with the kid. You might scour the plains in vain for the big Chief Wish-Heap-Dough. In his place is Mr. Little Bear, in the human habiliments of the Anglo-Saxon sect; and the leather of his shoes is patented and the loop of his necktie is copyrighted. For these things John Tom had grafted on him at college along with metaphysics and the knockout guard for the low tackle. But for his complexion, which is some yellowish, and the black mop of his straight hair, you might have thought here was an ordinary man out of the city directory that subscribes for magazines and pushes the lawn-mower in his shirt-sleeves of evenings.

"Then the train rolled in, and a little woman in a gray dress, with sort of illuminating hair, slides off and looks around quick. And the Boy Avenger sees her, and yells 'Mamma,' and she cries 'O!' and they meet in a clinch, and now the pesky redskin can come forth from their caves on the plains without fear any more of the rifle of Roy, the Red Wolf. Mrs. Conyers comes up and thanks me an' John Tom without the usual extremities you always look for in a woman. She says just enough, in a way to convince, and there is no incidental music by the orchestra. I made a few illiterate requisitions upon the art of conversation, at which the lady smiles friendly, as if she had known me a week. And then Mr. Little Bear adorns the atmosphere with the various idioms into which education can fracture the wind of speech. I could see the kid's mother didn't quite place John Tom; but it seemed she was apprised of his dialects, and she played up to his lead in the science of making three words do the work of one.

"That kid introduced us, with some footnotes and explanations that made things plainer than a week of rhetoric. He danced around, and punched us in the back, and tried to climb John Tom's leg. 'This is John Tom, Mamma,' says he. 'He's an Indian. He sells medicine in a red wagon. I shot him, but he wasn't wild. The other one's Jeff.

He's a fakir, too. Come on and see the camp where we live, won't you, Mamma?'

"It is plain to see that the life of the woman is in that boy. She has got him again where her arms can gather him, and that's enough. She's ready to do anything to please him. She hesitates the eighth of a second and takes another look at these men. I imagine she says to herself about John Tom, 'Seems to be a gentleman, if his hair don't curl.' And Mr. Peters she disposes of as follows: 'No ladies' man, but a man who knows a lady.'

"So we all rambled down to the camp as neighborly as coming from a wake. And there she inspects the wagon and pats the place with her hand where the kid used to sleep, and dabs around her eye-winkers with her handkerchief. And Professor Binkly gives us 'Trovatore' on one string of the banjo, and is about to slide off into Hamlet's monologue when one of the horses gets tangled in his rope and he must go look after him, and says something about 'foiled again.'

"When it got dark me and John Tom walked back to the Corn Exchange Hotel, and the four of us had supper there. I think the trouble started at that supper, for then was when Mr. Little Bear made an intellectual balloon ascension. I held on to the tablecloth, and listened to him soar. That redman, if I could judge, had the gift of information. He took languages, and did with it all a Roman can do with macaroni. His vocal remarks was all embroidered over with the most scholarly verbs and prefixes. And his syllables was smooth, and fitted nicely to the joints of his idea. I thought I'd heard him talk before, but I hadn't. And it wasn't the size of his words, but the way they come; and 'twasn't his subjects, for he spoke of common things like cathedrals and football and poems and catarrh and souls and freight rates and sculpture. Mrs. Conyers understood his accents, and the elegant sounds went back and forth between 'em. And now and then Jefferson D. Peters would intervene a few shopworn, senseless words to have the butter passed or another leg of the chicken.

"Yes, John Tom Little Bear appeared to be inveigled some in his bosom about that Mrs. Conyers. She was of the kind that pleases. She had the good looks and more, I'll tell you. You take one of those cloak models in a big store. They strike you as being on the impersonal system. They are adapted for the eye. What they run to is inches around and complexion, and the art of fanning the delusion that the sealskin would look just as well on the lady with the warts and the pocket-book. Now, if one of them models was off duty, and you took it, and it would say 'Charlie' when you pressed it, and sit up at the table, why, then you would have something similar to Mrs.

Conyers. I could see how John Tom could resist any inclination to hate that white squaw.

"The lady and the kid stayed at the hotel. In the morning, they say, they will start for home. Me and Little Bear left at eight o'clock, and sold Indian Remedy on the courthouse square till nine. He leaves me and the Professor to drive down to camp, while he stays up town. I am not enamored with that plan, for it shows John Tom is uneasy in his composures, and that leads to fire-water, and sometimes to the green-corn dance and costs. Not often does Chief Wish-Heap-Dough get busy with the firewater, but whenever he does there is heap much doing in the lodges of the palefaces who wear blue and carry the club.

"At half-past nine Professor Binkly is rolled in his quilt snoring in blank verse, and I am sitting by the fire listening to the frogs. Mr. Little Bear slides into camp and sits down against a tree. There is no symptoms of firewater.

" 'Jeff,' says he, after a long time, 'a little boy came West to hunt Indians.'

" 'Well, then?' says I, for I wasn't thinking as he was.

" 'And he bagged one,' says John Tom, 'and 'twas not with a gun, and he never had on a velveteen suit of clothes in his life.' And then I began to catch his smoke.

" 'I know it,' says I. 'And I'll bet you his pictures are on valentines, and fool men are his game, red and white.'

" 'You win on the red,' says John Tom, calm. 'Jeff, for how many ponies do you think I could buy Mrs. Conyers?'

" 'Scandalous talk!' I replies. ' 'Tis not a paleface custom.' John Tom laughs loud and bites into his cigar. 'No,' he answers; ' 'tis the savage equivalent for the dollars of the white man's marriage settlement. Oh, I know. There's an eternal wall between the races. If I could do it, Jeff, I'd put a torch to every white college that a redman has ever set foot inside. Why don't you leave us alone,' he says, 'to our own ghost-dances and dog-feasts and our dingy squaws to cook our grass-hopper soup and darn our moccasins?'

" 'Now, you don't mean disrespect to the perennial blossom entitled education?' says I, scandalized, 'because I wear it in the bosom of my own intellectual shirtwaist. I've had education,' says I, 'and never took any harm from it.'

" 'You lasso us,' goes on Little Bear, not noticing my prose insertions, 'and teach us what is beautiful in literature and life, and how to appreciate what is fine in men and women. What have you done to me?' says he. 'You've made me a Cherokee Moses. You've taught me to hate the wigwams and love the white man's ways. I can look over into the promised land and see Mrs. Conyers, but my place is—on the reservation.'

"Little Bear stands up in his chief's dress, and laughs again. 'But, white man Jeff,' he goes on, 'the paleface provides a recourse. 'Tis a temporary one, but it gives a respite and the name of it is whiskey.' And straight off he walks up the path to town again. 'Now,' says I in my mind, 'may the Manitou move him to do only bailable things this night!' For I perceive that John Tom is about to avail himself of the white man's solace.

"Maybe it was 10:30, as I sat smoking, when I hear pit-a-pats on the path, and here comes Mrs. Conyers running, her hair twisted up any way, and a look on her face that says burglars and mice and the flour's-all-out rolled in one. 'Oh, Mr. Peters,' she calls out, as they will, 'oh, oh!' I made a quick think, and I spoke the gist of it out loud. 'Now,' says I, 'we've been brothers, me and that Indian, but I'll make a good one of him in two minutes if——'

" 'No, no,' she says, wild and cracking her knuckles, 'I haven't seen Mr. Little Bear. 'Tis my—husband. He's stolen my boy. Oh,' she says, 'just when I had him back in my arms again! That heartless villain! Every bitterness life knows,' she says, 'he's made me drink. My poor little lamb, that ought to be warm in his bed, carried off by that fiend!'

" 'How did all this happen?' I ask. 'Let's have the facts.'

" 'I was fixing his bed,' she explains, 'and Roy was playing on the hotel porch and he drives up to the steps. I heard Roy scream, and ran out. My husband had him in the buggy then. I begged him for my child. This is what he gave me.' She turns her face to the light. There is a crimson streak running across her cheek and mouth. 'He did that with his whip,' she says.

" 'Come back to the hotel,' says I, 'and we'll see what can be done.'

"On the way she tells me some of the wherefores. When he slashed her with the whip he told her he found out she was coming for the kid, and he was on the same train. Mrs. Conyers had been living with her brother, and they'd watched the boy always, as her husband had tried to steal him before. I judge that man was worse than a street railway promoter. It seems he had spent her money and slugged her and killed her canary bird, and told it around that she had cold feet.

"At the hotel we found a mass meeting of five infuriated citizens chewing tobacco and denouncing the outrage. Most of the town was asleep by ten o'clock. I talks to the lady some quiet, and tells her I will take the one o'clock train for the next town, forty miles east, for it is likely that the esteemed Mr. Conyers will drive there to take the cars. 'I don't know.' I tells her, 'but what he has legal rights; but if I find him I can give him an illegal left in the eye, and tie him up for a day or two, anyhow, on a disturbal of the peace proposition.'

"Mrs. Conyers goes inside and cries with the landlord's wife, who is fixing some catnip tea that will make everything all right for the poor dear. The landlord comes out on the porch, thumbing his one suspender, and says to me:

" 'Ain't had so much excitement in town since Bedford Steegall's wife swallowed a spring lizard. I seen him through the winder hit her with the buggy whip, and everything. What's that suit of clothes cost you you got on? 'Pears like we'd have some rain, don't it? Say, doc, that Indian of yorn's on a kind of a whizz to-night, ain't he? He comes along just before you did, and I told him about this here occurrence. He gives a cur'us kind of a hoot, and trotted off. I guess our constable'll have him in the lock-up 'fore morning.'

"I thought I'd sit on the porch and wait for the one o'clock train. I wasn't feeling saturated with mirth. Here was John Tom on one of his sprees, and this kidnapping business losing sleep for me. But then, I'm always having trouble with other people's trouble. Every few minutes Mrs. Conyers would come out on the porch and look down the road the way the buggy went, like she expected to see that kid coming back on a white pony with a red apple in his hand. Now, wasn't that like a woman? And that brings up cats. 'I saw a mouse go in this hole,' says Mrs. Cat; 'you can go prize up a plank over there if you like; I'll watch this hole.'

"About a quarter to one o'clock the lady comes out again, restless, crying easy, as females do for their own amusement, and she looks down that road again and listens. 'Now, ma'am,' says I, 'there's no use watching cold wheel-tracks. By this time they're halfway to——' 'Hush,' she says, holding up her hand. And I do hear something coming 'flip-flap' in the dark; and then there is the awfullest war-whoop ever heard outside of Madison Square Garden at a Buffalo Bill matinée. And up the steps and on to the porch jumps the disrespectable Indian. The lamp in the hall shines on him, and I fail to recognize Mr. J. T. Little Bear, alumnus of the class of '91. What I see is a Cherokee brave, and the warpath is what he has been traveling. Firewater and other things have got him going. His buckskin is hanging in strings, and his feathers are mixed up like a frizzly hen's. The dust of miles is on his moccasins, and the light in his eye is the kind the aborigines wear. But in his arms he brings that kid, his eyes half closed, with his little shoes dangling and one hand fast around the Indian's collar.

" 'Papoose!' says John Tom, and I notice that the flowers of the white man's syntax have left his tongue. He is the original proposition in bear's claws and copper color. 'Me bring,' says he, and he lays the kid in his mother's arms. 'Run fifteen mile,' says John Tom—'Ugh! Catch white man. Bring papoose.'

"The little woman is in extremities of gladness. She must wake up that stir-up trouble youngster and hug him and make proclamation that he is his mamma's own precious treasure. I was about to ask questions, but I looked at Mr. Little Bear, and my eye caught the sight of something in his belt. 'Now go to bed, ma'am,' says I, 'and this gadabout youngster likewise, for there's no more danger, and the kidnapping business is not what it was earlier in the night.'

"I inveigled John Tom down to camp quick, and when he tumbled over asleep I got that thing out of his belt and disposed of it where the eye of education can't see it. For even the football colleges disapprove of the art of scalp-taking in their curriculums.

"It is ten o'clock next day when John Tom wakes up and looks around. I am glad to see the nineteenth century in his eyes again.

" 'What was it, Jeff?' he asks.

" 'Heap firewater,' says I.

"John Tom frowns, and thinks a little. 'Combined,' says he directly, 'with the interesting little physiological shake-up known as reversion to type. I remember now. Have they gone yet?'

" 'On the 7:30 train,' I answers.

" 'Ugh!' says John Tom; 'better so. Paleface, bring big Chief Wish-Heap-Dough a little bromo-seltzer, and then he'll take up the red man's burden again.' "

From WAIFS AND STRAYS 1917

Confessions of a Humorist

There was a painless stage of incubation that lasted twenty-five years, and then it broke out on me, and people said I was It.

But they called it humor instead of measles.

The employees in the store bought a silver inkstand for the senior partner on his fiftieth birthday. We crowded into his private office to present it.

I had been selected for spokesman, and I made a little speech that I had been preparing for a week.

It made a big hit. It was full of puns and epigrams and funny twists that brought down the house—which was a very solid one in the wholesale hardware line. Old Marlowe himself actually grinned, and the employees took their cue and roared.

My reputation as a humorist dates from half-past nine o'clock on that morning.

For weeks afterward my fellow clerks fanned the flame of my self-esteem. One by one they came to me, saying what an awfully clever speech that was, old man, and carefully explained to me the point of each one of my jokes.

Gradually I found that I was expected to keep it up. Others might speak sanely on business matters and the day's topics, but from me something gamesome and airy was required.

I was expected to crack jokes about the crockery and lighten up the granite ware with persiflage. I was second bookkeeper, and if I failed to show up a balance sheet without something comic about the footings or could find no cause for laughter in an invoice of plows, the other clerks were disappointed.

By degrees my fame spread, and I became a local "character." Our town was small enough to make this possible. The daily newspaper quoted me. At social gatherings I was indispensable.

I believe I did possess considerable wit and a facility for quick and spontaneous repartee. This gift I cultivated and improved by practice. And the nature of it was kindly and genial, not running to sarcasm or offending others. People began to smile when they saw me coming, and by the time we had met I generally had the word ready to broaden the smile into a laugh.

I had married early. We had a charming boy of three and a girl of five. Naturally, we lived in a vine-covered cottage, and were happy.

My salary as bookkeeper in the hardware concern kept at a distance those ills attendant upon superfluous wealth.

At sundry times I had written out a few jokes and conceits that I considered peculiarly happy, and had sent them to certain periodicals that print such things. All of them had been instantly accepted. Several of the editors had written to request further contributions.

One day I received a letter from the editor of a famous weekly publication. He suggested that I submit to him a humorous composition to fill a column of space; hinting that he would make it a regular feature of each issue if the work proved satisfactory, I did so, and at the end of two weeks he offered to make a contract with me for a year at a figure that was considerably higher than the amount paid me by the hardware firm.

I was filled with delight. My wife already crowned me in her mind with the imperishable evergreens of literary success. We had lobster croquettes and a bottle of blackberry wine for supper that night. Here was the chance to liberate myself from drudgery. I talked over the matter very seriously with Louisa. We agreed that I must resign my place at the store and devote myself to humor.

I resigned. My fellow clerks gave me a farewell banquet. The speech I made there coruscated. It was printed in full by the *Gazette.* The next morning I awoke and looked at the clock.

"Late, by George!" I exclaimed, and grabbed for my clothes. Louisa reminded me that I was no longer a slave to hardware and contractors' supplies. I was now a professional humorist.

After breakfast she proudly led me to the little room off the kitchen. Dear girl! There was my table and chair, writing pad, ink, and pipe tray. And all the author's trappings—the celery stand full of fresh roses and honeysuckle, last year's calendar on the wall, the dictionary, and a little bag of chocolates to nibble between inspirations. Dear girl!

I sat me to work. The wall paper is patterned with arabesques or odalisks or—perhaps—it is trapezoids. Upon one of the figures I fixed my eyes. I bethought me of humor.

A voice startled me—Louisa's voice.

"If you aren't too busy, dear," it said, "come to dinner."

I looked at my watch. Yes, five hours had been gathered in by the grim scythe-man. I went to dinner.

"You mustn't work too hard at first," said Louisa. "Goethe—or was it Napoleon?—said five hours a day is enough for mental labor. Couldn't you take me and the children to the woods this afternoon?"

"I *am* a little tired," I admitted. So we went to the woods.

But I soon got the swing of it. Within a month I was turning out copy as regular as shipments of hardware.

And I had success. My column in the weekly made some stir, and I was referred to in a gossipy way by the critics as something fresh in the line of humorists. I augmented my income considerably by contributing to other publications.

I picked up the tricks of the trade. I could take a funny idea and make a two-line joke of it, earning a dollar. With false whiskers on, it would serve up cold as a quatrain, doubling its producing value. By turning the skirt and adding a ruffle of rhyme you would hardly recognize it as *vers de société* with neatly shod feet and a fashion-plate illustration.

I began to save up money, and we had new carpets, and a parlor organ. My townspeople began to look upon me as a citizen of some consequence instead of the merry trifler I had been when I clerked in the hardware store.

After five or six months the spontaneity seemed to depart from my humor. Quips and droll sayings no longer fell carelessly from my lips. I was sometimes hard run for material. I found myself listening to catch available ideas from the conversation of my friends. Sometimes I chewed my pencil and gazed at the wall paper for hours trying to build up some gay little bubble of unstudied fun.

And then I became a harpy, a Moloch, a Jonah, a vampire, to my acquaintances. Anxious, haggard, greedy, I stood among them like a veritable killjoy. Let a bright saying, a witty comparison, a piquant phrase fall from their lips and I was after it like a hound springing upon a bone. I dared not trust my memory; but, turning aside guiltily and meanly, I would make a note of it in my ever-present memorandum book or upon my cuff for my own future use.

My friends regarded me in sorrow and wonder. I was not the same man. Where once I had furnished them entertainment and jollity, I now preyed upon them. No jests from me ever bid for their smiles now. They were too precious. I could not afford to dispense gratuitously the means of my livelihood.

I was a lugubrious fox praising the singing of my friends, the crows, that they might drop from their beaks the morsels of wit that I coveted.

Nearly every one began to avoid me. I even forgot how to smile, not even paying that much for the sayings I appropriated.

No persons, places, times, or subjects were exempt from my plundering in search of material. Even in church my demoralized fancy went hunting among the solemn aisles and pillars for spoil.

Did the minister give out the long-meter doxology, at once I began: "Doxology—sockology—sockdolager—meter—meet her."

The sermon ran through my mental sieve, its precepts filtering unheeded, could I but glean a suggestion of a pun or a *bon mot.* The solemnest anthems of the choir were but an accompaniment to my thoughts as I conceived new changes to ring upon the ancient comicalities concerning the jealousies of soprano, tenor, and basso.

My own home became a hunting ground. My wife is a singularly feminine creature, candid, sympathetic, and impulsive. Once her conversation was my delight, and her ideas a source of unfailing pleasure. Now I worked her. She was a gold mine of those amusing but lovable inconsistencies that distinguish the female mind.

I began to market those pearls of unwisdom and humor that should have enriched only the sacred precincts of home. With devilish cunning I encouraged her to talk. Unsuspecting, she laid her heart bare. Upon the cold, conspicuous, common, printed page I offered it to the public gaze.

A literary Judas, I kissed her and betrayed her. For pieces of silver I dressed her sweet confidences in the pantalettes and frills of folly and made them dance in the market place.

Dear Louisa! Of nights I have bent over her cruel as a wolf above a tender lamb, hearkening even to her soft words murmured in sleep, hoping to catch an idea for my next day's grind. There is worse to come.

God help me! Next my fangs were buried deep in the neck of the fugitive sayings of my little children.

Guy and Viola were two bright fountains of childish, quaint thoughts and speeches. I found a ready sale for this kind of humor, and was furnishing a regular department in a magazine with "Funny Fancies of Childhood." I began to stalk them as an Indian stalks the antelope. I would hide behind sofas and doors, or crawl on my hands and knees among the bushes in the yard to eavesdrop while they were at play. I had all the qualities of a harpy except remorse.

Once, when I was barren of ideas, and my copy must leave in the next mail, I covered myself in a pile of autumn leaves in the yard, where I knew they intended to come to play. I cannot bring myself to believe that Guy was aware of my hiding place, but even if he was, I would be loath to blame him for his setting fire to the leaves, causing the destruction of my new suit of clothes, and nearly cremating a parent.

Soon my own children began to shun me as a pest. Often, when I was creeping upon them like a melancholy ghoul, I would hear them say to each other: "Here comes papa," and they would gather their toys and scurry away to some safer hiding place. Miserable wretch that I was!

And yet I was doing well financially. Before the first year had passed I had saved a thousand dollars, and we had lived in comfort.

But at what a cost! I am not quite clear as to what a pariah is, but I was everything that it sounds like. I had no friends, no amusements, no enjoyment of life. The happiness of my family had been sacrificed. I was a bee, sucking sordid honey from life's fairest flowers, dreaded and shunned on account of my sting.

One day a man spoke to me, with a pleasant and friendly smile. Not in months had the thing happened. I was passing the undertaking establishment of Peter Heffelbower. Peter stood in the door and saluted me. I stopped, strangely wrung in my heart by his greeting. He asked me inside.

The day was chill and rainy. We went into the back room, where a fire burned in a little stove. A customer came, and Peter left me alone for a while. Presently I felt a new feeling stealing over me—a sense of beautiful calm and content, I looked around the place. There were rows of shining rosewood caskets, black palls, trestles, hearse plumes, mourning streamers, and all the paraphernalia of the solemn trade. Here was peace, order, silence, the abode of grave and dignified reflections. Here, on the brink of life, was a little niche pervaded by the spirit of eternal rest.

When I entered it, the follies of the world abandoned me at the door. I felt no inclination to wrest a humorous idea from those sombre and stately trappings. My mind seemed to stretch itself to grateful repose upon a couch draped with gentle thoughts.

A quarter of an hour ago I was an abandoned humorist. Now I was a philosopher, full of serenity and ease. I had found a *refuge* from humor, from the hot chase of the shy quip, from the degrading pursuit of the panting joke, from the restless reach after the nimble repartee.

I had not known Heffelbower well. When he came back, I let him talk, fearful that he might prove to be a jarring note in the sweet, dirgelike harmony of his establishment.

But, no. He chimed truly. I gave a long sigh of happiness. Never have I known a man's talk to be as magnificently dull as Peter's was. Compared with it the Dead Sea is a geyser. Never a sparkle or a glimmer of wit marred his words. Commonplaces as trite and as plentiful as blackberries flowed from his lips no more stirring in quality than a last week's tape running from a ticker. Quaking a little, I tried upon him one of my best pointed jokes. It fell back ineffectual, with the point broken. I loved that man from then on.

Two or three evenings each week I would steal down to Heffelbower's and revel in his back room. That was my only joy. I began to rise early and hurry through my work, that I might spend more time in my haven. In no other place could I throw off my habit of extracting humorous ideas from my surroundings. Peter's talk left me no opening had I besieged it ever so hard.

Under this influence I began to improve in spirits. It was the recreation from one's labor which every man needs. I surprised one or two of my former friends by throwing them a smile and a cheery word as I passed them on the streets. Several times I dumfounded my family by relaxing long enough to make a jocose remark in their presence.

I had so long been ridden by the incubus of humor that I seized my hours of holiday with a schoolboy's zest.

My work began to suffer. It was not the pain and burden to me that it had been. I often whistled at my desk, and wrote with far more fluency than before. I accomplished my tasks impatiently, as anxious to be off to my helpful retreat as a drunkard is to get to his tavern.

My wife had some anxious hours in conjecturing where I spent my afternoons. I thought it best not to tell her; women do not understand these things. Poor girl!—she had one shock out of it.

One day I brought home a silver coffin handle for a paper weight and a fine, fluffy hearse plume to dust my papers with.

I loved to see them on my desk, and think of the beloved back room down at Heffelbower's. But Louisa found them, and she shrieked with horror. I had to console her with some lame excuse for having them, but I saw in her eyes that the prejudice was not removed. I had to remove the articles, though, at double-quick time.

One day Peter Heffelbower laid before me a temptation that swept me off my feet. In his sensible, uninspired way he showed me his books, and explained that his profits and his business were increasing rapidly. He had thought of taking in a partner with some cash. He would rather have me than any one he knew. When I left his place that afternoon Peter had my check for the thousand dollars I had in the bank, and I was a partner in his undertaking business.

I went home with feelings of delirious joy, mingled with a certain amount of doubt. I was dreading to tell my wife about it. But I walked on air. To give up the writing of humorous stuff, once more to enjoy the apples of life, instead of squeezing them to a pulp for a few drops of hard cider to make the public feel funny—what a boon that would be!

At the supper table Louisa handed me some letters that had come during my absence. Several of them contained rejected manuscript. Ever since I first began going to Heffelbower's my stuff had been coming back with alarming frequency. Lately I had been dashing off my jokes and articles with the greatest fluency. Previously I had labored like a bricklayer, slowly and with agony.

Presently I opened a letter from the editor of the weekly with which I had a regular contract. The checks for that weekly article were still our main dependence. The letter ran thus:

> Dear Sir:
> As you are aware, our contract for the year expires with the present month. While regretting the necessity for so doing, we must say that we do not care to renew same for the coming year. We were quite pleased with your style of humor, which seems to have delighted quite a large proportion of our readers. But for the past two months we have noticed a decided falling off in its quality.
> Your earlier work showed a spontaneous, easy, natural flow of fun and wit. Of late it is labored, studied, and unconvincing, giving painful evidence of hard toil and drudging mechanism.
> Again regretting that we do not consider your contributions available any longer, we are, yours sincerely,
> The Editor

I handed this letter to my wife. After she had read it her face grew extremely long, and there were tears in her eyes.

"The mean old thing!" she exclaimed indignantly. "I'm sure your pieces are just as good as they ever were. And it doesn't take you half as long to write them as it did." And then, I suppose, Louisa thought of the checks that would cease coming. "Oh, John," she wailed, "what will you do now?"

For an answer I got up and began to do a polka step around the supper table. I am sure Louisa thought the trouble had driven me mad; and I think the children hoped it had, for they tore after me, yelling with glee and emulating my steps. I was now something like their old playmate as of yore.

"The theatre for us to-night!" I shouted; "nothing less. And a late, wild, disreputable supper for all of us at the Palace Restaurant. Lumpty-diddle-de-dee-de-dum!"

And then I explained my glee by declaring that I was now a partner in a prosperous undertaking establishment, and that written jokes might go hide their heads in sackcloth and ashes for all me.

With the editor's letter in her hand to justify the deed I had done, my wife could advance no objections save a few mild ones based on the feminine inability to appreciate a good thing such as the little back room of Peter Hef——no, of Heffelbower & Co.'s undertaking establishment.

In conclusion, I will say that to-day you will find no man in our town as well liked, as jovial, and full of merry sayings as I. My jokes are again noised about and quoted; once more I take pleasure in my wife's confidential chatter without a mercenary thought, while Guy and Viola play at my feet distributing gems of childish humor without fear of the ghastly tormentor who used to dog their steps, notebook in hand.

Our business has prospered finely. I keep the books and look after the shop, while Peter attends to outside matters. He says that my levity and high spirits would simply turn any funeral into a regular Irish wake.

Hearts and Hands

At Denver there was an influx of passengers into the coaches on the east-bound B. & M. express. In one coach there sat a very pretty young woman dressed in elegant taste and surrounded by all the luxurious comforts of an experienced traveler. Among the newcomers were two young men, one of handsome presence with a bold, frank countenance and manner; the other a ruffled, glum-faced person, heavily built and roughly dressed. The two were handcuffed together.

As they passed down the aisle of the coach the only vacant seat offered was a reversed one facing the attractive young woman. Here the linked couple seated themselves. The young woman's glance fell upon them with a distant, swift disinterest; then with a lovely smile brightening her countenance and a tender pink tingeing her rounded cheeks, she held out a little gray-gloved hand. When she spoke her voice, full, sweet, and deliberate, proclaimed that its owner was accustomed to speak and be heard.

"Well, Mr. Easton, if you *will* make me speak first, I suppose I must. Don't you ever recognize old friends when you meet them in the West?"

The younger man roused himself sharply at the sound of her voice, seemed to struggle with a slight embarrassment which he threw off instantly, and then clasped her fingers with his left hand.

"It's Miss Fairchild," he said, with a smile. "I'll ask you to excuse the other hand; it's otherwise engaged just at present."

He slightly raised his right hand, bound at the wrist by the shining "bracelet" to the left one of his companion. The glad look in the girl's eyes slowly changed to a bewildered horror. The glow faded from her cheeks. Her lips parted in a vague, relaxing distress. Easton, with a little laugh, as if amused, was about to speak again when the other forestalled him. The glum-faced man had been watching the girl's countenance with veiled glances from his keen, shrewd eyes.

"You'll excuse me for speaking, miss, but, I see you're acquainted with the marshal here. If you'll ask him to speak a word for me when we get to the pen he'll do it, and it'll make things easier for me there. He's taking me to Leavenworth prison. It's seven years for counterfeiting."

"Oh!" said the girl, with a deep breath and returning color. "So that is what you are doing out here? A marshal!"

"My dear Miss Fairchild," said Easton, calmly, "I had to do something. Money has a way of taking wings unto itself, and you know it takes money to keep step with our crowd in Washington. I saw this opening in the West, and—well, a marshalship isn't quite as high a position as that of ambassador, but——"

"The ambassador," said the girl, warmly, "doesn't call any more. He needn't ever have done so. You ought to know that. And so now you are one of these dashing Western heroes, and you ride and shoot and go into all kinds of dangers. That's different from the Washington life. You have been missed from the old crowd."

The girl's eyes, fascinated, went back, widening a little, to rest upon the glittering handcuffs.

"Don't you worry about them, miss," said the other man. "All marshals handcuff themselves to their prisoners to keep them from getting away. Mr. Easton knows his business."

"Will we see you again soon in Washington?" asked the girl.

"Not soon, I think," said Easton. "My butterfly days are over, I fear."

"I love the West," said the girl, irrelevantly. Her eyes were shining softly. She looked away out the car window. She began to speak truly and simply, without the gloss of style and manner: "Mamma and I spent the summer in Denver. She went home a week ago because father was slightly ill. I could live and be happy in the West. I think the air here agrees with me. Money isn't everything. But people always misunderstand things and remain stupid——"

"Say, Mr. Marshal," growled the glum-faced man. "This isn't quite fair. I'm needin' a drink, and haven't had a smoke all day. Haven't you talked long enough? Take me in the smoker now, won't you? I'm half dead for a pipe."

The bound travelers rose to their feet, Easton with the same slow smile on his face.

"I can't deny a petition for tobacco," he said, lightly. "It's the one friend of the unfortunate. Good-bye, Miss Fairchild. Duty calls, you know." He held out his hand for a farewell.

"It's too bad you are not going East," she said, reclothing herself with manner and style. "But you must go on to Leavenworth, I suppose?"

"Yes," said Easton, "I must go on to Leavenworth."

The two men sidled down the aisle into the smoker.

The two passengers in a seat near by had heard most of the conversation. Said one of them: "That marshal's a good sort of chap. Some of these Western fellows are all right."

"Pretty young to hold an office like that, isn't he?" asked the other.

"Young!" exclaimed the first speaker, "why—— Oh! didn't you catch on? Say—did you ever know an officer to handcuff a prisoner to his *right* hand?"